Valley of CHOICE

TRILOGY

One Modern Woman's Complicated
Journey into the Simple Life
Told in Three Novels.

OLIVIA
NEWPORT

SHILOH RUN PRESS

An Imprint of Barbour Publishing, Inc.

Accidentally Amish © 2012 by Olivia Newport
In Plain View © 2013 by Olivia Newport
Taken for English © 2014 by Olivia Newport

Print ISBN 978-1-63058-503-7

eBook Editions:
Adobe Digital Edition (.epub) 978-1-63409-196-1
Kindle and MobiPocket Edition (.prc) 978-1-63409-197-8

All scripture quotations are taken from the King James Version of the Bible.

This book is a work of fiction. Names, characters, places, and incidents are either products of the author's imagination or used fictitiously. Any similarity to actual people, organizations, and/or events is purely coincidental.

Published by Shiloh Run Press, an imprint of Barbour Publishing, Inc., P.O. Box 719, Uhrichsville, Ohio 44683, www.shilohrunpress.com

Our mission is to publish and distribute inspirational products offering exceptional value and biblical encouragement to the masses.

Printed in the United States of America.

Accidentally AMISH

Dedication

For Caleb and Cana, luminous in my life

Acknowledgments

So many bits and pieces come together to make a novel. Thanks go to Rachelle Gardener, my literary agent, who first pointed out a newspaper article about the Amish settlement near Westcliffe, Colorado.

One of my uncles has spent years on a quest for information about our family history. He was the one who first turned up information about Jakob Beyeler, which made me curious enough to weave a historical thread into the contemporary fabric.

I found Diane Klopp by clicking an Internet link of indeterminate reliability. At the other end of the link, Diane had a copy of a hard-to-find book and gladly supplied missing research details about land grants and property descriptions in Berks County, Pennsylvania. As it turned out, she knew the land well, having grown up on a farm that adjoined the Byler property of my ancestors.

Thanks go to Lorene and Julianna Hochstetler, representing descendants of the Hochstetlers whose family history quite likely intersected the Bylers' in some way. Their comments on an early draft mattered.

And of course thanks go to the Barbour team for seeing what this might be and making it possible for so many to read.

One

$\mathscr{H}$ is kiss was firm and lingering as he cradled her head in one broad palm.

"Annie," he murmured as he took in a breath. His hand moved to brush her cheek. He kissed her again.

Annie's stomach churned while her lips went on automatic pilot. Kissing Rick Stebbins was nothing new and, frankly, less exciting every time. But in the moment, it seemed the safest choice among miserable alternatives.

She pictured where her blue Prius was stashed in the parking lot behind the modest glazed-brick office building. A small red duffel lay on the passenger seat and a compact suitcase on the floor. The denim bag she had carried since high school, on the desk she was leaning against, held her laptop in its padded case. Car keys hung from a belt loop on her jeans. Her cell phone was in a back pocket.

Annie Friesen was ready.

Rick would never admit to what she suspected. More than suspected. She was no lawyer, but she knew it would take more evidence to make an accusation stick.

And Rick was a lawyer. *Her* lawyer. Her intellectual property

5

lawyer. If only he had not slipped that extraneous document between the pages of the last contract awaiting her signature in triplicate. Whatever she thought she felt for him dissolved with that test of her attention to detail. He was the one who failed. She would sign nothing more from Rick Stebbins.

Rick took another breath. The air he exhaled on her neck was hot, and his fingers moved down to the front of her neck, toying with the gold chain resting on her collarbone.

I am so out of here, she thought, and ducked her head to avoid further lip contact. She stroked his tie before putting her fingers lightly on his chest and pressing him away gently.

"I have work to do," she said, "a meeting tonight. I told you about it."

"You can be late." Rick put his hands on her elbows.

She had seen him when he did not get his way—the weight of his hand slamming the desk in frustration, the set of his jaw, the frenzy of work that ensued. This time Annie did not plan to be anywhere in sight. He would calm down once he accepted that his plan would never happen. And then they would be over.

Annie shook her head and squirmed out of his grip. "You're the one who said I have to protect my copyright at all costs."

"Isn't that what you pay me to do?" Rick asked. "Are you sure I shouldn't be with you tonight?"

To Annie's relief, he did not move toward her again. "I want to try the civilized approach," she said. "Barrett and I have worked together a long time. Surely we can still talk to each other."

"He's adamant the new program was his idea. He even retained his own counsel." Rick laughed. "I guess he doesn't trust me any more than he trusts you."

"Our relationship has been no secret to anyone working here." Annie picked up the denim bag and slung it casually over one shoulder. *But it's over now. That was your last kiss, buddy.*

"Don't sign anything I wouldn't want you to sign." Rick raised his dark eyebrows at her.

What he wanted her to sign was precisely the problem.

Annie opened her office door, stepped through, and waited for Rick to follow. She locked it behind him and concentrated on breathing evenly. No one would think twice about seeing them together at the end of the day leaving the building that housed Annie and Barrett's small company.

They were more than successful. The first financial security software program Annie wrote, which Barrett marketed, sold rapidly. First, small credit unions bought it, then large ones, then conventional banks. Before long, a firm specializing in serving the financial industry recognized their program for the gem it was and bought them out. Annie was twenty-seven and had more money in her bank account than her parents had seen in all their working lives—or would ever see. She and Barrett decided to open another company and see if they could do it again, this time with a program that used store discount cards to track grocery inventory movement according to customer shopping habits and product placement. They also served a number of local companies with website design and custom software. These clients provided a working lab. Sometimes the problems she solved on a smaller level became just what Annie needed to get past a glitch in the bigger project.

Annie just wanted to write software. She was happy to see Barrett get rich right along with her. He was brilliant with the marketing and sales side and had earned his share of the fortune.

But Barrett wanted it all. He couldn't write software to find his way out of his gym socks, in Annie's opinion, but now that she was on the verge of a breakthrough, he wanted to squeeze her out of the latest deal.

And Rick was helping him. Annie was sure of it. She couldn't prove it, but that didn't mean she was going to lie down and let it happen. She merely needed a few days where she could think clearly and make a plan to fix this mess.

Outside the building, she pushed the button on her clicker,

and the lights on her car flashed.

"Call me later?" Rick's brown eyes glimmered in familiarity and suggestion.

"It might be late." *More like never!*

"It's never too late if it's you."

Aw. He can say the sweetest things. Not.

Annie let him peck her cheek and then walked briskly to her car while he seemed to saunter toward his on the other side of the lot. She navigated out of the maze of look-alike buildings in the complex and pulled out onto Powers Boulevard, a north-south arterial. Early on a mid-July evening, the Colorado Springs sky was still a stunning blue. The rush-hour traffic that glutted Powers in late afternoons had thinned—as much as it ever thinned on Powers—to midweek moviegoers, diners, and chain-store shoppers. Annie whizzed past one shopping center after another, a progression that also thinned and gave way to industrial complexes.

She glanced in her rearview mirror and glimpsed Rick's bronze Jeep two lanes over and six cars back.

Maybe she should hire a private eye. Or another intellectual property attorney. Someone who had a clue what to do. But she could do nothing with Rick Stebbins hovering over her every move, waltzing into the office at his whim, and making plans for them every night. A room in a bed-and-breakfast in Steamboat Springs awaited her, but she had to slip off Rick's radar.

Barrett was waiting—supposedly—and Rick was following. He was not even going to wait for a report from Barrett, apparently. Annie may have been trusting and naive up to this point, but she was not going to walk into a trap now.

Would he hurt her? Annie did not intend to risk finding out.

Heart racing, she turned right just where Rick would expect her to turn and headed west around the south edge of the city. A few seconds later, his Jeep slowly made the same turn. If she deviated from the predicted route too soon, Rick's suspicions would go into high gear. And if she made the wrong turn, she would hit a dead end. Neighborhoods of Colorado Springs were not tidy little squares on a grid. They were full of curves and angles and cutoffs and one-way streets and dead ends. Annie had grown up in this town and had been driving her own car for almost ten years. At the moment, she wanted to slap herself for not being sure where these side streets would take her.

Annie jerked the wheel to the right and swung into a sedate neighborhood of lawns and front porches, as if decades ago builders were determined to recreate the Midwest in the high desert climate. She couldn't squeal her tires without raising attention, but she pushed over the speed limit as much as she dared.

A moment later, Rick's Jeep appeared. Was it her imagination, or was he following more closely?

Annie tapped on the GPS and glanced at the map showing her location. Rick had a system, too. It would take some doing to outsmart him.

She had to try.

Moving generally in the direction Rick would expect, Annie varied her turns, making several maneuvers in quick sequence as if she were knowingly zigzagging across town. The area was coming back to her now. In high school she had a track teammate who lived down this way. Annie used to come down here on weekends after she got her first car, her first real independence.

Think! Where is that place you used to go?

The Jeep narrowed the distance behind her. Annie pounded the steering wheel. Her phone sang Rick's tune, and she ignored it. A moment later, it announced a text message. She refused to look, instead making another sharp turn into a hotel parking lot.

This was it. The hotel had been new when she was in high school. Now it had a ready-for-remodel quality, but it still anchored her geographical bearings.

Another message zoomed in. Again she ignored it. She cruised around the back of the hotel, staying as close to the building as she could. This was not the place where Barrett was waiting, and it was

9

not where Annie had intended to go, but it would have to do. So far the Jeep had not followed her into the lot.

Annie pulled into an empty parking spot in the first row outside a back door of the building. She dropped the keys into her denim bag then pulled its wide strap over her head before picking up the small red duffel that held a change of clothes and a few personal items. This was not exactly going according to plan. The rental car was waiting for her in Castle Rock, where she would have brought the trail of her own car to an end by stashing it in a friend's garage. Now she would have to leave the suitcase and find another way to get there.

A glance over her shoulder reassured her that Rick had not made the same turn into the hotel lot.

Not yet.

She opened the car door, got out, closed the door behind her, and listened to it lock. Behind the hotel, a grove of aspen trees shuddered in the wind, their leaves twinkling in waning sunlight. And beyond that, if it was still there, was a lumber distribution center the local contractors used. Specialty woods. Trims, cabinets, that sort of thing. Annie used to go to the parking lot for purposes she would never have admitted to her parents.

The Jeep's headlights glared just as Annie reached the edge of the grove. She pressed up against a tree, knowing that a slender aspen would never fully hide her form. Golden aspens that were a spectacular sight on a sunny autumn mountain drive were not much use for hiding behind in the summer. Perhaps the growing shadows would disguise her, though, if she kept still.

Rick parked the Jeep. He got out. His dress shoes clicked against the pavement.

Annie wished for someone—anyone—to pull into the lot right then, or come out the back door of the hotel.

He stood at the edge of the grove now. Annie's denim bag bulged on one side of her, and her red duffel on the other.

Way to be inconspicuous.

"Annie, I know you're here." His bass voice resonated confident, calm. "It would seem we understand each other fully now."

Annie held her breath.

Rick advanced into the grove.

Annie suddenly itched at the base of her neck. And her hands. And her twitching nose. She refused to scratch.

"I don't know why you're running, Annie. Nobody wants to hurt you." Rick's silky timbre slithered between the trees. "We just want you to sign some papers and this can all be over. It's sound business."

More sound for him than for her. She had to disappear for the next few days so there could be no question of her signature on any documents.

He was three feet away from her. With one turn of his head, she would be done for.

Annie heaved the red duffel bag and hit her target, thankful for the weight of a hairdryer. Rick stumbled off balance for a split second, tripping over the bag and swearing. Annie ran through the grove. She heard his footsteps behind her, but the voice of her high school track coach rang in her ears, warning her not to turn her head to monitor a competitor's progress. The grove was not deep, and she was soon out of it and in the parking lot of the lumber center. Several trucks of various ages and sizes created a maze in the small lot. The first truck she spied, a red pickup with a long bed, had a tarp folded away from one corner with the back gate down. Annie hurtled herself onto the gate without breaking stride and pulled the tarp over her. Knees pulled against her chest, she wedged in between two neat stacks of lumber at the edge of the bed.

And held her breath again. Her lungs burned in fury.

Rick thudded past. "Annie!"

His volume startled her, but she did not move. Not one millimeter. His steps retraced their route.

Annie heard the shuffle of other footsteps. *Barrett!*

"Can we help you, sir?"

No. Not Barrett.

Rick stopped. "Looks like I need to come back when the place is open," he said amiably.

Annie could picture the grin that surely accompanied the comment. No doubt he had his hands in his pants pockets, looking friendly and harmless.

"They open at seven in the morning," the mystery voice answered. A pause. "Are you a contractor?"

Sure. In the dark-suit attorney's uniform Rick wore.

"I don't want to hold you up," Rick said. "I'll come back another time."

His footsteps tapped away. Annie took a real breath.

"Odd fellow, don't you think?" the voice said. "Dressed funny for this place."

Another man chortled. "You're standing beside a man in homemade clothes, and you want me to agree that a fellow in a suit is odd?"

Both men laughed. One of them yanked on the tarp and secured a corner onto a hook.

"I'm so used to you, Rufus," the first man said. "I don't think of you as odd."

"Well, you're a good friend, Tom. Let's go home."

"Let me just fasten everything down and we'll get on our way."

Go home? Where is home?

Annie winced as the truck's gate slammed shut so close the hair on her arms fluttered. She clutched her denim bag. The man tugged on the far corner of the tarp and hooked it in place. She did not dare reveal herself now. She couldn't be sure where Rick was. How would she explain herself to the truck's driver?

Two doors slammed, the engine turned over, and the truck backed up.

A third text message buzzed in Annie's back pocket. She didn't have room to reach for the phone.

Two

$\mathscr{P}$inholes in the tarp where the canvas threads were stretched thin suggested the sun soon would be fully set.

Without access to her cell phone, Annie could only guess at how long she had been squatting in the back of the truck between piles of lumber. Ten minutes? Twenty? The driver left behind city streets for a highway. Annie felt the acceleration and merging sensation that forced her body to lean to one side.

I-25.

But which direction? Even in daylight Annie used the view of the mountains to the west of Colorado Springs to orient herself. Under a tarp in a vehicle that made multiple turns, she had long ago lost any sense of direction. If they were on the way to Denver, she would know where she was when the vehicle finally stopped. From there she could go anywhere she wanted or needed to go. If they were headed south, getting out of Pueblo would not be as easy. Walsenburg would be impossible. Annie pictured herself on the side of the interstate with her thumb out.

She still clutched her denim bag to her chest, her arms now wedged in by her own knees. With her phone, she could give herself a hot spot Internet connection and work on her computer anywhere. At the moment, though, not being able to open her laptop meant the new software at the heart of her flight was being tested. If it withstood the hacking attempts Barrett was surely making at that moment, Annie would know it was secure. Barrett would not be happy when he discovered the changes she made a few hours ago—changes that took protecting her creative work into her own hands. How long would it be before she could decipher his efforts and know that her own work had done its job?

Getting her laptop open under these conditions was physically impossible. If she could get to her cell phone, though, she could get online and discern what Barrett was doing. Inch by inch, she twisted an arm away from her chest and down the side of her torso. She just needed to slip her fingers into her back pocket. She tipped her hip up as far as it would go.

No luck. Just wasn't going to happen. All she accomplished was scraping her forearm and making her shoulder sore.

She was cut off. Completely. Indefinitely. This had never happened to her before. In resignation, Annie leaned her head against the wood stacked on one side. Mentally she created a list of the first steps she would take as soon as the pickup stopped.

Wherever it stopped.

Lumber creaked with the sway of the bed. Exhaustion engulfed her.

The truck stopped. Annie bolted awake—with no notion of how long she'd slept.

Please, God, don't let me be in Texas.

A few seconds later, she heard the truck doors open and slam shut again.

"Are you sure you don't want to unload tonight?"

Annie tried to reconcile the voice with the ones she'd heard earlier and the names they exchanged in the parking lot. Rufus was the deeper voice, Tom the pleasant tenor.

"No Rufus, it's ten o'clock. That's late, even for me, and it's the middle of the night for you."

"Tom, I hate to tie up your truck," Rufus said. "I'm sure you have other loads to haul tomorrow."

"I'll meet you at my place first thing," Tom said. "We can go to the job site together. We'll have more help unloading there. It won't take long."

"I hate to say it," Rufus said, "but the load is probably safest at your place for the night."

"I don't understand why Karl Kramer doesn't leave you alone." Tom's voice spat irritation. "You do good work for a fair price."

"He doesn't think it's fair. He thinks I'm underbidding him to force him out of business."

"That's ridiculous."

"Tell that to Karl Kramer." Rufus's rich voice softened.

"I have half a mind to do just that," Tom said. "But I guess it won't be tonight. I'd better get home."

"At least let me get you a glass of lemonade before you get on your way." Rufus perked up again. "It's been a long, hot day."

"I would accept that gladly."

"Maybe some of *Mamm*'s peach pie?"

Tom hesitated. "I'd better not. Tricia has me on some new-fangled diet."

The voices drifted away after that, and Annie couldn't decipher what they said. They were only going for a glass of lemonade. She did not have much time to figure out where she was.

Annie fumbled in the dark for some sort of latch to release the gate. She couldn't find it. Finally, she ran her hand along the edge of the tarp until she found a hook, unfastened it, climbed over the gate, and hooked the tarp back in place. Crouching beside the truck, she took in her surroundings.

A barn. Definitely not Denver. About forty feet off was a sprawling two-story log home with a dim light emanating from one corner of the first floor. Annie didn't see any other lights,

15

though she saw the shadows of what looked like a chicken coop and some sort of workshop.

I am in the boondocks.

After a quick stretch, she reached into her back pocket for her phone. A touch on the screen brought it to life.

10:08.

Strong signal bars.

I must be close to someplace.

A horse neighed behind her, making her jump. Annie's eyes adjusted to the shadows, and the horse nudging the edge of a split-rail fence came into focus.

At least it's not a yelping dog giving me away.

But did she want to stay here? She would have to sit out the night and figure out where *here* was in the morning. Or she could get back in the truck, uncertain where she would end up. Tom's place. Where was that?

The horse neighed again at the same time that Annie heard voices returning.

"What does Dolly want?" Tom asked.

"Once she's in the barn, she'll settle down," Rufus answered. "I'll see you in the morning, Tom. Thanks again for hauling the load."

Annie's decision was made. She had no time to climb back into the bed of the truck. She had to get out of sight—now! She dashed through the shadows to the barn's door, slightly ajar, and slipped inside.

Tom got behind the wheel and started the engine. Rufus slapped the side of the truck as it rolled past him.

"Come on, Dolly," he said. "Time for bed."

Annie glanced around the dark barn. There was not so much as a nightlight. As if in response to her presence, a cow mooed and a second horse snorted. Annie had no idea if a barn had a back door, but she felt her way along the stalls, hoping for one nevertheless. Rufus was sure to notice his animals acting strangely. It was just too dark, though, for her to find an escape. The moon outside was barely a sliver, and the barn's walls were solidly built, admitting no light. The horse snorted again, and a tail swished against a stall wall.

The barn door whined slightly as Rufus opened it wide. Annie froze in place, out of options. With one hand, Rufus led Dolly, and with the other he reached into the darkness. A moment later a gas lantern cracked the shadows. Annie could see now that Rufus would have to walk past her to reach an empty stall.

Dolly pawed the ground with one hoof.

"Come on, girl," Rufus urged. "I'm tired. We have a long day ahead of us tomorrow."

Annie scanned the barn. A buggy. Two buggies, actually. A large black one and a smaller one, more of a cart. They looked just like the pictures in history books illustrating the nineteenth century.

Her head turned toward Rufus now. Violet-blue eyes gleamed in the lantern's light, and brown hair fell across his forehead under a hat. Annie blinked at the straw hat then assessed the rest of his clothing—a plain, collarless, long-sleeved dark blue shirt, sturdy black trousers with suspenders, heavy brown work shoes. Her eyes widened. He was *Amish*!

Rufus stopped his forward progress and stared at her.

"I'm sorry, Rufus," Annie stammered. "I can explain."

He stiffened. "How do you know my name? Did Karl Kramer send you here to cause trouble?"

"No! I don't even know Karl Kramer."

"I don't want to seem inhospitable, but what are you doing in my barn?"

"I need a place to stay for the night." Annie put her hands up, palms out. "I'll get out of your way first thing in the morning."

"How did you get here?"

"It's a long story."

Annie held still under the inspection of his violet-blue eyes. Finally, Rufus led Dolly down the center of the barn and into her stall. Annie held still as man and horse passed. Once the horse was

17

settled, Rufus closed the stall and turned back to Annie.

He crossed his arms across his chest. "I enjoy a good story."

"I didn't say it was a good story, just long." Annie's mind raced with questions of her own. "The truth is, I'm not even sure where I am."

"I can help you with that. You're in the San Luis Valley between the Wet Mountains and the Sangre de Cristos. In the daylight, the view is spectacular."

"I'm sure it is."

Rufus seemed in no hurry to leave. "You never said how you know my name."

"I heard you and Tom talking." Annie exhaled slowly.

"How do you know Tom?"

"I don't."

He pressed his lips together. "Perhaps you can give me the short version of your story."

Annie sighed. "I was. . .in a bit of trouble and had to hide."

"And?"

"I stowed away."

"In Tom's truck?"

She nodded.

"What kind of trouble are you in?"

"I'd rather not say," Annie answered. "If you want me to leave tonight, I will. Right now."

"And go where? How?"

Annie tilted her chin up. "I can take care of myself. I don't want to be trouble."

They stared at each other for a solid thirty seconds.

"I have an empty stall. I'll get you a quilt and some fresh hay," Rufus finally said. "But I'm not going to leave a gas lantern in the barn with an *English* who doesn't know to be careful."

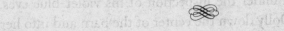

Rufus woke before the sun, as he had since childhood. As always, his mother already stirred in the kitchen downstairs. Even when they had first moved from Pennsylvania five years ago and the early weeks in Colorado were erratic and challenging for all of them, the rhythm that formed her forty-seven years hardly wavered. In a few more minutes, his sisters Sophie and Lydia would be up, along with brothers Joel and Jacob.

He got out of bed and dressed quickly, thinking of the mysterious guest in the barn. She was like Ruth, the same slender build putting skin on fierce determination. Rufus moved into the hallway, cocked his head to listen to the sounds below, and ducked into the small room where his sister used to sleep. On the hook behind the door, he found what he was looking for. He folded a deep purple dress and a white bonnet, then with quiet steps, he descended the stairs and slipped out of the house.

It was silly to think the *English* would want the dress. She wanted to leave, did she not? She had promised she would leave. Whatever happened to her the night before surely rattled her, but he was certain she was not the sort to be frightened in the daylight.

But something had compelled her to trust her welfare to a stranger's truck. He only wanted her to know she was welcome and it was safe to stay if she wanted to.

He did not wake her. She slept on the quilt, her arms around her bag, her hair the same color as the hay behind her head. She was an *English* woman, yet he could not shake the sense that she somehow belonged here in his barn. He watched as her long eyelashes fluttered in resistance to coming wakefulness.

Rufus laid the folded dress next to her hair spilled on the hay then went back to the house for his breakfast.

Annie woke abruptly with the distinct sense that someone had been there. She pushed herself upright and immediately checked her bag for her laptop then patted the bulge in her back pocket. Relief. Everything was right where it should be. Except her. She definitely did not belong here. Annie pulled her phone out and touched the screen. The three text messages she ignored the night before were now seven.

DON'T BE A FOOL, ANNIE.

YOU'RE THROWING EVERYTHING AWAY.

THIS IS NOT OVER.

She deleted the rest unread then checked her e-mail. Four messages, four taps on the DELETE option.

Then she saw the dress. The deepest, richest purple cotton cloth she had ever beheld, the color of an African violet bloom.

She was sure it had not been there the night before. Rufus must have brought it. But why? She reached for it and let the smoothness of its texture slide across her hands.

This time Annie heard the barn door open, and Dolly was nudging the stall door looking for attention. Rufus stood silhouetted in the opening, the rising sun behind his head brushing the sky pink.

Three

Annie lurched to her feet, dropping the folded dress and clumsily brushing hay from her clothing.

Rufus pulled the barn door nearly closed with one arm then moved toward her. "I brought you some breakfast."

"That was kind of you." Annie ran one hand through her hair, dislodging more hay.

Rufus set a tray on a small stool and backed away.

"Thank you." Tentatively, Annie lifted the dish towel that covered the tray and discovered hot buttered biscuits and a bowl of applesauce. "I found the clothes. Thank you for that as well."

He smiled. "You're being polite, but I don't suppose you can really see yourself wearing my sister's dress."

Annie liked the way his cheeks spread when he smiled—then she could not believe the thought had crossed her mind under the circumstances. He was Amish, after all. "That smells good." She picked up a biscuit.

"My mother is a very good cook."

Annie took a hefty bite. She had not eaten since breakfast the previous day, so extenuating circumstances or not, she was ravenous. She swallowed two large bites rapidly.

21

"Um, about the clothes?" she said.

Rufus shrugged. "It was just a thought."

"And thank you so much." She just was not sure what the thought was. "I promised I would leave first thing this morning."

He nodded. "I began to think about what made you run in the first place."

"I can't imagine what you must think of me."

"Maybe you have a good reason to be here. Perhaps it is *Gottes wille*. God's will."

Annie swallowed more of the moist biscuit and scooped a spoonful of applesauce. *God's will?* That thought had not occurred to her.

"You don't have to eat so fast," Rufus said. "I did not tell anyone you are here."

Annie forced herself to wait a few seconds before her next bite. "You've had your breakfast, I suppose."

He nodded.

"Are you even supposed to be talking to me?"

"You're in my barn. I'd say that gives me good reason."

"But you didn't have to feed me."

"It's the Christian thing to do."

"Thank you again. I'll get out of your hair in just a moment. How far will I have to walk to find. . ."

"Civilization?"

His arched brow made Annie look away. "I didn't mean anything. I'm sorry if I offended you."

He shook his head. "It takes much more to offend. We're about five miles from Westcliffe. I can take you. I'm going anyway."

"That's right. You're meeting Tom," Annie said.

"Whom you don't know," Rufus reminded her.

"I know he'll be waiting for you to empty his truck." Annie wiped her mouth on a corner of the dishcloth. "I don't want to hold up either of you."

"It's no trouble. I'll get the buggy ready."

Both horses neighed softly, and behind Rufus the barn door cracked opened slowly. A small boy shoved against its weight, gradually widening the gap.

Annie's eyes widened as well. Her gaze went back and forth between Rufus and the boy. The resemblance was remarkable. *His son.* Something in her sank.

Triumphant, the boy brushed the dust off his hands and for the first time looked inside the barn. He wore black pants and a white shirt. From under his straw hat, straight-cut blond hair hung over his forehead. He swirled one bare toe in the dirt of the barn floor and stared at Annie.

"I'm Jacob Beiler," he said. "Who are you?"

Rufus chuckled softly. "Good question."

"I'm Annie. Annalise, actually. It's nice to meet you, Jacob."

"Do you have a last name?"

"Friesen," Annie answered. "I'm Annalise Friesen."

"Are you from Pennsylvania?" Jacob asked, moving to stand next to Rufus. "I'm from Pennsylvania, but I do not remember Pennsylvania."

"I'm from Colorado," Annie said. "I've never been to Pennsylvania."

"Jacob was a baby when we moved here." Rufus rested a hand on Jacob's shoulder. "We've only been here about five years."

"Oh, I see." Annie supposed a wife would be the next character to enter the scene.

Rufus smiled again. "You didn't even know there were Amish people in Colorado, did you?"

"Well no," she admitted. "I don't come this way often."

"So why are you here now?" Jacob asked.

"Don't be nosy, Jacob," Rufus said.

"I'm not nosy," the boy responded. "*Mamm* says I'm just curious about everything."

"*Ya.* But don't be so curious about this. Have you had your breakfast yet?"

"I forgot," Jacob said. "The sky called me, and I wanted Dolly to see."

Another form split the glare coming through the open barn door. A woman paused to inspect the scene. "*Guder mariye.*"

"*Mamm*, Annalise is here," Jacob announced.

"*Ya*. I see that." The woman's floor-length dress was a deep turquoise under an apron that matched the purple garment still folded at Annie's feet. A white bonnet sat loosely on her head, the ties hanging down her chest. "I'm Franey Beiler. I see you have met two of my sons."

They're brothers! "I'm pleased to meet you as well," Annie said awkwardly. She stooped quickly and picked up her bag. "Perhaps I should leave now."

Franey looked from Rufus to Annie, but her face remained open, even amused. The hard edge Annie expected from an Amish mother who had just found her son in the barn with a strange woman did not appear.

"I'm sure you're wondering why I'm here," Annie said. "Rufus had nothing to do with it. I take full responsibility."

"I raised my son to give a cup of cold water to a traveler in need," Franey said. "Or at least a cup of *kaffi*. Do you like *kaffi*?"

Coffee? "Very much."

"I'm going to take her into town," Rufus said. "I have to meet Tom."

"Tom can wait ten minutes while our guest straightens herself out," Franey said. "Please come to the *haus*, Annalise." She gestured out the wide door toward the house. "Sophie should have been out to milk the cow by now."

Annie felt compelled to accept the invitation and fell into step beside a woman she judged to be about twice her age—or perhaps not quite that old. If Rufus was her son and Jacob was her son, Franey Beiler had spent a lot of years having babies. She must have had a handful by the time she was Annie's age.

In the house, Annie made a couple of false starts with the

water pump at the bathroom sink but finally succeeded at splashing water onto her face. She dug in her bag for something to tie her hair back and stared at her reflection in a small, dull mirror. If she didn't know better, she would not have guessed that the young woman who stared back was a successful software creator who already had made a small fortune.

Yesterday morning she woke in her own paid-for condo and drove to her own office in her own loan-free car. She had known the day would bring upheaval, but she had not expected to end up in the San Luis Valley preparing to ride in an Amish buggy.

Where in the world was Westcliffe, anyway? What would she do when she got there?

Annie didn't have a clue.

Safely behind the closed door, she opened her laptop. She pulled her phone out of her pocket. Within seconds, she found service and used it to give herself a hot spot connection to the Internet. A quick look at Barrett's web activity was all she needed for now. When she got to Westcliffe, she would figure out her next physical move.

She could see that Barrett had tried. Persistently. For a long time. But he had not hacked her system. Annie saw no activity in the last several hours and imagined Barrett and Rick had knocked some furniture around before deciding to sleep a few hours. They would try again. Determination was one of the qualities Annie admired most in Barrett.

Annie couldn't help opening a new search window and typing in the words "Amish bathrooms." She scanned through information that surprised her then laughed softly at herself. She was standing in an Amish bathroom, after all. Other than the lack of mirrors and excess lighting, the basics were there. Annie closed the computer and slipped it back into her bag.

In the hall, she smelled the rich fragrance of serious coffee and followed the waft to its origin. Despite its log exterior, the home was spacious with generous rooms flowing into each other. The simplicity of furnishings slowed her pace with their beauty. An armless rocker beckoned, and Annie let her finger trail along its curved back. She had not sat in a rocker in years. Over the dark, scrubbed hardwood floor, a handcrafted rug warmed the space with its rich hues of browns and blues. Simple maple tables accented the room, each one also clearly serving a purpose, holding a lamp or basket. A German Bible sat on its own stand, the large volume prominently displayed. Annie squeezed her eyes shut, trying to picture the last place she had seen her Bible.

"There you are," Franey said when Annie finally found her way to the kitchen. She handed Annie a steaming mug. "*Kaffi?*"

Annie sipped carefully to test the temperature of the coffee, grateful for the first swallow washing down her throat. Out the kitchen window, she saw a slim girl in a gray dress move toward the barn. She could not have been more than twelve or thirteen—Sophie, she supposed.

"Rufus said you're in trouble," Franey said.

Annie was startled by her directness. "Well, I. . .ran into an unexpected circumstance. I'm not sure it qualifies as trouble. I'll figure it out. I'm good at solving problems."

Franey nodded. "We don't have too many visitors from the outside in our *haus*, but I trust Rufus."

"I got myself into this mess," Annie was quick to say.

"It is not our way to turn our backs on someone who needs help."

"Thank you," Annie said again. She couldn't imagine how an Amish family could help her out of her muddle, but she did appreciate Franey's sincerity.

"The buggy is ready," Rufus said, saving her from having to muster a more complex response.

Annie took a deep swallow of coffee. "So am I."

A few minutes later, Rufus clicked his tongue to get Dolly moving. Annie shared the bench of the small green, cartlike buggy with Rufus. Behind the open-air bench was flatbed cargo space.

It would not accommodate nearly as large a load as Tom's truck, but Annie supposed Rufus used the cart frequently to haul loads of wood for whatever his work was. She pondered the network of leather strapping across Dolly's brown haunches, the animal's swinging white tail, and the smooth shafts of wood that connected the cart to Dolly's shoulders. With no experience to compare to, she had little vocabulary available for what she saw. The wooden wheels cranked in rhythm to the horse's pace. Annie turned her head slightly at the drift of an unpleasant odor.

Annie wondered if it would be polite to ask how long it took a horse and buggy to traverse five miles. Rufus carefully kept the rig to the side of the road, leaving ample room for cars to pass them. She watched the cars, one after another, and could not help noticing the empty passenger seats in most of them. Although Dolly seemed to keep up a brisk trot, to Annie the pace was torturously slow.

"You might as well enjoy the scenery," Rufus said. "I don't imagine you get to see views like this too often."

"Colorado Springs is beautiful, too."

"Somehow I suspect you don't see the views there, either." Rufus lifted one hand from the reins to gesture. "God's beautiful creation."

He was right. Other than glancing at the mountains to remind herself which way was west, she paid little attention to the landmarks of nature. Her eyes were on the road or on her computer screen or on her phone display. Her world spun around clicks and taps and memory and data patterns. Beside her, Rufus took in a deep draft of air, and Annie found herself doing the same.

"Is there a place in Westcliffe to rent a car?" she asked, recovering her purpose.

Rufus laughed. "The population is 417."

"Oh."

"There's always Silver Cliff, next door." He paused. "Population 523."

Annie flushed. She would just have to figure it out when she got there. She turned her head and looked in both directions, understanding she truly was in a rural mountain valley. Changing the topic of conversation seemed prudent.

"What brought your family to Colorado?"

"Look around. Land. Wide-open spaces. Pennsylvania is getting crowded, and land is expensive." Rufus paused for another deep breath. "I decided to try my hand out here, and my parents chose to come, too. I have younger brothers who will one day need land of their own."

"Was it hard to leave?"

He shrugged. "Two of my *brieder* are married and chose to stay in Pennsylvania. I know my mother misses them—and especially the *kinner*. She only hears about her grandchildren in letters. About fifty Amish families are scattered around the valley, so we do have company."

"Beiler." Annie crooked a finger under the gold chain at her neck. "I've heard that name somewhere."

"It's a common Amish name."

She shook her head. "I don't know any Amish people. I heard it somewhere else." She sat up straight. "It's my great-great-grandmother's name. That's what it is. Malinda Byler. I've seen it in the family Bible. She married Jesse Friesen."

"Do you have ancestors from Pennsylvania?"

"I don't know," she said. "I'll have to ask my mother."

He looked at her out of the side of his eyes. "Speaking of your *mudder*, does she know you're in trouble?"

Annie looked away from him. "I'll call her when I get a chance."

"You should go see her. A telephone is useful for business, but it's not a relationship."

"I will. I promise." *He's rather free with advice,* Annie thought.

Rufus turned the buggy on a new road. "We're almost there. If you don't mind, I'll stop by Tom's and let him know I'll be right back."

Annie spotted the red pickup from a hundred yards away.

"Something's wrong," she said. "The truck doesn't look right." It sat too low to the ground.

They both peered down the road. Tom stood outside his truck with a phone to his ear. Rufus urged Dolly to trot faster. Annie leaned forward as Tom turned and waved. He flipped his phone closed just as the buggy came alongside the pickup.

All four tires were slashed.

Four

In one practiced motion, Rufus pulled Dolly to a halt and jumped out of the buggy. Annie took a little longer to climb down with more care. She stood behind Rufus, who squatted beside the left rear tire. She had a clear view of the back of his neck, where brown hair met white collar.

Tucking his phone into his shirt pocket, Tom looked at Annie, questions in his eyes.

"I'm Annie," she said. "It's complicated."

"I would imagine so." Tom glanced at Rufus.

"Do you know when it happened?" Rufus slid a finger along the gap in one tire.

"I didn't hear anything," Tom said.

"They might have parked at a distance and come in on foot. Looks like a big knife to me."

"You're really not going to tell me why you have an *English* woman in your buggy?" Tom asked.

"I found her in the barn."

"Oh. That explains it."

"Before that she was in the back of your truck." Rufus stood up and flipped back the tarp. "My guess is she was wedged into

30

that space right there."

Annie nodded.

Tom's expression hardened. "Who are you? If Karl Kramer put you up to this, you're making a mistake."

"She doesn't know Karl," Rufus said. "She's harmless."

Harmless? Not exactly the word Annie would have chosen. If only Rufus Beiler knew her net worth and what she could do with a computer.

Tom twisted his lips to one side then turned his attention to Rufus. "It's time for you to get the police involved, my friend."

Rufus shook his head and stood up. "I understand if you need to report this because your property was damaged, but it is just not our way to get involved with the *English* courts."

"How many times are you going to let things like this happen?" Tom asked.

"As many as it takes, I suppose."

Takes for what? Annie wondered. "That's what Kramer is counting on," Tom said. "This nonsense is not going to stop as long as he knows that you won't do anything about it. He'll think all he has to do is outlast you, and you'll leave."

"The valley holds plenty of work for both of us. He will figure out I mean him no harm."

"You give him more credit than he deserves." Tom paced slowly around his truck, shaking his head.

"I'm sorry you suffered for your kindness toward me," Rufus said, "and I understand if you don't want to taxi for me anymore."

"Of course I'll taxi for you. I have insurance for stuff like this," Tom said. "But the police are not going to believe this was a random prank. I live too far out of town. It won't take a rocket scientist to trace this to the fact that I was hauling *your* lumber."

"*Es dutt mirr leed.* Again, I'm sorry."

"I'll be fine. It's you they're after."

"Who's after you?" Annie wanted to know. "Who is this Karl Kramer you keep talking about?"

Tom and Rufus stared at her.

"Okay, so I'm sticking my nose in," Annie admitted. "But after all, I'm standing right here. Am I supposed to cover my ears and sing while you have this conversation about an obvious crime?"

Tom glanced at Rufus. "She's got spunk."

If you only knew. Annie dug one heel into the dry soil.

"What would you suggest we do about the load?" Rufus asked Tom. "I was planning to take Annalise to town then come back to ride with you to the job site."

"Go ahead and take her in while I figure something out."

"Hello?" Annie said. "No one answered my question."

"It does not concern you," Rufus said.

"Maybe I can help." Reflexively, she armed herself with her cell phone. "What harm can come from telling me what's going on? I do rather well at getting the results I want."

"Somehow I suspect the result you wanted last night did not involve ending up in my barn," Rufus said.

"Low blow." Tom kicked a slashed tire, hiding a smile.

Annie was unfazed. "You have no idea what result I was seeking. I assure you I fully met my business objective last night and have ample resources at my disposal for my next steps. On the other hand, your business seems in peril, not to mention your friend Tom."

Tom extended a hand toward Annie. "We seem to agree on that point."

Annie shook Tom's hand. "I don't know all the background, but I agree that Rufus should talk to the police. Clearly this is not the first incident of this kind."

"Karl Kramer thinks he runs the county's construction industry," Tom said. "He is convinced he is losing business to Rufus's considerable woodworking skills."

"And he's not happy about it," Annie said, "so he misses no opportunity to let Rufus know how he feels."

"That about sums it up."

"Can these incidents be documented for legal action?"

"If Rufus would cooperate, they could be," Tom said. "But he says that is not the Amish way."

"It's not," Rufus reiterated.

"Tom, is this the first time you've been a target?" Annie asked.

"Other than the libelous muck that spews out of Karl's mouth, yes."

"Then perhaps we can capitalize on the fact that Karl crossed a line."

"We?" Rufus tilted his head at her. "I was under the impression you were leaving town."

Annie shrugged. "We can build a case against Karl that doesn't have to involve Rufus directly."

"I won't be a witness in court to anything," Rufus said.

"If Karl keeps this up, you won't have to be."

"I like this girl," Tom said.

"I promised to take you into town." Rufus ignored Tom's comment. "So I'm going to do just that." He gestured toward the buggy.

"You might as well go on to the job site after you drop her off," Tom said. "I've already spoken to my insurance agent, and they need an official report, so I have to call the police. I'm not sure when I can get your load out to you."

"Don't worry about it," Rufus said. "And I'll cover any costs your insurance doesn't pay for."

Rufus was tempted to urge Dolly to a faster pace to make up for lost time. His crew would be idle and expect to be paid for showing up on time.

"I think it's better if you don't involve yourself with the trouble here," he said to Annalise. "I may know someone in town who can help you get back to Colorado Springs today."

"What if I don't want to go back?"

He looked at her out of the side of his eye. "Are you running from something?"

"Of course not."

"Yet you felt compelled to take refuge in Tom's truck and my barn."

"It's not what you think."

"That depends on what you think I think."

"Don't play word games with me," Annalise warned. "I'm very good at them."

"You seem to be very good at a lot of things."

"I don't like to brag."

"You're definitely not Amish." Rufus chuckled. "May I speak plainly?"

"By all means."

"If you set aside your pride, you'll admit you were frightened last night. You're used to solving problems, but you're in a predicament you don't know how to get out of."

"No I'm not." *I know exactly what I'm doing.*

"Do you make a habit of jumping into strange trucks?"

"Of course not."

"So what happened?"

"It's complicated."

"So you've said."

"Well, it is."

"Fair enough." Rufus could not help noticing the way her gray eyes reflected the colors of the scene around them. "I can respect your privacy. Just do not feel you must solve my problems."

"You made your point, all right?" Annalise turned slightly away from him and gripped her phone in front of her.

"Good." He watched her for a moment. Thin strands of hair worked loose from the blue cloth tie and floated against her smooth white neck, intermittently airborne in the breeze the buggy's motion created. The gold chain around her neck glistened in the sun.

Rufus turned his eyes to the road, his blood pumping hard because of her presence. His life was predictable. Calm. Ordered. This outsider would never understand his way of living, no matter how much she poked her nose into his business. The best thing he could do for both of them was find her a ride back to where she came from.

Westcliffe still lay two miles ahead of them. Mentally Rufus inventoried the tasks and supplies available at the job site at the far edge of town. *Crew* was an overstatement for the two Amish teenagers who worked for him. He had hoped to frame in a new rank of cabinets in the family room of the private home he had helped to build, but he needed the long pieces in the back of Tom's truck. His mind wandered to cabinets ready to hang in other parts of the house and the sanding and staining still to be done on the downstairs mantel.

Beside him on the bench, Annalise cradled her cell phone in one hand and rapidly jabbed at it with the forefinger of the other. Her motions were too erratic to be dialing a phone number. She was going straight to the Internet, no doubt intending to become an expert in something or other in the next few minutes. During his *rumschpringe*, when he tried out some of the *English* ways of living before he was baptized, Rufus dabbled with the Internet. He knew how easy it was to get information quickly. Perhaps she was researching her options for getting out of Westcliffe and would know more than he did by the time they got to town.

Rufus wished he did not care that she was leaving so soon. But Tom was right. Annalise Friesen had spunk, something that compelled him to turn his head and look at her again.

"How much farther?" Annie raised her eyes to the road before them and shoved her phone into her back pocket.

"About two miles," Rufus said.

"Is it straight down this road?"

35

He nodded.

"You were right this morning," she said, inhaling. "I forget to look at the view."

"Sit back and enjoy."

"Actually, I'm wondering if I should walk the rest of the way." She met his gaze and saw for the first time the violet-blue dance of his eyes. "I just follow the road, right?"

"That's right. It would be hard to get lost at this point."

"Then if you don't mind, I think I'd like to walk." Annie tightened her grip on her bag and breathed in the mingled scents of roadside vegetation.

Rufus pulled on the reins, and Dolly slowed. "Are you sure about this?"

Annie nodded.

"It feels strange to just leave you on the side of the road."

Annie shrugged. "It's a beautiful day and a simple walk."

"You won't know where to go when you get there."

"They speak English in Westcliffe, don't they?"

"Of course."

"I'll be fine. I can take care of myself."

His Adam's apple bobbed up and then down as he swallowed his reply.

"I know you think I can't look after myself or else I would not be here," Annie said, "but I assure you, I'm fine. Thank you for the accommodations last night, and I hope Mr. Kramer comes to his senses soon."

"Thank you," Rufus said.

"Please thank your mother for me as well."

"I will. If you're ever down this way again, I'm sure she would enjoy seeing you. I know Jacob would."

The buggy stopped, and Annie climbed down. To be polite, she looked at Rufus, but she tried not to really see him, lest she decide to get back in the buggy just because he was there. The sensation shivered out of her.

"Look for Mrs. Weichert's shop on Main Street," Rufus said. "She sells some of my mother's preserves. Sometimes her daughter has business in Pueblo. She might give you a ride."

"I'll be fine."

Annie stood still and watched Rufus ease the buggy back onto the highway. Then with her bag slung over one shoulder, she progressed toward town in no particular hurry. Hues of green and brown and red she had never before noticed passed imperceptibly from one to the other. A breeze stirred in a pristine Colorado blue sky and ruffled her hair with a tender touch.

She was free.

She wasn't suspecting Barrett. She wasn't dodging Rick. She wasn't juggling three calls on her phone. She wasn't reading between the lines of a contract. And while it was not impossible for Rick to discover where she was—he could pull strings and find a way to track her—it was unlikely he was anywhere nearby.

Free. *Please, God, let it be so.*

Another mile down the road, a blue-and-red sign announced the presence of a roadside motel. Annie's eyes followed the direction of the arrow and saw the humble structure set back from the road and up a steep slope. The building was not large—perhaps twenty rooms—and the outdoor green-and-purple color scheme was hideous. Nevertheless, the place whispered her name. Giving into whimsy, Annie turned her steps toward the motel.

Her phone buzzed in her pocket. She paused with one hand ready to extract it.

Five

The screen announced, MOM/DAD. Annie answered the call.

"Where in the world are you?" Myra Friesen demanded. "I just want a peaceful cup of coffee with the newspaper, and the phone won't stop ringing."

"I'm sorry," Annie said. "I'm fine. No one needs to worry. Who called?"

"The police called about your car."

Annie grimaced. "What happened?"

"That's what they want to know. It was parked in front of a hotel but not registered to any known guest. So it got towed. Imagine my surprise when I sit down with my morning coffee and get that phone call. I had no idea you still had your car registered at our address."

"I've been meaning to change that," Annie said. "What did they do with it?"

"The towing company has it. They'll charge you for storage, you know, if you don't go get it."

"I don't think I can get it today." She could afford to store the vehicle indefinitely. At least Rick did not have his grubby hands on it.

"Where are you, Annie?" Myra asked again. "You sound like you're outside."

"I am." Annie licked her lips. "I had to go out of town for business reasons, but I'm enjoying the beautiful day."

"Your assistant called, too. She didn't say anything about a business trip."

"I didn't have a chance to tell Jamie before I left. I'll catch her up soon. Go back to your coffee."

"What about Rick?"

"What about him?"

"When he called, he seemed quite concerned that he did not know where you are. Considering how close you two have been, it was odd that he thought I would know your whereabouts when he doesn't."

Annie sighed. "Rick and I are not close now, Mom. I don't tell him everything."

"When I told him about the car, he was concerned something happened to you."

Yeah, right. He wishes.

"I'm fine," Annie said. "I just need to take care of a few things before I come home."

"You still haven't said where you are."

"It's better if you don't know, Mom. Trust me."

"That sounds ominous. Are you going to have to break my kneecaps?"

"Maybe. You know, the usual top secret stuff with a tech company in the cutthroat modern business world."

Myra laughed. "Next you're going to tell me not to bother my pretty little head about it."

"Something like that."

"I don't understand most of your techno-garble anyway. Do you want me to get your car out of hock? I could go to your condo for the extra keys."

"Don't bother. E-mail me the name of the tow company, and

I'll deal with it." After a pause, she added, "Use the private family e-mail address."

They were quiet for a beat, then Myra spoke, "Honey, are you really all right?"

"Fine, Mom. I'm fine."

"I love you."

"I love you, too."

After the call disconnected, Annie considered her phone. For years she literally never powered her phone off. Perhaps the moment had come. It might at least slow down Rick's search. With no doubt in her mind that it was only a matter of time before he wore down his contact in the police department and triangulated her location, she powered off and stuck the phone back in her pocket.

Her attention reverted to the motel before her. She had not stayed anywhere but a five-star resort in years. Her business dealings required a certain image of success. But this place was a portal to another world. No one would think to look for her here.

Rufus Beiler assumed she wanted to leave as soon as possible. Annie certainly had led him to that conclusion. But a nondescript motel in a place she had never been before might be exactly where she belonged now. The Steamboat Springs reservation had already gone to waste. Westcliffe might be just the place to set up a temporary headquarters and try to thwart the alliance that Barrett and Rick had formed.

Instinctively, she reached for her phone to log on and see if the two men she had trusted most—until a few days ago—had managed to do any damage in the last two hours. The black screen reminded her she had taken step one in cutting herself off from them.

Annie decided. Ten minutes later, she put seventy dollars cash on the counter in the motel's small lobby.

"We do take credit cards." The middle-aged woman behind the counter tended toward plump and battled gray. "Debit also."

"Cash is more convenient for me." Annie could not afford to

reveal any movement on her financial accounts right now. Rick knew too much about them, and Barrett could get into anything he decided to get into.

Except my program, she thought, *at least so far.*

"My name's Mo," the woman said. "Let me know if you need anything. Breakfast runs from seven to nine."

The room was modest and in need of fresh paint, but the owner clearly wanted to bill the place as belonging in the twenty-first century. The television was small, but it was a flat screen with basic cable channels. The high-speed Internet access would let her use her computer without turning on her phone. Annie plugged in both laptop and cell phone to juice them up.

Next she spent a few minutes scrambling the passwords of every online account she could think of, even minor sites she had no reason to believe Rick would be interested in tracking. She checked on the secure server that backed up her software program and breathed relief when she saw no evidence Barrett had hacked his way in, though she saw several new attempts that morning. Annie puzzled over what else she could do to ensure he would never succeed and clicked her way around the keys for another half hour. Then she stretched out on the bed and turned on the television to pass the time until computer and phone were fully powered. Idly, she searched "Amish in Colorado" and read several newspaper reports of the group's migration west. Every few minutes she glanced at the charging icons to monitor progress.

When she slammed Rick's head with the duffel back in the aspen grove, Annie surrendered personal items that would have kept her going for a few days. At minimum, she was going to need a fresh shirt and perhaps a baggy T-shirt to sleep in. Annie pulled up Google Maps and looked at the route between the motel and Westcliffe shops.

The walk to Westcliffe's quaint Main Street was an easy mile with the placid mystery of the Sangre de Cristo Mountains unfolding in constant view. Annie followed the gray highway across ground growth rolling in yellowish stripes before giving way to an irrigated green that signaled a town. A hazy memory niggled at her of a family trip to the Great Sand Dunes when she was small. Her intuition told her she was not far from where she played in a flowing creek with her sister while her mother sat in an orange lawn chair with her feet in the water on a beastly hot day. Other than that, Annie could not recollect being in this part of the state. Now the beauty crooked a finger at her, and she did not reach for the phone in her pocket even once.

Annie's pace slowed as she came into town and guessed at the ages of the stone and brick buildings that anchored it. A gabled church bell tower thrust a cross into the air, and Annie's feet turned in that direction without explanation. At the sight of it, a hundred years of history shivered through her, and she wondered if the residents who built the church could have imagined what she did for a living. The simple old-fashioned church stirred in her an impression of a place to belong. Before it became historic, this was simply a church where the community gathered.

The twentieth century had rumbled through the region, leaving in its wake signs that lit up and blinked, vehicles of various eras, practical business shelters, rehabbed houses, and ATMs. Yet the town stood poised in the past, weighing its future.

The ATM outside a stately bank gave her pause. How long could she stay afloat without resorting to a traceable electronic transfer of funds? She could not afford to lose herself in daydreams of scenery and history. She had a business to protect, and neither Rick nor Barrett would give up just because she managed to give them the slip. There was always her retirement fund. Rick might not think to track an IRA that she opened before she met him. The tax hit would be worth it if it meant she could halt Rick's aggression.

On Main Street, Annie found a couple of promising shops and rummaged for essentials. Surely it was only a matter of a couple of days, a week at the most, before she could safely return home. She would hire someone to help her, and in a few days she would stop

Rick and Barrett's attempt at legal thievery of her creative work.

Annie thought of Rufus. The offense against him was plain to see, and now it was spreading to his friend. Yet he refused to take action.

I've got too much invested, she thought. *I'm not giving up without a fight.*

She stood in the bright afternoon sunlight, unsure what to do next. Find food, she supposed. She could have a meal now and take something back to the motel for later.

A passing patch of purple made Annie lift her eyes from the sidewalk. Two Amish women, one middle-aged and one younger, exited a furniture store. Annie considered the sign that hung over the door and surmised it was an Amish business. The women smiled at her as they passed on the sidewalk then entered the same discount store Annie had just come out of. Annie watched their long skirts and sturdy shoes disappear from view—then chided herself for staring. No one else seemed to find the women's movements noteworthy.

An image of herself in the dress Rufus had left in the barn flashed through Annie's mind. It hardly seemed possible that only that morning she had woken to his peculiar offering.

Annie glanced around the street, stuffed her purchases in her shoulder bag, and scouted the environs for any sort of restaurant. She ate quickly at a sandwich shop, promising herself that when she was not under pressure to save her business, she would return to explore Westcliffe. On the way out of town, she noted the gas station with a couple of cars for sale and idly wondered how she could buy one without leaving a trail.

She shook the thought out of her head. *I have a perfectly good car. I just have to clean up this mess, and I can go get it.*

An hour later, Annie was showered and wearing her jeans with a fresh forest green T-shirt. A front porch ran across the length of the motel with Adirondack chairs scattered at irregular intervals. Annie settled into one with her laptop. The vista was nearly irresistible, but she forced herself to focus, compromising by working where the sun warmed her skin. If she could sort out a plan for dealing with Rick and Barrett, she would have plenty of time to relish the views.

Rufus spent the day sanding and staining detail pieces for woodwork around the house under construction and satisfying himself that the mantel was perfect. Tom showed up in the midafternoon with the new load, and the crew started on framing in the family room cabinetry. On his way out of town, Rufus took the buggy to an office building where the owners were dabbling with the idea of renovating and wanted him to quote on the job. He collected measurements, asked a few questions, and promised to make a formal bid. Perhaps if he focused more on remodeling rather than new construction, Karl Kramer would stop harassing him.

It was almost six o'clock when he let Dolly move at her own pace down the road toward home. His mind wandered to what awaited him at the farm.

Jacob could be a daydreamer. No one doubted the little boy's good intentions when he headed out for his chores, but often it fell to Rufus to double-check and make sure the animals had hay and fresh water and to look for eggs Jacob missed. His sisters, twelve and fourteen years old, were more dependable about milking the family's only cow and keeping up with churning butter and making cheese. *Daed* would have been in the alfalfa fields all day with sixteen-year-old Joel and no doubt would be soaking his sore feet by the time Rufus came through the door. *Mamm* would put down her sewing and check on the chicken potpie in the oven.

A mile out of town, Rufus happened to glance up from the road. Even from a distance he was sure of the slender form stretched out in the Adirondack chair, her hay-colored hair hanging loose as she hunched over a computer.

What was she still doing there?

44

Six

$\mathcal{A}$nnie rubbed her eyes and glanced up just in time to see Dolly *clip-clop* past. Was it her imagination, or was Rufus Beiler looking at her just before the buggy moved out of sight behind a tower of blue spruce?

Rufus Beiler.

Annie's hand moved to the phone in her back pocket. When she had spoken to her mother, she missed her chance to ask about the Byler name in her own family history. She hesitated over turning the phone on, but curiosity mounted, and she hit the speed dial number for her parents' house.

"Mom, it's me."

"Are you all right?"

"Fine, Mom. Relax. I just remembered a question I wanted to ask."

"What's that, honey?"

"I met someone named Beiler today, and that got me thinking about Daddy's grandparents. Wasn't there a name like Beiler in the family?"

"It rings a bell, but I'm not the best at keeping track of your father's side of the family tree."

"I suppose I could ask Daddy, but I don't think he keeps track, either."

"His grandparents died when he was a little boy. He never talks about them."

"But I saw the name somewhere. Malinda Byler." Annie spelled the name. "I think it was a maiden name. Are you sure you don't know anything?"

"Aunt Lennie gave us a book years ago," Myra said. "A genealogy mishmash that some distant cousin put together."

"That's it!" Annie said. "It had a black comb binding and a pink cover. I remember looking at it in high school."

"It must still be around here somewhere. You can look in the basement the next time you come."

Annie groaned. "Half the boxes down there don't have labels."

"Then you'd better hope the one you're looking for does," Myra said. "I don't have time to go digging, but if I think of it, I'll ask your father."

"Thanks."

"Still don't know when you're coming home?"

"Nope." Annie paused. "Mom, I may not be able to have my phone on much. Don't freak out if you can't get me. If something's important, just use the family e-mail."

"I worry about you, Annie."

"No need."

Annie ended the call then turned off her phone. She opened her laptop again and considered the screen. What were the odds of finding a competent and available intellectual property attorney in the San Luis Valley? She did not want glitz. Rick was well connected, so Annie wanted someone who was *not*, someone Rick would look right past. But this someone needed the guts to go up against Richard D. Stebbins and get the job done.

Cañon City, Walsenburg, Alamosa. How hard would it be to find a bus or catch a ride to one of those cities? Surely once she got there, she could rent a car and operate independently but still stay under Rick's radar. Annie looked through the Yellow Pages listings and clicked through to one link after another to study the scope and experience of each attorney. The list narrowed to three. It was too late in the day to phone an office number and expect someone would answer, but first thing in the morning, Annie would make the calls. In the meantime, she had to think through how to tell her story succinctly and with enough urgency to persuade an attorney to drop other work and jump on her case.

Annie clicked over to her e-mail, which she had not looked at all day.

Four frantic messages from Jamie, her assistant, time stamped at two-hour intervals throughout the day.

Fourteen messages of varying importance from clients with complex business needs for whom she did custom website work.

One message from a corporate partnership she did not recognize, making her heart lurch with dread that Rick was bringing in reinforcements. What was Liam-Ryder Industries, and what did they want?

Twenty-three Facebook notifications.

One terse message from Barrett underscoring that their business success was primarily due to his efforts.

She did not check Twitter.

Nothing from Rick. Annie was not sure if that was good or bad.

Annie answered one message from Jamie, assuring her that she was simply taking care of unexpected business, and gave instructions for responding to the more high-maintenance clients. She promised to be in touch soon. She ignored Barrett and did not even open the message from the unfamiliar corporation.

Somewhere behind her a cell phone rang. When she heard a man's vociferous swearing, Annie nearly jumped out of her chair. A door slammed, and a man in jeans and a blue work shirt stomped out of the room next to hers, a hammer in his hand. He brushed past her on the long porch. At the far end, near the lobby, Mo stepped outside.

"Hurry up, Jack," Mo said.

"I'm coming." His statement of the obvious weighed heavy with irritation.

"It's going to fall down! I told you hours ago I was getting nervous."

"I said I'm coming!"

Annie could not help watching the interchange. Jack made no effort to hurry his pace in response to Mo's agitated movements—which only made her more visibly disconcerted. When the crash came, Jack rolled his eyes and entered the lobby. Mo squeezed her head with both hands and moved down the porch toward Annie.

"He'll pitch a fit if I stand in there and watch what he's doing," Mo muttered.

Annie wondered if a response was required and finally said, "I hope everything is okay."

"He's just aggravated he had to pull the sink out of the room next to yours. I trust he's not disturbing you."

"I didn't even know he was there until he came out."

"He's the most cantankerous handyman I've ever had." Mo sighed. "I arranged for a carpenter to come tomorrow. I knew those shelves in the lobby needed work, but I didn't think they were going to fall apart today. I doubt Jack can do anything now but clean up the mess."

Annie nodded. "I hope it works out." She went back to inspecting her e-mail.

"Don't forget, continental breakfast from seven to nine every morning."

"Did Annalise sleep in the barn again?" Jacob Beiler asked in the morning over his bowl of oatmeal.

"No, Jacob," Rufus answered, "Annalise was our guest for only one night."

"If she was our guest, why did we make her sleep in the

barn?" Jacob waved his oatmeal-laden spoon precariously. "I don't understand why she was here."

"She just needed a place to stay for the one night."

"She's pretty."

The image of Annalise Friesen sitting on the porch in front of the motel lingered. Rufus wondered if she was still there. He would find out soon enough, he supposed. But he could not allow the lithe *English* woman to absorb his attention.

"Are you thinking about Tom's truck?" Franey ladled oatmeal into a bowl and handed it to her daughter Sophie, who passed it on to Lydia. Franey filled another.

"He had new tires on by the afternoon," Rufus said, "but it pains me that he suffered for helping me. I'm not sure I should ask him again."

"Don't you need his help?" Sophie asked.

"Yes I do," Rufus said. "I just don't want him to get hurt again."

"You pay him to taxi you, don't you?" Sophie said.

"Yes, of course."

"Then if you don't ask him to drive you, you won't be paying him, and you'll hurt his business."

Rufus tilted his head. "Maybe it's better if he only taxis for us when we have appointments, and he should not carry my lumber."

"That's up to him to decide," Lydia said.

"If you don't ask him, you'll have to find someone else," Sophie said. "And who will want to taxi for you if they think it's dangerous?"

Rufus looked from one sister to the other. "When did you two get so smart?"

"What is the dress for?" Jacob asked before shoveling more oatmeal into his mouth.

"What dress?" Franey asked.

"The pupel um," Jacob mumbled.

"Don't talk with your mouth full."

Jacob swallowed dramatically. "The purple one. I saw it in the barn this morning when I watered the animals."

Rufus blanched.

"What is he talking about?" Franey asked her eldest son.

"*Verhuddelt.*" A mix-up. Rufus pushed his chair back from the table. "I'll see."

He was out the back door before his mother or sisters could say more. Offering Ruth's dress to Annalise had been a silly gesture in the first place, but leaving the garment in the barn was sheer foolishness. Rufus went directly to the empty stall and picked it up, still neatly folded.

Rufus blew out his breath. *Hochmut.* His own pride would not let him walk through the house with the dress now and stir up another round of questions. In fact, he did not want to go back inside the house at all, preferring to let the incident fade from notice. Instead, he laid the dress between two buggy blankets on a shelf just inside the entrance to the barn.

Out of sight, out of mind, he told himself as he turned to take Dolly's bridle off the hook. He had work to do.

Annie squinted at the digital readout on the clock next to the bed. 8:36. She sat up immediately. The business day was well under way, and she was losing time with sleep. As she swung her feet over the side of the bed and raked fingers through her loose hair, a rumbling stomach reminded her that breakfast would end in less than a half hour. If she missed the motel's fare, she would lose even more time walking to town in search of food.

Annie pulled on the jeans and T-shirt from the day before, splashed water onto her face, ran a brush through her hair, and went in search of food, which theoretically would be available for another seventeen minutes.

Annie closed the door behind her, not bothering to lock it since she left nothing of value. She kept her shoulder bag with her at all times. Paranoid or not, she was not going to leave her computer unattended. She moved down the porch toward the lobby, unsure what to expect after yesterday's crash. Pieces of shelves lay stacked in one corner, and assorted tools suggested a carpenter was already on-site. Annie moved through the lobby toward the small dining room where she presumed breakfast awaited. Despite the noises in her stomach, food held little appeal, but when would she have another opportunity to eat? That depended on the result of phone calls she had yet to make and e-mails she had yet to read. The attorneys on her list were now ranked in order of preference. If she could get hold of them, she would interview all three by phone before making a decision, but she was determined to have someone on her side before the end of the day.

A few motel guests sat at small tables under the wall-mounted television, which was blaring morning news. A small girl played under a table, humming as she bounced a rubber ball. The food counter looked picked over, but the coffee's fragrance was robust. She drifted toward the dated fifty-four-cup urn just like the ones she used to see at church. She found a large Styrofoam cup with a plastic lid and instantly made the decision to take food back to the room. Eating between business actions was a familiar habit. A whole-wheat bagel smeared with cream cheese and a banana would round out a breakfast she was certain she could carry. At the last minute, she also dropped an apple into her bag for later. With the bag over her shoulder, coffee in one hand, and the bagel and banana in the other, Annie smiled absently at her fellow guests and headed back through the lobby.

When she saw Rufus Beiler line up his measuring tape on the wall, Annie's brain flashed the command to back out the other direction, and in that instant of hesitation, a rubber ball rolled from the dining room and under Annie's foot.

When her feet went out from under her, instinctively she let go of her breakfast and clutched her bag, making sure her computer would not take the first hit of the fall. Her head slammed the door frame between dining room and lobby, and when she hit the floor, she was flat on her back. Her first thought was whether she had smashed her phone. The next was that manufacturers of Styrofoam cups should make lids that stayed on during perilous descent.

"Ow! That's hot!" she screamed into Rufus Beiler's face as he kneeled over her. And then she understood why the old cartoons showed characters seeing stars when they hit their heads.

Seven

September 1737

She never imagined such a wicked wind, nor the number of times they would huddle in it, hardly able to breathe for its force and feeling as though their knees would buckle.

Verona Beyeler put one hand to her mouth and extended the other to touch her husband's elbow. She meant to hide both her horror at the sight and the nausea that hit whenever she came up on deck, as she steadied herself against Jakob's solid form. The ship rolled on the rhythmic, swishing swells of the North Atlantic, its sails strung at carefully calculated heights and angles. Verona avoided looking up at the towering masts for fear that dizziness would toss her over the railing. The day had been bright. Only in the last thirty minutes did the dismal overcast fittingly claim the horizon.

A gust snatched the corner of Verona's shawl, sending it flapping, and instinctively she let go of Jakob to retrieve it and clench it back into place. Jakob's head turned for a moment at her gesture, and then his eyes returned to the small shrouded bundle on the board. Verona tugged the strings of her prayer *kapp* to be sure it could not come loose as well.

Not another child. She did not know this child's mother

well, and for the moment she did not let herself feel the woman's heartache. As they stood among the dark-clad mourners, about a dozen, she felt the weight of the group. Sorrow turned to numbness rapidly on these occasions, which were far too frequent.

A man's voice droned words Verona did not want to hear. The wind swallowed most of them, for which Verona was grateful. The children began dying before the ship even left Rotterdam, starting with Hans Kauffmann's little girl. Five more died during the nine days in port at Plymouth. Now they were in the middle of the ocean, and the dying continued. The youngest children seemed the most vulnerable. Already more than twenty children had succumbed to measles and smallpox. Adults who would not forsake caring for their children fell as well. Hans Zimmerman's son-in-law died, depriving him not only of a beloved family member but a practical laborer with whom to homestead. Jakob and Hans were already conniving to claim land next to each other—now with one less man to work the acres.

According to Charles Stedman, captain of the *Charming Nancy*, land was still at least two weeks away, perhaps three. Verona's own five children occupied her hands almost constantly, but her mind was free to fill with dread.

The child on the board now could not be more than two years old. Lisbetli's age. If Verona had seen the bundle lying idly on the deck, she might have mistaken it for tightly wadded bedding waiting for the wash.

Two men picked up the board, balancing one end on the deck's railing. Fathers put on their hardened faces, and mothers pulled scarves up to hide quivering lips. The droning man pronounced his final words, and the two attending the board gently tipped the end up to an acute angle. The bundle lost grip and slid. A few seconds later came the slight splash, barely noticeable in the wake of the ship.

The mother's wail rent the air but was soon stifled.

Verona turned and once again reached for Jakob, this time

with a gasp. Behind them stood two of their daughters. At eleven, Anna was a help with the younger children, but at five, Maria demanded unceasing attention.

"How long have they been there?" Jakob asked softly.

Verona shook her head. Unless the girls could not see past the mourners, they would have seen the body go into the sea, not a memory she wished for them.

"The sickness is not a secret," Jakob murmured. "Anna is old enough to know what happens, and Maria will probably forget what she saw."

Verona was not so sure. As the funeral onlookers dispersed, she stepped across the deck as steadily as she could manage and reached her daughters.

"What are you two doing up here?" she asked.

"Maria got away," Anna explained. "Maria always gets away. She was halfway up the ladder before I saw her."

Verona planted a kiss on the top of Maria's head. "Go back below. It's cold up here, and the sun has gone away." She would not ask what they saw and make them unnecessarily curious.

"Can we come back later?" Maria asked.

"Maybe. If the sun comes out. Now go down to our berths." Verona touched both girls at the shoulders to turn them around and sent them back to where they had come from. "See if Barbara needs help with Christian and Lisbetli. *Daed* and I will be down in a few minutes."

She felt Jakob's presence behind her and turned to meet his gray eyes. "Tomorrow it could be Christian bundled up on a board."

"It won't be," Jakob said.

"You can't promise me that. He's been sick for two weeks."

"He's getting better or you would not have left him alone with Barbara," Jakob pointed out.

"If we had stayed in the Palatinate, he would not be sick."

"You don't know that," Jakob said. "The first children who got sick were probably infected before we boarded in Rotterdam. You know I'm right."

"But at least the children would have had fresh air and some decent food. That might have kept him well. Maybe it was a mistake to come."

Jakob took Verona's face in his hands and captured her violet eyes. "It was no mistake. We made this decision together. We cannot practice our faith in Europe without putting ourselves in danger. Christian would grow up to be drafted into one war or another, and I can't take that chance. We barely have enough money to make a fresh start now. If we had waited any longer, I hate to think what we would have faced."

Verona said nothing, her eyes no longer meeting his.

"William Penn's sons offer us a new life," Jakob continued. "The process takes time, but it is fairly straightforward. We can afford more land than we could ever hope for in Europe, even if others would have left us alone and let us believe what the Bible says."

"I have heard stories of people waking up in their berths to find someone dead beside them." Even thinking about it, Verona felt the feverish heat of Christian's skin as he lay next to her during her nightly vigil to assure herself he had not gone cold.

With one hand, Jakob gestured widely to the open sea. "There is no turning back, Verona. We have to see this through."

"At any cost?"

"Leaving Switzerland was the best choice for us. You know it was. Anywhere in Europe, life for true believers is unbearable. The Romans and the Lutherans will never accept the Anabaptists."

"We were both baptized when we were babies," Verona said. "Are you sure we had to be baptized again? Are you sure we have to separate from the world?"

"Why all these sudden doubts?" Jakob tugged at the strings of her *kapp*. "Have I ever asked you to believe something you did not know in your heart to be true?"

Verona shook her head. The bun of brown hair at the base of her neck wobbled.

"We chose this together," Jakob said. "We chose our faith. We joined the church because we wanted to. We chose this new life."

"I did not know it would be this hard." Verona's voice cracked. "And we are not even there yet." The dreary horizon now carried rain. She could feel it spattered in the wind.

"We will have *land*, Verona," Jakob said. "I will build you a beautiful home. I will open a tanyard. We will grow acres and acres of food for the children. William Penn's vision was for a place where people could come to live peaceably and worship according to their conscience. We will have a good life."

Verona swallowed hard. "If Christian dies—"

He put a finger to her lips and shook his head. "He won't. He will clear fields at my side. He will grow up to inherit our land and have a good life. Perhaps he will become the first Amish bishop to come of age in the English colonies!"

Verona smiled at the thought.

Jakob gently nudged her out of the path of two families approaching on deck.

"Even the Mennonites do not speak to us," Verona whispered.

"It's just as well. We separated from them for good reasons. What do we have to say to each other?"

Verona knew Mennonites slid their children into the sea just as the Amish did. Mennonite stomachs rumbled from hunger just as loudly as Amish stomachs. Mennonite babies whimpered just the same as Amish babies. She squelched her doubt about whether the separation had been for good reason and watched the progress of the Mennonite mothers, knowing they must share her fear.

None of the adults among the passing Mennonites turned their heads toward Verona and Jakob, and when one of their children smiled at her, a hand reached out and redirected his gaze.

Verona sighed. Perhaps Jakob was right. Perhaps it was just

as well. Twenty-one Amish families boarded the *Charming Nancy* along with the Mennonites. It was enough of a burden to bear the loss of Amish passengers. She was not sure she had room in her heart for the others. She supposed that not speaking to each other was one way of living peaceably together, at least for the weeks on the ocean.

"I'd better go check on Christian," Verona said, "and Lisbetli should be waking from her nap."

Jakob nodded. "I see Hans Zimmerman at the end of the deck. I want to speak to him. I'll be down in a few minutes."

Verona watched her husband stroll across the deck, his dark red hair showing the extra inches of the journey. She would have to trim it soon. When he greeted his friend, she turned her attention to the immediate task. Glancing into the opening she had sent her daughters down a few minutes ago, she gathered her dark skirt in one hand. With the other she gripped the railing that would guide her way down the ladder.

Though the Beyelers were a family of seven, they had only two berths, meant to hold a total of four people. Other families did the same. Some of the children were still small, so Verona wasted little energy feeling sorry for their lack of space. What meager belongings not in barrels in the cargo hold were crammed under the bottom berth—clothing, a few eating utensils, cloths for washing up in scarce freshwater.

Jakob was right, as he always was. The life that lay ahead held so much more potential than what they had left behind. They would miss their families, of course, but no one had suggested they should not go to Pennsylvania, a land of wide-open opportunity for anyone willing to work hard. She would be glad to be in the new Amish settlement, away from the threats that pursued the true believers in Europe.

At least their berths were curtained off with quilts, reminders of their families. The quilts offered some sense of privacy, though the makeshift separations did little to muffle the moaning of the sick or the impatient speech of a weary parent. Neither did they disguise the smells of hundreds of passengers packed into close quarters.

Verona brushed the heads of Anna and Maria, who sat on the floor with a handful of pebbles their only toys. Their prayer *kapps* were missing—again. She cringed at the thought of the scum beneath her daughters and promised herself she would sweep the floor around the family's bunks again before the day was over. Pushing aside the quilt hanging on the upper berth, she found Barbara, fourteen, sitting cross-legged at one end of the compartment, while Christian, eight, sprawled across most of the space.

His eyes were open, which made Verona's mouth drop open in relief.

"He's been talking a little bit." Barbara twisted the ties of her *kapp* in the fingers of one hand. "I gave him a few sips of water. I don't think he's as hot as he was."

Verona laid a hand against her only son's cheek and agreed with her eldest daughter's assessment. "Maybe we'll try a little broth for supper," she said, searching Christian's face for further confirmation of his recovery. He nodded just enough to give encouragement.

Lisbetli squawked from the lower berth. Anna jumped up from the floor and peeked behind the quilt. "She's awake."

Verona hoped Lisbetli would celebrate her second birthday on their new homestead. She smiled at the toddler, who should have been scooting across the berth determined to get down but was instead lying listless, glistening. Verona scooped her up and kissed her ruddy cheek. Was it warm, or was it her imagination?

Maria popped up and tickled the baby's feet. "*Mamm*, what are these red spots on Lisbetli's belly?"

Eight

Violet-blue eyes stared down at her. Annie stared back. Footsteps drummed across the brown-tile floor.

"Is she all right?" Mo knelt beside Rufus.

"My head." Annie gasped in pain.

"Don't move!" Rufus and Mo said in unison.

"She needs a hospital," Mo said.

"I'm fine," Annie insisted, unsure which hurt more—her back or her head.

"I'll call right now." Mo moved to the phone on the desk. "But it takes forever to get an ambulance out here."

"Who needs a hospital?" Annie said.

"Quite possibly, you." Rufus glanced in the direction she had come from. "I don't see what you tripped on. I was careful to keep my tools out of the way."

"It wasn't your tools," she said. *It was seeing you.* "I've been known to be clumsy at various points in my life. This confirms the theory."

Rufus plucked the rubber ball from behind Annie's knee. "Here's the culprit."

Annie moistened her lips and turned her head toward the

dining room, where forks, momentarily frozen in air, now resumed their purpose in the hands of hotel guests. Rufus rolled the ball back toward the little girl who stood staring at the scene.

"I'm calling an ambulance." Mo picked up the phone.

"No!" Annie said, surprising even herself with her volume. "Just give me a few minutes." Gingerly she tested one leg and then the other. Both bent at appropriate angles.

"There's an urgent care center much closer than the hospital," Rufus said. "Let me take you there. My little brother fell out of a tree once and needed an X-ray. They were very thorough."

"With all due respect, Rufus, the buggy is too slow," Mo said, "and you'll bounce her around like a broken bedspring. I'll take her in my car."

Annie pressed one forearm against the floor and shifted her weight to it, rolling to one side as she began to stand up. Her bag suddenly felt like a hundred-pound weight. As if reading her mind, Rufus slipped the strap over her head and off her shoulder then offered himself for support while Annie painfully sat upright.

"I'll bring the car around." Mo disappeared before Annie could protest further.

"You should let her take you," Rufus said. "Let *der Dokder* look."

Annie had to admit she had taken a solid smack. Pain radiated out from her spine in at least three places, and already the back of her head was tender.

"No more arguments," Annie said. "But I hope it doesn't take long. I have a lot to do today."

"First make sure you're all right."

"You don't understand."

"Considering how you ended up in my barn the other night, perhaps I understand more than you realize," he said, "but you need medical attention."

"I thought you people didn't believe in modern medicine." Annie lay back down on the floor with her head turned to one side. Lying flat was less painful than propping herself up.

"Who told you that?"

She tried to shrug and winced instead. "I don't know. Isn't electricity against your religion?"

"It is not that simple."

"You'll have to explain it sometime."

"Gladly. But right now you're going to a doctor."

Mo honked then jumped out of the green sedan parked outside the glass lobby door.

"I'm going to pick you up," Rufus said softly. "Very slowly. You tell me if it hurts too much."

She nodded as his arms slid under her knees and behind her shoulders. She looped her arms around his neck. Once upright, he took a few test steps toward the door.

"You okay?" he asked.

Annie nodded and leaned her head toward his chest for balance, her cheek brushing the soft black fabric of his shirt. He smelled faintly of sawdust and hay, but she was afraid a deep breath would stab her rib cage.

A cell phone rang, and Mo dug in her purse for it. "I can't talk now," Mo barked into the device.

Then she froze and listened. She held up her free hand, and Rufus halted.

Mo snapped the phone shut. "My mother is having some kind of crisis. I'm sorry, but I think I need to head over there right away."

"We'll take the buggy, then." Rufus resumed his careful pace but changed the direction slightly. "I've got you, Annalise."

She nodded against his chest and took a deep breath, not caring about the pain it caused. *I've got you, Annalise.*

Rufus stepped easily up into his cart as if he routinely carried around an extra hundred and fifteen pounds. "I'm sorry. This is not as comfortable as a car."

Annie winced as he set her in the seat. "My bag," she grunted.

"I have it."

The room was cold, and Annie was not fond of the beige printed cotton examination gown. *Some things are stereotypes because they are true,* she thought.

She had not persuaded Rufus to go home. Annie had imagined she could call a cab to get back to her room at the motel. Then she reminded herself where she was and that cabs might not be as plentiful as she presumed. Besides, she had to admit that moving any of her limbs involved pain. *"Accepting a little help is not a sign of failure."* Her mother said that all the time. Annie seldom acted like she believed it, but the fall left her with little choice. She pictured Rufus in the waiting room, guarding her denim bag. At least she had her phone, which she had taken custody of when a nurse helped her out of her coffee-sodden jeans. She searched "Amish medical care."

Rufus sat in the waiting room, sharing a vinyl seat with Annalise's bag. He felt the hard form of her laptop pressing against his hip. Rufus considered using a computer a couple of times in a public library to look up specific information but resorted instead to asking a librarian to help him find books he could carry home. It seemed so much simpler than learning how to communicate fluidly with a machine. He spoke English, High German, and Pennsylvania Dutch, but learning the language necessary to think like a computer did not appeal. What could possibly be on Annalise's computer to make her so attached to it when a live, wild, vibrant world was right before her eyes?

Still, the computer mattered to her, so Rufus would put it in her hands personally. He stood up to approach the reception desk cautiously.

"Excuse me, but can you tell me if Annalise Friesen is all right?"

The gray-haired receptionist glanced up at him. "Is she your wife?"

"No! She's. . .a friend who was injured. I brought her in. I just want to know how she is."

The receptionist glanced at her computer screen and hit several keys. "The doctor is getting ready to discharge her."

"When she comes out, she will come this way, *ya*?"

"Yes." The woman softened slightly. "I'll see if she'd like you to wait with her."

She was gone before Rufus could object, and when she returned a moment later to lead him to Annalise's room, he no longer wanted to object. When a nurse pushed the door open, Rufus hesitated in the door frame.

"You can come in," Annalise said. "They're about to spring me, but they say I can't go unless I have a ride. I guess that's you."

"I guess so." She was dressed in her own shirt and oversized pink sweatpants that made her appear frail. Though he had only known her a day, already Rufus knew Annalise did not tolerate frailty.

The nurse held a clipboard and flipped through forms. "Sorry about the wardrobe. It was the best we could do. Nothing is broken, but she may have a mild concussion. She might be a little sleepy and confused for a while, and it's better if someone is with her. The doctor says three days of rest. We've given her something for the pain."

Rufus nodded.

"Expect considerable bruising and tenderness." The nurse stuck the clipboard in front of Annalise. "Patient signs here."

"I feel loopy," Annalise said, though she signed the form as directed.

"That's why you need your friend." Now the clipboard was in front of Rufus. "Driver signs here," the nurse said. She reached over to a side counter and picked up a plastic bag to push into Rufus's arms. "Here are her personal items."

"Can she walk?" Rufus asked.

"I've got a wheelchair ready." The nurse stepped into the hall and returned in a few seconds with the wheelchair.

Annalise was going to need looking after. She could not go back to Colorado Springs in this condition, and Mo was running a motel, not an infirmary.

He would take her home, Rufus decided. He would not take no for an answer.

"She can stay in Ruth's old room," Rufus told his mother. "I know I am asking a lot, but I will try to be home more the next couple of days to help."

Annie listened in a vague, medicated haze. She did not recall agreeing to this arrangement and was not entirely sure who Ruth was or why her room was available, but she liked the idea of lying in a bed at that moment. She was on a sofa in the Beiler house and had a fleeting thought that she could no longer understand the conversation. It was as if Rufus and Franey had switched to another language. If she could just rest a few minutes, she could muster the strength to call the attorneys.

The conversation went mute.

When she woke, the sparse bedroom was dim, the only light coming in from the hall through the open door. The shadows formed themselves into Rufus's shape sitting in a straight-backed chair just outside the door, and gradually Annie's brain made the necessary neurological connections. This was Ruth's room at the Beiler house, and she had dozed the day away in the fog of painkillers.

"Rufus," she said. He was instantly on his feet. "Why am I here?"

"Because you need to be." He stood tentatively in the doorway.

"I. . .have business matters. . . ." She sighed, which hurt.

"You are in no condition."

She lifted a lightweight quilt and saw that she was wearing a nightgown.

"Do not worry," he said, "my sisters helped you change. Then they washed your things and put them over there." He pointed to a neat stack on top of a dresser. "I will go back to the motel tomorrow to get whatever you left."

"It's not much," she said.

"Yes, as I recall, you had little with you."

"I really do need to check on some things," Annie pushed herself to a half-sitting position. "Where's my bag?"

Rufus pointed toward the foot of the bed.

Annie winced as she leaned forward to reach her bag.

"You should rest."

"Fortunately, in my business I can work and rest at the same time."

"Does your line of work have something to do with why you ended up in the back of Tom's truck?"

"That has more to do with the people I chose to work with," she said, "and less with the business itself." Slowly, she managed to fish her phone from the bag.

"Must you do this now?"

"Let me just check my e-mail on my phone." She ignored Rufus's scowl. "You can come in."

Rufus stepped tentatively into the room.

Three messages from Jamie reporting on client actions.

Thirteen Facebook notifications.

Six client questions.

One from Barrett.

I am not a mobster, Annie. Let's sit down and talk this through. We've worked together too long for it to end this way.

Annie opened the site her family used for messages and found one from her mother.

You were right. Daddy says Jakob Byler came from

Switzerland in the 1700s. He doesn't remember much else.
We'll find the book the next time you're here. Maybe Aunt
Lennie knows more.

> Love,
> Mom

"Rufus," Annie said, "did your ancestors come from Switzerland?"

"Nearly three hundred years ago. That is a strange question to ask at the moment, *ya?*"

"I told you I had a Byler great-great-grandmother. Her ancestors came from Switzerland, too."

"I suppose it was a common name then, just as it is now." Rufus moved closer to the bed, glancing at the open door. "I'll get one of my sisters to help you."

"I don't need help. Tell me about your ancestors before I get loopy again."

"Our roots go back to Christian Beyeler, who was a child when he came with his parents to Pennsylvania. He grew up to be prominent among the early Amish in Lancaster County."

"I'll have to find out more," Annie said. "Meeting your family has made me curious. But first I have to deal with some pressing matters."

"Can I help you with any of these pressing matters?"

She lifted one shoulder and let it drop—and regretted the motion. "I doubt it. I run a tech company. Some personnel matters are heating up right now."

"Well, the company will have to run itself for a couple more days." Rufus took the phone from her loose grip. "Are you ready to try to eat something with your medication?"

Nine

October 1737

Christian Beyeler opened his mouth and sucked in a long, slow breath, filling his lungs with fresh air until he thought they might pop. Only that morning had he convinced his mother he was truly well and would not collapse if she allowed him to go up on deck without Barbara standing guard. He did not care that she only relented today because she was absorbed with baby Elisabetha. The little girl's spots disappeared at last, and the fever broke, but she was not taking water very well and was far from the cheerful, curious Lisbetli who entertained the family. His mother was up most of the night with the fussy child, trying to soothe every sound before it emerged to awaken other passengers. Christian closed his eyes and breathed a prayer for his baby sister.

The saltiness that hung heavy in the air across the Atlantic thinned now as the *Charming Nancy* navigated the channel into Philadelphia. The ship had entered Delaware Bay two days ago and was fighting the winds the last miles of the journey. Christian hoped for an early glimpse of Philadelphia. So far he had not seen more than lanterns along the shoreline.

Now the sun was shrugging away from the horizon and pinking up the eastern sky. Christian kept to the starboard side so he could watch dawn's hues meld into the waiting day. He moved toward the bow, determined to be the first one in his family to see Philadelphia.

His parents were doing a brave thing. Of that Christian was sure. Europeans had been moving to the Americas in fits and dribbles for two hundred years because they believed enormous profit lay in the new land, but Christian's father had explained that no one had attempted anything like William Penn's holy experiment. Christian's eight years were pockmarked by sores of exclusion because of what his parents believed. But in Pennsylvania, belief would be as free and abundant as air. He was as sure of that as anything he had ever known.

Jakob watched his second daughter climb the ladder from the third-class passenger quarters to the deck. Barbara had gone up ahead. He glanced over his shoulder at Verona, who sat on their lower berth with Lisbetli limply on her lap and Maria leaning into her shoulder. He had promised he would go up and check on Christian. Once Anna clambered through the opening at the top of the ladder, Jakob began his ascent.

In the time it took him to emerge on deck, the girls had wandered in separate directions. Jakob caught a glimpse of Anna going toward the bow and Barbara toward the stern. Christian was nowhere in sight. Jakob's instinct told him to chase the younger daughter. Anna always had a nose for where her only brother would show up. Barbara was fourteen, practically grown. She would know to return to their berths when the time came.

Jakob had to move quickly to keep up with Anna, dodging rigging, barrels, mops, and idle planks. He breathed a prayer of thanksgiving that the scourge that sent passengers into the sea had calmed. Verona thought the baby was still fragile, but Jakob believed that if she had survived this long, they were unlikely to lose her now. They were so close to Philadelphia. By the end of the day they should be on solid ground and out of the cramped quarters where disease thrived. Perhaps Verona would start to believe again that a better life lay ahead, not behind.

"Anna," he called, "wait for me." He recognized the posture of her reluctance, but she did stop and turn toward him.

"I see Christian." She pointed. "He's right up there, close to the bow."

Jakob followed the line of her finger and saw his towheaded son transfixed as he watched the Pennsylvania coastline with its evidence of settlements and promise of civilization. The boy looked thin, he realized. All the children did. Jakob was suddenly alarmed by his own acquiescence to what the journey had done to his family. Clothing hung on all their frames as if it were made for husky strangers rather than stitched by Verona's fingers for their familiar frames.

But it was over. They had survived. All of them. Many families around them bore sickness compounded by death, but the Beyelers were whole and present. Moving to a new life was not for the fainthearted. If they could survive the journey, they could survive homesteading their own land and living in the freedom of their own beliefs.

"Are we going to have real beds in Philadelphia?" Anna wanted to know.

Jakob stroked the back of her head. "You'll still have to sleep with your sisters, but at least the bed won't be riding the waves of the sea."

"Good."

They reached Christian. The three of them stood, wordless in a sacred moment, peering ahead and scrutinizing the view for any sign of the port city.

"Are we going to have a garden in Philadelphia?" Anna asked.

"No, not in Philadelphia," Jakob answered. "We will only stay there to get the papers we need. Then we will go to our own land. *Die Bauerei.* The farm."

"Will we have a big house?"

"Not at first. But someday, if God blesses us. We will be with other Amish families, and we will be grateful for whatever God gives us."

"Will Lisbetli have to be baptized?" Anna asked. "Will I?"

"Not until you are all grown up and decide to join the church."

"I'm going to join the church as soon as I can," Christian announced. "I already believe in my heart."

"I'm glad to hear that."

"There's Barbara." Anna pointed.

The ship listed to one side as it turned. Anna slid toward Jakob, but it was Christian who caught her.

Verona rubbed circles in the center of Lisbetli's back, a touch that had soothed the little girl since she was a newborn. With her other hand, Verona coaxed the baby to sip water from one of the three tin cups the family shared. Lisbetli had little weight to spare.

At her mother's knee, Maria picked up the loose nail she had gripped every day of this journey. Near the base of the berth's wooden frame, she scratched a mark into the wood.

"How many is that, *Mamm*?" Maria asked.

Verona did not have to think to answer. She had counted every day on the sea, too. "Eighty-three."

"That's a lot, isn't it?"

Verona nodded. "We're almost there. Try some letters now."

Maria put the nail down and poised her finger over the coating of dirt on the floor. "Sing, *Mamm*."

Verona began to hum a quiet hymn, adjusting first her *kapp*, then Maria's. The little girl made four tedious strokes until she formed an *M*. The truth was Verona recognized only the most basic words and could barely spell her own name. She would have to depend on the schooling of the older children to help Maria.

"I'm hungry, *Mamm*."

Verona had little food to offer. She unwrapped a napkin and

handed Maria the last piece of salted pork. The ship's rations had been far from adequate, and Verona early had formed the habit of saving some of her own meals for the inevitable request from one of her children.

"Let's go find *Daed*." The distraction might keep Maria from saying she was hungry again. Verona took her warmest wrap, and the three of them stepped over the baggage and personal belongings of other passengers to get to the ladder.

Maria had learned to do well on the ladder, but for Verona climbing with Lisbetli was always challenging. On deck, Verona squinted as her eyes adjusted to the growing light. She settled Lisbetli on one hip and took Maria's hand as they walked the deck scouting for the rest of the family. Even after eighty-three days on ship, Verona's legs were unsteady. This should be the last day, Jakob had told her. Verona hoped he was right.

Lisbetli seemed to perk up in the daylight, lifting her head off her mother's shoulder. Verona dared to hope that the baby would find her cheerful disposition once again.

Verona supposed she was one of the last to come above. It was not hard to decide where to go stand. The Mennonites were portside, and the Amish had gathered starboard. Her son would be on the bow. If Captain Stedman would let him, Christian would steer the boat.

When Jakob saw her, he opened one arm wide, and she stepped into its arc.

"I knew Christian would be at the front of the boat," Verona said.

"That is because he is looking forward and not back," Jakob said. "He is a wise little boy."

"Like his *daed*." Verona leaned her head against her husband's shoulder for a fraction of a second.

"How is the baby?" Jakob asked.

Lisbetli squirmed and reached for her father. Jakob took her in his arms.

"Does that answer your question?" Verona asked.

"This little one won't remember Europe," Jakob said. "She has only hope to look forward to."

They stood a long time on the deck. As the channel narrowed even further, Verona tried to remember the map Jakob once showed her and the slender, crooked finger of water that led from the Atlantic Ocean, through the Delaware Bay and to Philadelphia. Parents stood more erect, their countenances brightening. Children took their cues from the adults and began to point and squirm with increasing frequency.

"Is that it?" they asked again and again. "Is that Philadelphia? Is that where we're going?"

Christian kept his face forward, his features raised in determination to the breeze. His feet were planted squarely, shoulder width apart. He had no need of the rail. His body adjusted immediately to every shift in the ship's motion. Jakob took delight in his four daughters, but Christian, his only son, lit his face with a color that he did not reproduce for any other occasion.

We are humble people, Verona thought, *but surely it is not a sin to feel this way about your own child. Surely God knows the joy of an only son.* Her son was well. Her baby was well. In a few hours they would be in a city with markets and merchants and an October harvest of vegetables. Her tongue salivated at the thought of food not dried in salt, food that came directly from the ground and not through a barrel.

No one in the crowd wanted to surrender a position with a view of the approaching city. There would be plenty of time to go down and collect belongings later. After almost three months on the ocean, the families on board had eyes only for their new home, their new future.

Verona sighed and put a hand to her forehead to shield her eyes from the sun. Looking after five children and keeping their living area from becoming squalor, Verona had spent much of the journey below deck.

She turned her head and coughed once, a motion that sliced through her head. Determined not to pass out, she gripped the rail. *I'm just not used to the light,* she told herself when the throbbing behind her eyes made her want to empty her stomach. *The important thing is we're almost there.*

Ten

"No more lollygagging," Annie said to the empty room. She was stiff, sore, and slow moving, but she pulled on her jeans and T-shirt and sat up at a small table in the room, rather than on the bed.

She needed a phone—her own phone, preferably. It had been turned off for most of two days, but in the middle of her haze, Annie's systematic brain determined that if she disabled the global positioning feature on her phone, anyone trying to track it would face frustration. Triangulation with wi-fi alone would be a lot harder. She turned the phone on, tapped her way through several screens, and turned off the GPS. Annie let out a slow, controlled breath. At least she could use her phone freely.

Two days of dozing in concussive haze carried consequences. E-mails stacked up to the point it could take Annie hours to sort out the technical issues and respond to her regular clients. Jamie forwarded several inquiries from potential clients. Jamie also reported that Barrett was not spending much time at the office, and the marketing assistant was floundering for direction. The bank was calling with questions the bookkeeper could not answer. Three software writers who worked for the company were nervous.

Where are you? was the clear message. *What's going on?*

But Annie could not lose time dealing with the details when the entire company was at stake.

What would Barrett and Rick be trying to do now? That was the question. Jamie's report that the bank was calling the office suggested they were trying to move funds. Calmly, she logged onto the company's primary bank account and inspected recent transactions. So far everything looked routine. Her personal accounts seemed secure as well. So what were the questions?

Barrett and Rick couldn't turn back now. They were in too deep not to win.

The attorneys. Annie brought the list up on her laptop and dialed the first number on her phone. While she listened to the ring, she checked the charge indicators on both devices. Within a few hours, she would need a place to plug in, and she was pretty sure it was not going to be at Rufus's house.

An answering service responded for the first lawyer on her list and she left a message with basic information. She dialed the second number, and then the third. She got live voices on the line, but the attorneys themselves were unavailable. More messages.

Annie stared at the phone in her hand. Once the lawyers got her voice mails, they could play phone tag for days. She had to leave the phone powered on.

Other than the bathroom across the hall, Annie had not been out of Ruth's bedroom since she arrived. Her head turned toward the footsteps she heard in the hall now and saw the girl who had gone out to milk the cow.

She dug in her bruised brain for the name of Rufus's sister. Sally? Linda?

"I'm Sophie," the girl said softly.

That's right. Sophie and Lydia. "Thank you for all the help you've been the last few days."

"You're welcome. Rufus made me promise to check on you."

"I'm much better." Annie tugged her shirt straight and wondered what her hair looked like compared to Sophie's careful braids and pins. Wincing, she stood and began to pull the bedding into a semblance of order.

"I can do that." Sophie stepped swiftly to the bed and took control of the sheets.

Annie's hands rested on the quilt, pieces of blue and purple and green forming cubes that seemed to tumble over each other. The pattern made her slightly dizzy. She supposed it had a name. Later, when she had sufficient power, she would do an Internet search on "Amish quilts."

"*Mamm* will want to know you're up." Sophie smoothed the quilt into place. "I will walk downstairs with you."

Annie nodded. She stuffed her phone into her back pocket and hung her bag over one shoulder. Every step was pain. She couldn't drive a car even if she had one. But electricity was out there, just beyond the Beiler property.

Franey Beiler met her at the bottom of the stairs. "Annalise! I didn't know you were up. Would you like something to eat?"

"I don't want to be any trouble for you." Annie swallowed the urge to add that she needed electricity more than food right now.

"Go out on the porch," Franey said. "It's a beautiful day. I'll bring you a sandwich and a glass of tea."

"Thank you."

Sophie held open the screen door. "Please excuse me. I need to weed in the garden."

Sophie's soft words drifted with her gaze as she stepped outside. Annie watched Sophie join another girl—it must be Lydia, Annie realized—squatting in the garden. Standing still, Annie thought of her own sister, Penny, and a fragment of memory about digging in the backyard. For a few minutes, Penny had persuaded Annie that they could dig to China.

On the porch, Annie found a two-seater swing, its pine slats sanded smooth along the perfect curve of the back and seat. She had to admit it was still difficult to move around. If her mind were not on an impending need for battery power, she could have surrendered to the unobstructed view of the Sangre de Cristo Mountains and her own recuperation. Instead, the mountains reminded her of her remote location. The late-afternoon sun layered the view with shifting shadows, and Annie wondered anew what she had gotten herself into. Yes, the setting was bucolic. Yes, the mountains were stunning. Yes, the air was unsullied and the land animated in ways the city could never match.

But she had no place to plug in a power cord. And without a place to plug in, the rest of it did not matter.

Annie put the swing into tentative, gentle motion.

Sangre de Cristo. Spanish for the "Blood of Christ." It struck her as interesting that a religious group like the Amish would choose to settle in the shadow of such a religious-sounding name. Was that on purpose or just coincidence?

Was anything on purpose, she wondered, or was everything just coincidence?

Coincidence that Tom's truck was in the parking lot that night.

Coincidence that she got in it.

Coincidence that she ended up here. On Amish land.

Coincidence that Barrett was stabbing her in the back.

Coincidence that Rick chose Barrett and not Annie.

Coincidence that a fall cost her two days of fighting back.

Coincidence that her great-great-grandmother's name was Byler.

Annie typed "Jakob Byler" into the search screen on her phone.

Cemetery listings, genealogy forums, Amish settlements. Annie could not waste battery power clicking through the links right now. She could not even be sure this was the Jakob Byler she was descended from, but she was curious. She put the phone in her pocket, but the Amish settlement link lurked in her mind. What if this were the right Jakob Byler from her family line? Had he been Amish? Was he related to Christian Byler, Rufus's ancestor?

Franey came through the door just then with a plate and a glass. She set them down on a small table next to the swing.

Annie had to admit the sandwich—ham and cheese stacked on whole-wheat bread she was sure Franey had baked herself—enticed her. For that matter, Franey had probably made the cheese and smoked the ham.

"Thank you." Annie reached for half of the sandwich.

"I hope you'll eat more than you have the last few days." Franey sat in the swing next to Annie. "I was beginning to worry about you."

"I feel much better," Annie said.

"*Gut.* Now you can discover God's purpose in bringing you to our home."

Had Franey been reading her mind? Annie glanced at the view again, almost ready to believe she was here for a reason. But the reason would have to wait. She could not afford to be Rick's doormat.

"I have my own business, but I can work anywhere if I have a computer and a phone." Annie bit into the sandwich and discovered how hungry she was.

"Then no doubt you'll need electricity soon."

"Yes I will." Annie watched the girls in the garden. "You have lovely daughters. Do they always work so hard?"

"They are good daughters." Franey leaned back in the swing and smiled. "Your *mudder* must be worried about you."

"I spoke to my mother." Technically this was true, though Annie had spared her mother the details of her dilemma and had not mentioned her injury.

"Here comes Rufus."

Rufus turned into the long driveway from the main road. Annie watched as Dolly pulled the buggy to the habitual spot outside the barn and stopped. Rufus lowered himself from the bench and walked toward the front porch.

Annie flushed when she saw him looking at her.

"I'm glad to see you up." Rufus did not smile, but he caught her eyes with an ease she did not expect.

"What's that in your hand?" Franey asked.

"It used to be my favorite saw." Rufus sank onto a porch step below the swing and stared out at the mountains. "Someone snapped it in half today."

"Oh Rufus, I'm sorry," Franey said. "I hate that these things keep happening to you."

"I just left it for a few minutes." He examined the broken pieces. "I guess it doesn't take long for someone to step on the end and yank the handle up."

"Someone is watching you," Annie said. "Someone saw an opportunity and took it. It's a message."

Rufus sighed. "I try to be mindful about who is around when I'm working, but I cannot see everyone."

"What about your crew?" Annie asked.

"My crew? A couple of Amish boys. I can't see what they would have to gain from breaking my tools."

"You never know," Annie said. "Sometimes the people closest to you are the ones you have to worry about."

Rufus turned his head toward Annie. "Be careful, Annalise. You might be giving me a clue about why you're here."

At that moment, Annie's phone rang in her pocket. She sprang off the swing—then winced in pain. Looking at the incoming number, she said, "I have to take this." With one hand holding the phone to her ear and the other supporting a sore spot in her back, she went down the steps and toward the barn for some privacy.

No matter how far she wandered, Annie felt Rufus's eyes on her while she spoke to attorney number two. Franey got up and went into the house, but Rufus sprawled statue-like on the porch steps, his elbows propped two steps behind him. In one hand, the metal of the broken saw glinted in the sun. The slump in his shoulders distracted her enough that she had to turn away from him to explain her legal challenge to the attorney. A few minutes later, she breathed a sigh of relief and started back toward the porch. Rufus had not moved.

"Would you be able to give me a ride into town tomorrow?" she asked. "I just arranged a meeting."

"I leave pretty early," Rufus reminded her.

"I'll be ready." Annie sat next to Rufus on the step.

"Are you sure you're well enough for this?"

"I have no choice."

"You always have a choice," he said.

Annie raised her eyes to the view. "It doesn't seem that way in this situation. It's complicated."

"So you've said."

"Can I ride with you or not?" Annie tightened her grip on the phone in her hand.

"Of course."

"Perhaps it's better if I move back to the motel anyway."

"You're welcome here."

"Thank you. Your family has been lovely and accommodating, but I think I should go."

"To the land of electricity."

"Well, yes. Electricity connects me to my life, after all."

"Or cuts you off from it, depending on how you look at it."

Annie did not respond. She fixed her eyes on the Sangre de Cristos. As remote as the Beiler house felt from her real life, the mountains beckoned into deeper mystery.

"The tea your mother brought me had ice cubes," Annie said, "and the lettuce on the sandwich was crisp and cool. How. . ."

"Propane gas refrigerator," Rufus said. "We heat water with propane, too."

"And the lamps are all propane?" Annie mentally pictured the lamps in Ruth's bedroom.

Rufus nodded. "The wringer washing machine runs off a gas engine. In Pennsylvania, my mother had a blender that ran off of compressed air. We use generators. And you'd be amazed what we can do with a few car batteries if we really want to."

"But no electricity." Annie's fingers itched to type "Amish

electricity" into a search window.

"We don't connect to the electrical grid," Rufus said. "Too much of modern life comes too fast when you do that."

"I can only imagine what you must think of my life."

"I know very little about your life," Rufus said, "but it got you here. You have to wonder about that."

"Believe me, I do," Annie said. "I'm meeting with a lawyer tomorrow. I hope to sort things out soon."

"I hope you get what you want."

"Maybe he could help you, too," Annie said. "Surely what you're experiencing constitutes harassment."

"Talking to a lawyer will not get me what I want."

"If this Karl Kramer would leave you alone, you could get on with your life," Annie said.

"I'll get on with my life either way."

He turned his head to look at her. His wide violet-blue eyes sparkled in the sunlight. Annie's breath caught.

"What is it?" Rufus asked. "Pain?"

She shook her head. "Your eyes. I suppose you know how striking they are."

He tilted his head. "I'm told they are my grandmother's eyes, and her grandmother before that."

She felt his eyes on her then, considering her.

"It's good you're staying another night," he said. "How about if I take you to town tomorrow, you have your meeting and your electricity, and then you come back here for one more night? Just to be sure."

Annie nodded, transfixed. As much as she needed a dose of electricity, she wanted to return to this peacefulness.

He leaned forward and prepared to stand. "I'd better round up Jacob and check on the animals."

"Can I come?"

Eleven

*D*olly crunched the apple while Rufus stroked the spot between her eyes the next morning. He had hitched the larger buggy. It would be more comfortable for Annalise. Rufus still wished he could talk her into resting one more day. What was so important that it could not wait for her to be stronger tomorrow?

The sound of giggling made him lift his hand from Dolly's face and turn toward the barn. Jacob shot out of the structure with a grin on his ruddy face.

"Annalise doesn't know how to milk a cow." Jacob raised a hand to smother his laughter.

Annalise emerged from the barn, flanked by Sophie and Lydia. "I'm afraid it's true. I haven't been near a cow for twenty years—until now."

"I'm going to teach her," Sophie said. "You'll be back in time for the evening milking, won't you?"

Rufus raised his eyebrows. "I believe so."

"Let's start with just *touching* a cow, all right?" Annalise smiled. "I'm not making any promises."

She was at ease with his siblings, which brought unexpected

83

relief to Rufus. Her ponytail bounced in the morning light, and Rufus could hardly tear his gaze away. "We should be going."

Annalise took the hand Rufus offered, and he helped her up and onto the buggy bench. Having her there, beside him, as he took Dolly onto the road, made him grasp for conversation. He hoped for something they might find in common, but nothing took solid shape. Instead, he remembered her form in his arms as he carried her to the buggy outside the motel, and later up the stairs to Ruth's bedroom, her face close to his.

Rufus glanced at Annalise, and she smiled awkwardly, as if she were reading his mind. Both of them looked away.

He had to speak. "This meeting will solve your troubles, *ya*?"

She tilted her head. "I hope at least to have an ally by the time it's over."

"Then there is to be a battle?"

"Perhaps *confrontation* is a better word. It's complicated."

"Yes, I remember." She did not believe he could understand her business troubles. Perhaps she was right. "At least the cow will be waiting for you when this day is behind you."

She laughed. "That's bound to be a confrontation of a different sort."

"The *English* have farms," he said. "Surely you have some experience."

"I went to a dairy farm on a school field trip once. Six hundred cows. Machines everywhere."

"Perhaps your visit here gives you a different perspective of the quiet life." Rufus turned her head to see her face.

Annalise met his gaze with a smile. "It's quite tempting to consider that—on many levels. I will know more after this meeting."

The front left buggy wheel hit a hole in the pavement, and Annalise winced at the sudden dip.

"You are still sore," Rufus said.

"Yes, but clear of mind."

Annie chose a table in the coffee shop away from the commotion at the counter and sat in a chair facing the door. The power cord ran from her laptop into the outlet beneath the table. She eyed with satisfaction the icon on her screen that assured her juice was flowing. Her meeting with the attorney was not for two hours, but she had plenty of work to catch up on. She had not said much to Lee Solano on the phone the day before and was leery that someone immediately available and willing to meet her in a small-town coffee shop rather than his own office was desperate for work. What did that say about his practice? But the others had not returned her inquiry calls, making him her only option.

Housed in a beige brick building, the imitation Starbucks coffee and tea shop could have been anywhere in the country with roots from two centuries earlier. With a tall caramel latte within reach, Annie attacked her e-mail backlog. Scanning, she could tell which ones would be simple to answer. A good number she could easily redirect to her software writers. A few were starting to sound snippy about her lack of a timely response. One by one she placated the clients who depended on her technical services.

The company's ongoing bread-and-butter work was writing custom programs with focused objectives that clients identified for themselves. The solutions she found, however, eventually became joints and tendons of the consumer patterns software she now had stashed on a secure server.

On a typical day in the office, Annie would dispense with administrative tasks fairly quickly, motivated by the anticipation of working on the new project as many hours of the day as possible. Barrett would be in his office next door. He did less and less programming and more and more marketing and seemed happy with the arrangement.

Until a few weeks ago. The morning banter ceased. When Barrett refilled his coffee mug, he passed by her open door without a greeting. At the end of the day, he was out the door without stopping in to say good night. It was true he had a wife and baby at home, but that had never gnawed into his extroverted socializing before.

Annie missed the old Barrett.

The string of e-mail messages from Jamie, her assistant, kept Annie informed of routine matters. Jamie was a solid anchor whenever Annie traveled. This absence was no different. Some messages, however, carried an undertone that said, *Please call me.*

Annie wrapped her fingers around her cell phone, which had been turned off most of the time for days. As little as she knew about the Amish, she knew a phone ringing as constantly as hers did would be unwelcome. Now she turned it on. To no surprise, the voice-mail box was full and text messages nearly cascaded off the screen to the floor. Annie ignored them all and dialed Jamie's number.

"Friesen-Paige Solutions," Jamie said.

"Don't let on, but it's me," Annie said.

"How may I help you?" Jamie said evenly.

"Go next door to the doughnut shop. Call me from there."

Annie put the phone down on the table and stared at it, mentally picturing Jamie casually stepping out from behind her desk and leaving the suite then the redbrick building. It was nothing unusual for Jamie to make a doughnut run.

The phone rang, and Annie snatched it up. "Jamie?"

"Annie, what's going on? I opened an envelope from the lawyers today, expecting something routine. But you're named as a defendant in a suit, and Barrett is the plaintiff. Is this some kind of joke?"

Annie's shoulders slumped. "I wish."

"Did you and Barrett have a fight?"

"Not exactly," Annie said.

"Rick drew up these papers," Jamie said. "I thought you and Rick—"

"Not anymore. That's over."

"Oh. Sorry."

"Don't be. Listen, Jamie, I don't know when I'll be back to the office. I'm going to work from where I am for a while."

"And where are you?" Jamie asked.

"That doesn't matter." It was better if Jamie did not know. "I promise to stay in touch. Do me a favor and watch for any funny business on my credit cards or debit card."

"This all sounds very cloak and dagger," Jamie said.

"I'm just being careful."

"What should I do about the papers Rick sent over?"

"Scan them and e-mail them to me. Can you do that in the next few minutes?"

"Yes, of course."

"I've been through my e-mail. Any other fires I should know about?"

They talked for a few more minutes about routine matters. Barrett was staying away from the office, Annie was glad to hear.

"Thanks, Jamie," Annie said. "Don't forget to take doughnuts back to the office with you."

Annie ended the call. A lawsuit. So that is what it had come to. Barrett stopped talking to her, and Rick—who supposedly loved her—chose sides and cast her away.

Why would Barrett do this? He knew they had a good thing going. They were both making great money. He never once hinted that anything was wrong.

Perhaps Rick had been planning this for months. Their first date, the sweetness of their first kiss, the hunger in the ones that followed—maybe it was all about the company. And when Rick saw that she was too savvy to do anything careless—such as sign a document she had not read carefully—he turned to Barrett. With his affable, trusting nature, Barrett was an easy target. Any number of arguments coming from the mouth of the firm's legal representation could persuade Barrett to hack into Annie's work.

Annie steamed. To think that she had ever trusted Rick Stebbins, and even let herself care about him. Poor Barrett. No matter how Rick had lured him in, Barrett's pride would not let him back out now.

The main door to the coffee shop opened and a man in a gray suit entered. Annie stood and fixed her eyes on him. It wasn't a very good suit and did not fit well. The man pushed sunglasses off his face to the top of his balding head. In a few seconds, he figured out who his client was. They introduced themselves with a handshake, and Lee Solano went to the counter to buy the socially obligatory coffee that would entitle him to conduct business on the premises.

Annie had asked questions about his practice and experience the day before on the phone. Now she probed further. She had to be as sure as possible that Lee Solano was outside Rick's sphere of influence, and she had to feel confident he understood what was at stake in an intellectual property matter—now a lawsuit. When she was as satisfied as she could be under the circumstances, Annie blew out her breath and began her story. Lee Solano dutifully took notes with a cheap pen on a classic yellow legal pad. Just as she finished, a new e-mail dinged in. Jamie had sent the attachment.

Annie opened it and turned her screen toward Lee. "Can they do this?"

Lee squinted as he scrolled through the document.

"What does he want?" Annie asked.

"Everything," Lee answered quickly. "You must have some serious work going on. This Barrett fellow claims his creative contribution was the impetus leading to the work, and that without it the work would not exist. On that basis, he wants your name separated from the work, leaving him free to pursue legal agreements involving the work without requiring your permission."

"I don't understand. We're partners. We run a company together."

"He's making the claim that this particular work does not

fall within the boundaries established by your partnership. I would have to see your partnership incorporation documents to comment on that."

"But that's ridiculous." Annie took a gulp of coffee. "Barrett and I have worked together for years. We have different strengths, but we share the profit equally."

Lee shrugged. "Existing intellectual property laws were developed decades ago without any glimmer of application to software. Intellectual property used to be about words and music and art. Entries like software take some thrashing out in the courts. I'm afraid we're a long way from having clear application of the law under either copyright or patents."

"Where does that leave me?" Annie swallowed hard.

"We'll start with a countersuit," Lee said, "and I'll bury Mr. Stebbins in paperwork. But our best bet is to find some way to keep this from going to court. Don't worry, Miss Friesen. You've got someone on your side now."

Rufus spent the morning making sure the custom cabinets installed throughout the house under construction were exactly as ordered and that no damage had occurred to the black oak panels. A flooring company from Walsenburg was in the midst of installing carpets and hardwoods. It would not be long now before the family could move in.

Rufus collected his tools and laid them carefully in the back of the buggy. The two teenagers who worked for him were gone for the day. Rufus had a few fix-it jobs around town, and the Amish families in the valley always seemed to require a carpenter, but he needed another big job. Under his father's skill and Joel's help, the farm was doing as well as could be expected in the arid Colorado climate but not turning much of a profit. Coaxing growth from seeds in the ground seemed to require a different set of farming habits than in Pennsylvania. The dry air and soil left a lot for the

Beilers to learn about farming in the West, rather than in the long-tested soil of Lancaster County, Pennsylvania. Land might be cheaper in Colorado, but it was also more stubborn.

He was not unhappy with his business prospects, but lately they had grown thinner, making Rufus wonder what Karl Kramer was telling people about him. The Amish community was still small. Rufus needed jobs from the *English* to build a profitable business.

Rufus swung up onto the bench, picked up the reins, and directed Dolly into town. For a few minutes, he sat in the buggy in front of the coffee shop. He had heard of people who spent hours in coffee shops and could well imagine Annalise as one of them. After securing Dolly to a signpost cemented into the sidewalk, he reached under the seat for an item then pulled open the shop door.

She looked up almost immediately. And smiled.

Rufus pulled out the chair across from her and sat down. In his hand was his cell phone and the power cord. Behind a sober face, he gave in to amusement at her wide eyes.

"You're using a phone *and* electricity?"

"I promised to tell you our views on electricity."

"By using it in a public place?"

"Electricity is a useful form of power. We recognize that. We simply do not want electricity to become the focus of our lives by bringing it into our homes. That is the place of our families."

"And the phone?"

"Our district has a generous position on phones because we are so widely scattered. We are permitted to use phones for business and safety."

"But not convenience?"

"Convenience is for the individual. For us, the community comes first. If electricity or a phone carries us away from community, it also carries us away from God."

"I never thought of it like that." Annalise fidgeted with a pen on the table.

"You can ask any questions you wish."

"Thank you. Maybe when I don't have so much on my mind. . ."

"Of course. How did your business meeting go?"

She laid her head to one side, and her loose hair danced in the light as it fell away from her face. If he never married, he would never see a woman's hair fall away from her ear in just that way and be able to reach out and catch it.

"It went well," she said. "We have a plan of action." As if she could read his thoughts—for the second time that day—she smoothed her hair close to her head and tucked it behind her ear.

"And will this plan of action carry you home—to your own community?"

She pressed her lips together. "I hope so."

Annalise did not quite meet his eyes this time. "I promised Mo I would stop by the motel," he said, "but I can enjoy a cup of *kaffi* first."

They did not leave the coffee shop for another hour. When they reached the motel, Rufus helped Annalise down once again. Her pale complexion told him she was more tired than she would admit.

The door of the motel lobby swung open, and Mo emerged. "Well, if it isn't our star guest. How are you?"

Annalise managed a smile, Rufus was glad to see.

"How is your mother?" Annalise asked.

"Cranky as ever, but the crisis is averted for now." Mo turned to Rufus. "Just the man I want to see. I've had a vision of remodeling the lobby, and you're just the person for the job."

In the lobby, Annalise stood to one side and held her computer to her chest, glancing at him from time to time as Mo gestured and explained. Rufus hardly heard a word Mo said about the work.

"Do it!" Jacob urged.

Annalise grimaced. Rufus spread hay.

"*Die Kuh*," the little boy said, "and it's a very nice cow." He leaned his head into the side of the cow, next to where Sophie sat on a three-legged stool.

"Her face is pretty," Annalise said. Both of the animal's pink ears stood up straight. Between her eyes a white stripe divided a mass of brown.

"Touch her nose," Jacob said. "She likes that."

"Jacob," Rufus said softly, "if Annalise does not want to touch the cow, she does not have to." It was, after all, a texture bearing no resemblance to her sleek laptop keys.

"It's not that I don't want to," Annalise said. "It's just not as simple as it sounds."

"I must start milking soon," Sophie said. "Please don't startle her."

Annalise's hand moved, slowly, toward the white stripe. When the cow moaned, she flinched but immediately resumed her purpose.

Rufus smiled and tossed a pitchfork of hay into Dolly's stall, glad to see Annalise's determined spirit on display in a cow stall as well as a coffee shop.

Two slender fingers made contact in the space between the cow's eyes and nose, and a moment later, a full hand began a soothing stroking motion.

"It feels harder than I thought it would," Annalise said.

His sisters were giggling, and Annalise's laugh blended with the sound.

She relaxed. He saw it. Rufus leaned on his pitchfork and savored this image of Annalise Friesen in his barn with members of his family. Even the denim bag slid off her shoulder and nested in the hay as she now rubbed the sides of the cow's face with both hands.

Twelve

Annie wrestled dreams that night and woke more than once hoping for daylight to creep through the curtains in Ruth's bedroom. Finally, she sat up and turned on the propane bedside lamp. She was beginning to miss the pillow-topped mattress in her condo, surrounded by familiar possessions.

She had spotted three thrift stores in Westcliffe—which she found curious given the insignificant size of the town—so she had some options to find more clothing. It looked as if she would be here another few days while Lee Solano conjured whatever kind of magic he had in his power. For now, his instructions were for Annie to lie low and not show any response to Rick's legal maneuvers. Returning to Mo's motel would at least put electricity on her side. She was taking a break, she told herself, a short break that would save her business.

She threw back the quilt and stepped to the desk four feet away to power up her laptop. For now she ignored her e-mail, but she could not resist checking her secure server. It looked as if Barrett had been knocking around the edges of the project but had not gotten through the barricades she had in place.

Annie smiled. All this time and he wasn't making a dent. She touched a hand to her neck to finger the gold chain—and felt nothing but skin.

Panicked, Annie opened every drawer in the room and unfolded her paltry wardrobe. She dumped her denim bag onto the bed and separated the contents for inspection. Not finding the gold chain, she bolted to the bathroom across the hall, trying to remember everything she had touched in the last few days. Annie could not even remember the last time she had been sure the chain was around her neck.

She sank into the bed to wait for first light.

Rufus moved the envelope aside as he had done dozens of times already and rummaged for a pencil in his toolbox. The letter had arrived five days ago. Rufus was not sure he wanted to know what it said. Ruth repeatedly wrote to him in care of Tom and Tricia, so he could only conclude she did not want their parents to know of the letters.

What happened was between Ruth and *Daed* and *Mamm.* Rufus did not want to find himself in the middle. And he did not think it was a good idea to involve Tom and Tricia even just to deliver a letter that arrived at their home.

Ruth had taken almost nothing with her that day. Rufus was never sure if it was because she did not truly intend to go or because she did not want to be beholden to anyone, not even for a change of clothes.

Rufus missed her. Ruth was the sister nearest to him in age, though two married brothers filled the span between them. When he raised the question of moving to Colorado, Ruth was the first to say she wanted to go. His married brothers thought Rufus ought to at least find a wife before heading out for a new settlement. When his parents decided they were in favor of the move because it could mean land for their younger sons, Rufus's determination set in.

In Colorado, the chances of finding a wife among the Amish—
the only wife Rufus could accept—were far from encouraging. He
was already twenty-eight and was still required to keep his face
clean shaven and sit in church with the younger unmarried men.
If it was God's will for Rufus to be alone, so be it. He would still
work hard for the sake of his family.

Mo made it clear the previous afternoon that she was not
looking for bids on the work she had in mind. She wanted Rufus.
He had done enough odd jobs to prove he was dependable and
honest, she said, and she had seen his cabinetry craftsmanship in
the home of a friend. Mo was finished repairing falling shelves.
She wanted new ones. A new reception desk. New cubbies behind
the desk. Perhaps a new look for the small lobby that would appeal
to more upscale customers.

In his workshop across the yard from the barn, Rufus sketched
the lobby from memory before breakfast. A vision emerged as his
pencil skittered across the page, shading in cabinetry and a desk
with rounded, welcoming edges. The day before, Mo gestured widely
with her own ideas, but they were vague. Rufus's sketch would
accomplish her objectives and improve the traffic flow through the
lobby as well.

Engrossed in the task of putting his vision on paper, Rufus did
not hear Annalise approach the open door of his workshop.

"Hi, Rufus."

He turned toward her approaching brightness as he ripped the
page from the pad in satisfaction. "*Guder mariye*, Annalise. Are
you hungry for breakfast?"

"Famished," Annalise said. She looked around. "So, this is
where you work?"

Her shoulders and back looked less tentative. Her hair hung
loose, cradling her face in softness before draping her shoulders
with its sheen. Rufus turned his gaze away, abruptly aware of the
effect she was having on him.

"I am a simple cabinetmaker and carpenter."

She touched a small chest awaiting its lid. "It's beautiful."

Suddenly he wanted to give it to her, but he had promised it to Sophie.

"I'm missing the gold chain I always wear," Annalise said, her hand at her unadorned neck. "I wonder if you've seen it."

Rufus slapped his own head. "It's not lost. They removed it at the clinic when they were doing X-rays. Sophie found it in the bag when she washed your things. She was afraid of losing it, so she brought to me." Rufus suppressed the warmth that came with thinking about holding the chain in his hand.

"You have my chain?"

"It's in the buggy," Rufus said, "in a box under the bench. It did not seem right to have it in the house. Our women do not wear jewelry. I'm sorry I forgot about it."

"Can I go get it?"

"I will get it. Just wait here."

Rufus dropped his pencil and sketch into his toolbox and disappeared out the front of the building, leaving Annie standing alone in the workshop. She buzzed her lips and looked around for a place to sit down, settling on a low, rugged bench beside the door.

Curious, Annie tilted her head to try to look at Rufus's sketch, but he had laid it facedown. All she could see were the impressions of the heaviest lines making slight ridges in the back of the paper. An envelope obscured the bottom of the page. Annie did not have to look too hard to read the writing on the sealed message. The top left corner clearly said "Ruth Beiler" with an address in Colorado Springs. Annie recognized the street name. It was just off a major intersection she drove through several times a week.

Rufus came through the door. Annie stood and moved toward him. He opened a small plastic envelope and poured the gold chain into her open hand. She closed her fist around the gold, brushing his fingers in the process. Was it her imagination, or did his hand quiver just once?

"Thank you!" She opened the clasp and raised the chain to her neck. Her hands met at the back of her neck and buoyed her hair for a moment while she fastened the clasp.

"You're welcome." Rufus closed his own hand over the small plastic bag, now empty. "I'm sorry I didn't remember sooner. It seems to mean something to you."

"It's twenty-four-karat gold. I bought it when—" Annie stopped herself. Rufus would not be interested in how she celebrated making her fortune. "Never mind. Just thank you."

"We should go have breakfast."

"Yes." Annie paused. "I do have one question, though."

"Of course."

"Why haven't you opened that letter from your sister?"

Ruth Beiler flipped back to the beginning of the chapter in her textbook. After reading for forty minutes, she would be hard pressed to write a paragraph identifying the chapter's main themes. In four hours she had to be in class ready to take a quiz. Starting over was the obvious choice.

Thinking coffee might help her concentrate, she rose from the chair and moved to the wide ledge under the window that held a small coffeemaker and an electric kettle. Ruth's dorm room was compact, but it was private. When she first arrived, she tried living with a roommate, with disastrous results. The young woman assigned to share a room with her did not know what to make of someone with such conservative views and habits. Though they were both nursing students at the University of Colorado, they found little common ground.

In those days Ruth still wore her *kapp*. Now it hung on a hook by the door, and she had traded in her aproned dress for simple long skirts and high-necked solid-colored tops. Her hair was still in braids coiled against the back of her head. She stood out when she walked across campus or boarded a bus to go to her job at the nursing home, but becoming modern had never been Ruth's intention when she left Westcliffe.

Ruth scooped coffee into a fresh filter and poured water through the small coffeemaker. In a few seconds, the familiar dripping began. She absently tapped the top of the pot while she pondered what really kept her from studying.

If Rufus had read her letter and answered it right away, she would have heard from him by now.

And what if he never read it?

Ruth wasn't sorry. Her choice was not without consequence. She regretted the pain she caused. But she would choose the same again.

It was an impulse on his part to invite her, Annie was sure. And it was an impulse on her part to accept. Perhaps he regretted it. She would not blame him. Spiritual devotion had little to do with why she accepted, and neither did curiosity.

Little Jacob was glad to see her when Rufus brought the small buggy to pick her up on Sunday morning. The rest of the family would come in the larger buggy pulled by Brownie, the second Beiler horse. Jacob chattered away the miles between the motel and the farm where a cluster of six or eight Amish families would gather to worship.

Church, Amish-style.

Annie's Protestant upbringing included more or less weekly church attendance. She carried fond memories of going to church and the people who cared for her there. In high school, though, training for track competitions dominated her schedule, and then she went away to college. As an adult, her churchgoing habit was a long way from regular. A few months earlier, though, she had attended a friend's baptism. In her teen years, Annie always intended to be baptized, but the timing never seemed right.

She believed. Certainly she never decided *not* to believe. But getting an education and launching a career—and starting two companies—required focus. Time. Energy. Now she wondered if she had moved too far away from God for it to matter that she had not been baptized.

Supposing that God still spoke English, Annie decided to pray. After all, she was in church. *Please, God, make this mean something.*

Annie now sat on a bench in the back on the women's side of the room. Rufus gave her enough notice that she was able to rustle up a modest skirt among her thrift-store finds. People around her spoke German, including Rufus's mother and two younger sisters. The idea of going to church with Rufus should have made her think twice. If she had known the service would be in German and she would not even be sitting with Rufus, she might have thought three times.

Sophie leaned over and whispered into Annie's ear. Annie quickly tucked her gold chain under the top of her blouse. She had a lot to learn about Amish worship.

The women faced the men. Annie wanted to shift to one side and look for Rufus among the unmarried men—all of them younger than he was. Perhaps she could catch his eye. But she knew better than to wiggle in church. Rufus mentioned that the services tended to be long, but Annie never imagined he meant three hours and two sermons.

With no hint of modernity in the service, Annie supposed the Amish had always worshiped this way, even in the days of the first settlers to land in Pennsylvania. She made a mental note to do a fresh Internet search on "early Amish worship" as soon as it was appropriate to use her phone.

At last the final hymn began with a single male voice. Others gradually joined. Sophie shared a battered hymnal with Annie, but the page held only German words that meant nothing to Annie. Everyone seemed to know the tune.

Annie filed outside with the other women. It wasn't long before the transformation was under way to accommodate a meal for sixty people. Annie just tried to stay out of the way as men rearranged benches and women arranged dishes on three serving tables. Sophie and Lydia greeted friends they only saw every two weeks at church before being prodded to help with the food. Annie watched the constant movement, but she was at a loss for how to step in and help. Instead, she wandered farther away, past the row where the horses were tied and out to a fence around a field. In a brief episode of English, someone had mentioned that the host family grew barley.

In the middle of the commotion, Annie was relieved to find Rufus walking toward her.

"You might have prepared me a bit more," she said playfully.

"Would you have come if I had?" He looked over his shoulder, and she followed his eye toward men standing in a group.

She shrugged. "Now we'll never know."

"Was it torture?"

"Let's just say my High German is not any better than my Pennsylvania Dutch."

"When you learn one, you will no doubt learn the other."

When. He said "when." Annie soaked up his countenance. These were his people. This was his life. And he had honored her by inviting her to share it for these few hours.

"Are you hungry?" His face crinkled.

"Let me guess," Annie said. "Men eat separately from women."

"You are learning our ways well."

"The ways are new to me, but I have a feeling they are very old."

Rufus adjusted his black felt hat. "We do not rush into change."

"But you do change, don't you?" Annie gestured toward the house. "Lights, hot running water. This is not exactly camping out."

"We consider our choices carefully. Are they good for the family? For the community? Our old ways remind us that we live apart, separate from the ways of the world."

Annie resisted the impulse to raise her fingers to her gold chain. "Yet when I blundered in bringing the twenty-first century with me, you welcomed me."

"We welcome anyone who seeks truth."

Annie's reply caught in her throat. Perhaps he was right. Perhaps she wanted more from Westcliffe than a place to hide from Rick Stebbins. She could have gone somewhere else when she had the chance. And yet she was here.

"Maybe after lunch you could give me the abbreviated English version of the sermon."

"Which one?" He grinned.

"The one you think would do me the most good."

A voice boomed from beyond them. The only word Annie could pick out was Rufus's name.

"They need my help," he said.

She nodded, and he walked backward away from her, smiling. She again watched the activity, mesmerized by how little it must have changed in the last couple of hundred years.

Thirteen

October 8, 1737

I want to go right now." Maria pulled on her brother's hand.

Christian held his position solidly. "We can't. We just have to wait a little while longer."

"No more waiting!" Maria hollered.

Christian clamped a hand over her mouth and turned her around to face him. "Maria Beyeler, you hush," he hissed. "This is important."

This was no time for child's play. While he knew Maria was too young to appreciate the solemnity, Christian did not intend to miss the moment. The ship's deck was at capacity with families ready to debark after one last formality.

Captain Stedman lined up the men, sixteen years or older, and prepared them to march off the ship.

"Why can't we go?" Maria wanted to know.

"It's the law," Christian said. "First *Daed* has to promise to be a good subject to the king of England. We have to wait for him to come back."

"I'm tired of waiting." Maria stomped away, and Christian let her. He could see she was headed for their mother, standing only a few yards away. He was tired of waiting, too.

When the men began filing off the ship, the officials watched them carefully. Small boys were another matter, Christian realized. At the moment, no one cared what he did. His heart pounding in triumph, he found himself on the pier a few minutes later. He could see his father's height among the throng of men and ran sideways to keep up with the march yet not lose sight of his *daed*. The words the men spoke would mark their decisions to settle in the New World, and Christian wanted to see his father's face when he took the oath.

Christian felt his feet lift from the ground as his shirt tangled around his neck. "*Daed*!" he screamed.

A gruff, middle-aged man picked Christian up and set him atop a barrel on the pier. His red face spouted angry English words, and he shook his finger in the boy's face, but all Christian could do was shrug.

"*Daed*!" Christian screamed again before the man clamped his hand on Christian's mouth.

The man pointed toward what looked like a market to Christian—but they were selling people. Christian remembered his parents had said they were fortunate to have funds to pay for their passage, while others crossed the ocean as redemptioners who would work for years to redeem the price of their journey. Panicking, he struggled against the man's grip.

Christian managed to free his face. "Amish!" he shouted, "Amish!"

The man stepped back to look at him more closely.

And then Jakob was there, scooping up his son. He rattled at the man in German. The man screeched at him in English. Christian clung to his father, and Jakob hustled to rejoin the march before anyone could stop them.

"What were you thinking?" Jakob had a firm grip on the back of Christian's shirt.

"I just wanted to see you take the oath," Christian said.

"You almost got yourself sold as an indentured servant," Jakob said. "I'm sure he thought you stowed away on the ship. The men who run these shipping lines are not known for their mercy toward boys who are able-bodied workers."

"*Es dutt mirr leed*," Christian said. Triumph dissipated into shame. "I'm sorry. Please forgive me."

"I do forgive you." Jakob did not break stride. "But you must be more careful."

There was no going back now. Shamed or not, Christian would see his father swear allegiance to King George. The oath would be in English, which amused Christian, because his father knew only about two dozen words of the language, which he had picked up from the crew of the *Charming Nancy*.

At the courthouse, an official with a sheet of paper for reference began to call out phrases, which the men, whether Amish or Mennonite, in a collective rich bass, echoed.

We subscribers, natives and the late inhabitants of the Palatinate upon the Rhine and places adjacent, having transported ourselves and families into the Province of Pennsylvania, a Colony subject to the Crown of Great Britain, in hopes and expectation of finding a retreat and peaceable Settlement therein, do solemnly promise and engage that we will be faithful and bear true allegiance to his present majesty King George the Second and his successors, kings of Great Britain, and will be faithful to the proprietor of this province and that we will demean ourselves peaceably to all his said majesty's subjects and strictly observe and conform to the laws of England and of this province to the utmost of our power and best of our understanding.

A thunderous cheer rose from the men, Christian's voice among them. He caught his father's eye and grinned.

Verona was frantic when she discovered Christian gone, but Jakob managed to calm her when he returned to the ship with their son. Now the family stood in line to debark. As they inched forward, Jakob shoved the heavier barrel and the older children managed the lighter one together. Verona cradled the subdued Lisbetli and gripped Maria's hand as much as she could. In addition to the barrels, they had three small trunks that Jakob hefted easily one at a time and bundles the children carried.

This was what it came down to. Fifteen years of marriage, five children, a life of being ostracized for daring to stand by their beliefs, and what she had to show for it was right before her eyes in shades of gray and brown crammed into barrels and bundles. Everything she had for setting up housekeeping in a wilderness was within her reach.

On the ship, Verona had traded away a few items for things that seemed more pressing at the time. When Christian wanted a book of botany descriptions that no longer amused the Stutzman boy, Verona parted with a tin platter. When Maria fell in love with a small bucket, Verona parted with two wooden spoons. She could do so little to give her children pleasure during the months at sea. Trades among passengers seemed to provide diversion that made the journey less tedious. Jakob assured her they could find what they needed in Philadelphia. Ships came in every week bearing goods from Europe and the Caribbean, and he had budgeted funds for bedding and a few simple pieces of furniture.

Verona absently let go of Maria and put her hand to her own forehead, not sure whether it was her hand or her face that was clammy. The headache that began several hours ago had not abated, but the demands of getting the family ready to leave the ship left her no time to indulge in rest.

"Maria, come back here," Barbara called. "We have to wait in line."

Verona snapped to attention, only now realizing that Maria had left her sight.

"No more waiting!" Maria pouted. But to Verona's relief, she returned.

One by one the passengers filed past a makeshift table where their names were checked off lists. Jakob gave the sonorous announcement of his name and the names of everyone in the family. Barbara stood at his side, her eyes flicking from one set of papers to another and watching pens scratch and spill ink. Finally, Jakob turned and grinned at Verona, signaling their freedom.

"*Daed*," Barbara said, "they didn't spell our names right."

"What does it matter?" Jakob said. "We know our names."

"But the ship's list says *Biler*. And I saw a man write *Byler*." She spelled the difference aloud.

Jakob chuckled. "They've made us sound properly English."

It was not easy getting their meager belongings lowered to the dock. At one point, Verona handed the baby to Barbara because her own arms were too unsteady to carry her, much less help hoist the barrels and bundles. She wanted only to close her eyes and lie down. As soon as the first crate was upright on the dock, Verona sat on it and settled Lisbetli in her lap once again.

As anxious as everyone had been to get off the boat, now they looked lost. Verona's ears were unaccustomed to the sound of English coming from wharf workers, and her head hurt too much to try to make sense of the strange words. Passengers huddled with their earthly possessions and spoke their comfortable German. A few experimented with walking on solid ground again, while others sat on their trunks and looked around, trying to get their bearings. Verona sat with her back to the ship with its masts and sails and rigging. She was not sure what she expected of Philadelphia, but not this. Dozens of piers protruded into the Delaware River. Each was a hive of activity. Sailors roamed while stevedores moved goods off and on ships. Laborers pushed carts laden with goods. Horses pulled against the weight of wagons.

Beyond the docks, brick and clapboard structures looked solid, for which Verona was grateful, but also they were also foreign and unfamiliar.

Two mothers clutched each other in a moment of grief. Verona recognized them. Between them they had lost a husband and four children during the journey. Gratitude for the safety of her family stabbed her heart. Was it selfish to be glad her husband and children were walking around on the dock when so many had been lost? She squeezed Lisbetli tighter.

Jakob paused to catch his breath. Two barrels, three trunks, assorted bundles. Everything seemed accounted for. Around them, families gradually made their way off the dock at various paces. It was time for him to sort out his own family's next move.

"Where will we go now, *Daed*?" Anna asked.

"I have an address," Jakob answered. "An English Quaker family rents out houses to Germans and Swiss. We will be comfortable waiting there."

"No more waiting!" Maria stomped her foot. "I want to go to the new farm right now."

"Shhh." Verona beckoned the protesting child to her side.

Jakob tilted his head and considered his wife. He had expected her to be more animated upon arrival. She sat on the top of the barrel, gripping Lisbetli, staring without focus.

"We have to wait, Maria." Christian's voice carried an authority Jakob had not heard before. "It takes time to get the papers for the farm."

"How much time?" Maria wanted to know.

"That's hard to say," Jakob said. "First I have to apply for a land grant, and then we'll have to wait for a survey."

"I want to grow beets."

"I'm afraid you'll have to wait until spring to plant your beets."

"How long until spring?" Maria stamped her foot.

"About six months."

"I don't want to wait."

"You have no choice," Christian said. "*Daed*, we need to hire a wagon, don't we? Someone who can take us to the address?"

Jakob nodded. "It's a German part of town. Some of our families from the ship will be nearby."

"I'll go up to the road and find a wagon," Christian said.

"We'll go together," Jakob said. He was not about to let his only son run off unattended again. "Perhaps we can share a wagon with the Zimmermans."

Jakob hoped the information he received was reliable. If it was not, he would not know where to go. Although they came from England and not the Continent, the Quaker owners of the house had some sympathy for another religious group that simply sought freedom. Jakob carried a letter of reference from their sponsoring family in Rotterdam to ease introductions in the new land. The immediate challenge was to negotiate with a wagon driver. Jakob listened for every snatch of German around him.

Maria and Anna were stomping on the dock in glee, as if testing to see if it would remain solid. Jakob laughed, happy to let them dispel their excitement before corralling them into a wagon. Lisbetli began to whimper in her mother's arms, and Jakob reached for the baby.

"She's taking too long to get well," Verona said softly.

"She'll be fine." Jakob laid his cheek against the baby's head. "We're here now. Everybody is going to be fine."

"Maria, come back," Anna's voice called after her restless little sister, who had darted into the throng making their way up the dock. Anna turned to her parents. "I can't see her anymore!"

Jakob glanced at Verona, as if to ask which of them would chase Maria.

Verona paled and slumped. A second later, she slid off the crate, unconscious.

Fourteen

No matter how early Annie walked through the foyer to the dining room for breakfast, Rufus was already at work. He measured and calculated and sketched and spread wood samples around, evaluating the natural light.

Eight days.

Eight days since she fled the threat to her livelihood. Eight days since meeting the Beiler family and wondering about her own Byler family history. Eight days since she looked into those violet-blue eyes for the first time. Annie shook off the sensation that came with that memory. She had moved back to the motel, where Rufus had begun the remodeling project with steadfast attention to detail.

Lee Solano had hurled a wall of paperwork against Richard D. Stebbins and successfully postponed the court date assigned to the suit Rick filed. This gave Annie time to build a case to strike back. Rick stopped trying to contact her, and Barrett seemed to have ceased trying to hack her system. Annie breathed easier and had begun to use her credit card when she ventured into town.

Today Rufus was on his knees inspecting the back of the reception desk when Annie approached the lobby with her bag over her shoulder. She slowed her steps for a moment and watched him, wishing that she could see him in his workshop crafting form and function together.

"Good morning, Rufus," Annie said.

He nearly bumped his head getting himself turned around to greet her. "*Guder mariye.*" He gestured toward the desk. "It will take three men to get the desk out."

"Are you at that stage already?"

"No. I just like to be prepared when it's time."

"How is your family?" Annie asked.

"They are well, thank you. Jacob asks about you every day."

"He's a sweet boy. Give him my best greetings."

"Perhaps you would like to do that yourself tonight at supper." He tilted his head. "It would make Jacob happy."

"Then by all means." Annie would have accepted the invitation on any excuse. Was it possible that she missed the farm?

"We will go together from here at six o'clock."

Annie nodded. "That's fine."

Rufus turned back to the dilemma of how to remove the desk, and Annie went into the dining room to pick up an apple and a blueberry muffin to eat while she walked to town. Meaning no offense to Mo, who made passable coffee at the motel, Annie was holding out for the more robust offering of the coffee shop. In only a few days, she had formed the habit of spending her mornings there with her laptop.

Annie settled in with a mocha caramel grande nonfat latte and flipped open her computer. In a few seconds the Internet connection icon went solid and she was online, scrolling through her e-mail looking for messages from Jamie or Lee Solano. A grunt at the next table seemed just purposeful enough to make her look up.

"You have a cool computer." A teenage boy slouched in his chair, his knees sticks poking out of baggy green shorts.

"Thank you," Annie said, unsure if she wanted to encourage conversation. He looked to be about fourteen with a stereotypical adolescent chip on his shoulder.

"I really need a computer," the boy said, "but my parents say we can't afford it."

"Don't you have any computer at home?"

"Just a stupid desktop that's like, ancient. It's almost three years old. My dad says it's good enough for homework and he doesn't have money to throw around on a computer every time something new and better comes along."

Annie twisted her lips to one side. "I guess it can get expensive."

"No kidding. I've tried to find a job, but there aren't any around here. I'm not old enough anyway."

"Maybe something will turn up."

"I have two sisters. They spend more time on the computer than they do in the bathroom. I never get a chance."

"That doesn't seem fair." Annie sipped her coffee, her eyes on her screen.

"I know. My dad just says, 'Life's not fair.' Like that solves anything." He stood up. "Hey, can you watch my bag for a minute? I need a bagel."

Annie glanced at the backpack the boy left behind. An ID tag hung from the strap with a name and address in clear block letters. She did not even have to get up to see it.

She turned back to her laptop. A few clicks later, she smiled smugly to herself. One teenage boy was going to be very happy in about three days. What was the point of having money if she could not be spontaneous with it?

Rufus helped Annalise into the buggy promptly at six o'clock. She had changed into the same full skirt she had worn to church a few days earlier and a simple blouse. Rufus appreciated her attempt to be respectful of their lifestyle, but it would have been more convincing if her denim bag did not hang from her shoulder. His mother and sisters carried purses—sometimes backpacks—so the bag itself was nothing unusual. But anyone could tell it held her laptop. Why was she loath to leave it behind? Her cell phone was no doubt silenced but in her skirt pocket as if it were a third hand.

"What's the matter?" Annalise asked. "You're scowling."

"It's nothing."

"It's something."

He hesitated then said, "Your computer. You never go anywhere without it."

"I can't be sure it's safe if I don't have it with me," Annalise said. "Don't worry, I'm not going to sneak off to use it in the middle of dinner."

Was he wrong to wish she would confide in him?

"If I ask you about it," Rufus said, "you'll tell me it's complicated, right?"

"It *is* complicated."

They rode in silence for more than a mile. Then Rufus spoke, "It seems to me it takes a great deal of energy to grasp at the air as much as you do."

"What is that supposed to mean?"

"I'm sorry. I should not have said that." Rufus sighed. He felt the wall rise between them and changed the subject. "Jacob will be so glad to see you. It's a surprise."

"Tell me you told your mother you were bringing me home for dinner."

"How could I? I haven't seen her since breakfast."

"You have a cell phone."

"I only use that for business or emergencies."

"That doesn't sound very convenient to me," Annalise said. "What if it's a not a good evening for having a guest?"

Rufus laughed. "I know my mother well. And you have a lot to learn about our ways."

Annalise raised one hand to check the hair she had pinned down in a severe manner. Annalise was trying too hard to respect their ways. With a pang, he wished she would remove the pins and let her hair fall around her face. It would be beautiful in the afternoon light.

And immediately he felt guilty. To have such thoughts about any woman—if it was God's will for him to be alone, he could not have such thoughts.

"I hope you will enjoy a good home-cooked meal," Rufus said. "I imagine you have exhausted the restaurants in Westcliffe by now."

"Twice and three times over." Annalise laughed. "But I'm used to eating out. I'm afraid I'm not much of a foodie."

"A foodie?"

"I'm not much use in the kitchen."

"I see." He paused. "Would you like to be?"

"Useful in the kitchen?" She turned toward him and twisted up a lip. "I would need a committed teacher."

"Amish women are determined. My mother would teach you." He had gone too far, but he did not want to take back the words.

They rode another mile. This time Annalise broke the silence.

"Can I ask you a question?" she said.

"Of course."

"I thought Amish people didn't have anything to do with outsiders. I mean, I understand you can build cabinets for them to make a living. But why. . .I mean. . .me? Taking me in when I fell. Church. And now dinner with your family?"

Rufus swallowed. "People sometimes want to visit our church, and I've invited you to share a meal to make a little boy happy."

"Aren't you encouraging Jacob to get a taste of the big, bad world or something? Face it. I'm a technology addict. I'm the ultimate un-Amish. What must your family think about the last week?"

"I can see that you are in trouble," Rufus said. "You hide away in Tom's truck. You hire a lawyer. You do not let your computer out of your sight, and you jump if your cell phone rings. I may not live in the way of the *English*, but I can see what is plain before

113

my eyes. The Good Samaritan could not walk past what was plain before his eyes."

"Well," Annalise said, "Thank you for your concern, but I'm managing quite well under the circumstances."

"Managing? You're hiding. How is that the same thing?"

Her face blanched, but he was not sorry he challenged her. She did not know her own value. Three cars whizzed by them on the highway, leaving the buggy to quake in their wind.

"Those people should slow down," Annalise said.

Yes. And they are not the only ones.

Eli Beiler read from a German *Biewel* while food steamed on the table. The aroma of Dutch-spiced pot roast made Annie suddenly ravenous. Her eyes feasted on the beans and carrots from the garden, rich in color. The family bowed for silent prayers. When at last Eli said, "*Aemen*," Pennsylvania Dutch flew around the table with the passing dishes. Annie filled her plate and smiled.

"We have a guest," Eli reminded everyone. "We will speak English."

"My brothers in Pennsylvania have sent letters," Rufus explained quietly to Annie.

The conversation switched to English.

"Daniel says the new *boppli* looks just like our little Jacob at his age." Franey heaped mashed potatoes onto her plate.

"What did I look like when I was a *boppli*?" Jacob wanted to know.

"You were round and bald and slobbery," Sophie said, ignoring Lydia's elbow in her side.

"Matthew says the farm is doing well this year. He bought a new plow." Franey's face lit with a sheen Annie had not seen before. "And he and Martha want to come to visit. I wonder if Tom would be willing to drive all the way to Denver to get them from the train."

"We can ask," Rufus said.

Serving dishes clinked around the table, and Annie's plate filled rapidly. Although she could not understand the family jokes, clearly Sophie and Lydia were teasing each other, and Joel was quick to add to the banter. Jacob, sitting between Annie and Rufus, wove between speaking English to Annie and Pennsylvania Dutch to the family. Every few minutes, Annie was caught off guard when someone addressed her and anticipated a response.

"Annalise is interested in our family history," Rufus explained unexpectedly. "Her grandmother's name was Byler. Maybe there is a connection."

"Perhaps," Eli said. "We have a book you are welcome to look at."

"What sort of book?" Annie asked.

"Genealogy of our family name," Eli said. "Beiler is a common Amish name spelled several ways, but we suspect all the spellings go back to Pioneer Jakob Beyeler who came from Switzerland."

"I would love to see the book." Annie leaned forward to see Eli at the end of the table.

"Then you shall. I'm afraid the print is small and hard to read. You are welcome to take it with you and study it as much as you like."

"Thank you! I'll be careful with it."

"Let us know what you find," Franey said. "I don't think anyone here has ever looked at that old book."

Jacob wiped his face with his cloth napkin in dramatic fashion. "I don't understand what you're talking about. It's time for my chores in the barn, anyway. Can Annalise come with me?"

Faces around the table turned to Annie.

"I would love to." She looked over Jacob's head to catch Rufus's eye.

"It won't take long," Rufus assured her. "He just needs to check on water for the horses and the cow, and sweep the work area."

"Sounds great," Annie said.

Rufus shook a finger at Jacob. "I left my toolbox in the barn.

You stay out of it."

Jacob took Annie's hand and led her out the back door and down a path past the garden to the barn. Refusing her help, he pushed the wide door open by himself.

"This is where we found you," he said.

Annie smiled. "Yes it is."

"You were like a present for Rufus."

Annie felt the blush rise in her face and was glad Rufus was not in the barn. "Your brother was kind to me."

"Don't tell Joel, but Rufus is my favorite *bruder*. Matthew and Daniel don't count. They live too far away, and I don't remember them."

"You have a wonderful family, Jacob."

"I'm blessed," he announced as he reached for a broom.

"Yes you are," she agreed.

Behind them, a cell phone rang. Rufus's toolbox sat right inside the door on a low shelf. Jacob looked at the phone and twisted his lips. "It says, RUTH. She taught me how to read her name before she left." He turned away from the phone and began to sweep.

The phone rang several times then stopped. A moment later, it rang again, and again the caller ID announced, RUTH. Annie moved toward the phone.

"We're not supposed to answer it," Jacob warned. "She left."

"Left for where?" Annie asked. The phone rang again, and the sound seemed to send a neurological signal compelling her to answer.

"I'm not sure. But she's gone. We can't answer." Jacob moved deeper into the barn as the phone's insistence grated on Annie.

She snatched it out of the toolbox and flipped it open. "Hello?"

"Uh-oh," Jacob said, dropping his broom and running out of the barn.

"I'm sorry. I must have the wrong number," a voice said softly into Annie's ear."

"Hello, Ruth," Annie said. "You have the right number. I'll be happy to give your brother a message."

"Who is this?"

"My name is Annie. I met Rufus recently."

"Are you. . . Is your family one of the new families to come?"

"No, I'm not Amish," Annie said. "What would you like me to tell Rufus?"

"Tell him. . .tell him. . .just ask him to please read my letter. It's important."

"I'll make sure he gets the message. Hopefully you'll hear from him soon."

"*Danke.* Thank you. For answering. And taking a message. It's probably the best I could hope for."

Annie wanted to ask so many questions, but she squashed them. Before she could think of anything more to say, the call ended. Annie replaced the phone in the toolbox and sat alone in the barn. If Rufus could be such a Good Samaritan to her, then why couldn't he read his own sister's letter?

A moment later, Rufus stood in the doorway. "Jacob said you answered my phone."

"It was Ruth. She wants you to—"

"You should not have done that."

His voice had an edge she did not recognize. He was close enough that she could have reached out to touch him, but she stilled the impulse. Something clouded his eyes. Anger? Pain?

"She's your sister. She sounds. . .lonely or something." The tips of two fingers brushed back and forth along the gold links at her neck.

"She knows better than to call that number for anything other than business or an emergency." His tone was unbending. "I'm sorry you felt you should answer it."

"Don't you even want to hear what she said?" Annie pressed, frustration welling.

"As you like to say, it's complicated." He averted his eyes. "I should take you back to the motel now."

117

Fifteen

Rufus tugged on the reins to make Dolly turn into Tom's long driveway. That the red truck was parked outside the garage attached to the house told him he had not missed Tom. He watched the front door as Dolly ambled down the gentle slope. Rufus took Dolly and the buggy to the side of the driveway where Dolly could nuzzle the ground and waited. A moment of Tom's time was all Rufus needed, and if Tom's daily habits could be trusted, he would emerge from the house at any moment ready to begin his workday. When Rufus met Tom five years ago, he had run a hardware store in town—one where Rufus spent money on a regular basis. More and more, he left the hardware store in the hands of his capable staff and filled large blocks of time taxiing for Amish families and hauling assorted supplies for contractors. Rufus only wanted to be sure he was on Tom's schedule for tomorrow.

In the back of Rufus's buggy was a sample cabinet for Mo's approval. If she liked it—and Rufus was sure she would—he would need supplies from the lumberyard in Colorado Springs to build the rest. The owners were particular about their wood to a degree that Rufus appreciated, but it was worth traversing the distance to choose his boards from their lot.

Between a couple of odd jobs, building a sample cabinet for Mo, and updating his oversized accounts book, Rufus had not been at the motel for four days. He wondered now if Annalise was still staying there. The truth was he wondered about her more than once while he sanded white oak, mitered precise corners, and calculated income and expenses. Would she come through looking for breakfast just as he unwrapped the cabinet for Mo's inspection? Would her gold necklace lie against her skin under a T-shirt, or would a blouse open at the neck let the chain catch the light?

Dolly nickered, and Rufus shook the thought away. *What nonsense. I am spending far too much time with the* English. *If I'm not careful, I'll have something to confess to the whole church.* A silly ornamentation. That was all the chain was.

The front door opened, and Tom stormed out of the house.

Rufus jumped down from his buggy. "Tom, do you have a moment?"

Tom stomped toward his truck, a cardboard box under his arm. "Sorry, not now, Rufus."

Rufus strode alongside the truck as Tom opened the driver's door and nearly threw the box onto the passenger seat. "I just want to confirm the trip to Colorado Springs tomorrow."

"Yeah, yeah, we're good. I'll pick you up at seven." Tom sat in the driver's seat and fumbled his keys.

"What is it?" Rufus asked. "Is it Karl again?"

"Worse." Tom slammed the door.

Rufus jumped back when the engine roared. A few seconds later, a screech and a cloud of dust bore witness to Tom's fury as he pulled out onto the highway.

Annie did not have to order at the coffee shop anymore. The baristas saw her coming through the door and had a mocha caramel grande nonfat latte in process by the time Annie reached the counter to pay for it. She tipped generously and settled in at her favorite table to wait for someone to bring the completed concoction to her.

Annie punched the speed dial for Jamie.

"Friesen-Page Solutions."

"It's me," Annie said.

They ran through a few routine matters.

"I'll take care of things," Jamie said, "but I'm not sure I understand why you don't come home. Barrett is making himself scarce; you have a lawyer on your side. We haven't had so much as an invoice from Rick in a week. Why aren't you here?"

Annie sighed. The question was legitimate. "Things are working this way, aren't they? The work is getting done. I talk to clients every afternoon."

"You haven't talked to Liam-Ryder Industries," Jamie pointed out. "Shouldn't we at least find out what they want?"

"First, we should find out who they are," Annie said. "Have you got time for a little research?"

"Of course."

"Make sure they're not a legal firm in disguise."

"Okay. When can I tell people to expect you back in the office?"

"I don't know. Soon."

Jamie was right. Lee Solano had quelled the legal crisis for the time being. Barrett was behaving himself and leaving her system alone—no doubt trying to play the good guy who would appear sympathetic to a judge. Whatever his reasons, it did seem that matters were calm enough for Annie to show her face at the office. Yet she felt no particular urge to go home. Living in a low-level motel room with a wardrobe that quickly became redundant was not so bad, even without a car. She got plenty of exercise walking into town, cultivated a striking tan, and gaped every day at the Sangre de Cristos so close she could almost feel their ridged rocks and cushioning trees.

And Rufus Beiler was here. Annie would never say that to

Jamie, and of course it was a fantasy to think there could be something between them. Answering his phone had made that clear. But Rufus stood for something, and Annie was not finished finding out what it was.

Annie looked up at the duo bursting through the shop's door. "Jamie, I have to go. I'll talk to you later."

"That's the one," a teenage boy said, pointing. "She's the lady I talked to."

Annie had only seen Tom a couple of times, but she would not have pegged him for someone infused with rage. Behind him was the boy she had spoken to four days earlier. She wanted to smile, thinking of him getting the package, but the color of Tom's face suggested she temper her enthusiasm.

"Sorry," the boy muttered. "He found the box this morning and came and got me from my friend's house. I had to show him the laptop."

"You did this?" Tom said.

He set the cardboard box on the table hard enough to make Annie wince, considering the contents.

"I talked to this boy, yes," she said.

"This boy is my son, Carter Reynolds."

"I didn't know."

"Would it have mattered?"

"I'm not sure," she admitted.

"Annie, right?" Tom asked. His face flashed through six moods in a second but remained stern.

She nodded.

"You sent my son a computer? A strange boy you met in a coffee shop?"

"It sounded like it would be a help to the whole family to have another computer in the house," she answered evenly.

"This is a small town. Maybe we do things differently than a place like Colorado Springs, but around here we think it's odd for a complete stranger to take up with a child and give extravagant gifts."

"I didn't think of it that way." Annie blanched. "Everybody can use a computer. I didn't mean anything. . .predatory."

"Now that I see it's you, I believe that. But parents make decisions for their own kids."

"Of course." She glanced at Carter, who stood with his hands jammed into plaid shorts pockets, his shoulders folded forward.

"Not that it's any of your business," Tom said, "but we have our reasons for restricting Carter's computer access."

"I overstepped. I'm sorry." Annie met Tom's stare.

"Carter can't keep it." Tom nudged the box an inch toward Annie. "You may have innocent intentions, but we are trying to accomplish something else with our son. It does not include giving him an electronic appendage."

"I'm sorry. I don't know what else to say."

Tom's shoulders loosened. "I hope you can return it."

"It's no problem."

Tom turned toward his slumping son. "Come on, Carter. I'll take you home. Then I have work to do."

"I'm sorry for the inconvenience," Annie said.

Tom and Carter strode out of the shop, and Annie resisted the eyes of any spectators. Suddenly working outside on the motel's porch appealed.

Rufus saw Annalise coming with her arms full and stepped across the lobby to open the door.

"Thank you," she said.

She huffed through the door and unloaded her arms onto the reception desk next to the sample cabinet. Her eyes barely lifted from the box. Her fingers rested on one edge of it. "The cupboard is beautiful."

"You didn't even look at it," Rufus pointed out.

"I'm sure everything you do is gorgeous." She glanced at his workmanship. "Mo must love it."

"She seemed happy." He nodded at the box. "Is that something special?"

"It's a mistake, that's all."

Rufus had never seen that particular slant in Annalise's shoulders, a slope of surrender. "Annalise, what happened?"

He listened to her cryptic explanation of meeting Carter and impulsively giving him a computer. Rufus picked up a rag and needlessly brushed at absent dust on the sample cabinet.

"I'm sorry for how you must feel, but surely you understand Tom's point." He hoped his tone found the right balance of sympathy and realism.

"Yes, I understand Tom's point." Annalise spun to face him.

"You're bringing your ways into new territory," Rufus said. "Answering my phone. Pressing questions about my sister. Giving Carter a computer just because you can."

"You've made your point once again." Annalise rested both elbows on the desk behind her and glared. "I'm an idiot city girl bumbling around a small town—with Amish to boot."

Her phone rang before Rufus could respond.

Annie rolled her eyes as she answered the phone. How much worse could this day get?

"I hit pay dirt," Lee Solano said.

"What do you mean?"

"You're going to want to write this down."

"Just a minute. I'll put you on speaker and find a pen."

Glancing at Rufus, who discreetly stepped away when her phone rang, Annie pushed a button that brought Lee's voice into the lobby. She rummaged around the reception desk for a pen and flipped a registration card to its blank back.

"Take this number," Lee said.

Annie jotted down the digits then repeated them back to Lee.

"If you have any questions about what I'm going to tell you, call that number and ask for Jeannette. She'll tell you."

"Tell me what?" Annie asked.

"Where did Barrett go to college?"

"University of Northern Colorado, in Greeley." Annie wondered how that was relevant to the current crisis.

"That's what you think. That's what everyone thinks. The truth is he only attended two semesters."

"But—"

"It gets better." Lee's pitch rose. "He was expelled for plagiarism."

"What?"

"This should be enough to stop the suit." Lee spoke with pure triumph. "We just let Barrett know we have this, and he'll pull out of the suit."

"Wait. That would ruin him. It would throw doubt on everything he's accomplished."

"Isn't that the point?" Lee said. "He's the one who started playing hardball. Now you've got a fast pitch of your own."

"What if I don't want to throw it?" Annie thought of Barrett's wife and infant daughter. More futures were at stake than just Barrett's.

"You hired me to make this mess go away," Lee said. "This will do it."

"Yes, I suppose it would. But it seems. . .extreme." She was expecting legal proceedings, not extortion.

Lee laughed. "Don't you consider what he's done so far to be extreme? Quid pro quo."

"Can I think about it?" Annie tucked the phone number into her bag. "The court date is not for a month. What difference will a couple days make now?"

"There doesn't have to be a court date," Lee emphasized. "Not only do we make the suit go away, but we get Barrett to sign over his interest in the company. Whatever you want."

"I need some time." Annie's head spun with the implications of what Lee suggested. "I'll call you in a few days."

"I'm ready to jump as soon as you give the signal."

The call ended, and Annie looked up at Rufus leaning against the door frame. "I suppose you heard all that."

He nodded.

"It sounds pretty terrible, doesn't it?"

He folded a sheet of paper with deliberation. "Complicated, as you said."

"I didn't agree to anything." Annie adjusted the bag hanging from her shoulder.

"You're thinking about it. Is that not enough?"

"This is not the same as you and Karl Kramer." The trembling almost got the best of Annie as she returned her phone to a pocket. "You have no idea what's at stake."

"Don't I?" He let the silence dangle between them.

Annie picked up the box. "I should go to my room. I have work to do."

"Annalise." Rufus put a hand on the box to stop her. "I'm sure I sounded harsh earlier. I am not trying to be rude or to hurt you. But I think it is time for you to go home."

"I'm happy here. For now, at least."

"You're hiding here." He took his hand from the box and let it glide over the sample cabinet. "You're pretending at the small-town life and flirting with the Amish ways because of some possible connection three hundred years ago. You look things up on the Internet instead of living them. You can't be accidentally Amish. It's time to go home and figure out what you want from your life."

"I'll think about it."

"This gentleman is pushing you into an uncomfortable corner. Is this really what you want?"

"Maybe. Maybe not."

"Tom is taking me to Colorado Springs in the morning." Rufus picked up his toolbox. "I'm sure there's room for you in the truck."

Sixteen

Annie sat squished between Tom and Rufus on Colorado State Route 96, heading east. The urge to defy Rufus and insist she would go home on her own terms—and was perfectly capable of finding her own transportation, thank you very much—lasted about as long as an untied balloon let loose. The air went out of her, and she knew he was right. Jamie was right. Her mother was right. It was time.

Lee's voice ringing in her ears was the last push. She should try to talk to Barrett one last time. What Lee proposed was beyond anything Annie imagined when she hired an attorney. Annie wanted to stop Barrett—and Rick—but not shame him for the rest of his career.

Conversation on the drive was sparse. Annie wondered if it was always this way or if her presence between the two men muted them. She would have preferred to sit in the rear seat, but Tom had boxes stacked there, along with the battered suitcase Mo had given Annie to hold her thrift-store wardrobe. The denim bag also was in the back, along with the second computer, which Tom was gracious enough not to mention. Annie's phone was in her pocket. It was all she could do not to get it out and pull up a map of where they were going to track their progress. They rode for miles between signs of any businesses, following fence lines and warning signs about curves in the road. Clearly they were in ranching territory, though what the ranches produced was not immediately evident to Annie. Horses? Cattle? All she saw was hardscrabble for miles on end, pocked with random bundles of brush and patches of scrub oak.

A tree bent by lightning. A religious billboard. Crumbling log cabins. A boxcar parked miles from any track. No doubt Tom and Rufus knew these landmarks well. Then the road cut through the rock of the gently sloped Wet Mountains in the San Isabel National Forest. Her ears responded to the shifts in elevation with increasing pressure, but she was determined not to widen her mouth to make them pop. Ponderosas grew out of crags in a straight line toward the sun.

"It's a little different than your view of the trip in," Tom said.

Annie refused to blush. If she were not so beholden to Tom, she would have let him know she could hold her own in taunting banter. And Rufus had practically ordered her to go home. She said nothing.

"Well, enjoy the view," Tom finally said. "It certainly helps give a person perspective on what's important in life."

"My perspective on life is just fine." She couldn't help herself. "It may be a different life than yours, but it's a good life."

Rufus leaned ever so slightly into her shoulder. "Don't take everything personally. He only means to admire God's handiwork."

Another thirty miles passed in silence.

Signs for Colorado Springs popped up on the route, heartening Annie.

"Where did you say your car was?" Tom asked.

She gave him directions over the next half hour. When they pulled into the tow company's lot and Annie saw her Prius, relief she had not expected wrung through her. As much as she might try to convince herself she did not miss driving, the sight of her car, unharmed, made her adrenaline surge. A life she knew was within sight.

Except without Rick Stebbins. Definitely.

And without Barrett Paige. Probably. That part hurt.

Rufus got out of the truck to let Annie out then opened the rear door and removed her belongings.

"Are you sure you want us to leave you here?" He glanced around the lot. "You are not *naerfich*? Nervous?"

"I'm fine." She put her head through the strap of her denim bag and took the suitcase. "The office is right over there"—she pointed—"and I can see my car from here."

Rufus nodded. "Well, all right, then. It was a pleasure to know you."

The past tense stabbed. But he was right, as usual. She was not sure he would shake her hand, but she extended it anyway. "Likewise. I'm sorry I didn't get to say good-bye to Jacob."

"I'll tell him. He'll understand." He covered her hand with his, infusing sensation up her arm and straight to her heart.

She shrugged and took her hand back. "Yeah. It's not like I was going to move to Westcliffe or anything. Thank your mother for me. She was very kind. Your whole family, actually." She fingered the gold chain at her neck.

"Go see your own mother," Rufus said. "She must miss you after all this time."

"I will."

"I pray things become less complicated for you."

Annie moistened her lips. "I don't pray as much as you do, but I will try."

He got back in the truck. Tom waved and put the vehicle into gear. A moment later, Annie stood alone in the garage's lot.

She missed Rufus already.

Which was about the silliest thing ever to happen to her. *Please, God, give me my senses back.*

Annie drove straight to her office.

Jamie gasped when she saw her. "You didn't say you were coming!"

"It was a last-minute decision," Annie said. "Get everybody in here. I'll talk to all of you at the same time."

Annie took her usual spot at the head of the conference table in her office and waited for the others. Jamie returned with the three software writers, the marketing assistant, and the bookkeeper.

"So you all want to know what's going on." Annie folded her hands in front of her on the table. It was the only way they would stay still. "We're facing some changes. I doubt Barrett will be back, so I'll need to hire someone to fill his spot on the marketing side."

"What happened to Barrett?" Ryan, the marketing assistant, asked the question on all their minds.

"I wish Barrett well." Annie chose words carefully and with sincerity. "But he has different ideas about the business than I do, and it's almost certainly an irreconcilable situation. I intend to continue to grow the products and services we offer, and your creative contributions mean a lot to me."

"What about Rick Stebbins?" Paul asked.

Paul was the best software writer Annie had ever hired. "Mr. Stebbins and I no longer have an association of any sort," she said. "I have engaged other counsel from out of town for the time being, though I imagine I will look for a local firm when the dust settles."

As Annie talked, the sensation was as if she were telling one of those peculiar stories of people who claim a near-death experience on the operating table. She was talking. The voice was hers. The words were hers. She calmly answered questions with as much transparency as she deemed appropriate. But this was someone else's story.

Jamie, the last to leave Annie's office, closed the door behind her. The entire afternoon stretched ahead. She would be back in a few minutes with a turkey avocado sandwich and coffee, and Annie would dig in.

This was Annie's real life.

She knew right where Rufus was, at the lumberyard where this out-of-body experience began. He was selecting the wood that would become the front desk and cabinetry of a little motel outside of Westcliffe. She could see his hand brush along the grain of the wood as if to test it. He would get out his little notebook and short pencil and make calculations, and he would have his order ready to load when Tom returned from his own errands.

And somewhere in town was Rufus's sister Ruth. Based on the address Annie had seen, brother and sister were probably not more than five miles apart. The only difference was Rufus knew where Ruth was. Ruth had no idea her brother was so near.

Ruth Beiler hefted her backpack and was among the last to leave the lecture hall at the university. She could hear her mother's voice telling her to stop dawdling. Her small dorm room was a ten-minute walk, and already she dreaded the heat that would slam her as soon as she left the air-conditioned brick building. She missed the cooler mountain air of home, two thousand feet higher than Colorado Springs.

Home.

Where she could never belong.

If only Rufus would read her letter—and answer it. If only she had some news of her sisters and Joel and little Jacob. Sophie was the spunkiest of the bunch, but even she would not dare to send a letter behind their mother's back.

Ruth had not expected to be this lonely, certainly not after eighteen months. It was not as if she had time to sit around feeling sorry for herself. She carried a full course load even in the summer months and rode the bus to a nursing home, where she spent another twenty or more hours a week as a certified nursing assistant. She could talk to as many people as she wanted to during the day. And while many people looked at her oddly because of her conservative dress and the way she kept her hair fastened closely to her head, in some settings she found fragments of friendship. In a laboratory session, all that mattered was helping each other see what they were supposed to see on a microscope slide. At the nursing home, she worked regular shifts and saw the same people routinely. Occasionally in the break room, conversation that started over patient care shifted to personal plans. On Sundays she went up the road to the modern Mennonite church, and sometimes she managed to attend a young adult Bible study. Ruth forced herself to be more outgoing than her natural inclination and usually succeeded.

But it was not family. It was not home.

She was not baptized. She had not broken any promises. *Ordnung* did not demand that her family shun her. It was the way she left. She knew she hurt them, especially her mother. But did not *Ordnung* require them to forgive?

Out of long habit, Annie tossed her keys in the tray by the door and flipped on the lights.

Her condo was just as she had left it nearly two weeks ago. Well, not exactly. The cleaning service had been in for their regularly scheduled visit, so everything looked plumped up and squeaky clean. The rooms were cool. Annie had not changed the timer on the thermostat before she left. She winced at the wasted electricity but was glad for the relief from the heat now. She went straight into the bedroom to release her load onto the bed. She opened the small suitcase and gripped the paltry stack of clothes in both hands. They had come from a thrift store and were likely headed to another one. For now they would go on a shelf in her walk-in closet. She turned the light on in the closet and found a niche for them. For two weeks, she got by with a handful of clothing items. Now she stood amid racks of clothes she had not worn in a year or more. She had everything, from silk suits to little black dresses to workout clothes and jeans and sweaters.

Exhaustion closed in on her. Annie went into the bathroom, easily four times the size of the one at the motel, and turned on the shower with the custom showerhead she spent three days selecting. She peeled off her clothes and dropped them in the hamper then stepped into the steam.

She was out only a few minutes later. A luxurious hot shower failed to deliver the satisfaction she expected. Wrapped in a towel, she went back to the bedroom and found her oldest, softest pair of pajamas. She stared at the flat screen television mounted on the wall but had no urge to turn it on. An even bigger screen hung in the living room, but Annie didn't want to go there, either. She just wanted to get in bed.

The shabby suitcase still lay open on the bed. Planning to slide it under the bed, Annie moved to close it.

The book.

The genealogy book Eli Beiler loaned her lay in the suitcase. She should not have brought that home with her. What was she thinking? She supposed she could mail it back.

But she might as well finish exploring it. Annie removed the book, closed the suitcase, and slid it under the bed. Then she climbed under the bedspread and opened the book.

Lists. Dates. Random anecdotal recollections. The name of a ship, the *Charming Nancy*, thought to have carried the family of pioneer Jakob Beyeler to the new world.

Annie grabbed her laptop. With a few clicks, she had the ship's passenger list. There they were: Jakob and Verona, with Barbara, Anna, Christian, Maria, and Elisabetha. Real people who crossed the ocean in 1737. What circumstances greeted them when they got off the *Charming Nancy*? Annie sank into her pillows, thirsting for details she would likely never discover, but her imagination was already at work.

Seventeen

October 1737

She slept—too much, Jakob thought. Verona barely had been awake since they arrived in Philadelphia three days ago. When she woke, she insisted she was fine, just overwhelmed by the journey. Her smile did not quite persuade when she assured him she was glad to finally be in Pennsylvania after a year of planning and sailing. And then she dropped off to sleep again. Each conversation varied the theme only slightly. Jakob hardly dared to leave but at minimum had to find food, candles, and coal. Fortunately, their accommodations among German-speaking merchants made basic purchases far simpler than he had feared.

The house belonged to Quakers who once lived in it themselves before building a larger permanent home. Now it served as the entry point for one German-speaking immigrant family after another. The owners left several publications about William Penn and Pennsylvania in the house, and Christian already had spent hours poring over them, sounding out English words and trying to decipher from diagrams what the words might mean.

They occupied two small rooms, one for sleeping and one for cooking over the fire and sitting on crates to eat. The sleeping room had two narrow beds and assorted pallets on the floor. To let Verona rest, Jakob kept the children out of this room except at night. Near the fire in the front room, Jakob had pried open the barrel containing kitchen supplies, and Barbara had done her best to arrange them. She knew without being asked that she must try to produce meals at reasonable intervals and keep Maria and Lisbetli quiet. Jakob ventured out for a few minutes at a time to buy whatever they required for the next few hours.

Barbara took the other girls on walks three times a day. Lisbetli needed the fresh air, and Maria needed the physical activity. Anna was oddly quiet about the whole experience of arriving in Philadelphia and awaiting the next step, but she did what Barbara asked her to do to help. The girls were gone now, and Christian was reading again in the other room while Jakob watched Verona sleep.

She stirred. "Jakob?"

"I'm here."

She exhaled. "I should get up."

"You don't have to."

"I thought you would be gone."

"Where would I go?"

"To the land office. Last night you said you wanted to make your application today."

"I don't have to go today."

"Yes you do." Verona pushed herself up on one elbow. Slowly she raised her torso and swung her feet over the side of the bed. "I'm sorry I haven't been much help."

Jakob moved to the bed and sat beside her. "Don't talk nonsense. You're ill."

"I'm better now. Really. You have to go make the application."

"It can wait." He kissed the top of her head.

"There's no point waiting. The sooner you apply, the sooner we get land."

He couldn't argue with that. "I'll make you some tea. Perhaps by then Barbara will be back."

"You can take Christian with you. He's tying himself in knots waiting to see the city. He thinks I don't know, but I hear the way he talks."

An hour later, with Christian at his side and Barbara sitting with Verona, Jakob set out, expecting to find the land office easily. Most of the public buildings were on the main square on High Street at the center of the city.

As they walked, Christian tilted his head to listen. "How many languages do you think there are in Philadelphia?"

"At least Dutch, Swedish, English, French, and German," Jakob answered. "Probably a lot more. Settlers have been coming for a hundred years."

As they approached the square, Christian cut away from his father abruptly and stopped in front of a muscled gray horse. Jakob followed, patting the horse's neck and wishing he had an apple for her. If he had an apple, though, he would cut it up for his children.

"We're going to need horses, aren't we, *Daed*?" Christian asked.

"Yes we will."

"I want to help you choose them."

"When the time comes," Jakob said, though he knew the time would be soon.

"She's for sale," a voice said in German.

Jakob turned toward the man who emerged from a dim shop. He tried to make sense of the English words on the shop's sign.

"We have everything you need," the man said.

The words were German, but the accent was English.

"Horses, plows, barrels, ropes, beds, salt, flour, jerky. You are homesteading, yes?" the man said.

Jakob nodded. Was it that obvious? He put a hand on his son's shoulder, though Christian was well mannered and would not intrude on an adult conversation. Maria was the one who could never be quiet.

The man continued listing the items he had for sale, and Jakob understood. Homesteaders flowed through Philadelphia like a river. There was money to be made in supplying what they needed.

"I can get anything you need," the man said. "Just give me a list."

"Perhaps I will," Jakob answered. "But I don't even have land yet."

"Don't wait too long," the man cautioned. "The Penns are efficient. You might as well be ready when the warrant comes through."

Jakob patted the gray animal again and said, "Perhaps we will talk in a few days."

Jakob nudged Christian's shoulder, and they continued on their quest.

"Can we buy that horse?" Christian asked when they were out of the man's earshot.

"Buying a horse is an important decision," Jakob said. "We can't just buy the first one we see."

"She looks like a good horse to me."

"Yes she does," Jakob agreed. "I have a feeling we'll meet other men with similar businesses. You can help me find the best one to work with."

"Can I go with you to find the land?" Christian asked. "I promise I won't be any trouble."

Jakob shook his head. Christian had big ideas, but he was still just an eight-year-old boy. "I think it's better if you stay with your mother. We can't leave the womenfolk on their own, after all."

They found the land office, and Jakob realized how strategically the outfitting business was located. No doubt the pace of business in the center square swelled when ships disgorged immigrants and quieted in the weeks between arrivals. Jakob had spoken with Hans Zimmerman, the Stutzmans, and other Amish families from the *Charming Nancy* who had been to the land office already. A couple of families immediately succumbed to offers in the street. Though they were now well outfitted for the wilderness, they had very little means to sustain themselves for the weeks of waiting in Philadelphia. Jakob was keeping a tight mental inventory of every expense. He knew exactly how much money he had, but he was not sure how long it would have to last.

Hans Zimmerman was getting impatient. He wanted Jakob to ride with him to scout land as soon as the necessary permissions came through. Many of the settlers walked into the wilderness, but Hans was determined to take a horse. Jakob was going to need a horse as well, or at least a mule to carry gear.

The land office throbbed with activity. Jakob recognized families from the ship as he waited his turn for a haggard gray-haired clerk behind a desk to fire a series of questions.

"I am Jakob Byler, and I wish to apply for a land grant." Jakob spoke German.

Immediately the clerk raised an arm and signaled to a young man, who crossed the room to the desk. "German," the clerk said, pointing at Jakob.

"I will translate," the young man said in German. "We do this often."

Jakob nodded in relief.

While Jakob answered questions, Christian found pamphlets and picked out English words he had begun to recognize. When they left, Jakob felt confident he had satisfied the requirements of William Penn's sons, Richard and Thomas. The warrant would come through soon enough.

Verona was still sitting up when he returned to her after an absence of several hours, which encouraged him. When Jakob entered the room, Verona lifted her flushed face and smiled. Lisbetli sat on the bed with her, playfully tickling her mother's neck and giggling. Verona tickled in response, which sent Lisbetli into spasms of laughter.

"Mrs. Zimmerman was here," Verona said. "Hans has information on some land he wants to look at when you go."

"In Northkill?" Jakob asked.

"Irish Creek."

"The name certainly sounds more peaceable than Northkill."

Jakob examined his wife's face. Was she really better, or had she forced herself to stay awake because Mrs. Zimmerman visited?

"It's very close to Northkill," Verona said. "We would be near other Amish families."

Jakob nodded. "The Siebers are on Irish Creek. They came last year."

"I remember them," Verona said. "I always liked Mrs. Sieber."

"Perhaps someday we will have a real congregation," Jakob said. "Even a bishop." He paused. "I don't know how long I'll be gone. I hate to go off into the wilderness and leave you still in bed."

"I won't be in bed," Verona said quickly. "I'm so much better. Besides, we both know you have to go."

"I don't have to go right now with Hans."

"But you should. It's what you've planned all along."

"Winter is coming."

"All the more reason to go soon. Choose your land and be ready. When the papers come, you can engage a surveyor right away."

"And we pray that winter holds off long enough to get the survey done. Then we could move at the first spring thaw."

"So we will spend the winter here, then." Verona looked around the room. "I will make a home for us."

"When you are well, I will look for work," Jakob said. "Surely Philadelphia has tanyards."

"Not an Amish tanyard. Would you work for an outsider?" Verona asked.

"Will I have a choice? I must provide for my family. I'm only interested in honest work."

"Any tanner would be blessed to have you."

Jakob began to believe he could leave Verona safely. If she napped with the baby, she managed to be wakeful for most of the day. The Penn brothers approved his application for a land grant. By the time the papers were complete, she had organized the cooking and laid in food supplies. He and Christian chose a sure-footed horse with a mellow temperament and loaded leather satchels with bedding, warm clothing, and food. Hans Zimmerman did the same. Jakob and Hans consulted their maps and planned their foray into the thick forest northwest of Philadelphia.

They followed the Schuykill River as it meandered generally north, and turned west in the shadow of the Blue Mountains. When they could, they rode the horses. When the path grew steep or hidden, they walked laboriously. Hans constantly checked his compass, and in the end they did find Northkill Creek and several Amish families who had taken this sojourn the previous year. The Detweiler and Sieber families lived in cabins with stone chimneys and the evidence that their gardens had yielded well that year and stocked the root cellar.

When Hans and Jakob arrived, Mrs. Sieber did not hesitate to twist the neck of one of the chickens strutting in back of the house and prepare it for the pot. The eldest Sieber boy went to a makeshift smokehouse and came back with a skinned rabbit and squirrel. Jakob winced slightly at the offering, supposing the families did not enjoy meat every day, much less three varieties. He spied two rifles leaning up against the Sieber fireplace.

"Is the hunting good?" he asked.

"The boys do pretty well with Melchior Detweiler's boys," Sieber said. "They take down the occasional deer or elk, which feeds us a long time. Even a bear now and then. And they seem to get all the rabbit, grouse, and turkey we could ask for."

Jakob nodded, encouraged. He would have to teach Christian to hunt. First, he would need a gun.

By noon the following day, Jakob stood on land at the far west end of Irish Creek and knew he wanted to own it. He leaned against a black oak, feeling drenched in good fortune.

"Let's use this oak to mark our land," Hans said. "Our farms will join at this tree. Our families will join here as well."

Jakob nodded, smiling. Verona would love this view. The Blue Mountains sloped on the western horizon over woods that rose thickly from rich soil. They would have all the timber they needed. The creek would provide smooth stones to spark Verona's pleasure in the fireplace that would someday warm the home they would someday inhabit. A vision of a free life colored the expanse before him with one hint of shadow.

Jakob gestured toward the mountains. "Indian territory is on the other side of that ridge."

"I know," Hans answered. "But William Penn took great pains to build friendly relations. He paid the tribes for the land."

"William Penn has been dead for nearly twenty years. Things change."

Hans went silent.

Jakob continued, "Considering the threats we left in Switzerland and what we survived on the ship, I don't intend to lose anybody I love now."

"We must be careful and watch out for each other."

Jakob thumped the tree. "This black oak will remind us that this is no time to give way to fear." He once again scanned the view of his land then pointed toward a small natural clearing close to the creek. "There! Verona will want the house there!"

Eighteen

*B*arrett agreed to meet her. Annie had not been sure he would even answer her phone call, but he sounded amicable. Even wistful.

Annie pondered three outfits laid out on her bed. The goal was businesslike but friendly. Warm but firm. Finally, she put on a dark print skirt cut straight with a sassy flair at the hemline and a short-sleeved summer sweater in a shade of blue she knew Barrett was partial to. Her gold chain followed the neckline of the sweater in a perfect parallel curve. She would use a real briefcase today.

Annie closed her eyes, inhaled, then exhaled slowly. "Please, God, help me figure this out." She wanted to do the right thing—if only she knew what the right thing was.

In the middle of the morning, small clusters of people in business attire dotted the restaurant. In another couple of hours, the lunch crowd would surge through, but for now it was a quiet place to talk. Cutlery clinked occasionally, and voices ebbed and flowed with pleasant laughter and the buzz of getting down to business. Annie just wanted to hear straight from Barrett's mouth what he wanted out of their partnership. Sitting down together in a public place—without lawyers—might stir enough friendship to come to an agreement without going to court. And she would not have to ruin Barrett's future.

"I'm meeting a friend," Annie told the hostess. "His name is Barrett Paige. I don't see him."

The hostess checked the note on the seating chart. "Yes, he's here. He specifically asked for the back room."

She followed the hostess through the main dining room, breathing in the aroma of omelets and coffee and waffles and bacon.

Something was not right. Annie slowed her steps and sniffed. Aftershave.

Rick's aftershave. She had spent enough time close to him to recognize it.

Annie paused at a table and set her briefcase in a chair. "Excuse me," she said to the hostess. "Would you please tell my friend I'd like to eat out here?"

"It's no trouble to put you in the back. We've already set up."

"I prefer this spot." She pulled out a chair and sat down.

The hostess shrugged. "I'll tell him."

The scent grew stronger, and a moment later Rick Stebbins stood across from Annie, his fingers splayed on the back of a chair.

"Well, well, Annie Friesen." He leaned toward her. "Imagine running into you here."

Annie picked up her briefcase and moved it to her lap. "What are you doing here, Rick?"

"It's a popular place for business meetings."

"Barrett told you, didn't he?"

"Told me what?"

"Don't play games." Annie's pulse pumped harder.

Rick crossed his arms over his chest. "This is a public place. How was I supposed to know you would be here?"

"That's pretty thin, Rick." She met his flaunting gaze with a scowl. What had she ever seen in him?

"I just came over to borrow a chair." He rolled one out from the table and tilted his head toward another table. Two men in suits looked in his direction. "Meeting with new clients."

"How convenient."

"I believe you know how to reach me when you're ready to sign the papers Barrett asked me to prepare."

"Not gonna happen."

"I think you'll find your meeting has been canceled." Rick smiled as he rolled the chair toward the other table.

The hostess reappeared. "I'm sorry, miss. Your party seems to have left."

So this was how it was going to be.

Rufus looked up and raised an eyebrow. Karl Kramer sauntered from his car toward the motel and casually opened the lobby door. Rufus dipped the brim of his hat about an inch but held his pose in a straight-backed chair.

"I saw your buggy." Karl's hands were in the pockets of his blue work pants. "I heard you got some work going here."

"Yes, Mo asked for some cabinetry."

"Probably a new desk." Karl ran one hand along the nicked and notched front edge of the desk. "This one's been here about a hundred years."

"Yes, a new desk as well."

Karl glanced around. "I don't see tools or a crew."

"I am drawing up some final plans." Rufus looked past Karl Kramer to where he had left Dolly and the buggy. The horse seemed unperturbed, and the buggy was upright.

"When do you plan to install?"

"Mr. Kramer, with all due respect, I don't believe that's your business," Rufus said.

"I suppose it takes time to build. Handcrafted and all. You must take great pride in your work."

"We are humble people." Rufus spoke politely. "*Demut*. We do

143

not seek pride. I find satisfaction in my craft and hope it reflects the beauty of the Creator." Where was Mo? She had said she had the original blueprints of the building and dashed off to find them before Rufus could tell her he did not really need them. His own drawings were accurate, checked and measured three times. He just wanted her signature on his final quote. Then he would buy the remaining wood and start crafting cabinets in his workshop.

Karl thumped the desk. "It would be a shame if something happened. After all your hard work, I mean."

Rufus eyed Karl, his heart beating a little faster. "Why would something happen?"

"You just never know."

Mo entered the lobby just then and took up her position behind the desk. "You need something, Karl?"

"Just dropped in to chat with Rufus here."

"Rufus is busy." She held the blueprints out toward Rufus. "I'm ready to look at your numbers now."

Karl spoke. "Let me have a look at the blueprints. I can have a bid for you by the end of the day. We will install next week."

"Rufus and I have already come to an agreement, Karl. If you're trying to drum up business, this is the wrong place."

"Perhaps I'll drop by again after the work is done." Karl ambled toward the door.

Mo and Rufus said nothing more until Karl was out of the building.

"Is he threatening you?" Mo asked sharply.

"Not directly."

"Everybody in town knows Karl Kramer is gunning for you. I'll call the police."

"No," Rufus said. "That is not the way to solve our differences."

"He'd better not step foot in my motel ever again."

Annie sat in her office with the door closed, the phone in her hand. Lee Solano was on speed dial. Number nine.

On the phone just a few hours ago, Barrett sounded sincere. He wanted to talk. He didn't want to go to court. The whole mess was out of hand.

And now this.

It was all show. Barrett must have called Rick as soon as he hung up. Or perhaps Rick was in the room and heard the whole conversation. They probably had a good laugh.

"I'm being stupid," Annie announced to the empty room. "It's clear where Barrett's loyalty lies."

One little phone call to Lee. Not more than fifteen seconds. Everything would change.

The phone in her hand rang, startling her. Annie looked at caller ID.

"Hi, Mom."

"Hi, yourself. You haven't called for a week."

"Sorry."

"Where are you?"

"Back in town. Back at work."

"I'm glad to hear that. Everything okay?"

"It will be. I just need to make a phone call."

"Then I won't keep you. I've been thinking about that gene-alogy book you asked about. My brain is zoning in on where it might be. I wonder if you want to come over and help me move boxes around and find it."

"Sure, Mom. How about tomorrow afternoon?"

"After three. Stay for supper."

"I'll be there."

"You sound preoccupied."

"Just trying to find my stride again now that I'm back."

"You'll find it. You always do. I'll see you tomorrow."

Annie ended the call. She really did want to see the genealogy book. Though Annie had never heard of anyone in her family being Amish, she felt compelled to follow the trail of the Byler name.

She exhaled heavily, the phone still in her hand. She could almost see the scowl on Rufus's face at what she was about to do.

She had to.

She tried the peaceable route and it didn't work.

She had no choice.

Annie punched 9 on her phone, and an instant later Lee Solano came on.

"This is Annie Friesen," she said. "Do it."

"You're sure?"

"Yes." *No!*

She clicked off.

Nineteen

November 1737

The temperature took a distinct downturn by the time Jakob returned to Philadelphia ten days later. The sky looked as if a worn gray sheet containing the inevitable snow had unfurled behind the city.

Jakob was anxious to get back to his family with good news, but he was unprepared for what he found.

"*Daed* is home!" Maria squealed when Jakob opened the door. She jumped into his arms. His eyes scanned the room as he kissed the top of her head.

The bread on the table was hardened, and the fire in the hearth was dangerously close to going out. The flour bin was empty and the coal bin as well. The water bucket was depleted. Dishes on the rugged table looked as if they had not been scraped in three days. A rat feasted on food spilled in one corner.

"Maria, where is everybody?" Jakob worked to keep his voice calm.

"Bar-bar is sleeping. Anna takes care of Lisbetli now."

"Who takes care of you?" Jakob set Maria on her feet again.

"I'm big. I take care of myself."

Jakob tousled the girl's hair and led her into the bedroom.

Barbara was indeed in one of the beds, sound asleep. Anna sat on a pallet on the floor with Lisbetli, who was taking great delight in sweeping an area of the floor with a few pieces of straw tied together.

"*Daed!*" Anna hurtled at him.

Lisbetli stood and toddled toward him, and Jakob took her in his arms. He sat on the empty bed and motioned for Anna to join him.

"Tell me what happened, Anna. Where is *Mamm*?"

"It was time for Mrs. Habbecker's baby," Anna explained. "Mrs. Zimmerman said *Mamm* had to go and help because it was going to be a hard birth."

"But your *mudder* has been sick."

"She said that she is strong now, but I do not think she is. She sleeps too much."

"When did she leave?"

"On Thursday. In the morning."

Panic welled in Jakob. "But today is Saturday!" He glanced over at Barbara. "Is Bar-bar all right?"

Anna nodded. "She is sleeping. Lisbetli has been crying for *Mamm*. She does not sleep at night, and she will not let anyone hold her but Bar-bar. I try to cook, but I keep spilling things."

"And Christian?" Jakob asked.

"He just left to look for coal, but I don't think he remembers where you showed him to buy it."

"We must find your brother and your mother." Jakob stood. "Help your sisters get into something warm, please, and we'll go out together."

If Anna's account was accurate, Verona had been gone for two days. What would possess her to do that? Jakob racked his brain to remember where the Habbeckers had found accommodations. All he remembered was that it had not seemed near when he first heard of the place.

Jakob moved to the bed where Barbara lay and jiggled her

shoulder. He needed to see for himself that she was simply sleeping. She roused easily enough and sat up straight when she saw him. He let out his breath in relief.

"*Daed*! I'm sorry. I fell asleep." Barbara wiped one hand across her face and glanced at the waning light coming through the window. "I did not mean to sleep so long. Lisbetli—"

"Anna told me. Thank you for taking care of the baby, but I'm worried about your mother."

"Mrs. Habbecker—"

"She can't still be birthing two days later. I'm going to go look for *Mamm* and take the girls. Will you wait for Christian?"

Barbara nodded.

"I will get some water before I go."

The nearest Amish neighbors Jakob could think of were the Stutzmans, so he went there first. They sent him to Wengars, who knew how to find the Habbeckers. As he moved through the streets, his eyes scanned for Christian. Though Christian might return without coal, he had too fine a sense of direction to get lost. It was Verona Jakob was frightened for. Two days.

Verona dried her hands, unsure whether to surrender to grief or embarrassment. Either way, tears weighed in her eyes. The birth had not gone well. By the end of the first day, she was certain the child would not survive. Mrs. Habbecker was so spent she had stopped screaming with the pains, as if she also realized that her labor was in vain.

And then Verona collapsed. Caring for her own family exhausted her every day. Waiting more than twenty-four hours for a baby to be born without breath ultimately was beyond her. When she came to, having been tucked into a strange bed, another Amish wife was at her vigil post, and Mrs. Habbecker was pushing in grievous silence. Moments later, someone wrapped the baby and took him away, confirming Verona's fear.

Where? Verona wondered. He could be buried, at least. This child did not have to be put into the sea, leaving no trace of his existence. His grave marker might be small, but it would be more than the children who died in the crossing had.

Her own heart heaved in anguish for the Habbeckers even as shame washed over her for failing them at a crucial moment. Now two days had passed since she had seen her own children, and she finally found the strength to get on her feet again and help clean up after the birth before excusing herself as gently as she could. She did not even try to form words to speak to the Habbeckers. What could anyone say that would be of comfort?

Verona was settling her shawl around her shoulders when the knock came. She opened the door.

"Jakob!"

He stood in the door frame with two little girls, his face in question pose.

This was no place for the girls. Gathering the front of her shawl in one hand, Verona said a hasty good-bye to Mr. Habbecker and stepped outside.

"I was worried, Verona. The girls said you have been gone two days. The baby—"

She shook her head, and Jakob stopped. He understood.

"Can we see the baby?" Maria asked.

Verona hesitated. "Not right now." She reached out for Lisbetli, who let go of Jakob's neck and latched on to her mother's. Verona breathed in the scent of her child, her baby who was safe in her arms.

"You must be exhausted."

"I just wish I could have done something to help."

"You helped."

"I mean—"

"I know," Jakob said softly, "but that is in God's hands. You did what you could. God's will. . ."

Verona exhaled deeply. "I'm sorry for you to come home to this. But I am very glad to see you."

In that moment, she knew she might have accounted for the last few hours—her own unconsciousness. But she did not. And she would not. She saw the relief in his face that she was all right and imagined the possible explanations that must have run through his head when he discovered her gone for two days. She was fine. Jakob was home. They would go on from there.

Jakob filed a description of the land he wanted to claim at the first opportunity, as did Hans Zimmerman, and they began the next season of waiting. Jakob got rid of the rats that had taken shelter in their rooms against the deepening cold outside, and Verona determined to keep a spotless house and not give rodents further reason to seek sustenance there. Christian learned where to buy coal and where to draw water, and Barbara and Anna became as adept as their parents at striking bargains with the local merchants. Jakob found a place to board the horse—they had no grazing land or shelter for it beside the narrow house in a row of narrow houses—and set about finding work in a tanyard. Jakob located an outfitter he trusted and began to collect supplies they would need for homesteading, beginning with a wagon.

One by one the Amish families received their land grants and surveys. Some left for Northkill, believing they still had time to erect a shelter that could withstand the winter. Some hoped to form settlements in other counties.

The Stutzmans hosted a shared meal to bid the Buerkis farewell. Verona cooked that day to contribute to the meal but declined to go with the rest of the family.

"Are you all right?" Jakob probed.

Verona put a hand on his arm. "It's been a very busy time, and I'm tired. I don't know the Buerkis well, and I could use a couple of hours of quiet."

She felt the scrutiny in his eyes but remained firm, determined to give him no reason to think her choice to stay home was anything more than fatigue.

"All right," he said. "I will take the children so you can rest."

Jakob was amused by the way Christian hung on him all evening. After the meal, while the women cleared dishes and leftover food, the men spread their maps on the table. With candles positioned to light every corner, they took turns pointing to places where they had applied for land and calculating the distance between points. Most of them would be two miles or more from the nearest neighbor. Christian had been paying close attention to conversations over the last few weeks. He soaked up information about soil quality and tree density and water supply and wildlife and crop potential. Jakob smiled in pleasure when grown men began to ask his son, just turned nine, what he knew about the various locations where Amish families intended to settle. Christian even calculated with surprising accuracy how long each step in the land grant process took based on the experience of each of the settlers so far. Hans Zimmerman's survey was already under way. By Christian's estimation, his father should receive news any day now that his own application was moving to the survey step.

Jakob glanced across the room at his four daughters. Barbara soon would be fifteen. Before long he would have to entertain the thought of finding her a husband. In Europe she had gone further in school than any of his children could expect to go in this new world. In the last few weeks, he saw that Barbara was becoming competent both to keep a house and care for small children with attention and patience. Fleetingly he wondered if she would prefer to remain in Philadelphia. She was near enough to being grown that she could decide what she wanted. But he was not going to raise the question. He wanted her with him. He had not come this far to begin separating his family, and her best chance of finding a husband was among the sons of the Amish families moving to Northkill. More would come in the next few years. His daughters could marry men of their own people.

Verona stirred up the fire in the hearth to ensure it would be burning when Jakob returned with the children. Lisbetli was probably already asleep in someone's arms.

Verona had spoken the truth when she told Jakob she was tired. Her deceit was only in disguising the depth of her exhaustion and the frequency of the headaches that sliced through her eyes. The illness she carried from the ship had never fully left her.

And it would not.

She knew that as surely as she knew Mrs. Habbecker's baby would not draw breath. The vistas of the homestead on Irish Creek were not for her eyes, but she would not stand in the way of Jakob's future there with the children. The authorization to make the legal survey of the land would come any day, and she would make sure Jakob mounted his horse and rode off to meet the surveyor. Every detail of the survey must be accurate. There must be no question of the land Jakob was investing his life in, so he would want to be present to verify each measurement. Already Christian loved the land without even seeing it, and Maria was determined to plant beets. The Bylers would have their fresh, free life. But without Verona.

Verona carried her candle to the bedroom, where she undressed and got into bed. Tomorrow she would make Jakob ready to ride before the week's end.

Twenty

Annie stood at the bottom of the basement stairs and turned to her mother with widened eyes.

"Are you in a contest, Mom? She who has the most boxes wins?"

Myra slapped Annie on the arm. "Half of this stuff is yours."

"Is not."

"Is too. You never had room at the apartment. But now your condo has lots of space. You should take it."

"What if I don't want it?" Annie poked at a box with her name on it.

"Then why would I want it?"

"Well, I'm not here to go through my childhood mementos," Annie said. "Where do you think the book is?"

Myra led the way. "There's a pile of boxes in the back corner that came from Grandma Friesen's house."

"That stuff is still here?"

"It just never seems urgent to go through." Myra shrugged. "Speaking of mementos, did you bring any back with you?"

"Back with me?"

"From wherever you were. You never said where you were.

On your covert operation."

"It was just business, Mom." Annie turned her gaze to a tower of cardboard. "Not the kind of place you pick up souvenirs."

"You start with this one." Myra shoved a box toward Annie. "Can't you tell me now where you were?"

"Westcliffe. I was in Westcliffe."

Myra plunged a hand into a box. "As in speck-on-a-map Westcliffe?"

"That would be it."

Myra sucked in air. "You met somebody! You finally broke up with Rick."

Annie riffled through a box of her deceased grandmother's dresses. "Mom, why do you have Grandma's clothes?"

"Think vintage. And stay on topic."

Annie folded the box flaps down. "Rick and I didn't exactly break up, but the result is the same. He's history."

"And who is the future?"

"No one." Annie reached for another box. "You were right about Rick all along, that's all."

"Is he still your lawyer?"

"Nope."

"And you didn't meet someone else?"

Annie was slower to answer. "No."

"Annalise Friesen, you tell me the truth."

"I. . .met a family. They. . .befriended me."

"And?"

"And nothing."

"You're not telling me everything."

"Okay." Annie lifted her eyes to her mother's. "They are Amish."

"Amish!"

"They're not freaks, Mom. They just have their own way of living and believing."

"Of course. I'm just not sure what you would have in common with them."

"Circumstances sort of threw us together. I told you I met someone named Beiler." She paused to spell the name. "It was the Amish family." *It was the Amish family's son.*

"So you think those Beilers and our Bylers might be connected," Myra said.

"It just got me going down an interesting trail. There was a guy in 1737 named *Jakob Beyeler.*" She paused again to spell the name. "It looks like the Beilers are related to him. Maybe we are, too."

"Was he Amish?"

"Quite likely." Annie opened another box. "I'm sorting that out still."

"I've never heard any stories about any Amish ancestors. But you know who might know? Your great-aunt Lennie."

"But she lives in Vermont, and she can't hear on the telephone."

"You're in luck. If you hadn't stayed incognito for so long, you might have heard the family news. She's coming for a visit. She'll be here in a few days, and then she's off to California to see her new great-grandchild."

Rufus cleared the large worktable and wiped wood shavings away before laying out the carefully cut panels. He welcomed a few days in the workshop instead of on a job site. In the morning, his two sometime employees would arrive to help sand and assemble. They had talent—one more than the other—but would require close supervision. At odd moments, he wondered if it was worthwhile to pay for their help at this stage, but how else would they learn?

Beside Rufus, Jacob perched on a stool with his elbows on the edge of the worktable. "Am I going to be a cabinetmaker when I grow up?"

"Would you like to be?" Rufus flicked his eyes at his little brother.

"You make pretty cabinets. It might be too hard for me."

"It might be hard now, but I'll teach you."

"Who taught you?"

"*Daed*. And his *daed* taught him."

"When can I learn?"

"I'll tell you what," Rufus said. "I have some scraps from this project. I'll help you make a little box for *Mamm*'s birthday. Would you like that?"

Jacob sat up straight. "*Ya!* When is *Mamm*'s birthday?"

"In two months. We should have plenty of time."

The little boy stilled, his shoulders limp. "I wish Ruth could come for *Mamm*'s birthday."

"You miss Ruth, don't you?"

"Don't you?"

"Yes I do," Rufus answered quietly. "Every day."

"I know *Mamm* misses her."

"I'm sure she does."

"Do you think Ruth misses us?"

"Of course."

"Then why can't we see her? If I ask *Mamm*, she cries. No one will tell me."

Rufus put a man's long arm around a boy's small shoulders. "Do you remember when Ruth left?"

"A little bit. But *Mamm* told me to go to bed, and in the morning Ruth did not come down to breakfast."

"Ruth wanted to go, and *Mamm* wanted her to stay. That's why *Mamm* cries."

Jacob looked up at Rufus. "That's not the real story. But I guess I'm too little to hear the real story."

"It's real enough."

"Is it against *Ordnung* for me to still love Ruth?"

Rufus shook his head. "I don't think so."

"Is it against *Ordnung* for me to love Annalise, even though she's *English*?"

"Well, God tells us to love everyone."

"That sounds hard. But I do love Annalise. I guess she won't come back, either."

"No, I don't think so." Rufus was not going to lie to the boy.

"I wish I knew how to write better. I would write a letter to Ruth, and I would write a letter to Annalise. And I would tell them I love them just like God told me to in the *Biewel*."

Rufus was silent. The chance that Jacob would be allowed to mail such letters was almost nothing. But the moment seemed too tender to offer the boy an explanation that would not satisfy either one of them.

"It's almost time for supper," Rufus finally said. "Why don't you go see if *Mamm* needs some help?"

Rufus watched Jacob scamper across the yard and up the steps to the front porch. His thin form disappeared into the house. That little boy could be the closest thing Rufus ever had to a son of his own.

Rufus had filled his mind with Annalise, and his mind's eye saw her again, standing alone in a parking lot, armed with the contents of her denim bag. He said a prayer for her then for himself.

He turned back to his panels, the sound of Karl Kramer's steps across the motel lobby reviving in his ears. He almost wished he had a lock on the workshop door.

Annie's phone buzzed in her back pocket, and she took her hands out of a box of hand-tatted table linens. She recognized the calling number. Lee Solano.

"Hello."

"I went straight to your man Barrett."

"And?" Annie glanced at her mother and shifted to wander to another corner of the basement. Even there, she would be careful about her end of this conversation.

"He's backing down. Withdrawing the suit. Your genius is safe."

"Did he ask for something?"

"He still holds a financial stake in the company. He wants you to buy him out."

"That seems reasonable." Speaking calmly, Annie caught her mother's eye briefly. Her heart pounded.

"I recommend you sue for damages to reduce the amount."

"Oh, I don't think that's necessary." Annie smiled at her mother. "The matter seems to be equitably resolved."

"Don't you want to make him sweat a little more?"

"Has his representation spoken to the matter?"

"You mean Mr. Stebbins? I'm sure we'll hear about it when he finds out."

"Thanks for the update," Annie said lightly. "I'll speak to you soon."

Okay, God, why don't I feel better about this?

She shuffled back to her mother, who was still sifting through boxes. "Sorry. Business."

"Do you ever get to take time off?" Myra asked. "Were you working the whole time you were gone?"

"I'm running a company, Mom. That's a full-time commitment."

"But you have a partner. Can't he carry some of the load?"

Annie sighed. She would have to tell her parents sooner or later. "Barrett has decided to leave the company." That much was true. "I'm going to buy him out." Also true. "And Rick is going to represent Barrett while we sort it out." Probably true.

"Wow." Myra's countenance sagged. "I thought you and Barrett were getting along great."

"We had a good run. I guess he's ready for something new."

"You need some time off, honey."

"Maybe when this all gets sorted out." Annie ran her hands over a pile of old magazines. "Maybe I'll go back to Westcliffe. Find a front porch. Sit and look at the mountains."

"I knew it. You *did* meet someone in Westcliffe."

"No, Mom." Annie flipped open a random *National Geographic* from 1992.

"I haven't seen your face turn that color since the tenth grade." Myra grinned. "You didn't know that I knew Travis Carlton kissed you."

"Well, nobody has kissed me this time. Can we just look for the book?" Her phone buzzed again. "It's Jamie. I'd better take it."

"A courier just brought a package," Jamie said when Annie answered. "More legal papers."

Rick.

"Can you tell what it's about?"

"Let's see," Jamie said. "Something about a patent. In *his* name, in connection with. . .it's all mumbo jumbo."

"Thanks, Jamie." Annie felt her mother's unspoken questions even as she reassured Jamie.

"Aren't you worried?"

"I'll take care of it."

Annie ended the call and smiled at her mother. "I need to make a quick call. I don't want to bore you. Maybe I'll just run upstairs while I do it."

"If you don't come right back, I'm quitting," Myra said. "You're the one who wants the book."

"I'll be right back." Annie had already punched 9. By the time she got to the top of the stairs, Lee answered.

"It's bogus," Lee said after Annie explained what little she knew. "He can't patent something he had no part in creating. He's trying to edge in before your partnership legally dissolves so he can have a piece of the action."

"So he can't do this?" Annie paced across her mother's kitchen, where she used to sit and do homework.

"I'll have to see the papers, of course, but it sounds like a sneaky maneuver to me."

"Sneaky doesn't mean unsuccessful," Annie pointed out. "That's what lawyers do. No offense."

"I'm on your side, Annie. I'll do my best."

"How could he have these papers ready so fast?"

"Because they were already sitting on the corner of his desk. He's two steps ahead. Does he play chess?"

Annie groaned and put her face in one hand. "I never once could beat him."

"Well, I will. Just get me the papers."

"I'll take care of it right now."

She clicked off.

"Honey, are you all right?"

Annie spun to face her mother. "Just. . .a complication I didn't foresee. But my new lawyer is not worried."

Myra held up a spiral-bound book with a pink cover. "I found it."

"Oh, thank you!" Annie took the book in her hands and flipped to random pages. List after list of names, single spaced, filled a hundred pages.

"I'd better get supper going." Myra turned to the sink behind her, lifted the faucet handle, and ran water over her hands. "Pork chops in applesauce just the way you like them."

Annie grimaced. "I don't think I can stay after all, Mom. I need to run back to the office." She held the book against her chest. "Let me know when Aunt Lennie gets here. I promise to come to dinner."

Twenty-One

January 1738

"You must go," Verona insisted.

"We've only had the warrant two days," Jakob countered. "There's plenty of time for the survey."

"The weather is clear *now*." Verona would not give up easily. "Surveyors will be eager for winter work. If you do the survey now, we'll have no trouble with the papers come spring."

"You can always smell spring in the air."

"I don't smell spring, but I smell enough clear weather for the survey. It is the first day of a new year, Jakob. Celebrate by engaging a surveyor."

When Verona's deep violet eyes lit up in that particular shade, Jakob knew not to argue further.

So he found a surveyor well recommended for his efficiency and mounted his horse in the middle of winter to visit the land he had already come to think of as his own.

The next week, the surveyor did his work with Jakob pointing and describing and gesturing. They started at the black oak Jakob and Hans Zimmerman had leaned against together, and the surveyor marked three other trees as well. Jakob's land had corners now. Assured that the legal description would be filed as soon as possible, Jakob shook the surveyor's hand and watched the man pack away his brass and oak instruments, mount his horse, and head in the general direction of Philadelphia.

Jakob decided to stay another day and make his own sketches. The Siebers offered night shelter in their barn, but Jakob spent the daylight hours on his own land along Irish Creek. In winter sun, he dipped a quill and drew ink across thick paper. A great stone fireplace would anchor the house. He would carve the mantel out of black oak—plentiful on the land—with a table to match, both of them sanded and polished to a sheen. He sketched paths to the smokehouse, the icehouse, the barn, the stables. Pastures, crops, orchards, and gardens took form in black on white. Jakob drew a little square and wrote in it, "Maria's Beets." The creek bubbled through his drawing in the shade of black and Spanish oaks. A tanyard, farthest from the house in its own clearing, would supplement his income. If he could clear fifty acres of the 168 the surveyor had measured, the family would do well.

At first light the next day, Jakob closed the Siebers' barn door behind him and mounted his horse for the ride to Philadelphia. Verona had been right to insist he come, he reflected. Perhaps in as little as two months they would all come back together to Irish Creek.

"If my calculations are correct," Christian announced to his sisters, "*Daed* should be back in no more than two days."

Verona smiled as she stirred the stew in the pot hanging in the fireplace. She loved the feeling of having her children gathered in the warm room. Only three of them could sit on crates at the small table at one time, but they had acquired a couple of rickety chairs, and Lisbetli never stayed in one place very long anyway. Christian was rarely without a map anymore. Even Hans Zimmerman said that Christian knew distances and terrain better than most of the men. He had begun marking his maps with the names of

Amish families to indicate their future homesteads. To keep up with Christian, Maria was taking more interest in learning to read. Verona was pleased that Barbara, who had more schooling than anyone else in the family, made up lessons for the other children.

Verona gasped when the pain burst behind her eyes again. The ladle clattered to the floor as she put both hands to her temples. Though she closed her eyes, she felt Barbara and Anna lurch in her direction. Anna picked up the ladle, and Barbara caught her mother's elbows.

"I'm fine." Verona waved her daughters away. "It will pass in a moment."

"It's happening more often." Barbara did not let go of her grip. "Go lie down."

"Supper is almost ready." Verona reached toward the pot.

Barbara stopped her. "I will feed the children. Please, *Mamm*, lie down."

Verona feared that if she put her head to the pillow, she might never get up again. She would never get to tell Jakob about the new baby. Perhaps it would be better if he did not know.

Until the moment the horse buckled under him, Jakob had let his mind wander, dreaming of the homestead and fields rich with buckwheat, rye, and vegetables. By bedtime he would be sharing his sketches with Verona.

Suddenly his feet left the stirrups and his hands lost their loose touch on the saddle horn as his body flew off the mount. He landed on his back, inches from a tree trunk that could have cracked his skull. The breath went out of him, and for a moment he lay on the ground unsure whether he was capable of inhaling. Eight feet away, the horse neighed in protest and struggled to regain posture. To Jakob's relief, she did. He could see now the hole she must have stepped in with her left front leg, the soft depression camouflaged with wet leaves and broken branches. The horse limped in a small circle, and Jakob, still flattened, felt a swell of panic. If the horse's leg was broken, he did not even have a rifle to put her out of her misery. This was not a hunting trip, after all, and he had no other use to carry a gun through the wilderness. He would never shoot anyone, not even natives on the attack. And he didn't know how he would pay for another horse if this one turned up lame.

The immediate question was whether Jakob himself could stand. Pushing up on one elbow, he regretted the decision to take a deep breath. His hand went immediately to his rib cage. Once, years ago, he had broken three ribs. Instantly, he remembered the injury. With his fingers, he gently probed his side. If he was lucky, this time only two had cracked. Controlling his breathing, he managed to sit up and lean against the tree trunk he had come so close to striking. With quick, jagged breaths, he watched the horse.

Jakob clicked his tongue to call the horse to him, and she came. At first, he limited his evaluation to visual inspection of the fetlock in question. No bone protruded. Mindful of his precarious position, within easy kicking range and barely able to move, Jakob slowly reached for the animal's leg and ran his hand gently down the line of the bone. He felt no break. She seemed to favor the leg less with each step.

With a few minutes' rest, the horse would be fine. Jakob, on the other hand, winced at the thought of trying to mount in his present condition, never mind withstand the motion of riding. He studied the sky. Light would fail soon, and the temperature would plummet. Scanning the immediate vicinity, Jakob determined he could support a fire with deadwood for several hours if only he could manage to strike his flint hard enough to create the required spark.

Mrs. Zimmerman shook her head. "How long has she been like this?" She touched Verona's cheek.

165

"She only went to bed a few hours ago." Anna's face scrunched anxiously. "We asked if she wanted some stew, but she wouldn't wake up."

"She has been ill much longer than a few hours," Mrs. Zimmerman said.

"Since the boat." Christian stood in the doorway watching his mother sleep.

"She gets tired." Barbara choked on her words. "I try to help as much as I can so she can rest. Christian should not have bothered you."

"She is burning up with fever." Mrs. Zimmerman dipped a cloth in a bucket of water once again and turned to the boy. "Christian did the right thing to come and get me. Now he must go find my husband."

"What can Mr. Zimmerman do?" Anna asked.

"He knows the road your father would take back from Irish Creek."

Lisbetli wailed from the other room.

The fire burned low. Jakob examined the eastern sky for any hint of pink before deciding to put on more wood. His sense of time was gone, swallowed by catnaps he jerked out of without knowing whether he slept two minutes or twenty. Most of the night he was awake, partly in pain and partly on alert for the sounds of the forest around him. A squirrel's scamper, a twig's snap, the fluttering wings of a bird—it all made Jakob twitch. In the dark, he parsed every sound, making sure it belonged.

At the sound of hooves approaching, Jakob straightened his back with a silent wince.

A lone horse.

It could carry a single Indian.

The rhythm he heard was too rapid for the dark and getting louder.

Jakob slithered into the woods behind him. There was no time to kick dirt on the fire or untie the horse.

The hooves stopped. Someone dismounted and moved around the campsite.

"Jakob?" a voice called.

Jakob looked out from behind a tree to see Hans Zimmerman patting his horse's neck on the other side of the fire.

"Jakob? Are you here?"

"Yes!" Jakob called back. "I'm here!" With an arm cradling his ribs, he moved into Hans's view.

"What happened?" Hans rushed forward to catch Jakob's weight.

Jakob shook his head. "First, you tell me why you're looking for me in the middle of the night."

"Do you think you can ride?" Hans asked. "We have no time to spare."

"What happened, Hans?"

"It is Verona."

"*Daed*! What's wrong?" Anna cried when she saw her father.

Jakob, clutching his ribs, waved her off. "How is your mother?"

"She is not talking."

Maria threw herself at Jakob's legs. "Are you going to make *Mamm* better?"

Lisbetli screwed up her face and wailed. Christian handed her a wooden spoon, which she threw down, petulant.

"She wants *Mamm*," Anna said.

"I want *Mamm*, too," Maria said.

Hans, coming in behind Jakob, peeled Maria off of Jakob's legs and tipped his head toward the bedroom. "Go see her."

Jakob opened the door that had shielded the younger children from the sight of their mother. Closed off from the fire, the room was cold. Barbara sat on the edge of Verona's bed, and as Jakob entered, she pulled a cloth out of a bucket of water, wrung it slightly, and laid it across her mother's forehead. Then she moved out of the way, and Jakob took his daughter's vigil post.

"Verona, my love." He spoke into her ear.

Just when he thought she would not respond, she turned her head slightly, without opening her eyes. "Jakob?"

"Yes, I'm here."

The effort of trying to speak consumed her breathing. "Survey?"

"It's finished," he said. "We'll have the papers soon."

"Sorry." Her eyes opened to slits. She swallowed.

Jakob moved the damp cloth to her chapped lips for a moment. "Shh. Just rest."

"I cannot go." Her chest rose and fell in shallow rolls. "Promise me you will."

"We will wait till you are well."

She shook her head. "No. This is the end for me."

"Don't say that, Verona." Jakob laid his hand along her burning cheek.

"Love again, my love." Her eyes closed. "Don't be alone." Her chest fell and did not rise.

When he sketched his dream, it never occurred to Jakob to include a cemetery.

Jakob hired a wagon and, with Hans Zimmerman's help, took the pine box to Irish Creek. He would be gone at least five days, but Mrs. Zimmerman knew his heart and took the children home with her. Jakob could not bring himself to leave Verona in Philadelphia behind a church whose teachings she did not believe. He would tend a fire as long as it took to thaw the land enough to dig. She must be buried on Amish land.

Their land. The survey was a formality. It was only a matter of time before he could move his family to the home Verona wanted for them.

By the time Jakob returned to Philadelphia, Lisbetli had been inconsolable for a week, her usual compliant disposition shattered by the absence of her mother. She clung to her father's neck constantly, unwilling even to go to Barbara's arms. The little girl slept only when exhaustion overwhelmed and never for long. Jakob slipped out in the mornings—sometimes to Lisbetli's screams—to work at the tanyard, only to come home every night to a distraught toddler and a teenager with the face of a woman who knew pain. In a few days, Barbara would be fifteen. How could he ask her to mother her siblings? But how could he manage without her?

Jakob knew what the coming weeks would bring. For a while, Amish families would stop by with food or an invitation for one child or another to play with their children. But they were all marking time, and there were not many families from their ship left in Philadelphia. The true goal was to leave the city, to claim their land, to forge settlements where they could live apart and unencumbered by conflict over their beliefs. Wasn't that why they had come to the New World?

The survey came in. Jakob breathed relief that the choice to bury Verona on Irish Creek was without regret.

Love again, my love.

Twenty-Two

"I'm sorry, Mr. Beiler, but the bank officers have determined it's necessary to discontinue your line of credit."

Rufus squinted under his straw hat. This made no sense. "I wonder if there has been a mistake. Perhaps some confusion with another account."

The woman at the desk tossed her wavy black hair over one shoulder and made faces at her computer screen. "No, I'm sure it's the correct account. Would you like to set up a payment schedule for the outstanding balance?"

Rufus looked at her in confusion. He had opened his business account five years earlier when the Beilers first arrived in Colorado. A few months later, the bank extended him a small line of credit, and gradually over the years it grew with his business. Why would they suddenly withdraw it?

"We can convert the balance to an unsecured signature loan for a term of forty-eight or sixty months."

"I'm sorry." Rufus shook his head. "I don't understand. Is there some concern about my payment history?"

She pushed out her bottom lip and studied the screen again then clicked a couple of times on her keyboard. "The only information

I have is that the line of credit is discontinued. You'll have to talk to a bank officer if you want to know more."

"I do want to know more, please." Rufus fixed his eyes on the back of the computer monitor that seemed to determine the woman's statements.

"Please have a seat." She gestured to an imitation leather loveseat. "I'll see who is available."

Rufus sat, stunned. This had to be a mistake. Without a business line of credit, he would not be able to pay his employees—or himself—between payments from clients on bigger jobs. He would not be able to bid on any jobs that required more cash up front than he had in the bank. The new housing development north of town would be off-limits to him. The happy owners of the home where he installed custom cabinetry had given his name to two friends building in the new construction area. Both wanted bids, but already they were anxious to work with Rufus. Both—especially in combination—would require considerable cash outlay up front. The most he could ask from the customers was half of what he needed for supplies. Without a line of credit, it would be impossible.

Karl Kramer.

It was no surprise when the woman returned and reported that no officers were available, and perhaps he would like to come back next Wednesday to discuss his options.

No, he would not like to come back next Wednesday.

Rufus stepped out into the harsh end-of-July sun and wiped sweat from the hairline against his hat. In the heat, the weight of Karl's scheme fell against him, making Rufus anxious for the shade of the buggy. He barely even patted Dolly's face before taking his seat and picking up the reins. On the bench, though, he sat still, his chest heaving. "*Demut,*" he muttered. "*Demut.*"

Lord, this is impossible. Not my will, but Yours.

Ruth put her slight weight on the pad that automatically opened the sliding doors at Vista Valley Nursing Home. Every time she entered, she found the name of her place of employment ironic, and perhaps a contributing factor to her ongoing homesickness. Though she lived and worked and went to school snug against the foothills to the Rockies, she longed for the wide vistas of the San Luis Valley. Someday she would go back. That had been her plan all along.

Ruth walked briskly down the hall then took the corridor to the left, the one with the teal green stripe on the floor to direct visitors in and out of the wing where she spent twenty-five hours a week.

The nurse at the desk greeted her. "Ruth! Good. Mrs. Watson has been asking for you."

"Thanks, Angela," Ruth said. "Let me clock in, and I'll go see her."

In the break room, Ruth spun the dial on a padlock and opened her locker. She laid her purse on a shelf and picked up the comfortable white shoes she always left there. In a moment, she had changed her footwear and pulled on a smock. The other staff wore scrubs, but Ruth couldn't quite allow herself to don them and was grateful that—so far—the administration was sensitive to her religious leanings. Her skirts were simple and easy to move in, and the name tag on her smock clearly identified her as an employee.

When she was ready to go out on the floor, she slid her time card into the machine and awaited verification that it registered properly. It was precisely 6:00 p.m. Her shoes squeaked as she padded down the hall to Mrs. Watson's room.

The resident, sitting in a wheelchair, lit up as soon as she saw Ruth. "My favorite person in the whole place!"

"You're sweet, Mrs. Watson. I could probably squeeze in ten minutes of reading to you now, if you like, then more a little later."

"I know they don't pay you to read to me."

"They pay me to care for you, and reading does that. Besides,

I would come even if they didn't pay me."

"Now you're the one being sweet," the old woman said. "I was just thinking today about how long we've known each other."

"More than a year," Ruth supplied.

"That's how I reckon it, too. And in all that time I don't ever remember you taking a week off."

"No, I guess I haven't." Ruth picked up a couple of magazines from the end table. Mrs. Watson had particular reading tastes. "Do you want *BBC History* or the *Smithsonian*?"

"You don't have to read to me now, dear. I'm talking about a vacation for you."

"I'm fine, Mrs. Watson. I go to school year-round. There's not much time for a vacation."

"But you haven't been home in all this time."

"No," Ruth said quietly, "I haven't."

"Won't you have a break between terms at the end of the summer? If you request the time off now, surely they'll grant it."

"It can be hard to find a sub." Ruth flipped a few magazine pages.

"Nonsense. People take vacation days all the time. Don't you want to go home?"

"Very much."

"Then you should go."

Ruth smiled as she laid the magazines back on the table. "I have a few things to do. I should be back in about an hour to help you get ready for bed."

She slipped out of the room and leaned against the pale pink wall in the corridor. How could she explain to a sweet old lady like Mrs. Watson that she was fairly certain her mother did not want her to come home? Not after the way she left. Not after her *mamm* found her hiding and waiting for a ride on that day of all days. Her departure had wrenched an enormous wound through both mother and daughter. Ruth was not sure it could ever heal enough for her to be welcome on the farm again.

The roast beef was juiced to perfection. The sweet potatoes were mashed and baked with a golden brown-sugar crust. Garden-picked green beans and fresh red pepper slices splashed color across the table. Annie had lifted the buttermilk whole-wheat loaf from the bread machine herself not twenty minutes ago.

Even without the vegetables, Aunt Lennie would have added all the color the table needed. At seventy-nine, she moved more slowly than Annie remembered, but her determination faltered no more than it had twenty years ago. She made Annie smile every time she blew through town. A comfortable, sprawling two-story home in Vermont was home base, but Lennie always seemed to be on the way to somewhere, and Annie couldn't help but admire that.

After her father gave thanks for the food, Annie lifted the bowl and offered a spinach and strawberry salad to Aunt Lennie.

"Aunt Lennie," Myra said as she moved a generous portion of sweet potatoes to her plate, "Annie is doing some family research. We thought you might fill in some of the blanks."

Brad Friesen transferred a slice of meat to his plate. "I confess I don't know too much about the family history, other than what I remember about my parents—and you, of course."

"Most of what I know can't be proven." Lennie winked at Annie. "But I've stored away a tidbit or two. What would you like to know?"

"It's about your grandmother Byler." Annie smeared butter on still-warm bread. "Do you know anything about the Byler name further back?"

"Oh, there was an Abraham Byler and a string of Jacobs. Abraham was a sheriff, I believe. Malinda's father. Shot in the line of duty. But the Jacobs? I can't tell you too much."

"If Abraham was a sheriff, then I guess he wasn't Amish."

"Hardly. Why would you think that?"

"I didn't really." Annie stabbed three green beans. "It's just similar to the name of some people I met recently."

"Amish?"

Annie nodded.

"In Colorado?" Lennie clanked her fork and sat up straight. "Well, I'll be!"

"It's a fairly new settlement. Only a few families."

"So they're trying again." Lennie scratched an ear.

Annie perked up. "What do you mean?"

"Now, I told you, I can't prove any of this. Family lore says the Amish came to Ordway around 1910. A Byler cousin fell in love with an Amish girl and joined up. He got baptized and everything. He was going to live off the land and make a bunch of babies."

"You mean we really have an Amish relative?" Annie picked up a bite of roast on her fork but did not raise it to her mouth.

"Don't get ahead of me." Lennie put one finger on her chin as she thought. "Story has it that those poor folks never could get any irrigation out to their farms. After a few years, they packed up and went back to Pennsylvania. All except our cousin. Harold, I think his name was. Turns out he didn't believe all that much, and when the babies didn't come along, maybe he didn't love all that much, either."

"What happened?" Annie asked. Around the table, eating had stopped as everyone waited for the story. Lennie was the only one who systematically moved food from plate to mouth.

"Pennsylvania was the last straw," Lennie said between two bites of sweet potatoes. "What was left of the community was giving up and going home. Except Pennsylvania wasn't home for Harold. He disappeared the night before they were supposed to leave."

"What happened?" Annie pulled her phone out and started making notes.

"He turned up in California a few weeks later and never did come back to Colorado." Lennie tore a piece of bread in half.

"I haven't thought of that story for years."

"What about the Amish girl—his wife?"

Lennie shrugged. "Don't know."

Annie now had names to look for in her books. She tapped them into her phone. Abraham Byler. Harold Byler.

"What do you remember about your grandmother?" Annie asked, poised to enter more information into her phone.

"Malinda Byler? Not too much. Your grandma Eliza and I were little girls when she died. I remember she told us Bible stories on Sunday afternoons, and she could twist a chicken's neck faster than anyone I ever knew in all the years since." Lennie paused. "Of course, I don't see too many people twisting chicken necks these days. It's a dying skill." She laughed at her own pun.

Annie shook her head with a smile. Aunt Lennie was always the same.

"Her son Randolph was your father, right?" Annie asked, picturing the family tree she had sketched.

"Right. But she had other children. Most of them moved back to Arkansas at some point, but Daddy always liked the wide-open spaces of Colorado. I never thought I'd leave, either, until your Uncle Ted used his wiles to lure me to Vermont."

"It's amazing how geography brings an end to the story so fast," Annie mused. "Especially a hundred years ago."

"This is all fascinating," Brad Friesen said, cutting into his meat. "I should have paid attention long ago. But, Annie, why are you so interested now?"

Annie shrugged. "I just am. I've been so focused on getting where I'm going that I never thought much about where I came from."

"The Bylers are good stock." Lennie nodded emphatically. "Except perhaps for that character Harold. When you make a promise, you ought to stick to it, not run the other direction."

"Thank you, Aunt Lennie," Annie said. "You've told me things I might never have known."

"Yes," Brad agreed. "I'm glad you put us on your route west."

Annie picked up a red pepper slice and bit into its crispness. Moments divided families for generations. She had the urge to call her sister in Seattle for a long chat. And she had the urge to track down Ruth Beiler, no matter what Rufus thought. She was never going to see him again anyway, so why did it matter?

Twenty-Three

March 1738

Jakob tapped the paper twice and looked at his daughter sternly. "You must practice your letters, Maria."

Maria twiddled the quill between her thumb and forefinger. "I don't want to. I can't do it without *Mamm*'s songs."

Jakob had barely cleaned up from his half day at the tannery before Lisbetli latched onto him as she did every day. He shifted her now from one arm to the other. The toddler's head remained tucked under his chin during the whole maneuver. "*Mamm* would want you to do your letters, Maria. How else will you learn to read?"

"I don't care about any stupid books!" Maria threw the quill down, spilling the inkwell in the process.

"Maria!" Jakob righted the inkwell then lurched for a rag. The sudden motion made Lisbetli clutch his neck all the tighter and add a whimper to the commotion. Ink already soaked through the sheets of paper stacked on the table and dribbled off the edge before Jakob could slap the rag in place.

Maria leaped away from the table. "It's going to ruin my dress."

Jakob sighed and sat in a chair to sop up the mess.

"No. No down," Lisbetli protested, her predictable response

to the possibility that he might want to put her down for a few minutes.

Christian was gone to the livery to check on the horse, and the other girls were shopping for vegetables for the evening meal. Even if Barbara was home, Lisbetli would not release her father. She had been clinging to him for weeks, as if she was afraid he would disappear the way her mother had.

Jakob reached out a hand toward Maria. "Get your capes. We will go for a walk. It's not too cold out today. There is even a bit of sun."

"Where will we go?"

Jakob shrugged. "It does not matter. But I am going to need some new ink."

Maria hung her head. "I'm sorry about the ink."

Jakob tipped Maria's chin up and looked in her blue eyes. "I know you miss your mother. We all do."

They walked toward Market Street. Jakob scanned the pedestrian traffic every few yards, wondering if they would see the other girls. If Barbara managed to find beets, Maria's mood was sure to improve. Maria walked ahead of Jakob for the most part, and he let her wander at will. Occasionally Lisbetli would lift her head and point at something, but by and large she was content to mold herself to her father's chest as she had for the last two months.

The stationer's shop caught his eye, and he wondered why he had never noticed it before. It was in a row of narrow shops at the base of a three-story brick building close to the center square of town. He must have walked past it dozens of times. It was the laugh that caught his attention this time. The shop's door was propped open to welcome the springlike weather—though the danger of frost was not over—and as he walked past, a woman's lilting laughter lit the air.

"Maria," Jakob called as he slowed his steps and angled his head to look in the shop. Maria retraced a few steps and stood beside him.

Jakob watched a young woman behind the oak counter use a large sheet of plain brown paper to wrap a purchase for a well-dressed gentleman. The laughter drifted off, but a broad grin still cracked her face. Her chatter bore the familiar accent of Jakob's own birthplace in Bern, Switzerland. The customer seemed pleased with whatever he had said to elicit her convivial response as he tucked his package under his arm. Outside the shop, Jakob stepped clear of the doorway to allow him to pass.

"Are we going in?" Maria asked.

"Yes we are," Jakob answered, though he had not known until that moment.

Inside, the shop carried an assortment of writing papers, envelopes, inks, quills, and a few books.

"May I help you?" the young woman asked.

"I require a small packet of black ink powder, please." Jakob shifted Lisbetli in his arms.

"Your daughters are beautiful." The young woman pulled a jar of ink powder from a low shelf and laid out a sheet of paper to fold into a packet.

"This one is a little worn out these days." Jakob stroked Lisbetli's head.

The woman reached toward Lisbetli with curled fingers. To Jakob's shock, the little girl reached back, gripping the woman's hand.

"This is Lisbetli," Jakob said.

"So her given name must be Elizabeth." The woman smiled at the toddler. "My name is Elizabeth, too. Elizabeth Kallen."

"She is Elisabetha," Jakob said.

"Very similar." She reached across the counter and touched Lisbetli's cheek. "Hello, Lisbetli."

"I am Jakob Byler."

"It's a pleasure to meet you, Mr. Byler."

Lisbetli twisted in Jakob's arms and reached toward Elizabeth Kallen with both arms.

"Would you mind?" Elizabeth reached now with both of her own arms.

Jakob gladly surrendered the child across the counter. Elizabeth Kallen propped Lisbetli on one hip and tickled her with a finger under the chin.

"Do you have any books for children?" Jakob was not at all sure that the coins in his pocket would cover both the ink and a book—not to mention replacing the ruined paper still on the table beside the fireplace. Christian would not be happy to discover what his sister had done. Perhaps some of the sheets could be salvaged.

"I believe we have some illustrated folktales and a primer or two."

"Perhaps we'll look at a primer. Would you like that, Maria?" Jakob glanced up at Miss Kallen. "She is just learning her letters."

"Our books are all used," Miss Kallen explained, "so I believe you will find the prices reasonable."

She carried Lisbetli around the end of the counter and led Maria to the bottom shelf of a rack on the back wall of the shop. Jakob stayed where he was, watching his daughters. Maria apparently had forgotten that she did not want to learn her letters and held a slim German primer as if it were gold. Lisbetli had a thumb in her mouth and looked thoroughly comfortable in Miss Kallen's arms. Other than when Barbara twisted her baby sister from their father's arms so he could go to work, this was the furthest Lisbetli had been from Jakob since Verona's passing. Jakob used the moment to count his coins.

When he heard the baby's laughter, his eyes misted. Lisbetli hadn't giggled in so long. She popped her thumb from her mouth and grinned at Miss Kallen.

"We are moving to Irish Creek," he heard Maria announce. "There is no school there, and my mother died."

"I'm sorry about your mother," Miss Kallen said softly.

Maria's thin shoulders lifted and fell a few times before she continued, "I have to learn my lessons from my brother and sisters."

"I think you're probably a very good student."

"My brother especially likes maps. Do you have maps?"

"We get one every now and then."

"Try to find one with colors on it," Maria said. "Christian loves the ones with colors."

"Perhaps I will set aside the next one I see for your brother. You can remind your father to stop in again." Elizabeth Kallen glanced in Jakob's direction, and he couldn't subdue the upturn in his lips. Her tenderness with his children moved him more than he would have imagined.

And then he took back the smile. He had no business smiling at a young woman in a shop.

"We should go, Maria," he said. "Your sisters will be wondering where we are. We will take the primer home with us." He stepped toward Miss Kallen and reached for Lisbetli, freeing the woman's hands to seal the packet of ink.

When Jakob pushed open the door to their two small rooms, he found Barbara chopping onions and potatoes on one end of the table, and Christian scowling and scrubbing at ink stains at the other end. Anna sat on an upturned barrel near a window, staring out. Jakob supposed it did not much matter what was beyond the pane. These days she just stared for long stretches.

"I copied over the list, *Daed*," Christian said. "The old one was getting too hard to read. But the ink is nearly gone."

"You're an organized young man." Jakob reached into his pocket for the powder and dropped it on the table. Christian would know what to do with it. Lisbetli was stuck to him again, but he carried the hope that she would recover her childhood in the kindnesses of people like Elizabeth Kallen.

"I have three columns," Christian continued. "One column tells us the supplies we already have, like axes and hammers and pots. The second column is a list of things we absolutely need before we go. I put the bellows there. We can't go without those."

"When I get my wages next week, we'll go see the blacksmith," Jakob said.

"And the third column are things we can get when we can afford them."

Jakob leaned over the table and glanced at his son's lists, surprisingly neat and straight. The boy took the planning tasks so seriously that Jakob sometimes had to remind himself he was only nine.

A knock made all their heads turn. Christian hopped off his stool and opened the door. Hans Zimmerman stepped inside. The two men exchanged a greeting by lifting their chins toward each other.

"We're almost ready." Hans straightened his hat. "We'll be leaving in a few days."

Christian's eyes moved to his father and widened. Jakob nodded. His son was full of questions, but he knew better than to enter the conversation uninvited.

"There might yet be a blizzard." Jakob laid a hand on the top of Lisbetli's head.

"As the Lord wills," Hans replied, "but the Siebers have offered us shelter for the last of the winter. When the weather allows, we will begin clearing. We might still get a late spring garden in."

"I don't suppose we'll be far behind you. By Christian's reckoning, we will soon be outfitted ourselves."

"Would you like some coffee, Mr. Zimmerman?" Barbara asked. "It's fresh."

Zimmerman nodded. Jakob offered the best chair in the room to his friend and sat on a crate with Lisbetli in his lap.

"Christian, what news do you have?" Zimmerman asked as Barbara handed him coffee.

This was all the invitation Christian needed. He pulled his stack of papers out of his lap and reviewed the Byler progress in collecting homesteading supplies. Their wagon was stored with the man who kept their horse, and as they acquired items, Christian and Jakob secured them in the wagon. Christian had drawn his own scaled sketch of the farms emerging along Irish Creek: The Stehleys had arrived a few weeks ago and immediately claimed land west of the Bylers. Hans Sieber was to the south, and Hans Zimmerman to the west, beyond the black oak. Kauffmanns, Buerkis, Masts, and other familiar names had sprouted on Christian's map.

Jakob listened absently as Christian prattled on and Barbara cooked. The Amish community already on their farms would make sure each family had shelter as they arrived. Barns would go up quickly, followed by cabins. Although winter weather was still possible, more likely conditions would shift radically any day now. He should be excited to go—as excited as Christian. Jakob did look forward to being near Verona, but it would not be the same as being *with* her.

Love again, my love.

He was nearly fifty years old and moving to the wilderness with five children and a few other families. *Where would I find another wife?* he asked himself.

Jakob struck a deal with the blacksmith for hoes and tongs and an anvil. From the dry goods store, he bought yards of ticking and hired a seamstress to sew it into mattress covers. Verona would have wanted to do it herself, but it was too much to ask of Barbara and Anna. They labored enough by candlelight over their own clothing, simple dark dresses and practical aprons. He consulted his daughters about supplies for the kitchen and slowly but surely put checkmarks next to each item on Christian's list of essentials. Working less at the tannery, Jakob put his energy into filling the wagon and finding a second horse to help pull it over rugged terrain.

And he did much of this with his youngest daughter's arms around his thick neck. She seemed most soothed when he walked, so Jakob began to stroll in the late afternoons in weather that crept more certainly toward spring each day. Lisbetli would find enough solace to eat a good meal before falling onto her pallet exhausted. Unconsciously, his route settled into one that took him past the stationer's, and he found his steps slowing on that block.

One afternoon he heard the laughter again.

Lisbetli lifted her head. Before Jakob realized what she intended, the little girl wriggled out of his arms and slid down his legs to the ground.

She ran to Elizabeth Kallen, who squatted and opened her arms to receive the tiny, hurtling form.

Jakob followed his daughter.

Elizabeth smoothed loose hair and stood up with Lisbetli. "I was hoping you would come by."

Jakob's heart sped up. She wanted to see him?

"I have a map for your son," she said.

A map. For Christian. "How thoughtful of you."

"I understand it's very similar to one that William Penn used," Elizabeth explained. "I thought it might be of particular interest."

Jakob nodded. "I'm sure Christian will find it invaluable."

"I hope you will accept it as my gift." She held out the map.

Jakob's fingers closed around the map, brushing hers. "I should not infringe on your profit."

She shook her head. "It is torn on one end. We would not be able to sell it, so I thought your son might as well have it."

Lisbetli laid a hand on Elizabeth's face, and Elizabeth instinctively turned toward it and kissed the little palm.

Jakob's heart cracked open.

Jakob smoothed the quilt, one of Verona's last, at the front of the wagon right behind the driver's bench. He patted the pile. "Hop in, girls." Christian would ride at his side, and the girls would have their comfortable corner, where Lisbetli and Maria could enjoy a small space to wiggle. Tied to the back of the wagon, a cow nosed around in vain for a patch of grass. With the children in the wagon, Jakob took one last look around the two rooms, making sure they left nothing behind that belonged to them and took nothing that belonged to the Quaker owners. Traveling with a loaded wagon and leading a cow would require several days to reach Irish Creek. Gear to make camp each night hung from the rim of the wagon.

Jakob heaved himself onto the driver's bench and took the reins from Christian. "Ready to see Irish Creek?"

Christian nodded, his eyes wide in anticipation.

A slender form appeared at the side of the road, and Jakob blinked twice before he believed his eyes. "Miss Kallen! What are you doing here?"

"I suspected you were leaving today. I have something for Lisbetli." She held out a small, soft doll with a carefully cross-stitched face.

"You are too kind."

"May I give it to her?"

"Of course."

Elizabeth approached and leaned over the side of the wagon. Lisbetli popped her thumb out of her mouth and wiggled her fingers in a wave. When Elizabeth placed the doll in her hands, Lisbetli giggled shyly and held it tightly.

"Thank you, Miss Kallen."

"You're most welcome, Mr. Byler."

Maria leaned over and inspected the doll. "But it has a face, *Daed*! Our dolls don't have faces. It's a graven image."

"I hope I have not caused offense." Elizabeth laid one hand over her heart.

"Of course not." Jakob dared not offend her, either. "It is not our usual way for a doll to have a face, but Lisbetli loves it already."

Elizabeth looked crestfallen. "I have a lot to learn about the Amish ways."

"Christian," Jakob said, "why don't you thank Miss Kallen for the map she found for you?"

"It is a wonderful map." Christian bobbed his head sincerely. "*Danke.* Thank you very much for thinking of me."

"It was my pleasure." She looked from son to father. "May your journey be safe, Mr. Byler. You have my prayers."

"Thank you, Miss Kallen."

Elizabeth stepped back, and Jakob nudged the horses forward. He wanted to go, but she made him want to stay.

Twenty-Four

On Saturday morning, Annie sat cross-legged on her bed with a genealogy book on each side and her laptop straight in front of her. She looked from page to screen to page. Each source revealed twists on the spelling of family names and slightly different lists of descendants, but it all added up the same.

Jakob Beyeler arrived in Philadelphia with an Amish wife and five children.

His wife died.

He married again and had five more children, but no records indicated that this second wife was Amish.

Annie sank back against a stack of pillows. What a wrenching choice Jakob must have made. But somehow his older children remained Amish.

As she traced through the generations in the book Franey and Eli had loaned her, Annie found their names. At the time the book was assembled, they had one child. Rufus. A descendant of Jakob's first son, Christian Byler.

And she found her own name easily enough in the book her mother unearthed from the basement. A descendant of Jakob's second son, born to his second wife.

Beyeler. Byler. Beiler. Biler. Even Boiler. No matter how the name was spelled, the dates and random bits of information matched. It was all one family line that traced back to Switzerland in the eighteenth century and a countercultural religious group who simply wanted to live in peace.

Annie put her finger on Rufus's name and imagined the line completed with the siblings who followed. Daniel. Matthew. Ruth. Joel. Lydia. Sophia. Jacob.

She riffled the leaves of the bound book. Pages and pages of names and birth dates and death dates, each one a story. Most of them were gone from memory, but thick paper between plain brown covers collected the evidence of their existence. The pink-covered, spiral-bound book in which her own name appeared overlapped in the beginning with the record in the brown book. Quickly it diverged into a family line absorbed in mainstream culture and left behind increasingly distant relatives faithful to the Amish life.

Jakob's choice spawned two sets of descendants who would be hard pressed to find common ground three hundred years later. *Had he chosen for love?* Annie wondered. *Or necessity? How dearly had he paid for his choice?*

Annie's mind wandered to Ruth Beiler. Why had she left her family? What was really going on?

"Only one way to find out," Annie said aloud. She closed both books and moved them to the nightstand.

In her back pocket, her phone buzzed. Annie saw the caller ID: Lᴇᴇ Sᴏʟᴀɴᴏ.

What now?

"Did you get your bid in?" Tom asked Rufus. "The town council just gave the green light for remodeling the visitor's center."

Rufus hesitated and glanced around the house where he was installing a set of built-in bookcases with Tom's help. "I have some matters to work out."

"It's not a big job, but it seems like a good opportunity for you."

"It would be," Rufus agreed.

"Then why don't you bid on it?"

"It might not be the right time for me." Rufus dropped his hammer into the toolbox. "I've got the motel project and custom built-ins for two of the new homes. That will keep the crew busy."

"You can always take on more help."

Not if I can't pay them. "Tom," Rufus said, "do you know any banks you like in Colorado Springs?

"A few. Why?"

"I need to try a new place. Can we go next week?"

"Sure. Bidding is open for another three weeks."

Annie drove north on Rangewood toward the subdivision dominated by townhomes where Barrett lived with his wife, Lindsay, and their infant daughter. She slowed as she approached his street and eventually parked three doors down. Maybe he was home. Maybe if she did not make arrangements ahead of time, Rick would not be able to foil their meeting.

Annie had just about persuaded herself to present herself at Barrett's home when his garage door went up. A few seconds later, his green Subaru backed out. The car was filthy, which made Annie's stomach shoot acid up her throat. Something was not right. Barrett kept his car in impeccable condition. Had Rick done this to him?

If Barrett saw Annie's idling car, he gave no indication. He put the car in gear and roared forward, away from her.

Behind her steering wheel, Annie sighed. She glanced at the clock then put her own car in gear. One more stop might yet answer some questions.

Ruth turned a page in the textbook and encountered yet another list she would likely have to memorize and reproduce on a quiz. Music blared from the room on one side of her. Ruth could not identify the artist, and she did not care. It all sounded the same to her—deafening, bleating, clamoring. And constant. How did Amanda, the student in that room, find space for a thought? On the other side, through thin walls, Ruth heard dribbles of Tasha's phone conversation that landed in random intervals during slight lulls of the music. Every time she caught a snippet, she was surprised anyone could *still* be on the phone for that length of time.

Ruth called it artificial noise—sounds people chose to fill tender spaces but, as far as she could see, brought them no joy.

She began to hum one of the slow, soulful tunes from the *Aumsbund*, the music of her childhood, and simultaneously transferred the list in the textbook to an index card she could carry around and study.

The music went off abruptly, and Ruth heard footsteps in the hall that joined the five rooms of the dormitory suite. A sharp knock startled her.

"Somebody here for you, Ruth."

She scooted her desk chair back and went to the door. Opening it, she saw a woman a few years older than she was with blond hair and gray eyes. Jeans fitted her hips in smooth perfection. A white eyelet shirt with a slight suggestion of sleeves hung loosely above the jeans, revealing tanned arms. Ruth pulled on the cuffs of her own long-sleeved blouse.

"Ruth Beiler?" the woman asked.

Ruth nodded, straightening the plain blue skirt that fell nearly to the floor.

"I'm Annie. We spoke on the phone last week."

Now the voice registered for Ruth. A voice of compassion. "You answered my brother's phone."

Annie nodded.

"Please come in." Ruth stood back from the door. "I don't have

191

much to offer, but I can make tea." The music cranked up again next door. Ruth gestured with one hand. "And entertainment, of course."

"Is it always like this?" Annie asked.

"Only when Amanda's here." Ruth moved to the counter that served as her kitchen to make tea. Stilling the tremble in her hands that came with her visitor's presence required great focus. "How did you find me?"

"Your letter. I saw the return address on the envelope."

Ruth looked hopefully at Annie.

Annie shook her head. "No. Rufus has not read the letter."

Ruth's shoulders lost their ridge. "It's not the first letter. At least he doesn't send them back. So there's hope." She moved quickly to the bed and smoothed the woven cotton blanket. If only she had thought to take a quilt when she left home—not that there had been any time to think that night. "*Sie so gut.* Please. Sit down. I'm afraid I am out of practice at being a good hostess."

Annie sat down on the end of the twin bed. "Do you mind that I've come?"

Ruth shook her head and swallowed. "Not at all. But I don't understand who you are or why you've come." All she knew was that this stranger had seen her brother—perhaps her whole family—just days ago. Whoever she was, she was a welcome guest.

The music shut off, and a door slammed.

Ruth caught Annie's eye, and they both sighed relief.

"How do you know Rufus?" Ruth asked.

"I met him accidentally a couple of weeks ago." Annie let her bag slide off her shoulder and set it on the floor next to the door. "Then I got hurt, and he took me to your family's home for a few days. He was very kind—except when I said something about a letter he carries around."

"He carries it around?" Hope flowed in Ruth's veins.

"In his toolbox. I got the feeling he wanted it close."

"He was probably angry that I called his cell phone."

192

"I'm not sure Rufus gets angry." Annie twisted her mouth on one side. "But when he's disappointed, it comes through loud and clear."

"You seem to understand him well for. . .an *English*. Forgive me, but I can't help wondering about your friendship with my *bruder*. It's not like him."

"I know. It's odd. And 'friendship' may be too strong a word. Circumstances threw us together briefly. I don't expect to see Rufus again." Annie pressed her lips together momentarily. "On the other hand, I get the feeling you would like to."

Ruth's eyes filled, and the tremble rose afresh. She would not be able to withstand long.

"Ruth?" Annie's voice was barely audible.

"Why are they punishing me?" Ruth burst into tears. "I made a choice. It's a good choice. An honorable choice. I'm going to be a nurse and help people. Why can't they understand?"

Annie was on her feet now and wrapped her arms around Ruth.

"*Es dutt mirr leed*," Ruth muttered. "I'm sorry."

"We all make choices every day." Annie stroked Ruth's back, stilled the tremble. "You have to do what's right for you."

"That is not the Amish way." Ruth spoke into Annie's shoulder. "When you're Amish, choices have deeper meaning. You can't imagine what it's like."

"Help me imagine, then." Annie held her tighter. "I know I'm an outsider, but I do care."

"Most people just want to gawk at us." Ruth breathed in the unfamiliar scent of this stranger who had been with her family, hoping for the fragrance of home.

"I hope that's not what I'm doing. At least not anymore. Not after meeting your brother and seeing what matters to him."

Ruth pulled back from their embrace. "Are you sure there's not something between you and Rufus?"

"How can there be? I'm not Amish." Annie waved both hands

in front of her. "I was in a jam. He helped me, and I'm grateful. That's all."

Ruth dragged fingers across both eyes. She did not quite believe her guest. "Then why did you want to find me, Annie Friesen?"

Why indeed?

Annie lifted one shoulder and let it drop. "I don't understand what happened in your family, but I want to help." Ruth's resemblance to Rufus was strong—the same brown hair and violet-blue eyes and a more feminine version of his facial structure. Annie saw bits of Lydia and Sophia in Ruth's expressions, too.

"How?" Ruth turned to fiddle with mugs awaiting the boiling water.

"Well, I haven't figured that part out yet."

"Rufus would say you're interfering."

Annie nodded. "He made that clear."

"Still, you are here."

"I am. I'm used to getting what I want."

Ruth put a tea bag in each mug and poured water. "For some people, just wanting what they get would be enough. My life would have been easier if I were one of them."

"But you're not." Annie stood up straight for emphasis. "If I could make Rufus read your letter, I would. Jacob misses you, if that's any consolation."

Ruth smiled and handed Annie a mug. "I miss him back. He must have changed in all this time. Taller, I suppose. Reading."

"He read your name on the caller ID and was afraid."

Ruth sat in her desk chair, and Annie perched on the end of the bed again.

"I don't want Jacob to be afraid of my name," Ruth said, her shoulders hunched.

"Then we have to fix this."

"It's not so simple. What I did—"

"You made a hard choice, that's all," Annie said. "Something tells me you never meant to hurt anyone."

"I didn't!"

"I believe you." Annie saw Ruth's tears threatening another assault. "I know how important family is to all of you. I don't accept that whatever is between you and your mother must always be painful for you both."

"I did something awful." Ruth's words were a hoarse whisper.

"I'm good at solving problems. If you'll let me, I'll find a way to help you."

Ruth gulped tea, and then slowly she nodded.

"We'll make a plan," Annie said, "and go one step at a time. But first, I want to tell you something I learned because I met your family."

"What's that?"

"My family line traces back to the original Jakob Byler."

Ruth sat up straight. "So we're related?"

"Like ten generations ago and six times removed." Annie grinned. "But we might have a marker or two in our DNA to connect us."

"I can think of worse people to be related to. *Danke.*" Self-conscious, Ruth looked in her mug. "I need more tea. Can you stay for another cup?"

In the middle of the second cup, Ruth said, "I am trying to obey God. *Glassenheit.* Submission. That is our way."

"But if you submit to God by staying in school, you are not submitting to your parents or to the church."

"You understand." Hope caught Ruth's breath.

Annie shook her head. "Not really. It's hard for me to understand why other people get to make choices for you."

Ruth sighed. "The *English* think we spurn their ways. The truth is we are simply trying to choose God's way. That's all I'm doing."

"Even if it takes you away from your family?"

The pressure in Ruth's chest forced its way out through her

throat. "I don't like to choose between God and. . .those I love. But it seems to be the only way."

"I don't accept that." Annie shook her head widely from side to side. "I'm not as close to God as you are—at least not yet—but this doesn't seem right."

"Is it true what you said—that you're good at fixing things?"

"Absolutely. I'm going to help you."

Ruth closed her eyes and breathed out. "You are an answer to my prayer."

They drank three cups of tea. When Annie left and Ruth was cleaning up, for the first time in eighteen months, she did not feel alone. And an *English* was the reason.

By the time Annie turned the key in the lock at her condo, she wanted to see Ruth again. She wanted to see Ruth standing between her brothers or in the embrace of her mother.

She had to go back to Westcliffe. It was the only way to fix this.

Twenty-Five

June 1738

Jakob used both hands to grip the shovel's handle and send the implement's sharp edge into stubborn earth. Again. Again. Little by little the ground gave way. This day was like every other day in the nine weeks since they arrived on Irish Creek.

The land was dense with trees. They had their pick of fir and pine and spruce. The barn went up in a day with the help of the Siebers, Zimmermans, and Stehleys, all on adjoining Irish Creek land, and the Detweilers and others from Northkill. Then came the cabin, which was not large, because Jakob still dreamed of the real house he would have given Verona. But with a loft for sleeping, the family had more space than in the two rooms in Philadelphia. Even with no furniture to speak of, the determined older girls spread their mother's quilts around so the inside would feel like a home. As soon as Jakob and Christian cleared and turned enough land, the garden went in, and it was beginning to show promise that it would yield. Maria planted a square of beets and refused to let anyone else tend that section of the garden.

Jakob taught Christian to hold a rifle and aim steady enough to drop a deer. The animals browsed the black oak all over their land, so it was surprisingly easy to sight them. After a few sudden

197

movements that sent the wildlife scurrying before Jakob could lift a rifle, Christian learned to move with stealth through the woods. So far they had a bounty of meat—deer, rabbit, squirrel, wild turkey—but Jakob was looking forward to some vegetables.

They had cut dozens of trees already, some of them as tall as seventy-five feet. Oak and elm, sycamore and walnut stacked up to be crafted into furniture, planed for floor planks in the permanent house, or cut to warm his children at the hearth when winter raged anew.

For now Jakob did not want to think about winter. Early June sun gave lengthy light for felling and hauling logs, and the days would grow even longer through the summer. Soon he would yoke the horses and begin wrenching out the stumps scattered across the property. Then they could plow. Then they could plant more than a vegetable garden.

Whether he swung an ax, notched a log, joined a corner, or tucked Lisbetli into bed, Elizabeth Kallen hovered in Jakob's moments. He raised his face to the sun, closing his eyes to see her once more standing in the road while the wagon rolled past.

The flicker in the flame told Jakob he needed to seal yet another draft above the small window. The children were asleep in the loft, but Jakob had abandoned his bed in favor of these quiet moments alone with a pen in his hand.

Dear Miss Kallen,

For a long time, he got no further.

I have been remiss not to thank you more promptly for your final kindness toward Lisbetli.

But he had thanked her at the time. And it was only a rag doll.

> *How could you have known she would become as attached*
> *to the doll as she has?*

What he wondered most was how she had known where to find them. And why she had come.

> *Christian has plotted the homesteads on his map and*
> *refers to it often. Maria's progress in the primer is gratifying,*
> *and she writes her letters on a slate each afternoon. How*
> *thoughtful of you to suggest the perfect items for both of them.*
> *I admire your tender heart.*

The last sentence was far too forward.

> ~~*I admire your tender heart.*~~

Now he would have to copy the letter onto fresh paper. That being the case, Jakob supposed he might as well try out other phrases he feared to breathe.

> *I find myself thinking of you often.*
> *I trust this finds you well. I would hate to think you are*
> *distressed.*
> *Would you extend your kindness to an old man by*
> *allowing him to call on you?*
> *I know you are not of the Amish, yet your heart touches mine.*

He couldn't say any of those things. He drew lines of ink through the words.

Jakob laid his pen down and stood up, rubbing his shoulder. He took three steps back. *What am I thinking? She does not believe. This cannot be.*

Jakob moved to the fireplace and examined the embers. He had to leave enough burning to be able to stir up a cooking fire in the morning. Barbara had used the last log for supper. Jakob went to the door, intending to bring in enough wood for the day that would arrive in a few short hours.

When he came back through the door, he stopped in his tracks. "Barbara, what are you doing up?"

She turned to him from the table, a page in her trembling fingers.

"*Daed*, why are you writing this?"

Jakob took a breath and stepped toward the fireplace, where he deposited his load as quietly as possible. No other children need wake and hear this conversation. "That is a private letter, Barbara."

"I can see that."

"Then I ask you to respect my privacy."

"But you are writing to a woman. Are you going to marry her?"

"It is only a letter. She was kind to us."

"*Daed*, I understand if you want to marry again. Many of our people marry again quickly. But you have written right here that she is not of the Amish. How can you consider this?"

Jakob strode across the room and took the page from her hand. "Someday you will want to marry, Bar-bar. You will understand certain. . .feelings."

"Are you *in lieb*? Do you love her?"

Jakob did not respond.

"We suffered so much in Switzerland and Germany because of our faith. We came to this place—we watched *Mamm* die. For this?" She snatched the paper back and threw it down. "No, *Daed*."

Barbara turned and climbed the ladder to the loft without looking back.

Jakob blew out the candle but lay wakeful for long hours.

It was no surprise when Barbara disappeared with Lisbetli for a long time after breakfast. It was no surprise when Hans Zimmerman's horse maneuvered between black oak stumps and came to a stop where Jakob and Christian worked.

Jakob pulled out a handkerchief and wiped his forehead.

"Christian, go to the creek and bring us a jar of water."

"But we still have—"

"Just go, Christian."

The boy dropped his hoe, picked up the half-full water jar, and reluctantly turned his feet toward the creek.

When his son was out of hearing distance, Jakob spoke. "So Barbara has confided in your wife, and she is duly appalled at my behavior."

Hans slid off his horse. "We just want to understand, Jakob. Barbara believes you have intentions."

"How can I have intentions? I barely know Miss Kallen."

"You know we are meant to live apart, Jakob. 'Wherefore come out from among them, and be ye separate, saith the Lord.' Second Corinthians, the sixth chapter and verse seventeen."

"Separate from what, Hans? Am I to live separate from affection? Separate from a mother for a two-year-old who doesn't understand? Separate from someone who might free Barbara to consider her own future?"

"You know the community will care for your family," Hans said. "That is our way."

"You have a wife, and your children have their mother," Jakob countered. "The question has become far more complicated for me."

"You cannot go against *Ordnung*." Hans's jaw set firmly. "If you marry this woman, your life will change. Think of your children."

"I *am* thinking of them."

"Has the community failed you? Have we failed to encourage you in God's will? If we have, we will repent and help you to do the same."

"Elizabeth Kallen has the heart of God in her. I can see it in her eyes. Lisbetli knows this, too."

Hans scoffed. "Lisbetli is hardly more than a babe. But you have been baptized into the church. You cannot consider this step frivolously."

"I assure you that I do not," Jakob said. "But the fact remains that the number of our people is small. I am unlikely to find a wife among the Amish settlers here. Am I to grow still older while I hope that the next ship brings me a desperate woman widowed on the journey? Miss Kallen is a capable woman who would appreciate the challenges of homesteading and care for my children as her own."

"But would she join the church?" Hans challenged.

Jakob leveraged his shovel under a large stone, hefted it, and moved toward a pile of stones. "The stones here are smooth and well shaped. They will make a beautiful fireplace someday."

"Jakob, this is a serious question. Would she join the church?"

Jakob scraped at dirt. "I don't know."

"Would you ask her to?"

"I don't know."

"I don't think you've thought this through, my friend."

"I quite agree," Jakob answered. "Perhaps that is what I was trying to do last night when I wrote a *private* letter."

"She must join the church, Jakob."

Jakob plunged his shovel into the dirt until it stood upright. He turned to look his friend in the eye. "Must she? If I were to wed a woman like Elizabeth Kallen and give my children a mother in the middle of the wilderness, might I be answering a higher calling than the call to join the church?"

Christian returned with the jar of water. Jakob took a deep, cool draft. And Hans mounted his horse.

"Mr. Sieber is leaving tomorrow for Philadelphia to get supplies," Christian said a few days later over lunch. "We should give him a list."

Jakob nodded. "*Gut.* Make a list. I will take it to him this afternoon."

Barbara popped off the crate she sat on. "But we are supposed to go to the Stehleys' to welcome the latest families. Mr. Zimmerman offered to pick us up in his wagon since he comes right through our land."

"You take the children and go with him. I will meet you later."

Anna spoke up. "Is it true that you are going to marry the lady from Philadelphia?"

Jakob stiffened and glanced at Barbara.

"I'm sorry, *Daed*," Barbara said. "I thought Christian and Anna should know. They are old enough. They are not *boppli*."

He turned both hands palms up. "There is nothing to know."

"There might be." His eldest daughter clearly had her mother's stubbornness.

"I'm not going to give up the true faith." Anna was resolute.

"I would never ask you to," Jakob told her. "Your mother and I taught you to do the right thing. You must make the decisions of your own conscience."

Hans Sieber looked dubious when he saw how Jakob's letter was addressed.

"She is at the stationer's shop off High Street," Jakob said firmly.

"Should not the letter be addressed to the owner of the shop?"

"I do not wish to correspond with the owner."

Sieber raised his eyebrows.

"If you don't wish to take the letter," Jakob said, "I will ask someone else."

"We have been friends a long time, Jakob."

"This is why I trust you." Jakob met his friend's gaze.

Sieber nodded and added the letter to his satchel, along with Jakob's supply list.

Riding to the Stehleys' land, Jakob pondered how many days he should give Elizabeth to consider his carefully crafted words and planned his own departure for Philadelphia accordingly. The children could stay with the Zimmermans.

Twenty-Six

"I've got to get to the bank," Annie told Jamie. "They're expecting me promptly at ten."

"You can go just as soon as you sign this letter." Jamie laid a single sheet of paper in front of her.

Annie scanned the page. "This should do it. We're officially severing the company's relationship with Richard D. Stebbins, attorney at law."

"I can send it by courier, and he'll have it inside twenty minutes." Jamie tapped the paper on the desk with a triumphant index finger.

"Handy having a courier service across the street, eh?"

"Then sign the stinkin' page and make it official."

Annie picked up a black pen, with the thin rolling point she favored, and signed her name with flourish.

"Careful there." Jamie wagged a finger in warning. "The signature has to look right enough to be legal."

Annie laughed. "We're done with Mr. Stebbins. After I sign the documents to buy Barrett out, we can focus on moving forward."

Jamie picked up the signed letter and creased it in neat thirds before sliding it into an envelope. "I miss Barrett. It's not like him to just up and leave this way."

"I miss him, too," Annie said. And she did. Annie had withheld most of the story from her staff. Let them remember Barrett with fondness, she figured, even if they thought he lost his marbles for leaving. "I don't think I'll be long at the bank. The new attorney assures me he has arranged for the papers to be ready for signature when I get there."

"When you get back, I'll get Liam-Ryder Industries on the line."

Annie nodded. Liam-Ryder Industries had been patient for two weeks. She couldn't keep ignoring a prospective client with the deep pockets this company seemed to have.

"I'm calling the courier right now." Jamie stepped out of Annie's office to her own desk and picked up the phone.

Annie checked the list on her phone to see what else she had to do before she could go to Westcliffe sometime in the next few days. Eli's brown book was already on the front seat of her car.

Tom steered the red truck into the parking lot, pulled up in front of the building, and shifted into PARK. "Are you sure about this?"

Beside him, Rufus nodded. "It seems the most peaceable thing to do."

"It's a lot of nuisance for you to bank all the way over here. People would come to your aid if they knew Karl somehow got his fingers into the bank decisions. Give them a chance to help."

Rufus shook his head. "I am not trying to cause harm to Karl Kramer. I simply want to earn a living."

"I could come in with you."

Rufus smiled. "You're a good friend even if you are *English*. But I will be fine. I have my tax returns showing my business history and value. I can put up my share of the family land if I have to."

"Okay, then." Tom straightened behind the steering wheel. "I figure it will take about two hours to go see my mother. If you need a place to wait, there's a little garden area behind the bank. I'll look for you and honk."

Holding a soft, deerskin satchel, Rufus got out of the car and watched Tom's truck merge into the unforgiving traffic of Powers Boulevard, eight lanes across. He could not imagine driving a buggy in this town. All Rufus needed in Colorado Springs was a bank manager with a fair-minded sense of business practices. He stepped onto the sidewalk and paced over to the front door.

It was not far to the bank. Still, ever since Rick beat her to the restaurant where she was supposed to meet Barrett, Annie scanned the road whenever she drove. Rick could still try to interfere with signing papers. His grill could show up in her rearview mirror any moment.

But nothing was there. A bedraggled soccer mom in a white minivan. Businessmen with Bluetooth headsets in their ears and miniature offices spread across the front seats of the vehicles. Teens in aging hand-me-down cars heading for the movies. No bronze Jeep. No Rick.

Rufus entered the bank and asked to speak to a loan officer. He ignored the strange looks he always garnered when he came to town. Black suspenders pressed tracks into his white cotton shirt. Today he wore a black felt hat instead of his usual straw hat. Everybody who saw him did a double take and then politely acted as if it were perfectly normal to see an Amish man standing in the bank waiting patiently to apply for a business line of credit in Colorado Springs. Rufus was used to it.

"Mr. Endicott will see you now." Rufus was glad to duck into one of the offices and out of sight of the customers traipsing in and out of the lobby.

Barrett opted to sign the agreement in advance, so Annie knew she would not see him. She was just as relieved as he was to avoid a face-to-face meeting at this point. *What would he do now?* she wondered. He would have money, at least. But knowing Barrett, money was not the real question. He loved the frenzied din of a challenge. Lee Solano insisted on a thorough noncompete clause in the documents that dissolved the partnership, but Barrett could take off with his own ideas and build another company.

The branch manager was waiting for her when Annie entered the bank, and led her past a row of small offices with closed doors flanked by tall, narrow windows. The manager's office was larger and less cell-like. He slid a packet of papers across a smooth, uncluttered, glass-topped desk.

"Three copies of everything," he said. "Please sign all three, and I'll assemble one set for you."

Knowing she would sign in his absence, Lee had prepared Annie well for what the papers would be. Annie scanned each one to make sure it corresponded to what Lee directed and signed all three sets. In a matter of minutes, she had a manila envelope of documents in her hand and watched while the bank manager transferred funds as Barrett had previously directed. The company account showed considerably fewer assets, but Annie now held 100 percent of the company and anything it might create. She stood and shook hands with the bank manager, tucked her manila envelope under one arm, and left the bank.

He was waiting for her when she turned the corner on the sidewalk.

Rick Stebbins backed her up against the brick and crunched a piece of paper in her face. "How quaint. Sending a letter by courier. This means nothing."

"It means you have nothing to do with me," Annie answered evenly.

Rick pulled the envelope out from under her arm. "Is this what I think it is?"

"It's no business of yours." She smelled onion on his breath and knew where he had eaten his morning omelet.

Rick lifted the envelope flap and pulled the papers up a few inches. "So it's done, then. You and Barrett are no more."

Annie said nothing. His breath hovered over her face. She fought to keep her own breathing from turning ragged.

"You can't think it would be over that easily." Rick's brooding eyes held Annie's in a vise now. "Barrett was never the goal."

Annie felt his breath. He had never leaned in so close except to kiss her.

Rufus left the bank encouraged. He would have to wait for a letter confirming the line of credit, but the loan officer saw no reason not to think it would be approved. It was too early to expect Tom would be waiting. Rufus opted to wander behind the bank.

He stopped in his tracks. A man in a dark suit leaned against the brick with one arm, his face close to a woman's. At first Rufus thought he would disturb a romantic moment if he kept walking. *English* would kiss anywhere, after all. It did not matter who was watching.

The man's arm blocked the woman's face, but the color of her hair made Rufus suck his breath in. His eyes moved from her hair to assess her height and form.

Annalise. In trouble.

Rufus said nothing, just stepped right up to the pair and stared into the man's eyes.

The man jerked away from the brick. "What are you looking at?"

Rufus turned his eyes to Annalise. "Is everything all right, Annalise?"

"You know this guy?" Rick asked.

"None of your business," Annalise answered.

"Perhaps you should be on your way." Rufus spoke calmly and firmly to the man.

The man slapped an envelope against Annalise's chest. "I'm very good at what I do."

"So am I." Annalise pushed on the man's chest with one hand and gripped the envelope with the other.

The man glared at Rufus and got into a bronze vehicle and roared away.

Annalise was trembling now. Rufus wished he could gather her into his arms the way he had when she fell at the motel.

"What in the world are you doing here?" she said.

"It's good I came, *ya?*"

"*Ya,*" she answered then laughed at herself. "He wouldn't have done anything. He just tries to throw me off balance."

"He does a good job." Rufus glanced in the direction the man had driven. "I assume he is what you mean when you say, 'It's complicated.'"

She nodded. "Part of it. Most of it."

Rufus tipped his hat toward the garden behind the bank. "Let's sit down and watch something grow."

Annie let Rufus steer her to a bench positioned for admiring a bed of irises and daylilies. The irises had finished blooming weeks ago, but strong stalks almost as tall as Annie still foisted deep orange daylily blossoms upward. Annie thought absently that the flowers were the same kind her mother cultivated.

She sat next to Rufus on the bench, and though he kept a careful distance, his nearness overwhelmed her. If he held his arms open to her, she would fall into them gladly, hear his heart beating, savor the pressure of his embrace.

"Annalise, you're in trouble." Rufus planted his hands on his knees and leaned forward.

209

Annie shook her head. "No. Most of it is sorted out already. I have a lawyer. I just signed papers. That man is angry that he did not get his way." Annie tried to restore order to the documents still sprouting from the envelope in several directions. She put the tidied papers on the bench between them. "How do you do it, Rufus? How do you keep from striking back? I'm not trying to take advantage of anyone. I'm just fighting to protect what's mine."

"What does fighting solve?" Rufus leaned back. "Is what you call your own any safer now?"

Annie sighed. "You make it sound so simple."

"It is far from simple. But it is a choice to trust God's will."

He stretched one arm across the back of the bench, his fingertips now a mere inch from her shoulder. She ached for his hand to rest on there.

"I saved my company—for now—but I lost a friend in the process." Annie picked up the envelope, put the prongs through the hole, and fastened it shut. "I really tried to be peaceable, but he left me no choice."

"You always have a choice. The trouble comes when you judge the consequences and find some of them too high a price to pay."

His fingertips found their way to her shoulder, brushing up and down once and settling. She shivered in the heat.

"You don't even know what I chose, what I did." How could she expect Rufus to understand?

"I can see that what you chose did not make you happy. Or safe."

"Maybe you're right." The space between them called for closing. Annie inched over, laying the envelope on the other side of her. His hand rested firmly on her shoulder now. If he kissed her, she would let him. Even encourage him. "You know, in the *English* world, this is where you would kiss me."

"But that is not my world." Despite his words, he held his position.

He wasn't going to. She would have to do it.

Annie leaned into Rufus, one hand on his chest, and still he did not move. She found his mouth, and he did not move. She pressed into the softness, and he did not move, except to press back against her lips. Or was that her imagination? Warmth oozed through her as she waited for him to break the kiss. But he did not.

Her phone rang, and she jumped back to snatch it out of her pocket. Lee Solano.

"Hi." Intuitively, she strayed from the bench and turned her back to Rufus.

"Everything go okay?"

She ran her tongue over her lips, still tasting Rufus. "The papers are signed. It's done."

"No sign of Stebbins?"

"Well, he did show up, but I handled it."

"Harassment. Find a witness," Lee said. "We'll get a restraining order."

"Oh, I have a witness." Annie turned back to the bench.

But Rufus was gone.

A horn honked, and Annie raised her eyes to the red truck in the bank parking lot. Rufus pulled open the passenger door and got in.

Tom would carry Rufus back to Westcliffe. She had not even mentioned seeing Ruth or thought to return Eli's book. All she had wanted was that kiss, no matter what.

Annie sighed and pulled out her phone to look at her schedule. She was having dinner with her parents the next night and a meeting with Lee the day after that. Then came a day of client meetings. Something had to give.

Maybe Rufus would not even want to see her. Maybe he would not listen once she spoke Ruth's name.

Twenty-Seven

July 1738

Elizabeth Kallen yanked on a crowbar to pry the crate open.

"And what did this week's shipment bring us?" Rachel Treadway, whose husband owned the shop and provided Elizabeth with a small room at the back of his house as most of her compensation, barely lifted her head from her accounts.

Elizabeth grunted and wrenched on the crowbar one more time. The lid came free.

When Elizabeth moved in with the Treadways nine years ago, she did not expect to stay more than a few months. As the years passed, though, she thought less and less about living anywhere else.

Until recently.

Elizabeth reached into the crate and pulled out a tightly wrapped bundle of rose-colored paper in half-sheet size.

"It is a new color. There must be matching envelopes." Elizabeth carefully laid the paper on the counter and turned back to the crate. "Yes, here they are. The usual yellow and blue are here as well."

"Any ink?"

Elizabeth moved crumpled paper around the crate. "Blue and black."

212

Rachel groaned. "The artist over in Elfreth's Alley has been begging for purple and green for his drawings."

Elizabeth shrugged. "Only ordinary paper and ink today."

"We get more and more people asking us for books." Rachel waved the feather of her pen against her chin. "I wonder if I should speak to Mr. Treadway about adding a few more racks."

Elizabeth couldn't imagine where more racks could go in the narrow space of the shop.

"I heard that the Helton girl is finally getting married." Rachel spread several receipts on her desk. "She's nearly thirty. I know for a fact her mother had given up hope she would ever marry."

"Love has no timetable." As Elizabeth turned away, a bead of perspiration formed at the back of her neck and began its slow descent between her shoulders. "I'm thirty-two."

"Oh, but you're different. You have spunk. You came from Switzerland all by yourself when you were twenty-three, and things have worked out well, haven't they?"

Elizabeth nodded. "Well enough."

"We think of you as our own, you know."

"You've been very kind."

Elizabeth had not sailed from Europe to be a shopgirl, however. She was supposed to marry Dirk, who had moved to the New World two years ahead of her. He died in a lumber accident the day her ship left Rotterdam. But how could she have known? She spent two months at sea dreaming of a life that would never be.

She could have married, she supposed. It was not as if she never had another opportunity. But the Treadways, friends of her parents, had sheltered her in the first raw weeks of grief, and Elizabeth had not felt any urgency to move past her lost love.

And then she approached thirty, and passed thirty. Wives her age had five or six children. She had become an old maid who worked in a stationer's shop. After all these years, Robert Treadway trusted her to run the shop with Rachel while he devoted his own time to more lucrative business interests. She rather enjoyed chatting with customers, and she was free to spend her evenings quietly surrounded by books in her small room. On Sundays she went to church and dined with friends. It was not a bad life. If someone had asked, she would have said she was happy.

Until the day Lisbetli Byler reached across the counter and Elizabeth lifted her eyes to the face of the child's father.

Jakob stopped just short of the shop's door. The solid curve of the cobblestone beneath his feet reminded him he had come from a rough-hewn cabin to ask a woman he barely knew if she might leave the comforts of Philadelphia.

The letter had been delivered three weeks ago now. Had he allowed her enough time to consider?

With his eyes focused on where he was putting his feet, Jakob walked past the shop's open door. He would go see the cooper first for two new barrels to keep their foodstuffs in. Then perhaps he would go to the dry goods.

He stopped once again and looked back at the shop, its door propped open in case a breeze might stir in the street. On the farm, he would remove his jacket and work in shirtsleeves. But he could not call upon Elizabeth Kallen in his shirtsleeves.

He did not even know where she lived to make a proper call. He knew her only from the shop. Though he did not marry Verona until he was thirty-five, Jakob had little experience with these matters. His parents had joined the Amish when Jakob was ten. Since that time, he had barely even spoken to a woman who was not part of the church except to make simple purchases of items the Amish did not provide among their own.

He took a deep breath and stepped into the shop, certain that if she were horrified at the sight of him, he would know immediately and retreat without speaking. He would never trouble her again.

"Mr. Byler!" Sitting on a stool behind the counter, her face brightened with welcome. "What a pleasant surprise."

"I hope you are well, Miss Kallen."

"I am quite well, thank you. How is our little Lisbetli?"

Our little Lisbetli. Jakob couldn't help a smile. "She carries the doll with her everywhere she goes."

"I'm so glad. And Maria? And Christian?"

"Maria has learned to read quite a few words, and Christian is a great help with the work." He had written these things in the letter, but he would gladly say them again.

"I suppose you have come to town for supplies." Elizabeth stood. "What kind of paper and ink do you require?"

He had come all the way to Philadelphia to have this conversation, but this was not how he expected it to begin. Jakob's mind spun, confused. Had his letter not made it clear that his interest went beyond paper and ink? He had chosen his words so carefully. How could she not know?

Sieber. His neighbor might well have changed his mind about delivering the letter.

He blinked his eyes rapidly, feeling light-headed.

"Mr. Byler?" Elizabeth leaned across the counter. "Are you all right?"

The color drained from his face before Elizabeth's eyes.

"I wonder if you received my letter."

Elizabeth shook her head. "No, I don't believe we did. Were you trying to order a particular item?"

He looked as if he might stop breathing. Elizabeth grabbed her stool and ran around the end of the counter to offer it to him.

"Please sit down." She put a hand on his shoulder to urge him. "I will get you a cup of water."

Almost afraid to leave him unattended, Elizabeth pushed through the green velvet curtain that separated the main shop from the cramped space she and Rachel used as an office. Still hunched over accounts, Rachel sat at her small desk with a pen in her hand.

"Mr. Byler is here." Elizabeth took a tin cup off the shelf above the water barrel. "Apparently he sent a letter that did not reach us."

"Byler?" Rachel sat alert. "Isn't he one of those Amish people?"

"Yes, I suppose he is. But he's a paying customer."

"I think you should steer clear of him."

"I don't believe you've even met him." Elizabeth gestured to the main shop. "The poor man is out there having some sort of spell because we did not get his letter."

Rachel sighed. "We got the letter." She reached under her stack of accounts.

Elizabeth's eyes widened as she took the envelope. "This is addressed to me, but it is open."

"It might have been an order. But something about the handwriting made me uneasy. It is just not right."

"What is not right?"

"The things he says. He has no business making such a proposition."

Elizabeth lifted the flap of the envelope and slid the paper out.

Twenty-Eight

Two days later, Annie was in her Prius with an iPod full of her favorite bands cranking through the sound system. In comfortable navy slacks and a purple cotton shirt, she was ready to get down to business.

She liked Lee, and he had done a good job of dispatching her legal issues. She also liked the idea of throwing corporate work toward an independent attorney rather than a large firm. But his office was an hour away, and she was used to an attorney virtually around the corner. They would have to figure out how they were going to have a satisfactory professional relationship at a distance.

Annie parked outside Lee's unpretentious office in Cañon City, a second-floor suite in a corner building that likely did not exist three years ago. An hour later, she emerged into the sunlight, having agreed to a three-month trial of full corporate representation by Lee Solano. August had just begun. The searing heat of summer would persist for another six weeks. Wincing at the blast of heat that came from opening the car door, Annie sank into the seat and put the cooling system on maximum.

Lee had suggested she lie low for a few days. She persisted in her opinion that Rick would not hurt her physically, but Lee countered with the wisdom of not taking any chances while he sorted out the legal ground. Work from home. Stay away from the gym. Change where she shopped. Eat at someplace new. Use an uncommon route to everywhere.

An uncommon route to everywhere. That's what Lee said.

She was halfway to Westcliffe already. What was more uncommon than that? At least in Westcliffe she could step into the sunlight without expecting to see Rick Stebbins around every corner.

At least she hoped so.

Annie sat with the air, now hinting at turning cool, blowing in her face, and surveyed the environs of the office building and parking lot. She put the car into gear and rolled out of the lot and onto the street, where she made a complete turn around the block. Then she went to the next block and toured around a slightly wider radius in full alert, looking for any sign of a bronze Jeep with a small dent in the left front bumper.

No sign of Rick. He did have a law practice to run, after all. He could not spend all his time following Annie.

She exhaled with slow control. It was the middle of the week already. A couple of workdays—and then the weekend—in Westcliffe might be just what she needed to wait out Rick's fury. Her gym bag, tossed in the backseat, held workout clothes and two clean outfits. This time she would have a car in Westcliffe. Annie pulled over in a residential area, took out her phone, and shot a quick e-mail to Jamie with instructions to distribute her client meetings among the software writers and to set up the second phone conference with Liam-Ryder Industries for the following week. Then she let her mother know where she was going.

Besides, when Lee had found out she knew the name of the witness who had seen Rick confront her, he had prodded her to ask the person to stand by ready to recount what he saw. She neglected to mention the witness was Amish and lived in Westcliffe. Why should that matter? It only meant that her best chance of getting Rufus to agree to the plan was to go see him in person. She punched some information into her navigational system and hoped some of the scenery would look familiar.

An hour later, Annie slowed into the long Beiler driveway. The barn and the chicken coop were on the right, Rufus's workshop on the left, and the house straight ahead. It was a simple and efficient layout in the daylight, far from her first late-evening arrival. The view was comforting to Annie, and she thought of Ruth and what it would mean to her to see this place again. To be welcomed here.

She still did not know the whole story. Even after three cups of tea with Ruth, Annie knew the young woman was holding something back.

Annie shut off the engine, dreading the scorching instant that would come with opening her car door to the outside air. She looked at her denim bag on the seat beside her. It held her laptop, an e-reader, and several folders of legal papers. A fleeting impulse to grab Eli's book and leave the bag on the seat passed, and she reached to sling the bag over her shoulder and grabbed her iPod out of its slot at the same time. She couldn't leave valuable electronics in the car on a hot day like this.

When she cracked the door, Annie was surprised at the flutter of wind against her face. A couple of thousand feet in elevation made a difference. The day was warm, but the mountain air moved steadily. Still, she kept the bag on her shoulder and stepped out of the car.

"What am I doing?" she said under her breath. *Especially after that kiss.*

Shot through with doubt, Annie set her sights on the front porch. She went up the three wide steps and paused a moment at the swing where she had sat during recovery from her fall, where Franey Beiler tried to make her feel welcome, where Rufus sat with his broken saw, refusing to retaliate.

Sucking in a big breath, Annie knocked on the front door.

"Annalise!" Franey pushed the screen door open. "What brings you here?"

Annie held out the book. "I should have returned this before I left."

"Come inside," Franey urged. "I'll make some cold tea."

Annie shook her head. "Thank you, but I need to speak to Rufus. Do you know where he's working?"

"He's in his workshop. He's been working constantly on those cabinets."

"For the motel?"

"Yes. He's almost finished."

"Is it all right if I go find him?" Annie glanced in the direction of the workshop.

"Let me walk you out there." Franey fell in step with Annie on the path to the workshop. "Do you have business with Rufus?"

"Not exactly." Annie was not sure what she would say to Rufus. "I need to ask a question. A favor."

"I see. You are welcome here, Annalise," Franey said softly, "but I hope you don't have expectations about Rufus. He is a baptized Amish man. It is unusual for an *English* woman to take such an interest."

"I like to think of Rufus as a friend." Annie's heart rate surged. Had Rufus told his mother, of all people, about the kiss? "He showed me kindness more than once."

"I'm glad to hear you speak well of him, and our family enjoys you. But even an Amish mother recognizes a certain look in her grown children. Be careful."

Annie did not want to meet Franey's eye at that moment. She swallowed hard. "It's not like that."

"Isn't it?"

They were at the workshop. Franey pushed the door open, greeted her son, and revealed Annie's presence.

His shirt was open halfway down his chest, and both sleeves were rolled up to the elbow. Annie hesitated, embarrassed. The sight of him in that moment moved her more than all the shirtless men she had ever seen.

Rufus immediately dropped his awl and reached to adjust his shirt.

"I cannot get involved," Rufus said, after Franey left them and Annalise explained that he might help by giving testimony about what he saw. She had flustered him when she arrived, but not enough to make him do what she asked.

"But you saw him." Annalise leaned on his worktable with both hands. "He was right in my face. He's trying to ruin my business."

"He knows I saw him. I made sure of that." Rufus picked up a plane, though he was not sure what he meant to do with it.

"Right! So you could identify him if need be."

"I only meant to deter him from harming you. I cannot get involved with an *English* court case. How does that serve the cause of peace?"

"What about justice?" Annalise's face reddened. "Do you think I should let Rick Stebbins walk all over me the way you let Karl Kramer walk all over you?"

"Is that what it looks like to you?" Rufus carefully set down his plane and swiped his hands together to shake loose the sawdust trapped in the crevices of his skin.

"Well yes."

"Then I have failed." As much as it made sense to deny it, Rufus wanted Annalise to understand his ways in a way most *English* did not. She was so smart. Why could she not grasp this?

"What is it supposed to look like?"

"Jesus," he said softly. "It's supposed to look like Jesus turning the other cheek. Jesus loving His enemy."

"And if the enemy wins? If the enemy gets everything and you are left with nothing?"

"God will provide." If Annalise could understand this one truth, so many more of their ways would follow.

"That doesn't mean God does not expect us to work hard. You

221

work hard to make a living."

"God provides through the blessing of work. That is not the same as court battles and lawyers." Rufus picked up a rag and ran it across the worktable, knocking sawdust and bits of wood to the floor while Annalise was quiet. His words were soaking in, it seemed.

"Well, I didn't think you would testify, but my lawyer wanted me to ask."

Annalise leaned against a post at the end of the workbench. She had not expected to persuade him. Right next to her stood a stack of cabinets. She raised one hand to lightly follow the curved edge in the front design. "These are exquisite."

"Thank you." The moment he had hoped for was gone, but perhaps it would come again.

"Mo must be excited," Annalise said. "When will you install them?"

"I'll take them over tomorrow afternoon, and we'll begin installing the day after that. My crew is busy with something else right now."

He waited for her to bring up the subject they were avoiding, and after a couple more minutes of small talk, she did.

"I suppose we should talk about what happened the other day." She stopped fidgeting with the cabinets. "After. . .on the bench. I'm sorry."

She was five feet away from him, and still he could feel the warmth of her against his chest as he had on the bench. He wanted to put his arms around her then, and he wanted to now.

"Don't be. I'm not."

"You're not?"

He smiled at her surprise. "No." He occupied himself with hanging his tools in their respective spots.

"But—"

"Yes, but. I am an Amish man who wants to live simply, and you are an *English* woman whose life is *complicated*. I let myself feel my own loneliness for a moment."

"That's all it was? Loneliness?"

"That's all it can be, Annalise. I am not going to stop being Amish, and you cannot stop being *English*."

They stared at each other. Rufus knew she would have no words to raise against the simple truth he had spoken.

The door opened, and Jacob burst in. "Annalise! *Mamm* told me you were here. She says you can stay for supper if you want to. Please want to!"

Annalise looked from Jacob to Rufus, and Rufus nodded. He heard the choke in her voice when she answered, "I want to, Jacob."

"Do you like beets?"

She scrunched up her face. "Not very much."

"Good. Then I don't have to dig more." Jacob scampered off. Annalise laughed.

"I'm glad you're staying," Rufus said.

She nodded. "Me, too."

Annie had a "regular" chair at the Beiler table now. In addition to the beets, Franey Beiler served a ham-and-potato casserole and a salad of fresh garden greens. Rain pattered during the main meal, eventually rising to a steady sleepy rhythm.

"I hope it keeps raining all night," Lydia said.

"You just don't want to water the garden," Sophie said.

"It takes too many buckets. We need more rain."

"For the fields, too." Joel reached for the plate of bread. "Are you sure you cannot hire me, Rufus?"

"You have work on the farm," Rufus answered.

Eli cleared his throat, and Joel grimaced. "I love the alfalfa fields, *Daed*. But it might be nice to have a bit of real money now and then."

"God will provide," Eli said.

There it was again. Annie looked from Eli to Joel, two generations of Beilers sorting out what those three words meant.

Occasionally Jacob leaned in close to Annie to interpret what the family was saying in Pennsylvania Dutch. Jacob's English was very good for a small child who did not see all that much of the *English*. Rufus did not catch Annie's eye.

By the time Lydia and Sophie carried twin peach pies to the table for dessert, thunder jolted them all. The rain was a lashing whip now.

"Annalise," Franey said as she handed the visitor a slice of pie, "perhaps you should plan to spend the night."

"I thought I would see if Mo had a room at the motel," Annie said. "I plan to stay a few days."

"No point in going out in the storm. Ruth's room is just as you left it. You may stay as long as you like."

Now Annie did look at Rufus to catch his eye. He gave a nod. *Yes, stay the night,* it seemed to say.

"I'd love to," Annie said. "Let me help you do the dishes."

In the morning, Annie made a point to be up in plenty of time for breakfast. The last thing she wanted was Franey Beiler thinking she was a lollygagging guest. When Franey knocked on her door, Annie was already dressed and straightening the quilt, made of deep purple, blue, and green.

"Did you sleep?" Franey asked.

"Very well." Annie stroked the quilt, wondering how many years Ruth had slept under it. "The quilt is beautiful."

"It was Ruth's favorite," Franey said quietly. "My mother made it forty years ago. I used to keep it in the cupboard, but Ruth nagged and nagged for me to let her use it. I finally gave in, and then she was gone."

Annie swallowed hard. Would her next words bring comfort or sorrow? "I saw Ruth last weekend."

Franey's breath stopped as her eyes widened. "My Ruth?"

Annie nodded.

A second quilt hung over the foot of the satin black wrought-iron bedstead. Franey lifted it now and refolded it for no good reason. Annie hadn't even used it. "How is she?"

"She misses you."

"She knows where to find us."

"Would you like for her to visit?"

"I would like for her to come home. That's not the same thing, though, is it?"

Annie shook her head and held her tongue.

"It must seem to you that we are harsh toward Ruth."

"I don't know what happened," Annie said. "I only know she loves you."

Franey hung the quilt on the bedstead again with finality. "You're right. You don't know what happened."

Twenty-Nine

*J*acob gave her an I'm-going-to-be-mad-if-you-leave look, but after a breakfast full of chatter, Annie gathered her bag and headed into town. In her car, compared to the buggy rides of her last visit, the five miles zipped by. She parked on Main Street in front of an antiques shop. The sign on the door read, BACK IN 30 MINUTES, which amused Annie both because in Colorado Springs no business would risk missing a customer by closing in the middle of the day, and because the sign did not indicate when the thirty minutes began.

She waved her phone around in the air to catch a signal then checked her e-mail while she walked slowly.

"What are you doing?" Annie winced at her mother's typed words. *"What is this fixation you have with Westcliffe? Call me so I can talk some sense into you."*

Jamie had a list of questions. Annie considered walking three blocks down to the coffee shop to sit down and answer them. Would the barista still remember her beverage of choice, or had she already fallen out of favor?

And then she saw it.

She wondered why she had not seen it three weeks ago.

226

Perhaps it had not been there.

The FOR SALE sign pointed down the side street, directing her to the narrow green house toward the end of the block. She turned the corner, paced past three houses, and stood across the street. The house was two stories but barely wide enough for a decent living room. Probably a living room at the front, with an eating space and something that passed as a kitchen at the back, with perhaps two small bedrooms and a bath upstairs. Annie could not immediately detect where the stairs were, but she had a couple of guesses.

She doubted the whole house was more than eight hundred square feet of usable space. Her condo was three times that big.

This place was waiting for the big bad wolf to breathe too hard and blow it down. Her condo was brand new.

This would be Annie's idea of camping out, while her condo had every modern convenience.

The garage here looked like it was built to house a couple of bicycles. The condo had a reserved underground extrawide parking space.

Annie dialed the number on the sign and spoke to a real estate agent who assured her she could just go on in and look around. The back door was unlocked. The half-acre pasture behind the house was part of the property being offered. Water came from a well beneath the pasture. The realty office was at the other end of Main Street. Call if she had questions.

Annie's heart rate sped up as she strode down the driveway and found the three cement steps up to the back door. A wooden railing she was afraid to lean on enclosed the tiny porch. She paused to glance at the fenced-in pasture. "Horse property," they would call this on the outskirts of Colorado Springs.

The knob turned easily, and Annie stepped into the kitchen—she was right about the downstairs layout—and could see straight through the house to the place where she had stood on the street. The stairs, narrow and steep, rose from one side of the dining room. Downstairs, the walls were a cheery pale yellow. Though the place was empty, someone had obviously cleaned thoroughly and painted in hopes of persuading a buyer of the home's worthiness.

It was working.

Annie climbed the steps, almost afraid to hope for what she would find upstairs. A larger bedroom at the front of the house mirrored the dimensions of the living room, and a smaller one—about the size of her closet at the condo—sat over the kitchen. Neither one of them had a real closet, but the previous owner had left tall wardrobes probably deemed too difficult to bother moving. In the back bedroom, Annie pulled the latch of the wardrobe and imagined it filled with clothes from the condo.

Off the hall in between the bedrooms—papered in green and yellow stripes—was a bathroom with a claw-foot tub.

A claw-foot tub.

Annie had always wanted a claw-foot tub.

Gingerly she reached for the sink's faucet and turned a knob. The pipes rattled but produced clear water.

Rapidly, the picture began filling in. A copper pipe rose from the tub to a shower head. Annie would install a fixture from the ceiling to hang a shower curtain that enclosed the tub. She would do the bathroom in silver and pale pink. Eventually. Of course, the first job would be to make everything functional.

She was going to buy the place, not imagining there would be much competition if she offered just under the asking price. It was only two hours from the condo—a great weekend place. Something to fix up. A hobby. She needed a hobby. Everyone said she worked too hard, especially her mother.

Everyone. Who was everyone? Annie's work habits had cut her off from most of her friends a long time ago. Barrett was her buddy, and now he was gone from her life, taking with him his outgoing wife with whom Annie had always enjoyed spending time.

Annie stood in the upstairs hall, a whisper blowing through

her. She was meant to find this house on this day.

God's will. This house would be more than a hobby. She blinked against the picture taking form in her mind.

She walked through again, testing light switches and faucets. What she presumed was a broom closet off the kitchen opened to stone steps leading to a basement. Down the creaky stairs she found an ancient furnace and hot water heater. On the way back up, she noticed the shelf of cherry preserves and canned green beans. How long had they been there?

Yes, she was definitely going to buy the house. She would wait to tell anyone until her offer was accepted in writing. A cash offer would help speed the sale.

God's will.

Tires screeched through her dreams, but it was the pounding that made Annie throw back Ruth's quilt and leap out of bed. She was sleeping in her workout clothes. All the Beilers were in the upstairs hall at two in the morning, as Eli and Rufus scrambled down the stairs. Wearing shorts and a tee, Annie stood in the midst of the family waiting on the landing. When Rufus opened the front door, Tom's flashlight lit his face.

"It's your cabinets, Rufus," Tom said. "Karl got to them. Mo already called the police."

"I'm coming with you." Annie pushed past Sophie.

"Oh Annie," Tom said. "Do you have your car? Can you bring Rufus? I promised Mo I'd come right back."

"Absolutely."

Rufus was already on his way up the stairs to exchange a robe for real clothes. Annie ducked back into Ruth's room for jeans, shoes, and a sweater. Seven minutes later, they were in the Prius.

"This sounds really bad, Rufus." Annie backed up the car to turn around. "You just took those cabinets over there yesterday."

"Let's wait and see what happened."

"The police are going to be involved."

"That's Mo's decision, not mine."

"They're your cabinets. Your hard work."

Annie turned into the lane leading to the motel. Lights blazed across the scene. She spotted Tom's truck and two squad cars labeled CUSTER COUNTY SHERIFF. The other vehicles were unfamiliar—likely guests at the motel but perhaps also gawkers. She parked as close to the lobby entrance as she could.

Rufus was silent as he got out of the car and walked past a couple of women in shorts and sweatshirts. Annie followed closely, scanning for Mo.

An officer greeted Rufus. "I understand you are the carpenter doing the work here."

Rufus nodded, his eyes looking past the officer with the clipboard to the cabinets. Twelve hours ago, he left them stacked neatly in a suggestion of their final arrangement. Then he had covered them with pads and tarps. Now the pads and tarps were bunched in one corner, and blue and green spray paint splattered and squiggled across the exposed panels.

Annie squatted beside Rufus as he ran his fingers though the paint, barely dry. "Will it come off?"

"It should, but I'll have to sand and finish everything again."

"What about this?" Annie stuck a finger in a hole at the bottom of one front panel. Rufus's shoulders sagged.

"They used an auger," he said on a sigh. "Took a plug right out."

"Clearly it's premeditated." Annie pushed to a standing position, huffing in fury. "This is not the work of bored teenagers."

Rufus stood up. "See how many holes you find. I'd better check the desk."

Annie carefully examined all eight cabinets and found three more auger holes and one deep scratch, the kind a key made in the grip of determination. Rufus threw back the tarp from the new reception desk and found a long gouge across the top.

One officer was absorbed with taking Mo's report. Annie

listened in. Mo was asleep in her apartment behind the lobby. The lobby door was locked. Guests accessed their rooms from the outside. New guests arriving at odd hours could ring a doorbell that woke her, but it was uncommon for anyone to arrive past midnight. Mo heard nothing until an engine gunned. She called Tom, then the sheriff's office.

"This is the work of Karl Kramer," Tom insisted to the officer.

The officer turned his hands palm up. "Innocent until proven guilty. We'll investigate, but we can't arrest a person without something that smells like evidence just because you say he has a grudge."

The second officer questioned people standing in the parking lot, who turned out to be three motel guests and Tom's wife, Tricia. Nobody saw anything. One of them, who had been watching television, said she might have heard a truck, but she wasn't sure.

"We have breaking and entering, and we have vandalizing," the first officer said. "Mo, we'll do the paperwork in the morning. You can come by and make sure it's right."

"What about Rufus?" Mo turned toward Rufus, who was silent. "The ruined cabinets and the desk are his work."

"They were on your premises," the officer responded. "Check with your insurance agent."

Annie spoke up. "Someone drilled holes in the cabinet, someone who wanted to hurt Rufus. Not just anyone would have an auger lying around."

"You'd be surprised in these parts, ma'am."

"They didn't touch anything else," Annie persisted. "Not a drop of paint on the floor, not a scratch in any other furniture. Only Rufus's work."

"Annalise." Rufus voice came softly. "This is not necessary."

"Yes it is." Annie looked to Mo for support. "Whoever did this was not out to hurt Mo. They wanted to set Rufus back. They want him to bear the cost of righting this."

"Annalise, please," Rufus said.

The officer shrugged. "I'll make note that Mr. Beiler is a possible witness if we make it to court. And I'll have a conversation with Karl Kramer, see if he has an alibi that checks out."

"He wouldn't be stupid enough to do it himself." Annie balled her hands at her sides. "He'll say he was home in bed."

"I know you're frustrated, ma'am, but right now we don't have enough to charge anyone."

The officers left. The guests went back to bed. Tom and Tricia went home.

"I'll put on coffee. We'll sort out what's next." Mo disappeared into the motel's dining room.

"It's not fair!" Annie sank into a small armchair.

Rufus sat on the floor across from her and held one hand up tenderly on an unscarred side surface of a cabinet. "The damage is only on the surfaces that show."

"See! Karl thought this through."

"We don't know it was Karl."

"Don't we?" Annie sat forward, her back straight. "I bet you could tell me exactly what kind of auger makes that kind of hole, and I bet Karl has one."

"You have not even met Karl Kramer," Rufus reminded her. "I barely know him myself."

"If the police won't do anything, we have to take the matter into our own hands. We have to find proof."

"You know I'm not going to do that." Rufus did not move off the floor. "Anger will not rebuild the ruined cabinets."

Annie huffed. Rufus was nothing if not consistent.

It was well after three in the morning by then. Mo returned with steaming mugs of coffee.

The buggies began arriving at four.

Eli and Franey Beiler were the first. By six in the morning, eight buggies lined the lane, with horses nosing around for grass to nibble. When the day cracked open with light, Amish neighbors buzzed around the motel. Sawhorses and plywood planks created worktables. Tools and cleaning supplies emerged. Women put out food bright with color and wafting scents. Men carried the defaced cabinets out of the lobby and spread them on the makeshift workbenches, where they patiently awaited Rufus's discernment about which pieces of craftsmanship could be redeemed and which would be recreated. A group of teenagers, both boys and girls, eyed each other wistfully over the tops of their brooms as they restored order to the lobby.

Annie watched, flabbergasted. When she bought her condo, she couldn't even get anyone to help her move. But here, for Rufus, a couple of dozen people—no doubt with ample obligations of their own—rearranged their day to help one cabinetmaker keep his business on track. Inspired, she did what she could to contribute. Mo put on two large canisters of coffee to perk, and Annie rounded up mugs and arranged them on a rolling cart. Mo produced a tub of lemonade mix with a half dozen pitchers, and Annie went to work. For a good part of the morning, Annie kept the beverages flowing as sandpaper and skirts swished around her.

Around eleven o'clock, she leaned against a broad elm and slid down until she sat on its protruding roots. Wet blotches smeared her cheeks, tears leaking from her eyes against her will. *Please, God, make me understand what I'm seeing.*

"Annalise, what's wrong?" Rufus squatted beside her.

She startled, surprised he was so near. "It's beautiful. I can't believe what they're doing."

"This is our way. When one suffers, we all suffer. It's better together than alone. That is the body of Christ."

"I can see that. I just don't have anything like that in my life. I mean, I have my parents. But all these people dropped whatever they planned for today and came to help you. How did they even find out so fast?"

"They have phones. Someone decided this was an emergency." Rufus let his weight down on the ground and stretched out his long legs beside her.

They leaned against the tree trunk without words for several minutes, their eyes on the bustle of work. Perspiration gathered along her hairline. Annie ran her hands through her hair, wishing she had thought to grab something to draw it off her neck when she hastily dressed in the middle of the night. She swept her hair off her neck with both hands and held it up. The next instant, she felt Rufus's eyes on her. On her neck. She dropped her hands immediately, and her hair tumbled back around her shoulders and face. Annie scooped it behind her ears.

Beneath his hat and under his long sleeves, Rufus perspired as well. Annie breathed the scent willingly—the scent of honest work. She sat beside a man of trust and integrity.

Annie turned her head toward him. "Rufus, can I tell you something you will think is wildly ridiculous?"

Rufus half smiled and cocked his head at her. "What is that?"

"I bought a house yesterday. Here in Westcliffe."

He lifted an eyebrow. "That does seem out of character."

"There's something here that gives me a piece of my life I'm missing." Her eyes lifted above the Amish crowd to the mountain sheen.

"Knowing you're missing something is the first step toward filling the hole."

"So you don't think it's ridiculous?"

"That depends. I haven't seen the house yet." Rufus wiped his sleeve across his dripping forehead.

Annie laughed. "There's just something about being here. . . about you and your family and your people. You once said I was grasping at air. Seeing all this generosity makes me think I'm holding on too tight."

"You won't know if you don't let go."

"I'm not sure I can."

"If you are grasping at air, what are you really holding?"

"I haven't begun to tell you what I do for a living. I'm successful, Rufus. Wealthy, even." Annie turned to look at Rufus.

He raised a hand and drew his fingers across her damp cheek. "Have you heard the story of the rich young man in the Bible who came to Jesus?"

Annie's brain clicked through the stories she had learned as a child. "Jesus told him to sell everything and give the money to the poor."

"That's right. But he could not do it, not even for eternal life."

"People depend on me for their jobs, Rufus. Am I supposed to walk away from my own talent? From responsibility?"

"What does Jesus ask you to give up, Annalise? And what will you gain?"

Annie swallowed. "You always give me something to think about."

Rufus glanced up the lane. "We may be in the way of Mo's business. Here's a customer now."

Annie followed his gaze toward the woman sauntering toward the commotion. She jumped to her feet.

"Mom! What are you doing here?"

Thirty

$\mathcal{M}$yra Friesen scanned the scene. "Annie, what exactly are you involved with?"

"Isn't it beautiful?" Annie turned toward Rufus only to find he had stepped away, though he glanced over his shoulder to catch her eye.

"I had no idea your Amish fixation had gone this far." Myra planted her hands on her hips. "Is this some sort of barn raising?"

"Kind of. Vandals made a mess last night, and these people are all here to clean things up. What they're doing is amazing."

"Well, it's touching, I'm sure, but you're my concern. I'm worried about you, Annie. You've been vague about why you came to Westcliffe in the first place—I don't buy the line about business. What business could you have in a town this size? Why did you leave without your car? And now you're back here, apparently tangling with vandals."

"I'm fine, Mom. Can I introduce you to some people?"

"I stick out like a sore thumb." Myra wiped one hand along the thigh of her blue capris. "And so do you."

"You'll get used to it. And you don't have to meet everyone. Just a few people." Annie waved a hand toward the workers. "Just

236

the Beilers, the people I've stayed with."

"Oh. That's what this is all about. I suppose you found them in the books."

"As a matter of fact, I did. And I found Dad, too. And you and Penny and me."

Annie steered her mother to where Franey and Eli stood sharing a paper cup of lemonade at the end of one workbench. Eli had nearly finished scrubbing the paint off a panel and was getting ready to sand.

"Mom, I would like you to meet Franey and Eli Beiler." She gestured from the Beilers to her mother. "This is Myra Friesen, my mother."

Franey smiled pleasantly, and Eli nodded.

"It's nice to meet you." Myra awkwardly extended a hand in an indefinite direction.

"And you, too." Franey corralled Myra's hand and shook it, then guided it toward Eli's. "Perhaps I'll get to see how your daughter comes to be so spirited."

Myra looked around. "She has always had a mind of her own. I am trying to understand just where her spirit has taken her."

"She turned up in our barn in a most curious way," Franey said. "Our youngest was smitten immediately, so of course we took her in when she was injured."

"Barn?" Myra pivoted toward Annie. "Injured? Why do I think I'm not getting the whole story?"

"Mom, I'm fine."

Myra furrowed her forehead and glanced at Franey. "She's behaving in such an unusual manner lately."

"Daughters do that sometimes." Franey's voice instantly dropped to a murmur.

"Do you have daughters?"

"Three." Franey's response was barely above a whisper.

Eli offered the lemonade cup, and Franey took it—a little too eagerly, Annie thought. Before she could sort out what to say,

Rufus joined them then, sandpaper in one hand and soft cotton cloths in another.

"Everything all right?" he asked.

"Perfectly fine," Annie said. "This is my mother, Myra Friesen. Mom, this is Rufus Beiler."

"Hello, Rufus." Myra ran her eyes up and down his height. "I've just learned you have three sisters."

"And four brothers."

"Oh my. That's a houseful."

"Not everyone lives here." To Annie's relief, Eli spoke up. "Two of our sons are married in Pennsylvania. Our eldest daughter is also. . .away."

"Oh, then you can understand that I wanted to see where my daughter had taken herself off to without explanation."

Annie saw the color shift in Franey's face. "Mom, how about some lemonade? You've had a long drive."

"I could do with a bit of refreshment."

"I'll get you something," Rufus offered.

"No thanks." Annie avoided his eyes. The last thing she needed was for her mother to see how she looked at Rufus. "I'll get it. We should get out of the sun anyway."

Annie led her mother inside the lobby, which had been stripped bare, to where the rolling cart held half-empty pitchers of lemonade. She filled a paper cup, handed it to Myra, and proceeded to the empty dining room, where they sat at the end of a table.

"They seem friendly enough." Myra poured liquid down her throat.

"For Amish people, you mean?"

"For any people," Myra said flatly. "Must you think the worst of me?"

"I'm sorry." And she was. What was the phrase the Amish used? *Es dutt mirr leed.*

"You have to admit it's odd that you should take such an interest in them."

"Perhaps. But if the genealogy books are right, I very nearly could have been one of them."

"But you're not."

"No. Not by birth." Annie quickly gauged how far to push this conversation. "But what's wrong with being interested in learning about their way of life?"

"Nothing, I guess." Myra set her empty cup down a little too firmly. "Isn't it unusual that they should take you in? What was that business about being injured?"

"I fell and hit my head. I stayed in their home while I recovered. I'm staying there again now."

"Well, that's handy, what with how you feel about Rufus."

Annie's head snapped around to meet her mother's eye. "What do you mean?"

"I wasn't born yesterday. It's hardly your first observable crush."

Annie rotated her cup in her hands. "There's nothing between us."

"No, I don't suppose there could be. But when you look at him, I see more in your eyes than you ever showed for Rick Stebbins."

"I think we've established that you were right about Rick." Annie pinched a piece of wax-covered paper from the rim of her cup. "And you're right again. How could there be anything between me and Rufus Beiler? We come from different worlds." Even as she heard her own words, Annie did not believe them.

"I'm just looking after you." Myra patted Annie's twitching hand. "You're my baby girl."

Annie rolled her eyes. "I can look after myself, Mom."

"You've done very well for yourself. No one can argue with that. But in the last few weeks, you broke up with your boyfriend, dissolved your business partnership, and went incognito. A mother worries about these things."

If only her mother knew the extent of recent events. Rick Stebbins always one step ahead of her. Barrett's embarrassing secret. Kissing an Amish man in the park behind the bank. The narrow green house just off Main Street that would be hers in a matter of days. Yes, her mother would have plenty to freak out about if she only knew.

"As long as I'm here," Myra said, "you might as well show me around town."

"That will take about ten minutes." Annie stood up, grateful for the distraction.

They retraced their steps through the barren lobby and the bustling work zone and got into Annie's Prius. She backed up and did a three-point turn, watching the horses and buggies carefully. A couple of minutes later, they pulled out onto the highway.

"Who was that man in the gray Windbreaker?" Myra asked. "He didn't look Amish."

It was a warm day for a Windbreaker. "Fiftyish and balding?" Annie thought of Tom, the only *English* man at work on the cabinet panels.

"No." Myra shook her head. "Thirtyish and skulking. He got in that tan sedan that pulled out ahead of us. I noticed him when I arrived, but he didn't seem to be working. He stayed on the fringe of things."

Annie had not noticed. But she had a good guess. She squinted into the sunlight and reached for the dark glasses she always stored on the dash. In a moment, the tan sedan came into focus. She did not recognize it, but she closed the gap slightly and paced her speed to maintain an even distance. The turn onto Main Street and downtown Westcliffe came up on the right, but Annie continued past the intersection, keeping the sedan in sight.

"That looked like town to me." Myra craned her head to the right and back.

"Blink and you miss it." Annie pressed her lips together. "There's some new construction up this way that might give you an idea of the town's potential. People are building some nice homes. Rufus has a couple of custom cabinetry jobs there. His work is art."

They went past a sprawl of new homes and into a stretch of active construction. The tan sedan slowed, and Annie let off the accelerator slightly. When it turned into a construction zone, Annie drove past.

"There's not much more up here. We'll go back to Main Street." Annie pulled to the shoulder, waited for a minivan to pass, and swung the Prius around to head back toward town. As she passed the tan sedan, she looked carefully at the sign on the site.

Kramer Construction. Just what she thought.

"Mrs. Weichert runs an antiques store in town," Annie said. "Well, antiques and miscellaneous items of interest. We can stop if you like."

"No time. May Levering is expecting me for tennis this afternoon, and then there's some dreary fund-raising dinner that your father says I must attend."

Annie turned down Main Street and slowed. "Welcome to Westcliffe, Colorado. The signs tell you when it changes from Westcliffe to Silver Cliff, but it's not much." Annie pointed out the coffee shop, a thrift store, and the local newspaper office, then swung down a side street. Within four minutes, they hit the old schoolhouse, the historic Lutheran church, and a railroad museum. "That's about it." Annie turned again to head back to the highway. *Except the house I bought.* They were headed west toward the shimmering Sangre de Cristos now. "You can't beat the view."

"It's spectacular—I give you that." Myra twisted slightly in her seat belt to look at her daughter. "But somehow I still think it's not the view that pulls you here."

Thirty-One

Annie drove by the construction site two more times later in the afternoon. All she wanted to know was if the man she saw was Karl Kramer himself or someone who worked for him. Either way it was suspicious for him to leave a car up by the highway and take refuge in the trees while a couple of dozen people worked—and then drive to a place with a Kramer Construction sign. Once, she pulled over to the side of the road to take out her phone and do an Internet search on images of augers.

She seethed just thinking about it. Rufus would tell her to let it go. But Annie had some choice words spinning in her head that she would love to spit out at a prime suspect.

The day was over. Rufus would have to recraft four face panels, but the sides and top of the framing to hold the cabinets were salvaged. Patient volunteer scrubbing, sanding, and refinishing had cabinet surfaces looking as they were meant to be, saving him days of labor. Rufus was confident he had sufficient wood left to create the new front panels and the top of the desk. Mo fussed about how long the delay would take before Rufus could attempt installation again, but eventually she accepted the answer he gave.

Annie pulled her car into the long Beiler driveway. She turned in the gravel alongside the barn and negotiated her car to the back, where the structure provided a path of shade during the hottest part of the day.

As Annie walked around the barn, voices—in Pennsylvania Dutch—drew her inside. Rufus stood feeding an apple to Dolly while Lydia and Sophie gathered garden tools. They were all laughing about something. Annie hoped it wasn't her. When she stood in the open doorway, conversation switched to English.

"We should be able to pull the carrots soon," Lydia said.

"The beans just keep coming," Sophie said.

Somehow Annie thought the conversation must have been less mundane before she arrived.

"Do you want to help us in the garden?" Lydia said. "We're just doing a little weeding and looking for what needs picking."

"I don't know anything about gardens or how to tell if something is ready to pick." Annie took a step backward.

"We'll show you what to do." Sophie reached for her arm and pulled her deeper into the barn.

"Okay, then," Annie said. "Annalise Friesen at your service."

Jacob burst into the barn breathing fast. "A man is at the house looking for Annalise. *Mamm* said to see if she was here."

Annie saw Rufus stiffen. She sucked in her breath.

"What does he look like?" Rufus glanced at Annie and then back at Jacob.

"He's *English*. He's wearing a suit, and his shoes are really shiny. He came in a car that looks gold and brown at the same time."

"Bronze." Annie stepped even farther into the barn.

"Is he on the porch?" Rufus calmly fed the last bit of apple to Dolly.

The little boy nodded.

"Jacob," Rufus said, "I want you to walk slowly—don't run—back to the porch and ask the man if he would like to talk to me."

"Shouldn't I tell him Annalise is here?"

"Just ask him to talk to me. Do you understand?"

243

The little boy nodded.

Rufus turned Jacob's shoulders back toward the house. "Remember, slowly."

Jacob nodded. Annie watched the boy concentrate on moving slowly, his stride like that of a toddler.

Rufus, on the other hand, spun around. "Quick. In the dress." He turned to the shelves that held blankets the family used in the buggies in the winter and pulled out the dress he had left there weeks ago.

"That's Ruth's dress," Sophie said.

"Just help Annalise get it on." Rufus thrust the dress at Annie. "Get her hair up under the *kapp*."

Annie felt like a fashion model with a crew transforming her. Lydia dropped the dress over her head and rapidly pinned the front closure. Sophie removed Annie's shoes, rolled up her jeans, then grabbed Annie's hair—painfully—and punched it under the white *kapp*. With no hairpins to hold the hair in place, Lydia tied the *kapp* under Annie's chin

"To the garden, all of you." Rufus shoved a rake into Annie's hands.

By the time Jacob returned to the barn with the stranger, three young Amish women were working barefoot in the garden sixty feet away. One of them, in a deep purple dress, kneeled to pull weeds by hand, her back to the barn. Rufus assessed the man. Yes, this was the man from behind the bank. Rufus met him at the barn's doorway, leaning on a pitchfork.

"Can I help you?" Rufus crossed his arms.

The man laid his head to one side. "I'm looking for Annie Friesen."

"Her name is Annalise," Jacob said.

"Jacob," Rufus said calmly. "Thank you for showing our guest the way. You can go back to helping *Mamm* now."

"But—"

"Jacob, you must go."

"Yes sir." The boy turned to go, disappointed.

"Just a minute." The stranger glanced across the yard to the garden. "How many sisters do you have?"

"Three," Jacob said simply.

Rufus almost smiled at the perfection of it all. "*Mamm* is waiting for you, Jacob."

"I'm going, I'm going."

The two men stared at each other.

"I don't believe I got your name the last time we met." Rufus set his feet solidly shoulder width apart.

"Names don't matter." Rick's friendly veneer proved thin. "How quaint. Did she find you charming at the bank as well?"

Rufus shoved the pitchfork more firmly into earth. "Why have you come here?"

"I wanted to talk to Annie. I was told she might be at the Beiler place. I had no idea I would find you."

"Who did you speak to?" Rufus wanted to know.

"The woman at the motel." Rick waved a hand casually. "She's a little frazzled about something, but she said Annie was staying here."

"How did you find the motel?" Rufus asked.

Rick exhaled. "I'm not going to play twenty questions with you, whoever you are. I just want to talk to Annie. She is my fiancée. I'm worried about her."

"It did not appear that way to me the last time we met."

"Mind your own business. Isn't that what you people do?"

"Of course. But I would have to say that an *English* man standing outside my barn making demands is my business."

"Just show me where she is."

Rufus opened his arms wide. "Do you see her?"

Rick leaned to one side to peer into the barn. "Must be a dozen places to hide in there."

"You are free to inspect the barn," Rufus said. "Many people are curious about Amish ways."

Rick rolled his eyes. "Look, I'm not here for some lame tour."

"Then perhaps our business is concluded." Rufus met Rick's eyes. "In fact, I'm quite sure it is."

Rick pivoted and walked to his Jeep. On the way, he glanced around the property again. Rufus followed a few steps behind, smiling blandly until Rick got in his vehicle and turned the ignition. Rick reversed, turned around, and churned up clouds of dirt on his way to the main road. Rufus did not move until the car was out of sight.

When he turned around, Annalise had grabbed fistfuls of the purple dress and was hurtling toward him. Rufus pointed to the barn. Better to be out of sight, just in case.

She threw her arms around him the minute they were inside. "Thank you!"

"You're welcome." The weight of her against his chest. Her blond hair escaping the *kapp*. The sight of her in an Amish dress. Suddenly he wanted nothing more than to kiss her. Gently, he stepped out of her embrace before he could not stop himself.

"He must have followed my mother."

"Have you explained to her what is going on?"

"Not. . .every detail. I suppose I'll have to tell her something now." She paused, looked him in the eye. "Why did you hide me?"

Why indeed? "Was I supposed to hand you over to someone I know means you harm?"

"I'll call my attorney. He'll do something. I don't know what. But something." Annalise patted the dress fabric, no doubt looking for a pocket where her cell phone should be.

"You look stunning," he said softly. "I always knew you would. I guess that's why I brought you the dress in the first place."

Annalise's motion shifted to smoothing down the full skirt. Then one hand went to the *kapp*. "Am I doing this right? I notice your sisters leave their ties loose."

"Because their hair is braided and pinned up," he said. "It stays put."

"I'll have to learn to do that." She tugged, and the knot gave easily. With the *kapp* loosened, her hair tumbled around her shoulders.

A woman's hair. Who would have thought it could move him so?

"The dress fits." He soaked in the beauty of her. Her gold chain had worked its way over the round neckline. "I imagine it feels strange to you."

Her answer was slow. "Not as strange as you might suppose." She ran a tongue along her lips then pressed them together, holding her breath.

His own breath ran shallow. "In the *English* world, I suppose this is where I would kiss you."

"And in your world?" She stepped toward him and tilted her head up. Her *kapp* slipped off her head and hesitated at her shoulder before falling. Neither of them moved to stop it from hitting the ground.

"In my world, I very much want to," Rufus finally said.

Annalise laid a hand on his upper arm, sending him spinning. Her face was right there, and upturned.

Rufus stepped back, and Annie moaned, a sound she did not intend to release. He was not going to kiss her.

Rufus sighed heavily. "It would be wrong, Annalise."

"Would it? Maybe there could be something between us, after all, if we explore the possibility."

He shook his head. "That's not our way. The sight of you in Ruth's dress took me away for a moment. It gave me a picture of something that is not real."

Annie knew when a man wanted to kiss her. That part was real. A man's self-restraint at the moment of opportunity was unfamiliar, though. She took a step toward him. "I like the dress."

"You're playing dress up," Rufus said. "It's not you."

"Maybe it could be." Annie wanted to believe the words coming out of her own mouth.

"You don't know what you're saying." Rufus stepped back from her. "You've had a few Amish meals, been to church, admired some quilts. But you have no idea what it means to be Amish."

"I could learn."

"You would never choose it." Rufus looked away now. "It's not you."

"You don't know what I could choose." Her voice rose. "That's for me to decide."

"First, you have to understand what you are choosing between."

Annie bent over and snatched up the *kapp*. "Am I wearing Ruth's dress because she chose between? Even she couldn't choose your way."

Rufus exhaled. "She understood the seriousness of her choice."

"Then why must she be punished for it?"

"No one is punishing her."

"No one is speaking to her. No one even speaks *about* her. Is she being shunned?"

"Of course not. She's not baptized and has done nothing to deserve shunning."

"She believes she is following God's will. She misses you all so much."

He caught her eyes and held them. "You've seen Ruth, haven't you?"

"Yes. I can't believe you go to Colorado Springs as often as you do and you haven't seen her yourself."

"When she left, something broke," Rufus said. "My mother has never been quite the same. No one knew she was leaving. No one else was there when the moment came except my mother, and she won't talk about it."

"So you don't want to get in the middle of it? Is that it?"

"It's not my place."

"You've gotten in the middle of my problems several times now." Rufus sucked in his lips.

Annie took a deep breath before speaking. "What if I arranged for you to see Ruth? Would you do it?"

"Did you promise her already?"

"She doesn't know anything about it."

"I can't ask Tom to wait on me while I go off visiting. He's running a taxi service, and I pay for his time."

"I'll bring her to you," Annie said. "You name the place."

He turned away slightly and straightened some tools hanging on the wall. "I'm taking several pieces to the Amish furniture store on the north end of town next Thursday."

"I know where it is. What time?" Eagerness flushed through Annie at the thought of what this meeting would mean to Ruth.

"Three o'clock. I won't be able to wait past three thirty."

"You won't have to. I'll have her there at three." She could not fix whatever was broken between Ruth and Franey, but perhaps she could give Ruth her brother back.

"I can't promise, you understand," he said. "Some of this depends on Tom."

"You could call me."

"I only use my phone for business."

"She's your sister, Rufus. She needs you. At least read her letters."

"I'll try." He moved toward the door. "Be careful with the pins when you take the dress off."

She was alone in the barn then, wearing Ruth's dress. Slowly she felt for the pins Lydia had placed in the fabric and began pulling them out.

Thirty-Two

Ruth Beiler pushed the cart of empty food trays to the end of the hall where someone from the food services team would collect it. She was free to go on her own meal break, which meant she had a few minutes to study the posted schedule for next week.

When Annie called, Ruth immediately agreed to go with her to the furniture store on Thursday afternoon. But her normal shift at the nursing home began at three in the afternoon. She had to figure out which other morning CNA would be willing to stay late and cover the time Ruth needed. If she could just have an extra hour before she had to clock in, she could manage.

In the break room, in front of the posted schedule, Ruth filled a mug with coffee and lifted it to her lips while she mused the options. She raised a finger to Thursday's grid. Laura was out. She only worked during school hours and never stayed a minute past two thirty. Elisa was blacked out for the whole week on vacation. Heather wouldn't have child care for her two-year-old if she stayed past three.

"What's up?" Erin breezed in with the high-speed motion that carried her everywhere. Even when Ruth worked her hardest and fastest, she still felt like she didn't keep up with Erin, who now picked up a stack of magazines and grabbed a paper towel to wipe off the counter, all in one smooth motion.

"I have a schedule conflict," Ruth said. "I need to come in late on Thursday. I thought I'd just ask someone on the early shift to stay late."

"Naw. No one likes to do that. But I'll work the late shift if you'll work my early shift on Thursday."

Ruth nodded. "That would be fine. Thank you, Erin."

"You'd better go see Mrs. Watson. At least stick your head in before your break is over. She keeps track of these things."

Ruth laughed.

"And we have a new patient, Mrs. Renaldi." Erin set the magazines on the counter in perfect alignment. "She was in the rehab wing after a fall. She graduated out of there, but they're not sure she'll be able to live alone. The family wants to see how she'll do here first."

Ruth nodded, already feeling sad for a woman she had not met. Though she worked in a nursing home, she never quite adjusted to how easily families agreed it was the best place for their loved one. Growing up among the Amish, she never saw elderly family members living anywhere but with their families.

With ten minutes left on her meal break, Ruth padded down to Mrs. Watson's room and knocked lightly. "It's me, Ruth."

"It's about time." Mrs. Watson sat up in the armchair.

Ruth smiled.

"You're happy about something. I can tell," Mrs. Watson said.

"I'm happy to see you, as always." Ruth folded back the covers on the bed. Before long, it would be time for her to get Mrs. Watson ready for the night.

"No, it's something else. News from home, perhaps."

Ruth plumped a pillow and laid it in place. "Perhaps."

"Do tell."

"I'm going to see my brother on Thursday," Ruth said.

"Little Jacob?" Mrs. Watson asked.

"No. I wish he could come, too. But it will just be Rufus."

"The one you've been writing to?"

"That's right. A friend has arranged a meeting when he comes into town on business. It will just be a few minutes."

"It's a place to start."

"Yes, a place to start," Ruth echoed. And perhaps a place to finish.

Annie planned a long lunch break away from the office, figuring it would take about a hundred years to break even on all the days she worked through lunch. She snagged a primo parking spot outside the mall and entered the maze of shops through the chain bookstore, stopping to buy a coffee to carry with her. The usual department stores anchored the mall, and a couple of other furniture places had sprung up. She told herself she was just looking for ideas. After all, the purchase of the Westcliffe house had not even closed yet. Buying furniture to be delivered there would be jumping the gun. Still, what harm was there in looking?

By the time the tall, disposable coffee cup was empty, Annie's stomach gurgled, prompting her to think about eating. There was always the food court or the small café on the mall's upper level for something approximating real food. Annie's thoughts arced to her sister. Three years older than Annie, she had exactly the same face, everyone said, but Annie's eyes were gray and Penny's shimmered green. Most of Colorado Springs considered the café a decent place to grab a meal, but Penny always turned her nose up at it. Penny was a foodie who wanted to know that the cows she was eating had lived a good life. She would have known what exactly was growing in the Beiler garden with just a glance. Not like Annie.

Annie talked about taking time off to fly out and see Penny in Washington, but somehow it never happened. Penny breezed into town for two or three days at Christmas and then went back to her own life, with an occasional e-mail or phone call aimed at her family.

Annie laughed at herself when she thought of digging in the garden as if she knew what she was doing while Rufus fended off Rick Stebbins. She did call Lee Solano about the event. He pledged to choke Stebbins in legal actions. Annie was beginning to think Lee might actually get Rick off her back, though of course she would pay for it.

Sadness sluiced through Annie. She missed her sister. Penny was scrappy. She would have taken protecting her little sister into her own hands if she knew any of what was going on. Annie smiled at the thought.

They had not had a traumatic rupture in their relationship, but the truth was that Annie didn't speak to her sister much more than Rufus spoke to Ruth. Life diverged, and they let it. She put her hand on her phone, wondering what Penny would do if she called her in the middle of the day for absolutely no reason.

"Annie? Is that you?"

Annie blinked at the young woman beside her. "Lindsay!" She glanced at the stroller. "And the baby. How is she?"

Barrett's wife. Barrett's baby. In the mall.

"She's fine." Lindsay moved the blanket to allow Annie to see the baby's face. "She loves sleeping in the stroller, so I come here to walk. I have to do something about my baby fat."

"You look great." Annie took a breath. One of them would have to ask the obvious questions. "How's Barrett?"

Lindsay pushed the stroller back and forth with one hand. Then she broke into tears.

Annie's breath stuck for a moment. She was calculating how to get past the questions looming over them, and suddenly a sobbing new mother stood between her and the furniture stores.

"Lindsay?" Annie put a hand on Lindsay's quaking shoulder.

"He doesn't talk to me," Lindsay blubbered. "He says he made a lot of money when you bought him out, so we don't have anything to worry about. But I still don't understand why he wanted to sell his half when he was so happy working with you all these years."

Annie could not think of a thing to say.

"He says he's going to find something else to be passionate about, but he just sits in the house." Lindsay swayed at the hips with the motion of the stroller. "He hardly pays any attention to the baby, and I'm lucky if he says six words to me all day."

Annie gulped. "I'm sorry. I didn't know."

Lindsay stopped pushing on the stroller and dug in the diaper bag for a tissue. "I shouldn't dump on you in the middle of the mall. But I don't understand what happened. Barrett left the company, and then Rick didn't want to hang out with him, either."

"Rick doesn't want to hang out with him?" Annie tried to make sense of the statement.

"Barrett doesn't do anything he used to love," Lindsay said, "and I don't know what to do."

"I wish I knew what to tell you."

"You could tell me what happened. Why did it all fall apart?"

Annie's phone rang, and the baby squawked at the same time.

"It's the office," Annie said. "I'd better take it."

"Never mind. If I don't keep going, she won't go back to sleep."

"It was nice to see you." Annie spoke to Lindsay's back as she raised the phone to her ear. "Jamie, what's up?"

"The assistant of that guy at Liam-Ryder Industries has called three times." Annoyance rang in Jamie's voice. "He's in town just for the day before he flies out of Denver tonight, and he really wants a meeting."

"Tell them two o'clock," Annie said. "Let's just find out what they want once and for all."

By four o'clock, a plan formed in Annie's mind. She sat at the conference table in her own office and listened to the groaning tectonic shifts in her life. Jumping from one plate to the other was still possible, before they separated too far.

Lee Solano would have to be present at the next meeting with Liam-Ryder Industries. That much was clear.

This could happen fast.

And it could be good in so many ways. For so many people.

As the visitors left her office, Annie let her mind drift to a choice made three hundred years ago that ultimately brought her to this moment.

Thirty-Three

July 1738

They sat in Rachel Treadway's parlor, Jakob on a cushionless straight-back chair and Elizabeth across from him on a stuffed velvet settee.

"I'm so pleased you found time to visit Philadelphia again." Elizabeth's hands were crossed neatly in her lap. They spoke the familiar German of their childhoods.

This was Jakob's second visit in just a few weeks, leaving his farm and children in the care of others for days at a time. His choice to see her came at a high price. "We have much to discuss together," he said.

"Yes, I agree." *Ask me. I'll say yes.*

"The cabin is well stocked now. The children don't like to leave it."

She heard the nerves etched through Jakob's voice. "I would love to see your children."

"Especially Lisbetli?"

"Especially Lisbetli." *I would go back with you now. Ask.*

Jakob nodded. "That would make her very happy."

Elizabeth leaned forward, poured a cup of tea, and handed it to Jakob. "And your friends? Do they ask you to get their supplies also when you come?"

"I bring a list. It must be worthwhile to bring two horses and a wagon." He sipped his tea.

Elizabeth poured her own tea. "I see much to admire in the Amish."

He looked up. "Do you?"

I admire you most of all. "Yes." She added sugar and stirred her tea. Why did he not just say what was on his mind?

"We live plain and apart, you know."

Her heart bursting, she barely heard his voice. "Yes, I know. But you are strong people. Even when I was a child in Switzerland I could tell."

"Some would find our ways difficult."

"I suppose so." *Sip.* "Do any of your people ever choose to live otherwise?"

"It is very hard to do," he said. "It would be seen as a loss of faith."

"And would it be?"

"For some."

"And for you, Mr. Byler?"

"I am not as sure as I once was on that point." His teacup rattled, and he set it down.

"Do you think you will always live apart?"

She watched him swallow hard.

"I have been examining my faith for some time now. God works in mysterious ways."

"I have seen this to be true in my own life as well." Elizabeth hoped they were talking about the same thing.

"If God revealed His will, I would obey."

"As would I." Elizabeth sipped her tea. *I will say yes!*

"I have prayed that God would show His will."

"As have I."

"Very good."

Ask, she thought, *just ask.*

Jakob was silent. He picked up his teacup again. He took one delicate sip and carefully replaced the cup and saucer on the low table. "It is kind of the Treadways to provide for you as they have, but I wonder if you have thought of having a home of your own."

Finally. "Of late I have considered the matter with increasing frequency."

"And you are disposed to have your own home, Miss Kallen?"

She felt the hope in his words and answered quickly. "I am quite keenly so disposed, Mr. Byler."

"Ah. I am glad to hear this."

Jakob went silent again. Elizabeth poured another splash of tea into her own cup.

"I wonder if a particular religious atmosphere would make you uncomfortable," Jakob said.

Elizabeth chose her words carefully, mindful of what it was costing Jakob to have this conversation. "I believe each person must follow conscience, Mr. Byler. My faith means a great deal to me. I do not presume to judge another person. Only God sees the heart."

"I see. And do you have any particular aspirations for your home?"

"English." Her answer was firm. "I want my children to learn to speak English."

Jakob blushed. "Perhaps you would teach me as well."

"I would be happy to."

Jakob blew out his breath and dared to smile. "Perhaps you will speak to your minister, then. I wonder how much time you require to be ready."

Elizabeth nodded. "I will speak to the Treadways immediately so they can find someone else for the shop. I have very few possessions of my own."

"Thank you, Miss Kallen. You do me a great honor."

She smiled at his blush.

"You married Miss Kallen?" Maria's pitch rose with the realization. Her face broke into a grin as she looked at her siblings gathered around the table.

"*Daed*, no, you can't do this." Barbara stood up and moved to the hearth, where she gripped a blackened pot in both hands.

"It's done." Jakob glanced through the tiny window in the front of the cabin. "She's outside, anxious to see all of you. I expect you to make her welcome."

"She's a nice lady." Maria took Lisbetli's hands and clapped them together.

"Is she going to join the church?" Barbara asked accusingly, pot in hand.

"I don't know what she might decide to do in the future." Jakob knew this was not the last time he would hear this question. "I have not asked her to join."

"Then you're going to leave the church. You did not even wait for the bishop to marry you." Christian straightened in his seat. "You can't be Amish if your wife is not Amish. You're defying *Ordnung*."

"I don't want to stop being Amish." Anna's violet eyes—Verona's eyes—widened.

"I won't ask you to." Jakob touched Anna's trembling hand. "Neither will Elizabeth."

"Why did you marry an outsider?" Christian asked. "Don't you believe in our ways anymore?"

"The questions are not that simple, Christian." Jakob's eyes moved among the faces of all his children. "Elizabeth is eager to help us make a home."

"*I'm* making a home." Barbara set the pot on the table with a thud. "I'm cooking. I'm looking after the children. I'm mending your shirts. I never complain."

"You're doing a wonderful job, Bar-bar. But someday—soon—you will want to do those things for your own husband."

Anna scraped her chair back and began to pace around the room.

"I still don't understand." Christian leaned forward on the

table, his chin in his hands. "Do you not believe we must follow *Ordnung?*"

"I believe God has brought us to a new land for a purpose." Jakob leaned over and picked up Lisbetli from the crate she balanced on. "God has given us great opportunity. It is hard for all of us without your mother. God sent us Elizabeth to make it easier."

"But we keep separate from outsiders." Christian pushed back from the table. "How can we have an outsider living with us?"

"I hope she won't feel like an outsider." Jakob kissed the top of Lisbetli's head.

A gust of wind blew through the cabin. Jakob turned his head to see the front door standing wide open. He got up to close it. As he leaned against it to be sure it latched, he realized with a lurch how the door had come to be open.

"Where's Anna?" He spun around and pulled the door open again.

At the edge of the clearing, he saw Anna's dark apron disappear from sight into the black oaks. Elizabeth was already running after her.

Thirty-Four

Annie's laptop was open on the conference table on Thursday afternoon. In an open electronic document, presumably she was taking notes on the meeting with representatives of Liam-Ryder Industries and corporate attorneys. However, she spent more time glancing at the digital time display on the upper right corner of the screen than she did typing. If the meeting did not wrap up soon, she would have to leave anyway.

Twenty minutes. Fifteen. Twelve. Ten. Eight. Five. Three. One. She snapped the laptop closed and stood up.

"Gentlemen, I'm sorry, but I have another appointment, and it's impossible to reschedule." Annie scooped a stack of papers off the table and stuffed them into her bag. "I'm glad we've come to general agreement. Please feel free to use my office as long as you like to hash out the details of what we've been talking about. Jamie will assist you with anything you need."

"Excuse me, gentlemen." Lee Solano jumped up from the table and followed Annie out. She pulled the door closed behind them and looked at him expectantly.

"Are you sure about this?" Lee asked.

"I've never been more sure."

"But Barrett? I don't get it. We went to a lot of trouble to take him out of action."

"I know. At the time it seemed liked the thing to do."

"And now?"

"And now it seems like the time to make things right. I'm sorry for my mistaken judgment. Barrett was never the enemy. I should have known better than to think Barrett would try to steal my work. That was Rick."

"Don't forget the college plagiarism," Lee said.

"Which may or may not be true." Annie slung her bag over her shoulder. "I'm inclined to think somebody got the best of him then as well."

"You can't be sure."

"How can we ever be sure of what is in someone else's mind and heart? Maybe Barrett was already a victim, and we made it worse. If you could turn up that information, anyone could."

"Like Rick?"

"We broke Barrett's spirit," Annie said softly. "Now I want to put the pieces back together. I want to do the right thing."

"And Rick?"

She shrugged. "He doesn't figure into this new deal and hopefully never will. Barrett won't own the company. He'll just run it as a division of LRI. Rick will have nothing to gain by going after him again."

"This is happening fast." Lee drew a hand across his forehead. "I want to ask for some time to do due diligence. Find out who these people are."

"If you like. But they're on the New York Stock Exchange and made a profit the last seven quarters in a row."

"Let me be sure I understand the terms you're expecting." Lee readjusted his stance and rubbed his palms together. "First, you want to sell the company, including its major asset, which is the new program you've developed for tracking sales according to shopper patterns, product placement in stores, and web presence."

"That's right." Somewhere in Annie's brain, a giant clock ticked.

"Second, you want Barrett to receive a substantial offer to return and run the company, especially the sales and marketing he's so good at."

"Right."

"And you want everyone on staff to have guaranteed employment for at least two years with a bonus if they sign an agreement to stay for that period of time."

"Right again." Annie glanced toward the door. Lee had heard this all three times. She wasn't going to change her mind.

"The profits from the sale are to be placed in a trust that even you can't undo."

Annie took a deep breath. "Yes, that's right. We can talk more later. Right now, I really have to go."

"As your attorney, I have to say—"

"Later, Lee." Annie left the suite.

It was 2:23. She still had seven minutes to get to the corner where Ruth would be waiting by 2:30.

At 2:29, Annie pulled to the curb just shy of the corner and put the car in PARK. The clock in her dash clicked to 2:30 then 2:31 and 2:32.

At 2:38 Annie started to worry.

Ruth wasn't used to the daytime shift. Everything seemed to go wrong. She passed off charts to the wrong charge nurse and missed getting vitals on patients in a block of six rooms. She was still in the middle of helping residents dress when she was supposed to be helping them to their seats in the wing's dining area. And now she faced a mess of chocolate pudding and apple juice splattered across the tile because Mr. Green wanted butterscotch pudding and grape juice. With one sweep of his arm, he made sure no one could expect him to eat the substitution.

The clock at the nurses' station, large enough to see from yards away, said 2:37. Panic welled in Ruth. In the hall, she found a housekeeping cart.

"Mind if I take a couple towels?" she asked Tara, who pushed the cart. "I've got a small mess in here."

"Help yourself."

And then she saw him—a man who looked like Tom Reynolds. But what would Tom be doing here?

Familiar shoulders, the jeans and plaid shirt. He had just passed the nurses' station, striding toward the exit where automatic doors would wheeze open.

"Do you know that man?" Ruth tried to sound casual.

Tara glanced down the hall, two towels between her hands. "Sure. He comes a couple of times a month to see his mother, Mrs. Renaldi. But I think he changed his name."

"Reynolds." Ruth felt the blood drain from her face.

"Yeah, that's it. Know him?"

His name lodged in her throat as she saw the doors close behind him. For the first time, she noticed the red truck parked in the space nearest the door.

"Tara, do me a huge favor? Clean up the pudding mess in Mr. Green's room? I'm already late clocking out, and I have an appointment." Ruth put on her best pleading face.

Tara grimaced at the mess. "I guess so."

Ruth flew down the corridor. The doors opened slowly, with a hesitancy she found aggravating even on a good day. By the time she stepped outside, she saw only the back end of Tom's truck leaving the parking lot.

Groaning, Ruth ran back to the staff lounge to clock out and grab her purse. On her way out of the building, the clock at the nurses' station announced 2:44. He had a seven-minute head start. If he got there first, all her hoping would be for nothing.

Rufus sat in the office in the back of the Amish furniture store.

David, who ran the store, was flipping through pages of hand-written notes on a small yellow pad.

"I don't know why I write down half the stuff I do." David turned another page. "I'm afraid I'll forget something important. Then I can't remember what I thought was so important that I had to write it down."

Rufus attempted a laugh.

David riffled more pages. "I know I've got that special order in here somewhere. The lady was very specific about wanting matching end tables, and she doesn't want any shortcuts. Of course I thought you were perfect for the job."

"I'll be glad to take it on," Rufus said. *If you ever find your notes.* The little battery clock on David's desk said the time was 2:45. Now that Rufus had agreed to see his sister, every minute bonged in his head, a reminder of lost time. He imagined Ruth sitting in the passenger seat of Annie's car, the two of them pulling onto a busy street, stopping at a light, searching store signs.

Her packet of letters was safe in his bedroom, each one read at least three times.

"Oh, here it is." David tapped the page. "Yes, she admired the one on display. She'd like two, but slightly larger. She gave me measurements. Oh yes, she also wants a hope chest that matches."

"That sounds fine," Rufus said.

"How long do you think it will take? She was anxious to know."

"We'd better say six weeks."

"She'll want to hear four."

Rufus shook his head. "I can't promise that. We'd better stick with six."

"All right, six. I'll remind her that if she wants the best work, it takes time." David fished around in a desk drawer. "Let me write up the order on an official form with the measurements she gave me."

In the silence of David's concentration, the clock turned to 2:51.

Annie turned on the ignition as Ruth threw herself into the car.

"Sorry," Ruth said. "I just couldn't get away. I had no idea what the day shift was like."

"It should only be about twelve minutes." Annie put her foot to the accelerator. "We should be fine."

"I saw Tom Reynolds," Ruth said.

Annie scanned the view ahead, rapidly evaluating which route would be quickest. "Really? Tom was at the nursing home?"

"I didn't know, but his mother is there recovering from a fall. I guess he usually comes to see her during the day before my shift starts. He left before I did."

"Uh-oh. Maybe he had another errand."

They came to a major intersection, and Annie turned right onto the six-lane grid. Almost immediately she slammed on the brakes. Traffic in front of them was at a standstill. Two police cars crossed the lanes, barricading the northbound traffic.

"An accident." Annie leaned to the left to try to look around the congestion. Behind them an ambulance screamed at a searing pitch. The Prius shuddered as the emergency vehicle weaved past them at high speed.

Ruth moaned. "Can we go another way?"

Annie glanced in the mirrors. In a matter of seconds, vehicles sucked up any space to maneuver. "We're stuck."

Rufus gave David a price for the three pieces of furniture, knowing David would add another 15 percent to the number he reported to the customer. They agreed on some other pieces Rufus could make for David's showroom. Rufus would stop by again in two weeks with two cedar chests he was nearly finished with.

It was after three now. Rufus wandered through the shop one last time and then out the front door. A simple backless bench ran along the stone wall beneath the display window. Rufus took a seat and fixed his eyes in the direction he believed Annalise would come from, though he could not be sure. Across the parking lot, traffic flowed past in six lanes, knotting and unknotting with the rhythm of the well-timed traffic lights.

He wondered if Ruth had grown thin, how she supported herself, if she was sorry, if she was happy. He squinted as if he might find the answers in afternoon sunlight.

Rufus watched three cycles of the lights before the red pickup maneuvered into the parking lot and rattled Rufus to attention. Tom was back.

Tom opened the cab door, got out, and raised an eyebrow at Rufus. "Ready?"

"I guess I was daydreaming." Rufus stood up and glanced around the parking lot again, wondering if he should say something to Tom.

"Then let's get going," Tom said. "There's a parents' meeting at Carter's school. I promised Tricia I would be home for dinner so we could go together."

"Of course." The last thing Rufus wanted to do was inconvenience Tom or cause distress in his family.

The clock in Tom's truck said 3:17. They probably were not coming anyway, he decided. Annalise would not have waited until the last minute. Ruth must have backed out.

"I got lucky," Tom said, "and just missed a big accident on my way up. I heard it hit behind me. The southbound lanes should be fine, but I think I'll find another way out of town just in case."

"Whatever you think best." Rufus pulled the seat belt over his shoulder and snapped it into place. *God's will.*

They had moved barely twenty feet in ten minutes, but Annie had her eye on the entrance to a shopping center. If she could just make that turn, they could snake through connecting parking lots and come out north of the jam.

By the time they reached the entrance and Annie made the turn, Ruth burst into tears. The Prius was nimble and responded well to the frequent turns as Annie drilled through back alleys behind restaurants and box stores at a speed for which she deserved to be stopped by flashing lights.

They pulled into the furniture store parking lot at 3:24. Ruth jumped out of the car and ran inside without waiting for a full stop.

Annie parked properly and wondered if she should go in. She did not want to intrude on the moment of reunion between brother and sister, but her own pulse was rapid with the expectation of seeing Rufus. Just as Annie decided it was too hot to wait in the car, Ruth yanked open the passenger door and tumbled in.

"We're too late." She used the backs of both hands to wipe tears. "He didn't wait."

"He said three thirty!"

"Five more minutes?" Ruth said. "What difference could that make on a two-hour trip back to Westcliffe? He didn't want to see me."

"You don't know that for sure," Annie said. But she banged a hand against the steering wheel nevertheless. "We'll try again in two weeks. He comes every two weeks."

"Is this God's will?" Ruth swallowed hard and wiped tears from both eyes. "Maybe I'm not meant to see him."

"I don't know." What else could Annie say?

Ruth fished for a tissue in her purse and blew her nose. "Can you take me back to my room? I have a lot of studying to do."

Annie nodded and started the car.

Two weeks might as well have been eternity.

Thirty-Five

Annie's instinct was to call Rufus's cell phone. If it had been anyone else, she would have. Find out what happened. Make a new plan. That was why everyone had phones. The rules were different with Rufus, though. If Ruth wouldn't call, then Annie shouldn't.

She sat on her frustration for a week.

Then came the date for closing on the house in Westcliffe. Annie boxed up a few kitchen items, packed several changes of clothes, grabbed a blanket, and stopped by a housewares store on the way out of town for a decent inflatable mattress so she would have a place to sleep that night. The closing was scheduled at the bank at the edge of Westcliffe.

Annie knew the way now. She had been back and forth in daylight and remembered the changes from one state highway to another. She recognized the sequence of small towns—each clinging to its moment of history—that culminated in Silver Cliff and released into Westcliffe at the foot of the mountains. She would sleep that night in a house she owned outright in a town she had not known existed a few weeks ago.

She did the final walk-through with the real estate agent. Happily, the house was no more dilapidated than the day she bought it. Next came the closing, where she signed her name until her fingers cramped. At last the agent dropped the keys to the front door in Annie's hands. The key to the back door had been lost years ago, the owner claimed. If Annie wanted to lock that door, the locksmith in Silver Cliff would be happy to help.

Annie drove the few blocks from the bank to the house. She parked in the driveway and carried her suitcase in through the back door.

Sitting cross-legged on the floor of the empty living room, she opened her laptop and used her phone to give herself an Internet connection. With a few keyboard strokes, she was logged into her company's server and looking at everything she would have seen if she had been in her office in Colorado Springs. She could ensure no funny business happened before the business deal closed. Her cell phone signal was strong. Annie turned on the speaker, pressed Jamie's speed dial number, and set the phone on the floor.

"Did you really do it?" Jamie asked.

"I did." Even with no one there to see her, Annie could not help smiling.

"It sounds empty."

"I've got some serious shopping to do." Annie looked around, visualizing furniture.

"How long are you going to stay?"

"Just a night or two. Or three. I'm not sure."

"Mr. Solano called three times."

"I'll call him," Annie said.

"He sounded agitated. Is everything all right?"

"I'm doing my best to make sure it is." Annie looked around the room in satisfaction. "I'll check in again tomorrow."

She called Lee next.

"The papers are almost to the final draft stage," he said. "Are you ready to review them?"

"Anytime." Annie untangled herself to stand up and begin pacing through the house. "Are they pressing back on anything?"

"They're asking questions about why Barrett left, considering the nature of the offer you want them to extend."

"Make it work, Lee," Annie said simply. "It's a deal breaker."

"Really? Of everything that's on the table, hiring the guy who tried to rip you off is a deal breaker?"

"Yep."

"I've only known you a few weeks," Lee spoke through a sigh. "But I have to say, this is not where I thought we would end up when you first came to me."

"Things change. People change."

"You could ask for more money, you know. They would ante up."

"The offer is fine." She wasn't going to use the money anyway. "When everything is final, I want to be the one to talk to Barrett."

"You drive a hard bargain."

"Make it so."

Annie ended the call and leaned against the living room wall in the silence. Then she bent over to close her laptop and silence her phone. She did not even leave it set to vibrate or alarm. "Silent"—as close as she ever came to "off." Her eyes scanned the room and found nothing to land on. No electronic green lights glowing with reassurance of the steady flow of power. No cords dredging life from outlets toward convenience. No gizmos beeping urgent summons. No stacks of books and magazines she never got around to reading. Slowly, she lowered herself to sit again on the bare floor. Beneath her, oak planks pushed against her with their stories. Annie spread her hands on the wooden floor on either side of her and closed her eyes, letting her fingers trace slight ridges her feet would not have noticed. A vague coating of dust stuck to the crevices of her palm, and in the mustiness that stirred, she inhaled questions of past and future.

When she opened her eyes, she saw the inch-long weak raised wallpaper seam on one wall. Yellow paint did not quite seal the history behind it. Annie got up and walked toward the spot then scraped at it gently with a fingernail and looked closely. She could discern four—no, five—distinct stubborn layers of wallpaper that had resisted efforts to smooth the seam over the decades. Even Annie, with all her domestic challenges, had seen enough home decorating television shows to know the right thing was to remove wallpaper rather than add layers of paint or paper. She had a hazy notion that the process involved steam. But at the moment, she was grateful for the painted wallpaper. The stories of the house were still there, not whitewashed into oblivion. She was strangely curious to know what they were.

The house was nearly a hundred years old—but young compared to the stories rattling around Annie's brain. Jakob Byler and Elizabeth Kallen were an unlikely pair, as unlikely as Rufus Beiler and Annalise Friesen. Yet somehow they found a life together. *Were they happy?* she wondered. *Were they certain they made the right choice?*

In silence, Annie wandered through the rooms. In the kitchen, the stove and refrigerator were at least thirty years old, one mustard yellow and the other avocado green. Make that forty years. The real estate agent said they worked, but it was difficult to believe they were efficient. Annie leaned against the refrigerator and pushed, moving it just far enough from the wall to find the power cord and plug it in. The prompt reward for her effort came in the whir of a motor.

The dining room asked for a narrow table to be settled under the window, leaving space to walk through and access the stairs. Under the stairs, the wall was made of dark paneling, and Annie realized a door opened to storage space.

Over the next hour, Annie carried loads from her car and inflated her mattress. She arranged a few dishes on shelves in the kitchen, swept the wood floors, satisfied herself that the refrigerator was indeed becoming cold, however slowly, and hung towels in the bathroom. Her mind's eye saw furniture and window coverings and new kitchen cabinets.

She knew just who she would hire to build them. Surely Rufus would be willing. She would be a paying customer, after all, and she could pay him well.

Rufus. Ruth would hang like a curtain between them now. She couldn't just ask Rufus to build cabinets without first asking, *Why didn't you stay to see your sister?*

It was a good thing he did not have Annalise's phone number, Rufus decided, because he would be tempted to call it. Since the reason was neither business nor an emergency, it would be wrong. He had Ruth's number, but he never called it. If something happened to *Mamm* or *Daed*, he would use it. A mix-up about a meeting time was not an emergency that justified using a phone.

The remodeling work in the motel lobby was finished, including installing the replacement face panels and a new desktop. Rufus was now working on custom cabinetry for two homes in the new subdivision. The deadline was far enough off that he could spend time teaching his employees some of his craft, giving them a chance to create cabinetry and woodwork, not simply install it. He had just sent his crew home for the day and was getting ready to work on the tables for David's customer in Colorado Springs.

Rufus looked forward to times alone of careful, slow sanding, sensing the exquisite plane of pressure that would break open the beauty in the hardwood. Even a side table could reveal the artistry of the Creator through the grain of the wood. With each passing of sandpaper over the surface, Rufus breathed a prayer of thanksgiving for the blessing of work.

The workshop door opened and Jacob appeared. "*Mamm* says to ask you a favor."

"What would that be?" Rufus's hands hesitated to leave the rectangle of wood that would become the tabletop.

"She promised to take preserves to Mrs. Weichert's shop. She wants to know if you have time to do it."

Rufus carefully set aside the tabletop. It was a long way to town just to deliver preserves. But if his mother asked him to do an errand, she had a good reason. "Are the preserves ready to go?"

Jacob nodded. "Two dozen jars of peach preserves. I hope she saved some for us."

Rufus smiled. "She always does. Go tell *Mamm* I can do it right now. I need to go to the new job site anyway."

"I was planning to stay a few nights," Annie said into her phone. "I already made sure I can access the server from here. I don't need to come in."

Sighing, she listened to the plea from one of her software writers and regretted checking her messages. The project was due to the client in two days, and he was stuck.

"All right," she finally said. "I'll drive back tonight and be there first thing in the morning."

Before she left, she took some measurements of windows and room sizes. When she grew hungry, she reluctantly carried her denim bag out to the car and backed out of her driveway. She could stop somewhere for food on the way back to the condo.

Pulling onto Main Street, she saw Rufus's horse and buggy outside Mrs. Weichert's antiques shop. The buggies all looked alike to her, but Annie recognized the horse. When she saw the shadow in the door frame, she almost stopped.

Rufus looked at the passing Prius as it moved away from him. The car was unmistakable. Annalise had come to town and not tried to see him. Disappointment twisted into him.

But why should she see him? It was better that she didn't. He would write to Ruth and explain what happened. He hefted the box of preserves and took it inside the store.

In the buggy a few minutes later, Rufus nudged Dolly into the street and toward the gleaming mountains that still made him draw a deep breath every day, even after five years of daily greetings. At the edge of town, he turned north and drove past the sign that announced Kramer Construction and into the next cul-de-sac. Rufus had been careful to make sure his new customers were using another builder and not Karl Kramer. It was the end of the day even for the construction crews that labored long into the evening, and he saw workers collecting tools, readying to leave the site for the night.

Rufus tucked Dolly's reins in a crevice in the midst of a convenient pile of lumber. He crossed the dirt that might one day be a lawn or, given the climate, a Xeriscaped garden of rock and mulch and uncut natural grasses. Inside the front entrance, the stairs were roughed in and the downstairs space portioned by unfinished walls. Rufus had blueprints with specific measurements. Still, he liked to stand in a room and sense the life that might someday exist there.

"Hello, Rufus." The site foreman emerged from the would-be kitchen. "Is Tom hauling something here for you?"

Rufus shook his head. "No. I just need to get a feel for the place. I'm doing wall-to-walls in the family room and the master bedroom."

The foreman nodded. "Okay, then. You may be the last one out."

"I'll only be a few minutes. I promise."

Rufus heard the grind of engines outside as the crew started their cars.

He was glad the others were gone. It would be easier to feel the place, to stand where the windows would be and judge the light falling into the room. In the silence, he would hear the rustle of clothes against furniture, the scuff of slippers against the floor. He would see hands reaching for the cabinet knobs he was yet to create, fingers closing around them in a habit of a thousand repetitions. Rufus slowly paced the family room, standing still and silent several times.

Then he moved up the stairs to the master bedroom. One

wall opened out to a deck with a view of the mountains. Large windows on the opposite wall would no doubt reflect the vista. His cabinets would fill the far connecting wall. Rufus faced the wall now, his eyes closed.

A second too late, he realized he was not alone. He turned in time to see a pair of black work boots before he slumped into gooey murk.

Thirty-Six

July 1739

*C*hristian Byler loved the fields. The smell of wet earth, the rustle of eager corn in July, the sweeping bow of wheat in the wind—it was as if he felt the farm coming to life as his own bones and ligaments stretched. He was sure he would never forget putting crops in for the first time. His father sometimes fretted over what might go wrong—not enough rain, too much rain, hungry insects—but Christian savored each turn of dirt, every furrow, the mystery of seed covered in darkness springing to light.

Holding his straw hat in place, he ran now through the shortcut in the cornfield to where he knew his father would be judging whether the plants were of sufficient height for their stage of growth. He found his *daed* sliding off his horse at the far end of the field.

"How are the vegetables looking?" Jakob squatted and slid his hand under a cornstalk.

"Anna promises fresh beans for supper," Christian answered, "as much as we want." He leaned in to look over his father's shoulder, inspecting for insects boring through.

"Is Maria still sitting in her patch waiting for the beets to grow?"

Christian nodded. "She sings to them. She says it makes them happy."

"Seems to me they should be happy enough to harvest."

"Elizabeth knows how to make ink from beet juice. She promised to show us. Even Anna wants to learn."

Jakob moved to another plant and rubbed a leaf between his thumb and forefinger. "Elizabeth likes to try out everything she reads about. She's very creative."

"I wonder if the new baby will be creative." Christian hunched over to inspect a stalk for himself.

"Lisbetli will have to get used to not being the baby." Jakob paused to wipe sweat from his forehead.

"As long as Lisbetli can be with Elizabeth, she's happy," Christian said. "I still hope that someday Elizabeth will join the church—when we have a bishop."

"You could be waiting a long time for a bishop to come from Europe."

They moved another few feet to inspect plants, and Christian knew the conversation was over. His father had less and less to say about the church. The Amish families were cautious around Elizabeth—anyone could see that—but without a bishop to pronounce discipline, no one fully shunned Jakob for his choice to marry an outsider. The families needed each other too much.

Christian heard the flapping steps of someone running through the corn. He abruptly stood up straight.

"What is it, Anna?"

The girl breathed heavily and tried to speak between gulps of air. "Bar-bar says you must come. Right now!"

"Elizabeth?"

Anna nodded. "Her pains started only a few hours ago, but Bar-bar is already worried. She's afraid to be alone with Elizabeth when the baby comes."

Jakob stepped back to where he had left the horse and grabbed the bridle. "Both of you, quickly, get on." He picked up Anna, though she tended toward lanky at thirteen, and lifted her to the horse. Christian saw his father squat slightly with intertwined fingers and knew he was meant to step into the makeshift stirrup and swing himself behind his sister. "Tell Mrs. Zimmerman it's time." Jakob slapped the horse's rump as Anna took the reins.

As the horse began to trot, Christian looked over his shoulder at his father. He had never seen Jakob move as swiftly as he did now in the direction of the cabin.

"I want Elizabeth," Lisbetli said quite distinctly and adamantly.

"I told you," Jakob said, "the baby is coming. Elizabeth can't play with you right now."

"But I need her," Lisbetli whined and went limp as a rag doll across his lap.

"She can't play with you now." Jakob sighed heavily. He was on the cabin's small front porch with Anna, Christian, Maria, and Lisbetli. Barbara was inside with Mrs. Zimmerman. Bar-bar was sixteen now, old enough to learn something about birthing. How much longer would it be before she married and started birthing her own children? Several of the families had sons who must have noticed Barbara's industrious nature. Perhaps one of them would soon show interest.

Christian sat on the bottom step scratching in the dirt with a stick. Jakob never had to remind him to work on his sums, because he was constantly recalculating the number of acres they planted and the expenses that had gone into the effort so far.

Maria stood up. "It's too hard to do nothing. I'm going to talk to my beets. Call me when the baby gets here."

Jakob let her stomp off. Her garden patch was within sight of the porch. His eyes moved to Anna, who looked blanched and withered. When the next scream came from inside the cabin, he and Anna flinched at the same time.

"Take Lisbetli and go feed the chickens." Jakob gently dumped

Lisbetli out of his lap and then shoved open the door and went inside.

Mrs. Zimmerman appeared from behind the curtain that separated Jakob and Elizabeth's bed from the main living space of the cabin. She wiped her hands on a rag and shook her head slightly.

"What is it?" Jakob whispered.

"I don't think the baby is turned right." Mrs. Zimmerman kept her voice low. "It will take a long time to birth."

"Is Elizabeth in danger?" Jakob's heart pounded at the thought.

"They both are. You know that."

"You must do something."

"It is in God's hands, Jakob."

"You have been helping to birth babies for years," Jakob said. "You must know something you can try."

She shook her head. "I tried to turn a baby once."

"Then do that."

"It didn't help, Jakob, and the poor woman. . ."

Jakob forced himself to breathe. "Birthing was so easy for Verona. It was always a time of joy. Now this."

"Elizabeth is quite old to be having a baby for the first time." Mrs. Zimmerman shook her head again. "You must trust God."

"I cannot lose Elizabeth."

"You must trust. It's up to God."

Jakob pushed past his old friend and neighbor, past the curtain, past Barbara. Elizabeth lifted her eyes to his and held out one arm. He grasped her hand and fell to his knees at the side of the bed.

"Jakob, the pain! Something's wrong."

"Rest." He gripped her pallid hand in both of his as if in prayer. "Save your strength."

"I love you, Jakob Byler. I want you to know that before—"

He cut her off. "Before nothing. The baby will turn. The baby will come. We will have many years together."

She clenched his hand, her fingernails digging into him, and screamed.

A second scream, higher pitched, echoed—coming from behind Jakob. He turned to see Anna's whitened face.

"Anna, what are you doing here?" Jakob scolded. "I told all of you to go feed the chickens."

"This is all my fault!" Anna wailed and ran from the scene.

"Go to her, Jakob." Elizabeth gasped and waited for the height of the pain to pass. "She is such a confused child."

"I don't want to leave you."

They heard the cabin door creak open and slam shut.

"Go," Elizabeth said again. "Mrs. Zimmerman is here, and Barbara. I am not alone."

"No, I cannot."

"You must." Elizabeth untangled her hand from his.

Jakob looked at Mrs. Zimmerman, who only shrugged. Finally, he strode across the cabin and out the door. Fortunately, Anna had not gone far. He found her huddled under the front porch.

He squatted. "Anna, come out of there. I'm too old to crawl under porches."

At first he heard nothing, and then she scuffled across the dirt and into the light, hanging her tear-streaked, pale face.

"What is wrong, Anna? What is this nonsense about it being your fault?"

"It is. I did not want Elizabeth to come, and then I was so mean to her. And I did not want the new baby. I thought maybe she would leave if she did not have a baby."

Jakob took a controlled breath. "You are old enough to remember when Maria and Lisbetli were born."

She nodded.

"And neighbors have had new babies." Jakob leaned forward and grabbed Anna by the elbows to pull her out and into his embrace. "Sometimes birthing is harder than other times. It's not anybody's fault."

"But I thought such mean things!" Anna buried her face in his chest. "Before. . .before. . .I do not want Elizabeth to go away now because of me."

Jakob stroked her head. "It's not anybody's fault. Why would God punish Elizabeth for your thoughts?"

"Is it in God's hands?"

Jakob hesitated only slightly. "Yes it is."

"*Maam* used to say everything was in God's hands. But if that's true, why did *Maam* die? She loved God."

"You ask deep questions, Anna Byler. Perhaps it is not for us to understand God's ways."

Elizabeth screamed again, hideously. Anna gripped her father's neck. Suddenly she felt to him as small as Lisbetli.

The cabin door opened.

"*Daed*!" Barbara called.

"I'm here." Jakob stood so she could see him, pulling Anna to her feet as well.

"Mrs. Zimmerman is trying to turn the baby. It's awful. I can't stand it."

"Stay here with Anna." Jakob nudged Anna toward Barbara. "Let me go in."

"I never want to have a baby," Barbara said.

The shrieking stopped only long enough for Elizabeth to gulp and again gash the air with unearthly vehemence.

Christian took his younger sisters further from the house. He remembered when Lisbetli was born, and it did not sound like this.

And then came the aching silence during which anything could happen. Taking turns kicking a stone, Christian, Maria, and Lisbetli worked a jagged route back toward the cabin. At the porch, Christian caught Barbara's eye, but she said nothing. The five Byler children huddled on the narrow front steps ascending the porch.

And then the baby cried.

Anna was the first on her feet and pushing the door open. They tumbled into the cabin in a rolling mass, stopping just short of the curtain.

Their father came around the curtain and grinned at them. "It's a boy!"

"Can I hold him?" Anna, again, was the first.

"In due time," Jakob said. "Elizabeth has been through an ordeal."

Jakob returned to Elizabeth and drew a clean damp rag across her face, pausing to cradle one cheek. Mrs. Zimmerman wiped off the baby, wrapped him in a towel, and laid him in Elizabeth's arms before bundling up bloody rags in a sheet and moving away from the bed. Jakob straightened the bedding then pushed the curtain open to reveal Elizabeth propped up with the baby, swaddled in a small quilt, on her chest.

Anna took the first steps then halted.

"Come on, Anna," Elizabeth said, "come and meet your baby brother." She held out one arm.

Anna settled on the bed in the crook of Elizabeth's arm, and Elizabeth transferred the bundle of red squall to the girl's grasp.

"What's his name?" Anna asked.

Elizabeth looked up at her husband. "I'd like to call him Jacob."

Anna giggled. "It will be fun to have a little Jacobli in the house."

Christian watched as Anna cooed at the baby and tentatively explored his features with one gentle finger. It wasn't long before the other girls gathered around the bed as well, all of them anxious to meet their brother. Even Lisbetli climbed up on the bed and touched the baby's wrinkled wrist.

A boy. A brother.

Christian was used to having sisters—four of them. But a brother. He had been the only son. He was the one who worked beside his father in the fields, who kept the supply lists, who knew the trees that marked the corners of their land.

This new baby was not even Amish, yet he bore their father's name.

Thirty-Seven

*J*amie never interrupted a meeting for anything less than urgent. Annie raised her eyes in question when Jamie slipped quietly into her office.

"Excuse me." Annie nodded to the group gathered around her conference table.

Jamie whispered into Annie's ear. "A Ruth Beiler is on the phone, and she says it's an emergency. I tried to tell her you would return the call later, but she insists. She sounds like she's been crying."

"I'll take it at your desk." Annie stepped out of her office. She picked up Jamie's phone and punched the flashing button. "Hello, Ruth?"

"I'm sorry to call," Ruth said, "but it's Rufus."

"What happened?"

"Sophie sent a letter. No one has ever written, so I knew it had to be bad."

"Ruth, tell me what happened."

"Rufus was attacked. Three days ago. They took him to the hospital in Cañon City. Sophie said it was awful."

"We'll go to Cañon City." Annie was the one who had to be

calm. She knew that. "You and me. Can you get away?"

"I'm not working until day after tomorrow."

"Good. I'm coming straight over."

A pall settled on them in the car thirty minutes later.

"Will he even want to see me?" Ruth asked.

Or me? Annie thought. She said, "You should be there."

"My mother might not think so."

"I know your mother," Annie said, "and whatever happened between you, I believe she loves you."

"That doesn't mean she'll be glad to see me. You have to be Amish to understand." Ruth looked down at her long brown skirt. "She'll hate what I'm wearing. And Sophie will be in trouble for writing to me."

"Surely under the circumstances they would all want you to know what happened."

"You might think so."

They didn't speak for a long time after that. Annie followed the directions displayed by the navigation system in her dash. *You have to be Amish to understand.* The simple sentence tolled in Annie's head. She was fond of the whole Beiler family and curious about her own family roots. But no, she was not Amish.

Finally, the hospital was in sight. Annie found street parking close to the main entrance.

"You're coming in, aren't you?" Ruth asked. "Rufus will want to see you, won't he?"

Annie shrugged. "Not sure."

"I need someone." Ruth pleaded with those violet eyes that were just like Rufus's. "Please come in."

They walked through the sliding doors together and stopped at the information desk. Rufus was still listed as a patient on the floor just above them.

"Get off the elevator and turn right." The woman wearing a pink smock pointed. "There's a nice waiting room on the wing. They just redecorated."

When the elevator doors opened on the second floor, Franey Beiler stopped her pacing down the center of the hall. Ruth stared into her mother's sallow face. Everything in her heaved, and she barely avoided falling into a stagger. Annie hung back a little, moving just far enough to let the doors close behind her.

"You've come," Franey said simply in Pennsylvania Dutch.

Ruth stared at her mother's crossed arms, aching for them to open. She straightened her skirt and tugged at the sleeves of her pullover shirt as mother and daughter considered each other. She searched for a hint of forgiveness or understanding. Even a simple welcome would give her something to hold on to.

"He will be glad to see you." Franey's voice sounded haggard. Ruth wished her mother would reach out and hold her. Then she would know it was all right to reach back. If only she had thought to wear a prayer *kapp*. At least her hair was braided and pinned up.

Annie moved a little closer. "May I ask what happened?"

Franey pushed out her breath and moved her fingers to her temples. She switched to English. "Somebody hit him from behind then apparently pushed him down a flight of stairs. Tom found him, by God's grace. We're not sure how long he was there. Rufus doesn't remember much. Yesterday they took out his spleen. Several ribs are broken and he has a concussion. He's resting right now."

Ruth opened her mouth to speak, but the knot in her throat refused the passage of air. She forced herself to swallow and found her voice. "*Mamm*, this is so much for you to bear."

"If I hadn't asked him to take preserves to town, he might not have been there at all." Franey's voice cracked.

"It's not your fault, *Mamm*."

"God's will," Franey muttered. She gestured into the waiting room. "It's comfortable in here. Your father is sitting with Rufus now. We take turns."

In the waiting room, a little boy in a straw hat looked up from a book. His face split into a grin. Jacob hurtled himself into Ruth's arms, and she spun him around once. He was so much bigger than the last time she saw him. She soaked up the weight of him straddling her hip, the feel of his limber form fitting against her torso, the smell of his hair under her neck carrying the scent of home.

"I'm happy to see you, too, Annalise," Jacob said, "but I haven't seen Ruth in a really long time."

Annie smiled. "I understand."

"Did you bring her in your car?"

"Yes I did."

"*Danke.*" He nestled his head under Ruth's chin, knocking his hat off.

Ruth squeezed him and avoided her mother's glance. If *Mamm* disapproved of Jacob's enthusiasm, Ruth did not want to know.

Annie picked up the hat and reached for Jacob. "Why don't we go look at your book together so your mom and sister can talk?"

Jacob let Annie take him out of Ruth's arms and set him on the floor. She took his hand and led him to the far end of the waiting room. Ruth watched as they settled into a wide, stuffed chair together. Her cheeks burned, knowing her mother was looking at her. Finally, she turned to Franey.

"It's good to see you, *Mamm*," Ruth said in the easy language of her childhood.

"*Dochder*," Franey answered. Daughter.

A simple word that might have reassured Ruth instead stung. She was a daughter who disappointed her mother deeply. Ruth doubted her mother meant anything but that simple truth.

A reminder of the choice she did not make. Could not make.

Franey chose a chair, and Ruth sat beside her. "Elijah Capp has spent many hours here waiting with us for news," Franey said.

Elijah? Here? Another sting.

"He had doubts, too, you know."

"I do know." Ruth could hardly get the words out.

"But he was baptized that day."

Ruth had always supposed Elijah went through with his baptism. Even knowing his doubt and what it would mean that she did not follow, she let him do it. She had sealed both their fates that day.

They retreated into flaccid silence. Ruth sucked back her tears.

"Would you like me to take Jacob home?" Annie approached Ruth and Franey a few minutes later. She was no mother, or even a babysitter, but she could see the boy was getting wiggly.

"The girls are busy with the animals and canning." Franey rotated her slumped shoulders. "Joel is in the fields. They have no time to look after him."

"I'll stay with him."

Franey tilted her head and considered the offer. "He has some lessons he should be working on."

"I can do that."

"I don't know when I'll be home." Franey clutched a used tissue in one hand. "It's a long way to be going back and forth."

"Take your time."

Franey turned to her son. "You mind Annalise."

Jacob nodded. "They won't let me see Rufus. At least at home I can see Dolly."

"Do your chores."

He nodded again.

"Thank you, Annalise," Franey said.

"I'd like to see Rufus," Ruth said.

"I'll take you now." Franey stood to lead the way.

Annie caught Ruth's eyes and hoped her smile spoke reassurance. If Ruth's nervous state during the drive down was an indication, Rufus was not the most daunting mountain Ruth faced.

At the main doors on the first floor, Annie hesitated and

swallowed hard. Her stomach burned. She was leaving the hospital without seeing Rufus for herself. She'd been in enough hospitals to picture what it must be like for Rufus. He was the man so many depended on, and now he was lying in a hospital bed minus a spleen.

This did not have to happen. If Rufus had fought back even a little bit when Karl Kramer had been slashing tires, this might never have happened.

Annie settled Jacob in the backseat and made sure his seat belt was fastened. In the driver's seat, she adjusted the rearview mirror slightly so she could see him. "Have I ever told you that you have a great name?"

"Jacob Beiler is a great name?"

"Yep. Some very good men have had your name."

"*Daed* says it's a family name."

"You can be proud of your family."

"No I can't."

"You can't?"

"That would be *hochmut*. Pride is against *Ordnung*," Jacob said simply. "I think I'm going to like riding in your car. We can't have a car. That's against *Ordnung*, too."

Annie started the ignition.

At the Beiler house, Annie found the schoolwork Franey wanted Jacob to do, got him settled on the porch where she could keep him in sight, then stepped off the porch to use her phone. Somehow it seemed sacrilegious to use it in the house. Her eyes gazed at Rufus's workshop as she tracked down the number she needed.

"Tom Reynolds."

"Tom, this is Annie Friesen. I just heard about Rufus today."

Tom sighed. "He's in bad shape. I want to get over to the hospital to see him again."

"Tell me the police are involved now."

"Of course. I called 911 when I found him."

"And?"

"And not much. Because it's a work site, the place is crawling with footprints, so nothing stands out. So far they haven't found anybody who saw anything out of the ordinary. It's not like there's a neighborhood watch looking out for a bunch of half-built houses. But they're still talking to people who might not realize they saw something that mattered."

"Are they talking to Karl Kramer?" Annie paced in fury. "It's been three days. They should have arrested him by now."

"Nobody would like that more than I would," Tom said. "They just don't have any evidence."

"Somebody must have heard Karl threaten Rufus at some point."

"Maybe. But that doesn't mean Karl actually did anything."

"I'm going to talk to my lawyer," Annie said.

"Rufus would rather you didn't, I'm sure."

"Probably," Annie said, "but look where that's gotten him so far."

"Annie, leave it alone. The police are involved whether Rufus likes it or not. Give them a chance."

"Even if they press charges, he'll refuse to testify in an *English* court. We need evidence that doesn't depend on Rufus."

"We have to respect his wishes," Tom said. "I don't think he'd want you fishing around."

Thirty-Eight

Ten days later, Annie slowly pushed open the door to Rufus's room at the Beiler home.

"It's all right. I'm awake."

His voice, though weak, poured relief through her. "Your *mamm* said I could come up for your lunch dishes."

"Yes, I'm finished." Rufus was propped up in bed, but at least one of the pillows had escaped.

Annie moved to the side of the bed and gently pressed the pillow back into place. Rufus had eaten little from the tray. "Would you like something different to eat?"

"No thank you. I'm not very hungry. They keep bringing me food."

Annie smiled. "They want to help." *Just like I do.*

"How is the new house?"

"I have a long way to go with it," she said, "but I have no regrets."

"So this means we will see you. . .often."

"I believe so."

"*Gut.*"

"*Ya. Gut.*"

Rufus started to chuckle but winced.

He struck her as surprisingly well, considering what he had gone through barely two weeks ago.

"Lydia tells me you plan to attend church tomorrow," Annie said.

"She tells you the truth. They won't let me help with the benches, though."

"Your mother made me promise not to disturb your rest." Annie picked up the tray.

"I admit I'm ready for a nap. Thank you for coming. And for bringing Ruth."

Annie would have liked to pull up a chair and watch Rufus sleep, or if he stayed awake to be helpful so he would not have to move. But Franey's instructions had been strict.

Thank You, God. Thank You.

Downstairs in the kitchen, breads, cheeses, garden vegetables, and *schnitz* pies lined up in anticipation of the next day's congregational meal. Annie set the tray on the table. "Rufus is frustrated he can't help with the benches for church tomorrow."

"He's only been home a week." Ruth's hands were busy in the sink. "I tried to tell *Mamm* and *Daed* that they should let someone else take their turn to have church. But Rufus is determined to attend the service."

"Then I guess it's better it's here. All he has to do is come downstairs."

Ruth shook water off her hands and reached for a dish towel. "Thank you for bringing me home again."

"Your *mamm* seems glad to have your help caring for Rufus."

"He won't stay down much longer. He's threatening to go out to his workshop on Monday. The men who work for him have already been asking."

Annie carried Rufus's dishes to the sink and began to wash them. "What about you, Ruth? Are you going to church tomorrow?"

Before Ruth could answer, Eli Beiler entered the kitchen.

"The benches are almost set. Perhaps we could offer the men a cold drink."

"Of course, *Daed*." Ruth opened a cupboard and began taking down glasses.

Annie helped Ruth fill them with cold water and put them on the tray to carry into the wide rooms cleared of the family's furniture and filled with wooden benches. In her very *English* jeans and T-shirt, Annie stayed in the kitchen and let Ruth serve the men. But the door was open, and with fingers playing with the gold chain at her neck, she watched the way several men gathered to speak in hushed tones. The words that wafted toward her were Pennsylvania Dutch. As Ruth approached them, they straightened up and put on smiles. Even in another language, Annie recognized someone changing the subject of conversation.

"What were they talking about?" she wanted to know as soon as Ruth returned to the kitchen.

Ruth set down the empty tray. "I didn't hear everything, but I think it's about Rufus's medical expenses. Mrs. Troyer is having cancer treatments, so the fund is stretched."

"What does that mean?"

Ruth lifted one shoulder and let it drop. "They may ask families to contribute more."

"I hope everything works out." Annie tossed a dish towel on the counter. "I'd better go. I have an errand to run, and there's a lot to do at my house."

"Are you coming in the morning?" Ruth asked. "Please?"

"I'll be here."

Annie picked up her denim bag and went out the back door. She strode around the house to her car. With a little luck, she could get to the hospital before it closed. And with a little more luck, the business office would be open on Saturday.

Ruth sat in the back with Annie on Sunday morning. Both wore solid-colored, long skirts and high-necked blouses with no buttons, but still they stood out among the river of blues and purples and blacks. Ruth glanced at Annie to make sure she had remembered to tuck her chain under her blouse.

Worshipers stared not only at Annie, the visitor. Ruth felt the stares of families she had not seen in eighteen months, the last time she gathered with them for worship. For the most part, she avoided their eyes. This was not the time to explain to anyone why she left.

When the opening hymn began, Ruth's throat thickened too much to sing. How long it had been since she heard the timbre of unaccompanied voices slowly pondering the beauty of the High German words of worship. *Kommt her zu mir, spricht Gottes Sohn.* "Come to me," says God's Son, "all you who are burdened." Ruth let the hymn flow richly around her, adding her voice when she could gather enough air to sing a few words. The first stanza faded, and the second began. Ruth closed her eyes, wanting to believe the words that rose from the rows of benches. "I will help each person to carry what is difficult; with my health and strength He will win the kingdom of heaven."

Ruth held the hymnal open for Annie, who did her best to keep up with the German words printed in elaborate script without knowing the tune. Most hymns had ten stanzas or more. Hymn followed hymn for an hour's time. In between, the men whispered, "You sing," as they encouraged each other to begin a new song. In the custom that swarmed Ruth with familiarity, men humbly deferred to each other until someone at last intoned a long note. Ruth knew most of the hymns by heart, and as she sang them, she tried to forget she had been gone these long months.

But she had been gone. And she would be gone again. Ahead of her, sitting with the unmarried men and next to Rufus, Ruth saw Elijah Capp. He had to know she was here. How long would he wait before he approached her about the night that changed their lives? For the moment, Ruth wanted only to lose herself in the music and its assurances of God's help and presence.

The sermons followed. Ruth's body still remembered how to sit perfectly still for hours on the wooden bench. Next to her, Annie crossed and uncrossed her legs. Even Jacob, sitting a few rows ahead with their mother, was keeping still with more success than Annie.

Following worship, the men turned the benches into tables with practiced ease, and the women soon had the food laid out. The men of the church migrated to Rufus so that he could hardly get a bite in before receiving the well wishes of a representative of every family present.

Among the women, Annie seemed to mix in surprisingly well, a welcome visitor. She seemed more at home than Ruth felt. Even the minister and his wife called Annie away from the group for a private word on the porch, and Annie went without hesitation—even with a smile.

The smile faded, and Ruth saw Annie wander away from the gathering. Ruth followed her off the porch and across the yard toward the barn. Though Annie quickened her steps, Ruth caught up with her.

"What's wrong?" Ruth grabbed Annie's wrist to slow her pace.

Annie shook her head. Ruth could see the water in her eyes.

"Tell me," Ruth urged.

"The minister spoke to me—the one who gave the second sermon. I thought perhaps he wanted to welcome me. But what he was really doing was scolding me."

"For what? We've always welcomed visitors."

Annie sagged against the side of the barn. "I'm not just a visitor. I'm the *English* woman who paid Rufus's hospital bill yesterday."

Ruth's eyes widened. "The whole bill?"

Annie nodded. "Apparently it was a bad idea."

"The Amish care for each other," Ruth said softly. "When someone has large medical bills, the community takes care of them. Granted, it may be difficult because we don't have as many families as districts in Pennsylvania or Ohio, but we still are responsible."

" 'We'?" Annie asked. "You still see yourself as one of them. And I keep blundering on the outside. Why do the Amish say no to so many things?"

"Our life is not so much about saying no, but about saying yes and meaning it."

"But I have money. Plenty of it. Why shouldn't I use it to help?"

"Perhaps *because* it costs you so little," Ruth said gently. "Money does not answer every question."

Annie exhaled and looked at Ruth. "You understand the secret unwritten code better than I do, but you don't fit here any more than I do."

Ruth sucked in her lips before speaking. "No, probably not. But they are my family. My people. I have to figure it out."

"Well, so do I," Annie said, "just for different reasons."

Ruth nodded, not speaking.

"I think I'll go to my house." Annie dug the heels of her hands into her eye sockets. "I'm worn out from trying to be somebody I'm apparently not."

"Only you know." Ruth floundered for words of comfort.

"I'll pick you up in the morning to go back to town."

"I'll be ready."

Annie stood at the corner of the barn and looked back at the families eating lunch, still separated by gender. She watched Rufus. He sat up straight as he spoke and laughed with the other men, eating heartily among friends. This was his world.

Now he lifted his eyes to her across the yard. The quizzical look on his face sharply tempted her to go speak to him, but of course he was eating with the men. She would just make things worse by approaching him. She offered a weak wave and walked around the back of the barn to find her car.

She slowly maneuvered around the line of buggies with their black boxlike bodies. The horses were all in the pasture, Dolly's territory. She pulled out onto the highway feeling like a city girl through and through. Why had she ever thought she was meant to buy a house in Westcliffe?

Annie had managed to have some basic furniture delivered to the new house. She had a sofa to sit on in the living room with an ottoman to prop her feet on while she worked on her laptop. Mrs. Weichert's antiques store yielded a brushed brass floor lamp and a small oval oak dining table with four mismatched chairs. Both front and back doors had new locks. She let herself in the back door, dumped her bag on the table, and slouched into the couch with her laptop. On autopilot, Annie checked her e-mail, scanned through Facebook posts, rolled through Twitter, and clicked through a few blogs.

Nothing interested her. Her brain absorbed few of the words that reeled past her eyes. She opened up iTunes and played several favorite selections while she flipped through three of the unread magazines she had brought from her condo. Nothing made the jiggling in her knees stop.

Only one thing would help.

Annie went upstairs to the bedroom, where she still slept on an inflatable mattress while she shopped for a bed to suit the room, and pulled a pair of tennis shoes out of a box. She changed quickly into shorts with a sweatshirt and the shoes. The cul-de-sac was only a mile and a half away. An easy run. She hooked her house keys to her waistband and slipped one other item into a back pocket.

She was there in under twenty minutes. The crime scene tape was long gone from the house where Rufus had been attacked, a fact that infuriated Annie. She paused to stretch and catch her breath in front of the house, glancing around while she did so. On a Sunday afternoon, no crews were at work. Fairly sure she was unseen, Annie circled around to the back, seeking an unobtrusive way in.

The credit card in her back pocket came out and quickly earned its annual fee by slipping the back lock open. She was in the kitchen then walked through the hall to the stairs. The floor was tiled with large brown ceramic squares, and the stairs newly carpeted in a muddy beige. By the smell of it—she sneezed twice—Annie speculated that it had been installed only two days ago. There was no telling how many signs of Karl Kramer's presence the construction crew had covered. She opened a couple of closets and wished she had thought to bring a flashlight. Slowly Annie walked up the stairs, picking at the edges of the carpet. They were firmly tacked in place. Upstairs she easily found the master bedroom, where the attack happened. Her heart thudded in her chest when she saw that the padding was down, but the carpet was still in a roll at one end of the long room. She knelt and fished along the seams of the padding, determined to find something in the afternoon light. Inch by inch, she moved down the seams and along the edges of the room looking for loose spots.

On the third wall she found it. Something. A triangle of paper, barely an inch wide, was trapped between the wall and the carpet pad. With a gentle touch, Annie scraped one finger down the wall to get a grip on the paper and dislodge it. She groaned when she felt the edge rip away from a larger paper that was probably nailed down. But she had something. Holding it in her hand, she leaned back on her haunches. Handwritten letters—*ner*.

Or maybe half of an *m*—*mer*.

Written in black ink on a line. A signature.

Annie sensed a shadow cross hers. She jumped to her feet and moved toward the hall. "Who's there?"

She saw no one but in the stillness heard shifting weight, the creak of a step on subfloor in an uncarpeted room.

Thirty-Nine

Annie clenched the scrap of paper and stepped cautiously into the upstairs hall. Hardly breathing herself, she heard panting to her right. She stepped to the left and found the top of the stairs.

"What are you doing here?" a man's voice said.

Annie tapped down three steps rapidly then couldn't resist the urge to turn and look. The man she saw was dark, with black hair that needed cutting and a ragged mustache. He was older than the man her mother had spotted at the motel. Annie had always imagined Karl Kramer would look more businesslike.

"You're Karl Kramer, aren't you?" Annie surprised herself with the words and her own intuition. She moved down three more stair steps. "What are *you* doing here?"

"You should not be here."

He crept toward her with just enough persistence to drive her down another two steps.

"I could report you," Annie said.

"And have to explain yourself? I don't think so." He took the first step off the landing. "This is a small town. Everybody knows you bought that old house."

Two more steps and she was on the first floor, just as he took his second step down the stairs.

"The front door's unlocked," he said. "Get out of here."

Annie opened it, stood in the door frame with her hand on the doorknob, and turned toward the stairs. "If you hurt Rufus, I will find a way to prove it."

She slammed the door hard and ran even harder. It was still daylight. Anyone watching would see a young woman out for a Sunday afternoon run in the late August mountain sun. At the back of her house, Annie fumbled with her keys, breathless, and heaved herself into her kitchen. Inside, she leaned against the refrigerator and unclenched her fist. The scrap of paper was scrunched into the size and shape of a spitball, but she carefully unfolded every crease and pressed it flat.

Yes, she was sure now. It was *mer*, and it was a signature. Now all she had to do was find a sample of Karl Kramer's signature. Her laptop sat open on the ottoman, and she went to it to search for images of his contractor's license or title to a house or any kind of legal document that would bear his signature.

She came up with nothing. Her dreams that night shuffled documents and television crime show scenes together. She woke exhausted. But she had to pick up Ruth at six so they could be back to their lives in Colorado Springs before nine. At a staff meeting at ten, Annie would explain to her team what had been going on with the recent series of covert meetings.

Craving coffee, Annie pulled into the Beiler driveway. Rufus sat in a chair on the covered front porch. She had planned to simply wait for Ruth in the car without disturbing the rest of the family, but because Rufus was outside, Annie got out of the car and approached the steps.

"I didn't expect to see you out here so early." She leaned on the railing at the bottom of the steps.

"*Gut mariye* to you also," he said.

"Sorry. Good morning. But why aren't you still in bed, resting?" She moved up toward the porch.

"I have rested for two weeks. I want to work today."

"Aren't you pushing it?" Annie sat in a chair next to him and felt the warmth coming off his skin. She resisted the urge to put a hand to his forehead to see if the warmth was feverish. Outside, in the fresh air, he smelled more like himself instead of an arsenal of medicine.

"Work is a gift from God," Rufus said. "I simply want to receive His gift."

Annie decided not to argue the point. "I found something last night. I think it proves Karl Kramer was in that house. I just need to find a sample of his signature to compare and be sure." She told him about the scrap of paper.

Rufus turned slowly to look at Annie full on. "You went to that house?"

She met his violet-blue gaze and willed her thudding heart to slow. "The police aren't getting anywhere. I thought maybe some fresh eyes would see something they missed."

"You were foolish. You could have been hurt."

"I was investigating."

"You were trespassing."

"I didn't hurt anything."

"Didn't you?" His eyes turned back to the mountains.

"No. Besides, I wasn't the only one there. I've never met Karl Kramer, so I can't be sure, but I would bet my company that he was the man I saw in that house. Talk about trespassing. It's not his building project. The fact that he came back suggests he's up to no good."

"That logic is not exactly flawless."

"You know what I mean." Annie was not giving up easily. "What was he doing creeping around a house he is not even building?"

"I suppose you think he was looking for the paper you found."

"Could be. Most of it is still under the carpet pad."

"It's not your business, Annalise."

She reached across the chairs and put a hand on his forearm.

301

The muscles under her fingers tensed. "I care about what happens to you, Rufus. The sooner the police nail Karl Kramer, the sooner you can get your peaceful life back—without all these complications."

"I do want a peaceful life," Rufus said, "but you confound me more than anything else."

He withdrew his arm from her touch. His words silenced her, and a flush rose in her cheeks against her best effort to subdue it. Why was it so hard for him to see that she was trying to help?

"You must let it go, Annalise." Rufus sighed and leaned forward in his chair. "You can't control everything. You have to stop trying to win. You certainly do not have to win anything for me. That is a way of life from your world, not mine."

"I just want justice. God likes justice, doesn't He?"

"God *is* justice," Rufus said. "You don't understand that. You have been in our home. You have been in our church, among our people. You have even used your technology to study us. Still you do not understand. Just when I think you begin to grasp our ways, you take things into your own hands again."

"I'm just trying to help."

"I don't expect you to be Amish, Annalise, but I do hope you can respect our ways."

"I *do.*"

He shook his head. "Our life is grounded in submission, and yours seeks control. You can't have both."

Glassenheit. Ruth had used that word. Annie Friesen had never been very good at submission.

The front door opened, and Ruth emerged. Annie stood up.

"I hope you feel better soon. I've got some things to go control." Annie's dry tone sounded hollow even to her.

Rufus looked up at Ruth. "Did you say good-bye to *Mamm*?" he said, still speaking English.

She shook her head, and Annie realized how pale Ruth looked. "She's staying in bed late. I don't think she wants to talk to me."

"Neither of you is willing to talk about the one thing that

matters. You started something when you left," Rufus said, "and you are picking at a sore when you visit."

"I came back for *you*," Ruth said. "You could have died."

"And I thank you. But you came back again."

"To see how you are healing."

"You are training to be a healer. You will have to heal this thing between you and *Mamm*." Rufus leaned back and closed his eyes. The conversation was over.

Annie and Ruth got in the car and buckled their seat belts.

"Does Rufus always do this?" Annie asked.

"Do what?"

"Dump a pithy impossible challenge on people instead of just saying good-bye."

"He's hardest on people he cares about most."

Annie waited in the upscale downtown bistro for her mother. Once a month they met here for lunch. Generally they both pretended to review the menu, hunting for something new to try, and then both ordered the corned beef on rye they loved. It came with coleslaw they dissected, trying to discover the secret ingredient that made them want to buy a container to go—which they invariably did. In the fairer months, they ate outside at a small sidewalk table sequestered from passing pedestrian traffic by a iron fence. Annie had chosen a table in the shade.

When Myra arrived this time, Annie set her menu aside. "Let's just get the corned beef."

"Seems like the efficient thing to do." Myra had been shopping. She kissed Annie's forehead, and then she set a boutique bag on the sidewalk under the table. "Summer sweaters are 40 percent off."

Annie smiled. Myra loved to shop, but even more, she salivated over bargains. Annie's closet was full of bargains Myra had picked up over the years. Most of them Annie never wore.

The food came quickly. Annie suspected the waitress, who

served them every month, had put the order in to the kitchen before her mother arrived. She made a mental note to leave a huge tip.

"So you've been to the Amish place again." Myra corralled meat between bread slices.

"It's not the 'Amish place,' Mom. It's a quaint, historic small town with a few Amish families in the area."

"When do I get to see the house you bought?"

Annie swallowed a bite. "Let me get it fixed up first."

"I can't imagine what the kitchen must be like in a house that old."

Annie shrugged. "I don't do much in the kitchen anyway."

"I should have taught you better."

"You taught plenty, Mom. Penny learned, after all. She has food on the brain. I just thought other things were important."

"It's not too late to learn to cook."

"I suppose not."

"I could sew curtains for your new windows."

"I might take you up on that one," Annie said, "but you have to teach me. Did you know the Amish women make all the clothes for the family?"

"That's a little extreme, don't you think?" Myra sucked coleslaw off her fork, her eyes rolling in pleasure.

"I don't know. Maybe. But there's something appealing about the way the Beilers live—well, all the Amish, I suppose."

"What do you mean?"

"When I'm there, I hear sounds I don't hear in town. Instead of televisions and stereos, dishes clink around the table and milk makes that *whoosh* when it comes out of the cow. And I smell things I've always been in too much of a rush to notice. They have a reason for how they live. They hear the voice of God. They choose life instead of letting it happen to them."

"We all choose our lives," Myra said. "You chose to go to college. You chose to start a business. You chose your condo."

"Did I? The whole system is so competitive. Of course I started a business. That's what winners do."

"Annie, what are you talking about?" Myra put her fork down, laid her hands in her lap, and stared at her daughter.

"I wonder what it would be like, that's all."

"Living without television? Without electricity? Without that computer you use like an appendage?"

Annie spread coleslaw around her plate with a fork. "The trade-off might be worth it."

"You need a vacation. Let's go somewhere that has a beach."

"Mom. A vacation is not the answer. I've had a lucrative offer for the business. I think I'm going to take it. I could sell the condo. This may be the time to rethink my life." Annie shrugged. "And yes, the Amish may help me do that. They already have."

"Didn't you tell me that your friend Ruth left the Amish way after growing up in it?"

"She's still trying to figure it out. She's choosing something. Answering a call. It's very spiritual for her, even if it does come at a price."

"If you want to be more spiritual, maybe you should just go to church a little more often." Myra resumed eating. "We always went when you were little. We all got out of the habit. But when your dad and I go now, people still ask after you."

Annie nodded. "I might try that. But I might want more."

Myra's eyes narrowed. "You mean, like join the Amish?"

Annie pinched a piece of bread off the sandwich she had not eaten. "I don't know if I would make a very good Amish woman, but I wonder about it. I'm at least going to get serious about faith again and find out where it takes me." In her mind's eye, she saw herself standing in the purple dress in the barn. Rufus's scent filled her nostrils even now.

"Annalise Friesen, buying a weekend house near the mountains is one thing, but I've seen that look on your face before. You're seriously considering joining the Amish."

"I don't even know if they would have me, but what if I did?"

"Think about your family, Annie. Everything would change."

"Not everything."

"This is about that man, isn't it?" Myra said sharply. "He's got your brain scrambled."

"I admit Rufus—well, he's not like any man I've ever known. But I wouldn't do this just for him. I would do it for me. For my relationship with God to change."

Myra pushed her chair back and stood up. "I've lost my appetite." She tossed her napkin onto the table and picked up her shopping bag. "I believe it's your turn to get the check."

Annie's mouth hung open as she watched her mother walk away without looking back. *Great. Someone else fed up with me. Okay, God, what am I supposed to do with that?*

Forty

October 1747

Elizabeth flung open the green shutters and breathed in the view of the Byler farm from the kitchen window. Fall air snapped through on the breeze.

After Jacobli was born in the cabin, Jakob drew up plans for a house. When John arrived the next year, and Christian started sleeping in the barn because the cabin was so crowded, Jakob began stacking stones and smearing mortar. By the time Sarah arrived a year after John, the home was nearly finished. Joseph and David, Elizabeth was glad to say, were born in the bedroom upstairs.

The home was simple and functional, but compared to the cabin, it was spacious beyond Elizabeth's dreams. She enjoyed the roomy kitchen and the broad table large enough for the family to gather. Whether for meals, lessons, or conversation, the table was in constant use. The kitchen had a small hearth for cooking, but Elizabeth's favorite wall was in the main room. In the evenings, Jakob tended the fire in the wide wall made of stone harvested from the fields during the clearing years and matching the outside of the house. The black oak mantel seemed to give him particular pleasure. A rank of upstairs bedrooms sheltered all the children

307

with no more than two to a bed even when all ten of them lived at home. Now when Barbara's husband traveled overnight, there was plenty of room for Barbara and her toddler and infant sons to stay a few days.

Barbara married Christian Yoder, and Anna was engaged to his brother. Anna was already staying at Barbara's house most of the time because it was closer to the man she was engaged to—and whose family was planning her wedding.

Yoders. They arrived from Europe five years after Jakob. Already they were becoming a dominant family among the Amish settlers. The fact that their mother had been a distantly related Yoder made it easy for the Byler girls to gravitate toward Yoder sons.

Neither of the older girls even once wavered about remaining in the Amish faith. When an Amish bishop visited from another district, Barbara, Anna, and Christian were baptized. When he came again, Barbara married. The girls made their peace that Elizabeth would never join them and that their own father would be out of place in an Amish gathering. Christian, of course, held out hope that his father would return to the fold.

Elizabeth's only regret was that Jakob felt out of place at his daughters' weddings and chose not to attend. And someone else would host the celebrating families when Anna and Lisbetli married.

And Maria. What about Maria? At fifteen, she seemed in no hurry to join the Amish church, but Elizabeth did not want the teenager to make such a choice because of her.

At least there was Sarah. Perhaps by the time she was old enough to marry, there would be a proper church for her to marry in. Elizabeth did not even care if it were Lutheran or Presbyterian. Jakob would be there to see their daughter married.

Elizabeth smiled at what she saw from the window. Coming in from the vegetable garden, Lisbetli had Joseph by one hand and David by the other. Behind her, John and Sarah carried a basket of vegetables between them—most likely squash, Elizabeth thought. Not much was left in the garden at this point in the season. The cellar was well stocked for the winter.

"*Mamm*, I'm hungry!" David called out as soon as he spotted his mother in the window.

"You're always hungry," John responded.

It was true. At age four, David could keep up with Jakob or Christian at meals.

Elizabeth turned around and ran a rag over the table, wiping up the last evidence of lunch just before the children burst through the back door with their supper bounty. John and Sarah quickly disappeared into the other room, no doubt intending to be out of sight when Elizabeth vocalized the next chore.

"I thought Bar-bar would be here by now," Lisbetli said. The little boys freed themselves of her hands and clambered on Elizabeth, who dropped into a chair for support against their weight.

"I'm sure she'll come any minute." Elizabeth snuggled her little boys.

"Where's Maria?"

"Upstairs. She needed to put on a fresh apron."

"Are you sure you don't mind if I go?" Lisbetli asked. "The boys will be underfoot while you're cooking if I'm not here."

Elizabeth kissed both boys' foreheads and nudged them off her lap. "Lisbetli, the question is whether you want to go to the quilting bee. You're so helpful to me with the younger children, but you won't be a child yourself much longer. What do you want to do?"

"I don't want to hurt anybody's feelings." Lisbetli moved her fingers nervously across the back of a chair her father had made.

"Lisbetli," Elizabeth said softly. "You don't have to worry that you'll hurt my feelings if you decide to join the Amish church. Your father sacrificed something when he married me, but you are free to make your own choice."

"What if Maria decides to be baptized when the bishop comes

for Anna's wedding?" Lisbetli said. "If I don't join the church, I'll be the only one."

The only one of her mother's children not to stay true. Lisbetli did not have to speak aloud. Elizabeth knew—had always known—that the toddler she loved, now becoming a woman, would face the question.

"You are twelve years old, and today is only a quilting bee." Elizabeth pulled herself to her feet and examined the bounty the children had carried in. "You only have to decide what you'd like to do today."

"I do love to quilt," Lisbetli admitted. "I'm good enough that they'll let me do more than thread needles now. I'd like to make a baby quilt all on my own."

"A baby quilt?"

"For Anna. She's getting married in a few weeks. Maybe she'll need the baby quilt next year."

"That's a lovely thought. I have some scraps I can give you."

"Thank you." Lisbetli hesitated. "They have to be. . ."

"I know. Plain. They're left over from the dresses I used to make for you and Maria." As she spoke, Elizabeth adjusted the skirt of her own blue, flowered calico dress. Six-year-old Sarah was the only daughter she could dress in the prints and patterns she enjoyed. "I'm sure Anna would love to wrap a baby in a quilt made by Aunt Lisbetli."

"I've been thinking that maybe I should just be Lisbet now," the girl said. "It sounds more grown-up."

Elizabeth nodded. "I'll try to remember." She had to look harder and harder to glimpse the toddler who captured her heart.

"It's okay if you forget sometimes."

"Bar-bar's here!" John's enthusiasm rang from the other room.

Elizabeth heard the clatter of the buggy and went into the main room to look out the front door. Barbara wrapped the reins around a post and waved. A moment later she came through the door.

"Hello, everyone."

"Where are the babies?" David wanted to know.

"Anna is looking after them." Barbara looked at Lisbet. "She'll meet us at the bee."

Since Barbara hadn't brought the babies, David lost interest and wandered away.

"Where's Maria?" Barbara asked.

Clomping on the stairs answered the question. Maria appeared in a dark blue dress covered by a black apron that crisscrossed her back. She arranged her prayer *kapp* on her head.

"Where is your *kapp*, Lisbetli?" Barbara asked.

Lisbet's hand went to her head. "It must be on my bed."

"Then go get it. You can't go out with a bare head."

Lisbet dashed up the stairs.

The door swung open again, and Jakob came in with Christian.

"I thought the two of you went back to the wheat field after lunch." Elizabeth raised her cheek, knowing Jakob would brush his hand across it.

"Not yet. We had some work to do in the barn." Jakob obliged his wife with the gesture of affection. "One of the milk cows is acting strangely. If we're not careful, she'll dry up."

Christian lifted his hat a couple of inches and wiped his hand across his forehead casually. "Are the Yoders coming to the bee?"

Elizabeth suppressed a smile, but Maria was less discreet.

"Christian is *en lieb* with Lizzie Yoder." Maria grinned at her brother.

"Hush, Maria!" Jakob said sharply. But Elizabeth saw the twinkle in his eye. Anyone could see how Christian felt about Lizzie Yoder.

"It was an innocent question," Christian said.

"I do believe the Yoder girls plan to be there," Barbara said. "Perhaps I'll have opportunity to speak to Lizzie."

Lisbet thumped down the stairs, her black *kapp* askew on her head.

When his sisters were gone, Christian turned to his father. "*Daed*, on Sunday next week a visiting preacher is coming. We don't get to have church very often."

Jakob nodded. "I'll make sure you're free to spend the day."

"Thank you." Christian looked from Jakob to Elizabeth. "I would like to take Jacobli with me."

In the fracture of silence, Elizabeth felt the eyes of her four youngest children lift and settle on their father. "John and Sarah," she said to her two eldest, "please take the little ones to the table and help them learn to write their names." She looked at them in that way that forbade argument, and they quietly complied.

Jakob took a log from the stack beside the fireplace and methodically adjusted its angle before returning it to the pile. "Jacobli would feel out of place in Amish worship."

"He's only eight," Christian countered. "No one would hold your choice against one of your sons."

Elizabeth was on her feet. "You seem to forget that Jacobli is my son as well. He will *not* go to church with you."

"*Daed*, you've always said that all your children were free to make their own choices, each one according to his conscience."

"That's right."

"How can Jacobli choose something he has not experienced? Would it really hurt him to go to church with his own sisters and brother?"

Elizabeth stepped across the room and positioned herself between father and son. "Jacobli is too young. Your father and I will decide when he is old enough to visit the Amish."

"But there aren't any other churches around here." Christian gestured widely. "Isn't it better that he go to church somewhere?"

"I include religious instruction as a regular part of schooling my children." Elizabeth hated the feeling of heat creeping up her neck. "He is learning everything he needs to know about the love and mercy of God."

"*Daed*," Christian said, "this is your decision. You're the man of this house."

Jakob did not hesitate. "Elizabeth is right."

"But *Daed*—"

"I have made my decision, Christian. Will you check on the cow again in about two hours?"

Elizabeth let out her breath. Jakob had made his choice nine years ago. Never once had he disappointed her when Christian pushed him. And the older Christian got, though, the harder he pushed. If he wanted Jacobli this year, would he want John next year? Would he put Sarah in a *kapp* and apron the year after that? Elizabeth did not require an elaborate life, but neither did she think a church rule book should dictate what color her dress could be or how long her husband's hair must be. While she would never openly oppose them—for Jakob's sake—it seemed to Elizabeth the Amish went to unnecessary extremes.

Christian pressed his lips together and sat in the rocker Jakob had crafted when Sarah was a baby.

The door opened yet again, and Jacobli entered. He looked around. "Why is it so quiet in here?"

"No reason." Elizabeth turned to greet him by smoothing his dark red hair. "We were just having a discussion. Why is your face so sticky?"

He grinned. "I ran all the way up from the tannery. I have great news, *Daed*. Mr. Hochstetler and his boys have been out hunting. They got three deer and a bear, and they want to sell you the hides."

Jakob nodded with pleasure. "Soft deerskin will bring a good price."

"He's going to bring them in a few days," Jacobli said, "as soon as they get the meat off. Can I help you put them in the vats?"

"We'll see."

Elizabeth caught Jakob's eye. He knew how she felt about having Jacobli so close to the lime solution. How could something that could take the hair off a hide be good for a little boy? Nevertheless, Elizabeth loved seeing the pleasure in Jakob's eyes when their son grew excited.

313

"I think we should add some bark to the pit, *Daed*. But first we should take out the cattle hides from the Siebers. They've been in there three months already."

"You might be right about that." Jakob nodded.

Christian stood up and straightened his hat on his head. "Jacobli, you seem to know a great deal about tanning for an eight-year-old."

"I'm going to be a tanner when I grow up."

"It's messy business," Christian said. "Smelly and dangerous. Wouldn't you rather be in the fresh air?"

Jacobli shook his head emphatically. "The tannery is the place for me."

Christian sighed. "Give me the farm any day."

Jakob smiled. "Christian, you were just like Jacobli at his age. Have you forgotten your maps and charts and planting schedules?"

"Farming is the way of our people, *Daed*."

Jakob readjusted the same log again.

Elizabeth nudged Jacobli toward the kitchen. "Come on. I'll help you clean up."

Forty-One

Ruth loaded her backpack strategically. She did not want to lose valuable time shuttling back and forth between her dorm room and the library because of overlooked items. She had booked six hours of computer time. Her class schedule allowed her to work three eight-hour days back-to-back and have three days in a row to devote to her studies and still enjoy a Sabbath.

In the four days since Ruth left Rufus sitting on the front porch, tears spurted at unpredictable intervals. Mrs. Watson asked Ruth to read, but she had avoided the task because she was uncertain the lump in her throat would allow the formation of spoken words. She completely forgot the shower she promised to give Mrs. Bragg, and she mixed up dinner trays for several residents. Seeing Mrs. Renaldi on the wing reminded her of Tom Reynolds, which made her think of Rufus, and then her mother and the rest of the family.

Ruth braced herself for the weight of the backpack bulging with textbooks and notebooks for four courses. She had her hand on the doorknob when she thought to make a phone call. Lowering one shoulder, she slung her burden down long enough to find her cell phone tucked into the pocket of the strap.

"You sure you want to do this?" Lee Solano asked.

Annie exhaled and rolled her eyes. "You ask me that every time we speak to each other." They stood together outside the doors to a downtown bank. Walking through them would take her to the meeting at which she would sign papers that meant she was letting go.

"I have to ask," Lee said. "I've never had a client express such extreme wishes. I wake up in the night thinking I must have heard you wrong."

"You heard me right. This life is not for me anymore."

"Maybe someday you'll do another start-up."

Annie shook her head. "I've done it twice. That's enough."

"You're only twenty-seven," Lee said. "Don't paint yourself into a corner you can't get out of."

"You're in cahoots with my mother."

"Never met the lady," Lee said, "but it sounds like she has the smarts you used to have."

"Let's just do this." Annie pushed open the bank door.

Lee did not have to understand her choices. He was being paid handsomely for arranging the legalities. Beyond that, Annie was not trying to persuade anyone of anything. She wanted only to make a choice and see it through.

Lee pushed the elevator button, and they rode to the third floor without speaking. From there it seemed as if she were watching someone else's motions. Annie wore a blue silk suit and four-inch navy heels, the tried-and-true choices she relied on for business meetings of this caliber. Though young, female, and casual in an old boy's world, she was not some sort of teenybopper with a ponytail and chewing gum. But even as she shook hands and took her seat and tugged the bottom of her jacket straight, the weight of the purple dress in the barn draped off her shoulders, and it was soft cotton that she adjusted around her waist. She picked up a pen to sign documents with elevator music playing in the background and phones ringing and lights blinking, but she was sitting on the sofa in a hundred-year-old house, listening to sounds hidden in silence. Bearers of modern success surrounded her in a sleek conference room while outrageous numeric figures popped off the printed pages for something she could not hold in her hands, but she was on the Beiler front porch, sitting next to Rufus in the fragrance of a garden that proved where food came from.

Finally, the others left, with handshakes and claps on the back for a deal well done, and Annie was alone with Lee, holding in her hands a manila folder of legalese.

Lee picked up his briefcase from the floor and set it on the table to open it.

"Okay," he said, "now for stage two." He slapped a stack of papers on the table. "You can still back out of this part."

"I'm not backing out of anything." Annie picked up the pen again. "Where do I sign?"

"That's a pile of money in your hands," he said. "If you sign these, you're not leaving yourself much to live off of."

"I don't plan to need much. And there's still the condo. I told the real estate agent to lower the asking price by 15 percent."

He groaned. "Annie, please."

"I want it to sell quickly."

"The market is soft on high-end stuff like your place. You'll take a loss."

Deadpan, she looked at him.

"All right, I get it. You're not worried about money."

"In my recent experience, it's been more trouble than it's worth."

Annie paused only briefly over the signature line. The bulk of her assets would go into a holding account that could never revert directly to her. She needed more time to sort out just where it would go eventually. She couldn't just leave it without a purpose, like a forgotten trinket in a box. But it would never be hers for personal use.

Annie signed.

"You've been a great help in all of this, Lee. Thank you."

"You're welcome." He picked up the document and returned it to his briefcase. "The money should be transferred before the end of the day."

"You know where to find me if you have questions."

They exited the conference room, descended in the elevator, and stepped into the blinding Colorado sun. Annie squinted at her car parked across the street. Above the sounds of traffic, she recognized the vibration of her cell phone in the small purse she carried when she dressed up. Lifting the flap of the purse, she saw that the caller was Ruth.

"Hello, Ruth."

"Hi," came a diminished voice. "Do you think. . .could I. . . maybe see you today?"

"Yes, of course." Annie was eager to see how Ruth was. "I have one other meeting to go to right now. Should I pick you up later?"

"I can get a ride to your place," Ruth said. "I thought I could bring what I need to make dinner for you."

Annie smiled. "Yes. Absolutely. About six?" She dropped the phone back in the purse.

Now to talk to Barrett.

Sated with chicken stew and shoofly pie, Annie picked up a box of books and added it to the stack in the entryway.

"Are you really giving all this away?" Ruth followed with a second box.

"I didn't need most of this stuff living here," Annie answered. "I'm sure not going to need it in Westcliffe. I've tagged some furniture to take, with some bedding and practical items. But a lot of my things will find better homes elsewhere."

"I admire how ruthless you're being in packing things up."

"I've got time now." Annie grinned. "No job."

Ruth laughed. "How soon will you move?"

"I couldn't arrange for the furniture movers before next week, but I'll take some things this weekend by car."

"Oh good. I mean, that sounds like a good plan."

Annie paused, a roll of packaging tape in one hand and a permanent marker in the other. "Would you like to come with me, Ruth?"

Ruth straightened the top box in the stack then turned hesitantly toward Annie. "I can't leave things the way they are with my mother. Rufus is right about that."

The ashen face of her friend twisted Annie's heart. "Then we'll go together."

Annie padded down the hall in her bare feet to the bedroom. Ruth followed. The twin doors to the walk-in closet were wide open, though most of the closet's contents were strewn in piles around the room. In one corner a supply of flattened boxes awaited new lives of service. Annie picked one up, popped it open, and sealed the bottom with tape.

Ruth wandered to the bed and momentarily hung a soft pink cashmere sweater from her fingers. She folded it neatly then reached for a starched white shirt with a delicate string of blue and green flowers hand-embroidered down the front. "You have some very nice things."

"You know, you can have anything you want." Annie scribbled a label on a box. "If you need some clothes. Sweaters. A coat. Or a radio or a lamp or anything you see. A TV."

Ruth picked up a linen blouse, sat on the bed, and folded the blouse in her lap. "Thank you, but I would never be comfortable. I am still Plain at heart."

Annie put down her packing tape and sat next to Ruth on the end of the bed. She leaned into Ruth's shoulder. "I think your mother would be glad to hear you say that."

"Perhaps. But I have a lot to ask forgiveness for. And being Plain at heart will never be the same as joining the church."

"Perhaps if your family understood more about what you're doing, they would soften. You're doing something noble, in my opinion."

"Noble is too close to proud, *hochmut*. Is it humble? That is always the question. *Demut*. Am I submitting?"

"Well, how do you answer those questions?"

Ruth fingered the collar of the linen blouse. "If I submit to God, I can't be anything but what I am. If God created me to care for people, perhaps He also means for me to have the education to know how to do it."

"Rufus would be dead without people who knew how to care for him in a crisis," Annie said. "Surely your parents can appreciate that fact."

"I was not baptized." Ruth's voice was barely above a whisper. "So my choice to leave is not the greatest wound to my mother. It is the way I left that stabs her."

Annie wasn't sure she knew what Ruth meant, but the moment quivered too fragile for questions. She put an arm around Ruth's shoulder and leaned her head against Ruth's. "Talk to her."

In the silence, her advice echoed in her own mind. Perhaps it was true that her own choice to leave her life in Colorado Springs would not be her mother's greatest wound if she too did not leave well.

Ruth was the one to rupture the stillness. She stood and began folding vigorously. "We're going to need a lot of boxes."

"I can always buy more." Annie pulled a box closer to the bed and dropped in the linen blouse then a whole stack of shirts from the bed.

"Make sure you keep enough warm things for the winter. Westcliffe gets cold."

"I will."

"Does Rufus know you're doing all this?"

Annie grimaced. "He knows about the house but not that I sold my business and put my condo on the market."

"When do you plan to tell him?"

"I'm not sure it matters."

"Of course it matters."

"I don't want Rufus to think I'm doing any of this because of him." Annie expertly laid another strip of tape across a box.

"Are you sure you're not?" Ruth challenged.

"I'm not expecting anything from your brother, if that's what you mean."

"But you have feelings for him, *ya*?"

Annie dropped a trio of sweaters into a box. "It's hard not to," she admitted softly, "but that does not mean anything. He already said he does not expect me to be Amish. I am *English*. So what can happen?"

"He would not ask it of you, that is true," Ruth said. "But if you were to choose?"

"I don't know if I'm ready to choose to be Amish. And I don't think he believes I ever could. Besides, it would be wrong to make Rufus the reason."

"That is true."

"I've seen a different picture of life, and I wonder if it's meant for me. A life that does not ignore God." Annie taped a box shut and labeled it. "You and I are not so different. I never really asked what God wants of me before. Now I will."

Ruth laid a pair of wool trousers in the new box. "I wonder about our ancestor Jakob Byler. Growing up in the church, I heard stories about his son Christian, who is my ancestor. But now you discovered Jakob had a second family—your family. What made him choose as he did?"

"I'm sure it wasn't easy." Annie went into the closet and came back with a load of dresses on hangers. "I believe he arrived in Philadelphia an Amish man with a wife and five children. Then his wife died. There he was, in a new land—not even a country yet—with five children and a plan to homestead with a few other Amish families. It had to be tough. We have to put ourselves in his place and imagine the rest."

"And choose the best we can, just the way Jakob did."

Annie nodded. "I think so."

They folded clothes without speaking for a few minutes and filled two more boxes.

"So when are you going to talk to your mother?" Ruth asked.

Annie looked up and caught Ruth's eye. "Tomorrow. And then we'll go to the valley, and you'll talk to yours."

Forty-Two

December 1750

"One more day," Christian said to Lizzie Yoder, "and you'll be stuck with me forever."

"I don't want to be stuck with anyone else." Lizzie shivered under her shawl.

They sat in separate straight-back chairs next to each other on the Yoders' front porch. Early December sun looked brighter than it felt to Christian. It was probably selfish to keep Lizzie out in the cold, but it was the only place they could have a private moment. They were in plain view, but members of the large Yoder family thoughtfully managed to be occupied elsewhere.

"What a blessing to be ready to marry just when Bishop Hertzner has come to stay." Christian set his jaw in satisfaction. "Our children will grow up going to church every other Sunday, and not just when a visiting minister comes through."

"Christian, do you hope that God gives us a baby right away?" Lizzie looked at him shyly out of the sides of her eyes.

He reached over and patted her hand briefly. "We will be grateful for whatever God gives us. His will is certain."

Lizzie nodded. "Ours is the last wedding. All the fuss of the last few weeks will be over."

"I'm sorry we couldn't be first instead of the last of five," Christian said. "If only I had spoken to the bishop when he first arrived."

"It would have been prideful to insist on being first. Besides, what difference does a few weeks make when we have our whole lives before us?"

Christian twisted his hands together. "I wish I had finished our house. I didn't know we would have such difficulty getting the harvest in this year." He brightened. "But now we have our own land just a few miles away. Next year we'll have our own harvest."

"Do you really think so? Can we get enough acres cleared by spring?"

"I will chop down trees in the middle of a blizzard if I have to."

"I keep telling you I can help."

Christian shook his head. "You will be busy visiting and gathering the things we need for the house. We will spend a few weeks here with your family, then with the Kauffmanns and the Troyers and the Zooks. Before you know it, we'll be in our own home."

"I cannot wait."

Christian considered his bride-to-be. He had no doubt she was the prettiest of the Yoder sisters, but her devotion to the church had won his heart.

A wagon rattled into view and hurtled toward the house.

"Why is he driving so fast?" Lizzie rose abruptly, clutching her shawl against the wind, and moved to the edge of the porch. "My uncle! Something must be wrong—it may be my aunt."

She stepped to the front door, pushed it open, and screamed for her family. The answer came in a thunder of footsteps from every direction. When the wagon came to a halt only a few feet from the porch, Christian was there to grab the reins and steady the horses. Yoders swarmed around the wagon.

"Miriam!" Lizzie's mother pushed past and clambered into the wagon. Her sister looked nearly unconscious. "Adam, how long has she been like this?"

"Three days." Adam jumped from his seat into the back of the wagon. "She cannot hold anything down, Martha. She was determined to be well enough for the wedding tomorrow, but I am worried today. I could not wait any longer."

"Is she with child again?"

"She did not tell me," Adam answered. "But she must be. It is the only time she gets like this."

"Take her in the house. The room at the top of the stairs is ready."

Christian caught Lizzie's eyes. The room at the top of the stairs had been readied for them. He had not yet seen the preparations for where they would begin married life.

A tangle of arms lifted Miriam's limp form, cradling her as they transported her into the house. Stair-stepped small children climbed out of the pit of the wagon and raced each other around the house, oblivious to their mother's plight.

Christian was left holding the reins and stroking the horse's neck. Lizzie was frozen in place.

"I suppose I should put the horses in the barn." Christian found the horses' lead. "I'm sure they'll stay the night for the wedding tomorrow."

"Christian," Lizzie said, her face blanched, "they will stay far longer than that."

"Your aunt seems quite ill, but with your mother's care—"

Lizzie was shaking her head, her lips pressed together. "You don't understand. Miriam is with child. This happens to her every time. It lasts until she is at least four months along. With the twins, it was even worse. She'll be in bed for weeks. My mother will have to spoon-feed her. My uncle will have a terrible time keeping up with the cousins, so the little ones will stay here, too."

Christian considered these facts. "You mean, she will be in bed *here* for weeks?"

Lizzie nodded.

"She will be in. . .our bed. . .for weeks."

Lizzie nodded again. "Christian, where will we live after our wedding?"

Elizabeth used a long, thin washing bat to lift Jakob's shirts out of the barrel where she had left them in lye to soak out the stains. One at a time she plopped four identical white cotton shirts into a basket then bundled up assorted children's clothing and tossed them on top of the load. Lisbet was fourteen now, more than old enough to look after the children while Elizabeth sought creekside refuge. Elizabeth took her warmest cloak off the hook in the kitchen and arranged it around her shoulders.

"But it is cold out there." Sarah, nine, poked at the load with one finger. "Why are you washing clothes in January? Why not wait for spring?"

"Your *daed*'s shirts are dirty now." Elizabeth hefted her basket.

"Is Lizzie going with you?"

"No. This is Lizzie's baking day." Elizabeth's answer was quick. Lizzie was the reason she had decided to do laundry in the middle of January in the first place. Lizzie's second batch of buckwheat loaves sat on the table, rising in the warmth from the oven.

Outside, the slap of brisk air was welcome. Elizabeth started down the path to the creek. The water had frozen solid a couple of weeks earlier, but temperatures had risen again, and the creek yielded a sluggish flow.

A sluggish creek was good enough for Elizabeth.

It was not that Elizabeth disliked Lizzie. She was a perfectly lovely girl and well suited in temperament to Christian. Elizabeth was genuinely happy for the young couple. But Lizzie had been sheltered all her life from anyone who was not Amish and didn't seem to know what to do with Elizabeth, or Jakob, or Christian's half siblings. Over the years, Elizabeth certainly did not intentionally offend her neighbors. Most of them would speak to her in friendly ways. Mrs. Zimmerman helped her birth five babies, and Mrs. Stehley enjoyed borrowing Elizabeth's books. Elizabeth had learned to sew clothing for her Amish stepchildren, and mothers with younger children happily accepted her garments as serviceable hand-me-downs. Though Jakob repeatedly offered to bring her whatever she wanted from Philadelphia, in many ways Elizabeth lived as plain as her neighbors.

Lizzie did not say most of what she thought—Elizabeth was certain of that. It was Jakob whom Lizzie wordlessly condemned. Elizabeth was merely an unenlightened outsider. Jakob was the one who left the church when he married her. He was the one who put his children in the difficult position of choosing between him and the church. *How does he bear it?* Elizabeth sometimes wondered.

Christian was the third of the Byler children to marry into the extended Yoder family. The truth that their mother had been a Yoder was never far from Elizabeth's mind, nor, she suspected, from theirs. Newly married, Christian and Lizzie lived as separately as they could while sleeping under the same roof with Jakob and Elizabeth.

And now the bishop was here to stay. For the first time, the Amish families of Northkill and Irish Creek had an authority living among them permanently. Jakob seemed unconcerned, but Elizabeth wondered if the presence of a bishop would disturb the careful balance of their life together. Only a few hours ago, Elizabeth overheard Lizzie murmuring to Christian that the bishop should talk to Jakob. It would be best for everyone, Lizzie had said, if Jakob came back to the church and brought his family with him. If he repented publicly, no one would withhold forgiveness. It would be against *Ordnung* not to forgive.

At that moment, Elizabeth had knocked a pot against the table with particular swiftness, announcing her presence. She was *not* something to be repented of.

Elizabeth reached the creek and set down the basket. Closer to the water, the air was even more biting, but she did not care. Below a thin layer of ice, the water was moving. Elizabeth gripped her washing bat and broke the ice in one strike, creating an opening where she could rinse the clothes. One at a time, she swirled shirts and dresses and trousers in the frigid water and watched the dirt break free and flow downstream.

If only life were that simple, she thought. She picked up a shirt and wrenched the excess creek water from it.

By the time Elizabeth returned to the house, her hands were red and raw, but her nerves were settled. The aroma of Lizzie's baking efforts filled the kitchen, though the room was unoccupied. The trouble with Lizzie using the kitchen all day to bake was that Elizabeth could not feed her family more than cold meat and cellar fruit. Her own bread shelf did not offer much at the moment. Tomorrow would be her turn to beat and knead her bread dough and slide the loaves into an oven that took three hours to heat sufficiently.

For now, Elizabeth picked up the limp end of a rope and attached it to the nail on the opposite wall. If she left her laundry on the bushes outside, it would freeze before it would dry, so she hung it in front of the kitchen fire. Then she went in search of her children, wanting nothing more than to fill her arms with them while she dried off and warmed up.

As she passed the broad table, Elizabeth saw the mound wrapped in a dish towel. Laying her hand on top of it, she absorbed the rising warmth. She sensed someone was watching her and looked up. Lizzie leaned against the door frame leading to the main room.

"I thought you might enjoy some bread with your supper," Lizzie said. "I made plenty."

Elizabeth's breath caught. She was so cold, and she craved the heat of the fresh bread, even just a bite. "Thank you, Lizzie. It smells delicious."

"Mrs. Byler, I feel convicted that I have made you feel unwelcome in your own home. I hope you can forgive me."

Elizabeth hardly knew what to say. "Thank you, Lizzie."

"I promise to be more mindful of my actions," Lizzie said. "I do not want to appear ungrateful for your hospitality."

"You are Christian's wife. Of course you are welcome in his family home."

"The Kauffmanns will soon be ready for us. Christian says we are to move in three days."

Elizabeth shivered, and not entirely from the cold. Relief would come soon.

"Jacobli has built a wonderful fire in the other room," Lizzie said. "Come and warm up away from the wet clothes."

"Yes, I shall do that."

Lizzie moved out of the way, and Elizabeth stepped into the main room. The beauty of what she saw swelled and lodged in her throat. Lisbetli sat on a large rag rug with Joseph on one side and David on the other, the three of them with their heads bent together over a book Rachel Treadway had sent from Philadelphia. Sarah sat on her favorite window seat and stared out, just as Anna often had done in the cabin ten years ago. John and Jacobli were on their knees in front of the fire, poking at it with sticks and laughing about things that only brothers shared. The moment was worth every hardship they had endured.

"*Mamm*, come and get warm." Jacobli waved her over with a hand.

Elizabeth suddenly noticed how tall his form had become. Even folded up before the fire, his height announced itself. He was eleven, but she saw the man he would be soon enough. She perched on a low footstool in front of the fire, close enough to stroke Jacobli's head, and welcomed the flickering heat.

"*Mamm*," Jacobli said. "I think I want to meet the new bishop."

Her hand rested at the base of his neck now, trembling. "Have you spoken to your father?"

"Not yet. I wanted to tell you first. Lizzie says I would like him. He is very friendly, she says."

Lizzie. Of course she would be in league with Christian over the children's faith.

"We have always told you that when you were old enough, you could choose for yourself, according to your own conscience."

"Am I old enough?"

"What do you think?" Her heart pounded.

"I think I want to meet the bishop." Jacobli stabbed the fire with his stick.

He might as well have stabbed his mother's heart.

Forty-Three

"Can we park down here?" Ruth asked when Annie turned the car into the long Beiler driveway. "I'd like to walk up. She's probably in the garden."

Annie pulled to one side of the lane and turned off the car. "I'll give you a head start then see if you need anything."

"Okay. Thanks."

Ruth got out of the car and glanced back at Annie, the only friend who knew her in both worlds and felt the pull of both for herself. Then she drew a deep breath, puffed her cheeks in an exhale, and turned her steps toward the garden. Her mother was there, just as she had thought. Lydia and Sophie were supposed to look after the vegetables, but Ruth knew her mother did not regard the patch as a chore but as a place of solace. The Beiler children had learned long ago not to disturb Franey when she knelt there. She was as likely to be praying as weeding. On her knees now in the far end, Franey was picking out bits of growth that did not belong in the ordered rows and tossing them in an old basket. Remembering when that basket was new, so long ago, Ruth watched her mother for a few minutes.

"*Mamm?*" Ruth finally said.

Franey shifted her weight, putting one hand down on the ground to support the turn, and raised her face to her daughter. "Your brother is doing well. There's no need for you to go to all this trouble to check on him."

"That's not why I came." Ruth stepped forward. "I came for you."

"What does that mean, Ruth?" Franey stood now and brushed her hands together. Loose crumbs of black dirt tumbled to the ground, not back to where they came from, but to the new place where they belonged now.

"You're my *mudder*. I need you in my life."

Franey stooped to pick up her basket and the hand shovel she had used as long as Ruth could remember. She simply waited.

"I want to explain." Ruth moved closer, her toes at the edge of the garden now. "It might not change anything, but at least you will know."

She wished her mother would suggest sharing tea or sitting on the porch, but Franey was planted in the earth with her basket of weeds in one hand and her shovel in the other. Franey had done nothing wrong that day. Ruth was the one to deceive and disappoint.

Annie waited a few minutes before starting up the lane on foot. Instead of following to the garden, though, Annie took the path that forked toward Rufus's woodworking shop. The gray, brooding sky almost certainly held a torrent to unleash on the valley.

Annie pulled open the shop door and breathed a sigh of relief. "You're here."

Rufus looked up from his bench, where he was working on a hinge. "Why is it you never say good afternoon?"

"Sorry. Good afternoon."

"Good afternoon. I'm surprised to see you." He raised his eyes to her and straightened the front of his shirt.

Annie stepped closer to the workbench. "Actually, I'm moving into the house in town."

"Will you be coming down every weekend, then?" Rufus blew the dust off a hinge. He gripped a screwdriver in one hand, his eyes on her.

"I'm going to live here full-time." It wasn't the color of his eyes that transfixed her now, but the grasping that swirled in them.

"That sounds like a rash decision." Rufus set down the screwdriver and unrolled one sleeve toward his wrist, then the other.

"You're not the only one who thinks I've gone around the bend, but I'm sure it's what I am supposed to do." Annie put both hands on the workbench and leaned in.

"I suppose your technology allows you to run your business from here. You've been doing that already." Rufus gently lifted one cabinet and moved it to the end of the bench then put a new one, still looking raw, in the space in front of him.

"I sold it."

He looked at her. "The business?"

She had his attention now. "I sold it, and I'm not keeping the money."

Rufus stilled. "How will you support yourself?"

"I can live simply." Saying it, she believed it.

"And why are you doing this?"

"I know you don't believe me, but I want a different life."

"I did not say I don't believe you."

"You don't think I can do it, do you?"

"That is not for me to say." He put his hands in pockets of the tool belt around his waist and fished out another hinge. "I hope you can live simply enough to simply leave Karl Kramer alone."

"God's will, as you always say."

He shook his head. "Do not say that lightly, Annalise."

"I don't. I'm really, really trying to let go of managing everything my way."

Rufus picked up the screwdriver again, saying nothing. Annie saw several identical cabinets lined up on the floor awaiting hinges and front doors. This was work his crew could perform easily, yet clearly he intended to do it himself. Did he even have a crew anymore, or had his hospitalization and recuperation forced them to look elsewhere for employment? He looked tired—tired in body and tired in spirit. She wanted to sit with him and put her arms around him, draw his head down against her. She would stroke his brown hair, his clean-shaven cheek, his muscled arm, and he would close his eyes and rest.

But it could not be.

"I brought Ruth," she said abruptly.

He looked up at her again.

"To talk to your mother." She met his gaze. "To try to remove whatever it is between them. She thinks you are right about that."

Rufus set down the hinge and screwdriver then picked up a rag and wiped his hands free of the dusty evidence of his task. He repeated the motion more than necessary.

"You're thinking of going to find them, aren't you?" Annie crossed her arms over her chest.

Rufus tossed the rag onto the bench. "I am not sure how *Mamm* will respond."

"Who is trying to control things now?"

Rufus turned up one corner of his mouth. "Not control. Just be there."

"Can you imagine what I thought when I found you hiding in that outbuilding?" Franey did not take a single step out of the garden.

"I know," Ruth said. "It was wrong."

"Elijah Capp was in love with you."

Franey's voicing of simple fact stirred in accusation.

"I know," Ruth said. "I was not fair to him."

"He told his parents—our good friends—that he loved you, but he was not sure about being baptized." Franey's eyes fixed on Ruth.

"I told him he should not be baptized for me." Ruth slipped off her shoes. She felt the ground soften under her toes as she edged into the garden plot. "It had to be the decision of his own heart."

"But he thought you were going to be baptized. We all did. You took the instruction. You met with the bishop. I made you a new dress for the day. The church voted to receive you as a member— and Elijah, too. It was all set. Elijah loved you enough to put his doubts aside."

"I never asked him to do that." Ruth heard the breaking in her own voice.

"You didn't try to stop him," Franey said. "You knew what he was going to do, and you let him do it even as you planned your own escape."

"It was not an escape, *Mamm.*" Ruth took several steps toward her mother down a loam-layered row. She had not felt the give of earth beneath bare feet for a year and a half.

"It certainly looked that way. You knelt with the baptismal candidates when we bowed for prayer so the bishop could ask God's blessing on all of you. And when we opened our eyes, you were gone."

A sob rattled up through Ruth, forcing its way through her throat with a gasp.

"When they saw you were gone, no one would disturb the solemn occasion for the other candidates." Franey barely opened her mouth to speak now. "Certainly not Elijah. He was the first. The bishop came to him and poured the water on his head. Elijah made his promises, but you were gone. He sacrificed everything for you, and you spit on his sacrifice!"

"It was not that way."

"Wasn't it?"

"Elijah knew I had doubts. He knew I believed the Bible and trusted God, but he also knew I wanted to be a nurse. I couldn't choose!"

"But you did choose." Franey threw her shovel down and pointed at Ruth. "Afterwards, when we should have been rejoicing in your baptism and celebrating that you joined the church, we were tearing up the farm looking for you. Your father and I had no words for anyone. I'll never forget the way Mrs. Capp stared at me. What could I say? I could barely congratulate Elijah. He looked for you, too, you know."

Ruth swallowed hard. "No, I didn't know. I'm sorry I put you all through that. I should have just told you what I was doing. I corresponded with the university for months about how I could meet their requirements without a high school diploma. I didn't run on a moment's whim."

"I know it was no whim, because you arranged a ride with that *English* man who takes people to Pueblo."

"I knew I could get a bus in Pueblo."

"You were hiding in that shed. You had a suitcase. He knew exactly where to pick you up. The only thing you didn't plan was for your *mudder* to find you first."

Ruth felt a hand on her shoulder. She leaned back against the solid form of her brother. She knew then she could finish this conversation. Annie was beside her when the rain started in earnest.

"I didn't know until the last minute that I would really go." Tears flowed with rain down Ruth's face. "I didn't know what to say to you or Elijah or anyone."

"So you said nothing." Franey's voice barely rose above the patter from the sky.

"I would choose differently now," Ruth said. "I would tell you. I want to tell you now."

"Others have left, you know. You were not baptized. People would have understood. You would not have been shunned."

Rufus squeezed Ruth's shoulders, and Annie slipped a hand into Ruth's.

"*Mamm*," Rufus said, "I think Ruth is saying she's sorry."

"I want you to forgive me," Ruth pleaded, "for the way I left."

"Are you repenting?" Franey's question had an edge to it.

"I was thinking of myself, and that was wrong. I do repent of my selfishness."

"But not for leaving."

"Leaving was the right choice for me. I truly believe God wants me to be a trained nurse. I want to obey God's will."

"God's will." Franey gripped her basket with both hands now. "It's hard to argue when someone claims to know God's will in the matter."

The rain cast a shiver through Ruth. She squeezed Annie's hand.

"*Mamm*," Rufus said, "It's raining. Let's go inside and talk."

Lightning cracked the sky just as they reached the shelter of the porch, but they were drenched already. Inside, Franey said nothing to anyone. She handed them towels, disappeared for a few minutes, then sent everyone upstairs for dry clothing.

Annie opened Ruth's bedroom door and stared at two simple dresses lying across the Tumbling Blocks quilt, one blue and one purple.

With a nervous smile, she turned to Ruth, who was right behind her. "Your mother did this."

Ruth let her breath out hard. "I'm not sure what she means."

"I've had that purple dress on before, you know." Annie picked up the dress.

"It looks like you're going to wear it again," Ruth said. "You won't find any dry jeans hiding around here."

"You can help me do it right this time." Annie held the dress against herself. "How about you? Will it feel strange to wear one of your old dresses?"

Ruth picked up the blue dress and held it in front of her at arm's length. "It's just until we can get our clothes dry. Perhaps

337

it will reassure *Mamm* that I have not turned my heart away from God."

"And this one will tell Rufus I can make changes that take me closer to God."

Forty-Four

September 1757

Elizabeth wrapped both hands around her cup of steaming coffee and shared a corner of the table with Lisbet. Jakob and David were out milking cows. She had called once already for the others to come down to breakfast, but she relished the thought of a few moments alone with Lisbet, so she was not disappointed at their sluggish response.

"Tell me everything." Elizabeth leaned forward on her elbows. "It was the middle of the night when you and Jacobli got home."

"I've been going to apple *schnitzing* bees at the Hochstetlers' for years," Lisbet said, "but this was the most fun."

"Was Quick Jake Kauffmann there?"

Lisbet nodded, her eyes glowing. "Can I tell you a secret?"

Elizabeth smiled and set her coffee down.

"We're going to announce our engagement as soon as the harvest is in." Lisbet reached across the table and gripped Elizabeth's hand. "I really want you to be at my wedding in November. I can't get married without you, and I want to have my wedding in my own home."

Elizabeth unsuccessfully tried to swallow the knot in her throat. "I'll try, Lisbetli. I'll talk to *Daed*." Jakob did business with the neighbors and gave assistance when he could. But he had not been to a church event in all the years of their marriage, not even the weddings of his own children.

"I want *all* of my family there," Lisbet emphasized. "I wish. . ."

"You're thinking of Maria, aren't you?"

Lisbet nodded, tears springing to her eyes. "She should have been next, after Christian. Now we don't even know where she is."

"I'm sure she thinks of you often."

"If she didn't want to be baptized, she didn't have to. . ." Lisbet set her mug down hard. "Why did she think she had to run off like that?"

Elizabeth shook her head. She had no answer.

Lisbet swallowed her sorrow and forced a smile. "And Jacobli had better behave himself at my wedding."

Elizabeth rolled her eyes. "What did he do last night?"

"He was supposed to be peeling apples, but he gave Mrs. Hochstetler conniption fits by cutting faces into the apples and giving them names. Once they had names and faces, no one wanted to cut them up or crush them for cider."

"That sounds like my Jacobli."

"Then the Hochstetler boys started doing it. Mrs. Hochstetler took away their knives and sent them all outside."

Elizabeth gestured to the generous basket of apples and peaches gracing her table. "Are there any faces in this bunch you brought home?"

Lisbet laughed. "Mrs. Hochstetler threw the faces in the cider press herself before they could turn brown."

"How many bushels did you put out for drying?"

Lisbet shrugged. "I lost count. They just kept coming, so we kept peeling and paring. Their peaches are ripe, too, so that will be the next harvest. Jacobli is already scheming about what he can do with peaches."

Elizabeth tried to picture her eldest son frolicking with the Amish young adults. He was eighteen and attended their church services frequently, though not regularly. John had been a few times also but seemed less interested. Or perhaps the difference was that Jacobli could get along with just about anyone and John was more particular. So far, to Elizabeth's relief, Jacobli had said nothing about being baptized and joining the Amish church—though Christian and Lizzie raised the question frequently. He simply seemed to enjoy friendship with the neighbors. Jacobli's recent habit of wearing Amish clothing unsettled her, however. He hardly took off his straw hat anymore, as if he were trying on a choice.

Lisbet giggled again. "Mrs. Hochstetler kept making jokes about how many *schnitz* pies she would have to eat over the winter to keep her weight up."

"She's fatter than any woman in the valley!" Elizabeth said.

"Because she makes the best *schnitzboi* in the valley, too."

"The next time you see her, thank her for the basket she sent home with you. We'll have a feast for breakfast today." Elizabeth stood up and headed for the stairs. "I'd better get those sleepy heads up once and for all."

She stood at the base of the stairs and called her children's names one by one.

A deep, hoarse voice joined her with more urgency. "Jacobli! John! Joseph! Come down immediately."

"Jakob, what's wrong?" Elizabeth spun to face her husband who was standing in the door. David was right behind him.

"Where are the boys? Jacob! John! Now! David, bolt the door." The bolt thudded into place almost immediately.

"Jakob!" Elizabeth said again. She could count on one hand the number of times she had heard her husband raise his voice in the last nineteen years.

The weight of boys in men's bodies tested the stairs as Jacob, John, and Joseph thundered down in a gangly knot of arms and legs.

"Make sure you bring Sarah," Jakob boomed, and the girl

appeared at the top of the stairs.

Jakob was at the mantel now, pulling rifles off racks and stuffing them with gunpowder. He slapped one Brown Bess musket into Jacobli's hand and the next one into John's.

"Jakob!" Elizabeth put a hand on his arm. "I must insist you tell me what is going on. Why has it become so urgent to go hunting before breakfast?"

"We're not going hunting," Jakob said, putting a gun into Joseph's hands.

"But—"

"They shot John Miller in the hand," Jakob said rapidly, "while he was swinging an ax like he does every morning. Like we all do every day. Just chopping wood."

"Who would want to hurt John Miller?"

"We've lived in this valley for twenty years, most of them peaceful," Jakob said. "The Indians never bothered us until this ridiculous war between the French and the British. First the British build a fort in Northkill, and now the French have the Lenni Lenape shooting at us."

"But surely, Jakob—"

"Lisbet," Jakob snapped, "what time did you and Jacob leave the Hochstetlers' last night?"

"Late. After midnight. Once we finished with the apples, most of us stayed around talking or singing."

"*Daed*," Jacobli said, "what does that have to do with why you are handing out guns?"

"Or John Miller's hand?" Elizabeth added.

"The Indians took advantage of the moonless night." Jakob stood a rifle on its heel, gripped the steel shaft with both hands, and looked around the room. "You're all old enough to hear this. They attacked the Hochstetlers. I suspect it was not long after everyone left. By God's grace, you were gone already. The Indians set fire to the house. By the time neighbors saw the flames and got over there, it was too late to save anything—or anybody. The

Hochstetlers crawled out through a cellar window, but nobody could get close enough to help, not even when Mrs. Hochstetler was stuck in the window."

Elizabeth and Lisbet exchanged glances, regretting the banter about Mrs. Hochstetler's size.

"The Indians found them trying to hide. Mrs. Hochstetler was stabbed to death and scalped. One boy and the girl were tomahawked. Hochstetler and the other boys are missing. The neighbors saw the Indians ride off with them—after they torched every building on the land. Even their married son had to watch from across the field and could do nothing."

Elizabeth sank into the nearest chair. Sarah threw herself into her mother's arms. "What are you planning to do, Jakob?"

"I plan to assure myself that my children and grandchildren are safe. I'll ride all day if I have to. Jacobli and John, you're coming with me. Joseph and David, you're staying here. I know you're all good shots."

"Jakob, what are you saying?" Elizabeth could not believe her ears.

"We've never shot at anything we did not intend to eat," Joseph said.

"They are still boys." Elizabeth's pitch rose. "You cannot ask them to do this."

Jakob laid his hands on Joseph's shoulders and looked him square in the eye. "You're fifteen. We've raised you to follow your conscience. I hope you don't have to do anything at all, but if you do, I know it will be right." He turned to David, a year younger. "That goes for you, too."

Elizabeth rose. "I've heard rumors that Mrs. Hochstetler was not always kind to the Indians who came to her looking for food. Perhaps they chose her in particular. Perhaps the danger is past."

"I want to know my children are safe," Jakob said. "Christian and the girls' husbands—they would do what I suspect Hochstetler did. That man had guns in his house, and he knew how to use them. Why is his family slaughtered as if they did not have the means to defend themselves?" Jakob picked up his own rifle and stuffed his pockets with gunpowder packets and lead. "Bolt the door and stay away from the windows. If there's any danger, go out through the tunnel from the cellar. And take the guns."

Jakob and two of his sons rode their horses hard. He allowed himself a moment of relief when Christian's house came into view and appeared unharmed but pressed on to see for himself that Christian, Lizzie, and their three small children were alive.

He swung off his horse just as Christian swung open the door to his home.

"I see you've heard the news." Christian's eyes went to his father's gun. "You don't seriously think that using a rifle is going to solve anything."

"Is your family safe?" Jakob asked.

"We are unharmed, if that is what you mean."

Lizzie appeared behind her husband, baby Magdalena in her arms and Christli and Veronica clutching her skirts. The sight of his grandchildren slowed Jakob's heart rate.

"What if it had been your farm, Christian?" Jacobli asked.

"But it was not," Christian retorted.

"What if it were?"

"Our lives are in God's hands," Christian answered.

"I imagine that is what Hochstetler said to his screaming wife and children," Jakob said.

"They would not have been screaming," Christian answered calmly. "They knew they were in God's hands as well."

"I'm not certain this is God's way."

"*Daed*, in all these years, I have never heard you sound so *English*," Christian said. "In your heart, you are Amish. You cannot possibly be thinking of doing this."

"Don't tell me what is in my heart, Christian."

"If you shoot a man, will you have it in your heart to repent and ask forgiveness?"

Jakob ignored the question. "Please tell me you have prepared a place to hide. In the thicket perhaps, a dense place well away from the house where you could keep the children quiet."

Christian nodded. "Lizzie and I have talked about this, especially if something happens when I am away. We would never raise arms against another human being, but of course we would do all we could to avoid harm to ourselves."

Jacobli shifted in his saddle. "That's not true, Christian. You would not do all you could. Would you rather see your children toma—"

"Jacobli!" Jakob spoke sharply then lowered his voice. "Do you not see the children standing right there?"

Christian murmured to Lizzie. She took the children and withdrew into the house. Christian closed the door and strode over to the horses.

"You have been to our worship services," Christian said to Jacobli. "You have many friends among our people. You know our ways. I hoped that perhaps you would be ready soon to join the church yourself."

Jacobli shook his head. "I've hunted with the Hochstetler boys. Their rifles were right next to the door when I was in their home a few hours ago. Only their father would have forbidden them to defend themselves. If I had a wife and children, if I were in the place Mr. Hochstetler was in, I believe I would make a different choice."

"Your conscience would be forever smeared," Christian said.

"Perhaps," Jacobli said, "but my children would be alive."

"When everything is calm again, you will reconsider."

Jacobli reached for his straw hat. "I don't believe so. May God give you grace, Christian, but I am no Amishman." He tossed his hat on the ground. "*Daed*, we must find out if the Yoders are safe."

Forty-Five

Ruth removed the plain glass chimney of Annie's new lamp, turned the wick up slightly, and struck a match. The wick caught, and she replaced the glass.

"It's that easy," she said.

Annie nodded. "I guess even a techno-addict like me can learn to do that."

"This knob," Ruth said, demonstrating, "controls the flame size."

"Got it."

"It's a pretty lamp. You've found some real treasures in Mrs. Weichert's store."

"Her store seems perfect for a hundred-year-old house. I find myself wondering what the house was like when it was built. Maybe electricity had not even come this far out from the main cities. Maybe I'm not the first owner to light a kerosene lamp in this room."

"Maybe not."

Annie had added a cozy deep red armchair and a couple of end tables to the living room. The dining table shone with Ruth's labor of the last hour. Upstairs a new bed suited the proportions of Annie's bedroom. In the second bedroom, Annie had a small desk and a bookcase, but the main feature was a chair that folded out to a guest bed.

Ruth settled into the armchair. "I suppose soon you won't have reason to run back and forth so much. I want to be sure to thank you now for helping me reconnect with my family."

"It was my privilege." Annie toyed with the kerosene flame. "You'll be back, somehow. Remember, you promised to show me what to do with my floors."

"It's hard work to do yourself."

"Hey, I'm all about hard work."

Ruth saw the hesitation in Annie's face. "It's all right to talk about it, you know."

"Talk about what?"

"*Mamm* and me. We talked for a long time. I'm not sure she will ever accept that I am not going to be baptized into the Amish church, but she has managed to get past her hurt at how I left. I am grateful to you for that."

"And Rufus?" Annie asked.

Ruth tilted her head and twisted her lips. "I'm never quite sure what you're asking about Rufus."

"Is he well?"

"You know he is."

"And happy?"

"He's happy when you're around."

"That's nonsense." Annie fluffed a pillow on the sofa. "I have nothing to do with your brother's happiness."

Ruth shifted out of her chair and put a hand on Annie's arm. "You've been avoiding him. It's all right to talk to him."

Annie wriggled free of Ruth's grip to straighten papers on the coffee table. "There's nothing to say."

"I don't believe that."

Now Annie looked at Ruth. "It's impossible. He's Amish to the core. And I'm. . .well, not."

"But you're living more simply now."

"You know that's not the same as being Amish. Baptized Amish is what matters. Rufus says there's no such thing as accidentally Amish."

"Maybe you should think about it," Ruth said. "Not for Rufus. I don't mean that. But for yourself."

"Wow. Coming from someone who. . ."

"Ran out on her baptism," Ruth supplied. "You can say it. We both know I did it."

"Well yes," Annie said. "It seems ironic that you would suggest I think about becoming Amish."

"It wasn't right for me. It might be right for you."

"I have to take one step at a time," Annie said. "I have so much to learn. Being around Rufus confuses me."

"He's a good, good man."

Annie put her knees up under her chin and wrapped her arms around them. "Ruth, why has Rufus never married? He's quite old, isn't he?"

"I suppose so, in the Amish way."

"Has he had his heart broken?"

Ruth shook her head. "I don't think he's ever let it open far enough to break. Not until you."

Annie's feet thudded to the floor. "Now you're being ridiculous."

"Why not find out? Hire Rufus to build some cabinets for you."

"I plan to."

"After he finishes the cabinets, ask him to build you a table for a propane lamp. It hides the canister underneath. The kerosene lamp suits your house, but no one really uses them anymore."

"I'll keep that in mind."

"Then Rufus can help you with the soft spot in the kitchen floor."

"You're full of ideas." Annie tossed a pillow at Ruth. "Don't you have homework to do?"

"I suppose so." Ruth caught the pillow and rolled her eyes. "What time are we going back to town?"

"Why? Do you need some computer time?"

"It would help."

"Use mine. I think it might need charging, though." Annie moved into the dining room, picked up her laptop from the table, and pulled the cord out of her denim bag. "Whenever this place was wired, it was not for the Internet age. I only have two outlets in the living room."

"Maybe you can add more."

Annie reached behind the sofa and plugged in the laptop's cord. "I have a feeling that would lead to having the whole place rewired. I'm leaning in the other direction."

"What do you mean?"

"Other sources of energy."

"That sounds very Amish-like." Ruth still held the throw pillow to her chest, which warmed with an image of Annie and Rufus in this room together.

"I called a local company," Annie said. "They're sending someone out to have a look around and make some suggestions. After that we can head back to the Springs."

"That sounds fine."

Annie put the computer in Ruth's lap. "I'd like you to have this."

"Thanks for letting me use it." Ruth set the pillow aside and adjusted the computer on her lap. She would have to get used to how it felt, but the convenience of it sparked something in her.

"No, I mean *have* it." Annie lowered herself to the floor next to Ruth's knees. "I've been looking for the right time to give it to you."

Ruth's eyes widened. "You really are getting serious about changing."

Annie nodded, her fingers twisting in the gold chain in absentminded habit.

"But your computer! That's like giving me your arm."

"Not anymore," Annie said. "I've cleared all my old business files off. It's a good computer and not very old. You should get good use out of it until you finish school."

"I'm already grateful to you for so much, and now this!" Ruth's hand moved over the sleek casing.

"You made a hard choice that came at a cost," Annie said. "You should at least have the tools to do what you set out to do."

Ruth raised the lid of the laptop, her hand trembling with the thought that it was hers.

Annie pointed to a file icon against the blue background of the screen. "I did save some of the genealogy information. I thought you might be interested."

Ruth clicked open the file and scanned the documents Annie had gathered. "Do you still think about Jakob and Elizabeth? And the choices they made?"

"All the time! I imagine what their life must have been like. I'm used to everything being comfortable and convenient. They challenge me to learn that right choices come at a cost. You help me see that, too, you know."

"Me? All I did was hurt people I love."

"You followed God's call. And you're working on fixing the relationships. You remind me that perhaps I can avoid that mistake if I choose well."

A knock on the front door diverted the moment. Annie scrambled to her feet to pull the door open.

"Hello," a young Amish man said. "I'm answering your inquiry for an estimate on some gas lines and a generator."

"Yes, come in," Annie said. "This is my friend Ruth."

Ruth was on her feet, the color gone from her face.

"Hello, Ruth," the man said quietly.

"Hello, Elijah."

Forty-Six

June 1765

Elizabeth held her first flesh-and-blood grandson in her arms. Jacobli's *boppli*. They called him Jacob Franklin Byler. Chubby cheeks defined the shape of his face, fresh and red and squalling. She stroked the downy softness of his head. It had been a long time since she held a child only a day after birth. David, the last baby born in this house, was twenty-two.

"I think his hair will be dark red," she said to Jacobli, "the way yours was before it turned brown." One of the baby's eyes opened to a murky slit. An arm flailed loose from the swaddling. "How is Katie?"

"Resting." Jacobli closed the tiny fist in his own hand. "It was awful to see her in so much pain. The thought of losing her—"

Tears welled in Elizabeth's eyes, but she refused to release them. Instead, she focused on adjusting the baby's bundling.

"You're thinking of Lisbet, aren't you?" Jacobli asked.

Wordless, Elizabeth nodded.

"So am I," her son said quietly.

Somehow three years had crawled by since the day Lisbet labored. After four years of childless marriage, she was bursting with joy in the life she carried within her. The child slid easily

351

into waiting arms, but the bleeding was too rapid, and Lisbet died without ever holding her baby. Quick Jake insisted on calling the baby Veronica, after the mother Lisbet did not remember. He did not let Elizabeth see the girl often. Before her second birthday, Veronica caught croup and stopped breathing.

Elizabeth's being fractured that day.

Now Lisbet and her child lay in the earth beside Verona, and Elizabeth's own mother-heart was a constant seeping wound. Perhaps this child, a grandson who was truly hers, would stem the flow and lead her to the future once more.

"I'm so glad to have you and Katie here," Elizabeth said. And she meant it. Jacobli was a grown man, married. He could have gone anywhere.

"We wouldn't think of leaving you."

The tannery, which had been a second source of income for Jakob, was Jacobli's territory now. Over the years, he had expanded the lime vats and bark pits and learned to craft the raw leather into an array of useful items. Residents of the Northkill and Irish Creek settlements knew Jacob Byler's leather was unmatched even in Philadelphia. They were eager to sell him their hides then buy them back in the forms of saddles and reins and satchels and shoe leather and overcoats.

Jakob shuffled in from the kitchen. Every day, Elizabeth thought, he moved a little more slowly. She could hardly blame him. At sixty, she was slowing down herself, and he was seventy-eight. Only recently had he left the work of the farm to Joseph and David. He still presided, white haired, over the midday meal with detailed questions about the farm's operations and was always ready with advice, but he left the physical work to his sons.

"Can an old man hold his grandson?" Jakob asked.

Jakob settled in next to Elizabeth, and she gently laid the child in arms long accustomed to holding the bundled shape of a baby. Pleasure crinkled his weathered face, and Elizabeth felt herself go soft at the center, just as she had all those years ago when Lisbetli clung to her father's neck and he patiently waited for her to be ready to let go. Now it was Elizabeth's turn to cling. Aware that she was fortunate to have her husband still with her at his age, she did not want to think of letting go. She leaned into him, laying one hand at the center of his back and scratching in that place he liked so well.

"Christian and Lizzie are coming soon," Jakob said. "I suppose the others will be along before much time passes, too."

By suppertime, Elizabeth was exhausted. Her joints did not move as nimbly as they used to. None of Jakob's Amish children ever stayed long when they visited On this occasion, Anna was the first to come, and before she had been gone half an hour, Barbara arrived to inspect the new baby. Elizabeth welcomed them with platters of food and cool water drawn only that morning from the creek. John stayed a good part of the afternoon. Joseph and David peeked in between chores and availed themselves of the food. Sarah was the only one absent. She had planned months ago to come from Philadelphia when the baby was a month or so old. Katie remained secluded in her bedroom, only appearing at intervals to wonder what had become of her baby during these visits.

As it turned out, Christian was the last to come, and to Elizabeth's surprise, he came alone. Jakob was resting on their bed while Christian and Jacobli stood at the wide window gazing out on the farm as Elizabeth came and went from the kitchen, tidying up after the wave of visits.

"I am thinking of moving to Conestoga, or perhaps Lancaster," Christian said, staring out as he spoke. "My land is worth a good deal more than I paid for it, and I can easily get new land down there."

"But you've done so much work on your land," Jacobli said.

"That's why it is worth so much."

"You'll start over, then?"

Christian nodded. "It won't be as hard the second time. I'll have some capital to begin with. Still, it would be easier with help. You and Katie could come with us."

Jacobli laughed softly. "You never give up, do you, Christian?"

Elizabeth stacked plates left from the afternoon round of pie and carried them into the kitchen.

"It's good land," Christian said, "richer soil."

"I'm a tanner, Christian, not a farmer. What you mean is it's Amish land," Jacobli said. "I've seen the number of families that moved out after the French-Indian War and what happened at the Hochstetlers. Conestoga is farther from the frontier. Farther from the Indians. Further from the question of bearing arms on your own land."

"That has nothing to do with it." Christian put his hands on his waist, the stance he always assumed when he was about to be intractable. "If you saw the offers I have received on my land, you would understand why it is in my family's best interest to consider them seriously."

"You can't run away." Jacobli turned from the window to look his brother in the eye. "War is coming. The Stamp Act. The sugar tax. This nonsense about quartering British soldiers in private homes. Those things will still be true in Conestoga."

"I am not running away from anything." Now Christian crossed his arms on his chest.

"Does it not try your patience at all to think that the Crown expects the Colonies to absorb the debt of England's war with France?"

"The Amish have nothing to do with any war."

"War will follow you," Jacobli said. "And there *will* be another war."

"You cannot be certain of that."

Jacobli laughed aloud. "Perhaps living apart has insulated you too much. No one from the Colonies seems to be able to reason with Parliament. Even Benjamin Franklin got nowhere. The burden of taxes is growing too fast."

"We pay the same taxes anyone pays when we buy goods or file documents," Christian said. "We have no quarrel with that."

Elizabeth leaned against the door frame between the kitchen and main room, listening and wanting to believe Jacobli was wrong about a coming war.

"The time will come when the question will be far more complex," Jacobli said. "Sam Adams has organized the Sons of Liberty in Boston, and other cities are following suit. What if the Colonies go to war against Britain? What will you do then?"

Christian sighed heavily. "Do you ask these questions specifically to exasperate me?"

"Everyone in the Colonies must ask these questions. Do any of us know what we will do in the event of war?"

"The Amish will not fight. You know that. Our only concern is our own community."

"When the time comes, it won't be that simple," Jacobli said.

Christian uncrossed his arms and put one hand out to lean against the window frame. "So you have no interest in moving? Having your own land?"

"The tannery is a thriving business," Jacobli said. "And I won't go anywhere as long as *Mamm* and *Daed* are here."

Elizabeth caught Jacobli's eye and smiled. Her other sons were less predictable. Jacobli was the steady one.

"Conestoga is not as far as all that," Christian said.

Jacobli shook his head. "I am not Amish, Christian. You're my brother, and I love you, but we've made different choices." He raised his eyes again to the rolling land outside the window. "Katie likes the idea of something entirely new. Someday I might like to see North Carolina. I hear a man can build a good life for his family there."

Forty-Seven

February 1771

"He is gone." Elizabeth emerged from the bedroom, from the reek of death that had taken so long to come, and told Jakob's gathered children.

Earlier she had shooed them all from the room, wanting only to be alone with him, to feel the thickness of his hair grown long in the cold months, to put her hand in his and hold their intimacy between them, to press her lips on his. And she had not wanted spectators for any of that, especially not the whispering kind.

They all came, except Maria, who had never returned, and Lisbet, who awaited her father in the burial plot.

They came and they brought their children. Barbara and Anna even had grandchildren. They rotated in and out of the bedroom saying their good-byes. The number became too great for Elizabeth, and when it seemed to her that some were returning for a third good-bye, she banished them all to the outer room. The end was breaths away. In the final moments, she heard their murmuring hum from the corners of the house and ignored it, listening only for the air going in and out of Jakob's lungs. Elizabeth held his hand.

And then the ragged rhythm stilled and the hum became thunderous.

When she could no longer resist the creeping weight of his lifeless hand, their clasp fell off the side of the bed. She laid her head on his chest and listened to the emptiness.

Jakob was gone.

Only when Elizabeth was sure she could speak did she gather her skirts and walk into the main room. She spoke three simple words. Then without even a shawl around her shoulders, she walked straight through the house, out the front door, and into the February wind. Snow gave way beneath shoes made from her son's leather, while voices on the porch called to her to come out of the cold. She paced from the house to the barn, then to the smokehouse, then through the garden, brown and crunchy. "Maria's beet patch," the square of land at the far end of the garden, had long ago grown over but never lost its moniker.

Shivering and out of breath at last, she leaned against the stable, breathing in the hay that fed and warmed the horses. She and Jakob had built this together. It would never be the same. He was gone.

They assembled the next month for the onerous reading of the will, which Jakob had written just weeks after Jacobli's first son was born. Perhaps with Jacob Franklin's birth, his mind had moved to the next generation. Elizabeth imagined the conversations between father and son about looking after her. Christian had become surprisingly wealthy buying and selling land, which seemed to increase in value every month. It should have been no trouble for him to provide for her. But ultimately, Christian was not her son. She was not Amish, so Christian and Lizzie would never take her into their home. Not that she wanted to go there. She did not. Nor to Barbara or Anna or even her own John. Jacobli was the eldest of the children Jakob and Elizabeth shared, and it was his concern to do what he knew his father wanted.

A widow's seat, the will said. She would have the house and the stable and the garden. To continue an income, she would have the three cherry trees near the house and a meadow behind the barn, which the next owner—Jacobli—was obliged to plow for her.

Two rows of trees in the orchard.

Ten bushels of wheat and five bushels of rye each year.

The right to keep a cow and a hog in the field.

Jacobli was the only child mentioned with a particular grant in the will. All the children received a few pounds, but Jacobli was permitted to clear ten acres around the tanyard and build a house of his own. Katie would like that, Elizabeth knew.

Jakob had thought this through. He so clearly expected the land to be sold to settle his estate. But he also expected that Jacobli would be the buyer. Elizabeth would be comfortably cared for in the years without Jakob.

If she married again, she would lose it all.

Marry again?

No, she was not tempted, and Jakob had made sure she would not need to. Even if she were twenty years younger than her sixty-six years, she could not imagine another life with another man. She would see out her days in her widow's seat, surrounded by land she no longer owned but upon which they had built their life together.

He was gone.

Forty-Eight

Two weeks later, Elijah Capp turned the wrench on the last bolt behind the refrigerator. "That does it. This house would pass *Ordnung*."

"I'm glad to hear that," Ruth Beiler said. "I'll probably still have to teach Annie how everything works."

"I used propane and bottled gas whenever I could," Elijah said. "Seemed like the simplest thing."

"Thank you. I know Annie is so pleased." Ruth was determined to smile at him, despite the knot in her stomach that came with being in his presence. His familiar shrug. The way he was hinged at the shoulders and elbows and knees. The faint smell of oil perpetually sunken into his pores. The arms that had held her when no one was looking.

"We'll get through this, Ruth." Elijah turned to pick up his toolbox.

"I know it's been awkward," she said. "I wasn't expecting to see you when you first came to the house any more than you were expecting to see me."

"I'm glad Amos sent me out on that call," Elijah said. "I knew you were back in the valley sometimes, but I didn't know how to approach you."

"I can never tell you enough how sorry I am." Ruth found the nerve to look him in the eye. "We should have both said we wanted to wait another year for baptism. We might have figured out our doubts."

"I'm not giving up," Elijah said.

"On us?"

"That's right."

"But I'm not baptized into the church, Elijah, and I'm not going to be."

"I know."

The weight of contradiction hung between them. Ruth remembered what it felt like to have Elijah at her side—the security, the certainty of love. She shrugged off the sensation. "I won't be the reason you leave the church."

"You won't be."

"No Elijah, don't talk like this."

"You're the only one who ever understood me, Ruth. We can go back to that."

She shook her head. "No."

"Yes."

"I'm going back to school," Ruth insisted.

"I know. You should."

Ruth swallowed. "You were the only one who understood me, too."

"Then don't say no. We'll keep talking."

She looked at him a long time before she nodded.

They both jumped at the knock at the front door. Ruth moved swiftly to answer it, expecting to see the face of her brother. She was not disappointed.

Rufus smiled with half his mouth. "What are you up to, Ruth?"

"I thought you might like a tour." She pushed open the screen door and pulled him into the room. "This is the living room. Tell me what you see."

Ruth glanced through the house to the kitchen. The back screen door closed. Elijah was gone.

Annie saw Dolly and the buggy in the street and retreated into the dimness of the garage. She smiled to herself as she pictured what was happening in the house while she waited in the narrow, listing structure. Ruth would make Rufus look at every room—the living room, the dining room, the kitchen, then up the narrow stairs to the bedrooms and bathroom. The basement would be last. Rufus would look behind and under everything. What he saw would tell him more than any words she could muster.

Elijah Capp had been busy during the last two weeks. After walking through the house with him and hearing his observations about what changes were needed, Annie gave him a key and left the adaptations in his hands while she returned to Colorado Springs for final preparations.

Now Annie did not plan to return to her condo. Following her real estate agent's advice, she left enough furnishings for a potential buyer to imagine the place as a home. When the unit sold, the agent would sell or give away the furnishings. As a concession to her mother, Annie agreed to store the Prius at her parents' house rather than sell it at this point in time.

Curious, Jamie drove Annie and Ruth down, saw the house, poked around town, and continued on to weekend plans at the nearby Great Sand Dunes. On Sunday evening, she would return to ferry Ruth back to school. Sadness trickled through Annie in the shadows of her garage. She had not written a personal letter in years, but she expected to discover the virtues of the postal system very soon. She would miss Ruth too much not to write. Annie would keep a cell phone but planned to use it as minimally as possible. A second concession to her mother was a weekly phone conversation, but otherwise Annie would follow Amish practices about using phones only for business and emergencies. And at the moment, she had no business.

When Annie and Ruth saw what Elijah had done, they nearly

giggled. He was thorough, modifying everything from the heating system to the water heater to the aged major appliances. Nothing in the house ran on public electricity.

Annie smoothed her skirt for the fiftieth time and once again straightened the shoulders of the dress. Through the small window, she saw that Ruth was now leading Rufus down the three steps from the small back porch and following broken cement blocks toward the garage. Annie stood straight and got ready to smile.

Dear God, this seems crazy and right all at the same time. Be here, please.

A moment later, the garage door creaked open and a square of daylight framed Ruth and Rufus. Annie stepped forward.

"Annalise, what have you done?" Rufus said.

For a flash, she thought he was angry. Then she saw the smile twitching in his jaw.

"You're wearing the dress," he said.

Annie caught Ruth's eye as Ruth stepped out of the garage. "Ruth says I can keep it. It's the only one I have." She pulled up handfuls of purple cotton skirt. "But I'm going to find someone to teach me how to sew, and I'll make more."

Rufus laughed more heartily than Annie had ever heard him do. "You don't think I can learn to sew?"

He grinned and wagged his head. "I believe you can do anything you decide you're going to do. I suppose you're going to learn to cook, too."

"Yes I am," she said. "And next spring I'll plant a garden."

"Where is your car?" he asked.

"In storage."

"How will you get around?"

She turned around and pulled a bicycle away from the wall, another thrift-store find.

Rufus stepped over to the bike and took it by the handlebars. "It looks like a sturdy bike. Simple, practical. Useful baskets. Good tires."

"Of course. Did you think I would buy something fancy? Simplicity. Thrift. Humility. When I can't bike, I'll arrange an Amish taxi, just like you do." Out of long habit, Annie's fingers went to her neck, where she found only the simple curve of the dress.

Rufus's eyes followed her fingers. "Where is your chain?"

"I gave it away. It was a trophy of my old life. I don't need it anymore."

"Annalise," he said, his voice low, "I'm not sure what you want me to say."

"Say what you want to say." Annie put a hand on top of his on the handlebars.

"You must know I'm fond of you."

"You've never said so."

He paused. "I'm saying so now. But. . ."

"But there's no such thing as accidentally Amish." Annie finished his sentence. "I'm not playing dress up, Rufus. I don't know where this journey will lead me, but I know I have to take it."

"You really want to live as we do?"

"I want the faith I see in you. I want to understand what you value, how you make choices that bring meaning to your life."

"When I see you in that dress, I'm inclined to believe you." He leaned toward her slightly.

"Maybe you knew something that morning after I stole away in Tom's truck, when you first brought the dress to me."

He laid a tremulous hand against her cheek. "I knew you were beautiful sleeping in the hay. I knew I admired your spirit, even if you didn't know what you stumbled into. I knew I thought about you all night."

"Rufus." Annie wrapped her fingers around the hand at her cheek. "Let's figure out what this is."

"You are still *English*," he murmured.

She took a deep breath and let it out slowly. "I know."

"In the *English* world, this is where the kiss comes, *ya*?"

"*Ya.*"

"In the Amish world, too."

She stood expectant yet hardly daring to hope.

"Perhaps being certain is not necessary at every moment," Rufus said.

He bent to meet her, and she tasted his first sweet, lingering, freely given kiss.

Author's Note

This particular project brings me joy, because through it I have been able to explore my own family history. I am a descendant of Jakob Beyeler through the first son of his marriage to Elizabeth Kallen. The research process yielded certain historical hooks on which to hang a story, such as the passenger manifest of the *Charming Nancy*, the oath Jakob had to take in order to step onto a new continent, the property description of black oak that defined Jakob's property, the slaughter of the nearby Hochstetler family, Jakob's will describing his wishes for his surviving wife with particular detail. From there I imagined much of the story—what might have happened with my own ancestors and the choices they made that determined future generations. As I researched, I became mindful of the power of choice, and the contemporary story took form around that theme. Three hundred years after my ancestors arrived in Pennsylvania, the choices that shape our lives come in updated packaging, but they are essentially the same. We have the ability to say yes to what brings meaning and joy to our lives. May you embrace that choice on a daily basis.

olivia@olivianewport.com
www.olivianewport.com
@olivianewport on Twitter
www.facebook.com/OliviaNewport
Olivia Newport
c/o Author Relations
Barbour Publishing
1810 Barbour Drive
Uhrichsville, OH 44683

IN PLAIN
View

Dedication

For Sonja

Acknowledgments

It is hard to know how to say thank you to all the people who helped bring this book into being. My agent, Rachelle Gardner, believes in me, which probably spurs me on more than she knows. How blessed I am to call her friend as well!

I have no doubt about Barbour's commitment to make the book the best it can be. After all, they had the good sense to connect me with Traci DePree to work as editor on the Valley of Choice series.

My husband is always game to gallivant off somewhere with me, literally or cyberly, in search of information. Every writer should be so lucky.

And Sonja. What can I say?

Sometimes writing feels like a lonely enterprise, but when I lift my eyes from the screen I see a host of people cheering me on. I am thankful for each one.

One

Annie Friesen had a lot to learn about how to ride a bicycle in a dress that brushed her ankles.

The late-April day slushed with spring snow vacillating about whether to melt. Temperate Colorado mountain air beckoned a population sick and tired of huddling indoors all winter, Annie among them. Five miles stretched between her and the Beiler farm, five miles she was determined to traverse without depending on Rufus Beiler and his buggy to pick her up. She could walk or she could bike from her house in Westcliffe to the Beiler home, where Rufus's family expected her for supper, and she would surrender herself to their long arms of hospitality and acceptance. The moment to begin the walk and arrive on time had passed thirty minutes ago, though.

Annie turned the bicycle around in the narrow, century-old garage and assessed its readiness for the first outing of the spring. The tires seemed acceptable, the pedals spun appropriately when she kicked at one, and the brakes squeezed when cued. She walked the bike into the sunlight and laid it down on the ground while she heaved the garage door closed. Then she situated herself on the seat, straightened the heavy wide-knit navy cardigan she wore, and hiked up the skirt of her deep purple dress as far as a good Amish girl dared.

Annie was not a good Amish girl. At least not yet. She did not even always wear Amish clothing. After eight months of friendship with the Beilers and regular attendance at the district's worship services, she would have to rate her German as pitiful. She understood more every week, but she could not get her mind and tongue to cooperate in speaking. Private lessons were some help, though she often left more frustrated than when she arrived. Singing hymns from the *Ausbund* might as well have been reading a census listing, which meant she had a lot to learn about both patience and devotion. The *Ordnung* was a mystical obscurity she wished someone would translate to bulleted points in plain English. The hairstyles seemed severe—but only when she looked in a mirror, which she did less and less these days. The ties to her prayer *kapp* annoyed her whether she tied them or let them hang loose on her shoulders.

But she was trying. For one thing, she had given up driving her own car, which was up on blocks in her parents' garage in Colorado Springs.

Annie checked the strap on her helmet—a promise she made to her mother when she gave up driving—then put her weight on the top pedal and leaned into the bike's forward movement. The streets in town were wet but friendly enough for cycling. Once she got to the highway, though, Annie scowled at the sludge passing vehicles sprayed at her. She knew what the drivers were thinking because she used to be one of them. *What kind of idiot rides a bike on a high-speed road? If they can't go the speed limit, they should get off the road.* She was lucky if drivers moved three inches toward the center of the two-lane highway when they whizzed past her.

Rufus had offered to pick her up. All winter long he fetched her when she needed to venture beyond the confines of Westcliffe, where she worked on Main Street and lived on a side street. But Annie did not want to depend on Rufus for her every move until she learned to care for a horse and drive a buggy of her own. The promise of spring allowed independence, as far as she was concerned. Milder weather meant she could come and go as she wished, as long as she did not mind the rigors of riding or walking at high elevation. This first ride of the season made her want to lengthen her stride and let her feet hit pavement in heart-pumping rhythm. Did good Amish girls run cross-country?

By the time Annie turned into the long Beiler driveway, she was refusing to shiver in her damp sweater, and the sodden hem of her skirt was slapping against drenched stockings. The best she could hope to do was keep her headpiece on straight. The Beilers had taken her into heart and hearth as she was, but she still wished she could arrive without looking a mess once in a while.

Seven-year-old Jacob was the first to spot her, as he always was. He loped down the wide porch steps and across the yard with one hand holding his straw hat in place and his black winter-weight wool jacket flapping open. Annie checked to be sure he was at least wearing shoes, knowing that as soon as the ground dried up he would leave his boy-sized brown work boots neatly under his bed.

"Annalise!" The boy flung himself into her arms even before she could properly dismount. The bicycle tumbled on its side and she let it go in favor of his enthusiasm against her torso. Jacob knocked her slightly off balance, and her cell phone spilled from a sweater pocket. Jacob squatted to scoop it up. "Do you ever miss your old phone? I liked your old phone."

Her iPhone had been her lifeline to another world—e-mail, texting, Internet, Facebook, Twitter. She had done it all on her phone, and she never turned it off. She ran her whole company from that phone sometimes.

"I would trade a thousand phones just to know you." Annie wrapped her hand around the simple flip-style phone. This one was not even turned on. So far, in the last six months, Annie managed to avoid any emergency calls. Otherwise she only turned it on for her weekly calls to her mother, a compromise that helped keep the peace. Her parents had the number Rufus used for his woodworking business, so if one of her parents had a true emergency, they could reach her.

Annie glanced toward the house, ready for her pulse to quicken at the sight of Rufus.

"The Stutzmans are here." Jacob took her hand and tugged.

"Who?"

"The new family."

Annie managed a smile for Jacob's sake. She was expecting supper with only the Beiler family. They knew her well and patiently guided her through the path of learning Amish ways. The presence of another family, especially a new one, took the edge off her anticipation of the evening—and immediately she felt remorse at her ungenerous thought.

When Rufus Beiler heard the screen door slam behind his little brother, he lifted his eyes to the big window that looked out the front of the house. As it often was, Annalise's *kapp* was cockeyed, an unintended habit that made him smile.

"Excuse me," he said to Beth Stutzman, who hardly broke her chatter to breathe. "I'll be back shortly."

On his way out the front door, Rufus grabbed his coat off the rack. He met Annalise and Jacob halfway down the driveway.

"I told Annalise the Stutzmans are here," Jacob said.

"Thank you, Jacob." Rufus tilted his head toward the house. "Maybe *Mamm* needs your help."

"I hope she's all out of beets from the cellar."

"Jacob!"

"I'm sorry." The boy huffed. "I will be thankful for whatever is put in front of me to eat."

Rufus watched his brother start to kick the dirt beneath his boot and then think better of it. As the little boy clomped up the porch steps, Rufus laid his coat around Annalise's shoulders. She had, as she nearly always did, underdressed for the spring temperatures.

When she turned toward him and lifted her face in thanks, he wanted to kiss her right there. She was so lovely. Bits of moisture clinging to her face shimmered in waning sunlight. He barely kept himself from smoothing her blond hair back into place under her *kapp*.

"Stutzmans?" Her wide gray eyes questioned.

" 'Fraid so." He straightened the jacket around her.

"I'm not cold, you know." Her eyes smiled even if her lips were turning blue.

"So you often tell me." He would never admit he hung his coat around her so her scent would be on it when he wore it next.

"Anyway, Stutzmans," she reminded him.

"Just moved from Pennsylvania to join the settlement here."

"Did you know them in Pennsylvania?"

"Quite well. They are second cousins of my brother Daniel's wife and had a farm only four miles from ours." He paused and put his hand on her elbow.

"Oh. That's nice."

He heard the disappointment in her tone. "If you don't feel up to meeting new people tonight, I can take you home."

"Don't be silly. I'm here. The Stutzmans are here. I'm sure we'll get along famously."

Rufus was not so sure.

Instead of making a dripping entrance through the front door, Annie asked Rufus to walk her to the back door. She could slip into the kitchen and up the back stairs to dry off and straighten herself out. When she glanced in the small mirror in the bathroom, she rolled her eyes. Why did she seem to be the only Amish woman—well, almost Amish—who could not seem to wear a prayer *kapp* properly?

Under her thick sweater, the dress was surprisingly dry. She could do little about the hem of her skirt, which had plunged through one puddle too many. It would have to dry in its own time.

Downstairs, the table was extended to its full length and

Jacob was rounding up the last of the extra chairs from around the house. Eli and Franey, Rufus's parents, shared their home with five of their eight children. In between their eldest son, Rufus, and youngest son, Jacob, were Joel, Lydia, and Sophie, all teenagers.

Hospitality oozed out of Franey Beiler's bones, a trait that first brought Annie into the house last summer. Franey would not blink twice at accommodating seven extra people for dinner.

She suggested the Stutzmans sit where they pleased and the Beilers—and Annalise—would fill in. Annie's stomach heated as the tallest Stutzman daughter took the chair directly opposite Rufus. Annie pressed her lips together and took another chair. As Eli Beiler presided over the silent prayer at the beginning of the meal, Annie could not help but wonder about one empty seat. Joel Beiler was missing.

Ike and Edna Stutzman's daughters—Beth, Johanna, and Essie—seemed to Annie close enough in age that she would not be surprised to discover a set of twins among them. She guessed they were between nineteen and twenty-two. The boys—Mark and Luke—were younger, perhaps recently finished with eighth-grade formal schooling.

They were loud. *Laut.* Jacob had taught Annie that word.

Annie could not summon a more polite description that remained honest. The entire family spoke as if they were addressing a deaf grandfather, and one on top of the other. They were full of news of former neighbors in Pennsylvania, and Franey and Eli lit up in gratitude for stories of people they had lived so long among, including their own two married sons.

For Annie's sake, the Beilers often spoke English. The Stutzmans, however, made no such effort, beyond initial introductions. Pennsylvania Dutch flew around the table too fast for Annie to keep up with much of the conversation. Jacob sat beside her, as he always did when she came to dinner. Occasionally, he leaned toward her and offered a brief translation, which helped Annie to smile and nod in appropriate lulls.

Annie did not need translation to see that Beth Stutzman

directed many of her remarks at Rufus in a way that forced him to respond. *She must be the eldest,* Annie decided. Johanna and Essie made no effort to compete with their sister but instead sat quietly, observing the conversation and smiling benignly. Beth would have been finishing the eighth grade when Rufus left Pennsylvania, when he was a grown man already. But now she was grown up—and quite pretty, Annie had to admit. Had Beth Stutzman swept into town and thought she would snag Rufus Beiler on her first evening?

Jacob leaned toward her and whispered. "The Stutzmans are going to stay with us for a while. They want to paint their house before they move in. I hope they will let me help paint."

Annie smiled. "I'm sure you're a very good painter."

"No one ever gives me a chance to try."

Annie reached over and scratched the center of his back then laid her arm across the top of his chair, angling toward Rufus as she did so.

Despite the decibel level and Beth's brazenness, the evening was drenched in friendship going back generations. Annie could see for herself that these were not like the unfamiliar families in Colorado Springs who intersected each other's routines at swim classes and soccer matches for three years until someone transferred to a new job. They shared each other's days and nights, and various branches of their families had intermarried. Ike and Edna had come west for many of the same reasons Eli and Franey had come six years earlier. Unlike the Beilers, though, the newcomers had a community ready to welcome them and give them aid.

Even after six months of living as plainly as she could, and despite her dress and *kapp*, Annie felt very much the *English*. And she had been at the Beiler table enough times to feel the undercurrent that grew between Eli and Franey as conversation rose and fell and Joel failed to appear. Annie glanced at Rufus, catching his eye in a fleeting connection before Beth launched into another story meant for Rufus's benefit. The evening was nothing like what Annie craved when she had started out on her bicycle.

Eli's eyes, Annie noticed, moved between the clock and the front door.

Joel was going to have some explaining to do.

Two

*J*ohanna Stutzman and her brother Mark sat on either side of Joel's empty seat. As the meal progressed, both seemed to absorb a share of the available space, as if they no longer expected someone would arrive to occupy the chair.

Annie regretted putting so much food on her plate. She felt left out of the rapid, reminiscent conversation in the language she still struggled to learn, and whenever she looked at Eli, her anxiety for Joel heightened. Both factors dimmed her appetite.

This was not the first time Joel had been late for dinner, she knew. That only made things worse. Had he not known the Stutzmans would be there? If he had, would he have made an effort to be present?

The creak of the front door's hinges raised eyes around the table. Joel entered and closed the door carefully behind him. A still-growing seventeen-year-old, his trousers inched off his ankles as he turned to face the gathering at the table.

"Ah, Joel." With just two words, Eli's voice bore through the chatter.

"I'm sorry, *Daed*." Joel moved toward the table, his back erect. He brushed a bookcase, and a cell phone clattered to the polished wood floor.

"Hey, that's just like Annalise's." Jacob clambered out of his chair and picked up the phone.

"Jacob, get back in your seat." Eli's eyes remained on Joel.

Jacob handed the phone to Joel and obeyed his father.

"It's Carter's phone." Joel took his own seat. "I forgot he gave it to me to hold."

"We'll talk later," Eli said. "Just turn it off and put it away."

Annie winced on Joel's behalf. She saw Joel reach under the table and fiddle with the phone, which was indeed on. Eli was not going to embarrass Joel in the presence of guests—even old family friends—but even if the phone was not Joel's, Eli would want to know what his son was doing with it.

"Carter is the son of Tom Reynolds." Speaking English, Rufus deftly explained. "You'll want to meet Tom as soon as possible. He does a fair bit of taxiing and hauling for our people, and he doesn't mind the distances involved in our district."

"That's good to know." Ike Stutzman's voice was deep and commanding. "I heard that because of the distances, your district allows the use of telephones."

Oops. Annie caught Rufus's eyes and saw the flicker of dismay that his effort to deflect the conversation had been short lived.

"That's true," Eli said, "but the concern is for safety, not convenience or amusement."

His expression was not lost on Annie, so she had no doubt that Joel understood perfectly.

"Carter's dad was out looking at the new recreation area," Joel said. "He took some pictures."

Oops again. Not the best topic of conversation Joel could have introduced to take the heat off himself.

"No one has made any decisions about the use of that property," Eli said.

"What property is that?" Ike's inquiry sounded idle enough.

Annie pushed peas around on her plate. At least they were not beets. She stood in solidarity with Jacob on the beets question. She was relieved to hear Rufus's voice again.

"The county owns a few acres not far from here," Rufus explained in English. "There is some thought to developing a park. The organizers would like volunteers to offer their labor in order to keep costs to a minimum. They have invited everyone to participate."

"Even the Amish?" Edna Stutzman asked from beside Franey. "Surely they understand that we live apart."

Rufus tilted his head. "The park would be for everyone to use. If everyone shares the load, then everyone benefits as well."

"But this is an *English* project, is it not?" Ike thumped the table as he persisted with the distinction.

"Well, yes, I suppose," Rufus said. "It was the idea of Tom Reynolds and a few others. They propose a simple shelter from rain and sun, a children's play area, and trails for families to use."

"But this is an *English* project," Edna repeated.

Annie did not need a translation for the consonants spitting from Edna's mouth when she said *English*. She reached up and tugged on the two strings of her *kapp*, a habit developed over the last six months in nervous moments. While she was living largely plain until she decided whether to join the Amish officially, Annie resented Edna's inferences about the *English*.

"Do you often cooperate with the *English*?" Edna bristled as she broke open a biscuit.

"The *English* are our neighbors here," Rufus said, persisting in English. "When do you hope to move onto your farm?"

And that was it. He let it go and moved on.

Annie stifled a sigh. How did he do that? Just let things go when the tension mounted?

Relief blew out on Franey's breath, Annie noticed. She was not opposed to a park. She was not even opposed to working with the neighbors. Franey simply did not want to get involved with that particular plot of land. Annie did not know why.

It had something to do with Ruth. Annie knew that much. Annie missed Ruth. Rufus's sister would have known how to navigate the emotions in the room.

Franey's reticence about the land proposed for the park.

Joel's running around with Carter Reynolds and the boys from town.

Eli's need for order.

Even Beth Stutzman batting her eyes at Rufus.

Annie was glad that she could picture where Ruth was—the roadways of Colorado Springs bearing the buses Ruth rode to work and school, the university she attended, the small dorm room she lived in. Even though she knew Ruth was sure of her choice, Annie felt Franey's sadness.

Franey stood up. "How about dessert?" She smiled around the table. "I have peach pie, apple schnitzel, and rhubarb crisp."

Rufus's sisters Lydia and Sophie took the cue and began clearing the table. Annie did the same.

The Stutzman daughters rested comfortably in their chairs. Beth even put her elbow on the table, set her chin in her hand, and leaned toward Rufus. Annie shoved down the resentment that welled.

Humility, humility, humility, she told herself. No matter what she thought of their manners, she would serve them with a smile.

Rufus remembered the Stutzman girls differently. Perhaps it was because they were so much younger than he was that he never paid close attention to them when the families lived near each other in Lancaster County. They were taller now, more filled out. Beth's hair was much the same color as Annalise's, he observed. He supposed that her forwardness would wear off soon enough when she saw that he did not return her feelings, and when she met some of the other families who had sons looking for wives.

He looked at Annalise across the table. Concentrating so hard to follow conversation in Pennsylvania Dutch exhausted her, he knew, and the evening's exchanges had been particularly rapid. Several times during the evening he had switched to English in an effort to include her, but clearly the Stutzmans were not used to using English at home and inevitably switched back within a few sentences. As they told stories of Lancaster County, their enthusiasm spilled out in a torrent of Pennsylvania Dutch.

Annalise smiled at him in an expression he had come to know meant, *I'm tired and I want to go home.*

Rufus pushed back his chair. "It's been good to hear so much news from home. Now I think I'd better make sure Annalise is home before it gets later."

Annalise stood. "Thank you, Rufus. I do have to open the shop early tomorrow."

"You work in a shop?" Edna asked. "What sort of shop?"

"Antiques, collectibles, odd and ends," Annalise said. "It's right on Main Street."

"They sell some of my jam," Franey said. "Weekend visitors seem to like it."

"Beth makes excellent jam," Edna said, smiling at Rufus.

Rufus nodded politely and stood up. "I'll take Annalise home now."

"Let Joel take her," Eli said.

Rufus stopped in his steps. He always took Annalise home. In fact, often the quiet ride home was the part of an evening he looked forward to most. Talking freely with Annalise, holding her hand, hearing the way she laughed when only he was around. Rufus would not counter his father, though, especially in front of guests.

Eli lifted his chin toward Joel. "Stop on your way back and return Carter's phone, please. I don't want it in the house."

The phone could have waited until the morning, Rufus thought.

"I'll walk out with you." Rufus gestured toward the front door. "It will take Joel a few minutes to bring the buggy around."

Annalise followed him to the front door, where she retrieved her half-dry sweater. He read the mixture of disappointment and gratitude in her face when they stepped out under the porch light and she turned her face to him.

"I'm sorry," Rufus said. "I thought we would have some time to talk."

"Me too. But we must respect your father."

Rufus sighed gently. "You are learning our ways."

They descended the steps together.

"I really do have to open the shop early," Annalise said. "Mrs. Weichert is going into Cañon City to visit an old rancher's house. The family claims some of the pieces have been in the family for well over a hundred years. They may be an easy sell to the weekend antiquers."

"Will you be at the shop all day?"

She shook her head. "She promises to be back before noon."

"Then you'll be back here tomorrow?"

"My Saturday quilting lesson is the highlight of my week. Wouldn't miss it."

He nodded in satisfaction. "I'm sure I'll see you."

They walked halfway down the driveway to where her bicycle still lay on its side.

"I should check your brakes," he said.

"The brakes are fine. The tires, too."

"It can't hurt to double-check."

"It's fine, Rufus. You're sweet, but I built and sold two high-tech companies. I think I can keep a bicycle in working order."

Joel arrived with a horse and the small cart.

"You should have brought the buggy," Rufus said. "It's getting cold."

"I thought this would be easier to put the bike in." Joel was already gripping the frame in two places and lifting the bike into the cart.

"This is fine," Annalise said. "I'm not cold, you know."

Rufus smiled. "So you often tell me."

"You two can hold your smiling contest later," Joel said. "Let's get this over with."

Rufus did not much care for his brother's attitude, but this was not the time to challenge him. He turned to Annalise and offered a hand to help her up into the cart. "I'll see you tomorrow."

"Right after lunch."

"Have you got the phone, Joel?" Rufus asked.

Joel raised the reins. "I'm not an idiot."

"I know you didn't want to do this." Annie gripped the seat. Joel was letting the horse have a little too much head.

"Don't worry about it." He did not turn an inch in her direction.

He was seventeen. Annie had never been an Amish boy, but she did remember seventeen. She let an entire mile roll by before she spoke again.

"You and your father are going to work this out."

"Work what out?"

"This thing between you. That keeps you from talking to each other."

"I don't know what you're talking about."

Another mile.

If Joel did not choose to be baptized and join the Amish church, it might just take Franey around the bend. His older sister Ruth had already left home without joining the church, and while the relationship between mother and daughter had tenuously stitched itself back together over the last few months, Annie was sure Franey was not ready to go through that again with another child.

"I'm not Ruth, you know," Joel said.

How did he do that? "I didn't say anything."

"You don't have to. I'm not stupid. I know *Mamm* wants me to be baptized, the sooner the better."

"You have to do what is right for you."

"Look where that got Ruth."

"Still. It's true."

Another mile. Two more to go.

"I'm going to be baptized," he said. "I'm just not on a time schedule. There's no hurry unless I decide I want to get married."

"True enough."

"And I'm not getting married any time soon."

"I'm sure you know what you're doing."

"About as much as you do."

Everybody she knew back in Colorado Springs thought she needed a good shrink. Sell her business for millions of dollars and park the money where she could not touch it? Give up modern technology? Move into a decrepit house one-third the size of her custom-built condo and immediately get rid of the electricity? Take classes—in German—to learn the Amish faith?

"I stumble through one day at a time," she said.

"It seems to me you've got a pretty good grip on things."

"Smoke and mirrors, I assure you."

"I'm Amish," he said. "I'm not supposed to know about magic tricks."

Annie elbowed him and laughed. They turned off the main highway and onto Main Street heading east. A few blocks later, Joel turned the horse north.

"Lights are on in your house," he said. "Did you leave them burning?"

Annie leaned forward. "No."

"Well, somebody did."

The living room was well lit. Annie wondered if there were such a thing as an Amish thief. Who else would know not to reach for a wall switch?

Joel slowed the horse and reached to extinguish the lantern hanging from the front of the cart.

"I guess I forgot," she said.

"You don't forget, Annalise. Even I know that."

They stopped in front of the house. "Should we call 911?" Annie pulled her phone out of her sweater pocket and flipped it open. Westcliffe was the seat of Custer County. A county sheriff's car would be just minutes away.

"I can't just leave you here." Joel put a hand on Annie's arm.

They watched the house for a few silent seconds.

"I'm going in with you," Joel finally said. "But turn on the phone just in case."

Three

oel looped the reins around the mailbox at the curb. Staying in the shadow of the house, Annie led the way up the driveway and around the back of the house.

"How do you think they got in?" Joel's whisper might as well have been a megaphone.

Annie put a finger to her lips and stepped onto the small porch outside her back door. With one hand still gripping her cell phone, she slowly lowered the handle on the screen door. Ready to wince if the contrary spring at the top betrayed them, she opened the door inch by inch and slipped into the opening. Joel was right behind her when she tested the knob on the main door. She was sure she had locked it when she left, but it turned easily now.

Inside, her fingers found the edge of the counter and she felt her way along it across the small dark kitchen. A shadow crossed the light seeping around the edges of the swinging door between the kitchen and dining room. Someone was definitely on the other side—and moving around.

"I can't see anything." Joel's feet dragged on the floor.

"Put your hand on my shoulder. Watch out for the trash—"

But Annie's hushed warning was too late. Joel stumbled and sent the metal can clanging across the floor. She halted and froze.

Joel's tumbling weight against her back nearly knocked her over.

The door from the dining room opened. "Annie, is that you?"

The air went out of Annie so fast she almost whistled like a balloon. "Mom!"

Annie reached for the small propane lamp she knew was at the end of the counter and turned the switch. Her father now stood behind her mother in the doorway. Myra Friesen looked from her daughter to the young man behind her.

"This is Joel," Annie said. "Rufus's brother. Joel, these are my parents, Myra and Brad Friesen."

"Hello, Joel," Myra said.

"It's nice to meet you." Joel nudged Annie. "Everything's okay, *ya?*"

She nodded. Whatever brought her parents to her home without prior arrangement was nothing she needed Joel for. "Thank you for seeing me in."

"I'll leave the bike on the side of the house."

"*Danki.*" Thank you.

The screen door slammed behind him, and Annie closed the solid inner door. Then she righted the trash can, grateful she chose the covered model when she outfitted her kitchen.

Myra glanced around the kitchen. "You've done a nice job making something of this room. . .with its limitations."

"Thank you. Mom, what's going on? How did you even get in?"

"You've got a tree in the backyard just like the one at home. It even has the same low branch—good for climbing. It was simple enough to think you'd hide a key there like we do at home."

"Busted. Where did you stash your car?" If she had seen their sedan, she might have spared a few extra heartbeats moments ago.

Myra set the house key on the counter. "We figured your garage was empty, considering your car is in our garage at home."

Home. Was her mother going to work that word into every sentence? Annie let the comment pass and instead gestured to the dining room. "Why don't I make some coffee and you can tell me why you're here?"

Along with the coffee, Annie produced half a chocolate cake. They sat at the oval table up against the window in the dining room.

"Mmm. Delicious!" Myra jabbed her fork in for a second bite of cake. "Is this from a bakery in town?"

"No. I made it."

"You made this? You never used to like to bake."

"I'm trying a lot of new things these days." Annie nudged a small pitcher of cream toward her dad, who she knew would want a generous portion.

"Well, I miss some of your old habits." Myra licked chocolate off her top lip. "Like calling your mother."

"I call you every Saturday and we yak the charge out of my phone." Annie twirled her fork, balancing a piece of cake. "I would have called you tomorrow like always." So why were they here?

Brad cleared his throat. "We're here on a special mission."

"Which is?"

"Penny is coming home." Myra looked at Annie hopefully.

Annie had not seen her sister in almost a year and a half. Though Annie had gone to Colorado Springs for Christmas, at the last minute Penny had to cancel her flight from Seattle and missed the holiday.

"When does she arrive?"

"Tomorrow night."

"Tomorrow!" Annie set her mug down. "Why didn't we find out sooner?"

"We found out last Saturday. She called right after I got off the phone with you. I meant to send you a note, but I never got to it. I'm just not used to communicating the old-fashioned way, I guess."

Annie wondered how many times she and her mother would have to go around this loop.

"I wanted to leave a message on your phone," Myra said, "but you have all these rules about what is a true emergency."

"It seemed the simplest thing to drive out here," Brad said.

"I'm sorry I wasn't home." Annie reached for the pot and warmed up her coffee.

"We can take you back with us in the morning," Myra said.

"You're staying the night?"

"Certainly. Not here, of course. We've already checked in at Mo's."

Annie nodded. Mo's motel. Where they had electricity. And complimentary Wi-Fi.

"I'm sure you'll be comfortable there." She paused. "I'm not sure about going back with you, though."

Myra's fork hit the bare plate. "But you have to. I told you. Penny's coming. It's hard for her to get away."

"It might be hard for me to get away on short notice, too, Mom."

"But Penny's only going to be here for a few days. She's coming all the way from Seattle. Can't you come seventy-five miles? I'd like to have you both home at the same time."

"I know, Mom. I'm not sure about tomorrow, that's all. I'll have to figure out my work schedule."

Myra waved a hand. "You don't even need that job."

"I need work for reasons other than money."

"If you need something," Brad said, "you let me know."

"Don't be silly, Brad." Myra pushed her empty plate away. "She has more money than you and I can ever dream of."

Annie groaned. "Mom, we've been through this. I only have what I made when I sold my condo. I have to be careful. It has to last me indefinitely. All the profits from the sale of the business went into a charity foundation. I can't touch it."

"Your compassionate humanitarianism is admirable, but why you left yourself in need, I'll never understand."

"I'm not in need," Annie said. "I'm just living more simply, and it's good to have work."

"But in an antiques store? Why don't the Amish rules let you make money with what you know how to do—technology?"

"This is what I want, Mom. You have to accept it."

"But they put such value on family. We're your family. Surely they would want you to see your sister."

"I do want to see Penny." Annie missed her sister, who had not written so much as a thank-you note in at least five years. They used to communicate by texting most of the time. Annie had written two letters explaining the changes in her life, but she heard Penny's reaction only through their mother on the phone. "How long will she be here?"

"Just until Thursday. It's a short visit. You must come home."

"Please come," Brad said. "We can have dinner together a few times and catch up."

As determined as Annie had been over the winter to live without electricity and a car, and to learn to cook her own food instead of ordering takeout every night, she would be lying if she said she did not miss her family. But Mrs. Weichert was counting on her to look after the shop in the morning, and Franey Beiler was expecting her tomorrow afternoon.

"I'll figure something out." Annie's eyes suddenly ached to close, and she clamped her jaw against the urge to yawn.

Brad stood up and started stacking dishes, a habit Annie had always admired in her father. If she did not stop him, he would take the dishes into the kitchen and insist on washing them.

"That's a beautiful shelf." Brad glanced at a white oak shelf fixed to the wall beside the dining room window.

"Thank you. Rufus made it."

Brad inspected the carved pattern along the front ledge. "He's quite skilled."

"I know." Pride flushed through Annie, and she reminded herself. *Humility, humility, humility.*

"And these books?" her father asked. A dozen or so volumes in various colors and thicknesses populated the shelf.

"Various genealogy books," Annie said. "Several have come from Amish families, but the rest have come through the antiques shop. Mrs. Weichert doesn't mind if I take them."

"Are they all about the Beilers?"

Annie shook her head. "Most of them are not. I've gotten interested in the whole idea of tracing the generations back in any family."

Brad pulled a slim black binder off the shelf and opened it. "Is this the book you found in our basement?"

"Yep. That's your Byler roots, going all the way back to Jakob Beyeler in 1737."

"I thought it had a spiral binding," Myra said.

"I figured it would hold up better in a notebook with page protectors."

"That's a nice thought."

"That red volume is all about the Bylers of North Carolina."

"Are we related?"

"I'm pretty sure. I'd like to spend more time studying the family lines than I have."

Brad chuckled. "I'll let you give me the abbreviated version, but I admit I find it fascinating that my mother's family may be related to the very people you've become so attached to here."

"Me, too." Annie covered a yawn. "Sorry."

"We're all tired." Myra stood and picked up the coffeepot and creamer. She disappeared into the kitchen, still talking. "We'll pick you up for breakfast. Not too early, though. How about eight thirty?"

"Sorry, Mom. Mrs. Weichert is going to an estate sale in the morning. I have to be in the shop."

"Will it matter if you're late? How many customers do you get, anyway?"

Annie had to admit traffic was slow most days, but Saturday was likely to bring weekend lookers. "I promised her, Mom. She's counting on me."

"Well all right, then. We can have lunch in that quaint bakery down the street before we head back to town."

"Let's figure that out tomorrow." Annie stifled another yawn.

"Will you have your phone on?" Myra looked as if she already knew the answer.

Annie wondered why her mother insisted on pressing the question. "I'm sure I can get a message to you at Mo's. I'll use the phone in the shop."

"But you'll definitely go home with us as soon as you're free?"

"Mom, I do want to see Penny. I'm just not sure about tomorrow."

Four

October 1774

"Push!"

At her mother-in-law's command, Katie Byler grunted and bore down.

In the other room, Jacob heard the urgency in his mother's voice and the resolve in his wife's guttural response. It would not be long now.

Jacob soothed one of the twins by jiggling the child on his knee. He welcomed the other to lean against his leg. At two, the twins were too young to know what caused their *mamm* to make those sounds, and he saw terror in their round, ruddy, silent faces. At seven and five, their older brothers, Jacob Franklin and Abraham, remembered the twins' arrival and were less concerned about the event.

Four boys, all of them sturdy and healthy. Katie wanted a girl this time. A little sister.

Jacob's own sister was supposed to come from Philadelphia to help, but Katie had gone from uneventfully stirring the morning porridge to digging fingernails into his arm in the space of four minutes—three weeks earlier than anyone imagined. All the boys had been tediously late, even the twins. So with or without Sarah's presence, this baby was coming. It was all Jacob could do to send seven-year-old Jacob Franklin sprinting across the acres to fetch his grandmother from the big house. Soon after her arrival, Elizabeth Byler pronounced the child would appear before lunch. Jacob could not see how it was going to take even that long. Katie's scream melded into the wail of the new baby protesting an abrupt arrival into the chilly room.

"A girl!" Jacob's mother called.

Jacob stood and thrust the reluctant twins toward Jacob Franklin. He had to see for himself that Katie was all right.

At the bedroom door, he stopped and smiled. Katie was already grinning. She eagerly caught his eye.

"A girl," she said.

"A girl!" Jacob softened in satisfaction. Their daughter continued her objections while her grandmother wrapped her in a towel and placed her on Katie's chest. Katie counted fingers and toes as she had with all their children. Jacob moved closer to the bed.

"She has your forehead, Elizabeth." Katie gently rotated the child to get a good look at both sides of her face.

"Perhaps not my best feature." Elizabeth discreetly positioned a clean rag under Katie to await the afterbirth.

Jacob soaked up his wife's pleasure, glimpsing the depth of her yearning for a girl after four boys.

"Her aunt Sarah has four brothers," Katie said. "Your sister will have to teach this little one how she survived."

Jacob put his massive hand around the back of the baby's head. "For starters, Sarah never once let us take advantage of her."

His mother laughed as long-past years lit her eyes. She had borne five children but mothered ten, taking into her heart Jacob's older Amish half siblings.

He knew the story well. Both his parents had told it often. More than thirty-five years ago, after surviving a treacherous sea journey without losing anyone in their family, his five older siblings were abruptly left motherless in Philadelphia, their father crushed in loss. And then Lisbetli found Elizabeth's heart in a stationer's shop, and Elizabeth found his father's heart. The bookish woman of the city married the homesteader and moved to the wilderness, where she labored with five children she could call her own no matter what.

No matter what.

His Amish siblings loved her. Jacob believed that. Who could not love Elizabeth Kallen Byler and her gentle, self-sacrificing ways? Yet she refused to convert to the Amish faith, and for that the Amish siblings put on her the weight of luring their father away from the church.

And now this woman who had loved them all moved about the room cleaning up and delicately setting aside a bucket and soiled cloths. Her movements were swift and efficient, as she made sure Katie was as comfortable as possible. She stepped to the other side of the bed and pulled a quilt up over her daughter-in-law then paused to lay one last damp cloth across Katie's forehead.

His father had made his own choice. Jacob had no doubt. And his mother made hers.

The others were gone now. Lisbetli was in her grave, and Maria disappeared years ago, run away to who knew where. Unwilling to raise arms in skirmishes with Indians or the French, Christian sold his land and moved to the Conestoga Valley, farther from the frontier. Land the Amish had labored to clear and make farms of was now quite valuable, so other Amish families followed Christian, including Jacob's half-sisters Barbara and Anna. Eventually many of the Amish settled in a reconfigured Lancaster County, while Jacob remained on land that became part of Berks County.

"We should write to them." Katie looked up at Jacob, reading her husband's mind as she always had. "Your sisters will want to know about the babe."

Jacob nodded. "What would you like to call her?"

Katie shifted the infant into Jacob's arms. "Her name is Catherine."

"That's a big name for a little one."

"She'll grow into it. They all do."

A wail from the front room reminded them that Catherine's four older brothers were unattended.

"I'll go, Jacobli. You should be here now." Elizabeth laid a small quilt over the child nestled in his arms, quieted now. Jacob recognized it. All his children had slumbered under it in newness, warmed by a token of their grandmother's love.

Elizabeth left the room, and Jacob handed the baby back to Katie.

"I'll stoke the fire," he said. "It's too chilly in here for a babe."

Katie pulled the bedding up to where she held the child against her chest.

"Then I'll get you some food," Jacob said. "And tea."

"Your brothers will be along soon, I suppose," Katie said.

Jacob nodded. "By now John will have noticed I'm not at the tannery today. He'll call Joseph and David in from the fields."

"Your family does rally around a new babe. I have to say that about them."

"You might say a great deal more about them, but God has graced you with forbearance."

She laughed. "They are my family, too," she said. "Send them in as soon as they come. Sarah should be here tomorrow."

Tomorrow. Jacob was relieved it was not next week after all.

Magdalena Byler stood at the end of the lane, shading her eyes with one hand. Nathanael was late. If pressed, she would have to admit he was late habitually, but no matter when he turned up her heart quickened. He was twenty-two to her seventeen years. If they spoke to the bishop soon, they might yet marry before this year's wedding season passed.

The approaching cart stirred up dust before she heard the clatter of horses' hooves and wagon wheels. Nathanael would have come on foot. This must be Nicholas, the *English* who carried mail from Lancaster to the outlying farms twice a week. Magdalena raised one corner of her shawl to spare her lungs the whirling dust.

Nicholas waited till the last moment to pull on the reins, just as he always did.

"*Guder mariye*, Nicholas. Good morning. What do you have for us today?"

He passed her a bundle of envelopes tied together with string. "One is from Berks County."

"My *onkel*." Magdalena pulled the knot out of the string and began to flip through the stack. She paused when she recognized the blockish lettering of Jacob, her father's younger half brother. "It must be news of the baby."

"You can tell me all about it next time," Nicholas said. "Nothing going out?"

"Not today. *Danki*, Nicholas."

The horse resumed its trot. Magdalena scanned the road again, looking for any sign of Nathanael. Nothing stirred on the horizon. She was tempted to tear the end of the envelope, but it was addressed to her father and his wife. After one more glance around, she chose to take the letters to her father. Nathan could find her there.

Her parents had brought the family to the Conestoga Valley several years earlier. Her mother's death, just two years ago, stunned them all. But Christian Byler, her father, lost little time in marrying again to another Yoder daughter. Now he and Babsi coddled a baby of their own. With three brothers and three sisters, Magdalena had thought herself too old to become a sister again, but of course no one could resist baby Antje's blond curls and violet-blue eyes.

Magdalena decided to go to the barn rather than the house. Her father was sure to be there. She was curious enough about *Onkel* Jacob's news to want her *daed* to open that letter, even if he read the rest when he was sitting comfortably in his chair by the fire. Magdalena found him right where she expected, standing in the hayloft with a pitchfork in his hands. When he saw her, he thrust the implement upright into the hay and leaned on it to look at her.

"*Onkel* Jacobli has sent a letter." Magdalena waved the entire mail packet up for her father to see.

Christian Byler wiped his hands on his pants then carefully maneuvered down the sturdy ladder to the main floor. At forty-five, he still seemed robust to Magdalena. He did not ask younger men to do what he was not willing to do himself. The end of his brown curly beard rested against his chest as he took the stack of mail from Magdalena.

She had laid Jacob's letter on top. Her father now carefully broke through the end of the envelope and extracted a single sheet of paper.

"*Maedel*. A girl," Christian said a moment later. "They're calling her Catherine."

Magdalena smiled. "A pretty name. When did she come?"

"Nearly three weeks ago. Sarah is there now. All is well." Christian looked up. "I thought you were to walk with Nathanael Buerki this morning."

"I am."

"He's late."

"I know."

"Are you sure you want to spend your life waiting on this man?"

Magdalena nodded. Nathanael's perpetual tardiness bothered her father more than it did her. "He is worth it."

"You had better be sure."

"I am."

"You could have been married last year. He has his own land with a cabin. It's not the house you're used to, but it would serve you well for now."

"The cabin is fine. We'll marry when the time is right." Magdalena hoped it would be soon. "I'd better go back up to the road to wait for him."

Nathan was there when Magdalena reached the end of the lane again. He looked over his shoulder as he hustled her down the road.

"What's wrong, Nathan?"

"Patriots," he said. "I saw a gang of them on the ridge."

"They could be there for any number of reasons," Magdalena said. "One of their meetings, perhaps."

"I had a bad feeling, Maggie. From up there they can see the road in both directions. You never know when they will drop down."

"I don't understand why they cannot leave us alone. Is it so terrible that the Amish want to be neutral and peaceful?"

"Ever since the Patriots dumped tea in the Boston Harbor, there is no such thing as neutral in their minds." Nathanael slowed his steps and reached for Magdalena's arm when she got a few steps ahead of him.

"You said they were on the ridge," Magdalena said.

"I think they've moved," Nathan whispered.

Magdalena gasped and clutched Nathanael's hand as four young men lunged from bushes beside the road.

One of the men broke from the others and sliced between Magdalena and Nathanael, knocking her down at the side of the road and pinning her shoulders there. She stared into his gray eyes. He was Stephen Blackburn. His family had arrived in the Conestoga Valley the same year hers had. They were hardly more than children when they first met. He was *English*, but he had never threatened harm.

"Don't try anything." He gave her shoulder an extra shove; then he stood up.

What did he think she would try? She was Amish. She would not strike him or purposefully cause him harm. And neither would Nathan.

The foursome now circled a frozen Nathanael.

"Have you considered the hypocrisy of your position?" Stephen taunted. "Your people came to America seeking freedom, but now that the British threaten the freedom of all the colonies, you will not stand up against persecution."

Magdalena watched Nathanael's Adam's apple descend in a slow swallow.

"We are peaceful people," Nathanael said. "We would be hypocrites if we were suddenly to take up arms."

"There will be a war, you know," Stephen said. "You will have to decide whether your allegiance belongs to Britain or America."

"My allegiance belongs to God alone."

"But you live in Pennsylvania. You must have some sense of patriotism."

Nathanael did not answer. Still tasting dirt, Magdalena was afraid to move.

Stephen slapped Nathanael sharply on one side of his face. "Are you going to turn the other cheek to me?"

Nathanael did not move. Stephen slapped him again, this time with the back of his hand. Nathanael stumbled back a few steps but did not lose his balance.

"How does that feel?" Stephen jeered. "Are you holier now because you turned the other cheek?"

A sob shuddered through Magdalena. She was on one knee now, trying to stand on rubber legs.

"Take him," Stephen said, and two others twisted Nathanael's arms behind his back.

"Where are you taking him?" Magdalena tried to catch Nathanael's downcast eyes.

"Hypocrites need to learn a few lessons in basic loyalty. Let's just say we're taking him to a school where he can learn."

"Please, we mean no harm to anyone." She stood firm on her feet now, her stomach turning itself inside out.

Stephen shoved Nathanael in the back, sending him stumbling into the bushes. He rotated toward Magdalena. "Don't try to follow. It will only make things worse."

Five

October 1774

At the pounding on the front door, Magdalena sprang to her feet. Across the room, her father stiffened.

"It's the men who took Nathan," Magdalena said.

"Let's not jump to conclusions," Christian answered. "Stay out of sight."

"*Daed*, they'll hurt you, too."

Christian turned from the mantel toward the door. "Maggie, take your little sisters and go into the kitchen. Babsi is there."

Magdalena shepherded Lizzie and Mary to the kitchen, grateful her other siblings were away from the house.

Her stepmother looked up from rolling a piecrust. "What's wrong?"

Magdalena shook her head. "Nothing."

"Somebody's at the door." Little Mary climbed up onto the bench at the table.

"*Daed* thought you might like some company." Magdalena took an apple from the basket on the table and handed it to Mary, hoping it would keep her quiet.

Babsi looked at Magdalena, doubt written across her face, but she said nothing. Avoiding Babsi's gaze, Magdalena glanced across the room to see baby Antje nestled in her cradle. The latch was off the back door. If they had to, they could all get out quickly.

"Magdalena!" Her father's voice boomed from the other room. "Magdalena! Come!"

She raced across the kitchen, pushed open the door, and launched into the spacious main room. Her brother Hans, at thirteen still growing into his man's body, was lowering Nathanael into a chair.

"I found him up the road," Hans said. "He's beaten up pretty badly."

Magdalena collapsed at Nathanael's feet, grateful he was back even if he was wounded. She had whispered prayers from her bed through the watches of the night. God had been gracious to answer her pleas, and she now murmured words of gratitude.

"Hans," her father said, "you'd better ride to tell his family. Magdalena, get some rags and a basin of water. Let's see how bad it is."

Magdalena forced down the knot in her throat. Babsi and the girls watched wide-eyed from the other end of the room. She pushed past them to the water barrel in the kitchen and filled a basin then grabbed some clean cloths.

"It's not so bad," she heard Nathanael say when she neared him again. But she did not believe him. The strain in his voice told her that even breathing pained him. Outside the house, Hansli's horse gathered a gallop.

Magdalena knelt on the floor and dipped a rag into the water then gently pressed it to the cuts on one side of Nathan's face. His eye was black and swollen. Dried blood traced its path from his cheekbone down the side of his neck. She moved the rag, moistened again, to his swollen lips. A ragged tear in his shirt— the kind created only in violence—exposed the bruises that had already formed. Hardly more than a few square inches remained untouched across his abdomen.

When she leaned back on her haunches, covering her mouth in horror at what he had been through, her father moved in and gently began peeling Nathanael's shirt off.

"Mary," Christian said, "go get a clean shirt from my wardrobe. Magdalena, see if there is *kaffi* in the kitchen."

Babsi took over cleaning Nathanael's wounds. Magdalena roused herself and went in search of coffee, though when she returned she could see that the cuts in Nathanael's lips made it impossible to know how to offer it to him. He managed a swallow and allowed Christian to lean him forward and put a fresh garment on him. In time, Nathanael put his head back on the chair and was asleep.

"Nathanael may be chronically tardy," Christian said, "but he is a good man. He does not deserve this."

Magdalena's tears came now. "What can we do, *Daed*? Is this what it means to be peaceful people?"

"I will ride to Berks County," her father said, "and talk to Jacobli."

"What can *Onkel* Jacob do?"

"He is surprisingly well connected. He might know who is behind these attacks."

"And then?"

Christian rotated his wrists and held his palms up. "We try to have a peaceful conversation."

"With the men who did this?" Magdalena could hardly believe her father would suggest an encounter.

"With their leaders," Christian said. "With men who know the difference between a British officer and an Amish farmer."

"I'm going with you." Magdalena saw in her father's face the understanding that she was not asking permission.

"The cows are milked, the boys are asleep, and the fires are stoked at *Mamm*'s." Jacob rubbed his hands together over the flame in his own kitchen. He looked from his wife to his sister.

"You look pretty pleased with yourself." Katie was nursing the baby in the only comfortable chair in the kitchen.

"And why should I not be?"

"Sarah, are you sure you wouldn't rather stay up in the big house with your mother?" Katie asked. "There is more room there, and it is so much more comfortable. You've been a great help, but the baby has settled into a routine, and I can manage through the night."

"*Mamm* seems to like her own routine," Sarah said from the table, where she was writing labels for the next day's canning efforts. "But I will see about spending a few nights with her before I go home to Philadelphia. I worry about her rumbling around that big house all by herself so much."

"We see her every day," Jacob reminded her. "And David is still living there. She's not alone."

"I just worry," Sarah said. "She hasn't been the same since *Daed* died. It's been four years."

"What is four years after all the years they had together?" Katie said quietly.

"You're right. I can't help feeling anxious for her sometimes." At the neighing of a horse, Sarah looked up. "Are you expecting someone?"

Jacob shook his head.

Katie smiled at her cooing babe. "Perhaps it's just one of your brothers coming for another look at my beautiful Catherine."

Sarah scooted her chair back and went to the window. Jacob joined her. Shadows from the end of day lay across the yard between the house and Jacob's tannery. Jacob pushed the curtain out of the way for a better look.

"Well, I'll be," Sarah said.

"What is it?" Katie moved the baby to her shoulder to burp.

"It's Christian." Sarah turned wide eyed to Katie. "And I think that's Magdalena with him, though of course I haven't seen either of them in years."

Katie stood to peer out the window for herself.

"Someone had better open the front door," Jacob said.

Jacob bought the family property when their father died, expanded the tannery Christian had detested as a boy, and built his own small home nearby. Christian had not been to Irish Creek since Jacobli put on the addition to shelter his growing family. The profile of the house in the shadows was pleasing.

Christian supposed it would have been easier to go to his stepmother's house. She certainly had more space to accommodate unexpected houseguests, and she would welcome them. Perhaps he and Magdalena would still end up there, but he would not sleep tonight until he laid before Jacob the injustice his associates had done.

What Christian did not expect was to see Sarah framed in light when the front door opened. Guilt stabbed his gut. He had business in Philadelphia from time to time, but he had never taken the time to see what had become of his younger half sister. He told himself he was not sure of her address since her marriage, but at the moment that excuse sounded thin even to him.

When Sarah opened the door wide, Jacob and Katie were there as well. They all seemed to stare past him, and their jaws dropped.

"May we come in?" Christian asked.

Sarah inhaled sharply then said, "Of course. We're surprised to see you, that's all. Both of you."

"Yes, welcome," Katie was quick to add. "We're eager to hear your news." Her face was turned toward Christian, but her eyes fixed on the young woman behind him.

Christian followed Katie's line of sight. "You remember Magdalena," he said. "She has some interest in the matter that brings me to Irish Creek without the courtesy of a letter first."

"You're welcome anytime." Jacob laid a hand on his brother's shoulder. "Magdalena, you've grown since we last saw you."

Christian looked quizzically at their three hosts.

"Do you not see it, Christian?" Sarah finally said as she gathered their wraps.

"See what?"

"Magdalena is a striking young woman," Jacob said. "She looks just like Maria at that age."

Maria. Christian had not let himself think about his missing sister for years. Had she really run off with that young *English* trapper as everyone supposed, or had she fallen victim to foul play? Had they given up looking for her too soon? If she had come to harm, he would not forgive himself for failing to protect her. And yet if she had run off, it was surely because of his pressure for her to be baptized and join the Amish church. Neither alternative was comforting.

Christian found his words. "I suppose to a father, a daughter's face is her own, but of course I see the resemblance."

Sarah stepped forward and embraced her niece. "You were just a girl when I saw you last. I'm so glad you've come."

"Would you like to see the baby?" Katie held her daughter out to Magdalena, who accepted the squirming, cooing bundle.

"I'll make some coffee," Sarah said. "Have you eaten? Sit down and tell us why you've come so urgently."

Sarah and Katie went into the kitchen, but the door between the rooms remained propped open.

"It's the Patriots," Christian said. "Of late they make it exceedingly difficult to remain people of peace. The British are not much better, but it's the Patriots who have just beaten up Magdalena's young man."

Katie gasped. "I'm sorry to hear that."

"I am, too," Jacob said. "I've been warning you for years that there will be a war."

"I have come to see that you are right," Christian said, "but I do not see how berating Amish young men will resolve the tensions between the Crown and the colonies. Are the Patriots any closer to their goal because they have attacked Nathanael Buerki?"

"War seems to blur the lines of morality," Jacob said.

"If war comes, the Amish will not be part of it. Why should we be pressured—with such extreme means—to take up sides?"

Sarah and Katie returned with a pot of coffee and a platter of bread and cheese. Sarah put some on a plate and offered it to Magdalena.

"Magdalena," Sarah said, "you have barely said a word."

"My father speaks for me," the young woman finally said. "I have been baptized and hope to wed in the Amish church. I want only to live plainly and at peace with everyone."

"I don't know what to say," Jacob said. "Neutrality is going to be virtually impossible." He turned to his sister. "Sarah lives in Philadelphia. The talk is in the streets all the time. Philadelphia is to be the capital of a new nation."

"The General Assembly's official position is for Pennsylvania to oppose independence," Sarah said. "The representatives are mostly Quakers who oppose violence. But few expect that position will hold. When you walk the streets, you can feel the energy for revolt. It flows through all the colonies."

"You must know someone you can talk to, Jacob." Christian's tone grew insistent. "Do what you must. Our father raised us both to listen to our consciences. This would not be the first time you've acted in good conscience when we have not agreed. But violence toward innocent young men? How can Patriots object to the Crown forcing them to pay unjust taxes, yet turn around and attempt to coerce Amish men to betray their beliefs?"

Silence fell over the room. Katie poured coffee.

"They shouldn't," Jacob finally said. "Such actions are contrary to the very notion of freedom."

"Then talk to somebody. I know you have influence here that extends into Lancaster County." Christian gestured at Magdalena. "We will not raise a hand against our attackers, but there must be a peaceable solution."

Jacob and Sarah looked at each other.

"Perhaps between the two of us," Sarah said, "and my husband, of course, we may make some inroads regarding the plain peoples."

Several windows glowed with lamplight as Magdalena approached the big house with her father. She had warm memories of this place.

She remembered Elizabeth, who was not her grandmother but loved her as if she were.

She remembered the broad pleasure on her grandfather Jakob's face when her father brought his children to visit—briefly.

She remembered that her parents were always ready to go home before she was. Magdalena's own mother was kind to Elizabeth, but in a stiff way that Magdalena did not understand even as a child. Her stepmother had never met Elizabeth and was not likely to.

"It's not too late," her father used to say to *Dawdi* Jakob. "If you repent, the church will forgive."

Older now, Magdalena saw that her father had never given up hope that *Dawdi* Jakob would return to the Amish church and bring Elizabeth with him. He loved them both so deeply.

But it did not happen. And now the Bylers who were Amish wanted only peace, while the Bylers who were not Amish were close to the center of the Patriots' revolution.

Six

"I should at least stop by and explain." Annie wiped her hands on her jeans on Saturday morning then picked dust left by her half day's work out of her T-shirt.

"Isn't this the opposite direction than we want to go?" Myra raised an eyebrow.

Seeing her mother standing in Mrs. Weichert's eclectic shop took some getting used to for Annie. Myra wore lightweight designer slacks in a hard-to-match shade of blue that she nevertheless managed to match. With the casual shirt and sweater, she looked as if she had idly thrown the outfit together on a Saturday morning. Annie knew the skill that level of shopping required.

Six months earlier, Annie gave away a walk-in closet full of clothes like that. Now she wore jeans to work because Mrs. Weichert counted on her for lifting and shoving and keeping some order in the storeroom. Her small collection of dressy tees and polo shirts rotated with her work schedule and her new simple life in a hundred-year-old house a few blocks away. The only two dresses hanging in her wardrobe were Amish dresses. She wore them when she visited an Amish family or gathered with the Amish congregation. Annie was determined to sew the next dress herself.

Business in the shop was brisk enough to pass three hours easily. Mrs. Weichert had returned from the estate sale with a tall dresser, a writing desk, and three lamps. Annie had helped unload them and situate them in the storeroom for closer inspection later, finishing just as her parents arrived.

"Franey is expecting me," she said now. "I told you about the quilt. We work on it every Saturday."

"You could call her."

"Mom. Please." Her mother knew the guidelines for using telephones.

"It seems to me this simple life of yours is a little complicated."

"It's only five miles." Annie searched her mental files seeking a route to the Springs that did not require backtracking and making the detour total ten miles.

"I suppose we have no choice. We'll swing by your place to get your things, make this one stop, then we'll be on the road. You'll have time to relax before Penny arrives."

Annie did not remember agreeing to go. But she had not said she wouldn't, so thirty minutes later she sat in the back of her parents' Toyota—new over the winter—and rested her arm on a small canvas bag containing a couple changes of clothing.

She really wanted to spend the afternoon quilting. Penny's plane was still six hours away from touching down.

And there was Rufus. Almost two weeks had passed since their last real conversation, and she missed him.

Outside the car window, trees hastened toward blooms while snow still whitened the slopes of the Sangre de Cristo Mountains. Annie sometimes rode in someone else's car on this road, but her winter in the valley had taught her the rewards of patient observance. Even as the Toyota bore down on the road, something in Annie wanted to scream for her father to slow down even though he was not going all that fast. It was just too fast for the moment.

Inside the car, Myra Friesen listed more possibilities for family fun than the chamber of commerce. Penny was only staying five days. And if Annie knew her sister, Penny was already filling her calendar with catch-up coffee meetings with old friends.

Everything was changing with her parents' sudden personal intersection into Annie's simple life. The whole day. The next week.

Memories stirred. Two successful companies. Technology that set new industry standards. Seizing change and using it for her own advantage. Life in the fast lane.

The choice she made six months ago after she stumbled onto the Beiler family farm to give it all up. The choice her own family did not understand. They might never, she realized.

Annie leaned forward, gripping her father's seat in one hand and pointing with the other. "See the lane? Turn left. It's a long driveway."

Brad Friesen slowed the car and made the turn. Gravel ground under the tires as he let the natural grade of the lane draw the vehicle toward the house.

Annie spotted Franey in the garden. She put her window down and waved. Franey returned the wave then let her hoe drop into the dirt. She made her way toward the vehicle, arriving just as the car came to a stop and wiping her hands on a flour-sack apron.

"You remember my parents? You met once last summer, out at Mo's."

"Yes, of course." Franey leaned in the window and gave the welcoming smile that greeted all guests to her home. "You must come in for some refreshment."

"Thank you. That would be lovely." Annie was out of the car before her mother could protest, though she saw the way her parents looked at each other and slowly exited the car. "Don't you want to see the quilt, Mom? You gave me some scraps for it, remember?"

"Why, yes, that would nice." Myra turned to Franey. "We just have a moment, though, so please don't put yourself out."

"It's no bother. We have a houseful right now anyway." Franey waved an open hand toward her home. "Please come inside."

Annie scanned the wide yard for any sign of Rufus. Even

just a moment alone would bolster her. He was nowhere in sight, though. The door to the workshop was shut tight with no lights showing in the windows. The barn was closed, but Annie realized two horses were missing from the pasture where they usually grazed while they were not out pulling buggies.

"The men are out looking at the work that needs to be done on the Stutzmans' house," Franey said.

Annie held her breath against the urge to sigh and stepped toward the house. "Sorry, Dad. Guess you're stuck with girl talk."

Brad Friesen took his daughter's hand, and Annie returned the squeeze that had always been their secret reassurance.

Inside, Franey said, "Please make yourselves comfortable. I'll clean up a bit and get some iced tea." She disappeared into the kitchen.

Annie watched her mother's eyes move around the room. She knew the questions behind her gaze. The first time she came into the Beilers' home Annie whipped out her iPhone and tapped in an Internet search on Amish bathrooms. Even though her mother had been in Annie's home, which used alternate sources of energy rather than electricity, the curiosity factor was sure to be high in an authentic Amish home.

"It seems quite comfortable." Myra tentatively selected a seat on a sofa and signaled to Brad that he should sit beside her.

"Relax, Mom. I'll get the quilt."

Annie went to the cedar chest under the wide window framing a view of the Sangre de Cristos. Though she grew up in the foothills of the Rockies and had barely noticed them when she lived in the Springs, Annie did not tire of the peaks she now saw every day. She snuck a look while she lifted the lid of the chest and gathered a bundle of Amish hues into her arms. Leaning up against one end of the chest was the lap quilting frame she used each week. Annie picked it up, still reluctant to concede that she could not spend the afternoon quilting.

Across the room Annie dropped the frame into a chair and used both hands to spread the quilt out in the open space, making sure one corner landed in her mother's lap.

"You made this?" Myra slipped one hand under the blue corner and let the fingers of the other hand graze the stitching.

Annie nodded. "It's just nine-patch squares. Nothing fancy to start with. Franey said I could use a treadle machine, but I wanted my first quilt to be handmade."

"The colors are lovely." Myra's expression softened.

"Do you see the brown?" Annie smiled. "That's the dress you made for Penny when she was in the play her senior year."

"I remember. And the dark green is the curtains we used to have in the kitchen. You and Penny were so little then."

Annie pointed to a patch. "There wasn't much of this pink, but I wanted to use it somehow. It was Franey's idea to put it at the center of each nine-patch."

"Did I hear my name?" Franey entered with four glasses of tea on an unadorned wooden tray. She bent slightly for the Friesens to get hold of the drinks then set the tray on a side table and picked up a corner of the quilt still held together with long, evenly spaced basting stitches. "Our Annalise is learning quickly."

Annie sucked on her bottom lip as she watched her mother's reaction to the endearment in Franey's words.

"Annie masters everything she puts her mind to," Myra said, her smile fading and brow furrowing. "It started when she was three and a half and decided to do handstands."

"It is an admirable quality," Franey said. "God blessed us richly when He sent her into our lives. But I'm sure you feel the same way."

Myra reached and covered Annie's hand. "And we hope to have her with us for many more years."

Now Annie sucked her top lip.

"We would love to have you visit us any time you come to Westcliffe to see Annalise," Franey said.

No one but Annie and Penny would recognize the miniscule straightening of Myra's spine, the movement that came just before her mama bear roar.

Annie stood quickly. "My parents surprised me with the news

that my sister is coming home for a few days. They are hoping to have us all together."

Franey raised her eyebrows and turned her lips up. "Yes, you should do that."

The sound of rapid steps brought Edna Stutzman and her three daughters down the front stairs.

"Whose quilt is that?" Beth took the corner of the quilt from Myra's lap.

"These are our houseguests," Franey said. She made introductions quickly. "Annalise was showing her mother the work she has done on her quilt."

"That it explains it then," Beth said. "It is the work of a beginner. At least she's trying hard."

Annie swallowed a retort. *Humble, humble, humble.* "Franey is teaching me every Saturday."

Beth pulled the yardage through her hands in three swift tugs. "I could work on this in the evenings for you. It has potential."

Franey gently lifted the quilt from Beth's hands and folded it properly. "It can wait until Annalise has time. After she spends a few days with her family."

Annie met Franey's eyes. On the sofa, her mother shifted in agitation.

Ike Stutzman put his finger to a chin buried in beard.

Rufus remembered that Ike had been doing that since he was a young man with neither wife nor beard. Ike had a pronounced cleft in his chin and his finger fit there nicely. Rufus was not the only boy to imitate the gesture with a snicker when he was Jacob's age. Doing it once in the presence of his father, though, halted the fun. A month doing the chores of three boys persuaded Rufus that imitation was not all that amusing. But he smiled now at the thought that Ike still put his finger in his chin when he was thinking.

"It sounds like fine land, of course." Ike nodded. "And you

make a good point about participating in community decisions if we are to also benefit from the outcomes."

"I'm glad you see it that way." Rufus nudged the team to a brisker pace. Annalise should be at the house by now, working on her quilt.

"However, in this case it seems a frivolous matter, and I would have to advise against it."

Eli's voice from the bench behind them saved Rufus from having to respond. "Ike, you just got here. You have plenty of other things on your mind."

"It seems like a simple enough matter," Ike said. "We have an abundance of God's handiwork here. Our people do not need hiking trails to see that."

Eli nudged Ike's shoulder. "Perhaps you would get to know some of your neighbors in the process."

Ike's sons also were in the back of the wagon. Rufus wondered where Joel was—again. Joel could at least extend friendship to Mark and Luke while the Stutzmans were their houseguests. Joel's new habit of disappearing from his work in the family fields had reached disconcerting frequency. His father was sure to step in soon.

The horses knew to turn into the lane.

"We have visitors," Eli said when the house came into view.

Ike huffed. "*English.*"

"Our neighbors nevertheless."

Rufus took in the scene. A late-model silver Toyota, spanking clean, parked close to the house. If Annalise was there, she was not alone.

Franey laid the quilt on top of the chest and looked out the window. "The men are back. I should pour more iced tea."

"I'll help you." Annie ignored her mother's helpless gaze, picked up the tray Franey had set aside earlier, and followed Franey into the kitchen. If Rufus put the horses away and came in through the back door she could see him, even if for just a moment.

Franey moved swiftly around the kitchen, setting out glasses, filling them with ice, and pouring cold tea. Annie dawdled with a stack of cloth napkins, running thumb and forefinger over the folded edge of each one before laying it on the tray.

"Don't worry. Rufus will be along." Franey lifted the tray and held it out to Annie.

Annie let out a sigh and returned to the front room to serve the men. Her mother still sat on the sofa, looking unsure of where to let her eyes settle. She was trying not to stare. Annie gave her credit for that much. Her father stood to shake the hands of Eli and Ike, comfortably meeting their gazes.

Ice clinked in glasses as conversation turned to work the Stutzmans needed to do on their new house to make it suitable for an Amish family. Talk of painting made Annie realize she had not seen Rufus yet. While she mentally speculated about where he might be and half listened to talk of propane appliances, she cocked her head for the sound of steps in the kitchen. As long as Annie did not meet her mother's eyes, Myra would not interrupt to urge their departure.

Finally she heard the screen door chink into its framed notch. Excusing herself, Annie picked up several empty tea glasses and headed for the kitchen. Rufus was at the sink washing his hands.

"You've had a busy morning." Annie moved to the sink and set the glasses down. Standing beside him, she looked up.

He rewarded her with a smile. "Looks to me like you've had a change of plans yourself."

Her shoulders sank.

"What is it? Aren't you happy to see your parents?"

"I should be happy. My sister is coming home. My mother wants me to stay with them for a few days."

"Well, that's good. You haven't seen your sister in a long time."

"Not since before. . .all this."

"Last summer, you were the one who persuaded me that I should see my sister Ruth after a year and a half of silence." Rufus reached for a dish towel and dried his hands. "I hate to see you fall into the same trap. You should go."

"I don't know why I'm so nervous. I made a choice. Once we see each other face-to-face, I know Penny will understand." She wanted him to raise his hand to her cheek. Or cover her hand with his. Or smile again. Or something.

He reached into a cupboard for a glass and poured the last of the tea into it. And yet he said nothing more.

"Well," Annie finally said. "They're waiting. I guess I should go."

He nodded then dumped the cold drink down his gullet.

When she heard the swish of skirts, Annie turned to see Beth standing in the doorway to the dining room. She crossed her arms on her chest, suddenly self-conscious that she was wearing jeans and a tee.

Beth smiled, her eyes fixed on Rufus. "I'm glad you're back. But don't get too comfortable. Your *mamm* and my *mamm* suggest that you give me a tour of the area this afternoon. Once I know my way around, I'll be able to help with errands."

Annie glanced at Rufus, who caught her eye. "I've just put the horses away," he said.

"But it's a fine day for a ride in an open cart. Little Jacob would love to go with us. He's such a beautiful boy." Beth smoothed her rich blue dress.

"Perhaps Lydia and Sophie would like to take you," Rufus said.

"They seem to be busy today." Beth tugged one prayer *kapp* string.

Rufus shifted his weight.

He was going to do it. Annie heard it in the way he softly cleared his throat. Rufus was going to take Beth Stutzman on a tour.

She broke her pose. "I should see how my parents are getting along."

Seven

Ruth Beiler let her overstuffed dark green backpack plop onto her narrow bed. She rolled her shoulders, trying to urge out the hunch of nine hours in the university library staring at textbooks and computer screens.

The corner of the letter stuck out of the tall zippered compartment on the side of the bag. Looking at it, Ruth pressed her lips together. Then she turned her back on it, going instead to the narrow counter where she kept an electric kettle. She rattled the kettle.

Empty.

Ruth walked across the four-room suite to a sink and filled the kettle.

"Hey, Beiler!"

Ruth looked up to see the young woman who had moved into the suite in the middle of the spring term. Lauren sat on the love seat in the common area with her booted feet propped up on the coffee table. As usual, she wore fatigues. Though the brown T-shirt fit snugly, the camouflage pants generally were baggy and held in place by a belt.

"Hi, Lauren. Did you hear from your brother today?"

Lauren tipped her blond head in a practiced gesture. "Yep. He has a month's leave before being reassigned for his new tour. I'll see him next weekend."

"I'm so glad for you."

Lauren stood, and Ruth saw once again the uneven gait that had resulted from a fractured kneecap—and which kept Lauren out of the army herself. Her father, an officer stationed at Fort Carson in Colorado Springs, had served three tours in Iraq. Her brother, stationed out of North Carolina, had been abroad for most of the last two years.

Despite Lauren's enthusiasm for all things military, she was Ruth's favorite suitemate. Neither of them dressed to fit in. Lauren favored her army clothes, and Ruth dressed in long skirts and modest blouses.

Ruth lifted the full kettle. "I was about to make tea. Want some?"

Lauren shook her head and let her feet thud to the floor. "My study group is meeting in a few minutes. I should get my junk together and go."

"Another time, then." Ruth stepped toward her room. "It would be good to chat."

"Tomorrow night."

Ruth looked up again. "Tea tomorrow?"

Lauren shook her head. "Let's go out. Dinner will be my treat."

"Oh." Ruth could not find a place to fix her eyes, except on the kettle in one hand. "I probably should stay in. I have an exam on Tuesday morning."

"You need to let loose, Beiler. Just relax for a change. Between your classes and your job at the nursing home, you never take a minute for yourself. Let's get a decent meal."

"Maybe we should decide tomorrow." Ruth had never been out on a Sunday night, except for the singings at home. Going to a restaurant did not seem like keeping the Sabbath.

Lauren laughed. "When my parents say something like that, they mean no. But I'm not going to let you get away with that, Beiler."

Ruth rubbed the end of a sleeve between thumb and forefinger. "We'll talk about it tomorrow."

Back in her room, she plugged in the kettle, took a tea bag out of the box, and dropped it in a mug.

The letter tugged at her.

Elijah's tight, meticulous script had brushed her heart when she removed the envelope from her student mailbox. It was not his first. In the last six months, he had written four times and he lost no opportunity to make plain his undimmed affection for her. More than affection. Love. The difference was that this letter was the first since she replied to one of his.

Almost as soon as she pushed her letter through the slot in the sidewalk mailbox, Ruth regretted it. She had not written anything particularly personal, certainly not a true expression of her own feelings. But writing at all would encourage Elijah, and that was wrong. He was a baptized member of the Amish church, and she had run out on her baptism.

Run out on Elijah. Run out on the future they dreamed of.

How he could still feel anything for her after that, she would never understand. There was no going back. While she still felt plain at heart and lived simply, she would never go back to the Amish church. God had made her to be a nurse, and she intended to answer the call. She refused to be the reason for Elijah to break his vows to the church.

The kettle whistled, and Ruth once again turned away from the unopened letter.

Penny's flight was fourteen minutes early.

Annie stood between her parents just beyond the security line on the main level of the twelve-gate Colorado Springs airport. Her mother had been tracking Penny's flights on her phone since before she left Seattle. In front of them, an eager three-year-old sighted his grandmother among the disgorgement of plane passengers. Calling and running toward her, he violated the security zone. Though his father snatched him back, it was too late. The alarm blared, startling everyone. The boy wailed briefly but instantly settled when his grandmother reached for him.

Business travelers looking for drivers holding signs with their names.

Families dragging strollers and diaper bags.

Solo passengers looking lost and weary.

And people like Penny, who strode at a confident clip pulling pilot cases behind them and knowing exactly where they were going.

In the moment that she hugged her sister, Annie was glad she had come home with her parents. She did not often admit to herself that she missed Penny—especially since she had given up using a cell phone and e-mail—but she did.

"Did you check a bag?" Brad Friesen asked his eldest daughter.

Penny tapped her carry-on. "Everything's in here."

Brad took over towing the bag. Myra had one arm around Penny's shoulder as they stepped side by side onto the escalator that went down to the exit. Annie pulled up the rear, feasting her eyes on this family she loved. Her throat thickened with the thought that her choices might well separate her from them.

Sumptuous. That was the only word Annie could think of to describe dinner at the downtown restaurant. In the candlelight, her mother's face lit with the bliss of having her family together. Myra had raised two daughters to be independent and take care of themselves. When she shared a table with them once again, though, a newness flushed across her face. Sitting across from Myra, Annie realized how much she loved seeing her mother look this way.

"I have presents," Penny said as soon as they passed, satiated, through the front door of their home.

Annie smiled. Penny never came home without gifts. Annie used to think it was because Penny felt guilty for living so far away. Over the years, though, she came to see that generosity spilled out of most of what Penny did. Why she had not realized this as a child, Annie did not know. She supposed she was too busy being the competitive little sister.

Penny unzipped a front pocket of her bag and extracted several small packages. To her father she presented a soft leather e-reader cover case.

"We both know you want it," Penny said.

While Brad turned the cover over in his hands, Penny handed Myra a small bottle of perfume.

Annie knew the bottle had not come cheap. She used to buy the same scent herself. Myra raised her eyebrows and flashed Penny a smile.

Then Penny turned to Annie. "I saw this and thought of you. You're the only one I know who has the figure for this dress."

Annie gulped. A dress? She had not worn any dress but Amish dresses in so long she hardly knew what it felt like. Her hands trembling slightly, Annie took the lightweight flat package from Penny. How could she possibly wear anything Penny gave her now?

A gasp shot past Annie's best intentions as she raised the dress by the shoulders and saw how it shook out and found its drape. It was silk. Good quality silk. A rich red in color, the dress had a modest V neckline and cap sleeves. At the waist, the fabric overlapped itself and gathered to one side, where a small gold buckle was the only adornment.

"Oh, Penny!"

Myra slid a careful hand against the back of the dress, and Annie watched her mother's face. Was it only a few hours ago that she had laid her clumsy quilt in her mother's lap? Suddenly everything about Annie's new life seemed frumpy and unskilled.

"It's spectacular, Penny." Annie handled the dress gently, cautious to keep it on the white paper it had been wrapped in rather than let it brush against the roughness of her jeans. If she snagged it, Penny could not take it back.

"It will look spectacular on you," Penny said.

"Penny, it's so generous! And gorgeous. But I don't see. . .well, under the circumstances, it would not be practical for me to keep it."

"It won't hurt to try it on."

Penny raised her eyebrows. Annie knew that look.

"Just try it on," her mother urged. "Those black heels you used to love are still in the closet of your bedroom."

"I'll help you put your hair up," Penny said.

Annie closed her eyes briefly before saying, "Okay." For a few minutes she could go back in time to the sisterly habits of fifteen years ago. What harm would it do?

Thirty minutes later, Annie stood in front of the full-length mirror attached to the closet door of her childhood closet. She hardly recognized herself.

For the last eight months, she had let her hair grow uncut. She wore it either in a ponytail or braided and twisted back in the disciplined Amish style Franey taught her. Penny had swept it high on her head, leaving tendrils to frame her face. The dress fit as though Annie had been the model for the pattern. Cool, sleek silk against her skin set off sensory reactions she thought were long gone. The bodice covered well, yet left no doubt of the form beneath it. The skirt fell just above her knees. When she stepped into the black heels, the muscles in her calves found old memories.

"You. Look. Fantastic." Penny grinned.

Annie grimaced but said, "I do, don't I?"

"You have to show Mom."

"You go ahead. I'll be right out."

Penny left, and Annie tried out several angles in the mirror. If only Rufus could see her now.

Annie had never had trouble getting a man to kiss her if she wanted him to—until Rufus. She waited weeks—even months—between kisses, then afterward, invariably, he seemed sorry. He did not say he was sorry, but why else would he wait so long before doing it again? If he saw her now, he would come close and brush a tendril from her face and bring his lips close to hers. His hands would go to her waist as his mouth found hers.

Annie shuddered, ashamed. The image in her mind was everything Rufus was not. How could she even consider trying to make him kiss her like that? She pulled one pin, and then another. Her hair tumbled free around her shoulders.

"What's taking so long?" Penny stood in the doorway. "Wow. I think I like your hair down even better."

Annie did, too. Setting her hair loose only made her miss Rufus more sharply.

"Come show Mom."

Annie complied, feeling every bit as beautiful as her family told her she was. What she had not expected was to love the feeling.

Her father had been the first to fade, and her mother soon followed after securing agreement from everyone to attend church in the morning. They had not been to church together as a family in—Annie was not sure how many years.

After their parents turned in, Penny ensconced herself on Annie's bed and leaned against the wall with a bowl of popcorn.

Annie straightened the red dress on the hanger and put it in the closet. She rummaged through the old clothes. "I didn't think we'd be going to church. I didn't bring anything to wear."

"Excuse me! Did you not just hang up a smokin' hot dress?"

"For church?"

"Why not? No plunging neckline. No bare shoulders."

Annie moved a few more hangers before admitting that everything in the closet was, well, too high school. Why hadn't her mother given this stuff away years ago? "I could probably wear nice jeans."

"You're wearing the dress, girl. It will turn a few heads."

"Maybe I don't want to turn heads." Annie let her hand drift over the red silk one more time before closing the door.

Penny tilted her head back and dropped several popped kernels into her mouth. "So how serious are you about this Amish thing?"

"I'm figuring that out."

"I don't think Mom is taking it all that well."

"No kidding."

"Is it Rufus? Is that it? You can't be with him if you're not Amish?"

Heat crept up the back of Annie's neck. "Well, that's part of it." With more notice that she would see her sister face-to-face, she might have prepared her words better. "But it's more."

Penny shifted on the bed, meeting Annie's eyes.

"I was wired into everything before I met the Beilers," Annie continued.

"Technology, having it all. Lots of money. But was I happy?"

"I guess I've been gone too long," Penny said. "I didn't know you were unhappy."

"I didn't know myself." Annie picked up a throw pillow left from her adolescent purple phase and sat on the bed. "It hasn't been easy to unplug, but most of the time I think it's worth it."

"Most of the time?"

Annie licked her lips. "I have moments. But simplicity has more moments."

"Can't you just live a simpler life without giving everything up? No law requires you to own a big-screen TV. What's so evil about electricity?"

"No one says it's evil. But electricity—or texting constantly or owning a car—means you can escape to another place at a whim. The thing that makes the Amish strong is the community that brings them together, because they can't leave at a whim."

"Dad doesn't seem too rattled, but I don't know how you'll ever persuade Mom."

"I know." Annie fiddled with mementos from college that still lay on the dresser. "If I do become Amish, I don't want it to be just on the outside. I have to find out if I can really see the world as the Amish do."

"And if you can? Then you can be with Rufus?"

Eight

July 1775

*N*o matter how old she got, Magdalena never got used to
the feel of a *kapp* on her head at the height of summer. Once
she got clear of the house, she stopped to set the basket of quilt
remnants on the ground and remove her *kapp*. If corn had eyes
instead of ears, perhaps the hearty crop would tattle on her. As
it was, Magdalena could brush undetected through rows of her
father's corn almost as tall as she was. After she crossed the creek
onto the land that belonged to Nathanael's family, she would put
the *kapp* back in place.

The quilt fabrics were a ruse. Magdalena did not even enjoy
quilting. It was a fact of life. Somebody had to piece together a
family's bedding, and no Amish woman would think to marry
without at least rudimentary skill. Magdalena had learned early
and well from her mother before she passed. Only last year
Magdalena was hard at work on the quilt she hoped would cover
the bed she and Nathanael would share as man and wife. She
finished it, stored it carefully in a cedar chest, and waited for his
proposal.

Yet, after the attack, the wedding season passed with no
further mention of marriage from Nathan's lips. In another couple
of months, this year's couples would begin having their banns

read at the close of worship. No doubt every other Sunday would herald some new pair. Everyone acted as if they did not know who would become engaged, but of course the banns were seldom a true surprise.

Magdalena stopped in the middle of the cornfield and rubbed the heels of her hands into her eye sockets. Hard. She had hoped for last year—or this year at the latest. Nathan had his own land and was a wise farmer who learned well from the experience of his father and uncles. His farm was not large by standards of the Conestoga Valley, but it was a solid start. Everyone said he had a gift for the land, just as Magdalena's father did. Their families cared for each other. No one would stand in the way of their marriage.

Except the Patriots.

Nathan never talked about what happened that day. At first, Magdalena told herself he needed more time. When he was ready, he would tell her what happened, what they had done to him, how awful it had been, how he had refused to retaliate, how he stood strong as a peaceful man of God. She would comfort him and be proud of him.

No. Not proud. *Ordnung* did not allow pride in any form.

She could care for him and tell him he did the right thing.

But Nathanael never talked about the experience, not to Magdalena and not to anyone. Rather than looking forward to marriage and living in his own house, Nathanael seemed increasingly content with the room he had shared with his brothers growing up. As the youngest, he was the only one left living under their parents' roof, and he showed no restlessness with the arrangement.

Magdalena bunched up her *kapp* in her hand and threw it against the ground. With the ties splayed in two directions, it looked pitifully innocent, and Magdalena instantly filled with regret. Repenting, she snatched it out of the dirt and put it back on her head.

She did not know how to pray anymore.

She straightened her dress, took several deep breaths, and

adjusted the basket of cloth on her hip. Nathanael's mother would appreciate the gift of the scraps. Magdalena made up her mind right then that even if she did not get to see Nathanael, she would not regret bringing the gift. It was not too late to make it a sincere offering.

"How is he?" Magdalena asked when Nathan's mother welcomed her into the summer kitchen half an hour later.

The older woman shrugged. "He's been out to the fields this morning, but he's back now. I heard him talking to his father about the extra help they will need to get the harvest in."

"Surely they still have a few weeks to sort that out."

"Between the two farms, it's a great deal of work," Mrs. Buerki said.

What she did not say was that her youngest son did not always carry his share of the load anymore, but Magdalena understood. In the summer kitchen, they were far enough from the main house to speak freely, but after ten months, little remained to be said about Nathanael.

Despite the heat of the hearth, the summer kitchen's limestone walls kept the structure reasonably cool—for which Magdalena was grateful after her walk in the sun. A door propped open at each end allowed the air to move.

She set the basket of fabrics on the worktable. "I thought you might want to go through these and see if you can use anything."

Mrs. Buerki's eyes brightened. "Did I tell you I'm to be *grootmoeder* again?"

Magdalena's eyes widened as her heart sank. Another of Nathanael's brothers was having *kinner* before she and Nathanael were even married. It was probably Obadiah and Esther, but she could not bring herself to ask. "Then you'll need to start a new quilt," she managed to say. "There's plenty here for a babe."

The gray-haired woman smiled briefly. "Go on in the house, Maggie. He'll be pleased to see you today, I think."

Magdalena nodded and stepped out into bright sunlight again. She crossed the yard and tapped lightly on the open door at the back of the main house. "Is anyone home?"

"In here." Nathan's voice sounded bright, but she knew that his tone was not always a promise of his mood.

She loved him. She could not imagine not loving him. Though Nathanael usually seemed glad to see her, he had not asked her to ride with him to a singing since before the attack. Whatever hope for the future they held between them last year had weakened like coals spread too thin. Nathanael was jumpy and wild eyed at times, sparking the nickname Nutty Nathan l. No one ever called him that to his face, of course, but Magdalena fumed nevertheless.

Nathan sat at the table beside a cold hearth, and Magdalena took a seat opposite him.

She could not stay long. She wished she could sit all day with him even if he did not speak to her again, but her chores would not allow such indulgence. Her older brother and sister were married now and in their own homes, leaving Magdalena to help with the younger children. Babsi was with child again, though so ill that the midwife feared the child would come far too early to survive.

For now, she decided to give herself half an hour to sit with the man she loved.

"Are you hungry?" Magdalena asked. "I am sure your *mamm* would not mind if I fixed you something to eat."

He shook his head then turned to gaze out the window.

"You must be tired from being in the fields in the sun." Magdalena searched his face for any encouragement.

Nathan crossed his arms and cradled his own elbows. "You are kind to come."

"Of course I came."

"I know I disappoint you, Maggie."

"No, you don't. You couldn't." She reached across the table, but he did not grasp her hand.

"Are you sure you want to do this?"

Jacob met Sarah's gaze and answered evenly, "Yes."

"It could be dangerous," she said. "Your movements may come under scrutiny."

"I am aware."

"My husband will help you however he can."

"Emerson is a fine man, Sarah."

"I've always thought so. But there's *Mamm* to think of."

"I'll be careful. *Mamm* will be in no danger."

"You may be overstating your case." Sarah tugged at the canvas covering the load in Jacob's wagon. "I hate to think what might happen if you get stopped."

"Who would stop me? The British have their hands full trying to keep their grip on Boston. That only makes our work more imperative. We must move while we have opportunity."

" 'Our work'? Is that what it is now?"

Jacob leaned forward and kissed Sarah's cheek. "We're in this together, you and I."

"Christian will be horrified."

Jacob's jaw hardened. "Last year he came here with Magdalena and asked me to do something."

"I hardly think this was what he had in mind."

"The question must be resolved so we can get on with our lives. Boston is only the beginning. If we let the British have Boston, we're done for." Jacob swung himself up into the wagon's seat and picked up the reins. As he pulled away from Sarah's stately Philadelphia home, he resolved to return to his own land the long way—by way of the Conestoga Valley. It was better to stay off the main thoroughfare between Philadelphia and Berks County anyway, and honesty was the best route with his brother as well.

Christian flipped back the canvas and flicked his eyes toward Jacob. "That is a great deal of saltpeter."

Jacob nodded.

"You can only have one end in mind for such a load."

Again, Jacob nodded.

"Jacobli, this saltpeter will produce far more gunpowder than your household requires. Remember that I once hunted the hills of Berks County alongside you."

"If you want me to state my intentions, I will." Jacob cleared his throat. "Though we differ in our acts of conscience, I don't intend to deceive you."

"You're making gunpowder for the Patriots." Christian slapped the canvas back in place then caught himself. He would not allow Jacobli's choices to provoke his temper.

"The colonists *are* going to fight the Crown," Jacob said. "But they can't hope to be successful if they must continue to depend on the French for gunpowder. We must have our own supply."

Christian's belly heated. He prayed regularly and fervently for Jacobli and all his siblings to find the way of peace. Would God never answer?

"The land behind the tannery is more than suitable for a powder mill," Jacob said. "It's a good distance away from any other families, and it will be easy to hide the operation if need be. Having the creek so near is an advantage as well."

Christian could hardly bear the thought. Beautiful Irish Creek, once a thriving Amish settlement, was reduced to this.

"*Daed* swore an oath to the Crown you now defy," Christian said. "I was there that day. I heard it for myself."

"*Daed* could not have foreseen the events of the last thirty-five years." Jacob was unbending. "I thought you were not taking sides."

"I'm not." Christian swallowed his frustration. Jacob had always had a way of using Christian's own words to provoke him. "Of course I shall remain neutral."

"Christian, this is the best way to put an end to the kind of danger your Maggie's young man faced."

"By arming the perpetrators? I fail to see the logic."

"We will put an end to this war before it can spread beyond Boston. The Patriots will have what they want. Establishing a new nation will leave them little time to harass peaceful Amish farmers about their lack of loyalty."

"Peaceful Amish farmers are very loyal, Jacob. It's only that we seek to serve a higher power."

"My gunpowder will ensure that you can continue to do so." Jacob stared at Christian, unmoved.

"You'd better go, Jacob. I don't want Magdalena to see what you have in your wagon."

Nine

Annie wore the red dress to church.

She scrounged up a pair of shoes with lower heels and tamed her hair demurely with a silver clip at the base of her neck, but she wore the dress.

The Friesens sat together in a pew about halfway back in the sanctuary. When Annie was young, the family attended church a couple of times a month. During high school, her training program and track competitions almost always interfered with church events aimed at teenagers. She had a few friends who had gone to the same church, and they had stayed in touch in a general way. But since she had given up Facebook and Twitter, she no longer tracked the path of their lives. And explaining her new life to anyone? Complicated.

The lively contemporary music, with a six-piece band and a concert-quality sound system, made Annie feel out of practice. She tried to sing the unfamiliar songs, but she could not bring herself to clap as others around her did. Her months of worshipping with the Amish had left their mark. The time to sit for the sermon came as some relief. And at least the sermon would be in English. She would not have to strain to follow High German.

This was a church week for the Amish in the hills around

Westcliffe. Annie wished she had missed an off weekend instead. The congregation would sing hymns. Long hymns. Slow hymns. Time-to-think hymns. And then two of the men would give sermons.

Brushing aside the image of Rufus sitting among the men, Annie reached for a Bible in the rack in front of her and found the passage listed in the bulletin. Wedged between her mother and her sister, she felt both of them looking at her out of the side of their eyes. Annie did not give them the satisfaction of turning her head. She had a lot to learn about the Bible, and she might as well take advantage of an English service. Rufus often referred to a Bible verse and Annie hardly ever knew what he was talking about. She could change that if she tried.

They stood for one last song, and that was when Annie saw him. Randy Sawyer. What was he doing here? Across the aisle, he turned his head toward her and smiled. Annie jerked her head back to the large screen displaying the words of the song. When the music ended, and the pastor gave a final blessing, Annie stretched out the process of returning the borrowed Bible to its place. If she had been alone, she would have exited the pew at the far end, but with no escape from the path her family was taking toward the center aisle, she was face-to-face with her college boyfriend ninety seconds later.

"Are you visiting Colorado Springs?" She shook Randy's hand awkwardly and stepped away from her family. Thankfully, they continued greeting other people down the aisle, and would not hear her awkward fumbling.

"I live here now," he said. "New job." He named a technology firm she knew well and pulled out a business card.

"Oh. The Springs is a beautiful place to live." She could not help looking at the fingers of his left hand. No ring. She hated that she did that.

He nodded. "You look beautiful yourself."

Annie flushed and moved one hand down the silky skirt. Randy Sawyer had never needed a silk dress to want to kiss her—

and much more. She moistened her lips, unsure what to say next. The crowd thinned around them.

"I've heard that you've done quite well since college." Randy put one hand in a pocket.

Annie nodded. Randy did not seem nearly as unnerved by this encounter as she was. Had he selectively forgotten their frequent furtive quests to find some place on campus to be alone, and what they had done when they found those places?

"I read that you sold your business last year," he said, "but I lost track of what you went on to next."

She lifted her shoulders slightly. "I'm slowing down. Trying to enjoy life."

He smiled. "If the reports I heard are anywhere close to true, you should be able to enjoy life quite comfortably."

She had no response. What was she supposed to say? *I gave away my fortune and despite what this dress might imply, I'm thinking of becoming Amish?*

"Annie," he said, "I want you to know that I've grown up since college. I know we didn't always make the best choices in our relationship, and I'm sorry."

She put her hands up, palms out. "We made those choices together."

He nodded. "It's good to see you, Annie. Be happy." He leaned in and kissed her cheek.

Buried sensations stirred. Annie's breath caught as she watched her first love turn and walk up the aisle of the church. She closed her fingers over his card.

Rufus sank into the Adirondack chair on the front porch, closed his eyes, and inhaled deeply. The spring mountain air heralded late-afternoon rain. If a storm rolled through, Rufus wanted to be right in that spot to watch it. The porch was deep enough and the overhang broad enough to keep storm watchers dry.

He opened his eyes to conduct his daily study of vegetation

on the slopes of the Sangre de Cristos. Evergreens and snow kept shifting colors on the mountains all winter long, but rushing weeks of spring left pale green hues that Rufus waited for all year. On the Sabbath, with the worship service and shared meal finished, he could sit as long as he liked breathing in the fragrance of a new season.

Rufus grimaced slightly at the sound of the front door opening behind him. Clattering footsteps meant at least some Stutzmans were among the entourage about to burst into his peace. Rufus was still getting used to the added commotion in the house.

His mother appeared—and right behind her Beth and Johanna Stutzman.

"There is a singing tonight, *ya?*" Franey looked at her son expectantly.

"*Ya, Mamm.* At the Millers'."

"*Gut.* It will be a good time for the Stutzmans to get to know other young people."

Beth pushed past her sister. "I would love to go. It would be the first singing in our new community."

"I'm sure you would be welcome," Rufus said.

"Then it's settled," Franey said. "Rufus will take you in the big buggy."

Rufus startled and sat up a little straighter. He felt too old for the biweekly singings and seldom went. His mother knew that. More than a year had passed since his last time.

Before Annalise.

Franey began to count on her fingers. "Rufus, Beth, Johanna, Essie, Lydia, Sophie, Joel, Mark, Luke. You'll need both buggies. Joel can drive the smaller one with the boys and you can take the larger one with the girls."

Rufus blinked blandly, seeing no gracious way out of this. "I suppose we should plan to leave about five."

Franey and Johanna withdrew into the house. Beth settled into the chair beside Rufus. "This will be the first singing ever for Mark and Luke. Perhaps they are too young to think of pairing off, but they can at least meet some of the other boys."

Rufus refrained from pointing out that the other boys would be older than Beth's brothers, as would the girls. He supposed it could not hurt for all the Stutzman children to at least learn the names of others they would worship with every two weeks.

"I didn't know it would be so beautiful in Colorado." Beth's eyes were on the mountains.

"It's a different kind of beautiful than Pennsylvania."

"I think it's spectacular. It's a wonderful place for a new settlement."

Beth's face glowed with enthusiasm. Rufus wondered whether to believe her.

"We've had to learn to farm differently," he said.

"Of course it will be hard work." Beth nodded earnestly. "But the land is beautiful, and my parents are so pleased that they will be able to help Mark and Luke have property of their own when the time comes. I hope my brothers can find something half as beautiful as your land."

Rufus was not blind. Beth was the prettiest of the Stutzman sisters. Not a hair was out of place on Beth's head. Her *kapp* perched perfectly, and her clear eyes and rosy complexion brightened any room she entered. She also was an expert quilter and had prepared last night's dinner for fourteen all on her own. More than once his mother had mentioned in Rufus's hearing how helpful Beth was around the house while her family stayed there, which was high praise for only two days' time.

He knew his mother liked Annalise, but did she think he did not have it in him to choose her over an Amish girl? Whatever she was afraid of, pushing Beth Stutzman on him was not the answer.

A vocalist and a four-piece band all crowded onto a small performance stage in one corner of the restaurant.

Ruth Beiler's heart pounded harder than the beat of the music. She was in a restaurant on the Sabbath.

Lauren took her to a small artsy restaurant downtown, which somehow increased Ruth's sense of guilt. Twice already Lauren had been mistaken for a soldier by people eager to thank her for her service to their country. Lauren was quick to explain that wearing fatigues was her way of showing support for her father and her brother, but she basked in conversation about the military with anyone. Ruth hoped Lauren's family members would be safe, but beyond that she hardly knew what to say. Her family never spoke of the military, and Lauren seemed to speak a language foreign to Ruth. Munitions and weaponry and incendiaries and military acronyms and abbreviations.

"See? Isn't this better than being stuck in the dorm?" Lauren stabbed her blackened trout and moved an ambitious bite toward her mouth.

Ruth let out her breath and smiled. Sabbath or not, she was here. She might as well enjoy it.

When Ruth ordered a salad, she expected a modest bowl of greens. Instead she faced a plate heaped with fresh spinach, red peppers, feta cheese, and grilled salmon.

And she liked it. Her fork crunched through a pepper slice and into four spinach leaves. As Ruth lifted it to her mouth, she wondered how difficult it was to grow spinach in Colorado. Ruth knew she could buy fresh spinach at dozens of grocery stores or farmers' markets in Colorado Springs. Still, the ingrained question of growing her own food, as her family always had, popped up at odd moments. Perhaps someday she would live in a place where she could serve as a nurse and still grow vegetables. She missed her mother's garden.

"I know you take the bus around town," Lauren said. "You could borrow my car if you ever get in a jam."

Ruth swallowed hard. "Thank you, but I don't have a license."

"No license?"

"I do have a permit." Ruth savored the tang of vinaigrette on her tongue. "A friend at work was teaching me, but her husband got transferred to Kansas City."

"Well, we'll work on that starting tonight. You can drive home."

Ruth inhaled. "No. I would be too nervous. I've never driven in the dark."

"Everyone has to learn to drive at night." Lauren maneuvered her fork with one hand and tapped the other on the tabletop in rhythm with the band's beat.

Their conversation dangled as the music's presence filled the room. Ruth realized she was tapping a foot. The music, a ballad of lost love, tugged its soft beat out of her. She watched the drummer, and her foot met his tempo. The vocalist sang with her eyes closed and a fist over her heart, as if she were singing her own heartbreak.

Ruth thought of the words in Elijah's letter, the most candid of all the letters so far. *So far.* How could she consider continuing this correspondence? She would surely break his heart.

Again.

Ten

"Y ou're going out?" Two days later, Annie set the last of the lunch dishes in the sink and looked at her sister.

"I'll be back before dinner." Penny took a set of keys off a hook. "Mom said she couldn't get out of her committee meeting, but Mrs. Metzger is picking her up. I figure I can use her car."

"To do what?"

"Gonna catch up with Mahalia. She has the scoop on everybody from high school."

"Oh. Okay." Annie had not thought she would find a moment alone during this visit. Suddenly the afternoon yawned wide.

"It's already Tuesday. My visit will be over before I blink twice. I'd better grab the chance while I have it." The keys jangled in Penny's hand. "Did you want to go somewhere? There's always your car."

"I don't drive it. You know that. It's up on blocks."

"Nope. It's in the garage right next to Mom's."

"But the tires are probably low on air."

"They looked fine to me."

Penny led the way into the garage, pressed the button to lift the garage door, and got in the new silver Toyota. Annie waved as Penny backed out. Annie's blue Prius was indeed in the garage.

When had her father taken it off the lifts and filled the tires?

Back in the kitchen, Annie stared at the lone key still on its hook.

Rufus dipped his brush in the paint and stroked a muted seafoam shade onto the trim around an interior door.

"Did anybody talk to Elijah Capp?"

The sonorous voice of the bishop rose above the hum of people working to get the house ready for the Stutzmans to inhabit. Rufus glanced around the dining room, where three young Amish men were painting walls. They did not interrupt their rhythms. Rufus leaned around a ladder to see Bishop Troyer standing in the living room with his sleeves rolled up and his thumbs hooked in his suspenders.

"Elijah is coming this afternoon," someone finally said. "He doesn't think it will take very long to do the conversions. Not more than two days."

The bishop nodded. Rufus dipped his brush again. With a crew of a dozen Amish men, the painting progressed swiftly. Rufus had set aside his own work for the day, as had all the others. This sacrifice meant the Stutzmans would be in their own home soon and not living among a deluge of paint cans, ladders, and spackle tools.

Rufus glanced around. Where was Joel? he wondered. Joel was supposed to come down as soon as he and Jacob looked after the animals.

And what about Mark and Luke? This was to be their home, but they were nowhere in sight.

Neither Eli nor Ike had said anything about their missing sons, but Rufus could not help watching the pair of fathers closely for signs that they noticed the absence of the boys as the morning wore on. The women would come with lunch soon.

"I hear Elijah is eager to take up with the *English* on their project to make a park."

On the surface, Old Ezra's words were a simple remark, but Rufus heard their meaning.

"The project has merit." Eli Beiler wiped paint off the side of his hand.

"Bah!" Ike had his mind made up. "Ezra is right. It is an *English* project."

"It doesn't have to be."

Rufus smiled slightly at his father's persistence. Eli could be every bit as stubborn as Ike.

Gideon and Joshua stopped their brushes and turned toward the conversation. From across the room, Samuel and Levi did the same. Opinions rushed through the discussion.

"We should mind our own business."

"They invited us to help. We will offend if we don't."

"They do not yet understand what it means that we live apart and have nothing to do with the *English* ways."

"We'll be using the land. Why should we not help care for it?"

"We use it only if we choose to. We can choose not to."

"I still say we should mind our own business. That is our way."

"That land is right between several Amish farms. Of course they want our cooperation."

"No need to be uncharitable."

"Who is in charge, anyway?"

"So far, it is just talk. No one is named as leader."

Rufus dipped his brush yet again and continued working on the trim.

"The word in town is that Karl Kramer wants to have a hand in it," Old Ezra said.

"Karl Kramer! He hasn't had a kind word to say about any of us since we got here. I cannot believe he wants us to share in the work."

"All the more reason to mind our own business. I don't trust Karl Kramer."

"I've never even met the man."

"Don't think he wants to meet us. Don't forget what he did to our Rufus last year."

Rufus stiffened.

Ike moved toward Rufus. "What is this business about?"

"It's nothing," Rufus said.

"He tried to kill you," Old Ezra said.

Ike raised his eyebrows.

Rufus dabbed at the wall. "He is just uncertain about us because he does not know us."

"And if we live apart as we should, we don't have to know him."

"Rufus," the bishop said, "I'd like to hear what you think about this."

Rufus set his paintbrush down and turned toward the center of the room. Every eye was on him.

"I think," he said, "that undoubtedly we will use the land. Our young people, in particular, look for recreation—a picnic, a hike, a safe place for outings or courting. Even if a new park were not situated between several of our farms, we would use it. Many of the people in town are happy to have us here. Almost everyone in this room hires Tom Reynolds for taxiing and hauling, and he is one of the people who would like to see a new park. Since they have invited us, I see no harm in responding to the gesture of friendship."

For a few minutes, the room was still and silent. Then a few boots shuffled. The bishop cleared his throat but did not speak.

"If Rufus were in charge, I would do it," Gideon said.

Around the room, murmurs of agreement buzzed. Rufus stifled a sigh. He had no intention of leading anything.

"There's an enormous boulder smack in the middle of that land," Samuel observed. "Are they planning to move it?"

"It's too big to yank out with a tractor."

"There's always dynamite."

"Or leave it alone."

"It's a mistake to get involved." Ike crossed his arms.

Rufus dipped his brush and reached for the trim above the door.

Old Ezra gripped a ladder and moved it to a new spot. "Where is that younger boy of yours, Eli? He's tall enough that he could be of some help around here."

Annie spun on her heel and left the kitchen. No point standing there staring at the key. She had not driven her Prius in six months. The only reason she still owned it was to placate her mother's hope that her lifestyle change was temporary.

The house was empty. Even the cat was nowhere in sight. Her mother's committee meeting would consume the afternoon. Her father seldom was home from work before six. Penny would gab the afternoon away with her childhood best friend.

For the last three days, Annie had used electricity freely. When she walked into a room, she flipped the light switch without thinking about where the power came from. When the dishwasher was full, she turned it on. When the telephone rang and she was nearest to it, she answered. She stayed up late and watched two movies with Penny, complete with microwave popcorn. When her mother's computer froze, Annie knew just what to do to get it going again. Her hair hung freely around her face and shoulders, and she was glad for the furnace that fired up when the overnight temperatures dipped below forty. She did not think twice about the photos her mother snapped constantly. Annie wore comfortable jeans—except for the red dress—and not once did she have to stumble over choosing the right German word or get hopelessly lost in a dinner conversation.

It was surprisingly easy to be at home. Comfortable. Automatic. And in this situation, being *English* was the most peaceful option.

Annie could find something to read and pass a quiet afternoon until her family returned.

Or she could do what she most wanted to do. See Ruth Beiler. At least she could try.

Annie pulled a finger across the spines of books on the third shelf in the family room. She turned off lights where no one was sitting and straightened the pillows on the sofa, which she and

Penny had left in disarray during their morning sister talk. But Annie was simply passing through the family room, and she knew it. Her cell phone, with Ruth's number in it, was in the canvas bag she packed when she left Westcliffe. Now she went to the closet, opened the bag, and removed the phone.

Then she sat on the bed. As automatic as so many things felt in the last few days, this was different. She lived the *English* life for the sake of peaceful hours with her family, not expecting them to adjust their lives to her choices.

But this. This was a different sort of choice. She knew Ruth Beiler now used a cell phone daily—even texting.

Ruth might not answer, though. She might be at work or in a class or studying in the library with her phone silenced.

And if she did answer—and had some free time—Annie would be making her next choice simply by turning on her phone now.

She would take the Prius's key off the hook, get in the car, and drive to Ruth's dorm across from the main university campus.

Annie sat for ten minutes with the phone in her hand, still turned off, and her lips pressed together. This was not an emergency by any stretch of the imagination. But she'd had no warning she was going to come home, so she could not arrange a visit by mail. Ruth was so close, yet so far.

Finally, Annie flipped the phone open and composed a short text. AM IN TOWN. FREE THIS AFT?

She pushed SEND then held the phone in her hand, unsure whether she wanted it to vibrate.

It did. YES! WOULD LOVE TO SEE YOU. HOW?

BE RIGHT THERE. *SEND.* Turn the phone off. Flip it closed.

Annie jammed the phone in a back pocket just in case she had a true emergency in the course of the afternoon. She stuck her driver's license and some cash in another pocket and moved swiftly toward the kitchen. If she slowed down, she might feel the guilt.

The car key fit into her hand in a familiar mold.

Eleven

"I'm a failure at being Amish!" Annie flopped onto Ruth Beiler's dorm bed, landing on her back with her arms splayed over her head. "I sent you a text when it was not an emergency, just because I wanted to see you. And I drove over here in a car I still own." She did not want to admit aloud to wearing the red dress or the number of movies she had seen in the last three days. Or her reaction to Randy Sawyer.

Ruth nudged Annie's feet over to make space to sit on the end of the bed. "I ran out on my own baptism. I win the Rotten Amish contest."

Annie laughed and sat up. "Maybe I'm not meant to be Amish. I love my simpler life—most of the time—but three days at home with my parents and look what I've done. Is that all it takes to break my resolve?"

"Your family is *English*, Annalise. You are not baptized Amish. You have done nothing wrong."

"Are you sure?"

"Yes, I'm sure."

"Good. Because I'm not. How can I expect my family to honor my choices if I can't honor them myself?"

"We all choose every day." Ruth leaned her shoulder against

445

Annie's. "I made a huge choice when I left home. Outwardly, leaving meant I was choosing not to be Amish. On the inside, though, I have to choose every day to stay here and stay in school. Even after two years I have trouble belonging in this world."

"I think you've done very well." Annie raised her hands to tick off her points." You're a good student, you use a computer, you have a job, you found a church, you're getting along with your mother."

Ruth got up and began to tidy the university-supplied desk next to her bed. "And I dress like a nerd, I still braid my hair, I don't see the point of reality TV, and other students don't know what to make of me other than helping them in a study group."

"I assure you, reality TV is no great loss." Annie leaned forward with her elbows on her knees.

"It would be something to talk about, that's all." Ruth snapped closed the rings of an open binder. "When are you going back to Westcliffe?"

"I'm ready to go now, but I have to get a ride." Annie put both hands up. "I drove here, so I have to drive back to my parents' house, but after that I'm hanging up my keys again. I repent!"

Ruth smiled and laughed softly.

"What's so funny?"

"You're beating yourself up about driving, and I'm learning to drive."

"What!" Annie sat up straight.

Ruth nodded. "I've had a permit for a long time. I have to carry some kind of ID that *English* will accept. A couple of friends have given me a few lessons."

"See! You do have friends. Someone who will teach you to drive and still speak to you afterward is the truest friend of all."

"The first one moved away." Ruth laughed. "Maybe that was her way of saying the lessons were not working out."

Annie swatted Ruth's shoulder.

"The second one is from a military family and is a woman on a mission."

"I like her already."

"Mostly I've steered away from any busy streets and have only driven in broad daylight, but Lauren let me drive her car home from downtown at night."

"Lauren?"

"My new suitemate. She wears army clothes all the time, but she looks at me like I'm a regular person."

"You *are* a regular person."

"I don't understand half the stuff she says. Body armor and assault weapons and explosives. Apparently in her family, that's dinner table conversation."

"I'd like to meet her."

"I wish she were here now. Another time."

"Let's go driving." Annie jangled the key to her Prius. "We'll go out on the interstate."

Ruth shook her head. "I'm too nervous. I'm used to the speed of a horse."

"Just picture a *lot* of horses. Galloping. We'll stay in the slow lane, I promise."

Annie met Ruth's eyes and saw the gleam of desire. With a grin, Ruth clutched the key in her hand and slung her purse over her shoulder.

Ruth gripped the steering wheel at nine and three, amazed yet again at the sensation of freedom. The car was not hers, and she did not have a license. But in that moment she could choose where to go, and getting ready did not involve the tedious process of harnessing horses or checking their shoes.

"It's not so different from driving a buggy," Annalise said. "You have to be aware of everything happening around you on the road. React appropriately with your feet rather than reining in the horses or pulling on the buggy's brakes."

Ruth nodded. Annalise was right. Even on the bus or in someone else's car, Ruth found her body reacting slightly to what she saw around her. She knew what it felt like when a driver took a fraction of a second longer to slow than she would have liked. Pedestrians ready to step off a curb put her on full alert even as a passenger. She recognized when a driver did not slow down enough for a turn and her own body fought the centrifugal force that pressed her against the inside of the passenger door.

Still. Driving. What would her mother think? Even Rufus did not drive a car, not even to haul what he needed for his work. He hired Tom Reynolds for that.

She negotiated out of the dorm parking lot and onto Austin Bluffs, heading west toward the mountains. Annalise murmured encouragement as Ruth adjusted to the speed limit and moved her eyes frequently between mirrors and the view out the windshield.

"You're enjoying this, aren't you?" Annalise answered Ruth's smile with one of her own. "It's a cultural milestone, Ruth! You're driving!"

"Yes I am." Ruth pressed her lips together in focus. They crossed over Nevada Avenue, and she saw the signs for I-25. Choosing north would take them toward Monument. Choosing south would take them toward Pueblo. And toward Westcliffe.

"We can go where you want to go," Annalise said.

Ruth smoothly entered the interchange that would glide the car into the northbound traffic.

"Don't slow down," Annalise said. "Accelerate to enter traffic at a steady speed."

Ruth nodded, blew out her breath, and checked mirrors. Even she knew that her first experience of merging onto the interstate was perfect. Sitting back in the seat, she let out her breath.

"How far shall we go?" Annalise asked. "Monument? Castle Rock? Denver?"

Ruth shook her head. "Not Denver. That's too far." *Too far from what*, she asked herself. Too far from her dorm room? Too far from the valley where her heart longed to be?

They went past the exits, many of them marking places Ruth had never visited in a routine that alternated between classes and

25

work shifts, punctuated on Sundays by attending a nearby church. Though she had left the San Luis Valley region, her world was contained in a simple framework.

The sky shone blue and broad and bright before her. The Rockies rose bronze and unyielding on her left. The car rumbled softy forward over gray wideness.

Ruth liked the immediate response to even slight pressure on the accelerator.

She liked the effortlessness of steering a vehicle, compared to the slow, awkward maneuverings of a team of horses.

She liked adjusting the seat to fit her.

She liked being enclosed and keeping the temperature comfortable.

She liked the speed.

Ruth glanced at her passenger. "Annalise, I'm going to say something I've never said before in my entire life."

Annalise smiled slowly. "Can't wait."

"Wheeee!"

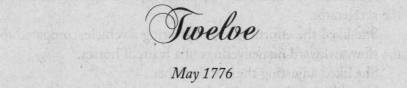

Twelve

May 1776

Christian heard the rustle of the corn and looked up, alarmed. The sound came too fast, the steps too heavy and too many. Instinctively he turned his head toward the house, though it was too distant to see from his western field. Despite his first impulse at the breakfast table that morning, he had agreed Magdalena could take the small cart for a half day to visit her friend Rebekah. No doubt she would also drop by Nathanael's family farm. That meant Babsi was home alone with the smallest children—and heavily pregnant.

Christian dropped the knife he was using for digging out weeds and stood up straight. A moment later, three men drew their three horses to a halt in front of him.

"Good morning, gentlemen." Unafraid to look them straight in the eye, Christian assessed them in turn.

"Which way did they go?" One of the riders had trouble stilling his mount.

"They? I assure you I have been alone in my field all morning." Though he refused to look at the path they had taken, Christian knew the intruders had flattened countless ears of corn. These men were British sympathizers. He had seen them before.

"Four treasonous Patriots came this way," the man said.

"We saw where they turned off the road. They cannot have gone anywhere else."

Christian shook his head. "I have not seen them."

"They turned into your field not four minutes ago. You are hiding them."

Christian made a wide sweep with one arm. "I'm growing corn, gentlemen, as I do every year. That is all. I hardly think I would be able to disguise four beasts and their riders in a half-grown cornfield."

"How do we know you would not give them aid?" As the man's horse continued to strain against the reins, the hilt of his sword glinted in the sun.

"I have nothing to do with your dispute."

"Dispute! Man, do you not understand that this is war?"

"I have nothing to do with your war, either. I only wish to live at peace with all men."

"You delude yourself, good sir. If you are not for us, you are against us."

"I am against no man." Christian spoke with calm. "If I might be permitted, I ask you to kindly take care of my crop on your way back to the road. It may provide your sustenance one day."

"We are not going anywhere until we find the traitors."

Christian stepped to one side. "Then I will not detain you further."

"If we find these men in your field, we will be back for you. Your Amish pretensions do not deceive us."

"It is not my intention to deceive you. I speak truth when I tell you I have seen no Patriots come through my land."

The man snorted. "Soon enough you will have to choose a side. If you don't choose wisely, you will be as traitorous as they."

Christian said nothing. What good could come from antagonizing them?

At the crack of a whip, the horses thundered through the corn.

Jacob had had enough of the rain for one day. No doubt the farmers of Pennsylvania were happy for some moisture in their fields, but once he left the stone-paved streets of Philadelphia, the risk of a wagon wheel bogging down in muddy country roads would make the trip home to Berks County tedious.

For the moment, though, Jacob did not want to be anywhere else but in the city where his parents had met.

He had come to Philadelphia on a routine supply trip, with lists from a few of his neighbors and plenty of space in his wagon for any saltpeter that might have found its way to the city in an unrecorded manner. Only a few hours ago he was eating breakfast in his sister's kitchen. The simple note from his brother-in-law came by messenger. Nearly giggling, Sarah read it aloud. *Come to the State House. We will make history today.*

When Jacob and Sarah arrived at the brick-towered State House, they could not get anywhere near the building, nor catch any sight of Sarah's husband. Drays, coaches, and chaises congested the streets around the State House. Pedestrians from every neighborhood of the city swarmed the flat brick sidewalks. Despite the steady rain, hundreds—then thousands—pressed in to plant their feet in the yard behind the State House.

"There's Emerson." Sarah pointed, and Jacob saw her relief at the sight of her husband in the throng.

Even in her layers of petticoats, slender Sarah was nimble enough to twist among the crowd and devise her own path to the other side of the yard. Jacob, requiring more space to maneuver respectfully, kept his eye on the crimson dress his sister sported that day. Her feathered hat made her easy to spot. A step or two at a time, he crossed the yard politely, catching snatches of conversation in the process.

"Pennsylvania needs an assembly that represents the will of the people."

"We're here to show we mean business. We're through being

bullied by the British or our own Assembly."

"By the end of the day, the Assembly will be out on their ears. We'll have men of vision running Pennsylvania."

"Is it true?" Jacob asked as soon as he reached Emerson and Sarah. "Is the Assembly to be ousted?" He wiped rain from his eyes and strained to bring into focus the scene unfolding before him.

Emerson nodded. "How fortuitous that you are in Philadelphia just now. I knew you wouldn't want to miss this, not after all the risks you've been taking for the cause."

Sarah glanced around. "Are you sure you ought to speak so forthrightly, Emerson?"

Her husband threw his head back and laughed freely. "This is a Patriot crowd if ever there was one. We are among like-minded souls."

"Can they really throw out the Assembly?" Jacob asked.

"The Assembly did themselves in. Clearly the people want them to vote for independence at the new Continental Congress. Since they refuse to commit themselves to such a path, the people will take matters into their own hands."

"I hope there will be no violence here today," Sarah said.

Emerson shook his head. "Let's hope it is only the noise of a determined crowd."

The chanting started then. "Independence now! Independence now!"

"There must be three thousand people here." Despite the sheltering brim of his hat, rain once again streaked Jacob's face.

"My guess is closer to four thousand," Emerson said. "I could hear the chanting from my office three blocks over."

"Imagine what it might have been if the weather were fair." Sarah gripped her brother's forearm. "Look! One of the assemblymen is trying to speak."

From their position across the yard, they could not make out the man's words, but the booing that followed left no doubt of the crowd's sentiment. Nothing he said placated the throng, and nothing short of mass resignations would satisfy. Jacob opened his mouth to speak again then abruptly took in breath and held it.

Was it even possible that he saw what his mind registered?

He squinted against the drizzle and wiped his eyes on his coat sleeve. The crowd swallowed the figure that had caught his eye just a moment ago. What had he seen? A woman. No, a man. If it was a woman, it seemed unlikely, and if it was a man, it was impossible. It had been so long, and she—or he—was far enough away to make Jacob distrust his own vision.

Jacob stepped away from Sarah and Emerson—as much as the crowd would allow—and tried to follow what he had seen, but the shifting mob obscured his view at every step. When he found a clear break in the multitude, whatever he had seen was no longer there. He squeezed his way back to Sarah and Emerson.

"Jacob, what is it?" Sarah asked.

He turned to her, uncertain whether to put into words what made no sense as it flashed through his mind.

"Jacob," Sarah said again. "You look as if you've seen a ghost."

"I just may have," Jacob said.

"Someone you know? You do business with a lot of people in Philadelphia now."

He shook his head slowly. "Not business. And someone you know as well." He turned to lock eyes with his sister.

"Oh?"

"Maria." Jacob exhaled the name. "I think I saw Maria."

"How can that be?" Emerson asked. "You've always said she disappeared when she was barely grown."

"She did," Sarah said. "We never knew what happened. No one knew she was unhappy, if that's what she was. I was only seven or eight myself. Jacob, you can't have been more than ten. Christian was not married yet. Are you certain?"

"No. It was someone in men's clothing. Drab, ordinary fabrics. A hat pulled down low. But the face! It was like looking at Magdalena, only twenty years older."

Sarah's eyes locked on his. "Jacob, do you know what it would mean to *Mamm* to find Maria?"

Jacob nodded.

"What can we do to find out if it is Maria?" Sarah turned to her husband. "Emerson, you must help."

Emerson turned his palms up. "How? I never met Maria. I've never even met Magdalena. And I certainly did not see whoever Jacob thinks he saw—which may have been a complete stranger."

"But if it was Maria—"

Jacob put a hand on his sister's shoulder. "Emerson's right. I'm not even sure what I saw. The rain distorts many things."

"But if it was Maria, then she is here in Philadelphia. We can ask around. You have connections. Emerson knows a lot of people. We could at least try for a few days."

Jacob shook his head. "Katie is due to have the new baby in a few weeks. I promised this would be the last trip for a while. This is no time for me to linger in Philadelphia. "No, it couldn't have been her.

The crowd thundered again.

"That's it," Emerson said. "They're demanding a new government, and I believe we're going to get it. The Assembly will have no choice but to vote themselves out of existence because of their own incompetence. When the Continental Congress meets next month, Pennsylvania will vote for independence."

From where Magdalena sat, she could see Nathanael clearly. He always sat in the same place during church. No matter whose home the congregation met in, Nathanael managed to put himself along the outside edge among the unmarried men. Magdalena learned long ago that she could sit on the same outside edge, in the facing women's section, and see Nathanael clearly during most services.

Nathan helped his father work both their farms, but he had never moved into his own cabin. Just last week Magdalena had stopped in at the cabin and saw that someone was squatting there. Though Nathan's mother had outfitted the cabin with basic supplies when he acquired the land, anyone passing through now could see it was untended. What was to stop someone from taking up occupancy?

Mrs. Buerki often invited Magdalena to supper, where she sat next to Nathan and smiled as she passed dishes around the table. Nathan was polite and ate well. He seemed to find some pleasure in her silent company after meals. As far as anyone knew, he slept well at night. His family said he was the first one to wake in the morning and out to the barn to tend the animals. If asked a question, he answered as simply as possible, but never discourteously.

But he was not *her* Nathanael any longer. Magdalena wondered if it would be worse to give up hope that he would return to her, or worse to be certain he never would.

It had been a year and a half. In a few weeks another wedding season would begin—the third since she and Nathan talked of marriage. Magdalena was tempted to stop stitching linens for her chest. What was the point?

She sang the last hymn with half a heart, feeling as if it were moving at half the usual ponderous pace of the hymns from the *Ausbund.* This one had fourteen stanzas, and they would sing them all. Once it had been one of Nathanael's favorites, and whenever they sang it she would catch his eye with a shy smile.

This time, as soon as the final phrase of the hymn dissipated into the air, Magdalena stood and swiftly moved out of the congregation, out of the house, out of the close air that was strangling her next breath.

She ran, and she did not answer the voices calling her back.

Thirteen

If you do what I ask, you can see for yourself." Annie, with her feet up on an ottoman in the living room, tilted her head and snared her sister's eyes.

"I don't know, Annie." Penny tossed a pillow at Annie.

"Please." Annie caught the pillow. She intended to milk her little-sister status for as much as she could get. "You could see my house. Meet my friends."

"You mean meet Rufus."

"Well, yes, but others in his family as well, if we catch them at home."

"I'm afraid I'll stare."

"You won't. I know you have a lot of questions about what I've been doing the last few months. If you come and stay overnight—"

"Whoa. Overnight?"

"Yes, overnight. You can see what my house is really like, even at night. You always say you like to visit people where they live so you can imagine them in their own homes."

"By 'always' you mean I said that once when I was thirteen."

"And maybe one other time when you were seventeen. Pretty please?"

"It's Wednesday. It's my last full day here, Annie. I fly out tomorrow afternoon."

"Come on, Penny, you've seen all your friends. We've had family meals coming out our ears. Frankly, I think Dad would like his peace and quiet back."

"You're the noisy one."

"Am not."

"Are too." Penny sighed. "If I'm back in time to have lunch with Mom before my flight tomorrow, it might work."

Annie swung her feet from the ottoman to the hardwood floor with a thud. "Perfect. I'll go pack."

"We can't take Mom's car, you know," Penny said.

"I know. We'll take the Prius, but you drive. I'll send Ruth a text."

"Ruth?"

"Ruth Beiler. If we're just going overnight, she'd probably like the chance to see her mother."

"Are you even supposed to be texting her?"

"So now you're the Amish police?" Annie laughed and opened her phone. "Last time. I promise."

"Why did Ruth Beiler leave if the Amish are so phenomenal that you're trying to get in?"

"It's not a question of 'getting in,' Penny." Annie nimbly thumbed in the text message to Ruth. "It's following a calling. It's choosing something, rather than being run over by the stampede of everybody else."

"Are you sure you're not just choosing Rufus?"

Annie set her phone down on the cushion next to her to await Ruth's response. "Would it be so terrible if I were?"

"Since I haven't met him, I reserve judgment."

"Thank you for being fair. But no, I don't think it's just about Rufus. Maybe I belong with the plain people even if I don't belong with Rufus."

"Annie, if you join the Amish, am I even ever going to see you again?"

"Of course you will." Annie answered quickly, but the color was gone from Penny's face. "They're not some kind of cult that brainwashes kids and cuts them off from their families."

Annie watched as her sister swallowed hard. Then Penny sucked in a ragged breath.

"It will be all right, Penny," Annie said. "We'll still be sisters. We may just have to get better at writing letters."

"Won't they ask you to believe a bunch of crazy stuff?"

"What do I believe now, Penny? That's the bigger question. What kind of faith do I have? Do I make choices that have anything to do with Jesus, or do I buy into thinking I deserve everything at my fingertips?"

"Surely those aren't the only two choices."

"Perhaps not. I'm still asking a lot of questions."

"I go to church," Penny said. "There's plenty to believe without being so drastic about it. Why can't you join a normal church?"

"Who decides what's normal?"

Penny pushed the pillow off her lap. "Never mind. Let's just do this."

A couple of hours later, Ruth opened a rear door of the Prius and settled into the backseat. Annie made the introductions. Penny was polite, but she made no effort to strike up a conversation with Ruth. Every minute or two, Annie saw Penny glance in the rearview mirror and she wondered if Ruth were looking back, inspecting her sister at regular intervals. Ruth and Annie's occasional murmurs softly infused the awkwardness that settled over the car. *One step at a time*, Annie told herself. Penny did not have to love Ruth today. But Annie did wonder what tomorrow's drive back would be like, when Penny and Ruth would be alone in the car.

Rufus knelt and fished through his open wooden toolbox, not finding what he wanted.

"What have you lost now?" Mo, owner of the motel, put one hand on her hip and gazed down at Rufus.

Rufus looked up, pushed his hat out of his eyes, and gave a halfhearted smile. "Does it seem to you that losing things has become a habit?"

"Yes, I seem to hear you rummaging in that toolbox more often these days."

"I prefer to believe I haven't lost anything. It's a matter of not anticipating what to bring with me from my shop. I did not anticipate needing a small corner chisel."

"I can offer you an ice pick."

Rufus smiled and shook his head. "I'll manage somehow. Thank you again for the new project."

She waved him off. "This place is a perpetual remodeling effort. I'm lucky you're available." Mo picked up a pile of fresh towels and headed down the hall.

The only chisels Rufus had with him were too large and awkward for the fine corner work he needed to do. The task would have to wait for another day. He doubted anyone would notice if he did not tap off the barely visible overhang at the end of the closet, but he wanted the work to be right.

He stood up and wiped his hands on a rag then swished the rag over the trim he had been bent over. Another doorway across the hall was waiting for its custom trim installation. Spring air gusted through the propped-open front door of the motel and threatened to take his hat. As Rufus picked up his toolbox, he heard a horse whinny—and it was not his. He grimaced as he craned around a corner to see what other Amish person had business at the motel.

Beth Stutzman. Driving her family's brand-new buggy.

She did not have business at the motel, he knew, except to find him. The temptation to step quietly out of sight flitted through his head. Instead, he stepped into view. "Hello, Beth."

Beth grinned, making her seem a little too enthusiastic to see him. She carried a thermos.

"I thought you might like something cold to drink." Beth unscrewed the lid, which doubled as a cup, filled it with the liquid, and handed it to Rufus.

"That's kind of you." He took a swift swallow—lemonade, it turned out to be—and handed it back to her. "What brings you out this way?"

"I wanted to see if I could be any help to you."

"You would not happen to have a small corner chisel in your apron?"

"No, but I'll be happy to go fetch it for you." Beth's face lit up. "Did you leave it on your workbench?"

He had not expected that response. "Do you know what one looks like?"

"Of course. My father uses a corner chisel all the time."

That answer made sense. Ike Stutzman was the first person to demonstrate how to use a corner chisel to Rufus two decades ago.

"Mine is part of a set of small tools wrapped in a leather pouch," Rufus said. "But it's not urgent. I'll bring it the next time I come."

"Nonsense. You're here now. You might as well get the job done. I'll be back before you know it." She thrust the thermos at him and swished her skirts back through the lobby and out the front door.

Round-trip, the errand was eight miles. Then she would have to scour his workbench to find the packet of chisels. Most of an hour would pass before she returned.

It was too late to stop her now.

Franey was sitting on the front porch of her home when they drove up. Her face lit when her daughter stepped out of the Prius, and Annie saw the curiosity that piqued when she and the driver emerged as well.

"What do we have here?" Franey asked as her daughter kissed her cheek.

"*Mamm*, this is Annalise's sister, Penny."

"Welcome to our home," Franey said. "I am so glad Annalise took the opportunity to visit with you."

Penny flashed Annie an unsettled look before saying, "Thank you. Me, too."

"When Annalise left on Saturday, I had not imagined I would have the pleasure of meeting you. Your sister has been a delight to our family."

"She seems very glad to know you as well." Penny looked around the yard. "It's beautiful here."

"Won't you come inside?"

Penny's eyes widened, and Annie took the cue. "No thanks. I just wanted you and Penny to meet. I'm going to show her my house and where I work."

"Annalise has a lovely little house," Franey said.

"I am only here overnight, *Mamm*," Ruth said. "Penny will drive me back tomorrow."

"The Stutzman sisters are sleeping in your room, but I can put up a cot in Lydia and Sophie's room for you."

A few minutes later, Annie was back in the passenger seat of the car. She rolled her gaze toward Penny. "Isn't Franey great?"

"She seems very nice."

"Of course she's nice. And she would not have bitten you if you had accepted her hospitality."

"Hey. I'm being a good sport. Don't push it." Penny put the car in reverse and looked back over her shoulder at the lengthy Beiler driveway.

"It's easier to just turn around," Annie said, "and drive out going forward."

Penny glanced at her then put the car in DRIVE. "I suppose you've had a lot of experience figuring this out." She twisted the steering wheel sharply to the left.

"I'm here a lot. Of course, I'm not usually in a car."

"I'm not sure who Franey was happier to see, Ruth or you."

"Ruth is her daughter."

"And you might be. . .well, you know." Penny pulled out onto the highway and headed toward town.

"Just drive."

"Are we really going to drive all over tarnation hunting for Rufus?"

"He's probably at the motel. It's four miles."

"That's one of their buggies, isn't it?" Penny carefully steered around an enclosed black buggy headed in the same direction.

"Yes. I'm not sure who." Annie twisted in her seat, but she could not see the driver.

A few minutes later they parked in front of the motel. Annie saw Rufus's buggy off to one side. The horse was unhitched and wandering on a generous tether, so Rufus must have been there a long time.

As she slammed the passenger door, Annie looked over the top of the car at her sister. "You behave yourself."

Penny smiled in that way that Annie did not quite trust.

They entered the motel. From behind the desk, Mo looked up. "Who do we have here?"

"This is my sister, Penny."

Mo's eyebrows went up a notch. "Bringing her to meet Rufus?"

"Maybe." Annie tilted her head.

Mo waved them on through. "I won't tell anyone! He's just down the hall."

"Thanks, Mo."

Penny elbowed Annie. "She treats you like a couple already."

Annie pushed back with her own elbow. "Behave."

And there he was, his white shirt stretched across his broad back as he expertly placed pieces of trim he had crafted in his workshop on the Beiler land. Annie slowed her steps, wanting just to watch him and breathe in the fragrance of his artistry as it took form.

Penny stubbed her toe on a stray chair, and when it scraped the floor Rufus turned.

His face brightened.

"Rufus, I want you to meet my sister. This is Penny."

Rufus brushed a hand against his trousers before offering it to Penny. She took it then glanced at Annie with upturned lips. Annie allowed herself a slow breath of relief.

"It's a pleasure to meet you," Penny said with perfect manners. With one finger, she traced the carved pattern in a piece of trim. "Your work is beautiful—everything Annie said it was."

"I trust you had a relaxing drive down." Rufus caught Annie's eye before dipping his hat at Penny.

"I had no idea this part of the state was so gorgeous," Penny said.

Annie felt as if she were watching from the outside. Her *English* sister was chatting with the Amish man who had made her rethink her life. She had harassed Penny into coming. Now, though, her blood pulsed faster. Annie wanted Penny to like Rufus. She wanted Penny to see everything wonderful that she saw in him. She wanted Rufus to see past Penny's *English* exterior and believe she was a wonderful sister. When she met Rufus's gaze, and the familiar warmth flushed through her, she saw delight in his violet-blue eyes.

The lobby door clattered open, and Annie turned toward steps that progressed firmly in her direction.

Beth Stutzman stood there, and Rufus's eyes moved to her expectantly.

"It's not there. I looked everywhere." Beth Stutzman's gaze moved to Annie. "Oh, hello. Annalise, is it? I almost didn't recognize you dressed like. . ."

Annie swallowed and moistened her lips before responding, but Rufus broke in. "Beth, this is Annalise's sister, Penny Friesen. And Penny, this is Beth Stutzman, an old family friend. She was kind enough to go look for a tool I neglected to bring today."

Annie felt her sister's eyes on her, as if saying, *Old family friend? Sure.*

"It's the oddest thing, though," Beth said. "I definitely know what a corner chisel looks like, and I promise you, it is nowhere in your workshop. The whole set is missing."

"I'm sure it will turn up," Rufus said.

"I'll help you look again later," Beth said. "But I wanted you to know right away that it's lost."

Annie's brow furrowed. Since when would Rufus send Beth Stutzman to look for tools? She caught Rufus's eye then looked away quickly at the slight paling of his complexion. The concern— and the triumph—in Beth's face were unconvincing, but Annie preferred to sort out her questions with Rufus later. In private.

"Why don't we go?" Annie nudged Penny. "We don't want to get in the way here."

Fourteen

Ruth knelt in the garden. Late afternoon was her favorite time to fill her hands with the mystery of the earth. The garden was dormant now, still readying for its summer yield. In a few weeks, when her sisters worked the soil and planted, the family would see the promise of nourishment for a new year. Weeds were already pressing their way to the sun, though. One by one Ruth picked them out, being sure to get the roots, and tossed them into a wheelbarrow.

A few feet away, her mother wielded a hoe, splitting clots that had formed over the winter and pounding the fragments into smooth soil. The rhythm was familiar to both of them. Whether in Pennsylvania when Ruth was young or during the last six years in Colorado, Ruth and her mother had chased out the evidence of winter and prepared to feed the family. Until two years ago. Ruth pushed the thought out of her mind and imagined her sisters working in the garden. They would do the weeding and watering as the vegetables grew. For yet another year, she would not be there to see the plants sprout.

Ruth watched her mother work, envying the contentment she saw and the simple companionship of silence. Finding a ride from Colorado Springs was worth the trouble to see these simple moments of pleasure in her mother's face.

"Annalise wants to have a garden," Franey said. "She has never had a vegetable garden."

"She'll enjoy it. She's so curious about everything."

"Plenty of the *English* grow vegetables." Franey raised the hoe several feet before thudding it through a stubborn clot repeatedly. "But gardening will have special meaning to Annalise. For her, it's part of learning our ways."

"Yes, I suppose so." Ruth wrapped her fingers around a weed already six inches high and yanked.

"Annalise is persistent about her quilt, too. I suggested she start with a lap quilt, but she was determined to make something she could put on a bed."

"She is used to aiming high."

"As long as success does not lead to pride, doing your best is an excellent quality."

"*Demut*. Humility. This is not always easy for Annalise."

"*Demut* is not always easy for any of us." Franey winked. "After all, no one makes a better schnitzel than I do."

"*Mamm!*" Ruth laughed at her mother's pride. *Hochmut*.

"I'm teaching Annalise to cook our traditional foods. She never cooked much at all, you know, before moving here."

"She was too busy running a company."

"She's trying hard to change and understand our ways. And she learns so quickly."

Ruth stuffed weeds deeper into the wheelbarrow. She loved Annalise, too, but she had not expected the garden conversation to be all about her. Where was the contented silence she used to share with her mother, or the soft humming of hymns from the *Ausbund*?

"Rufus says Annalise has room on her land for a small barn," Franey said. "I think she should learn to drive a buggy soon."

Ruth hid a smile at the memory, just a few days old, of Annalise teaching her to drive a car. Would Annalise think managing a horse and buggy was as easy as driving a car?

"She wants to begin making her own clothes. I told her perhaps over the winter."

"But it's only spring now," Ruth said.

"Gardening, cooking, quilting, driving—she has plenty to learn for now."

"She won't want to wait that long."

Her mother never asked Ruth about what she was learning. Pharmacology, pathology, health care ethics. Franey had made her peace that Ruth was pursing higher education, but apparently even talking about her courses was too *English*.

But Annalise, it seemed, could do no wrong. Jealousy warmed Ruth's chest.

"Canning." Franey stood still and looked over the garden plot. "When we're just planting, I seem to forget how much will grow. I'll need all the help I can get canning everything for the winter."

"Well, you won't miss me because you'll have Annalise." Ruth tossed an entire clump of dirt instead of knocking the small weed loose from it.

"Ruth Beiler, what has gotten into you?" Franey leaned on her hoe and stared wide eyed at her daughter.

"I'm sorry, *Mamm*." And she was. Ruth had chosen to leave. She had chosen to miss the rhythm of planting and growing and harvesting the family's vegetables. She had chosen to surrender the closeness of her family to her own future, away from them.

Franey slowly resumed slicing into the soil with her hoe, but her vigor had dissipated.

"Forgive me, *Mamm*. I should not have said that. I should not even have thought it."

"We should go and see how Lydia and Sophie and the Stutzman girls are coming along with supper." Franey grasped her hoe and carried it toward the house, where she leaned it against the back porch railing and disappeared through the door.

Ruth slowly stood, brushed dirt from her skirt and gripped the handles of the wheelbarrow.

After dinner at a small restaurant on Main Street, Annie put her key in the lock of her back door and turned it. She stepped aside to let Penny enter first. They each carried an overnight bag.

"Maybe I should have taken you in through the front door," Annie said, "but this is how I usually come and go." She turned a knob on a lamp at one end of the counter and a clean light illuminated the simple kitchen.

Penny looked around. "It's. . .quaint."

"The house is a hundred years old, Penny. So yes, the kitchen is small. It's all small, and I've come to love it."

"Do you cook much?"

"All the time now. Not the kind of cooking you do, of course. But you'll be glad to know I'm going to have a garden this year. I know how strongly you feel about fresh food."

"Amish or not, a garden is a great idea. I may make a foodie out of you yet."

"Rufus has drawn it all out. He's going to come and turn the soil for me." Soon, Annie hoped. "Let me show you the rest of the house."

Annie led the way into her small dining room, which opened into the living room. She paused several times to turn on lamps.

Penny inspected the cabinet beneath one of the living room lamps. "That's beautiful." She opened the door. "A propane tank?"

Annie stoked the tabletop. "Rufus's handiwork. Propane is a common way to provide light."

"Among the Amish, you mean. It's sort of like camping."

A fire started in Annie's stomach and burned its way up. "Look, Penny, I asked you here to show you my home, my life. Don't make fun."

Penny laid three fingers across her mouth and stared at Annie, silent. But Annie knew what her sister's expression meant.

"Ever since we picked up Ruth today," Annie said, "you've been acting weird."

Penny put a finger to her own chest. "I'm acting weird? You're the one who gives up electricity and moves to the boonies, and I'm acting weird?"

Annie exhaled. "I understand you need some time to take it all in."

"This man had better be worth it," Penny said. "You might tell yourself being Amish is not just for him, but you'd better be sure. You're changing everything. I mean, hey, Annie, just because you found we had one Amish ancestor doesn't mean you have to go back in time."

"I'm not going back in time, Penny. I'm just choosing a simpler way to live. Simpler values. A faith that asks me to measure my decisions more carefully."

"In the end, you're still choosing Rufus Beiler. So you'd better be sure. Don't think I didn't notice your reaction when Beth Stutzman showed up. You're not sure."

Penny was right, of course. Annie was not sure she was the right wife for Rufus. Someone like Beth Stutzman would know how to be an Amish wife who brought no disgrace or embarrassment to her husband. Annie moved to the stairs.

"I'll go get your room ready," she said. "Make yourself comfortable for a few minutes."

Upstairs, Annie opened a chair that unfolded into a twin-size bed and stretched sheets across it. She moved to the small desk and stacked up the papers there, clearing a surface for Penny to use. While her hands were busy, her mind also whirled. Sitting in the desk chair, she pulled open the bottom drawer and riffled through file folders. Her fingers settled on one folder, and she paused to think.

When Annie heard Penny's footsteps on the stairs, she made a rapid decision.

Fifteen

The night was deep when Ruth left the sleepy house. Even the Stutzman girls, who seemed to giggle behind their teeth more than Ruth remembered, had settled in for the night. She had taken a flashlight from the kitchen drawer, and now she turned it on and aimed at the path. Even without a light, though, her feet knew the way. Clouds hung low, a curtain hiding the stars. Her frame ached to lie against the solidity of the broad rock and stare into forever.

She wore her brother Joel's warm jacket because it was handy on the hook next to the back door. The flashlight beam bobbed ahead of her steps. Ruth moved swiftly, remembering the tree root she once tripped over and the low branches of an evergreen, the depression in the ground that often collected water, and the bushes with hidden spurs. Ruth's parents had no idea how many times over the years she had escaped to the rock, whether by light of sun or moon.

With two families under the roof, fragmented conversation had bounced around the rooms during dinner and games. If she was hearing right, this might be the last time she could find solitude at the rock. At the very least, because of the park improvement project, the acres around the rock would be more populated. And at the very worst, the rock would be blasted. Its pieces could be used to outline a footpath with no hint that they had stood united and unmoved for eons.

If she walked briskly, Ruth could reach the rock in twelve minutes. On a cloudy night, Ruth estimated fifteen. She moved through trees to a clearing, and there, even under a dull, dim sky, the rock beckoned. The boulder stood more than five feet high and spread six feet long and nine feet across. Ruth knew where to put her foot on the rear side of it in order to heft herself to the top in two wide climbing steps. The flashlight turned off, she lay flat on her back and stared up.

Without the ornamentation of stars, the view lacked the unfathomable sense of infinity. Instead, clouds veiled the secrets of the sky, leaving Ruth to ponder the shroud around her own life.

On this rock she had imagined her future as a public health nurse. On this rock she plotted to escape her own baptism and go to college. On this rock, she chose to break Elijah's heart.

Now she lived in the in-between, sure of her life calling to nursing, but not yet qualified to carry it out. Sure that leaving the church was the right decision, but not truly finding her place among the *English*. Sure that she could not drag Elijah away from his promises, but not able to keep him out of her heart. She should not have answered his last letter. She should not even have read the last letter. He was getting brazen.

A glimpse of one star would reassure her that it was not for nothing.

The rock was cold, as it always was. Eventually the chill seeped through Joel's jacket, through Ruth's sweater, through her skin. Ruth gripped the front panels of the coat and held them tightly around her, but in truth she did not mind the cold. Inhaling, she took in the fragrance of spring, the murkiness of apple blossoms carried on a breeze jumbled with the smell of mud in the damp earth below. Surely rain would come before the night was over.

Ruth flinched at the sound of a cracking branch. The night was too cloudy to cast a shadow, but she knew someone was there.

She sat up and turned her head in the direction the sound had come from.

"Ruth? Are you here?" The voice was a solid sort of whisper.

Ruth fumbled for the flashlight and pointed it toward the voice. "Elijah?"

He emerged from the nearest tree.

"What are you doing here?" Adrenaline surged into Ruth.

"I might ask you the same question." Elijah found the footholds and climbed onto the rock. "Turn off that light."

She clicked the flashlight off and lay flat again. "I don't get many chances to come here anymore. I hear they may blast this rock to smithereens."

"Not if I have anything to say about it." Elijah lay down beside her.

The hammer in Ruth's chest pounded harder, faster. More than two years had passed since she and Elijah used to meet at the rock in daytime innocence—and nighttime guilt.

"Elijah," she said staring into the gray again, "how did you know I was here?"

"I didn't."

"Do you come often?"

The length of his silence confounded her.

"I feel you close when I come here," he said. "This is where I first knew I loved you."

Ruth's pent-up lungs deflated. "Elijah, I'm sorry I answered your letters. I was thinking of myself and not what is good for you."

"My feelings are the same, Ruth. *You* are what is good for me."

"We can't keep going around this circle, Elijah. We can't be together."

"You made your choice. I could make mine."

"No! Not because of me. You've been baptized. They would shun you. I would always know what I took from you."

"I hope," he said, his voice low as he turned his face toward hers, "that you would always know what I gave willingly."

They were not more than twelve inches apart. A familiar

tremble began when she felt his breath, warm against the cold, mingling with her halting respiration. He raised a hand and grazed her cheek and neck then settled on her shoulder. Ruth could barely feel his touch through her layers of clothing, but memories roused, and she closed her eyes and breathed in his smell.

Ruth heard Elijah shift his weight, putting himself up on one elbow and turning his whole body toward her. He shielded her now from the chilled breeze, casting a stillness between them. When she opened her eyes, his face was right where she thought it would be, so close to hers that she could barely focus on his features. He was going to kiss her. It would be sweet and ardent and complete. She moistened her lips and swallowed in anticipation.

A star glimmered through the fog above them. Ruth rolled away from Elijah and sat up out of his reach.

Sixteen

June 1776

"General Washington has fallen back time and again." Joseph moved mashed potatoes around on his plate. "If he doesn't have a victory soon, we're going to lose Philadelphia."

John reached toward the basket in the center of the table and helped himself to a thick wedge of bread. "Washington has had his share of victories."

Joseph let his fork clatter against his plate. "Not lately. I don't think you appreciate how precarious our position is."

Jacob observed that while one brother's analysis of military realities caused him to leave food on his plate meal after a meal, the other's unflagging enthusiasm for the cause fed his appetite. He glanced at his mother and winced. At least their wives had already taken most of the dishes to the kitchen to wash up.

"I think I'll go help the girls." The Byler matriarch rose from her chair. "I never know where I'll find things when someone else cleans up."

Jacob waited until the broad door closed between the main room and the kitchen. "You know *Mamm* does not like when you talk about the war at the dinner table."

"I cannot help it," Joseph said. "I must do more."

"Your crops help feed the militia. You play an important role."

"You and John could look after my land."

"We have our own fields, and the tannery and the powder mill."

"I know. But all the powder in the world will not matter if Washington does not have enough soldiers."

"Washington is a better general than you give him credit for," John said.

"We are all trying to do our part, Joseph." Jacob tapped his fingers on the tabletop. "You cannot take the weight of winning the war on your own shoulders."

They heard the wagon and sat alert.

"That will be David," Jacob said. He crossed the room to open the front door in time to see David sling down from the wagon seat and hitch the horses to a post. He raised his eyebrows in question as his youngest brother stomped the dust off his boots before entering.

David shook his head. "I delivered the load just as we planned, but I did not find much to haul back."

"How much?"

"More coal and brimstone than saltpeter."

Jacob tilted his head and sighed. "I have some saltpeter left from May. Perhaps we will be better off than we think."

David reached inside his shirt. "I have this as well."

"From Sarah?" Jacob took the envelope.

"I did not get to see her, but she left the letter with her maid."

Jacob laughed. "She's using her maid for subterfuge. There is no telling what Sarah would do right under the nose of a British officer if she had the chance." He opened the envelope and scanned the note. "Thomas Jefferson, eh? She says he is the best man for the job."

"Apparently he has a knack for wordsmithing," David said. "I'm sure the rest of the Congress will hack his effort to pieces, but somebody has to get something on paper."

Jacob could not help but wonder if Sarah had made any inquiries that might lead to Maria. If she had, she did not mention them.

"Is there any food?" David asked.

"There's bread on the table. I'll see what else is left."

As David sank into a chair, Jacob pushed through the door to the kitchen and scanned the room. "Where's Katie?"

"I sent her to lie down on my bed," his mother answered. "The poor thing is worn out. The new *boppli* will be here soon. I sent all the children upstairs."

"David is home."

"And hungry, I suppose." Elizabeth held out a hand, and John's wife put a plate in it.

"Of course." David always wanted food.

Elizabeth moved to the pie cabinet, where the leftover food sat, and began to fill the plate.

"I think I'll go check on Katie," Jacob said.

On his mother's bed, Jacob found his wife turned on one side with a hand on her swollen belly. She smiled when he appeared in the door frame.

"I noticed you did not eat much." Jacob sat and massaged Katie's arm from elbow to wrist.

"Indigestion."

"That's what you said before Catherine, and before the twins. It went on for days."

"I know. It won't be much longer."

"Catherine needs a sister."

Katie nodded. "I want to name her Elizabeth. Do you think your mother would mind if we called her Lisbet?"

He leaned over and kissed her forehead. "She would be honored to share her name, and pleased that you want to remember my sister." He stroked the back side of her hand. "Would you like to go home to your own bed?"

"After I have a nap. Do you mind waiting?" Katie snuggled her face into a pillow.

In the end, his mother insisted on putting the children to bed upstairs so Jacob would not have to disturb Katie to take her home. She would need her rest before hard labor began.

John and Joseph collected their families and rumbled off the homestead, which had become a productive farm in the last thirty years. Jacob's mother occupied a widow's seat—the house and a few acres around it, where she kept chickens and sometimes a pig, and had a couple of cherry trees. Though he built his own house near the tannery after his father died and Jacob owned the rest of the land that had once been his father's, he would provide for his mother as long as she lived. David still resided in the big house, hesitant to buy his own land because he dreamed of North Carolina.

"After independence," David said often, "America will open wide." It would not be long now, Jacob hoped.

Mother and son sat on the front porch together admiring the stars.

"I'm sorry the boys are not more careful about their war talk," Jacob said.

Elizabeth let a long moment lapse. "Until the day your father died, Christian hoped he would return to the Amish church and peaceful ways."

"*Daed* was a peaceful man, but he would do whatever was necessary to protect his family."

"I am not Amish," Elizabeth said, "but that does not mean I love war."

"I know. I hope you do not think any of us loves war."

"I am a mother of four able-bodied sons. Of course the thought of war distresses me. And do not think I cannot guess what is really in those wagons you send David out with. You could not possibly be tanning that many hides."

Jacob chuckled. "No, *Mamm*."

"Just remember that the British soldiers are sons and husbands and fathers as well."

"What does this mean?" Magdalena wanted to know. "Are we citizens of this new nation whether we want to be or not?"

"It does not change our lives," her father answered. Gently he took the newspaper from her hands and folded it. "Why are you reading this? We have nothing to do with any of that. You know this, Magdalena." Where did she even get this newspaper? News of the Declaration of Independence had reached the countryside outside Philadelphia within a day. He could not shield her from that, but she had no business reading an *English* newspaper. Calmly, Christian sat on the top step leading up to the broad front porch of his home.

"How can you say it has nothing to do with us, *Daed*? These people took Nathanael from me. And now they want to force me to be a part of their new nation?" Magdalena paced in the dirt at the bottom of the steps. Her youngest siblings tumbled in the grass beyond her.

"We live separate, Magdalena," Christian said. "Apart. Peacefully. We give our allegiance to God. Force is not a part of our lives."

"Tell that to Nathan."

"Magdalena!"

She stopped pacing, crossed her arms, and turned to face him. "I'm sorry, *Daed*. I mean no disrespect. They attacked Nathanael and he has never been the same. I know the men who did it."

"One of them was shot in the battle at Lexington. The ways of force did not help him."

"You know Nathanael was not the only one they bullied," Magdalena said.

"The Patriots bully anyone who is not a Patriot." It was simple fact, Christian thought.

"But they *especially* bully the Amish."

"They understand an enemy," Christian said. "The British are an enemy, and they believe they must fight an enemy. But they do not understand neutrality. They do not understand loving their enemies."

"The British are not much better. Look what they did to your corn."

"They harmed only a small fraction of the crop."

"Were you really there when your father swore allegiance to King George?"

Magdalena seemed to be calming, he was glad to see. "I was not supposed to be. I was a disobedient little boy who snuck off a ship and into a strange city. I put myself and my family at risk because I wanted to see my *daed* take the oath. But yes, I was there."

"He promised allegiance to the Crown. Did that duty die with him? Or are we bound by it as well?"

"Magdalena, you are full of questions tonight." Christian was not surprised. Of all his children, Magdalena was the most spirited. She had grown into the image of her missing *aunti* Maria in more ways than one.

"If I have to choose a side, I choose the British," Magdalena said.

"But we will not choose a side. You understand this, *ya?*"

She did not answer.

"Take the little ones inside to clean up for bed, please," Christian said.

Magdalena called the children, and they rambled up the steps, pausing to kiss their *daed* on their way into the house.

In a month or so Babsi would bear their second child. After two miscarriages following Antje's birth, Babsi was particularly anxious to hold this child in her arms. When he was a boy, Christian's parents left Europe because of the proliferation of wars. They did not want their only son to grow up and be forced to serve in an army. That was why his father swore allegiance to the king of England. Pennsylvania was a free land. But could it now remain free and be peaceful while his own children grew up?

A few days later, Jacob held his own declaration of independence. Lisbet lived up to her name and even looked like his mother. This squalling bundle was the first of his children—the first of his family—to be born in the United States of America, rather than a British colony.

Jacob kissed his new daughter's cheek, grateful she would grow up in a free nation.

Seventeen

"Did you sleep?" Annie handed Penny her largest mug filled with hot coffee.

Eyes closed, Penny inhaled the steam. "I didn't think I would, but I did."

"Must be the mountain air." Annie gestured to the dining room table. "I made blueberry muffins."

"From scratch?"

"From scratch."

"I'm impressed."

"You should be." Annie picked up a muffin and bit into it.

"You have hot water in this joint? I need a shower."

"We are a five-star camping facility. But me first. I know how you dawdle."

Upstairs, Annie showered and dressed. Then half listening to the sounds of Penny's progress, she opened the folder she had retrieved the night before and stuck an envelope in the bag she always carried. An hour later, with Penny at the wheel, they rolled into the Beiler driveway.

Ruth was ready, sitting on the porch with her small bag and her head back against the top of the Adirondack chair. She looked weary to Annie. When Ruth spotted the car, she leaned forward and lifted herself out of the seat.

Annie got out of the car and met Ruth coming down the porch steps. "Excuse my bluntness, but you look like a truck hit you."

Ruth rubbed one hand over an eye. "I didn't sleep."

"Your next visit will be more restful. The Stutzmans will move out and you'll get your room back."

Ruth shook her head. "There's just so much to think about when I come here."

Annie considered probing, but Ruth moved toward the Prius and did not meet her eyes. A car door slammed, and Annie saw that Penny had gotten out and was walking toward them.

Annie pulled an envelope out of her bag. "Ruth, before you go, I have something for you."

Ruth twisted at the waist to look at Annie. "You do so much for me as it is."

"I want to give you some papers." Annie slipped a form out of the envelope and unfolded it. "This is the title to the Prius. I've signed it over to you."

"What?" Ruth's sluggish steps froze.

Penny came near. "Yes, what she said. What?" She took the paper from Annie's hands. "You really did sign over the title to Ruth Beiler."

"You have to take it back," Ruth said.

Annie shook her head. "Nope. I already put your name in and signed."

Penny handed the paper to Ruth. "Looks legal to me."

"It may be legal," Ruth said, "but it's crazy."

"Why?" Annie set her jaw in challenge. "You need a car."

"I've been getting along without one."

"It's stressful to get around in Colorado Springs without a car. You can't do that indefinitely. You have a permit, after all."

"For ID purposes," Ruth said.

"Then why have you been learning to drive?"

Penny's eyebrows went up. "You've been learning to drive?"

"Shh. Not so loud." Ruth glanced toward the house. "My

mother doesn't know and this is not the way to tell her."

"Of course not." Penny lowered her voice. She turned to Annie. "But what about insurance? Repairs?"

"It's still under warranty for two more years." Annie handed the envelope to Ruth. "The papers are in here, along with enough cash to put insurance in your name for the next six months."

"But your *car*," Ruth said.

"*Your* car." Annie blew out a breath. "I've been thinking about this constantly the last few days. And about what I did on Saturday. I can't have the car sitting there, tempting me, making it so easy. I would always know I could get it whenever I want. You need it. I don't."

Penny looked from Annie to Ruth. "You really have a permit?"

Ruth nodded.

"Then this is yours." Penny dangled the Prius key in front of Ruth.

Ruth softened. "I don't know what to say, Annalise."

"Just drive carefully."

"I will," Ruth said. She looked back toward the house. "But not until we're out of town. I don't need to rub it in *Mamm*'s face."

"Then let's hit the road," Penny said. "We'll drop Annie off and get going."

Annie shook her head. "I don't have to be at the shop until two o'clock. I'm going to hang around here awhile. Maybe work on my quilt."

"I'm sure *Mamm* would love that," Ruth said.

Something in Ruth's tone sounded off to Annie, but Ruth was already putting her bag in the car so the moment for conversation passed. Annie hugged her sister then waved good-bye as Penny turned the car around and aimed for the road. What would Penny and Ruth find to talk about? she wondered. Or would they be content with silence? She hoped not.

Annie turned, went up the steps, and crossed the porch. Tapping lightly on the front door, she turned the knob with the other hand. She glanced over her shoulder and across the clearing to Rufus's workshop. Franey would know if Rufus was around.

No one was in the front room. Jacob would be in school, and Joel should be out in the fields with his father. *Franey, Lydia, and Sophie must be scattered in the house,* Annie thought, *or perhaps in the barn.* She heard no sound of any of the Stutzmans, either. Perhaps they were busy readying their own home.

Annie moved to the cedar chest under the window. If she had a few minutes alone, she could surprise Franey by making some progress. Her palms stroked the polished finish of the chest. She imagined Rufus's hands insisting on perfection in his craft. The touch of the solid chest that he had labored over started a tremble in her fingers. She wished Rufus would feel that way about the quilt she labored over. Annie knew it was far from perfect, though. Perhaps this would not be the quilt he admired, but the next one, or the one after that. Her throat thickened. How long would it take before she could offer Rufus what he deserved in a wife?

Maybe never. Even if she could learn to be perfectly Amish, she had done things in her past she was not sure she would ever want to admit to Rufus.

Penny's words knocked around in Annie's head. Was she sure becoming Amish was not just for Rufus? She could be wrong. With a sigh, she lifted her eyes to the ceiling. *Lord, make me sure. I'll go or I'll stay. Just make me sure.* But at the thought of a future without Rufus her chest heaved in protest.

She had begun to lift the lid when she heard the familiar weight on the outside steps.

Rufus opened the front door, an empty tumbler in his hand that he intended to refill in the kitchen.

The cedar chest's lid thumped closed. Annalise spun around and smiled at him. He loved her smile. Today, though, it left him doubting her state of mind.

"So our sisters are off together," Rufus said.

Annalise nodded. "They may spill all our secrets to each other."

"More likely they'll stare at each other for an hour or so."

"No doubt." Annalise moved toward him and reached for the glass. "Let me pour you a cold drink."

He let go of the glass but did not miss the tremor in her hand. "Just finishing a few odd jobs." He looked around. "Is no one home?"

"Not that I can tell," Annalise said.

She turned toward the kitchen, but he touched her wrist then held her hand. "I don't really care about the drink. We haven't talked in ages. I want to know how you are."

She was trembling. He was sure of it. And her eyes were puddles.

"How was your visit home?" He nudged her gently to the sofa and sat down beside her.

Her lips moved through about twenty poses without settling on words.

"Complicated, eh?" he said.

She nodded and put her hands up to the sides of her head, squeezing. "My family doesn't understand what I'm doing. Sometimes I think I don't understand what I'm doing myself."

Now the tremble was in her voice. He took her hands in his and lowered them to her lap, holding them there. Under his fingers, he felt the resistance slide away. He waited a few more seconds, holding her with his eyes, urging the tension from her.

"You're listening," he said, "and trying to obey."

She took a deep breath and exhaled heavily. Her hands, still under his, relaxed.

Rufus raised a finger to her lips. "You don't have to explain everything now." He traced her lips, lightly, barely touching them. In the months he had known her, he could count on one hand the times he had kissed her. But he had lost track of the number of times he wanted to kiss her. If he gave in every time he wanted to—every time she wanted him to—he would not be thinking of her good, but only his pleasure.

The tremble was in her face now, and he knew he should stop. If he did not, he would move his hand to her hair, and his face close to hers. This woman, this *English* who dared to take up Amish ways, turned him inside out.

He brushed the back of his hand across her cheek and moved away from her. "I can take some time away from my work," he said. "Let's go for a walk."

Her eyes brightened, the puddles cleared. "Yes, I would like that."

He heard the faint rattle of a buggy turning down their lane, and his mind rapidly indexed who it might be. The horse's steps were solid, the trot steady. The axle of the buggy creaked. Ike Stutzman almost had not bought the buggy because of that creak.

When the front door opened, Annalise stood up. Rufus rose and turned to see Beth come through the door.

"Oh, good," Beth said, "you're not busy. *Daed* asked me to come fetch you. He wants your advice about some cabinets in the new house. He wonders if you might be able to repair them."

"Perhaps I could come by later in the afternoon."

Annalise moved out of his peripheral vision, but Rufus forced himself not to glance at her in Beth's presence.

"He was hoping you could come now. If you don't think you can fix them, then he'll tear them out today. He doesn't want any more delay in making the house ready for us to move in."

"*Ya*, I suppose every day matters. You go on, though. I'll get my tools and bring my own buggy."

"I would be happy to take you." Beth took a step toward him and smiled. "I'd love the company."

"I may need my buggy to go on to a job site anyway." Rufus stepped back. "Let your *daed* know I'm coming and I'll be right there."

"If you insist."

He let out a sigh when she retreated through the door. When he turned, though, Annalise was not in the room.

Rufus went through the house to the kitchen, where Annalise

487

was washing the tumbler he had carried in.

"I'll come right back," he said. "We'll take that walk."

She shook her head. "I'll just walk back to town. I have some thinking to do." She set the glass in the dish rack.

Rufus regretted not kissing her when he had the chance.

Eighteen

*I*f he had just kissed her, she would feel better. Annie had not expected Rufus to kiss her, though, because he hardly ever did. Still, if only he had.

Annie hit the button on the cash register and the change drawer kicked open, nudging her just below the ribs. She counted back change to a customer who left happily with a small silver-framed mirror Annie had priced and set out only two hours ago. When Mrs. Weichert returned, she would be pleased to hear of several sales that made the day profitable. Two other couples still lingered in the shop, unusual for a Thursday afternoon. Annie picked up a rag to wipe down an empty shelf before she began bringing knickknacks from the back room to fill it.

Of course Rufus was not interested in Beth. Annie knew that, even if Beth did not. But the undefined nature of her own relationship with Rufus left her feeling uncomfortably exposed. She did not have to be Amish to see that the community would love to see him married—to an Amish woman. Beth Stutzman would be a better Amish wife than Annie could ever hope to be.

Annie blew out her breath and rattled her lips. A buzzing sound escaped. Oops.

489

"Pardon me," she said to a startled customer who was approaching the counter. "May I help you?"

The customer led her to the back of the shop where yellow-paged tomes stood in formation in trim uniforms on neat shelves. The books the shop carried did not qualify as rare, but they were anywhere from forty to eighty years old. Novels, biographies, histories, and genealogies beckoned from decades past. Annie sometimes got distracted with them herself, pausing to read when she was supposed to be organizing. Certainly they were more noteworthy than the unsorted hardbacks in the several thrift stores in town. The customer already had three books in his hands. Annie focused on helping him find the final volume he sought then returned to the front of the store to ring up yet another sale.

She needed to stop thinking about Rufus. That was all there was to it. She had work to do.

The bell on the door jangled as the remaining customers left the shop without purchasing anything. Annie pulled a clipboard from a shelf below the cash register and traced a finger down the task list Mrs. Weichert had created for the week. Alone in the shop, Annie could not disappear to the back room longer than it took to bring items to the front. She went back and forth a few times, wiping down each item as she put it on a shelf, always listening for the bell.

And she was not thinking about Rufus. Not much, anyway. But he still owed her a walk, and she intended to collect.

When the door opened next, a medley of tenor and bass voices drowned the bell. Annie looked up. A mass of gangly teenage appendages stampeded as a herd through the door. Out of the center of the creature they had become, three crates emerged and hit the floor in thuds.

"Hello, Annalise."

Joel Beiler came into focus. Mark and Luke Stutzman stood on either side of him, and behind them were Carter Reynolds and Duncan Spangler. Somebody thumped fingers rhythmically against a denim-leg drum, but Annie could not see who. It had to be one of the *English*. At the random thought that Amish cloth did not make that sound, Annie blinked twice.

She tossed her dust rag on the front counter. "Hello, boys." She glanced at each one in turn. "What do we have here?"

"Amish stuff." Carter Reynolds peered at his phone and moved his thumbs into action on its buttons.

"Mrs. Weichert said Mrs. Stutzman could sell things on commission." Joel pointed a foot toward a crate. "Carved boxes, small wooden buggies. Some quilting."

"I see." Annie bent and lifted a lap quilt off the top of one crate. Rich colors in a complex pattern with small pieces, exquisite stitching. "It's beautiful."

"My sister Beth made that one," Mark Stutzman said.

Of course she did. Annie dropped the quilt, unfolded, back onto the crate. "We'll have to go through and price everything individually."

Mark produced a sheet of paper folded down to a square. "*Mamm* put on here what she would like to sell them for."

"I see." Annie unfolded and inspected the page. Mrs. Weichert would likely add another 20 percent, but the items would still be priced attractively. The word *Amish* on the labels would raise the curiosity factor. Amish items tended to move quickly on the weekends.

Carter elbowed his way past the Amish boys. "I'll help you carry them to the back." He set his phone on the counter and bent down.

"Thank you, Carter." Annie squatted, briefly riffling through the contents of a crate before grasping its sides. She felt her own cell phone escape her back pocket just as she stood again. It hit the floor. "Can someone grab that? Just set it on the counter."

She followed Carter into the back room, and Joel trailed with the last of the crates. Annie wondered about the motley assortment of boys who had arrived together. Joel was slightly older than the others, with responsibilities of his own. How did he come to have a free afternoon to spend with *English* boys? Carter's father often provided taxi service for Amish families. From what Annie observed a few days ago, though, she did not think Joel was interested in befriending the Stutzman brothers. Yet here they were, all together. Joel's face was as blank as a whiteboard. She could discern nothing from watching him. And Duncan? The Spanglers were neighbors not too far from her house off Main Street, but she knew little about them. Annie supposed Duncan and Carter went to school together.

"Did you bring a buggy into town?" Annie picked up a carved wooden buggy.

"We came in the back of my dad's truck," Carter offered.

"How will you get home, then?" Her eyes turned to Joel.

Joel glanced out the shop's window. "Tom said he might have to run back our way later. Or we can walk."

Annie nodded. It was not as if she could offer them a ride, by car or by buggy.

"Let's go," Mark called from the front room.

Annie wondered what they could be in such a hurry about, but the boys, once again silhouetted by the afternoon sunlight, morphed into one creature with entangled legs that managed to amble out of the shop. She watched them for a moment through the display window as they traversed Main Street in a black huddle. They did not pause to examine any windows but rather moved purposefully, leaving Annie pondering again what united the five of them.

Ten minutes passed before Annie encountered the cell phone on the counter. She knew immediately it was not hers—the scratches on the front cover were not right. It had to be Carter's.

She flipped the phone open just to be sure. It lit immediately with a hideous screen saver no doubt hacked from a video game Carter was not technically old enough to purchase.

With the phone in her hand, Annie stepped out to the sidewalk and looked up and down the street. The boys could be anywhere by now. Surely Carter would try to use his phone and realize the mistake. She needed to close the shop in twenty minutes. Would they come back by then? Even if she could justify the situation as an emergency—which it was not—calling her phone to alert Carter was pointless. Her phone was not turned on.

Annie went back inside the shop and sat on the stool behind the counter. The phone buzzed with a text message. Out of long instinct she flipped it open again. MOM SAYS BE HOME FOR DINNER. The message must be from one of Carter's sisters.

Sometimes Annie thought giving up her cell phone was harder than surrendering her computer. Her iPhone had been such an easy connection to any information she wanted. The phone she had now, identical to Carter's, was capable of connecting to the Internet but she did not carry the service. Did Carter's parents let him have an Internet package on his phone? she wondered. Pressing her thumb in a quick sequence answered her question.

His Internet history twisted her gut. She was being nosy, she knew. Not an admirable quality in an Amish woman. But she saw what she saw, and now she would not be able to ignore it. Why was a fifteen-year-old boy from a small town looking for that kind of information?

Annie cleared her throat. She powered the phone off, slapped it closed, and jammed it in a back pocket. Her lips worked in and out six times.

She had faced temptation and lost—again. Just for a moment she remembered running her life from her phone.

Temptation led to knowledge, though.

To seek help for the boy, she would have to admit she poked around in Carter's private business.

Maybe it was nothing. She had searched for stranger topics herself, just out of curiosity.

But maybe it was something.

Nosy or not, and almost Amish or not, Annie was going to find out what those boys were up to.

The hands on the clock ticked slowly toward four thirty, when Annie could close the shop. The boys would have almost thirty minutes' head start. She would sprint the four blocks home, grab her bicycle, and start asking questions around town. Five teenage boys on foot could not disappear without leaving a trail.

One thought made Annie press her fingers against closed eyes. If Joel was involved in this, Franey would tremble to her core.

Nineteen

Rufus hitched up the lightweight open cart to Dolly, his favorite horse among the three the Beilers kept. Under the cart's seat, as always, a basket held apples. Rufus grabbed one and pressed it against Dolly's lips, smiling as she snatched it with her teeth and crunched. He swung up into the driver's seat and took the reins in his hands.

The front screen door thwacked closed. Joel was supposed to fix the broken spring three days ago. Someone was sure to get hurt if it went unattended much longer. Before turning his head toward the porch, Rufus knew the footsteps crossing it were his mother's.

"I'm looking for Joel." Franey stood at the base of the steps, one hand on a hip and the other shading her eyes. "He should have been in from the fields by now. They've only just planted the alfalfa. How much weeding could there be to do? If he'd said he was irrigating I might believe he is still out there."

"Would you like me to ride out to the field to find him?" Rufus's stomach sank at the thought of chasing after his wayward brother rather than accomplishing his errand.

"No. You have things to do. I think I should ask your *daed* to speak to Joel. But if you see your brother, bring him home with you."

"Yes, *Mamm*. I will see you for supper with or without Joel." Rufus nudged the horse forward.

Dolly found her trotting rhythm as soon as he turned out onto the highway. Time was tight. Rufus clicked his tongue to see if Dolly had any canter in her.

When he pulled up in front of the construction trailer that served as the office of Kramer Construction, Rufus tied Dolly securely to the closest tree, climbed the three narrow makeshift steps up to the trailer, and opened the door. Just inside, a young woman lifted her eyes without moving her head. Her fingers held their place above the keyboard.

"I would like to see Mr. Kramer, please." Rufus looked her in the eyes. Her frown made clear she knew who he was. And she knew how the man who signed her paycheck felt about him.

"He's on the phone." The woman's fingers resumed their patter.

"I'll wait."

There was no place to sit. File cabinets and stacks of blueprints cluttered the space. Rufus spread his feet apart slightly and crossed his hands in front of him. The thin walls of the trailer did little to disguise the animation in Karl Kramer's voice behind a closed door. Whatever the deal was, Karl intended to have his way. His price. His schedule. His crew. Rufus focused his eyes on the back of the woman's computer monitor and tried to hear more of her soft keys clacking than the voice in the other room.

When the voice fell silent, he thought she might look up. Because she did not, he cleared his throat.

"Just a moment." She leaned toward the monitor, squinted, and made two quick corrections. "I'll ask Mr. Kramer if he is available to see you."

Not, *I'll tell Mr. Kramer you're here*. The difference was not lost on Rufus as she slipped through the office door and closed it behind her. On the other side the voices were low, indistinct.

She returned perhaps ten seconds later. "Mr. Kramer is unavailable. He has a number of matters to attend to before the town meeting tonight. Perhaps another time."

Rufus was not surprised in the least, though he was fairly certain that these were not the same words Karl Kramer used to express his decision. "My business is *about* the meeting tonight," Rufus said. "It is important that I see him."

Her smile was vacant. "I'm afraid that's not possible." She took her chair again. "Can I help you with anything else?"

"No. Nothing else, thank you. Only this one thing." Rufus did not move.

"Perhaps if you were to make an appointment for some time next week."

He shifted his weight to one leg. "The afternoon is nearly over. I will just wait and have a word with him on his way out."

"I'm afraid he was quite specific that he did not want to see you, Mr. Beiler." She turned over a stack of papers and moved her fingers back to the keyboard.

Rufus counted to ten.

Then he counted back from ten.

Then he turned, took two steps, rapped three times, and opened Karl Kramer's office door himself.

At home, Annie changed into a sturdy pair of tennis shoes and made sure she wore a sweatshirt with a hood. April afternoons could turn chilly without notice. She zipped up, rolled the bike forward, and jumped on. The boys had headed east on Main Street, which meant they could have crossed the vague line between Westcliffe and Silver Cliff.

It was probably nothing. She hoped it was nothing. Just a teenage boy curious about a question in the news. But even what she scanned before shutting down the phone seemed like more than idle curiosity to Annie, and she wanted to be sure. After all, it could be dangerous. She pedaled down Main Street, stopping at a few of the shops to duck her head in and ask if anyone had seen the boys. One of the perks of living in a small town was that people were likely to know the boys and whether they had been around. Sometimes it seemed to Annie that the town had all-seeing eyes.

She traced them for most of a mile before information petered out. Her last stop was a gas station.

"Hello, Hank." Annie pulled up to the air pump alongside a service bay and fiddled with it. She pushed a couple of squirts of air into her rear tire. "I wonder if you've seen some boys. Kind of a strange bunch. Amish and *English* together."

Hank laughed. "Dressed in black?"

"Last time I looked."

"They were here." Hank wiped oil off his hands onto a cloth. "They were hanging around the diesel pumps."

Annie's stomach tightened. Diesel fuel?

"The only one who looked old enough to drive was Amish," Hank said. "If they had bothered to bring a can, I might believe somebody needed gas for a tractor. But it wouldn't take five guys to carry a can. They're getting nothing from me. I shooed them off."

Annie swallowed. "Did you happen to see which way they went?"

Hank waved his rag down a side street. Annie hopped back on her bike.

Even though they had a half hour's jump, they were still on foot when they left the gas station.

Annie pedaled into the wind, scanning the flat acres of the valley between the Wet Mountains and the Sangre de Cristos as she moved from town streets, around aging buildings at the edge of town, to broken asphalt and gravel stretches. Every now and then, someone stepped outside to check a mailbox or fill a garbage can or rake a flower bed.

Across a field, she spotted a mass of black that seemed to shape-shift, first a stretched line, then a compact ball, then a straggling string. She pedaled harder. They were cutting across open field—easier on foot than on a bike. Twice Annie lost her balance when she hit a stubborn rise of earth with insufficient momentum, her ankle taking the impact of catching herself on one foot. Annie debated abandoning her bicycle to move more quickly on foot, but she dreaded the thought of having to find her way back to retrieve it from under a random scrub oak. Annie rode when she could and walked beside the bike when she could not pedal safely. Keeping the boys in view while lugging the bike pushed her heart rate up higher than it had been in a long time.

Finally she was close enough to call out. "Joel!"

The black mass thinned as one figure paused and turned. The others slumped along, unperturbed. Annie resolved to succeed at keeping her balance on the old bike and swung a leg over its seat. She forced the top pedal down and threw her slight weight into making it rotate.

Joel heard her, she was sure of it. He paused, after all, and looked back across the field at the sound of his name. But he had turned back to follow the others. Annie saw them disappear one by one, at random intervals, but because of the rise in the hill and the distance she could not see where. She pedaled yet harder—and tumbled to the ground. Splayed in the dirt with the bike three feet away, Annie gobbled air. When she managed to get upright again and assure herself that it did not hurt to move, Joel was out of sight.

Annie kicked the bike's front tire and left it lying in the dirt. Then she muttered, "Humble, humble, humble."

On foot, she scrambled to where she had last seen the boys. Without the eye-bending rise and fall of terrain, she saw now where they disappeared. A slight slope hid their final steps, but only one destination was possible.

A construction site. Or at least some kind of storage site.

It was fenced and surrounded by a tent of thick plastic. Annie sidestepped along the fence line looking for an interruption to the boundary, any place they might have slipped under a loose flap of plastic sheeting or squeezed around a post.

"Hey!"

The booming voice nearly stopped her heart. "What are you doing here?"

Annie expelled breath then allowed a measured amount of air back into her lungs as she turned around. She did not recognize the tall, deeply tanned man. "Just out enjoying the countryside."

"This is a hard hat zone." He knocked his knuckles against his own head covering. "And it's private property."

Annie raised her hands, palms out. "Not looking for trouble."

Twenty

Hard Hat Guy gestured with one thumb that the conversation was over. He pointed Annie back the way she had come.

Annie smiled pleasantly. "Have a nice evening."

She backtracked to where her bicycle had betrayed her and yanked it upright. Scanning the view once more, she saw for the first time the tracks of mashed weeds. Twenty feet away were the twin ruts trucks must have used. Following the boys earlier, she had descended the knoll at the wrong angle. The truck route would have been doable on the bike. She heard an engine catch and watched the man in the hard hat steer his truck onto the makeshift road and head in the other direction.

Good. The coast was clear. It took more than a guy in a hard hat to deter Annie Friesen.

On her bike again, Annie rode in the tracks down to the fenced area and around to the other side. If a construction site had a front, this was it. She approached and held still, certain that if the boys were inside she would hear them. Nothing. No shuffle. No murmur. A cat brushed her leg as it emerged through the fence. It shot off in a typical feline manner, but Annie figured the cat saved her some time looking for an opening. She laid her bike down and squatted to peer through the tear in the plastic sheeting.

Stacks of bricks. Bags of cement. Piles of lumber neatly arranged by size. Twin green wheelbarrows. Rolled rubber edging.

What was so secretive about that? Annie did not see what Carter might have been looking for, but other than some odd storage she did not see any sign of actual construction, either. She might have been strolling the aisles of a home improvement store. Relieved not to find anything more sinister, she straddled her bike again.

She still had Carter's phone.

Rufus closed the trailer door behind him, having come to a fragile agreement with Karl Kramer. He would do everything he could to prove he meant what he said.

Next he would have to persuade a few more people that he had not lost the good sense God gave him. He untied Dolly, led her in a half circle to get turned around, and headed the cart toward home. He needed a good meal before the evening meeting.

Annie spotted Joel, perhaps a mile later, his lanky height in relief to his surroundings. He was on a footpath that ran parallel to the highway in stretches and disappeared at other times. This time she did not call his name. She just pedaled harder.

He was alone when she reached him and cut him off by riding just past him, then bringing the bicycle to an abrupt halt in his path.

He met her eyes but said nothing.

"I know you heard me." Annie planted her feet on either side of the bike and removed her helmet.

"I wasn't sure you were calling me," he mumbled.

Yes, he was. Annie let it pass. "Where is everyone else?"

"Heading home for supper, I guess. Carter and Duncan have homework."

"And Mark and Luke?" Why wouldn't the Stutzman boys be

with Joel if they were all returning to the Beiler home for the evening meal?

"Not sure. I think they went to find their *daed* for a ride. I decided to walk."

At that rate, he would be late for supper again. Annie reminded herself she was not his mother. Joel was seventeen. He knew what he was choosing.

"What were you all doing at that storage site?"

"We weren't." Joel answered quickly. "It's just a shortcut."

That was the longest shortcut to nowhere Annie had ever seen.

She pulled Carter's phone from her back pocket. "Carter picked up the wrong phone."

"No wonder it wasn't ringing constantly." Joel put out an open hand. "I'll get yours back for you."

Annie swung her arm back, moving the phone beyond Joel's reach. "That's all right. I'll hang on to this one for now. I know how your father feels about having cell phones in the house."

She watched him, looking for a sign that he knew what was on the phone. The wobble in Joel's nod was unconvincing.

"By now Carter has probably figured out the mistake," Joel said. "I'm sure he'll want to trade back as soon as he can."

"No doubt. He can come by the shop."

Joel scuffed a step away from Annie. "I should probably get going."

Annie did not move. "What's going on, Joel?"

"Excuse me?"

Joel did not have the same wide violet-blue eyes several of his siblings had. His were brown. Annie never could read brown eyes. She stared into them and found no hint of anything amiss, but she did not believe it.

"How is Carter getting along these days?"

Joel spread his feet and stood solid. "The *English* make everything so complicated."

Who was he talking about?

"Joel, I looked at Carter's phone. At his Internet history. I saw what he was looking up."

"Carter is always looking at his phone. He sends texts and plays games. I don't pay attention."

"So you don't know what he was looking up today?"

He moved to get around her. Annie let the bike roll forward to block him again, relieved that he was reluctant to lie outright.

"Joel," Annie said, "if Carter's in trouble, you want to help him, don't you?"

"Carter is just *English*. They don't know how to let things be."

Again with the doublespeak about the *English*.

"I think you know what's on his phone."

"You make too much of it."

"Do I?"

Brown eyes or not, Annie was ready to stare down Joel.

Rufus slowed the cart, looking for a safe place to pull over and be out of traffic. His tug on the reins halted Dolly.

"Joel!"

Joel and Annalise both answered his call with their glances. Though Joel was on foot and Annalise had her bicycle, Rufus suspected he had interrupted more than a random encounter between friends.

"Joel, *Mamm* was looking for you. She'll be wondering where you were. I'll take you home."

"She does not have to worry about me." Joel gripped the side of the cart's seat and prepared to heft himself up.

"It's a matter of simple respect to tell her if you need to leave the farm."

"I'm not a child, Rufus."

Rufus turned away from his sulking brother and took in the sight of Annalise. Dirt smudges on her jeans. The gray sweatshirt, unzipped, falling off one shoulder. A haphazard elastic band slipping out of her hair. Disheveled. Annalise at her best, in Rufus's opinion. "You look like you could use a ride home."

Annalise sat on the bike, her hands gripping the handlebars, one foot on a pedal, the other ready to push off. "I'll be fine."

She always said that. So independent.

"It will only take me a few minutes to ride a couple of miles," Annalise said. "You should take Joel home."

She would manage, Rufus knew. And it was better if he did not imply that she needed his help. Still, he wished he had time to take her home.

"Are you going to the town meeting tonight?" Annalise asked.

"Yes." Rufus perked up. "And you?"

She nodded. "At the elementary school, right?"

"Yes, I believe so."

"Then I'll see you there." Annalise smiled.

"I'm sorry we did not have our walk, Annalise."

"There will be other days."

Joel swung himself into the seat. "We'd better go or we'll both be late for supper."

Rufus turned back to Annalise. "May I pick you up for the meeting this evening?"

Her eyes flickered bright. "That would be lovely."

Again, she glanced at Joel. Rufus followed her eyes. What was going on between those two?

"Then I'll see you in a couple of hours," Rufus said.

Annalise nodded and shoved off. Rufus watched her pedal in the opposite direction; then he nudged Dolly forward.

"Joel," he said, "is there something going on that I should know about?"

"Just drive."

Twenty-One

After supper, Rufus took Dolly down Main Street pulling a buggy, rather than the nimble cart he used for daytime errands. With the sun gone down, the temperature dropped, and the buggy was warmer and dryer. Rufus wanted Annalise to be comfortable, even though the ride to the elementary school was only a mile from her home.

He turned left off Main Street a block early, made two right turns, and pulled up in front of Annalise's narrow house aimed back toward Main Street. Her head bobbed in the front window just before she pulled the curtain closed and put out the light. A moment later, she locked the front door behind her and followed the path of concrete stepping-stones, hardly more than rubble, that led to the street. More than once Rufus had offered to clear the crumbling steps and pour Annalise a new walkway. So far she refused. She had fallen once over the winter, but even then she insisted that a new walkway would ice over just as easily as the old one.

Rufus dropped from the bench at the front of the buggy and offered a hand to Annalise. He was never sure if she would accept his assistance or walk past him to heave herself up into the buggy.

Tonight she accepted, and he squeezed her hand slightly in the process. Her dress was not Amish, but she wore a modest dark

506

skirt and sweater rather than jeans. She had gotten pretty good at braiding her hair and pinning it close to her head. He liked her hair down, but of course he would not tell her that.

"I was surprised to find you with Joel," Rufus said once they were moving.

"He was there on the path when I came along on my bicycle."

She flashed him a smile, yet it disappointed him. He knew her smiles. This one said, *I'm not going to talk about that.*

"He should have been at home." Rufus let the sway of the buggy nudge his shoulder into Annalise's.

"So I gathered." Annalise was watching the road, turning her head in both directions at the corner.

She still had the instincts of an automobile driver, Rufus thought. He did not suppose anyone ever unlearned how to drive. She had not said anything for weeks now about learning to drive a buggy. He waited for three cars to pass before giving Dolly rein to turn left onto Main Street and follow the way to the school.

"*Daed* is becoming impatient with Joel," Rufus said. "My brother Daniel used to do the same thing—disappear for hours and see no wrong in it as long as his work was done."

"Daniel straightened out, didn't he?"

"Only because Martha Glick came along. Daniel was smitten hard, and she does not put up with nonsense."

Annalise laughed. Something at the center of Rufus melted every time a lilt escaped her lips. Daniel was not the only Beiler brother to be smitten. But Martha was Amish. The solution had been simple. Daniel and Martha shared a faith and a community that included their families. Annalise's choice would be more complicated.

"I am afraid *Daed* will not be so patient this time," Rufus said. "Joel needs to think about his choices more seriously."

She did not answer. He wondered again what she knew.

They reached the school. Rufus steered Dolly to the edge of the parking lot where she would be out of the way.

"Looks like a good turnout for the meeting." Annalise accepted his assistance down from the buggy.

His was the only buggy, though. Not many Amish men would leave their farms and families for a town meeting, especially in the evening. His own father did not. Still, Rufus had hoped some would come.

Inside the school gym, a few rows of plastic chairs beckoned. Rufus and Annalise sat together. It was an odd sensation to be next to her in a group of people. In church, the most he could hope for was a glimpse of her among the women, across the wide rooms of hosts' homes. Rufus estimated about forty *English* had come—and thirty-five of them were speaking into cell phones, reading cell phone screens, closing cell phones, putting away cell phones.

Annalise used to be like that. He doubted she even had her cell phone with her tonight. People could change. Rufus liked to think so, at least in Annalise's case.

Tom Reynolds stood behind a table at the front of a group of chairs and cleared his throat heavily.

"Thank you all for coming," Tom said as the thin crowd settled. "As you know, this is not an official town meeting. It's just a conversation. A few of us have had some ideas for a project, and it seemed wise to invite others into the discussion. If you wish to speak, just raise your hand and I will call on you one at a time."

Tom scanned the gathering as heads nodded then recapped the idea for creating a recreation area on acreage the town owned. "The likelihood is the town council will make the project official, provided the community is willing to help. The project is outside the town's budget, though, so funding will be minimal. If the idea does come to fruition, it will be because the community makes it happen."

Rufus glanced at Annalise. She seemed to be listening intently. He wished they had sat farther back. He could not tell who might have come in late and sat down behind him.

Karl Kramer, for instance.

As soon as Tom Reynolds invited comments, Mo was up on her feet and standing in the aisle.

"We must have strong leadership," she said. "Someone who knows what he's doing. Someone who has the right skills for the sort of project we're undertaking. I propose that we ask Rufus Beiler to head it up."

Murmurs rose, and feet shuffled, but Mo held up a settling hand. "I know some of you are still unsure about the Amish in our community, but you all know Rufus Beiler. He does excellent work. You could trust him with your life." She turned to nod at Rufus.

"Why aren't any of the other Amish here?" someone asked. "If they are not going to support this, why should we put one of them in charge?"

Rufus winced.

"Tell them." Annalise elbowed him, whispering. "Explain how the Amish stay home with their families in the evening."

He shook his head.

Mo was still in the aisle. "You can't ask for a more dependable man than Rufus Beiler." She pointed around the gathering. "I know some of you have hired him to build your cabinets and to make furniture. When he accepts a project, he commits to excellence."

"Too bad you're not running for president." Annalise covered her mouth to hide her grin.

"Perhaps we should hear what Rufus has to say," someone suggested.

It was as if a wind blew through the place and turned every head toward Rufus.

He stood slowly, his hands on the back of the empty chair in front of him. "I suspected something like this might come up." He paused. "I recommend we include Karl Kramer in leading this project."

Annie heard the collective gasp.

"Karl Kramer!" Mo put both her fists on her hips. "You can't be serious. Karl Kramer would be the first person to wish the Amish would disappear from Westcliffe and all of Custer County."

"I did not say it would be without challenge." Rufus's fingers drummed the chair's back.

"He tried to kill you last year," Mo said. "If Tom hadn't found you on that construction site, you might have bled to death."

"We don't know that Karl was responsible for that."

"The police dropped the investigation because you would not press charges."

"The past is the past," Rufus said. "I bear no grudge toward Mr. Kramer. I think we both have seen there is work enough in this valley for the two of us—and others. I have already spoken with Mr. Kramer, and he has agreed to be coleaders."

"You and Karl Kramer?" Tom Reynolds's voice quivered in confusion. "You are proposing that you and Karl would work together?"

"I am."

Objection welled in Annie. Over the winter, she had tried hard to understand Rufus's refusal to press charges against the man who almost certainly attacked him. But Jesus said to turn the other cheek, as Rufus always reminded her. Instead of revenge, Rufus steered his own livelihood away from projects that would aggravate Karl, even sacrificing jobs that would have turned a good profit.

Keeping peace from a distance seemed to be working. So why would he voluntarily step within reach of Karl's slap?

"Rufus." Annie reached over and touched his hand, which still thumped the chair. He dropped his hands to his sides, away from her touch.

Annie grimaced at the sight around them. Voices erupted, people talking over each other. Mo looked like she was ready to punch someone. Here and there others stood to have their say.

Tom held out both hands to settle the crowd. "Let me suggest that this would be a good time to take a break. There are coffee and cookies in the back. We can reconvene in fifteen minutes."

Mo hurtled toward Rufus. Others swarmed as well. Annie

found herself snared under a web of swinging elbows. She scooted over one plastic chair at a time until she came to the end of the row. There she stood up to consider the crowd around Rufus.

These people liked him.

They trusted him.

They clamored for him.

Rufus stood patiently in his black trousers and collarless jacket, his hat on his head. If he were married, he would have a beard. No doubt it would grow long and curly, like his father's, and cover the space of chest where his shirt formed a white V under his chin.

On the surface he had nothing in common with these people.

Nothing in common with *her*. The thought unsettled her.

Annie moved slowly toward the table in the back where refreshments were set up. She never drank coffee this late in the day anymore. That was her old life. She might still be tempted to use her phone and drive in Colorado Springs, but staying up all night drinking coffee and working no longer held allure. Drifting toward the meager refreshments merely gave her a chance to think. Annie picked up a thickly frosted sugar cookie, which she knew for a fact came from the bakery on Main Street, and retreated to a corner.

Rufus's proposal stunned her. Work with Karl Kramer? Yet she could see the wisdom. If Rufus Beiler and Karl Kramer could work together, the Amish and the *English* might truly find their balance with each other. But without funding, Rufus's effort might come to nothing.

Every problem had an answer. At least one, and probably more. It was just a matter of finding the most efficient one.

It was coming to her, taking shape, finding focus. Just because she no longer owned a high-tech business did not mean she could not sift through solutions. By the time Rufus disentangled himself and stood at her side with a steaming Styrofoam cup, she had manipulated the factors to a pleasing conclusion.

She turned her face up to him. "I want to help, Rufus."

"Everyone is invited to help." He sipped his coffee.

"When I sold my business, I put all that money in a charitable foundation. It's not for my personal use. But this project would be perfect."

As usual, his face did not give him away. Annie plowed ahead.

"They'll settle this question of who should lead the project, and it will be you and Karl, together. You'll insist on the partnership, and because they want you so much they'll take Karl in the deal."

Rufus raised one eyebrow.

"The next issue will be money," Annie continued. "Tom already said the town doesn't have any. If money were not an issue, this recreation area could be done really well, and everyone would be happy to be part of it. I can do my part by arranging the financial end."

His eyes softened now. "Annalise, you have a kind heart. But it's not that simple."

"Why not? I wouldn't be using the money for personal reasons."

"But you would still be controlling it."

She shook her head. "Not if I set up a special account with the bank for you to access. The money would go there. I would have nothing to do with it." She waved her hands, nearly dropping the cookie. "You and Karl could decide together how to spend it."

"Annalise—"

Tom's voice interrupted him as Tom called the meeting back to order.

"Please don't suggest this," Rufus said, "not until we have a chance to talk more."

She stared into his violet-blue eyes and knew he would never agree, but for now she nodded. "Excuse me. I need to talk to Tom before he starts again."

"Annalise, please, do not speak to him about money tonight."

Annie ducked past Rufus, pulling a phone from her pocket in the same motion. She flipped it open, thumbed a few buttons, and cleared the Internet search history. By the time she reached Tom across the room, her intentions shifted. She held out the phone.

"Carter must have my phone," she said. "If you don't mind, ask him to bring it by the shop."

Tom tucked the phone in his shirt pocket. "I'm going to have to hang his phone around his neck. Or take it away from him. I'm not sure which."

"He was helping me when he set it down. Anyone could have picked up the wrong phone."

Tom scanned the room. "We'd better get started again."

Annie returned to her seat next to Rufus.

When the meeting reconvened, Mo reluctantly agreed to the arrangement Rufus suggested, and others agreed. Karl and Rufus would run the project—including raising the needed donations of materials, labor, and money.

The ride home was quiet. Rufus pulled on the reins in front of Annie's house, set the brake, and turned on the bench to face her.

"Thanks for the ride." Annie knew she was muttering but she could not help it. Why was it so hard for Rufus to understand that using the money in her foundation could benefit everyone in Westcliffe? She started to get down from the bench.

He put a hand on her shoulder. "Annalise, why do you think the *English* buy my furniture and cabinets?"

In the dark, she could not see his eyes. What was he really asking? "You do beautiful work. I don't have to be Amish to see that."

"Other people produce their merchandise more quickly, for less money."

"But it's not as good. There is value in your craftsmanship. It will last."

He nodded. "It is the Amish way. We build to last. Furniture, families, communities. There are no shortcuts."

"I don't see why generosity would undermine the Amish way." Heat crawled up the back of her neck.

He picked up one of her hands. "Sometimes the solutions must come from within the problem."

Twenty-Two

Aweek later Beth Stutzman laid another thick slice of pork roast on Rufus's plate. The third one. Fortunately, her father had already scraped the last of the mashed potatoes from the serving bowl.

Rufus smiled blandly into the beam of Beth's face.

She sat on his right. On his left was Johanna, and across the table sat Essie. Their uniform hairstyle accentuated the similarities of their features, differentiated only by different eye colors.

The Stutzmans were living in their own home—and not a minute too soon, which was an opinion Rufus kept to himself. When Beth invited him to dinner as a way to say thank you for his help in readying their home, he assumed his whole family would be there. He came straight from Mo's motel after installing some trim. Even then, he assumed his family would arrive in the second buggy at any moment. Only when he saw how the dining room table was set did he realize he had been singled out for the invitation.

"Tell us what you've been working on, Rufus." Ike Stutzman tore a corner off a slice of bread and steered it into his mouth. "The girls tell me you make beautiful end tables."

"I do have several orders for custom tables." Rufus politely pushed his fork through the tender pork. "I'll be taking a load to Colorado Springs next week."

"Do you make tables for the *English*?"

Rufus swallowed another bite, unsure of the shading of Ike's question. "Many *English* appreciate our value in both beauty and usefulness. It is not against *Ordnung* to do business with them."

"I suppose not."

Stifling a sigh, Rufus ate yet another bite of pork roast. "You seem to have settled in well here."

"I miss your family already," Beth said.

With her hair pinned perfectly and her posture flawless, Beth exuded competency at everything she put her hand to. Rufus resisted her gaze. "I'm sure we will see each other," he said.

"I have a feeling I will find myself wandering to your place in the afternoons, looking for a way to be helpful."

"I'm sure there will be plenty to do here," Rufus said. "You'll get used to a new routine soon enough."

"But our view is not nearly as lovely as yours."

Rufus nodded politely. It was not possible to have a bad view of the Sangre de Cristos from anywhere around Westcliffe.

"Where are the boys tonight?" he asked.

Edna Stutzman waved one hand. "Oh, you know, *rumschpringe*. They are having their running around time."

"They have made friends with some town boys." Beth seemed eager to share the information. "Your brother introduced them."

Rufus's eyebrows lifted a notch. Joel was introducing Amish boys to town boys?

"The boys have talked about *rumschpringe* for years," Edna said. "They just need to get it out of their system. We're sure they will settle down when the time comes."

Rufus nodded. Mark and Luke struck him as a little young for *rumschpringe*, not even old enough to attend Sunday night singings. Not old enough to consider courting. They were barely out of school. *English* boys their age would still be looking forward to high school. Amish boys should be taking up a man's share of household chores, especially in a family just moving to a new farm.

But Mark and Luke Stutzman were not his sons.

And neither was Joel.

"Were you pleased with the outcome of the meeting last week?" Ike stabbed his fork into the last of the green beans on his plate.

Rufus recognized the seasoning in the green beans. They must have come from his mother's cellar, canned from last year's garden bounty. Franey would have made sure the new family lacked nothing.

Including him, apparently.

He roused to answer Ike's question. "I'm pleased that community support seems to be growing. Even in the last week, more people have come forward and said they want to help."

"Are they *English* or Amish?"

"Both. I am only trying to do what is right."

"Then perhaps it will work out. You are an honorable man."

Ike's look of approval moved from Rufus to Beth. Rufus resisted the urge to squirm.

"I made pie," Beth announced.

All three daughters stood and began to stack dishes. Rufus saw no way out.

Forty minutes later, after insisting he could not eat a second slice of blackberry pie, Rufus climbed into the buggy and told Dolly to take him home.

If only he and Annalise could have a quiet, uninterrupted meal. They needed to do better than snatch a few minutes at a time.

"The estate did not look too promising. I'm not sure what's in the boxes," Mrs. Weichert told Annie on Friday afternoon. "I made an absurdly low offer for the whole lot, unseen. I did not expect they would accept it."

"Let's hope there's an amazing find in one of them." Standing beside the truck bed full of boxes and crates, Annie wriggled out of her unzipped sweatshirt. Drenched in the sunshine of a May sky, she jumped at the chance to work outside.

"I pulled up next to the trash bin on purpose," Mrs. Weichert said. "Use your own discretion. Feel free to chuck whole boxes if you don't see anything we can use."

"I'll get right to work." Annie hefted herself up on the open tailgate.

"I need coffee."

"Fresh pot ten minutes ago."

Mrs. Weichert disappeared through the shop's back door. Annie went to work. She estimated at least thirty boxes and crates of various sizes, all of them securely sealed. She pulled a box knife off her belt loop and went to work. Slashing open the first six boxes within reach revealed assorted books, handmade crafts, a porcelain figurine collection, dishes, fabric scraps, and throw pillows. Annie could see already that she would have to go through every box to find the one item that might make it to the shelves. Another batch would make a local thrift store very happy, and the rest was headed for the Dumpster. She immediately set aside the box of fabric scraps, wondering if there might be anything in it that could find its way into an Amish quilt.

Annie lost herself in the work. Two boxes held evidence of a lifetime carving habit and another a colored-glass bottle collection. Annie set aside a box of books for closer inspection later. A box of photographs made her pause long enough to find a place to sit.

There were almost exclusively black and whites, some of them professional portraits, and some reaching back decades. Perhaps even a hundred years.

Annie turned over a stack of photos and flipped through looking at the backs. A few had partially legible notations of names, places, and dates. For the most part, though, they were unmarked.

Probably the last person who might have known who these stern faces belonged to was gone. Words like "Mother" and "Uncle N after the war" did little to bring these lives into twenty-first-century memory. Someone was giving away an entire family history because no one was left to remember it.

Annie thought of the lists of names that traced her family and Rufus's. Three hundred years ago they shared an ancestor. Now they had an occasional unsubstantiated story, or a rare photo from her family. A year ago she had paid attention to none of it. Now she could not imagine boxing it all up to sell to a stranger willing to haul it away.

She let out the heaviness that had gathered in her chest and wiped an eye with a knuckle.

"Annalise, are you all right?"

She turned at the shoulders to see Elijah Capp standing at the end of the truck, a toolbox hanging from one arm. "Hello," she said. "Yes, I'm fine. Just sorting all this stuff."

"Mrs. Weichert called about a plumbing problem."

Annie nodded. "The sink in the back room. It's not draining well. I don't think it's anything too troublesome."

"I'll take a look."

"Thank you, Elijah." She raised her eyes to meet his. He seemed to hold words in his throat that he could not bring himself to say. "Is there something else?"

"I don't know if Ruth told you she saw me," he finally said, "when she came down with you a couple weeks ago."

"No, she didn't say anything." Anyone could see Elijah Capp was still twisted in heartbreak.

"I know she's not coming back." Elijah ran his thumb and index finger along the brim of his hat. "But she's not over me."

"Well, Elijah, I think you're right. On both counts."

"She's wrong if she thinks I can't make my own choice. I wish she would make room for happiness."

Annie moistened her lips. She was not sure she understood what he was talking about—and if he were planning something, she was not sure she wanted to know what it was. She sliced open another box. "What are you saying, Elijah?"

He shifted his weight and shrugged one shoulder. "Ruth and I are not any more unlikely than you and Rufus."

Annie stopped, midmotion, and turned her whole body toward Elijah. Squatting in the dust in her jeans, picking through the remains of an unknown life with her hair once again tumbling out of its ponytail, she felt about as un-Amish as she had at any moment in her life.

"At least you and Ruth have the past together," she finally said.

"That's not good enough for me." Elijah's jaw set.

"Still, it's something." Annie's legs ached from squatting. She stood up and looked down at Elijah from the truck bed. "Sometimes I think Rufus and I are getting close, but I always manage to disappoint him with what I don't understand about being Amish."

"Is that how you think he feels?"

"Doesn't he?" Annie doubted Rufus talked to anyone about his feelings, so how would Elijah know?

"He's not disappointed. He just doesn't know what to do with you."

"Because I'm *English*? Because he has no business getting involved with me?"

"Because you do the unexpected."

Annie blew out her breath. "That must frustrate him no end."

"I think it pleases him no end."

"I don't know if I can ever follow *Ordnung*. Rufus deserves to be with someone who understands his life."

"He deserves to be with someone who *is* his life."

Air rushed into Annie's throat far too fast, and she turned away.

Elijah shifted his toolbox to the other arm. "I'll go see about that stopped drain."

Annie smoothed out the purple Amish dress on her bed. It had once been Ruth's dress. Ruth, someone who knew how to be Amish.

Annie had done so well over the winter.

She learned to cook. She *would* learn to quilt properly. Her ears throbbed with Pennsylvania Dutch and High German. She learned to pray. Sort of. And she had broken the spine of her Bible with wear.

Then she went home and wore that stupid red dress—still hanging in the closet of her childhood bedroom.

When she put it on, she slid into old skin, where everything fit. Nothing about her life since had fit right.

Annie dropped her T-shirt and jeans to the floor and pulled the purple dress over her head. Her fingers had become nimble with pinning the pieces of the dress in place. She yanked a brush through her hair, pinned up the blond mass, and put on a prayer *kapp*.

She did not have a mirror in her bedroom. The only mirror in the house was the small one in the bathroom. But she still had her imagination, and it served her well in forming a mental picture of herself.

Perhaps her own ancestors had looked not so different from this. Plain dresses. Tamed hair. *Kapps* on their heads as they sought to discern humility and peace as a way of life.

The rap on the door sounded distant, as if it came through the centuries rather than simply up the stairwell. Annie almost did not move, not willing to surrender the moment. But the sound came again, more insistent.

There was no time to change. Besides, it was no secret to anyone in town that she sometimes wore Amish clothing. Annie clutched purple yardage in her fingers and descended the stairs.

She opened the front door. "Rufus!"

"Hello, Annalise." He stood with his hands crossed in front of him at the wrists. "I am more than a week delayed, but I thought perhaps we could have that walk."

Annie smiled and laid her hand in his open palm.

"Am I taking you away from something?" Rufus allowed himself to squeeze Annalise's hand as they started down the crumbling sidewalk that she had not allowed him to fix. Yet.

Annalise shook her head. "I was just planning a quiet evening at home."

"I see."

"You're wondering about the dress, aren't you?" Annalise said. "You've seen me wear it plenty of times."

"When you come to supper, or church." Rufus inhaled her scent, her nearness. "But in your own home?"

"It makes me feel peaceful. Helps me think."

"And your thoughts tonight?"

"I haven't felt so peaceful lately. Being Amish. . .well, it's not as easy as people think." Annalise raised brimming eyes. "And I've missed you."

"Things will settle down now," Rufus said. "The Stutzmans are in their own house. Life will go back to normal."

"I hope so."

"You have nothing to worry about, Annalise."

"Don't I?"

"No. No one holds a candle to you." Rufus squeezed her hand again.

"Let's take a very long walk, then." She squeezed back.

"What do you have in the way of garden tools?" he asked as they reached the street and fell into rhythm with each other.

Annalise sucked in a smile. "For my garden? I'm afraid I don't have much to work with."

"Why don't we walk over to Tom's hardware store? Jacob is going to need something that suits his size to break up your soil tomorrow."

"Tomorrow?"

"I thought my brothers and I could do the tilling while you're quilting."

"Oh, no you don't. I want to be there."

Rufus paused his steps, forcing Annalise to stop and look at him. "Let me do this for you, Annalise."

She started to protest further but put a hand to her own mouth. "*Demut*. I don't have to do everything myself."

Twenty-Three

"I saw you out walking in that purple dress." Mrs. Weichert moved a set of figurines and cleaned the glass shelf beneath the small statues.

Annie tilted her head to one side as she ran a thumb along a row of forty-year-old books on Monday. "It was a nice evening for a walk."

"I suppose a lot of people think you're crazy, but I think you look darling in those dresses."

Darling? Not exactly Annie's goal. "I wonder if we should give up on some of these books. They don't seem to be selling."

"It takes time. We'll get a lot more weekenders once summer is in full swing." Mrs. Weichert rearranged figurines. "Everybody wonders if you're really going to become Amish."

Annie's reply caught in her throat. She dislodged it and let it slide down.

"It's wonderful to see a young person willing to make a sacrifice," Mrs. Weichert said.

Annie reached back with both hands and tightened her ponytail. "Maybe I should bring those dishes out of the storeroom. It's a complete set, and only a couple of tiny nicks. You almost can't see them."

The ceramic dishes had been one of the best finds in the truckload of boxes Annie had sorted through the previous week. They dated back to the 1970s, but the earth tones looked surprisingly contemporary. In the storeroom now, Annie turned over one of the bowls to find the manufacturer. A name etched in a brown circle was not quite readable. A signature served as a logo, but she could not decide if the vowel in the center was an *A* or an *E*.

The old impulse surged to reach for her iPhone and get on the Internet. She could not do that any longer, but she could use Mrs. Weichert's computer. The laptop was anachronistic in this shop of vintage and antique items, but it served a needful business purpose. Annie moved to the small desk, opened the laptop, and tapped a thumb on the track pad. At least once a week she used a computer to help in her work. Annie's deft navigation of the Internet had yielded price-setting information beyond Mrs. Weichert's knowledge on several occasions. Even some of the Amish used computers to run their businesses. But for Annie, the automatic movements her hands made, the sleek keys under her fingers, and the familiar sensation of her eyes on the screen—it all taunted, whispering from shadows.

Annie woke the computer, and a search box appeared. Her fingers hovered over the keyboard. Finally, instead of the craftsman's name, she typed two words. *Randy Sawyer.* A list filled the screen. She narrowed the search with the name of the company her old flame was working for now, and in an instant his smiling professional photo and bio burned through her gray eyes.

She closed the search box and took a deep breath. What was she doing?

Could she really make this sacrifice, as Mrs. Weichert called it?

It should not feel like a sacrifice. Should it? She should not be wondering about Randy Sawyer. Should she?

Her walk with Rufus on Friday was three days old now. Annie had seen him briefly at his home on Saturday, where he insisted that she stay with his mother and quilt while he dug her garden.

On Saturday evening, she sat on her back porch and inhaled the fragrance of turned earth, the fruit of Rufus's labor with Jacob. On Sunday, she looked up twice from the shared meal after the service to catch Rufus watching her. The violet focus of his eyes stirred a creeping warmth in her before he diverted his gaze.

No, *sacrifice* was the wrong word. Whatever choice lay before her would not feature what she left behind, but rather what she took hold of. And Rufus Beiler was the person who made her want to take hold.

Exhaling, Annie opened the search engine again and soon found the dishes on the Internet. Early seventies, a midwestern manufacturer, designed by an artist who found local fame in other mediums. A limited edition. Only five hundred sets had been cast in the particular color combination stacked a few feet away from the desk. A complete set of eight was definitely of value. Mrs. Weichert should hold out for a good price. Annie carried the dishes out to the shop and began wiping them clean and arranging shelf space.

The bell on the shop door jangled. Glancing up, Annie recognized Colton, the young man who worked in the hardware store Tom Reynolds owned.

"You got any of that Amish jam?" Colton asked. "My wife wants some."

Mrs. Weichert pointed to the shelf that supported glass jars both Franey Beiler and Edna Stutzman had canned. The man slid jars around with two fingers. Annie supposed he was looking for a particular fruit his wife had requested. Peach and blackberry were all he would find, though.

"It's all over town that Karl Kramer is on a tear." Colton picked up one jar of peach and one of blackberry and moved toward the counter.

"What is he knotted up about this time?" Mrs. Weichert tapped the electronic cash register.

"Apparently he keeps close count of his fertilizer bags." Colton extracted a wallet from his back pocket. "Three bags are missing from a place where he's been stockpiling supplies. Rumor is it's some sort of commercial grade with higher ammonium nitrate."

Annie's hands stilled.

The cash register beeped. "I don't know why Rufus wants to work with that man," Mrs. Weichert said. "You never can tell what little thing is going to set him off. He probably miscounted."

"Who wants to steal fertilizer, anyway?" Colton asked. "This is ranch country. Everybody has some."

Not everybody, Annie thought. Not teenage boys who did not want to raise suspicions by inquiring about ammonium nitrate levels in the fertilizer at the hardware store one of their fathers owned.

That morning, before he left his workshop for the home where he was installing cabinets, Rufus checked every hook on the wall the third time. The set of small chisels was not there. Now, in the wide yard beside the new home, he emptied his toolbox in the back of the buggy, though he had done this before as well. If the leather case did not turn up soon, he would have to bear the expense of a new set. For now, he chose a larger chisel and replaced the rest of the tools according to the careful arrangement that characterized his toolbox.

Rufus turned at the sound of a car spewing gravel. He put a calming hand on Dolly's rump. The car screeched to an abrupt halt, bouncing forward with unspent momentum before settling. Karl Kramer leaned out of the driver's side window.

"If we're going to work together, you have to give me a phone number." Karl shook a finger at Rufus.

"What's wrong, Karl?"

"I can't meet this afternoon. Somebody is stealing fertilizer from me, and I intend to find out who it is."

"Who would steal fertilizer?"

"If I knew that, would I be chewing the fat with you now?"

"Tomorrow, then," Rufus said. "I hope you sort things out soon."

"I intend to. Whoever did this is going to be sorry."

Karl pulled his arm inside the car and accelerated. With his hand on Dolly's neck, Rufus watched Karl's car hurl down the road much faster than it should have. He hoped Karl would calm down before they met again. If the project derailed because Karl could not let go of a couple of bags of fertilizer, Rufus would have little success convincing anyone to give Karl another chance.

"Annie, Rufus is here for you."

Annie stuck her head around the corner from the desk in the storeroom where she had been making notes about the newest inventory. Her ponytail sagged and she was fairly sure a smudge covered one cheekbone, but she smiled anyway.

"I thought you had a meeting." Annie entered the main shop and tucked a perpetually rebellious strand of hair behind her left ear.

"Canceled."

Rufus's lips did not turn up, but Annie caught the hint of dance in his eyes. She looked at Mrs. Weichert.

The shop owner waved a hand. "Yes, you're through for the day. Go on, you two."

"I'll drive you home," Rufus said when they stepped out on the sidewalk.

"It's only four blocks."

"We'll take the long way."

Annie took the hand Rufus offered to help her up to the buggy seat. Outside the bakery across the street, two women watched. Annie felt their stares, and she turned her head to smile at them. Curiosity on the faces of onlookers no longer made her self-conscious.

"I'm not sure Westcliffe has a 'long way,'" Annie said.

"We'll invent one."

Rufus guided Dolly past the turn onto Annie's street, going several blocks and then turning the opposite direction. They zigzagged up and down the streets, past the historic Lutheran church and the old schoolhouse, past the small railroad museum and the newspaper office. Each time he had an opportunity to turn in the direction of Annie's house, Rufus went the other way.

"I suppose in your *English* world this is not much of a date," Rufus said, his eyes forward.

Is that was this was? "This is better than an *English* date," Annie said. "I'm glad to see you."

"Karl is making a fuss about some missing fertilizer."

Annie let three houses pass before she spoke. "Rufus, suppose someone in the Amish community was involved."

"Why would any of our people be involved? We don't steal and our sources of fertilizer generally are more. . .natural, shall we say?"

She smiled. "Well, then, not directly involved. Just theoretically."

"If theoretically someone knew about this?" He leaned toward her.

"Yes. Theoretically."

"Then theoretically someone ought to speak to the elders. But not theoretical elders. Real ones."

Annie nodded. Thinking of Joel, though, complicated her thoughts. She did not for a minute believe Joel would be involved with theft.

"Do you know something?" Rufus asked.

She squirmed. "Not exactly." A false accusation would do needless harm. She chuckled as they went past the same corner for the fourth time. "People are going to think you've lost your mind if you keep driving in circles."

"Theoretically I would hate for that rumor to get back to my parents."

"Then theoretically, I suppose you should turn left at the next corner and take me home."

In front of her house, Rufus helped Annie down. She stood for a moment to stroke Dolly's neck.

"Thanks for the ride home." Annie drank a deep breath and

let it out in contentment. "I could make coffee. We could sit on the step."

And then she saw her.

Beth Stutzman clomping down off Main Street toward them. Annie pressed her lips together.

"There you are!" Beth called to them from half a block away. "I've been trying to catch you all over town. Why were you driving as if you didn't know where you were going?"

"Hello, Beth," Annie said.

"Hello, Annalise." Beth's gaze barely moved in Annie's direction, instead focusing on Rufus. "I was hoping you could give me a ride home."

Rufus caught Annie's eyes.

"You *are* going home now, aren't you?" Beth asked, looking from Rufus to Annie and back again.

Beth's tone grated even as Annie erased her vision of coffee on the front steps with Rufus. "I'll see you later," Annie said.

She saw the sink in his shoulders as he nodded at Beth. "*Ya*, I'm heading home."

He politely aided Beth's ascent to the buggy seat, climbed up beside her, and picked up the reins.

Theoretically, Rufus did not look very happy with Beth's request. Theoretically, Annie was pleased to know he would rather have sat with her on her front step for a few more minutes.

Annie turned back to the house. The missing fertilizer was not theoretical, and neither was Annie's memory of the Internet history on Carter Reynolds's phone.

If only Joel were not being so evasive. The consequences could be far from theoretical.

Twenty-Four

September 1777

$\mathcal{M}$agdalena chose to walk. One of the Stutzman sisters, who had married a Yoder distantly related to Magdalena, had a new babe. Magdalena had offered to do some mending so the new mother could rest and enjoy the child. She knew her own talent with a needle. The couple's mending had stacked up during the heaviness of pregnancy with an older child to care for. Magdalena's repairs would hold for a good long while.

The couple's farm was four miles away. Calculating both the walking time and the visiting time, Magdalena reckoned she had the better part of three hours away from the house, perhaps even four. Magdalena much preferred setting her body in motion and raising her face in the warmth in the sky to wiping noses and shooing children out of the kitchen. The brutality of summer heat had eased, but the days still brimmed with sun. She would cut through the paths that joined the back property boundaries and stay off the main road, and she would have hours for uninterrupted thoughts while she carried the mended garments to the Yoders.

Babsi's baby had come as well. A boy. They named him Jacob, for his grandfather. The name had been in the Byler family for several generations already, and of course it made Magdalena think of her *onkel* in Berks County, and his son Jacob Franklin.

The miles between Lancaster County and Berks County were far from insurmountable, but the two branches of the Byler family had less and less in common. Magdalena supposed that in another generation they would hardly know each other.

If only one of these little Jacoblis could be hers—hers and Nathanael's. He did not come right out and say he did not plan to marry, but anyone could see he had lost interest. He was content. Too content.

It stabbed her sometimes, that he could lose his love for her.

Magdalena pushed out air and moved the old flour sack filled with mended garments to the other shoulder.

She did not see them until she crested the small hill, hardly more than a mound. And if she had not turned her head at that angle at that precise moment, she might have missed them altogether. Against the slope, four men sat on the ground, huddled around a patch of something. Leather? Paper? She could not be sure.

Magdalena did not realize her feet had stopped moving until she caught his glance. Eyes large and brown stared at her. No hat restrained his shaggy brown hair. They locked eyes while he jumped to his feet. His motion caused the others to look up as well. She heard the slap as rifles moved to their hands, and she froze. Never before had she seen a gun aimed at her.

"I'm sorry," Magdalena muttered. "I won't disturb you." She took a few steps.

"Halt!"

When she turned again, the first man was moving toward her. "What do you have in the bag?"

Magdalena licked her lips and swallowed. "Mended clothing. For a friend."

"Show me."

Magdalena dropped the bag off her shoulder and spread the top edges. He riffled through a few layers with one hand, his musket at the ready in the other.

Who did they think she was? Magdalena wondered. And who were they? She watched their movements, curious.

"Do you come through here often?" he asked.

"No, not often." Magdalena twisted the top of her bag closed.

"Why are you here today?"

"I felt like walking. Usually I take a cart on the road." She realized now that two of the men wore jackets in shades of red. Not British uniforms, but nevertheless a suggestion of their sympathies. She took a step back and saw fire in his eyes.

"I should be on my way." Magdalena slung the bag over a shoulder.

The man turned and spoke over his shoulder to the others. "Bring the paper."

A younger man—surely no older than fifteen, her brother Hansli's age—picked up the paper they had huddled around. He took five uphill strides and was beside her.

"You will carry this for us."

She met the first man's gaze and fingered the strings of her *kapp*. "I am Amish."

"I know. That's why you are perfect."

"I do not understand."

He pointed. "On the far side of that ridge is a boulder. It looks a little like a bear cub from a distance."

Magdalena stood still, anticipating. She knew the ridge well. Patriots had been gathering there for more than two years.

Now he folded the paper as he talked. "It's a simple task."

"I am Amish," she repeated.

"No one will look in your bag."

"You did," Magdalena pointed out.

"But not because I suspected you. I saw an opportunity."

"Amish do not take sides in a war." Even as she spoke the words, her belief in them trembled.

"When you get to the rock, look to the south. You will see a small cabin."

Nathan's cabin. Magdalena exhaled and inhaled three times before speaking. "What will happen to the men on the ridge if I do this?"

"What will happen to you if you do not? The battles are spreading. Your General Washington is going to lose Philadelphia any day."

"He is not my General Washington," she said. "The Amish have no generals."

"It will be better for you if you are on our side when Philadelphia falls. It won't be long before the countryside is under British control once again. Your theory of neutrality will not hold up then." Without asking permission, he took the bag from her shoulder and plunged his hand inside, pushing the letter to the middle. His fingers came out empty. "Inside the cabin you'll see a shelf with jars of preserves on it."

Mrs. Buerki's jars of peaches and beans, long forgotten. Magdalena's heart thundered as she realized the squatters in Nathan's cabin were British sympathizers.

"Put the letter under the third jar from the left."

"That's all?"

"That's all."

She held his brown eyes as she raised her bag to her shoulder. "And if I should happen to pass this way again?"

"Then perhaps we will happen to talk again."

"The Israelites could not make bricks without straw, and I cannot make gunpowder without saltpeter." Jacob pulled his leather apron over his head and flung it against the stone wall of the tannery.

"The French are very close to having a fresh supply of powder at Washington's disposal." David sat hunched forward on a barrel, his hands tucked under his thighs.

"That's not much help now." Jacob pulled a forearm across the sweat on his forehead. "The British are marching toward Philadelphia, and they seem to be getting ample help from sympathizers in the countryside."

"Our officers need harnesses and saddles as well as powder. You're making those as fast as you can. It's a great help, Jacob."

Jacob exhaled and gazed at his youngest brother. "I couldn't do it without you. But if we lose Philadelphia—"

"That won't be the end of the war. We will keep fighting!"

"Sarah is in Philadelphia. She will refuse to leave, you know."

"I know." David put his hands behind his head and stretched his back.

"Joseph is going to enlist any day," Jacob said.

"I know that, too."

"This is hard on *Mamm*."

"Did you ever tell her you saw Maria?"

Jacob shook his head. "I *might* have seen Maria. Why break *Mamm*'s heart all over again if I was wrong?"

"You're right." David raked his hands through his hair. "I'd better go. This time my wagon really is full of potatoes to feed hungry bellies."

Magdalena slipped out the back door, her prayer *kapp* hanging loose around her neck and a shawl around her shoulders. The midnight sky was clear, the moon bright. This brought both comfort and anxiety. She could see her way, but she would have to remember to stay in the shadows. It would be easier once she was away from the clearing around the house and barn.

She had lain for hours in her bed, waiting for the settled sounds of sleep to come from every room. The new baby fussed himself and his mother into exhaustion, and Magdalena did not dare leave her room until the shuffling behind Babsi's door stopped.

But she was out now, and she allowed herself one deep breath before turning her feet swiftly toward her goal. Twice before she had done this, her heart pounding as she flung herself through gradations of shadow in darkness. Instead of moving up the lane to the main road, Magdalena crept through the back garden and across one fallow field. Beyond it she found the cover that taller crops, though picked bare, would provide.

She never read the letters, although they were not sealed. She simply carried them from one destination to another according to Patrick's instructions.

Patrick. She'd heard one of the men call out his name, unaware she was near. She had not yet spoken hers to him, and he had not asked.

Soon she was across the second field. Dry corn husks crunched under her feet. Every sound magnified, every step thudding, every sweep of her hemline crackling in the dirt.

She froze.

Her steps were not the only sounds she heard.

Magdalena ducked into what was left of the corn row and dropped flat to the ground. She turned her head toward the sound and saw a boot.

A brown boot. The sort Amish men favored. A second boot came into the frame of her vision. Both feet turned toward her and stopped.

"Magdalena, get up."

She bolted upright. "*Daed*! What are you doing out here?"

"Magdalena, get up out of the dirt."

She took her father's outstretched hand and pulled herself to her feet.

"Maggie, what are you doing?"

"I was going for a walk."

"Do you find the moonlight romantic?"

"No! If you think I'm meeting a man, please put your mind at ease. There is no one."

"Let us walk together back to the house, then."

"Did you follow me?" Magdalena's fingers wrapped around the folded paper hidden under her shawl.

"Yes, I did."

"But why?"

He puffed air softly. Magdalena knew that sound. Her father would not be distracted, not when he obviously found her actions suspicious.

"Magdalena," he said, "would these midnight forays have

anything to do with the British sympathizers?"

"Why would you ask that?"

"I would not be the first farmer to suspect they have been camping on my land. Please answer my question."

Magdalena could not tell a full-blown lie to her father. "It is only a few letters. I do not even know what they say."

She winced when her father took her elbow, not because it hurt but because she knew she had pushed his tolerance too far. When he turned her toward home, she did not resist.

"Maria, we are Amish."

"Maria?" She blanched. Her *daed* never mixed up names. "I am Magdalena."

"I'm sorry. Sometimes you remind me of my sister." He relaxed his touch on her elbow. "We are Amish. We do not get involved in these affairs. Force is not our way."

"I am not forcing anyone," she said. "It is just letters."

"And how do you know one of these letters will not change the war?"

The thought made her heart quicken. If she could in some small way contribute to bringing an end to the Patriot uprising, she would feel she had done well. She pushed regret for pride out of her mind.

They walked home without talking. Magdalena gripped the letter, already scheming how she might break away in the morning while her father worked in the field they now traversed. He would watch her closely, but he could not keep her in sight every moment of the day and night.

Philadelphia fell before the end of the month. The day the news reached him, Jacob sat up alone in the middle of the night pondering its implications. British troops, with ample gunpowder, marched the streets where his parents had met and where his sister now lived.

Jacob tapped the table with one finger. He was not going to

give up. He had what he needed for a small batch of powder in the iron kettle behind the tannery. In the morning he would carry coals from his own kitchen to light the fire and heat the saltpeter to crystals. He had plenty of lye for boiling the brimstone in linen rags, and red cedar was stacked up outside the tannery for burning. Pounding the mixture into dust would take days.

Jacob rubbed a thumb against the edge of the table, remembering the feel of the silky fine powder that would result from his labors. Perhaps he would use the saltpeter to make a smaller but more powerful batch. He might not have as much as he wished, but General Washington was welcome to whatever he did have. Jacob liked to imagine his gunpowder causing the explosion that would shoot off a cannon.

And he would have to get a message to Sarah and Emerson. David might have some ideas how. If he could get the message through, his sister would offer reliable details about events in Philadelphia.

Twenty-Five

Whether she wanted to admit it or not, Annie half listened to the traffic outside the shop the next morning hoping to hear Dolly's clip-clop. Rufus worked more and more often doing custom work in the subdivision springing up north of town. He created cabinets in his workshop on the Beiler property, which meant he could go days—or even weeks—at a time without needing to come into town. Eventually he had to install his handiwork, though, and Annie liked to think he would look for a reason to meander down Main Street.

When the clip-clop came, however, it was not Dolly but Brownie, and the buggy carried not Rufus but Joel and the Stutzman brothers. From her position at the cash register, Annie saw all three teens drop from the buggy's bench and walk around to the back to unload several crates.

"Did you tell Mrs. Stutzman you wanted more of her jams and handmade goods?" With no customers in the shop, Annie spoke freely to Mrs. Weichert.

"I don't see any harm in keeping a few of her things. Franey Beiler doesn't do blackberry jam, and it seems to be popular."

"This looks like more than a few jars of jam."

Joel held the shop door open now, while Mark and Luke

538

carried crates. Mrs. Weichert's eyes widened slightly and Annie stifled a smirk.

"Our *mamm* sent in a wide selection," Mark said. "She said you may choose what you would like to keep and we will pick up the rest the next time we are in town."

"My goodness, your mother has been busy. This is quite a bit more than I was expecting," Mrs. Weichert said. Mark moved toward the counter with two crates. Luke had two more.

"We'll get the rest, then," Mark said.

"There's more?"

Behind the crates, Annie snorted then generated a cover-up cough as the brothers stepped out to the buggy.

Mrs. Weichert brushed her thumbs across a quilted pillow sham. "Joel, perhaps you could help Annie take these to the back room. We'll have more space there to go through everything."

Annie was not so sure. The back room was strewn with assorted finds from three separate estate sales, all awaiting cleaning and pricing. But when Joel complied with Mrs. Weichert's request, Annie did the same.

In the back room, Annie set down the crate she carried and slid it up against a wall. "I suppose Carter and Duncan are in school."

"Yes, I suppose they are." Joel nudged two more crates snug up against the first.

"Seems like the bunch of you have been spending a lot of time together."

Joel met her gaze. "Not all that much."

Annie peered at a wooden birdhouse with a single hole in the front. "I wonder if one of the boys made that."

"Might have."

"I guess everybody has heard about Karl Kramer."

"I don't pay much attention to him," Joel said. "His fuse is too quick."

Now why would Joel be talking about a fuse? Annie heard the bell on the door jangle and Mark's soft voice, his words indistinguishable.

"I'll get the rest," Joel said.

As he turned away, Annie wondered how it was he had time for mundane errands for the Stutzmans when undoubtedly he had chores of his own. It was the middle of the morning, at the height of spring. On a farm. Annie found it hard to believe he did not have work waiting for him at his father's side. Surely the Stutzman boys could have brought their own buggy into town.

Joel returned, his arms full.

Annie smiled, daring him to keep looking so glum. "I'll make more room." She pushed a mostly empty oversized box out of the way.

"This is the last of it."

"I hope Mrs. Stutzman appreciates your help. I'm sure you have a lot of other things you could be doing."

"My morning was fairly clear." Joel brushed his palms against each other, spewing dust. "It is our way to be helpful."

"Yes, of course. I of all people understand Beiler hospitality."

He looked at her, and the corners of his mouth went up, but the gesture did not convince Annie.

"Is everything all right, Joel?" She spoke before she meant to, laying a hand on his forearm.

"Of course. Why should it not be?" He moved out of her touch.

Was that irritation in his tone? Defensiveness? Simple fatigue? Slow and subtle was not going to work. Annie changed tactics.

"What do you know about Karl Kramer's missing fertilizer? Or what do your friends have to do with it?"

"I'd better go."

Joel touched the brim of his hat in a way that made clear Annie would get no further reaction from him.

"Joel, if the boys are getting themselves into trouble—"

"Good-bye, Annalise."

Rufus stood at the end of Annalise's short front walk and tipped his head back far enough that even the brim of his hat did not filter the streaming sun. Annalise sat on her front stoop, her legs stretched out, eyes closed, face raised. Her hair, hanging loose today, draped her shoulders. He was certain that she had not cut it since the day he met her.

And the thought of what that meant made him smile.

She opened her eyes just then, and he saw the joy chase through them before she composed herself.

"I couldn't remember if you were working only half a day," he said.

"I'm off until Thursday. Where's Dolly? I didn't hear you coming."

"I left her grazing. I'm working nearby."

"Are you sure it's safe to leave her unattended?"

"Karl Kramer and I have come to an understanding, if that's what you mean," Rufus said. "But my crew is there."

"Just in case. Okay." Annalise scooted to one side of the step and reached for a plastic container behind her. "I have sandwiches. Ham and cheese?"

Rufus lowered himself to the stoop beside her and accepted a hefty half sandwich. He could not ask for a much more public place than her front yard. Tongues might wag about how much time they spent together, but no one could accuse them of being secretive.

"Tom and I are going to Colorado Springs tomorrow." Rufus rotated the sandwich in his hands, planning his assault on its girth. "I think you should come."

"Really?"

Rufus nodded. "You should see your mother more often."

"Oh."

The sag of her shoulders told him he had said the wrong thing. "Annalise, she is still very anxious about what you are doing here. She needs to know you are not turning your back on her."

"Of course I'm not." Annalise picked at the crust of her own sandwich, the other half of his. "I just don't know what else I can say to explain things to her."

"Just be with her. Let her see that she raised a wonderful, capable woman with strong values. That she isn't losing you."

He heard the edge of hesitation in her breath.

"I'm going to shop for tools, and Tom is going to visit his mother in the nursing home," he said. "We would be back by suppertime."

"How about seeing Ruth?"

"Your mother, Annalise. You need to see your mother. Call her from the shop."

She took a big bite, purposely occupying her mouth, he thought. When she swallowed hard, he knew he had persuaded her.

Lauren was there on the sofa when Ruth entered the suite. Ruth dropped her backpack beside Lauren and plopped into the chair opposite the sofa.

"You should have let me pick you up from work." Lauren peered over the top of her laptop and her glasses at Ruth.

"It seemed like a lot of trouble. You're in the middle of a paper."

Lauren scoffed. "I suspect my professor is a closet pacifist. No offense. I know you're the real thing."

"No offense taken."

"My professor keeps making me tweak my subject, thesis, sources—the whole thing. He won't admit he just doesn't want to read a paper about incendiary devices and military munitions."

Ruth laughed. "He doesn't want to admit that you know more about it than he does."

"You got that right."

Ruth put her head back, closed her eyes, and breathed out her fatigue. Finding Lauren in the suite always heartened her. Their other suitemates, rarely there, kept to their own rooms. Without Lauren's encouragement, Ruth would do the same. More than once, though, as she lay alone in her bed she grinned at the unlikely friendship between an Amish girl and a self-taught munitions specialist. Ruth understood most of what Lauren talked about now.

An entire new vocabulary sorted itself out in Ruth's mind, finding categories and relationships in a peculiar grammar. Weapon numbers and abbreviated names and schematics inserted themselves into conversations about study groups and coins for the laundry. Ruth still was reluctant to believe she would ever have much use for this particular set of words.

"We should do a driving lesson," Lauren said. "No point in having a car and letting it sit in the parking lot."

"Whenever you're ready."

"Admit it, you like driving." Lauren snapped her laptop shut. "Let's go now."

Ruth did not stifle her laugh. She had been lonely for so long after leaving the valley of her family's home. It was good to once again be with someone who knew her well.

"I'll get the key."

Tom Reynolds was cranky.

His mood rarely faltered this much, but Annie almost wished she were riding in the open bed of his truck instead of wedged between him and Rufus. Before they left Westcliffe, Annie toyed with seeking counsel from both men while the three of them were captive to the road. What if something were going on with the boys? Tom and Rufus could sort it out. In only minutes, though, Tom's disposition clamped her mouth shut.

Tom twisted the steering wheel in a sharp turn. "Carter has too much unsupervised time. When summer vacation comes, he'll have way too much free time."

"He's a good boy, Tom," Rufus said.

"When he was little, Trish and I could not leave him alone for a minute or he'd get into trouble." Tom accelerated. "Can't you keep him occupied on your crew, Rufus? You wouldn't even have to pay him."

Annie blocked out most of Tom's tirade, unwilling to offer Carter up for sacrifice at the moment. She gripped the seat when he took turns a little too fast. She glanced at Rufus every few minutes, admiring his calm responses.

But, no, this did not seem like the time to mention to Tom that his son might be building a bomb and that his Amish friends—including Rufus's brother—might be helping him. She could not be sure, and maybe she was wrong, and she did not want to make false accusations, so never mind. *How do you know?* he would ask. *Because I'm nosy and jump to conclusions and I have no proof,* she would have to say. She did not want the Amish to dub her Nosy Annalise.

They pulled up—finally—in front of Annie's parents' home. With Mrs. Weichert's permission, Annie had used the phone in the shop to alert her mother that she was coming and to make sure she would be home. When Annie got out of the truck, Myra Friesen was already standing in the front door frame.

"I'm not so sure about this," Annie muttered in that moment when she was wedged between the truck and Rufus standing at the open door.

"It's the right thing."

Visions of the red dress flashed through Annie's mind. She would only be home a few hours this time. Surely she could not get into trouble in one afternoon.

No. She wouldn't. She just wouldn't. In fact, she would put that dress in the trash herself.

Her arm brushed Rufus's as she moved past him, and his fingers fluttered for hers.

A rare gesture. He knew how much she needed it.

"When I come back, I will come in and say hello to your mother." As he spoke, Rufus waved at Myra, who returned the gesture with the delay of reluctance.

Twenty-Six

"I only wish you were staying longer." Annie's mother squeezed her tight. "I made brunch."

"Quiche Lorraine?" Just the thought triggered Annie's salivary glands. Her mother's quiche, a family weekend staple during Annie's childhood, was a dish she would like to learn to make now that she was determined to cook properly.

"With a fresh spinach-cranberry salad I still have to put together." Myra turned toward the kitchen.

"Almonds?" Annie followed her mother.

"Of course."

"I took all this for granted growing up." Annie perched on a stool at the breakfast bar, where she could smell the baking quiche and imagine it rimmed by a perfectly golden crust. Her mother would know precisely the moment to remove it from the oven. "The next time I come, maybe you can teach me to make your quiche."

"I'm glad to hear there will be a next time." Myra opened the refrigerator and rapidly transferred an array of ingredients to the counter.

"Of course there will be a next time, Mom. You're being dramatic."

"I might argue that you're the one with the flair for drama of late, but let's not quibble." Myra dumped a bag of spinach in a colander. "Oh, before I forget, there's some mail for you on the sideboard in the dining room. Some of it looks important."

Annie doubted important mail would be coming to her parents' home. She had been living in Westcliffe for eight months now, and mail came to her house. "Probably junk."

"I don't think so. You'd better look at it." Myra brushed her hands on a dish towel. "I'll get it."

"Mom—"Before Annie voiced her protest that she could fetch her own mail, Myra whizzed past her into the dining room and quickly returned.

"This does not look like junk." Myra tapped the envelope that sat atop a clothing catalog and a bank advertisement. "Isn't that the company you sold to?"

Annie picked up the flat manila envelope, imprinted with the logo of Liam-Ryder Industries. "Yes. It's probably some formality, a notification the government requires."

"I may not be a corporate executive, but that doesn't look like a form letter to me. Open it." Myra picked up a knife and let it drop through a cucumber in six quick taps.

Annie tore the envelope open. "Are you making dessert?"

"I have some Bosc pears. I was going to do something fancy, but I ran out of time."

"We can just eat them fresh." Annie slid a letter out of the envelope.

"I have caramel sauce."

"That would be good, too." Annie scanned the embossed page in her hand. How in the world had Liam-Ryder Industries tracked her down to her parents' address? And why? The sale of her software company, including its intellectual property assets, was final months ago. She let her breath out slowly as she read more carefully.

"What do they want?"

"I'm not sure."

Continued partnership with L-R Industries.

Two years of exclusive creative work.

Operate from the location of her choice.

A financial package that made Annie look twice.

Liam-Ryder Industries had bought her company and her innovative software to track and analyze shopping habits for individuals according to several variables. Now they wanted her, too.

Her next creative challenge could be the next software advance to transform the service industry. Annie turned the letter, the envelope, and the junk mail facedown on the breakfast bar.

"I don't know why they're sending me mail here. Can I help you with the salad?"

"Would you rather have raisins instead of cranberries?" Myra opened a cabinet and pulled out a box. "I have the golden kind you always liked."

"Cranberries are fine." Annie slid off her stool. "Let me make the salad."

The home phone rang, and Myra answered. From her mother's end of the conversation, Annie could tell Myra had launched into another community fund-raiser project. Myra's promise to track down a catering list took her out of the room. Annie picked up the knife her mother had abandoned and cut a few more slices of cucumber and considered beginning on the water chestnuts.

She glanced back at the letter from Liam-Ryder. The amount of money they were offering approached obscene levels for only two years of work. The president of L-R Industries had not said exactly what they wanted her to do—that would have been risky to put in writing, she supposed—but Annie knew he would not have approached her if the challenge were not stimulating.

The chase.

The hunt.

The conquest.

That tempted her more than the money. Curiosity made Annie's brain click through its gears. She laid the knife down and picked up the letter again then read it for the third time at a pace that allowed her to speculate on between-the-lines innuendos. Temptation crept through her, as seductive as the red dress had been. Abruptly she opened the door to the cabinet beneath the sink and dropped the whole pile of mail into the trash. She was chopping water chestnuts when Myra returned.

"Sometimes I think it would be easier to skip the chicken. We all just pretend it doesn't taste like rubber," Myra said. "Why don't we just ask people for money and save everybody a lot of time and fuss? It seems like we're always feeding someone's ego with these dinner events."

Annie pinched her shoulders up and held them there. "Maybe you don't have to plan them anymore."

"Believe me, I'm tempted. Your father insists the social contacts are good for his business." Annie was afraid that if she sliced any faster, her bounty would include a fingertip.

With the swiftness of long habit, Myra tore off a paper towel and wiped up the widening puddle beneath the colander of spinach on the counter. She opened the cabinet door to toss the soggy towel into the trash.

Myra picked up the letter. "Throwing away your mail so quickly?"

"It's nothing I'm interested in." Annie reached for the letter, intending to crumple it this time.

Myra raised her arm and stepped back, keeping the letter out of Annie's reach and already reading. "Annie! This is an amazing opportunity!"

"Under other circumstances, yes, it would be." Annie resumed chopping.

"But two years, Annie. Then you could be comfortable and never have to worry about money again."

"I already don't worry about money."

"Surely you're allowed to make a living. After all, you haven't actually joined the Amish. It's not too late to back out."

Annie swallowed and laid the knife down carefully before turning to her mother. "Mom, I don't want to back out. That's the last thing I want."

Color evaporated from Myra's face. "I thought you were just thinking about things."

"Well, I've been thinking for quite a while now. It might be time for me to do something more definite."

Myra moistened her lips and twitched her chin. "I read somewhere that the Amish are allowed to use computers as part of their businesses. That's all you'd be doing."

Annie shook her head. "You know it would be much more than that for me. My relationship with computers is a different life, a different set of values than anything the Amish could ever imagine or justify."

Annie felt it when she used Mrs. Weichert's computer at the shop for more than a quick search for information. She felt it when she picked up Carter's phone and looked at his Internet search history. Months of disciplining herself not to depend on the gratification of instantaneous information would melt into a river of slime running through her life if she considered L-R Industry's offer.

"I can't, Mom," she said.

"You could if you wanted to."

"But I don't want to. And I don't want to want to."

"Are you and Rufus getting serious? Is that it?"

"Honestly, I'm not sure what we are, Mom. That's not the point. I want to live more simply, with deeper values."

"There's nothing wrong with the values your father and I taught you."

"I didn't say there was, Mom. Maybe I need to understand them better. Maybe I'm just choosing something more overt. More definite."

"Then it's his family. His mother."

"Franey? What do you mean?"

"You're closer to her than you are to me."

"Oh, Mom."

"Don't deny it. You didn't want to come home while Penny was here because you didn't want to miss your quilt lesson with Franey Beiler. You're replacing me. How can I have a place in your life if you go Amish?"

" 'Go Amish'?"

"You have a family, Annie. Why are you turning your back on us?"

Annie dug the heels of her hands into her eyes.

"You've done that since you were a toddler," Myra said. "It's as if you made up your mind not to cry and so you just won't. I bet Franey Beiler doesn't know that about you."

"It's not a contest, Mom."

Myra gasped and lurched toward the oven, slamming the door down and reaching in with a dish towel as her hot pad. She set the quiche on the stovetop.

"Look at that. I've never burned a quiche before in my life. This crust is ruined."

They ate without saying much. The crust was darker than usual but far from ruined. After wedges of fresh pear, they agreed they would take a walk around the neighborhood. It did not escape Annie's notice that her mother chose a route that took her past her old elementary school, past her childhood best friend's house—though her friend had moved away years ago—and past her middle school. Annie felt every tortuous tick of the afternoon's minutes until it was time for Rufus and Tom to return.

When the red truck pulled up, Annie was already waiting outside in one of the two chairs her mother left year-round on a flagstone patio. She had said good-bye to her mother a few minutes earlier. Now she jumped up and crossed the driveway before Rufus could get out of the truck.

"Let's go home," she said through the open window.

"I was going to greet your mother." Rufus gestured toward the house.

"It's not a good time." Annie lurched into the cab.

Twenty-Seven

On Saturday, Annie parked her bicycle at the bottom of the steps leading up to the Beilers' front porch. The front door creaked, and Jacob Beiler pushed the screen door open wide.

"*Mamm* said you would be here soon."

"Well, here I am."

Annie never could manage to suppress a smile at the sight of the little boy who had attached himself to her nearly a year ago. While Rufus's feelings toward her mystified her at times, Jacob never gave her a moment's doubt. She straightened the fullness of her dress and reached up to make sure her prayer *kapp* had not escaped her head during the ride from town.

Jacob let the screen door slam behind him. "*Mamm* said to tell you she would be right back. Sophie is supposed to be in charge of me. I keep telling *Mamm* I don't need anyone to be in charge of me."

Annie climbed the porch steps and gave Jacob's shoulder a quick squeeze. "So your *mamm* is not here?"

"You're supposed to get everything out and get started." Jacob turned and led Annie into the living room and toward the chest he knew held her quilt-in-progress.

They both turned at the sound of steps coming through the dining room.

"Good morning, Annalise." Sophie nodded with her greeting. "I'm sorry I must steal Jacob back from you. He has not finished his work in the kitchen."

"Of course." Annie put a hand on Jacob's back and nudged him toward his sister.

"Make yourself at home," Sophie said. "You know you are always welcome here."

His shoulders slumped, Jacob trudged after Sophie into the kitchen. Annie lifted the lid on the cedar chest, savoring the touch of Rufus's workmanship in her fingers. Saturday morning quilting sessions illumined her weeks. Annie had missed too many of them recently. Franey Beiler was a skillful, patient teacher. Perhaps she found more to commend in Annie's work than it deserved, but her kindness crafted hope in Annie. As she lifted the quilt out of its safekeeping, Annie listened for the familiar cadence of Franey's steps across the hand-scrubbed, broad-planked flooring.

Her mother's words from three days ago oozed through Annie's mind now. Was there any truth in them? Annie certainly had not set out to replace her mother with a relationship with Franey Beiler. But did Franey somehow see Annie as a replacement for the daughter who had fled her own baptism rather than join the Amish congregation? Franey taught Annie skills she had taught her own daughters—including Ruth. Annie could bake a decent loaf of bread without a recipe and a tasty apple schnitzel if she paid close attention to the steps of the process. She was in Franey's kitchen often enough at mealtimes to learn more about cooking than she had ever tried to absorb from her own mother. She knew Franey liked her. Loved her, even. So did Eli. If she decided to formally join the Amish, they would welcome her as part of their family regardless of what became of her relationship with Rufus. But would she be a consolation prize? A peculiar comfort to offset Ruth's decision?

Annie shook the thought out of her head. The quilt was in her arms now, and she also snared the small basket that held threads and scissors and templates. She moved to the sofa to take her usual seat, remembering the block she was working on two weeks ago. A hoop still held it taut, as smooth on the bottom as it was on the top.

It took only seconds for Annie to see something was not right. Someone had been working on her quilt.

Someone who used fine, even stitches.

The block was finished—and flawless. Her own stitches, which she had wrestled with for four hours last week, had been picked out with a delicate touch that left the cotton fabric unblemished. Meticulous stitches replaced her work. Each length of thread was exactly the same measurement, equal distance apart, and pulled through with faultless tension. Annie flipped the quilt over and ran her fingertips over the back of the square. She found no knots visible to the eye or available to touch, only the same perfection on the underside that the quilt top boasted.

Fury roiled, then grief. If she quilted every day for a year, she could never replicate that precision.

But perfect as they were, the stitches spoiled her quilt. It was *her* quilt.

Moving off the sofa, Annie spread the quilt open on the floor, squatted, and crept around all four sides, lifting the unbound edges at intervals. Many of the squares were still basted in place to keep them from moving during the quilting process, but even an unpracticed eye could see the difference between the work she had done under Franey's supervision and the expert stitching that now shone from the block in the quilt hoop.

Annie looked more closely. The thread was not hers. The color match was closer than her choice had been. How was that possible?

She would have to give up. Abandon the violated project. Forget she ever tried to learn to quilt.

Certainly she would never be able to look Beth Stutzman in the eye—she was sure the work was Beth's. Even though everyone knew that Annie's amateur stitching did not measure up to the standards of the rest of the quilts in the Beiler home, no one else would have suggested undoing her efforts. How Beth found the time during the last two weeks, Annie did not know. The Stutzmans were not even living in the Beiler home anymore.

Annie grabbed the quilt with both hands, hurled it at the open cedar chest, taking no effort to be tidy, and stomped out the front door.

Rufus heard the screen door slam from across the yard and through the open workshop window. He set down his plane and stepped outside in time to see the burst of a rust-colored dress flashing across the yard, past the garden, and into the barn.

He found Annalise there a few minutes later.

On her knees in the end stall with her back to the door, she tore at the pins holding her hair in place. Her *kapp* was already in the straw. He watched, his breath fading, as her blond hair escaped the braids and shook loose. Her shoulders rose with the sudden, noisy intake of air of one caught up in weeping and forgetting to breathe.

"Annalise."

Instantly she was on her feet. She spun toward him, her hair settling around her face and draping across her chest. Both hands now tried to eradicate the evidence of her tears, but Rufus had never seen her eyes so full.

Annalise Friesen did not cry. She solved problems.

"Annalise, tell me what happened." He took a step toward her.

Standing in a shaft of light shed by the window above her, she opened her mouth but closed it without speaking. Again her shoulders heaved.

Rufus lightly touched her shoulder. "Talk to me, Annalise."

She blew out air and breathed in three more times before she could form words.

"Everything is a mess, and I don't know how to clean it up."

"What are you talking about?"

Annalise rolled her eyes, a gesture Rufus had seen a few occasions before.

"You name it," she said, "and it's a mess."

"You'll have to be more specific."

He wanted to take her in his arms and still her quaking. To feel her racing heart—surely it was racing—and count the moments until it quieted. To stroke her forbidden hair.

"My mother, for starters," she said. "I didn't tell you half of what happened on Wednesday. She's petrified I'll become Amish." She clenched the fabric of her skirt. "And look at me, standing here in this dress. What am I supposed to do?"

"I'll speak to her, if you like."

"And say what?" Her gray eyes dared him. "Will you tell her that you don't care for me and I should not become Amish on your account?"

"You shouldn't," he said quietly, knowing that he was ducking her arrow.

"See, I've made a mess with you, too. What am I doing here, Rufus?"

"You wanted to live a simpler life."

"You have to know it's more than that."

Slowly, he nodded. "I do know. And it is more."

Her tears glistened, welling again. Rufus wanted to wipe them away with his own fingertips. But he did not move. "It's Saturday. You came to quilt, I'm sure. So why are you out here?"

"Because I can't quilt, and everyone knows it."

"You are learning. *Mamm* says you are doing well."

"Clearly someone else has another opinion."

"What are you talking about, Annalise?"

She gestured toward the house. "Go look for yourself. Someone's been working on my quilt and doing a far better job than I could ever hope to do."

"Why would someone work on your quilt?"

"You tell me! Is this an Amish tradition I haven't heard of yet? Is it some secret of *Ordnung* that no one has written down for me? Maybe I should just quit the whole business."

Rufus closed the short distance between them and gripped

her elbows, demanding her eyes meet his.

"You don't mean that," he said.

"Don't tell me what I mean."

"You've come too far, worked too hard, to let this spew out of you."

"So now you're judging me, too. Great."

"I am not judging you, Annalise. But I am going to kiss you."

Her shoulders relaxed as a gasp parted her lips. As he leaned in to take her mouth, one hand moved up her arm and found the back of her neck, under the hair he loved to see hanging loose. His fingers traced her hairline then strayed into the thick waves. The other arm went to the back of her waist to pull her closer, and he felt no protest. Lips soft and yielding responded to the searching pressure he offered.

Rufus broke the kiss at last but stood with his forehead against hers. "Better?"

Her breath came out slow and long. "I'm sorry. I guess I've been more confused than I realized."

"I know we need more time to be together. To talk."

Annalise nodded. "There is something else I need to talk to you about."

"Of course."

"It's about Joel. And Carter. I'm messing that up, too. I'm not sure, but—"

When he heard the noise of the door opening behind him, Rufus straightened, stepped away, and turned. Joel stood in the gap of daylight, leaning his weight into the side of the barn door to slide it open all the way.

"I need Dolly," Joel said, "if you're not planning to take her out."

Rufus turned his palms up. "I'm not going anywhere."

Joel pushed up the latch on Dolly's stall and stepped in. "*Daed* was looking for you a few minutes ago."

"Do you know what he wanted?"

"No." Joel reached for Dolly's bridle on its hook.

Rufus licked his lips and glanced at Annalise. "I suppose I'd

better find out what he wants."

She nodded.

He reached a hand out a few inches, but she made no move to take it, leaving him no option but to go without her.

Annie moved out of the empty stall and toward Joel.

"It's not what you think," she said, restraining her wild hair and wishing she had picked up the prayer *kapp*. Why were Rufus's kisses always pilfered from disappointment?

"It's not my business." Joel busied himself checking the leather of the reins.

"I've had a bad day."

"That happens to all of us. I'm sure you will sort it out."

"Rufus was. . .well, you know, trying to help."

"I told you it's not my business."

Annie pressed her lips together, considering her next words. "I've been wanting to talk to you about Carter. The Stutzman boys, too."

Now he turned his head toward her, lifting an eyebrow. "It's my turn to say that it's not what you think."

"Is that my cue to say that it's not my business?"

Joel gave no answer.

"If someone gets hurt," Annie said, "I will regret saying it's not my business."

"The last thing I want is for anyone to get hurt." Finally he stilled his hands and turned to face her. "Do you trust me, Annalise?"

"Of course, but—"

"No buts. Yes or no."

It was Annie's turn to hold her answer as Joel led Dolly out of her stall and into the daylight.

Twenty-Eight

A year ago, in Colorado Springs, on a Sunday afternoon, Annie would have pulled on shorts and a T-shirt, hoping for sun in late May. Here in the mountains, even the afternoon cradled cool night air. Over the deep rust dress, Annie wore her thick navy blue cardigan.

Annie locked up the house, going out the back door to where she had left her bicycle leaning against the sagging back porch. She tied her *kapp* in place and hiked up her skirt as far as she dared to keep the hem out of the path of the bike's chain. All afternoon she practiced smiling and speaking polite Pennsylvania Dutch sentences. This time at least she had advance warning that the Stutzmans were coming for Sunday dinner at the Beilers'. When she closed her eyes and remembered the scene from the day before, Beth's unblemished stitches in *her* quilt still rankled. But Annie loved Franey. She loved all the Beilers. She loved being in their home. She was not going to let Beth Stutzman take that away from her.

Thirty minutes later Annie coasted to a stop in the Beiler driveway and assessed the scene. The Stutzman buggy had not yet arrived. All three of the Beiler horses were in the pasture.

She moved across the yard then paused on the porch, her

shoulders lifting and falling as her breath recovered from the mountain ride. Surely by now one of the Beilers had put her quilt away properly in the cedar chest.

"Annalise, is that you? Come here."

Franey's tone carried a note of anxiety that Annie did not often hear from this calm Amish woman. Annie opened the door and stepped into the house. Franey was in the living room, holding her quilt out. She gripped the finished block in her hands.

"What happened?" Franey's perplexed eyes squinted.

Annie did not answer. Franey had to know how the quilt square had come to be perfect.

"This is what made you disappear before our lesson yesterday." Franey expelled air. "I knew Beth was spending too much time here. She came in the afternoons, while I was in the garden, even after her family moved."

"I should have told you." Annie stepped across the room and took the quilt from Franey's arms. "I was stunned when I found it and thought about quitting. But I am not a quitter."

Annie met Franey's eyes. She saw the slight smile begin in one corner of her mouth.

"No, Annalise Friesen, you are not a quitter."

"I am not going to give up quilting, but I am not going to look at those stitches every time I pick up that quilt for the next twenty years." Annie jabbed at the center of the hoop. "Those stitches are coming out."

"*Demut*," Franey said.

"What are you saying?" Annie's voice rose with indignation. "Do you mean that humility requires me to let Beth Stutzman ruin my first quilt?"

"Is it pride that makes you want to pull out the stitches?"

"There's a difference between being humble and being humiliated." Annie's retort came low and firm. Surely even the Amish could see the distinction. "I'm going to pull it all out if it takes me the next six Saturdays."

They stared at each other. Annie heard Jacob humming to

himself in the other room.

"It won't take that long," Franey finally said, "because I am going to help you."

Annie grinned. "Thank you."

"First, I am going to have a word with Beth when she gets here tonight."

Annie reached out and put a hand on Franey's arm. "Don't do that. We'll work on the stitching next time, but making a scene tonight will just spoil everyone's evening."

"I would have a private word."

"Still, it is the Sabbath, after all."

"Of course." Franey blew out her breath and folded the quilt properly. "Let her be surprised when she sees the quilt finished."

Annie giggled. "I am trying to practice *demut*, but you are making it hard!"

Franey grinned and squeezed Annie's hand. They turned at the sound of a buggy. The Stutzmans had arrived.

Rufus glanced several times toward the end of the table where Joel sat between Mark and Luke at the Beiler supper table. That all three teenage boys were present surprised Rufus. He had heard enough mumbling from Ike Stutzman over the last few weeks to know that Mark and Luke were missing as many family meals as Joel. Tonight Eli presided over the table that united Stutzmans and Beilers with great satisfaction. The older boys sat at one end with Ike and Edna, then Stutzman and Beiler girls were around the middle of the table. At the far end, Rufus, Jacob, and Annalise sat near Franey and Eli.

The older boys whispered among themselves, heads together. Joel shook his head. More than once, Rufus saw.

Franey picked up an empty dish. "Let me get some more potatoes."

Across the table, next to Annalise as usual, Jacob leaned forward toward Rufus. "Is the rock really going to be in the way?"

"In the way of what?" Rufus asked.

"The new trail." Jacob glanced down the table. "That's what they're talking about, isn't it?"

Rufus smiled. "Why did God give you such good hearing?"

"He just did." Jacob grinned. "They say you'll have to take the rock out."

"No, I don't think the boulder will be a problem."

Jacob laid his fork down and kicked the legs of his chair. "Is it true *English* have better schools than we do?" Jacob asked.

"Not better," Rufus answered, "just different. Our people learn what they need for a satisfying life."

"But is it better?"

"Why all the questions?" Annalise said, patting Jacob's back.

"I just wondered."

"Well, you'd better eat, or your *mamm* won't be happy with you."

Franey returned with more potatoes and fresh basket of rolls.

As the little boy picked up his fork, both Rufus and Annalise glanced at the older boys. In between passing dishes around the table, the boys huddled with low voices. Something about their demeanor discomfited Rufus, and he looked from one father to the other expecting at least gentle chastisement. None came. Instead, smiles abounded for the Stutzman girls, who had each contributed a dish to the evening's meal.

Ten years ago it would have meant nothing more than friendship for the Stutzmans and Beilers to share a meal in the home of one family or the other. Now Rufus knew better. The girls had grown up in those ten years. Marriage prospects were considerably slimmer for them here in Colorado, as they were for Rufus himself. Every time Rufus had a meal with the Stutzmans, all three daughters paraded their homemaking skills. Rufus suspected that since he had not made any overtures toward Beth, Johanna now thought there was hope she could attract him. She smiled at him with a new expression tonight—several times.

Rufus turned his gaze away, offering no encouragement. Annalise sat across the table. Yesterday's kiss still lingered on his lips. She deserved better than to have to sit quietly and watch him find the fine line between discouraging the Stutzman girls and sinking to rudeness himself.

By the time his mother was offering coffee with Beth's blackberry pie, Rufus had made up his mind.

"I could use a walk after that fine meal," Rufus said. "Ike, perhaps you'd like to stretch your legs with me." Annalise's brow furrowed, and he saw her catch herself and make her face placid again even as she watched his movements. It was time he set things right.

The older man dipped his head as he glanced to his wife. "Of course."

They walked toward the Beilers' alfalfa fields. "We got here too late to prepare for the spring seeding," Ike said. "Just barely. But we have the early fall seeding to look forward to. We could still have a nice crop this year."

Rufus nodded. He locked his hands behind his waist. "I wanted to have a word in private, Ike."

"Oh?"

Rufus saw the hope in Ike's eyes. He shook his head. "I'm sorry, Ike, but I must tell you I don't lean toward the attentions of your daughters."

"You are just getting to know them," Ike protested. "We've only been here a few weeks. They are not the little girls you left behind six years ago."

"Clearly. But still, I would not like to think that any of them might mistake my intentions, for I have none. We are old family friends. I mean no harm to anyone, but your fine daughters would do well to turn their attention elsewhere."

Ike's thumb and forefinger stroked his beard. "I see."

"I hope you do, Ike. Your girls respect you. They will listen if you provide guidance."

"Of course they would. There can be no question of that. But I am sorry to hear you feel this is necessary."

"It's best for everyone, I believe."

"It's because of that outsider."

Rufus squelched a sigh. Though it still irked, Ike's response was no surprise. "This has only to do with me, I assure you. Please do not blame Annalise."

"You defend her quite quickly, I notice."

"Annalise needs no defending."

"I understand your reluctance about the younger girls, but Beth is mature enough to be a wife."

"I'm sure she is, and I hope she will meet someone soon."

Ike huffed. "Well, then. I suppose you are no more particular than you have ever been, or you would have married before you left Pennsylvania."

Rufus put his hands out, palms up. "I felt I should tell you. If you like, I will speak to Beth."

"She is still my daughter and under my care. I will speak to her."

Rufus turned his steps back toward the house. "Perhaps we should have a last cup of coffee."

Rufus discovered the boys had left to take a walk as well. In the living room, sitting among the Stutzman sisters, Annalise looked desperate for rescuing. At least he would get to drive her home.

On Monday afternoon, Annie tooled around town on her bicycle with a list of errands. Mrs. Weichert had decided to run an ad for a 20 percent off sale in the newspaper. She insisted on delivering the ad the same way she always had—an old-fashioned piece of original art, which her daughter had created with careful lettering. Annie tried to explain that the newspaper would likely scan and digitize the ad anyway, but Mrs. Weichert was not interested in the conversation. She seemed to prefer living in the century in which most of her shop's goods had originated.

Once that was delivered, Annie crossed the street and went down a couple of blocks to the narrow storefront library. The sturdy but kind librarian had called the shop earlier in the day to let Annie know her interlibrary loan book had arrived from a university in Indiana. Annie had found a notation referencing this book in a footnote of another equally obscure title that had come through the shop serendipitously more than six weeks ago. The deeper she got into Beiler—or Byler—genealogy, the stronger its vortex churned. Who knew what the new title would reveal?

Last, Annie had promised Mrs. Weichert she would return before closing time with a three-cheese grilled sandwich from the coffee shop to serve as Mrs. Weichert's dinner before she spent the evening doing inventory, for which she had refused Annie's offer of help.

In Annie's experience, the coffee shop catered to the morning crowd with a burst at lunchtime before an afternoon lull. To her surprise, the coffee shop was bustling at ten minutes to five. She placed an order and paid for it—adding a sandwich for herself—and sank into a brown leather love seat as she waited. At least four orders were ahead of hers, and while friendly enough, the staff did not specialize in speed. The waiting time would allow her to explore the genealogy book and determine if it would yield information about her ancestors.

Annie had done enough reading in coffee shops to block out the voices clattering around her. She turned the library book in her hands, drawing in its age on her breath. Carefully she opened the front cover. After scanning the table of contents, Annie flipped to a chapter in the middle of the book and traced her finger down the center of several pages. Finally she came to a list of names, descendants of Christian Byler. *Magdalena. What a pretty name*, Annie thought, refreshing after generations of Barbaras and Elizabeths and all the variations of those names. She did not know where her own name had come from—she would have to ask her mother—but *Annalise* made her feel connected to the *Annas* that seemed to turn up in every generation of Bylers.

Annie glanced up at the counter, just to be sure the sandwiches were not ready, as the conversation behind her compelled her attention.

"Carter, your dad has been looking for you all afternoon."

The voice belonged to Colton, the man who worked for Tom Reynolds at the hardware store.

"Um, I had something to do after school."

Carter Reynolds.

Annie did not move her head, but she stopped seeing words on the page as she listened to the exchange.

"He's pretty annoyed that you didn't call," Colton said.

"I guess I should skip the latte and go home." Resignation rang through Carter's tone. Nervous resignation.

Annie touched the look-alike phone in her back pocket that Carter had returned to the shop.

"If I were you, I'd call him now," Colton said.

"Um, I guess."

"Don't you have your phone?"

"Actually, no."

"He's not going to like it if you lost your phone again."

"I know where it is. I just don't have it with me."

"The only reason he lets you have a phone is so he can stay in touch with you."

"I know. I just had to use it for something today and. . .left it there."

Annie nearly turned her head to look at Carter. Why the vagary?

"Maybe you should go get it," Colton said.

"Um, I can't really. Besides. . .it might not still be there."

"Why not?"

"Um. . .a friend needed it. For a science experiment."

Annie raised her head out of the book.

"You're not talking sense." Colton sighed. "Here. Use mine."

"Thanks."

"Oh, just a minute. Let me turn off the alarm. It's about to go off."

A cell phone alarm. Missing fertilizer. Boys playing with science. This was not good.

Annie smacked the library book shut and maneuvered out of

the love seat as quickly as she could. How fast could she pedal out to the rock where Elijah Capp and Ruth Beiler used to meet?

Breathless when she arrived, she was not the first one there. When Annie saw Karl Kramer's car, she pedaled faster, supposing she could get closer on the bike than he could get with his car. She could not make herself believe the boys had a target in mind. Karl was climbing the path that was meant to be a trail soon, a path that would take him straight to the rock with its broad flat surface perfect for stargazing.

When she was within twenty yards of him, she let the bike fall away from under her and threw off her helmet.

"Stop!"

Karl stopped, but only for a moment. "I'm looking for something." He took three more long strides.

"I know. But you have to stop."

"Don't tell me what to do."

"Why did you come here, Karl?"

"I'm working with Rufus to make this into a park. You know that." His face contorted in aggravation.

Annie moved cautiously forward, her eyes scanning for small clues, her heart thudding. She hoped she was wrong.

"Yes, I know," she said, "but why now? Why did you come now?"

"If you must know, I got an anonymous tip about my missing fertilizer."

"It's only a few bags, Karl."

"I'm inclined to slap the next person who says that. The principle of the thing is at stake—someone took what belonged to me. I won't stand for that."

"It was probably just some kids seeing what they could get away with." She took a few steps forward and to one side, where she could get a better view of the boulder.

"I can see that. This place is loaded with fresh footprints." He gestured to the ground.

The boys. How many of them? Had Joel been here?

Still Annie searched, wondering if a group of teenage boys

would have the math and science skills required for what she suspected. She doubted Carter and Duncan could have done this on their own, but she had heard the Amish claim that their eighth-grade education was comparable to a conventional high school diploma. Did they teach chemistry? Circuitry? Physics? Perhaps. Elijah Capp astounded her with what he understood about circuitry and ignition, and he had never used electricity in his life.

Mark and Luke Stutzman had once blasted rock in a Pennsylvania meadow.

And Joel. How had he dared to ask her to trust him if he knew this was going on?

She guessed that Duncan Spangler would do anything on a dare.

Carter Reynolds was naive enough to be talked out of his cell phone. In the intrigue of the moment, he would not think about how he would explain its absence to his parents later.

"Karl," Annie pleaded. "Please. You have to stop."

"I am not going to be the butt of somebody's practical joke." Karl kept moving.

Annie saw it then. The fertilizer. The wire. The cell phone with a network of wires taped in place.

"Karl!"

Annie was too far away to see the first vibration of the cell phone. The flash made her cover her eyes.

Twenty-Nine

October 1777

"Is he gone?"

Jacob turned to see his mother standing at the entrance to the tannery. Elizabeth seldom came to see where he worked, though he had labored side by side at the lime-filled vats with his father since he was a child. No one was with her. She must have walked all the way down from the big house unaccompanied.

Jacob sighed heavily and put down the blade he was using to trim excess leather off a bridle. "Yes, Joseph left."

Though he was sure his mother knew the truth before she asked, Jacob's heart pinched when her face fell.

"He tried to say good-bye," she said, "but I wouldn't let him."

"Joseph will come back, *Mamm*," Jacob said.

"Do not make promises that are not yours to keep, Jacobli."

He had no response.

"Losing Philadelphia was the last straw, I suppose." Elizabeth rubbed her palms against her skirt.

"He thought he could be more help at General Washington's side than here. David will finish Joseph's harvest. John will take his animals for the winter."

She stiffened. "I see, then. You boys have it all worked out."

"He was going to join the militia in any event, *Mamm*. We're

569

just trying to make sure his family does not suffer."

"Of course. Perhaps I'll invite Hannah and the children to come stay at the big house, at least for the winter."

"I think they'd like that."

"I would be glad to have the *kinner* around. I can help with the little ones." Her hands moved up and down her thighs. "What will Washington do next?"

"I don't imagine he will walk away from Philadelphia without a fight."

"So there will be another battle. Soon."

Jacob stepped tentatively toward his mother. "I don't see how he can avoid it."

"Where?"

"Perhaps Germantown."

"And this is what Joseph wanted to do."

He saw the shudder in her shoulders. "Yes, *Mamm*. This is what Joseph chose. We've lived with danger all our lives. He is not afraid."

"That is what worries me. Because he is not afraid, he will take greater risks."

Jacob wrapped his arms around his mother. "*Mamm*, he has to do this."

"I suppose if you were not making gunpowder, you would follow."

Jacob was silent, feeling for the first time how thin his mother had become in the last year. Why did he not embrace her more often? He would have noticed sooner. "There is no point in imagining *if*," he said. "I am here. David and I are working together on something that matters to the Revolution."

"Then perhaps it is John I should worry about." Elizabeth pulled away from him. "And Sarah! She's as bad as you boys. Now she's trapped in Philadelphia, and it's too dangerous for any of us to go see her."

"It's an important cause, *Mamm*."

She covered her nose with one hand. "I have never liked the

way this place smelled."

Elizabeth pivoted. Jacob let her walk away, but he followed for a few steps into the sunlight outside the dark tannery. He almost called out to her to go visit Katie for some lunch, but Elizabeth had already chosen the path that would take her back up to the big house.

Magdalena let the old gelding pull the cart at his own speed. She needed time to think. The farms were clear of soldiers now. Both Patriots and British sympathizers had abandoned their local rivalries in favor of the armies amassed around Philadelphia. General Washington's attempt to take back Germantown, five miles north of the city, tightened the British grip on the capital. The untrained American soldiers lost themselves in the fog around the quiet hamlet. They stumbled into defeat rather than marching to victory.

Now it was the middle of October, and many speculated that the warfront would be quiet through the winter. Unpredictable weather made a march of any distance unlikely. Magdalena had been to the cabin twice since the Battle of Germantown and found nothing there but the dusty jars of preserves. She would never know if any of the letters she delivered had any bearing on the skirmishes around Berks County, much less Germantown or Philadelphia. No doubt by now Patrick and the others were serving in a British regiment with proper uniforms and exulting in the vice strangling the colonies' capital. The Patriots would be forced to give up and the whole matter would be done with.

The gelding slowed a little too much, so Magdalena clicked for him to pick up his pace. She did have legitimate errands at three other farms this afternoon. The Bylers were well known for their apple cider, and Babsi was sending a jug to every family that had helped feed this year's apples into the press. As always, Magdalena would stop in at the Buerkis' before heading home. She wavered between hope and relief every day. She always hoped Nathan would be at the house and she could once again search his face for signs that he loved her. When he was not there, though, at least for one more day she savored the reprieve of not seeing the answer she refused to accept.

She knew that the girls she had gone to school with whispered behind her back. They were married and producing children. Magdalena could have been married, too, they thought, if she would accept the truth that Nathanael was never coming back to her. The war around them had no bearing on the availability of Amish men. A half a dozen would have been interested in Magdalena with even slight encouragement from her.

But none of the men was Nathanael, and they knew not to invite Magdalena to ride with them to a singing or apple schnitzing.

If Magdalena ever married one of them, it would not be for love.

"Come on, Old Amos," Magdalena said to the horse who was slowing down yet again. "We can't sit here in the middle of the fields all day." She nudged the horse, but he took only a half dozen steps before stopping.

Old Amos deserved his name. *Daed* paid little for the animal four years ago because the horse was already ancient. Hardly worth what it cost to feed him, he was no use for anything more than drawing the lightest cart on the simplest errands. Magdalena tried again to get him to move forward, but Old Amos neighed and stayed put. Magdalena would have to get out and lead him. Perhaps with her weight out of the cart he would be willing to pull the jugs of apple cider. Grabbing the halter on both sides of the animal's face, Magdalena leaned away from him.

And then she saw what had made him stop.

The red coat was ripped in at least three places, and the white breeches were ground brown with mud. She supposed his hat was lost in battle, and he carried no weapon. He lay on the ground, unmoving.

A true British soldier. He must have come from the battle at

Germantown, but that had been days ago and miles away.

Magdalena let go of the horse's halter and took three steps toward the side of the road, where the ground sloped and pebbles skittered under her feet. When she saw the unkempt dark hair, she thought for a moment it was Patrick finally in the uniform he dreamed of. But it was not him.

The soldier's eyes were closed, but his chest seemed to lift slightly. Or at least she thought it did. She would have to get closer to be sure. She scratched her way down the hill about twenty feet then stopped once more to watch his chest.

Yes, he was breathing.

And bleeding.

When his eyes popped open, Magdalena gasped. They stared at each other for a frozen moment.

"Can you speak?" Magdalena finally asked. She knelt at his side and gingerly began to inspect him.

"Yes," he said.

In that one word, she could tell he had come from England and not one of the other colonies.

"Where is the wound?"

"My belly. Are you a Patriot?"

She met his eyes then shook her head.

"A sympathizer, then," he said. "I suppose that is good, though I don't care anymore."

He did not recognize the meaning of her Amish prayer *kapp* and she did not correct him. She had never called herself a sympathizer, but perhaps she was one.

Magdalena undid the last remaining button on his coat and gently separated the shredded red wool from his bloodied shirt. Pushing up the once-white shirt, she exposed the wound—and nearly had to turn away as the contents of her stomach rose to her throat. The hole in his side had been bandaged hastily with cotton strips that nearly fell apart at the touch of her fingers. Fresh blood oozed. Magdalena pulled her shawl off her shoulders and grimaced as she pressed it against the wound.

"I have a horse and cart up on the road. Do you think you can stand?"

"I've come all the way from Germantown, haven't I?"

"I'm astounded you've managed to come so far." She helped him sit up and tried to determine the best way to support his weight. It seemed unfeasible that he had been roaming the Pennsylvania countryside in this condition, yet here he was. Gray skinned and prone, but alive.

"I'm not going back," the man croaked.

"No one here will ask you to. Let's try to stand."

"War is a hideous thing. I am not going back."

"Don't worry about that now." Magdalena glanced up the hill at Old Amos and the cart. She put one of the soldier's arms around her shoulder, gripped his dangling wrist, and sucked in a deep breath. She stood, pulling him upright alongside her.

Magdalena had never heard such a scream as the one that roared from his lungs now. By the time she managed to get him up the hill and draped him across the cart, he was unconscious.

Magdalena turned the horse and cart in the narrow road and headed toward home. The apple cider deliveries would have to wait for another day. By the time she pulled the cart up as close to the front porch of her family's home as she could get, assorted family members had gathered. She caught her father's eyes as they carried the soldier inside the house and laid him on the table. Babsi went to work cleaning the ragged wound. Magdalena's younger sisters scurried from the water barrel with clean rags, while her brother Hansli stoked the fire that warmed the room.

"Magdalena?"

She turned toward her father's voice.

"Do you know this man?"

"No, *Daed*. I only found him and wanted to help."

He nodded slowly. "You did the right thing to bring him."

"I was not sure you would welcome a soldier in the house," Magdalena said.

"He is not a soldier now, only a man who has lost a great deal of blood."

Magdalena exhaled abruptly and heavily. She had not realized she was rationing her own breath.

"I thought you wanted to be neutral," she said.

"I am neutral. Today I will help this British soldier, and if tomorrow a Patriot turns up on our porch in need, I will help him also. Neutrality does not mean we turn our backs on humanity."

"Thank you, *Daed*."

"You are pale," he said. "His blood is all over you. Go clean up."

"I should help take care of him," she said.

"You have done your part."

Magdalena nodded but could not tear her eyes off the soldier. She wanted to believe that had he been a bleeding Patriot foot soldier, she would have done the same thing.

But she was not sure.

Thirty

Rufus was in the small cart. He almost had not come.

The message that summoned him was vague, cryptic, unsigned. It sounded like some sort of mistake. A note had turned up in his toolbox that afternoon. It could have been for anyone. But something about it made him think he would regret disregarding it. He twisted his torso to look at the open toolbox behind him. The note fluttered loose and escaped the buggy on the breeze. Rufus reached for it and missed. Dolly continued to trot forward. It was probably nothing, but he cared about the rock and wanted to be sure he would see nothing unusual there.

Instead, wide tire tracks rutted through the grass—fresh tracks, prompting Rufus to signal Dolly to speed up. He passed a bicycle tumbled in the weeds. Annalise's bicycle.

Rufus had never heard a bomb, but he imagined it would sound just like the blast that split the air

"Annalise!"

Annie fumbled with her phone as she charged the last few yards up the incline. By the time she squatted next to Karl, splayed on his back, she had it open, but her thumb slid off the power button

three times before the device began cycling on. For a few seconds, she was terrified it would not find a signal.

"Karl!"

No response.

"Karl, can you hear me?"

Finally her trembling finger pushed the buttons for 911. With her free hand, Annie thumped Karl's shoulder, trying to rouse him. Her eyes scanned for blood—which seemed minimal. What she saw were burns. And beyond Karl, weeds smoldered and flared. Annie dropped the open phone, leaped over Karl, and stomped on flames. They spurted up in new spots as fast as she could kick dirt on them. A more heavily grassed area might already have been out of control. The wind was calm, though, and loose dirt abounded. Both factors worked in her favor. Annie shed her jacket and used it to smother bouncing sparks.

"Karl!"

Still no response.

Rufus spotted Karl's car, and terror welled. He thought he had made progress with Karl. Why would the man lure Annalise up here? Whatever story he had concocted had to have been good.

Unless there was no story.

Unless Karl had not lured Annalise at all.

Unless Karl got the same sort of ambiguous, handwritten message that had drawn Rufus to this moment.

Annie was far from certain the ground cover would not spark again when she turned back to Karl, who lay silent and still. Once upon a time, Annie had been certified in first aid. A for airway. B for breathing. C for…C for. Cardiac something. No. Circulation.

"You have dialed 911." A crackly distant voice bore into Annie's awareness. "Do you have an emergency? We are unable to fix your location."

The phone! Annie snatched it up to her ear. "Don't hang up!"

"What is the location of your emergency?" the 911 dispatcher asked.

Annie glanced around. "I don't know the address. I'm out behind the Beiler farm, where they're thinking about making the new recreation area."

"What is the nature of the emergency?"

"An explosion. I think somebody tried to blow up the big rock." Annie leaned over Karl and turned her ear to his mouth. "Karl Kramer is injured. He's breathing, but he's unconscious."

Annie pressed fingers into Karl's neck to look for a pulse.

"Help is already on the way," the dispatcher said. "Do you have any reason to believe drugs or alcohol may have played a role in this incident?"

"No. I mean, I don't think so."

"Are any weapons involved?"

"You mean other than the bomb?!" Annie's heart galloped in her chest.

"Please remain calm, ma'am. I have already dispatched an emergency team. The information you give me now will assist them when they arrive. Tell me about the victim and the injuries."

Annie took a deep breath. "Fortyish. White male, five ten, 180 pounds."

"Very good. Is he conscious yet?"

Karl moaned again. Annie put a hand against the side of his face, and his eyes opened. Anger flared in them.

"Yes," she said into her phone. "He's coming around."

"How long was he unconscious?"

"From as soon as the bomb went off, I guess. Till now." Had it been two minutes or ten? Annie had no idea.

"Can he speak?"

"Karl, can you hear me?"

He groaned. "Whoever did this is going to pay."

Rufus threw down the reins and sprinted the final distance. Annalise was hunched over Karl Kramer. He squatted beside her and automatically put a hand on her shoulder. He expected trembling, but she was steady and strong.

"Help is coming." Annalise laid her hand on Karl's chest.

The burn marks on Karl's arms made Rufus flinch. Who could have done this?

Karl breathed heavily. "They blew me up with my own fertilizer."

"Shh. Don't upset yourself." Annalise's hand moved in a soothing circle on Karl's chest.

"It's too late." Karl rolled his eyes.

"What is he talking about?" Rufus asked.

"It's complicated," Annalise answered. "I tried to stop him."

"You knew about this?"

"Of course not. I just figured it out a little too late. I had no idea he would be here."

"Are you all right?"

"I'm fine. Karl is what matters. We have to keep him awake."

"I am awake." Karl punctuated his words with hostility. "My arms are on fire. Somebody is going to pay."

Karl shifted his knees, as if to roll over and try to rise.

"Don't move," Annalise said, the pressure of her hand deepening against Karl's chest. "They said you shouldn't move."

"Nobody tells me what to do."

Annalise glanced at Rufus. "They said he might have a concussion. He was unconscious for several minutes."

"They aren't doctors," Karl said. "They just answer the phone."

"They're trained for emergencies. We have to follow their advice."

"They're taking their sweet time."

A siren wailed in approach.

"Karl, you listen to Annalise." Rufus spoke more sharply than he had in years. He stood up. "I'll run up to the road and flag them down."

Rufus moved through trampled weeds, dodging trees and small boulders and holes that could reach up and twist an ankle. He saw only what the future might have been if Annalise had been a few steps closer to Karl Kramer just moments ago, and its vacant blackness sliced through him.

Thirty-One

The next morning, Rufus walked out to the big rock. When his family first came to the valley and purchased hopeful acreage with a stunning view, it was not long before they discovered the big rock. They used to come for Sunday afternoon picnics. His brother Jacob was only a year old at the time of the move. One of the toddler's first recognizable utterances indicated the rock, big as half a room and flat. The field below was low-lying vegetation for which they had not known the names. His sister Ruth found a book at the library, and gradually they learned to identify the strange plants distinct from anything they had known in Pennsylvania.

Now Rufus stood on the rock and looked down on the scene. Yellow plastic tape cordoned off the space where he found Annalise with Karl Kramer yesterday.

Crime Scene. Do Not Cross.

A crime scene practically on Beiler land. Annalise was as close to being a Beiler as anyone else in the valley, and she seemed to be at the heart of whatever happened.

No one was sure what transpired. The fire department had drenched the smoldering brush to ensure a gust of spring air could not revive the flames. And though officials would not issue their written report for several days, it was clear that an explosion caused the brush fire that left a black scar below the rock.

Now everyone knew where Karl Kramer's missing fertilizer had been. But why?

And why was Annalise there?

Rufus heard a truck motor and glanced up to see Tom maneuvering his red pickup as close as he could before getting out and taking the final stretch on foot. Tom stopped at the yellow tape. Rufus waved a greeting.

"I suppose you're here with the same questions I have." Tom shielded his eyes as he looked up at Rufus.

Rufus nodded. "The area has been carefully combed."

Tom asked, "Have they questioned Annie yet?"

"I don't know. I haven't seen her today." Last night had not seemed like the time to press her for details.

"She's not going to work at the shop today, is she?"

Rufus shrugged. "You know Annalise."

Tom exhaled. "Sometimes I wonder. How about you? Have they questioned you?"

"Not officially. It's not unusual for me to go past here. I promised to give a statement today, but I know nothing especially helpful." Rufus was climbing down the side of the rock. "Do you see anything from down there?"

"I heard they found remains of a cell phone. Bits of wire." Tom kicked up dirt.

Rufus maneuvered down to the ground and began circling to where Tom stood.

Tom crossed his arms on his chest. "Someone planned this."

"But did they mean to hurt anyone? Maybe they got more than they bargained for." Rufus ran his thumb and forefinger around the brim of his hat. "Karl's being the victim—well, it is not good news for the project."

"Some would say he deserved it."

"And they would be wrong. No one deserves stepping into a bomb."

"Well, it's a good thing for Karl that whoever made this bomb didn't have a better idea what they were doing." Tom put both hands on his hips, a familiar gesture. "Rufus, I know how much you hate getting involved in legal matters, but I don't see how you're going to dodge this one. Annie was here when it happened, and you were here moments later. The sheriff's office is not finished with either of you."

"One step at a time," Rufus said. "I'd like to see how Karl is and what he remembers. Can you drive me to Cañon City?"

Annie sat at her dining room table with a cup of strong coffee, a pad of paper, and a pen. She alternated sipping the coffee and chewing the top of the pen as she considered what she had jotted on the pad.

Carter lost his phone. More than once. So what?

What she overheard yesterday in the coffee shop was not incriminating without reading something into it.

Someone sent a message to Karl, but she did not know who.

Joel asked her to trust him. Several times. Why did she feel like she had made a mistake in doing so?

But what action could she have taken? She had no proof of anything—especially after she deleted Carter's Internet history before returning his phone.

Annie dropped the pen on the pad. She could talk to Joel. She could talk to Carter. She could talk to Tom. She could seek out an Amish elder. She could talk to the sheriff.

"Friesen, you've lost your edge," Annie said aloud. "If you were capable of making a decision, you would have done it by now."

The knock on her front door provoked a gasp and spilled coffee. Annie scampered to the kitchen for a towel. "Coming!"

Before opening the door, she looked out the front window. Sophie Beiler stood on her front stoop, a basket in her arms. Annie opened the door.

"*Mamm* is so worried about you." Sophie offered the basket.

"She's afraid you're not eating."

Annie peeked under the edge of a towel. "So she made cookies?"

"And blueberry muffins," Sophie said. "She just wants you to be okay."

"Come on in."

Sophie set the basket on the coffee table. "*Mamm* also wants to know if you called your mother. She said to tell you that this qualifies as an emergency."

"Um, no." Annie gestured that Sophie should sit down. "I'm not hurt. There's not really anything to tell."

"That's what *Mamm* said you would say. I'm supposed to insist. Where's your phone?"

Annie patted her jeans pocket. No cell phone bulge. "I'm not sure." She glanced at an end table, then into the dining room. "I must have left it upstairs."

"Shall I get it for you?"

"No. I'll look later."

Sophie tilted her head and lifted her eyebrows.

"Okay," Annie said. "I'll look now."

Searching the small rooms upstairs did not take much time. Annie returned empty-handed.

"I lost my cell phone. That may be the first time in my life I've spoken that sentence."

"Maybe you left it at the hospital. Or in Tom's truck."

"Yes. I'll have to check around." Annie sat on the sofa across from Sophie and lifted the lid on a small box at the end of the coffee table. She extracted a note card. "I think I will just write my mother. It will be less dramatic that way, less for her to worry over."

"You know your own mother best."

Annie's hand gripped a pen and hovered over the card. "So what is everyone saying? I can imagine the buzz."

"Oh, we don't have to talk about that."

"I want to know." Sophie's hesitation made Annie more determined.

"Well, no one knows what happened. The *English* say it was the work of Amish, which is ridiculous. The Amish say it was obviously the work of the *English*. Amish are nonviolent, after all."

"But they do occasionally have to remove an obstacle in a field by force, don't they? So they can plow and harvest easily?"

"Yes, that is true."

"Amish can understand explosives without being violent toward other people."

Sophie said nothing.

"You're holding something back," Annie said. "What is it?"

Sophie raised her shoulders. "A couple of people may suspect you."

"Me!"

"You were there. You understand these things. You could have made the call that. . .that. . ."

Annie rescued Sophie from having to finish that sentence. "I was an expert in a lot of things before I came to Westcliffe, but I promise you explosives was not on the list."

"I don't believe it, of course. No one at our house does."

"I should hope not. Do you know what happened to my bicycle?"

Sophie grimaced. "Joel looked for it when he went for Dolly and the cart, but the police said it was evidence."

"Evidence of what?"

"Well, maybe not evidence. But something to investigate."

Annie slapped her torso against the back of the sofa. "Great. Now I have no transportation. I suppose they have my book, too."

"Your book?"

"I picked up a genealogy book at the library yesterday before everything happened. It came all the way from a university in Indiana. I'm sure it was in the basket."

Sophie removed the towel and nudged the basket toward Annie. "I do have one more question from *Mamm*."

Annie reached forward and pinched a wedge out of a large chocolate cookie. "Yes?"

"Please come home with me. Lydia is shopping for a few things, so we have the buggy. *Mamm* wants to see for herself that you are all right." Sophie paused for a breath. "She thinks of you as her own daughter, you know."

Annie's throat thickened. She would be sure not to repeat Franey's sentiment in her letter to her mother.

"Please?" Sophie said. "We all want you to come. You can stay the night."

Annie shook her head. "No, I want to sleep in my own bed."

"Supper, then." Sophie cocked her head. "Rufus should be there."

Ruth twisted her backpack around. Even though her phone was set on vibrate and tucked in a side pocket of the bag, she heard its distinct insistent tone above the rhythm of the bus pulling out of the stop. She did not have to look at the caller ID. It was Elijah Capp. This was the fifth time he had called in the last three hours.

She pulled the phone from the pocket and wrapped her fingers around it, waiting for it to stop buzzing. Elijah deserved a face-to-face conversation, but so far she had not even been able to answer his last several letters. In her mind, she crafted phrases but was dissatisfied with every version. When she found the right words, perhaps she would have the courage to put them on paper. A letter he could hold on to might encourage him more to find his own path. Or hurt him more.

The bus lumbered to the next stop. Ruth stood and slung the backpack over one shoulder, awaiting the sucking *whoosh* of the doors parting at the bottom of the rubber-coated stairwell. The bus driver, who had been letting her off at this stop for two years, nodded a good-bye into his enormous rearview mirror. Ruth took the steps lightly, as she always did, and the doors suctioned closed behind her.

She could easily imagine what Elijah had to say. He had said everything before, after all. Perhaps she did not have anything new to say, either.

Ruth put her key in the lock of her suite and leaned into the door with one shoulder, a motion of habit. Inside, as she slid a key into the door to her room, she listened for activity in any of the other three rooms. She tossed the backpack and the keys onto her bed, with a fleeting thought that Elijah might be surprised at how thoroughly she was acclimated to the assumption that someone would try to steal her belongings.

"Boo!"

Ruth spun around and grinned. "Hi, Lauren. How is your Tuesday going?"

"I'm ready to blow this joint."

Ruth rolled her eyes and shook her head. "Do people really say that?"

"I'm people. I say it."

"What's the munitions report for the day?"

"My dad Skyped my brother today, then called me. He hasn't blown up anything even for practice in more than three weeks. He's getting antsy."

What would Elijah think about this conversation? The peaceful plain people hardly had use for a word like *munitions*, but it tripped off Ruth's tongue almost daily now.

Lauren punched the air. "You said you were going to do this. Are you ready?"

"Well, maybe—"

"Oh, no, no, no. There will be no withdrawal tactics now. Bring your identification documents and cash for the fee. They don't take plastic."

"All right," Ruth said. "Just give me a couple minutes to freshen up."

Lauren closed the door on her way out. Ruth went to the dresser, unpinned her hair, brushed it, and pinned it up again in a matter of seconds. From her bottom desk drawer she took the required documents then fished in her backpack for her small wallet.

She flinched when her phone buzzed yet again, but she ignored it. A moment later, though, she heard the notification that someone had left a message.

Elijah would no sooner leave a message on a phone than he would drive a car.

But he had. Something was wrong. She just knew it. She lifted the phone to look at the screen. Four unanswered calls. A rock formed in the pit of her stomach.

Finally Ruth accessed her voice mail. The rock turned hot. "Lauren!"

Joel was not there for supper. Annie heard the sigh in Eli's voice after the silent prayer at the beginning of the meal.

"He'll come around," Franey said softly in Pennsylvania Dutch. "He must."

Eli scowled into the bowl of peas and carrots.

Rufus was missing as well. As much as she loved Franey—and the whole Beiler family—Annie could not help but be disappointed.

"He went with Tom to see Karl." Franey seemed to read Annie's mind as she passed the mashed potatoes. "They've been gone most of the day."

Annie nodded and held the bowl of potatoes while Jacob served himself.

"Don't take more than you'll eat," Franey cautioned her youngest.

After supper, Sophie and Lydia were clearing the table, having refused Annie's offer of help, so Annie took her unfinished note card to the living room. Determined to tell her parents the truth about what happened, she did not want to be dramatic. Just the facts. She was still chewing on the top of her pen with the note in her lap when she heard Tom's truck. With a glance toward the empty dining room, Annie crossed to the front door and met Rufus on the porch.

On Saturday he kissed her, after months of holding back. On Sunday he drove her home with murmurs of assurance that Beth Stutzman meant nothing to him. Yesterday he held her hand in the ambulance and all the way home in Tom's truck. It all felt so long ago. She wished she could run into his arms now, feel his heartbeat, his hand at the back of her neck. Perhaps he would take her home again. He could let Dolly slow her pace, as he held the reins with one hand and her fingers with the other.

He gave her a tired smile. "Hi."

"Hi," Annie said. "How is Karl?"

"Okay. It won't be long till he's released. The burns looked worse than they are." Rufus leaned against the house, next to the door. The porch light spilled over him. "At least that's what the nurse said when she came in to change the dressings. I doubt she was supposed to tell us even that much."

"Did he say what happened? Why he was there?"

Rufus shook his head. "The nurse said someone from the sheriff's office had been there, but Karl was asleep from the pain medication."

"He sounded really angry yesterday," Annie said.

Rufus nodded. "He still is, when he's awake. He's not going to let go of this."

"Can you blame him? Somebody put him in the hospital. He has a right to know what happened."

Her words hung in the air, and she regretted them. This was Rufus. Last year somebody put Rufus in the hospital—probably Karl Kramer—and Rufus had let it go. Only pride, *hochmut*, demanded rights. Humility, *demut*, did not.

Annie stifled a groan. She was never going to learn to be Amish at this rate.

Rufus closed a hand over the fist that held her pen. "What are you writing?"

"A note to my parents. I have to tell them, but I am not ready for a phone call."

"I understand. Just be sure to sign the note."

She tilted her head, questioning.

"I suppose I will have to tell the police about the note I received." Rufus scratched the back of one ear.

Annie's pulse pounded. "What note?"

He squeezed her fingers. "One that I suspect is very similar to the one that prompted Karl to go out to the rock."

"Rufus! Why didn't you say something last night?"

"Too much was going on. And I don't have the note. It blew out of the buggy on my way out to the rock—before I realized it could be important."

"Who would want to hurt both Karl and you?" Not Joel. Certainly not Joel. Holes like Joel made swiss cheese of Annie's flimsy theory.

She savored the sensation of his hand around hers. If someone was trying to hurt Rufus, her investigation was far from over.

Thirty-Two

March 1778

"We never clear this part of *Grossmuder*'s garden. Why are we doing it this year?"

Jacob looked at his son. At thirteen, the boy had recently announced he no longer wanted to be Jacob Franklin, but simply Franklin. The decision amused Jacob and Katie, but they made the transition with surprising ease. Franklin hoarded pamphlets published by Benjamin Franklin no matter what the topic. Over the winter he seemed to grow four inches in his arms and legs and now was almost as tall as Jacob.

Jacob reached down with a broad hand and pulled out a tangle of withered bindweed from summers past. "It's too overgrown. We should have done this years ago." He filled both arms with weeds and heaped them on a pile he would burn later.

"Are we going to plant this part?" Franklin wanted to know.

"Maybe. When I was a boy we used to grow beets in this section." Maria's beets. That was what it had been. Jacob made no effort to hide from his children that he had a sister who disappeared decades ago, but rarely did anyone speak her name.

"I don't much like beets." Franklin yanked on a vine that was as long as he was tall.

"We don't have to plant beets. It's up to *Grossmuder*. Even if she does not want to plant anything, we should clean it up."

Franklin straightened and gestured down the hill. "Were you really born in that old cabin?"

"Yes, I was. My parents felt fortunate to have that shelter in the homesteading days." Jacob used the structure to store assorted farm tools now.

"And now we're a new country!" Franklin wrapped a thick, thorny, knee-high weed with a rag then gripped it with both hands and pulled. The weed surrendered its existence. He held it up. "I got the whole root." Franklin tossed it on the burn pile.

Jacob smiled and nodded.

"That's what we have to do with the British," Franklin said. "We have to get rid of the whole lot of them. As soon as I'm old enough, I'm going to fight."

Jacob sincerely hoped the fighting would be over long before Franklin could enlist, though he had heard of boys as young as fifteen finding a place in the militia. Franklin's voice had already deepened, and he had the height of a man.

"Do not glamorize war," Jacob said. "It is ugly business."

"But it's your business, isn't it?" Franklin yanked another weed. "It seems to me, it's the business of all red-blooded American men some way or another."

"Men," Jacob said, "not boys. You are thirteen and needed on the farm."

"I won't always be thirteen."

"And I hope there won't always be a war."

"We have to win, *Daed*. We can't stop until we win."

Jacob knelt and raked his fingers through the earth of a square yard cleared of weeds. Enough talk of war. "It's warm enough and the soil is soft enough. We should turn the earth once we get it cleared."

"Today?"

Jacob heard the implicit moan in his son's question, but he ignored it. "Go on down to the old cabin and get rakes and shovels."

"Yes, sir." As reluctant as he sounded, Franklin did as he was told.

Jacob let dirt sift through the fingers of both hands. The weeds were coming out easily enough. Whether or not he had really seen Maria on that rainy afternoon nearly four years ago, it was time to reclaim the plot of land where she talked to her beets whenever she felt anxious.

"*Daed!*"

The cry startled Jacob to his feet. This was not the timbre of a boy calling information to his father over a field. Jacob sprinted across the clearing and crashed down the hill to the cabin. Jacob saw what had caused his son to halt about ten yards short of the cabin. Wrapped in a man's wool coat and beaver fur hat, a form slumped against the door.

"We'd better see who it is," Jacob said.

The form moved and slowly stood. The hat dropped away in the process, and the coat fell open.

She was thin and pale and thirty years older, but her black curls tumbled as they always had. Her visage lacked the fullness of the image in Jacob's memory. If her face looked this thin, he hated to think how lean the rest of her must be. The baggy men's breeches made it hard to tell.

"Maria!"

Her eyes widened in surprise. "Jacobli, is that you?"

He folded her into his arms, breath to speak gone from him.

"*Daed?*" she whispered in his ear.

"Gone."

He felt her shoulders drop, even under the heavy coat.

"How long ago?" she asked.

"Nearly seven years."

She pulled back from him, shaking her head slowly, her curls jostling. "I never heard."

How could she have known? No one in the family knew where to find her—or whether she wanted to be found. Relief at seeing her alive flushed through him, but why had she come now?

"The boy is yours?" Maria said.

"My eldest. Jacob Franklin."

"Just Franklin." The boy's voice bore an irritated edge.

"Franklin," Jacob said, "meet your *aunti* Maria."

Maria laughed. "I like your name."

Jacob had always relished Maria's laugh above all his siblings'. He grinned broadly.

Franklin eyed the visitor cautiously. "She's one of the Amish aunts, right?"

Jacob looked toward Maria. "I guess not anymore."

"Not for a long time." Maria's eyes moved from Jacob to Franklin. "Someday I will introduce you to Mr. Benjamin Franklin, if you like."

Franklin gawked, making his father chuckle briefly. Jacob squinted as if to focus on the details of his sister's presence.

"Are you injured?" Jacob asked.

She shook her head, curls floating free. "Just weary."

"Franklin," Jacob said, "go up to the big house and get your *grossmuder*."

"Yes, sir." Franklin turned and started up the hill.

Maria's face was a question.

"Yes," Jacob said. "Elizabeth still lives. You must see her."

Maria sucked in a breath. "After all this time, why would she want to see me?"

"Because she loves you."

"I would understand if she never forgave me."

"If you think that, you have forgotten who she is."

"I thought I would find Christian here," Maria said.

"Ah. Forgiveness may not be as forthcoming from him."

"Where is he?"

"He moved to the Conestoga Valley years ago. Many of the Amish did. Their land here in Berks County was worth a considerable amount after they made real farms of the wilderness. They made enough money to start again in Lancaster County, farther from the frontier."

"Bar-bar and Anna? And Lisbetli?"

"Barbara and Anna also have gone to Lancaster County with their husbands," Jacob said. "As far as I know they are well. The names of their grandchildren make a long list. Even a few great-grandchildren have come along."

Jacob reached for Maria's hand, and she gave it to him. He breathed several times as he gathered his words. "Lisbetli went on to eternity. She is buried beside your mother. And *Daed*."

"But she was the youngest!" Maria keened, sinking slowly to her knees as her wail let loose.

Jacob weighted her shoulder with both of his hands, feeling the pulse of her sobs.

Finally she looked up. "What happened?"

"She birthed a child and did not recover."

"And the babe?"

Jacob hated to dishearten Maria's hope. He shook his head. "She fell ill when she was very young. She lies beside Lisbetli."

Maria stood up and wiped tears with the back of one hand, wandering a few paces from Jacob. "I've missed so much."

Jacob's heart swelled in his chest in the midst of this stunning conversation. Maria was the lost piece in the Byler family. He had to ask the obvious question. "Why have you come now?"

Maria met his gaze. Her voice, when it came, was small. "I am exhausted. I wanted to come home."

"And you have." Jacob closed the few steps between them and wrapped his arms around Maria again. She had not gotten much taller than he remembered—though he had grown from a little boy. The top of her head against his chest did not even reach his chin.

Footsteps disturbed their embrace. Jacob stepped back and turned his sister around. Elizabeth stood at the base of the hill, breathless with disbelieving eyes.

Thirty-Three

"Are we almost finished?" Annie set her jaw and glared at the officer on Wednesday morning. "I have to work today."

"Just a few more questions." The officer consulted his notes. "Did you see the note you say Karl Kramer received?"

"I didn't say he got a note. He says he got a note. No, I did not see it."

"And the one Mr. Beiler received? Did you see that one?"

Annie straightened in her chair. "No."

"But you were aware he received one?"

"He told me last night. I didn't know on Monday."

The officer twisted both lips to one side. "Do you have any knowledge of who wrote the notes?"

"No, I do not." Annie slumped. He was fishing. She was itching to get out of the sheriff's office and do some fishing of her own. If she turned up any proof, she would be back.

The officer tapped his pen on his notepad.

Annie opened her arms, palms up. "May I please have my bicycle? I'd like to be on my way."

"I'm afraid that's not possible."

"Why not?"

"We're not finished with it. That's why." He barely looked

up from his paperwork.

"What exactly do you need the bike for?"

"We found assorted tire tracks on the scene."

"The hill was too steep. I left the bike at the bottom. I told you all this." Frustration brewed in her gut.

"When we're finished with the bicycle, you'll be the first to know."

Annie spied the interlibrary loan volume in between a notepad and a file folder. "May I at least have my library book back? Do you have any idea what the fine is for losing an interlibrary loan? Surely you don't think an old history book is complicit in the explosion."

"Sarcasm will get you nowhere, Ms. Friesen."

She scowled and met his gaze. Without taking his eyes off her, the officer reached to one side and extracted the book from the stack of paperwork.

"We'll be in touch," he said.

Annie grabbed the book before he could change his mind. "Find out who hurt Karl Kramer. It wasn't me."

She pulled the note to her parents from her back pocket and marched down Main Street to the post office. With a groan she realized she had just missed the daily mail pickup.

Annie shoved the note through the letter opening, scowled, and set her course for the shop.

"You can't let this go on, Rufus."

Rufus tapped the cabinet hinge with the rubber mallet. "Mo, I know the explosion rattled everyone. I cannot control the way people feel. Perhaps they just need time."

"Don't be silly. People listen to you."

"I'm a simple Amish cabinetmaker." He nudged the hinge once more.

"Marv Hatfield said he wants to drop out. If we lose Marv, we lose both his sons."

Rufus dropped his mallet into his toolbox and wiped his hands on a rag. He was installing cabinets in a newly constructed home. Mo was not even supposed to be on the premises. Rufus glanced around, relieved that the general contractor was nowhere in sight.

"Alicia Paxton is the environmental guru of the whole town," Mo said, "and she thinks it's dangerous to proceed."

"I'm sorry to hear that."

"So do something before we lose every cent of funding along with all the donated labor."

"It only happened the day before yesterday," Rufus said. "We have to wait for things to settle down. The sheriff will find whoever was behind it. Perhaps people will reconsider then."

"They think it's because of the Amish, that they set the bomb."

Rufus raised an eyebrow under the brim of his hat. "It is not our way to make bombs out of fertilizer and a cell phone."

"People are saying it was a bad idea to join forces, that it's better if the Amish and the *English* live separately."

"That is the Amish way, after all," Rufus said.

"How can you say that? You've been behind this joint project all along."

"I still am. But it is true that it has been our way to live separately for hundreds of years."

"Are you dropping out, too?" Mo widened her stance, a hand on her hip.

"I promise to talk to them." Rufus set aside the thought of Ike Stutzman's vehement opposition. "But I am not going to move forward without Karl."

Mo groaned. "Oh, Rufus, why can't you let that go? If we hadn't involved Karl, maybe the explosion would not have happened in the first place."

"The man has burns all over his arms and neck."

"I know. And I feel bad for him, as rotten as he is. But we can't risk the project for him."

"We have time," Rufus said. "While Karl is healing, we'll keep talking."

Mo sucked in her lips. "You don't think Tom Reynolds will back out, do you?"

Rufus adjusted the tilt of his hat. "I couldn't say."

By Wednesday afternoon Annie's cell phone had been missing for two days. She picked up the telephone in the shop and dialed Tom's number. No, he had not seen her phone in his truck.

She hung up and pulled a phone book from beneath the counter, found the number, and dialed the hospital in Cañon City. Following a system of automated prompts, she finally reached a nurse in the emergency room who left her on hold so long Annie was about to hang up and start over again. In the end, though, the lost and found box did not yield Annie's phone, either.

The shop door jangled, and Annie switched to customer alert mode. But rather than customers, Mark and Luke Stutzman entered.

"Our *mamm* asked us to see what you've decided to keep in the shop," Mark said.

Annie gestured to the shelf Mrs. Weichert had arranged. "The blackberry jam does well, and the embroidered pillowcases."

"I'll tell Beth. She is the one who makes the pillowcases."

Of course she was. Miss Perfect Stitches. Annie forced a smile. "Well, if she has more, I'm sure Mrs. Weichert would like to have them. They've been popular."

"We can take anything that is in your way," Mark said.

"Mrs. Weichert is not here, but I'll look in the back room."

Annie crossed the store, vaguely aware that the boys were following at their own pace. In the storeroom, she riffled through Edna Stutzman's crates.

Well, Edna's work and Beth's. Maybe the other girls had contributed something, but Annie suspected the superior stitchery that customers had been admiring was Beth's. A full-sized quilt had lasted barely two days on display, despite a price even Annie thought was outrageous.

Some pot holders and small wooden toys had not sold, and Mrs. Weichert had returned them to the back room. Annie placed them in a crate and applied her own discretion to finish filling it. The sound of shuffling just beyond the door told her the boys had finally come to the back of the shop, where she knew they would wait politely. She picked up the crate, pausing to gain a firm grip.

The boys were speaking rapid Pennsylvania Dutch to each other. Annie strained to understand something. She had been hearing this language in the Beiler home and around tables after church services for eight months, and if pressed, she was capable of bits of polite conversation with speakers who indulged her with a reduced speed. But the words spewed too swiftly from the boys. Annie understood only fragments that did not seem to connect logically.

But one word was unmistakable, and she heard it four times. *Joel.*

And another. *Phone.*

Behind Annie, the building's back door opened to a rush of spring air.

"I saw the buggy," Mrs. Weichert said. "I figured the boys were here."

"I was just gathering some things that aren't selling."

Mrs. Weichert ran a hand over the contents of the crate. "You've chosen well. I'll talk to them." She took the crate from Annie's arms.

At the back of the shop, the boys switched to polite English.

The shop's phone rang, and Annie moved to the counter to answer it.

"Come get your bike," the caller said. "We're finished with it."

Thirty-Four

Annie lowered her bicycle to the ground in the same spot where she had left it two days ago. She took the hill faster this time, curious to see what the spot looked like now that the crime scene tape was gone. Finding her lost phone among the singed brush seemed unlikely, but she had nothing to lose by looking.

She stood on the hill, staring at the rock, and wondering what the boys could have thought they were accomplishing by trying to blast out a chunk of the hillside with a homemade bomb.

Unless they accomplished exactly what they intended.

She hated to think any of them were capable of hurting Karl—and certainly not Joel. It just did not make sense.

Annie kicked around in the dirt. Rain the previous evening had wiped out footprints and washed blackened brush into stripes down the incline. She set her feet squarely in the place where Karl Kramer had lain, and memory sparked. Her hand had still clenched the phone when she boarded the ambulance. She had it when she answered questions in the emergency room. After that, she was unsure.

Wandering back toward her bike, Annie wondered if the sheriff's officers had found anything useful among the footprints and tire tracks that had crowded the ground. Sophie's revelation that Annie was under suspicion for the explosion simmered in her mind. When Annie reached her bike, she yanked it up with fresh determination. If Joel had something to do with this, she was going to find out. And for Carter's sake, Annie hoped that what she suspected was not true.

Securing her helmet, Annie put the bike in motion and let gravity pull her down the slope and back on the main road. Hours of daylight remained at this time of year, plenty of time to pedal to the storage site and look for anything that might be have changed since the last time she was there. Grateful to be on pavement again rather than in the uneven brush of the hillside, Annie pedaled harder.

Lost in her thoughts, she did not hear the car approach from behind. She felt its wind as it whizzed by—a little too close for comfort—and she gripped her handlebars more firmly.

It was a blue Prius, just like the one she used to own. The vehicle slowed ahead of her, and in watching it, Annie lost her concentration. She strayed off the pavement onto the gravel shoulder, where she lost her balance. Putting out one foot, Annie managed to avoid toppling, but it was not a gracious moment. She got off the bike and pushed out her breath. Ahead of her, the blue Prius stopped abruptly on the side of the road.

The driver's door opened. Ruth Beiler got out. Annie grinned.

"Whatever you were thinking about the crazy driver, you can keep to yourself." Ruth beamed and dangled the car key. "It's all true, but just don't say it."

"You're driving!" Annie laid the bike down to embrace her friend with both arms. "I assume you're doing it the legal way."

Ruth laughed. "Of course." She pulled her wallet out of her skirt pocket and extracted a long rectangle of paper. "The State of Colorado made it official yesterday."

Annie glanced at the car. "Yesterday? And you drove all the way down here by yourself?"

"When I heard what happened, I knew I had to."

Ruth bent her head in toward Annalise, admiring the sheet of paper that gave her the freedom to stand on this road at this time.

"My friend Lauren gave me driving lessons," she said. "I was nervous about taking the road test, but she said I was ready."

"And she was right!" Annalise leaned against Ruth's shoulder. "I'm so glad to see you. Does your mother know you're coming?"

Ruth shook her head. "Only Elijah knows."

"Elijah?"

"He called and told me what happened to Karl, and that you and Rufus were there."

"It wasn't really an emergency. Rufus and I are fine."

"Elijah didn't know that when he called. He just knew you were at the hospital. I think it rattled him that it happened at. . . our rock."

"I didn't know you were speaking to Elijah these days."

Ruth looked away. "I'm not. Not exactly."

"What does 'not exactly' mean?"

A car rumbled past, and Ruth step farther off the side of the road. "Elijah writes, and I don't answer. I did for a while, but it's wrong, so I stopped."

"Why is it wrong?"

Ruth shook her head. "It can't be anything. I was not fair to him when I left on our baptism day. He only got baptized because he thought I was going to do it, and then I left. Now he's baptized, and we can't be together."

"Are you sure?"

"I'm going tell him once and for all."

Annalise tilted her head to one side. "You've said that before."

Ruth kicked a rock. "I know. But it's wrong. I have to stop it before we do something Elijah would have to confess to the elders."

"You're trying to protect him?"

Ruth nodded.

"Because you care for him?"

Reluctantly, Ruth nodded again. She hoped Annalise would not comment on the blush that that warmed her face and neck.

"Elijah is a grown man," Annalise said. "He can make his own choices."

"I don't want him to choose to leave because of me any more than Rufus wants you to choose to become Amish because of him."

"This sounds like a conversation that shouldn't be happening on the side of the road."

"Why are you here, anyway?" Ruth asked, pointing down the lonely highway.

"I lost my phone."

"And?"

"And I just wanted to go back and see where it happened again. I'm trying to make sense of it. I have pieces, but they don't add up."

"Where are you going now?"

Annalise hesitated, but Ruth waited.

"Well," Annalise said, "since you have your driver's license and a car, maybe you'd like to give me a ride."

"Anywhere," Ruth answered. "What about the bike?"

"I happen to know how to put the backseat down in that car. We'll jam it in somehow."

Ruth followed Annalise toward the Prius, where Annalise swiftly pulled a couple of levers.

"Are you sure about this?"

Annie pushed the car door closed and glanced across the open space ahead of them. "Sorry to drag you so far off the road, but I knew the Prius could handle it."

"I'm sure you know more about the car than I do," Ruth said, "but what are we looking for?"

"I'm not sure. Clues."

"Clues?"

"Just follow me."

"Why did we have to park in the trees?"

"You'll see."

Annie led the way, hearing the hesitancy in Ruth's steps.

"I don't think I've ever been here before," Ruth said. "How can that be?"

"I think that's what they're counting on."

"Who's 'they'?"

"I hope I'm wrong, but I have to be sure."

After a couple of minutes, the fenced area came into view, still covered in thick plastic sheeting. "I think Karl Kramer uses this place for storage," Annie said.

"It doesn't seem very convenient," Ruth observed.

"That's one of the pieces I haven't figured out." Annie scanned the area for guys in hard hats. "The coast is clear."

They circled around, while Annie tried to remember where the loose flap was that had given her access the last time.

"Annalise, I'm not sure about this," Ruth whispered.

"Here." Annie punched a hand through a slit, pushed aside thick plastic, and ducked through the fence. "Coming, Ruth?"

Ruth's head appeared. "What is this place?"

"Hurry up." Annie reached out and tugged on Ruth's wrist.

"Ow!"

"Shh."

"What are we doing here, Annalise?"

"There has to be something here."

"Like what?"

"Just look for something that doesn't belong."

Annie dragged her fingers along a pile of flooring under-layment and a carton of four nail guns. Next were two rolls of plush gray carpet and neat upright row of windows in three sizes, and beyond that a half dozen enormous rolls of black roof sheeting. A skid of concrete blocks seemed especially out of place. Ruth had taken her own path through the maze of construction supplies. Annie could see the top of her head as she moved along a makeshift aisle.

"Ruth? Are you finding anything?"

No answer.

"Ruth?"

"You'd better come here."

Thirty-Five

Annie hustled around a stack of two-by-fours to kneel beside Ruth. "What is it?"

Ruth's arm was wedged between piles of three-inch PVC pipes banded in sets of six. When she pulled it out, her hand gripped a neatly folded cloth. When Ruth unfolded it on the ground, Annie saw that it was a shirt—an Amish shirt. Between its layers was a small case holding four small chisels.

"Joel's shirt!" Ruth said softly.

"Are you sure?"

Ruth nodded. "I remember the fabric. It was the only time *Mamm* tried dyeing cloth herself. She wasn't happy with the irregular color. She just made the one shirt. The rest went into quilts."

Annie fingered the fabric between thumb and forefinger. "The quilt on your bed has some of this."

"Right. Jacob's quilt, too."

"I think these tools belong to Rufus." Annie put the thought out of her mind that Beth Stutzman knew more about chisels than she did.

Ruth nodded. "He uses them for fine work."

"He replaced the set the last time he went to the Springs

because he couldn't find it." Annie put her hand under the shirt so she could take the tools without touching them, wondering if fingerprints could be lifted from steel. She was not taking any chances. She folded the shirt around the set again. "We can go now."

"What are you going to do?"

"I have to talk to Joel."

"But Joel wouldn't have anything to do with the explosion."

Annie saw the protest in her friend's eyes, even in the dimness of the plastic shelter. "I'm afraid that remains to be seen."

Annie asked Ruth to drop her off at the end of the field where Joel was supposed to be working. Together they lifted the bicycle out of the Prius.

"Shouldn't I come with you?" Ruth said.

"I think it's less complicated if I go alone."

"Well, if you're sure. . ."

"Go on to the house," Annie urged. "Your *mamm* will be glad to see you."

Ruth winced. "Not if I show up in a car."

"I told her I gave you my car."

"That's different from seeing me actually driving it."

"You have to tell her eventually."

Ruth nodded. "Right now, though, I want to go find Elijah. Don't tell anyone you saw me."

"Okay." Annie reached out and squeezed Ruth's hand. "Find a way to tell me how your talk goes."

Annie watched Ruth strap herself into the car and navigate carefully back to the road. Then she put the bundle in the basket on her bicycle and began to pedal across the field.

She found Joel right where he was supposed to be, kneeling to inspect a row of alfalfa that would be ready for harvest in a few more weeks. He stood as she approached. Annie took the shirt from the basket and laid her bike down.

Joel reached for the garment, and Annie moved it out of his grasp. "I'll be curious to hear what you have to say about this."

"It's an old shirt that *Mamm* gave to Edna for her boys," Joel said. "I have nothing to say anything about it."

Annie opened the shirt and revealed the tools. "How can you not say anything about this?"

"I am not accountable to you, Annalise." His eyes hardened.

"Would you rather explain this to the elders?" It was the worst threat Annie could think of at the moment.

Joel was unflapped. "I asked you to trust me, Annalise. I thought you did."

"That was before a bomb went off, and before I found your brother's missing tools."

"Why were you looking?"

Annie pressed her lips together and blew her breath out her nose. "I was there, remember? I was the one who saw what happened to Karl Kramer. I was the one checking to see if he was breathing. That gives me some rights."

"Rights. Not very Amish of you."

"A man has been injured, Joel. Give me a reason not to go straight to the police with what I suspect." Annie wrapped the shirt around the tools and used the sleeves to tie a vicious knot.

"Suspicions are all you have. What you need is a confession." Joel put one hand on the bundle. "I will fix this. I just need a little more time." He spread his fingers to take the shirt from her.

She snatched it back. "How much time?"

Joel looked up and swallowed hard. "Three days."

"Everyone hopes the police will get to the bottom of things before then. Including me."

Joel spread his hands. "I might not need three days. "

"I don't know if ultimatums are very Amish, either, but here's the deal." She untied the sleeve knot, opened the case, and removed the smallest chisel. "You get the shirt and the case. And three days. If you don't fix this by Saturday, then I will."

The moment Ruth pulled off the highway onto Main Street, she regretted the decision to drive into town. Old habits tugged. In fine weather, she and Elijah used to walk into town on any errand they could scrounge up in exchange for the miles of conversation. In chill or damp, they took a buggy and often Jacob. Periodically they would turn their heads toward each other in shy smiles. Their mothers seemed not to mind the hours they spent together. And why should they? Ruth and Elijah were sixteen when they found the wideness of their common ground—old enough to think of marriage. If their mothers had known how often they spoke of life beyond Amish bonds, they might have been less generous in assigning errands in town.

Ruth was startled by how much it pleased her to have a car. And a driver's license. These possessions made this trip into town inaugural. Until Annalise's gift of the Prius, Ruth never entertained car ownership. She still thought of herself as living plain. But now she would save hours every week by not having to arrange her life according to bus schedules, and she could go wherever she decided to go.

And that was the very thing that made owning a car objectionable to her own people. Independence of will. Pride of ownership. Ruth gripped the steering wheel, determined that driving a car would enrich her life, rather than subsume it.

She drove the length of Westcliffe's primary street, turning around only when she reached the sign that welcomed her to the adjoining community of Silver Cliff. Even before she glanced at the dashboard clock, Ruth knew she had most of an hour before she was supposed to meet Elijah. She could not bring herself to get out of the car, though. If she spoke to anyone, the conversation would drive straight to awkward and complicated. The *English* shopkeepers would assume she was more like them now than she actually was. Amish neighbors would say nothing impolite, but their lips would press together in disapproval.

Ruth made a series of left turns that took her to the short street Annalise lived on. She parked and turned off the engine in front of the narrow green house. She was not sorry she had come to see for herself that Annalise was all right. She had been calling Annalise's phone for two days and getting no answer, so finding Annalise on her bicycle on the side of the highway liberated her from what she had let herself imagine. A lost phone was all that kept Annalise from quelling Ruth's fears herself. And it was right to speak to Elijah face-to-face and impress upon him that he must stop contacting her. She only hoped she would be strong enough when she sat beside him on the rock.

And then there was Joel. Annalise had refused to allow Ruth to stay with her to confront Joel together. Ruth's imagination could not conjure a believable explanation for the tools wrapped in Joel's shirt. And Joel certainly had no business amid the stored construction supplies.

Ruth pushed the button that lowered the driver's side window a couple of inches. Fresh air blew across her face. Closing her eyes, she leaned her head back, imagining being with Elijah in just a few minutes with the words in her mind still too unformed to speak.

A rap on the window startled her.

Ruth sat up straight, straining against the seat belt, and saw her little brother's face pressed against the glass.

"Jacob!"

"See, *Mamm*," Jacob said, "it is Ruth."

Ruth released the seat belt and got out of the car. She knelt and let Jacob wrap his arms around her neck.

"He insisted he saw Annalise's car on Main Street," Franey said. "He was halfway down the block before I caught him. Then he said it was you in the car, not Annalise."

Ruth stood, stifling regret. "Hello, *Mamm*." She stepped forward to kiss her mother's cheek.

"So you are driving." Franey shifted a shopping bag to one hip.

"Yes."

"When I heard that Annalise gave you the car, I was not sure you would accept it."

"It was a gift. I would not want to be ungracious." Ruth scratched a temple.

"You know I am very fond of Annalise, but I am afraid she does not understand that she is complicating your life with such a gift, rather than simplifying it."

"I am already finding it to be a practical gift."

"You have always said you would remain plain at heart even though you want to live and work outside our community." Franey's shoulders dropped as she moved her head slowly from side to side.

"I still feel that way."

"But driving a car, Ruth. I don't understand." Franey wrapped both arms around the sack.

Jacob tugged at the back door. "Can I have a ride?"

"Jacob, no." Franey put a firm hand on her son's shoulder and pulled him away from the car. "Ruth may have her reasons, but this has nothing to do with you."

"Maybe another time," Ruth said.

"Please don't encourage him," Franey said.

"Maybe Ruth can drive us home," Jacob said. "Then we won't have to wait for *Daed*. He's taking a long time."

"Jacob, be patient. We should wait for your father to finish at the hardware store." Franey glanced back toward Main Street. "The house is open, of course. Ruth can go on ahead and we'll see her for supper."

Ruth winced. "I'm sorry, *Mamm*. I can't stay. I only came to be sure Annalise was all right. Elijah told me what happened. I'll speak with him, and then I have to go home. I have to be at work at six in the morning."

Ruth appreciated her mother's effort to smile through her disappointment.

"I'll come again soon, *Mamm*. The car will make it so much easier to come back more often."

"Next time I want a ride!" Jacob said.

Ruth stroked the back of his head. "We'll see what *Mamm* says."

"Let's go, Jacob," Franey said. "Maybe your *daed* has something for you to carry."

" 'Bye, Ruth!" Jacob waved and started trotting up the street. Franey followed.

Ruth sank back into the driver's seat. Every choice she made seemed to dishearten her mother. Her thoughts turned to Elijah. She had to face him and disappoint him as well.

He was waiting for her on the rock. He sat at the front ledge with his legs dangling, and she approached from behind. His stocky frame tilted back, his weight on his hands a few inches behind his shoulders. Suspenders striped his white shirt, and the black hat on his head was slightly off tilt, as it usually was.

She loved him.

But he deserved a better love, one that did not tear his life apart.

As she hoisted herself up the final incline and onto the rock's flatness, he heard her. He dropped one shoulder, turned his head, and grinned.

"Hello." Ruth stood on the rock, looking at the scar on the ground below them. "Were they really trying to blow up our rock?"

"No one knows for sure, since no one knows who was behind the explosion."

"It's been three days." Ruth moved toward the center of the boulder. "What's taking so long?"

"It's a small town. You cannot go around making accusations until you are sure. That kind of damage can never be undone."

"I suppose not." Ruth did not like to think of anyone accusing Joel of anything—and certainly not this.

Elijah pushed up to his feet and stood beside her. "I'm glad you came."

Ruth slid a step away from him. "Elijah, I don't want to hurt you."

"Then don't. Don't say it."

"We can't keep going around this circle pretending that there will be a happy ending."

"We can have a happy ending if we want it."

"You know it's not that simple. If we're not careful, we'll be the ones causing damage that cannot be undone. I should know. I seem to be pretty good at it already."

"Don't chastise yourself." Elijah reached out and touched her elbow.

"Elijah, please."

He moved closer, wrapping his arms around her. She buried her face in his neck and let the tears come. The security of him. The warmth of him. The scent of him. The sureness of him. When he put his thumb under her chin to tilt it up, she did not resist. Could not resist.

The kiss lasted a long time. Finally Ruth pushed away.

"We should not be doing this."

"I love you, Ruth. There's never going to be anyone else."

"Yes, there will—but not as long as we have anything to do with each other. It's not fair to think we can be friends. And it's outrageous to think we can be anything more. If you can get me out of your mind, you would have a chance to find the kind of love you can build a life on."

"How do you know what I want, Ruth? How do you know what I'm willing to do? Do you think you are the only strong one?"

"I'm not sure that what I did was strong, Elijah. If I were strong, would I be here now? Would I have wanted you to kiss me?"

"Ruth, you've punished yourself enough over the last two years. You can stop."

"I'm not punishing myself," she insisted. "I only want the best for you. I don't want you to go through what I've been through, and I can't come back. I'm not coming back. You have to accept that."

"I do accept it."

She met his eyes, dark and probing. "No," she said. "I will not be the reason. Please don't write to me, Elijah. Don't call. It's best this way."

Thirty-Six

March 1778

"M*amm*," Jacob said, "Maria has come home."

When she did not answer immediately, apprehension flashed like lightning. Jacob felt it, and then it was gone. Whatever questions roiled in his mother, she would not turn her back on Maria.

He glanced at his half sister, who seemed less certain of Elizabeth's forgiveness.

Elizabeth's face contorted its way from blanched to flushed. "I remember the day you came in the bookshop with your father and Lisbetli. You were five years old."

Maria laughed nervously. "More than forty years ago. Lisbetli chose you before the rest of us did."

"Both of you were beautiful little girls, and I wanted nothing more than to stand alongside your father and watch you grow into women."

Jacob heard the breath go out of Maria. "I told *Daed* we would see you again," she said.

"I waited for you to come back to the shop then, and I've waited again all this time."

When his mother and sister were in each other's arms—sobbing—Jacob breathed his own sigh of relief. He turned to his son, who had watched the interchange with his mouth hanging half-open.

"Franklin, go get your mother. Use the wagon to bring everybody up here quickly."

"Everybody?" Maria echoed. "How many are there?"

"Four boys, two girls," Jacob answered. In another situation, he might have mirrored the polite inquiry with one of his own. But he would have to save his curiosity about Maria's family for another time. "Go, Franklin."

The boy turned and scuttled down the hill.

"Come, Maria," Elizabeth said, "let's go to the house."

An hour later, Jacob confined himself to the main room of his mother's house, savoring the comforting presence of his children. He sat in the chair nearest the fire to be sure none of the little ones came too near the grate. Catherine nestled in his lap, and the baby dozed in the same cradle Jacob himself had slept in so long ago. Joseph's two children squabbled at his feet, but Jacob paid no mind. He was listening to the sounds coming from the kitchen, where Elizabeth heated water over the small hearth for the tub and Maria gasped with delight at the luxury of a hot, unhurried bath. Jacob's wife, Katie, and Joseph's wife, Hannah, huddled in the kitchen looking for ways to be helpful.

Katie came out of the kitchen and glanced around. "Where's Franklin?"

"I sent him to ride out to John's and find David in the north field." Jacob paused to plant a kiss on top of Catherine's head. "Getting a message to Sarah is more complicated. And Joseph? I don't know where he is."

"We haven't had a letter since before Valley Forge," Katie said. She wiped her hands on her apron. "Hannah tries not to show it, but she's frantic."

"How's Maria?"

Katie laughed, the sound that cracked Jacob's heart open every time.

"Underneath all those clothes was a layer of dirt thick as window glass," she said. "But it's coming off little by little."

"I hope she'll tell us her story."

"Don't rush her, Jacob. She's been gone thirty years. She will need time."

Her counsel was wise as always, and Jacob nodded.

"I'm on my way upstairs to find her a dress," Katie said. "Your *mamm* says Sarah leaves a couple of work dresses here. Maria is too short for Elizabeth's clothes."

Another thirty minutes passed before Maria appeared in the main room, shyly tugging at a faded calico dress that hid her thinness. A girlish ribbon at the base of her neck temporarily tamed her long black hair. Behind her, Katie, Hannah, and Elizabeth stood like ladies in waiting. Jacob rose to greet the entourage.

"I have not worn a dress like this in a long time," she said. "I hardly know how to walk."

What had she been wearing? Jacob wanted to know. He swallowed the question and smiled.

"Ethan would be pleased, I think," Maria said.

"Ethan?"

"Her husband," Katie supplied.

Apparently more had transpired in the kitchen than a thorough scrubbing.

"I've been in one disguise or another for years," Maria said. "A wagon driver, a farm wife, a dairy farmer on milk runs. Usually in drab colors and fabrics that no one would notice."

Jacob tilted his head. "Perhaps a brown tweed jacket and breeches, and a hat pulled down low over your face behind the State House? The sort of thing no one would notice in a steady rain?"

He watched Maria's eyes widen.

"Yes, I was there in the State House yard that day," he said. "With so many people there, I couldn't move quickly enough to follow you."

She gasped. "I cannot believe it. You knew I was in Philadelphia?"

"I was not sure I could trust my eyes," he said, "and Sarah did not see you at all."

Elizabeth stepped forward and gripped Jacob's arm. "You never told me!"

"I did not want you to be disappointed."

"Knowing she was alive—that's all I would have needed."

"I'm here now," Maria said, "and I'm ready to tell you where I've been."

Jacob gestured for everyone to sit. Katie and Hannah shared the settee, each one first bending to pick up a toddler. Elizabeth sat in the rocker Jacob's father had made. Maria stood at the stone fireplace, one hand on the black oak mantel with fingers tenuously exploring its familiarity.

"I remember when *Daed* found this piece of wood," Maria said. "He knew it would be perfect here."

Jacob had been too young to remember. At the moment, he wanted to hear a piece of more recent history. She let her fingers trace over a few of the ridges of stone rising from floor to ceiling then turned to face her expectant listeners.

"Ethan came to Irish Creek when I was sixteen. He was only here a few weeks. An *English*. He hired himself out for odd jobs. I met him one day when I was visiting at the Stutzman farm and he rode through looking for work."

"They would never have hired him," Elizabeth said. "Not the Stutzmans."

Maria smiled. "You are right. But it was all the introduction we needed. I followed him, and we walked along the creek. It was love. I was *in lieb*." She raised her eyes to Elizabeth. "Suddenly I understood why *Daed* would consider leaving the Amish to marry. But I was Amish. Barbara and Anna and Christian were Amish. I was next. I was supposed to be baptized."

"We all thought you wanted to join the church," Elizabeth said.

"I suppose I would have, if I had not met Ethan. Then it did not seem as if keeping the family happy was a good reason to take such a step. I wanted to explain to Christian. I knew he was the one who would be most hurt. We could have worked it out in time, I think. But Ethan wanted to keep moving, and he wanted me to come with him. He did not propose anything unseemly. He said we could go to Reading and be properly married. Then we would go west."

"I do not understand all the disguises," Jacob said.

"That came later." Maria turned and held her hands out to the fire's warmth. "We did go west. Ethan did not take me anywhere I did not want to go. I knew adventure was waiting for us, and we found it."

"Where did you end up?"

Maria laughed. "We did not end up anywhere. We moved around western Pennsylvania and into Ohio. Trapping. Selling furs. Helping people outfit to go even farther west. God did not bless us with children, and perhaps it is just as well. That left us free for our new work when the time came."

"New work?"

"We did not hear about the citizens of Boston dumping tea into the harbor for a long time. But as soon as we learned of it, we wanted to be part of forging this new country. By the time we got to Boston, fighting had broken out. Boston was not the only place in trouble."

"New York?" Jacob asked, trying to recall the early turning points in the war. "And, of course, Philadelphia."

"And many places in between," Maria said. "Our experience in the wilderness suited us well for moving behind enemy lines, posing in all sorts of roles." Her voice thickened. "But we often worked separately, with a common base. When Philadelphia fell to the British, Ethan got trapped in the city, and I was beyond the British line. I haven't seen him in months, and none of my connections has heard anything about him. I was at Valley Forge all winter, on the fringes of Washington's camp."

"Valley Forge?" Elizabeth sat up straight. "The last we heard, Joseph was at Valley Forge."

Maria shook her head. "I didn't know. Who knows if we would recognize each other if we were face-to-face."

"He should have come home." Elizabeth sank back into her chair. "Washington has done nothing but try to survive the elements."

"Joseph is an officer, *Mamm*," Jacob said. "He cannot leave his post simply because he would be warmer at home."

"It's brutal," Maria said. "Not enough food for the soldiers, much less all the people following the camp hoping to find work. Clothing is in short supply, illness in long supply." She turned her gaze to Elizabeth. "I finally had enough. If I could not be with Ethan, or do some good for the cause, then the suffering is pointless."

"So you came home," Elizabeth murmured.

"The siege can't last forever," Jacob said. "General Washington has not given up. Abandoning Philadelphia would be tantamount to abandoning the United States."

Maria sighed heavily. "I know. But it's hard not knowing what happened to Ethan. Before now, I never realized how hard it must have been on all of you when I left."

Jacob watched Maria's eyes drift around the room, then back to Elizabeth's and settle there.

"I would have tried to sneak past the British lines," Maria said, "but I'm fairly certain someone betrayed me. The British were warned to watch for me. And I was so tired. I *am* so tired. A hot bath—do you have any idea how long it has been? Years! I'm weary of not eating. I'm weary of sleeping on the ground in the cold."

Elizabeth stood up and wrapped Maria in her arms. Jacob met his mother's pleading eyes over his sister's shoulder.

"I cannot promise anything," Jacob said, "but we have some connections of our own. When David gets here, I will talk to him.

Perhaps we can get word to Sarah. She might know somebody who knows Ethan."

Maria laughed nervously. "What a rebellious bunch we all turned out to be. Christian must be scandalized."

Jacob watched his mother blossom in Maria's company. On the first morning, they walked to Lisbetli's grave, where they shared a long cry. Elizabeth cooked meat as fast as Jacob could hunt it and pulled potatoes and vegetables from the cellar at rates reminiscent of the days she was feeding ten children. She insisted Maria sleep late in the mornings and drop off for a nap whenever she wished. Often when Jacob climbed the hill to the big house in the late afternoons, Maria slept on a mat in front of the fire, and Elizabeth watched over her, stitching a new dress for Maria or making over an old dress of Sarah's. Maria seemed to fatten up by the day and moved with increasing energy. She took long walks with her nieces and nephews, surprising Jacob with visits to the fields or the tannery.

Jacob measured Maria's return to health carefully and with pleasure. However, he did not forget that she had come to Irish Creek expecting to find Christian, her only full-blooded brother.

"It is time, you know," Jacob said one day when Maria sat at the kitchen table in the home he shared with Katie.

"Time for what?"

Her eyes told him she knew the answer. "I will take you to Christian," he said. "You will enjoy meeting his daughter Magdalena. She looks just like you."

Maria looked away. "They probably think I am dead. Considering what I have been doing, perhaps it is better that way."

"No, Maria." Jacob spoke softly. "Bar-bar. Anna. Christian. They all deserve to know what became of you."

"If I never saw them, how would that change the way things are now?" Maria said. She stood up and began to pace the kitchen.

"Because now I know," Jacob said. "David knows. John knows. *Mamm* knows. Our *children* know. You can't ask us to conspire to deceive the rest of the family. And besides, that is not the point."

"What do you mean?"

"You came here to find Christian. It is time you did."

Thirty-Seven

Annie had plenty to keep her busy while she waited for Joel to prove his word. However, Rufus's chisel would remain within reach every minute. Rufus would believe her account of how she came to have it. If Joel was smart, he would not take three days.

On Thursday, she prepared for her first sewing lesson. Annie had never been to the home of Betsy Yoder before, but the house seemed especially suited to the task of hosting a group of women with their sewing projects. By the time Annie pedaled to the Yoders', several buggies stood outside the home, horses hitched to split-rail fencing. Annie's fabric was folded neatly and laid into the basket hanging from her handlebars. By the end of the day, she hoped, the fabric would be cut according to Franey's pattern and Annie would have some notion of how the pieces would go together to form a dress.

Inside, the Amish women greeted her politely, offered refreshments, and suggested a table Annie could use to lay out her fabric. Franey soon appeared with her pattern and hovered while Annie flipped and turned pieces, looking for the most efficient way to lay them out. The process was not entirely foreign to her. Myra Friesen knew her way around a pattern, and Annie had witnessed her going through the basics of ironing the fabric flat, arranging pattern pieces, pinning them down, and carefully cutting. In her software-creating career, Annie had often mentally rotated three-dimensional objects and looked for how the pieces fit together. She did not imagine fitting together sleeves and bodice front and bodice back and skirt and waistband fitting was so different. The women watching her cut remembered aloud the first dresses they had made—some with fondness and some with frustration.

Edna and Beth Stutzman arrived just before lunch and seemed to take over the room with both conversation and their own projects. When she decided to participate in this day, Annie had steeled herself to expect the Stutzmans. If she was seriously considering becoming Amish, she would have to find a way to be gracious toward the Beilers' old friends, no matter what Beth had done to her quilt.

Beth crossed the room where Annie stood at the cutting table. Annie raised her head and looked Beth in the eye with a smile. Beth smoothed her skirt and looked the other direction. Annie managed not to roll her eyes.

Sandwiches and salads appeared on a long narrow side table in the Yoder dining room. Annie set aside the puzzle of fabric, leaving Franey at work while she left to fix a plate. She sat off to one side, where she could quietly marvel at her own involvement in an event such as this one. A year ago she had not even heard of Westcliffe, Colorado. Her own family history was a blur that did not interest her. She was wealthy and likely to become more wealthy. Her life was a string of conveniences and serial immediate gratification.

On the outside, Annie hardly recognized her life now. The inside was another matter. When familiar impulses welled, the challenge of forming new responses loomed. *Humility, humility, humility,* Annie reminded herself, even as she followed Beth's movements around the open, connected rooms.

Beth filled a plate. Annie watched her situate a chair where she could see clearly around the ragged circle.

"It's terrible what happened to that man Karl Kramer." Beth

rearranged the pickles on her plate. "I've heard he's not a nice man at all, but it's awful that someone would want to hurt him."

Murmurs of agreement rose around the room.

"The *English* don't understand our peaceful ways, I suppose." Beth paused to take a delicate bite out of a turkey sandwich. "Certainly I will never understand why they feel the need to blow each other up." She shifted her head toward Annie and raised one eyebrow.

Annie forced food into her mouth to keep herself from speaking. Someone had put too much mustard on the ham sandwich. The spicy kind. It stung her tongue, and her eyes watered.

"The *English* police will sort it out," someone said.

"It does seem to be taking a long time," someone else observed. "I'm not sure I understand why. It's been three days."

"Many people would have a motive against Mr. Kramer."

"They have several suspects, I heard," Beth said. She gave Annie a colorless smile. "But I believe one in particular is coming to the forefront. At a time like this, I take comfort in belonging to people of peace."

Annie nearly choked on the bread she was stuffing in her mouth.

"I understand you are very technical, Annalise." Beth had both eyebrows raised now. "What kinds of explosions have you been involved with?"

Annie licked her lips and turned to Mrs. Yoder. "The sandwiches are delicious." She chewed harder.

"If it were an Amish matter," someone said, "we could take it to the bishop. I'm sure he could get to the bottom of it."

"But of course this is not an Amish matter." Beth took another bite and glared again at Annie. "Annalise, even as an outsider to our ways, you can see that it is plain silly to think our people had anything to do with this unfortunate incident."

Annie filled her mouth again.

Beth picked up a pickle slice. "The bishop's time would be better spent reminding our men of their duty to the community."

Chew. Chew. Chew.

"Rufus Beiler, for instance," Beth said. "Why would he wait as long as he has to obey God's will and marry?"

A couple of young women giggled. Annie drew in a long, slow, spicy mustard breath.

Edna Stutzman spoke up. "You are right as usual, Beth. I will speak to your father myself, and he will speak to the bishop. Rufus Beiler is a dear young man, and we should not sit by idly while his faith weakens."

Annie's chewing slowed. Picking on her was one thing. But picking on Rufus? No amount of *demut* would allow her to listen to any more of this drivel.

The bishop. She swallowed. Yes, Bishop Troyer.

Annie took her plate to the kitchen, gathered up her dress pieces, expressed her gratitude to the hostess, promised Franey she would talk to her soon, and looked Beth in the eye one last time.

This was the first time Annie ever pedaled to the Troyers' farm, and she misjudged the miles. By the time she arrived, wind had stung her face red and dirt streaked the hem of her dress. Even under a helmet—which she had come to realize was not a very Amish device—her *kapp* was hanging behind her head, hair straggling out of its pins. Annie paused at the gate that marked the bishop's yard and tried to put herself back together before knocking on the front door.

The bishop was a minister, right? She could talk to him confidentially and make him aware that certain members were using the sewing day to spread gossip. Maybe she would not even need to name names. Just raise a concern. She was not a complete snitch, after all.

Mrs. Troyer welcomed her, and Annie gratefully accepted the offer of a glass of water. Sipping it, she sat alone in an unadorned parlor while the bishop's wife went to fetch her husband. Annie used the time to catch her breath as well as collect her thoughts.

She would not have to accuse anyone of anything directly. A few plain facts would reveal whether he leaned toward any particular conclusion—on both gossip and explosions.

A few minutes later, bearded and attired in a black suit, the bishop greeted Annie with a smile.

"Annalise, I am so glad you've come."

Had he been expecting her? she wondered. Maybe he knew more than she realized.

"I thought you would be the right person to talk to about all this," she said.

"Of course. I did not realize you knew about the classes yet. I did not want to presume you were ready until you came forward."

Classes?

"Baptism classes will begin in four weeks," the bishop said as he took a seat across from her. "We usually meet while the rest of the congregation is worshipping."

Baptism classes?

"Well, of course, I've been thinking about it," Annie said. The bishop seemed so delighted to see her. How could she tell him she thought some Amish boys were not living up to the peaceful reputation of their people? Or that the women of his flock were gossiping?

"Your case is unusual, of course." The bishop planted his hands on his knees and leaned forward. "The other baptism candidates are all younger and have grown up in Amish homes, so I hope you will feel free to ask any questions at all. I'm happy to answer them."

"Thank you. That's good to know." Annie squirmed in her chair.

"Baptism is an important step in our church. If you feel you need extra sessions to understand our faith, I'm sure we can arrange them."

"Thank you. I know your time is valuable." Her repeated gratitude encouraged his smile. Annie's brain fumbled for a way to change the subject.

"I want you to feel fully convinced of our ways of humility and submission before you're baptized."

The door from the kitchen opened, and the bishop's wife appeared. "I am sorry to interrupt," she said, "but the bishop is already late for a previous appointment."

The bishop stood. "Annalise and I have had a good talk. She is going to join our new baptism class."

Thirty-Eight

Annie waited.

She heard nothing from Joel on Thursday. In her mind, the conversation with Bishop Troyer replayed, and she kept hitting the STOP and REWIND buttons to listen again. Baptism had been the last thing on her mind when she showed up at the bishop's house. Was it *Gottes wille*, God's will, that the discussion had taken such a turn and she had not regained control?

Mrs. Weichert had scheduled her to work Friday morning. Annie opened the shop earlier than scheduled. If Joel was looking for her and did not find her at home, he would come to the shop. At the very least, she hoped he would give her some clue that evening when she joined the Beilers for the evening meal.

Annie was not sure if the ticking she heard was from a clock at the back of the shop or her own brain measuring out Joel's delay. By 11:00, no one else had come into the shop all morning. She sat on a stool behind the counter, hunched over her interlibrary loan genealogy book.

Pioneer Jakob Beyeler, immigrant from Switzerland in 1737, spawned two family lines. Rufus and Ruth descended from Christian, Amish leader of the eighteenth century. Annie descended from Jacob II, as he was known in the genealogy books—

not Amish. The original Amish settlements in Pennsylvania surely were seeking a reprieve from the persecution of Europe. But July 4, 1776, must have changed the North American climate for the Amish. War. The notion of the decisions Pioneer Jakob's sons must have faced during the Revolutionary War intrigued Annie, propelling her search through the book for any mention, any scrap of a mention, suggesting the political affiliations of her ancestors.

The distraction was successful. Another hour and a half passed in silence. When the shop's bell finally announced a customer, Annie startled and nearly fell off her stool.

Rufus nodded at the three *English* men standing in the middle of the aisle at Tom's hardware store and stepped past them as politely as he could. He had only come in for some sandpaper. He took five packages, in three different grits, off the racks and moved toward the front of the store. Tom was at the counter dumping change into one of the two cash register drawers.

"I'm not used to seeing you in here." Rufus laid the sandpaper on the counter.

"It's still my store," Tom said. "I lost Colton to the lure of the big city. He gave me barely three days' notice and moved to Pueblo."

"Sorry to hear that. I liked him."

Tom picked up the sandpaper. "Are you putting this on account?"

"If you don't mind."

The trio from the aisle migrated forward.

"You're Rufus Beiler, aren't you?" one of them asked.

Rufus turned. "Yes, that's right."

The man extended a hand. "Hayes Demming."

Rufus shook his hand. "Nice to meet you."

"We've been wondering when you're going to get that community project moving."

Rufus glanced from one face to another. "No doubt you heard Karl Kramer was injured. He needs time to heal."

"We were all set to help. Still want to."

"I appreciate that. I'm sure Karl will as well."

"I've been talking to businesses around town," Hayes said. "Every day more people are on the fence. If you wait much longer, you won't have the help you need."

"We must wait for Karl," Rufus said firmly. "I gave him my word we would work together."

"That was before the explosion. Do you really think he expects the entire town to wait for him?"

"I don't presume to know what he expects," Rufus said. "I only know what I promised."

"The window is going to slam shut," Hayes said. "I'd hate for the whole project to go bust after all the hard work that has gone into it already."

"I hope that does not happen." Rufus picked up his sandpaper.

"Rufus," Tom said, "perhaps you should reconsider. There's a lot at stake."

"Talk to Karl," Hayes suggested. "It's your project more than it is his. Maybe he'll understand."

Rufus tilted his head. "I don't think we should be bothering Karl right now—certainly not to ask him to back out."

"He wouldn't be backing out so much as stepping aside. If he really cares about the project, he'll want it to move forward."

"When the time is right, it will move forward."

Hayes shook his head. "Okay, but don't be surprised if it's you and Kramer carrying the whole load."

"Thank you for the conversation, gentlemen." Rufus touched the brim of his hat.

The men drifted back down the aisle.

Tom pushed the cash register drawer closed. "Are you sure, Rufus? This is no time to be stubborn."

"*Gottes wille*," Rufus said softly. God's will. He picked up his sandpaper and stepped out into the sunlight.

A flash of Amish black caught his eye, and he blinked in the direction of the moving form.

Joel.

Rufus made up his mind in that moment. Joel was not his son, but someone had to talk to him.

Rufus moved quickly down the sidewalk. Only when he was close enough that Joel could not claim not to have heard him did Rufus call out his brother's name.

Joel stopped and turned.

"I did not know you were planning to come into town," Rufus said. "I would have asked you to make a few purchases and spared myself the trip."

"I didn't plan," Joel said. "Something came up."

"Oh?" Rufus wrinkled his forehead. "Is everything all right in the fields?"

"The fields are fine." Joel shifted his weight.

"Is everything all right between you and *Daed*?" Rufus nudged Joel a few steps down a side street.

"Of course."

"*Daed* has been very patient with you." Rufus crossed his arms over his chest. "Perhaps even to the point of indulgence."

"I get my work done." Joel moved his brown eyes to scan the street in both directions.

"What are you looking for, Joel?" Rufus did not waver.

Now Joel's eyes fastened on Rufus. "It's nothing."

Annie left the shop mumbling, *Demut, demut, demut.* She had finally convinced Mrs. Weichert to send her weekly ad to the newspaper in electronic format, and now the editor claimed the file had corrupted and insisted Annie must come to the publication's office and straighten things out. She tucked a printed copy of the ad in a folder just in case and set out down the block.

Two black hats, brims nearly touching to form a single platform, made her stop. She took two steps back and pressed herself against the brick wall of a shop to listen.

"It's nothing," Joel said.

"It does not seem like nothing, Joel," Rufus said. "You miss a lot of meals. You go into town without telling anyone. You don't seem interested in the farm. I see the looks *Daed* and *Mamm* give each other at dinner."

"It's nothing," Joel repeated. "Everything is under control."

"What is it that you have to control?"

Annie inched closer. Rufus had asked the question that haunted her. She felt the outside of her jeans pocket for the shape of Rufus's tiny chisel.

"I'm sure you have things to do." Joel was made of rock. He was giving his brother nothing to speculate about.

Now Annie's hand slid into her pocket, where her fingers gripped the chisel's handle.

"You're right. I do have things to do," Rufus said. "But we will finish this conversation later."

Annie had never heard Rufus be so firm with Joel. As she saw Rufus's shoulders turn, Annie ducked into the shop whose wall she had been holding up. She turned her back to the front window, busied herself looking at a row of mismatched teacups, and waited for the brothers to walk their separate way on the street. When she stepped back onto Main Street again, she headed to the newspaper office with the ad.

Then she would find Joel.

As she expected, she solved the technology glitch at the newspaper in a matter of seconds. She left the print copy of the ad as a backup. The whole transaction took no more than four minutes. Joel could not have gotten far.

In jeans and sneakers, it was simple enough to power walk a few blocks, detouring down a side street to avoid passing Mrs. Weichert's shop for the time being. She caught up with Joel as he ducked into the coffee shop.

This was the place where the puzzle pieces had fallen into place just a few minutes too late only four days ago. Annie tugged on the glass door and followed Joel in. A moment later she touched his elbow.

Down the block, Rufus set the packets of sandpaper under the seat of the small buggy. Only then did he remember his promise to his mother to bring home coffee beans. He glanced toward the coffee shop, smiling at the notion of taking his mother the gourmet beans she would never buy for herself.

Outside the plate glass window a few minutes later, Rufus paused. Shielding his eyes from the sun's glare, he peered through—and saw Joel.

And Annalise. They stood close together, their faces somber.

And Annalise was holding the tiny chisel from the set he had lost weeks ago.

Slowly, Rufus opened the door and stepped into the coffee shop. He approached Joel and Annalise.

"Tomorrow." Annalise thrust the chisel toward Joel. "Period. No discussion. Or I use this."

Joel turned, met Rufus's eyes, and strode out of the shop. Rufus did not try to stop him. It was Annalise he wanted to talk to now.

She looked shocked to see him and shoved the chisel into her pocket.

"That looked like a serious conversation."

"Yes, it was."

Rufus sucked in his bottom lip then pushed it out. If Annalise had been wearing an Amish dress, she would not have been able to hide anything from him. Did she understand the isolation that came with keeping a secret?

"Annalise, why do you have one of my lost chisels?"

She puffed her cheeks as she blew out her breath. "Rufus, can you trust me for one day?"

"And my chisel?"

"I promise you will have the whole set back tomorrow. Just trust me."

He did trust her. He was less sure about Joel. The two of them were up to something.

"Tomorrow, then."

At four o'clock on Saturday afternoon, Annie shoved a rake into the garden soil Rufus had tilled for her two weeks earlier. Nothing was planted yet. She was not accomplishing anything in particular, other than keeping herself distracted.

Four o'clock. If Joel thought she was going to wait until the stroke of midnight before taking action, she would not hesitate to straighten him out. She pounded the points of the rake into the ground three times with particular fierceness.

Two more hours. That was the absolute outside limit.

Annie did not hear the car pull into her driveway in front of the house, but she did hear the doors slamming. Joel would have a lot of gall to show up in a car. She let the rake drop and stormed around the side of the house. Her parents' silver Toyota was parked in the driveway.

"Mom! Dad!"

"You scared us half to death with that note." Myra charged toward Annie and gripped her around the shoulders. "We came as soon as we got your letter."

"I'm sorry. I was trying not to scare you." Annie stepped out of her mother's grasp and lifted a cheek to her father's kiss.

"You used to be familiar with an invention called the telephone." Myra inspected her daughter from head to toe. "Surely getting caught in an explosion qualifies as an emergency."

"I know. I'm sorry. I should have found a phone." Annie wiped her hands on her jeans.

"You should *carry* a phone."

"Daddy, isn't this your golf day?"

"I was headed to the golf course when your mother showed me the note."

"I ruined your golf game. I'm a crummy daughter."

Brad Friesen shook his head. "No, you're not. Puzzling, perhaps. We're just grateful to see that you're all right."

Myra held out an envelope. "Liam-Ryder Industries is still after you."

Annie propped her rake up against the green shingle siding, brushed her gloved hands together, and took the envelope. She would open it later. At some point she would have to tell them with finality that she was not interested.

"Come on inside," Annie said. "Let me clean up and I'll tell you what happened—though I told you most of it in my letter."

While Annie washed up, her mother brewed a pot of coffee. Annie found a box of crackers in the cabinet and sliced up some cheddar cheese and an apple she had meant to eat two days ago and arranged everything on a platter. Then starting at the beginning, she told her parents about the day of the explosion. The task was more difficult than she imagined, since she decided to leave out information about her own suspicions or her deal with Joel.

"It's entirely unfair for anyone to accuse you." Myra was adamant.

Of course Annie agreed.

"Brad, perhaps we ought to drop in at the sheriff's office. Where do you suppose that would be?"

"Mom, please don't. The police don't seriously suspect me. It's just rumor, and it will blow over."

"You can still come home for a while," Myra suggested.

"Mom," Annie said quietly, "I am home."

Mother and daughter locked eyes. Only a rap on the front door pulled Annie's gaze away. She got up to answer the knock.

"Franey!" Annie glanced over her shoulder at her parents sitting on her sofa. It would be rude not to invite Franey in. With an inward wince, Annie stepped aside. "Mom, Dad, you remember Franey Beiler."

Brad was on his feet and extended his hand, which Franey shook.

"I only just heard," Franey said, turning to Annie. "You never said a word, you sneaky thing."

"About what?" Annie asked.

"The baptism classes, of course." Franey pressed Annie against her chest. "I'm so pleased. I'm sure Rufus will be delighted, too."

Annie stepped out of Franey's embrace and smoothed her hair with both hands.

Myra cleared her throat. "Annie, perhaps we should offer Franey some refreshment. I'll be happy to help you in the kitchen."

"Please sit down," Annie said, gesturing to the chair she had vacated. "We'll be right back."

"Baptism classes?" Myra hissed in the kitchen. "When were you going to mention that?"

"I can explain, Mom. I went to see the bishop about something else, and everything got mixed up. I didn't know it was going to happen."

"You seem to have agreed to join the classes." Myra composed herself, swallowing hard. "I know enough about the Amish to know that baptism means you are joining the church."

Annie straightened her shoulders. "Yes, that is what it means."

"You could be baptized in our church at home, you know. You don't have to join the Amish to be baptized."

"I know. But to join the Amish church it is required."

"But this is what you want?"

Annie nodded slowly.

The door opened, and Brad stuck his head into the kitchen. "Franey has just invited us all for supper. I said yes."

Thirty-Nine

April 1778

The rhythm of a team pulling a wagon gathered in the distance, eventually disturbing Christian Byler's prayer thread and causing him to open his eyes as he sat in his favorite outdoor chair. Amish clatter, Patriot clatter, British clatter—it all sounded the same at this stage. Over the years his wife's suggestion that he cut down the tree at the end of their lane became more insistent, but so far Christian resisted. Whatever came down the road would come whether they could see it or not, and their response would be the same. So why sacrifice a tree whose wood they did not need?

The ruckus slowed enough that Christian knew the wagon would turn into his lane. A moment later, he recognized Jacob in the raised seat. The woman beside him was not Katie, though. Christian had not seen Jacob's wife in years, but a woman did not change her frame and coloring.

Christian stood and waited for the wagon. Jacob pulled the team to a stop, set the wagon's brake, and jumped down. Christian's eyes never left the woman, who was slower to descend. Jacob said nothing but simply stepped aside.

Christian had seen those black curls on only one woman's head. "Maria," he murmured.

She smiled awkwardly.

The dress she wore was not Amish, but he had long ago given up that hope. Was she alive? That had been the specter question, and now he had his answer.

"You certainly took the long way back from the creek," Christian said, a smile forming at one end of his mouth.

"In the end, though, I came home." Maria moved slowly toward him.

All the moments Maria missed crashed through Christian. His entire marriage to Lizzie. The death of Lizzie. His wedding to Babsi. The births of all his children. The baptisms of his older children, all of whom honored him when they chose the Amish way for themselves. The close community of families who understood their old ways. The young men who might have courted her.

Christian swallowed hard. She was here now. Maria was here.

"You must come inside," he said. "Babsi—my wife—will want to meet you."

Within an hour the house was full. A couple of the children went running to find the others in gardens and fields and barns. Christian's married children rolled into the farm in wagons of their own, with their offspring raising the noise level in the yard. To them, Christian knew, Maria was more folklore than family. She was the mysterious sister who disappeared and was never found. She was the one about whom everyone wondered but few spoke.

Christian watched Maria's every move—the sweep of a hand familiar from childhood, a laugh matured but as easily provoked as in years gone by, the hair that refused taming, the violet-blue eyes of their mother.

Magdalena was on foot, as usual. She preferred the simplicity of walking where she wanted to go. Walking alone for miles every day pressed her anxieties out through her extremities. And if she took a little longer than usual for an errand, no one remarked. If occasionally a loaf of bread or a jar of preserves or a jug of cider did not make it to its intended recipient, so be it. It went to good use.

With the British army garrisoned in Philadelphia, demand for food and basic supplies multiplied. At first, Magdalena diverted the occasional bag of flour or corn. At the harvesttime last fall, this was easy enough to do. Over the winter, she watched Nathanael's empty cabin. His family still tried to farm some of his acreage, but no one paid attention to the structure. When Magdalena offered to dust the place from time to time in case Nathanael should decide to move into it, no one objected.

No one believed Nathanael would move into the cabin. Not after three and a half years. If he did not marry, he would not move from his parents' home.

So Magdalena gathered foodstuffs there. Brazenly, she carried hot coals from her own family's hearth and built a fire in Nathan's cabin, where she cooked three dozen loaves of bread and four cakes before passing them to a farmer whose name she did not know. He took a wagon of goods to the outskirts of Philadelphia, where British troops were eager to have them.

To Magdalena, the ease of it all was flabbergasting. Did her Amish dress and prayer *kapp* truly provide such unsuspecting protection? Or was her safety confirmation she was doing God's will?

The injured British soldier from last fall had disappeared long ago. He was not ungrateful for the care the Bylers offered, but he wanted only to be safe well away from the war. Magdalena always supposed he had gone farther west. He seemed not to care that he might never see his country or family again.

Her steps took Magdalena into the family's lane now. The wagons were familiar—her own siblings and aunts were here. But why? Why all at once? She had been gone only a few hours. Surely this gathering was unplanned.

Daed. Panic propelled her into a run.

She burst through the front door into a swarm of cousins and nieces and nephews. Laughter. Food. Children's games. These were not signs of sorrow or concern. Magdalena let out a long breath.

"Magdalena!" her father's voice boomed. "Come and meet your *aunti* Maria."

Aunti Maria? The lost aunt? Magdalena swallowed air and followed her smiling father into the kitchen, where the chatter and clatter of women at work oozed familiarity. Several pots hung in the hearth.

"Maria," Christian said, "Magdalena is here."

Magdalena watched the woman at the hearth turn, a large wooden spoon in one hand. She smiled.

"She looks just like you, Maria," Christian said. "Don't you think so?"

"I have not seen myself in a proper glass in many years," Maria said, "but you flatter me to think I was ever as beautiful as this young creature."

Magdalena flushed. The Amish did not talk this way. She never saw her own reflection in anything but a clear pond, and it would have been prideful to think herself beautiful.

She met the glowing eyes of her aunt with hesitancy behind her own smile.

Jacob settled into a chair on the porch. Christian had done well for himself in Lancaster County. Several real estate transactions yielded good profit for him. The spacious home sheltered his large family with ease, and the land around it prospered in provision year after year. Most of the farms that bordered his land were also Amish, which seemed to deepen Christian's contentment.

Christian silently occupied the chair next to Jacob. Most of the visitors had left. Maria was still in the kitchen showing Babsi and Magdalena how she cooked in her years on the frontier. The two brothers looked out on the remains of the setting sun.

"I suppose I will head home at first light," Jacob said.

"Thank you for bringing Maria to visit."

The finality in Christian's tone made Jacob squirm. He leaned forward, his elbows on his knees, and his hands dangling. "Visit?"

"I love my sister," Christian said. "Seeing her again has filled an empty spot in my heart. But she cannot stay here."

"So you've made up your mind after one long afternoon together?"

"She honored me with honesty. If she had come straight from the frontier with no political opinions, it would be different."

Jacob exhaled. "She's your sister, Christian. Your full-blood sister."

"And she's a Patriot zealot."

"You might say the same of me."

"You do not seek shelter in my house," Christian said.

"I'm here tonight. I've been here before."

"You go home to your gunpowder every time. When you drive past the farms, no one wonders what is under the canvas in your wagon. But Maria. A zealot is not something she does. It is something she is."

"And that compromises you?"

"We live apart, Jacob. We are neutral. I will not put my family at risk for Maria's cause."

Magdalena tired of watching Babsi and Maria cook after everyone had left. What was so unusual about roasting squirrel? Magdalena abandoned the household's best spoon in a basin of gray water and went out the back door to the stables. She wanted to check on the old gelding. They asked little work of the beast anymore. Magdalena wondered how much longer her father would tolerate sustaining an animal that did not earn its keep.

She stroked the gelding's neck. She would have to stay away from the kitchen for a long time to avoid making small talk with a stranger late into the night.

The door creaked open, and her father and aunt entered the stables. The tone arising from their mingled approaching voices sent Magdalena ducking into the hay. Revealing herself now would prove awkward. Instead, she squatted out of sight.

"Christian, try to understand," Maria's soft voice pleaded.

Magdalena heard the supple slap of leather against the wall, the familiar sound of her father rearranging bridles hanging on hooks inside the door. He always did that when he had to say something that he did not wish to say.

"It would only be trouble for all of us," her father said, "including you."

"It's been so long," Maria said. "I did not expect you to send me away as soon as I got here."

"Maria, I cannot put my family at risk."

"What about God's will?" Maria challenged.

"What about it?"

"If it is *Gottes wille* to keep your family safe, I doubt I have the power to endanger them."

Magdalena choked on the thought of the danger she might have brought to her family.

Christian exhaled heavily. "You haven't changed in all these years. You always were a vexing child."

"Don't make light, Christian," Maria said. "I'm alone. I want my family."

"You have Jacob. He shares your sympathies."

"I had hoped you and I had a bond that transcended wartime sympathies."

Magdalena listened to feet shuffling in the hay.

"You can't stay, Maria. That is my final word. You have admitted your history with the Patriots."

"And if I were supporting the British?"

"It would make no difference."

Magdalena pressed a fist against her lips. Her aunt was the enemy. There was no more gentle way to put it.

Her father, of course, had no enemies. The war had nothing to do with him.

But it had plenty to do with Magdalena.

And it had plenty to do with Maria.

Magdalena wished her aunt no harm. But she could never be

on the side of people who had stolen her future with Nathanael. She was glad to hear her *daed* be so firm that Maria must leave.

Magdalena had lived her whole life without knowing her *aunti* Maria. She saw no reason to change course now.

Forty

$\mathscr{F}$raney rode with the Friesens in their car, leaving Lydia, Sophie, and Jacob to take the buggy home. Annie sat in the backseat beside Franey. Every effort her mother made at polite conversation stabbed. Franey reached over and squeezed Annie's hand. Annie appreciated the gesture but withdrew her hand quickly, lest her mother turn her head and see.

Brad turned off the highway into the Beilers' long driveway and parked the car close to the house. As the foursome went up the steps to the front porch, Franey chattered about what she planned for supper and how pleased she was the Friesens were joining them. Franey pushed open the front door. Annie saw the split-second halt before Franey continued into the house and held the door open for the others.

"It looks like we'll have a roomful of guests," Franey said, motioning to the young men in the living room. "I would like you to meet the sons of our dear friends, the Stutzmans. This is Mark and Luke, with my son Joel."

Annie swallowed hard. Joel. Sitting between Mark and Luke on the sofa, the brims of their three identical black felt hats forming a stiff line. Joel held a bundle in his hands, and Mark and Luke looked far from pleased to be sitting in the Beilers' living room.

"Ike and Edna are on their way over," Joel said. He glanced at Annie, who transferred the glance to her parents.

"Is something wrong, Joel?" Franey asked.

Annie nudged her mother's elbow. "Why don't you sit over here?" She gestured to two comfortable chairs positioned apart from the main seating area and breathed relief when her parents complied. Annie watched Franey's face, her heart racing in anticipation of Joel's revelation.

"Mark and Luke have something they need to say." Joel measured his words. "Let's wait for Ike and Edna."

"We have guests," Franey said. "Annalise's parents. I wonder if Ike and Edna might come another time."

"It can't wait," Joel answered.

Annie perched on the arm of the chair her mother occupied and wondered if the tremble of her veins would pulse through the furniture.

She wanted Rufus to be there. If the boys were going to confess, she wanted him to hear for himself. And she wanted his strength in the room when the explosion came—when truth collided with expectations.

What had Rufus heard about her baptism classes? she wondered. Would he be pleased, as his mother was, or would he wonder why she had not told him herself?

Sitting beside and slightly behind her mother, Annie could not see Myra's face. But she recognized the posture, the tightness of concentration in the way Myra leaned her neck forward a few inches and held her head straight up. She did not intend to miss anything.

Rufus, where are you?

Annie heard the back door open, and she turned her head to listen for steps coming through the kitchen. Eli appeared in the dining room and stilled his steps to take in the scene in his living room. Annie heard another set of footsteps—the right ones now. Rufus entered and stood beside his father. She breathed a measure of relief.

Eli and Rufus roused at the same moment and moved across the rooms to greet Annie's parents with warm handshakes and kind greetings. Rufus glanced across the room at Annie again. He started to move toward her, and her breath caught.

A vehicle roared to a stop outside. At the sound of slamming car doors, Rufus detoured to the front door and pulled it open. Tom Reynolds stomped up the porch steps. Behind him, Carter Reynolds was less enthusiastic about this visit to the Beilers'. Annie watched the boy carefully. When he stepped inside the house and saw the Stutzman brothers, his eyes widened and his shoulders tensed.

"Good," Tom said. "All the perpetrators are here."

"Perpetrators?" Eli said. "That's a strong word, Tom. Come in and sit down, please."

"You'll understand in a minute, Eli." Tom sat in Eli's favorite armchair and pointed for Carter to sit in its twin. They faced the sofa, where Mark and Luke both began tapping their feet in jerking rhythms.

"What is it, Tom?" Franey asked. She stood behind the sofa, facing Tom.

Rufus, at last, moved to stand beside Annie.

"I looked at my cell phone account online," Tom said. "I always look over the lines my kids are using just to be sure no one is abusing the privilege of having a phone. Usually I'm flabbergasted at how many texts Carter sends or how much data he uses. This time there was practically nothing. Carter's line hasn't been used all week."

Tom reached into a pocket and pulled out a phone, a simple old-fashioned phone that flipped closed.

"Carter," he said, "why don't you tell everyone what you told me about this phone."

Carter looked at his lap. "It's Annie's. I found it in my dad's truck. She left it there when he brought her home from the hospital the day of the explosion."

Tom waved the phone in the air. "This is the phone I've seen lying around the house. I thought Carter was being forgetful about carrying it."

At the sound of a buggy clattering to a stop outside, Annie dipped her head to look out the window. "It's the Stutzmans."

"Perfect timing." Tom crossed his arms across his chest. "Perhaps we'll wait for them before we continue."

Franey opened the door. As soon as Ike stepped inside, with Edna right behind him, he demanded, "What is going on here? An *English* drove up to our house in his car and said he was your neighbor. He handed me a message practically ordering us to come."

"I sent that," Joel said from the sofa.

Annie leaned forward and whispered to her parents, "Maybe we should move to the dining room, out of the way."

"What is that boy doing with your phone?" Myra wanted to know, but she surrendered her chair to Edna Stutzman and moved with her husband to the dining room table. Annie leaned against the partial wall that separated the dining room from the living room. Once again, she met Rufus's gaze across the room.

Tom Reynolds continued his inquest. "Some of you know that Carter and Annie Friesen have the same model phone. They got them confused once before. I'm going to let Carter tell you what happened to his phone and why he tried to pass Annie's off as his."

Every set of eyes in the room fixed on Carter Reynolds. He worked his lips in and out for a good twenty seconds before he formed any words.

"We used mine as the alarm for the bomb."

The gasp that went up did not include Annie. Her shoulders sagged with the truth that she had been right.

"Joel tried to tell me not to get involved," Carter said, "but I wouldn't listen."

"Get involved with what?" Eli Beiler asked.

Carter pointed limply at the boys on the sofa. "They wanted to blast out the rock. They said they knew how to do it, that they'd done it before in Pennsylvania."

"We *have* done it before," Mark Stutzman said.

Ike's fingers were working his beard. "We once blew a boulder out of a wheat field. Is that what you are referring to?"

Mark nodded. "We watched carefully."

"It was Duncan's idea," Luke said. "He dared us. He didn't think Amish boys would be smart enough."

"Duncan Spangler?" Tom said. "Carter, you didn't mention Duncan earlier."

"He always says mean things about the Amish."

"He dared us," Luke repeated.

"I didn't want to do it," Mark said. "Luke is the one who stole the tools. And the fertilizer."

Annie let her breath out as Joel unwrapped Rufus's missing tools.

"Luke!" Ike barked. "Explain yourself!"

Luke picked at a worn spot in his trousers. "I just wanted to look at the tools. I was going to put them back. Then I realized I could use them to attach wires to the phone."

"Where did you get the wires?" Ike asked.

Mark glanced at Tom.

"From my hardware store," Tom said. "They didn't need very many feet. It would be easy enough to snip a length off the roll in the back of the store."

Luke nodded.

Annie straightened up and faced the boys on the sofa. "So you did steal Karl Kramer's fertilizer?"

"It was the easiest way," Luke said. "We wouldn't have to answer any questions about what we needed it for, and his storage was already halfway out to the rock."

"Annalise," Rufus said, "the small chisel?"

She swallowed, moistened her lips, and nodded. "Yes, I have it. I found the whole set in Karl Kramer's storage area. I told Joel. . . well, the truth had to come out."

Myra Friesen cleared her throat. "Annie, what is this all about?"

Annie met her mother's eyes then moved her glance to Rufus before continuing.

"When Carter and I mixed up our phones a few weeks ago, I saw his Internet history. He was looking at ways to make bombs. I know it was wrong of me to look at his phone, and maybe I should have said something, but just looking at the Internet didn't mean he was going to do anything."

"It wasn't me!" Carter slid forward in his chair. "They took my phone. They said they were allowed to use the Internet because they haven't joined the church. I didn't know what they looked up."

Annie believed Carter—almost. "But you knew about the fertilizer, and you knew they wanted to use your phone to set off the explosion."

Carter nodded.

"So why didn't you get your phone back?" Tom wanted to know.

"I didn't realize they meant the phone would be part of the explosion. Then I didn't know how to get it back. I was afraid I would accidentally do something to set off the bomb."

"We should never have let you run around with these *English* boys," Edna Stutzman said. "We never dreamed they would influence you this way."

Annie rolled her eyes. "Somebody got hurt," she said. "Karl Kramer is recovering from burns."

Rufus cleared his throat. "And the messages to Karl and me?"

"We wanted witnesses that it worked. That's all." Luke's voice had flattened. "You and Karl are in charge of the project. We figured you were going to take the rock out anyway."

"We had made no such decision," Rufus said quietly.

"And why does Kramer keep those supplies out in the middle of nowhere, anyway?" Luke asked, his voice finding its edge again. "I wouldn't be surprised if they were all illegal. Stolen."

"Contractors always have leftover supplies. And that is not the subject of this conversation," Tom said with surprising calm. He turned to Annie. "Perhaps you should continue, Annie."

Around the room, faces crunched in puzzlement.

"I knew something was wrong, but I didn't have all the pieces," Annie said. "I couldn't tie anyone to the fertilizer, for instance. And you can't accuse someone based only on Internet search history. I used to look up all kinds of crazy stuff. It didn't mean I was a terrible person. But people were saying I had something to do with the accident, so I went to Karl's storage site looking for clues to find the truth. Ruth and I discovered the tools wrapped in Joel's old shirt."

"Ruth has something to do with this?" Franey burst out.

"No." Annie's answer was immediate and final. "She knew nothing about it. I just asked her for a ride that day, and to help me look for clues. She recognized the fabric as Joel's shirt. Otherwise, I would not have known who to go to. I confronted Joel, and he asked me to trust him."

"We'll have to call the sheriff's office, of course." Tom was not leaving room for discussion. "If no one had been hurt, that might be different, but even Karl Kramer deserves justice."

"It's only a *rumschpringe* prank," Edna Stutzman said, though she glared at her sons.

Tom's expression did not bend. "It's a crime."

Outside, another car squealed to a stop and a car door slammed.

Forty-One

This time it was Franey who went to the window. "It's Mo."

She pulled open the front door once again, and the innkeeper stomped in.

"Where's Rufus?" Mo's progress stopped as she swept the room with her eyes. "Well, this is an odd bunch to find together in the Beiler house."

Ike Stutzman stood up. "Our visit is concluded." His wife and two sons rose and followed him, wordless, out to their buggy.

Annie glanced at her stunned parents, still sitting at the dining room table, before she crossed to the window at the front of the house. "I think he's angry, but it's hard to tell."

"Ike Stutzman would never let anyone be sure of the answer to that question," Rufus said.

"What does he have to be angry about?" Mo asked.

Annie glanced at Rufus.

"Let's not concern ourselves with that at the moment," Rufus said. "Why have you come all the way out here, Mo?"

Mo pointed a finger at Rufus. "Because of you! And I warn you, I am probably not as skilled as Ike Stutzman at disguising my anger."

"Why don't you have a seat?" Rufus suggested.

"No. I'll do a better job of staying mad if I stand up!" Mo's hands went to her hips. "You've got to get off your high horse and get this project moving."

Rufus calmly took a seat next to Joel on the sofa. Annie watched him from the window.

"I plan to go visit Karl soon and see what his progress is," Rufus said. "Perhaps his doctor has said when he will be well enough to work."

"That could still be weeks. We can't wait that long." Mo gestured toward Tom. "Speak up, Tom. I know you agree with me."

Tom cleared his throat. "I do agree with you, Mo. But it's Rufus's decision to make."

"Oh, come on, Tom, you can be more persuasive than that!"

Silent, Tom held his palms up.

"The police will figure out who is behind that explosion," Mo said. "The important thing is that we don't let an unfortunate event stop our momentum. I've heard nothing to suggest it would be dangerous to keep moving, but of course we can be more vigilant if that will make people feel better."

Annie saw the glances being exchanged around the room. Some of them were aimed at her.

"I want some answers, Rufus Beiler," Mo said. "I'm not leaving until I get them."

Annie grimaced and caught her mother's eye. Crossing back to the dining room, she leaned in and whispered to her parents, "Let's go into the kitchen."

"Perhaps we should just be on our way," her father suggested once they were behind the closed kitchen door. "It hasn't turned out to be a good time to visit."

"I'm so sorry about all this," Annie said. "I had no idea it would all come to a head this way. I'm sure this is not what Franey had in mind when she invited you to supper."

"It's all right," Brad said, "but we are in the way, and I would not want to hold Franey to her invitation under these circumstances. Another time."

Annie nodded. "I'm sure she would understand. I'll speak to her after everything calms down."

Myra drew her spine straight. "You two have lost your minds if you think I'm leaving now."

"But, Myra—"

Myra cut off her husband's thought. "I am not expecting supper, of course. But look what our daughter has been in the middle of. How can we just walk out before we know the outcome?"

"I'll call you," Annie said, "later tonight."

"And where is your phone?"

"I'll get it from Tom. I'll tell you everything."

Myra calmly pulled a chair out from under the kitchen table, sat down, and scooted the chair in.

Annie swallowed. "Okay, then. I'll start some coffee."

Annie found the pieces of the stainless steel stovetop drip coffeemaker in the dish rack and assembled it, placing it on the stove. She reached into a cupboard for the coffee.

"You seem to know your way around another woman's kitchen," Myra observed.

Annie opened the coffee. "They always tell me to make myself at home." *I'm one of the family,* she wanted to say but had the good sense not to.

The back door opened and Lydia, Sophie, and Jacob tumbled in.

"What's going on?" Sophie asked. "We just saw the Stutzmans leaving. Ike was driving a little fast, I thought."

"There are three *English* cars in front of the house," Jacob pointed out. He looked at Myra and Brad with wide eyes. "And two *English* people at the table."

"These are my parents, Jacob," Annie said. "Mr. and Mrs. Friesen. You've met them before."

"Oh. Nice to see you again."

"Mom, Dad, you remember Rufus's sisters, Sophie and Lydia. Jacob is their littlest brother."

Myra smiled pleasantly, and Brad offered a handshake to

Jacob, who returned it with manly enthusiasm.

"Annalise," Sophie said, "what is all this commotion about?"

"There's no short answer," Annie said softly. "I'm sure you'll get the whole story."

"We've never had three *English* cars here before," Jacob observed. "Maybe it's a new world record for an Amish family. But it would be against *Ordnung* to be proud of it." He slid into a seat across from Myra and asked her, "Is one of those cars yours?"

"Yes," Myra said, "the silver sedan."

"Mr. Reynolds drives the red truck, right?" Jacob kicked a table leg in rhythmic repetition.

Sophie put a hand on his shoulder—a little tightly, Annie thought.

"Don't ask so many questions, Jacob," Sophie said. "And stop kicking the table."

"Sophie," Annie said, "would you mind making this pot of coffee for my parents? I'll take Jacob out to check on the chickens and see if we can get the wigglies out."

"Certainly." Sophie moved swiftly to the stove and lit it.

"I'll be back in a few minutes," Annie assured her parents.

Out on the back porch, Annie gulped air. Too much was happening that she could not control.

Rufus listened patiently and managed to mollify Mo with the promise that they would speak again after he had been to visit Karl. With that assurance, she got behind the wheel of her dated green Chevy sedan and negotiated her way back to the road.

That left Rufus looking at Eli, Franey, Joel, Tom, and Carter.

"I smell coffee," he said. "Perhaps we should all have some."

"Good idea," Franey said. "I'll get it."

"I'll do it, *Mamm*. Just sit and relax."

He believed Carter's naiveté. Giving him a cell phone was meant to make his parents feel more secure while they gave him more independence. Rufus doubted Carter would have thought to research bomb making if not prodded by someone else.

In the kitchen, he found Sophie sitting quietly with Myra and Brad Friesen, who were both drinking coffee.

"Where has Annalise gone?" he asked after greeting them.

"Out with Jacob," Sophie supplied. "He was not going to quit asking questions. I suppose she could see I'd had my fill of him for one afternoon. Mr. and Mrs. Friesen have told me a little of what has been going on here."

"It's been quite an afternoon," Rufus said. "Sophie, if I could prevail on you to take the coffeepot out to the living room, I'd like to talk to Annalise's parents."

Rufus invited the Friesens to walk with him away from the house, away from the commotion. They walked across the open yard behind the Beiler home, and he led them on the wide path that meandered from the house and would eventually come out at the big rock. He did not plan to take them that far, though. There was no need to heighten their anxiety by taking them to the place where they all might have lost Annalise.

"I'm grateful to have a few minutes to spend with you," Rufus said. "I wanted to speak to you about Annalise."

"Yes?" Myra's response was guarded, perhaps even suspicious.

"I know her choices have seemed odd to you." Rufus chuckled. "They seem odd to me, too."

"I hope you are not pressuring her in any way." Myra batted at a dangling branch.

"I assure you I am not."

"She seems fond of you," Brad observed.

"I hope so. I am fond of her." Genuinely. Deeply.

"If she changes her whole life for you, and you reject her, how will she ever get over that?" Myra's tone splintered.

"I don't want to hurt Annalise." Rufus stopped on the path and turned to Brad and Myra. "I don't want her to change for me. I haven't asked her to do that. Please believe me."

"So you are going to reject her!"

"No, I—" Rufus began to respond, but Brad interrupted him.

"No, Myra, you've got it wrong." Brad fixed his gaze on Rufus. "This young man loves our daughter enough to stay out of the way of her choice. It's the only way she can be sure. Have I got that right?"

Rufus nodded.

"So she's not getting baptized because of you?" Myra asked.

Rufus swallowed hard. "I had not heard that she was getting baptized at all."

"We just found out ourselves," Brad said softly. "She's going to start the classes."

Annalise was planning for baptism? Rufus's heart beat faster as he smoothly turned the trio around and headed back toward the house. "The classes will be an opportunity to ask questions. It will be good for Annalise to listen to the answers."

"I don't want her to feel pressured," Myra said.

"Myra," Brad said, "have you ever known our daughter to do something she did not willingly set her mind to?"

Myra grunted. "No. She has always been headstrong."

Brad extended a hand, and Rufus shook it. "Rufus, I'm beginning to understand what Annalise sees in you. There is much to admire. If you two decide you have a future, I know you will have her best interest at heart."

Annie stood outside the chicken coop while Jacob sprinkled feed around and giggled at the hens that pecked the ground in response to his gift.

She blinked twice when she saw her parents and Rufus emerge from the path in the back. Her stomach clenched at the thought of the three of them together without her.

"Will I get to talk to your *mamm* and *daed*?" Jacob threw another handful of feed.

"I hope so. I know they would like you."

Annie looked again at Rufus and her parents. This time, she

saw peace in her father's face, and the weight of anxiety was gone from her mother's posture.

"Jacob," she said. "How would you like to talk to my parents right now?"

Forty-Two

Only once had Rufus been to Karl Kramer's office in the construction trailer that had been at the same location for at least five years. Twice Rufus visited Karl in the hospital. And now, after a quiet observance of the Sabbath the day before, he was on Karl's personal property for the first time in a rural area outside of Westcliffe. Rufus did not know Karl kept horses. When he saw them on Monday morning, he made Tom stop the truck so he could get out for a closer look. At least a dozen nosed around in the field before him, and he supposed more grazed in the pasture beyond his view.

"I wonder if Karl has ever thought about selling horses to the Amish." Rufus leaned on the top rail of the fence.

"It's a hobby, I think." Tom sat in his truck with the door open.

"I had no idea. It could be a profitable hobby. If Karl weren't so busy resenting us, he would see the opportunity under his own nose." Rufus paused. "I'm sorry. That was unkind."

"You're certainly doing your part to close the gap. Come on. Let's get this over with."

Inside the house a few minutes later, Karl was alone. After admitting them reluctantly, he moved with some care, but Rufus was encouraged to find him mobile and using his hands. They sat in a large central room, and Rufus told the story that had unfolded on Saturday.

"You're telling me we know exactly who is responsible for this?" Karl's face reddened under the healing burns. The set of his jaw made Rufus's stomach sink.

"We are telling you what the boys said," Rufus said.

Karl jammed a finger in the air toward Tom. "And your boy was in the middle of this?"

Rufus put his elbows on his knees and leaned toward Karl. "Carter did not understand everything that was happening."

Karl thrust his finger toward Rufus now. "If you're telling the truth, it's the Amish boys who knew what they were doing."

"Although they failed in their goal, yes, they seemed to have the best understanding of the science and math necessary." Rufus paused. "We're here today to ask your forgiveness."

"Forgiveness!"

Rufus nodded and glanced at Tom. "I'm sure the parents will want the boys to make their own apologies as well."

"Forgive this?" Karl held his arms out in front of him, burns still healing under dressings. "You can't be serious."

Annie twisted her lips to one side in thought. On a sheet of notebook paper on her dining room table, she wrote down all the facts that had emerged from two days before. Then she numbered them and rewrote the list in a way that accounted for events in the order in which they must have occurred. Next to each event, she jotted the initials of the boys involved at each stage.

In all the commotion, Luke Stutzman had raised a curious question. Why did Karl Kramer store construction and landscaping supplies so far from his office or the areas where he was actively building? Annie's experience with construction was limited, but it seemed to her that the collection was more systematic than left over.

Annie chewed on the top of her pen now. On another sheet of paper, she began to sketch what she remembered from her surreptitious visits. Neat rows of fence posts, cement bricks, carpet rolls, unopened five-gallon paint cans, tubs of grout, a stainless steel double kitchen sink, pallets of bricks, bags of cement, landscape edging.

Black market? she wrote. But that made no sense, given what was there.

Skimmed? Quite possibly.

Stolen? Annie circled this word. It would be just like Karl Kramer to steal from other contractors if he thought they were cutting in on his business. After all, last summer Karl arranged for someone to knock Rufus unconscious and then mutilated brand-new cabinetry Rufus was about to install.

"He's still up to his old tricks," she said aloud as she threw down her pen.

The sympathy she had been feeling for Karl Kramer over the last week dissipated in an instant. Maybe he got what he deserved after all. But what would happen to all the stolen goods now? Karl Kramer could still get away with his shenanigans.

Annie went upstairs and put on running shoes. What would she do for exercise, she wondered, when she adopted Amish dress all the time and could no longer wear running shorts and tennis shoes?

Rufus doubted it could be good for Karl to be this worked up. Perhaps they should have made sure a visiting nurse would be in the house when they brought this news to Karl. Rufus had heard that someone came every other day to check on Karl, and that his ex-wife even stopped by to help change dressings.

Karl winced in pain as he spread his fingers in haste. "I want the names of all those boys. Don't even think about trying to protect any of them."

"We don't seek protection," Rufus said. "The boys know what they did was wrong."

"Even Carter understands he got mixed up in something he shouldn't have," Tom added.

"Write down their names, and the names of their parents. This will be a matter for the sheriff's office. I intend to pursue the case to the fullest extent of the law."

"Of course that is your prerogative," Tom said. "We have not hidden this from the sheriff. Rufus and I spoke to him Saturday night and again this morning."

"Then why hasn't he arrested the whole lot?" Karl demanded.

"The boys say they never meant to hurt anyone. That part was accidental, and frightened them into silence. The real point is that the sheriff has very little physical evidence."

"He has their confessions!"

"He is making a point to talk to all the boys today to take their statements," Tom said. "But he told us this morning that his officers did not get any useful footprints or tire tracks from the scene. Of course there are no fingerprints."

"Get to the point, Tom," Karl barked.

Tom raised a shoulder and squeezed it against his neck. "He's not sure he could make a case."

"That's up to the district attorney's office."

"Of course it is. But the court will appoint a separate attorney for each boy," Tom said. "The lawyers will jump on the lack of physical evidence and the contradictory statements from the boys about who was doing what. The confessions likely will be thrown out as coerced."

"Since when did you take up the practice of law?"

"I'm just telling you what the sheriff said."

"The sheriff is not the district attorney." Karl glowered across the room. "Why are you really here?"

Rufus glanced at Tom. "For just what we said—forgiveness."

Annie's run took her to the edge of a field where a tent of plastic sheeting sheltered assorted contractor supplies. From the cover of trees, Annie watched a pickup truck back up to the shelter. The driver got out, released the tailgate, and began unloading.

Annie crept closer while he had his back turned, ducking behind a set of boulders. The man wore a hard hat, and Annie recognized his bulk. He was the same man she encountered the day she discovered this stash. She had gotten past him that day, and she would get past him again.

Better yet, she would not even try to get past him. No doubt he was a wealth of valuable information if she could pry it out of him. Annie retraced her steps into the trees, mussed her hair a bit more, and set off at a controlled jog. She cut right across the field and came to a stop at the back of the truck. Her breathing sounded heavier than it really was.

"Hello!" she called to the man. Close up, she could see he was transferring one-hundred-pound bags of sand as easily as if they were paper plates stacked and ready for the trash.

He paused and examined her. "I told you before to stay away from here."

"I know. But when I run past here I can't help being curious about what it is. Kind of a strange place to stockpile supplies, if you ask me."

"Who asked you?"

"Well, no one. Good point. I guess I just have natural curiosity."

"Curiosity killed the cat." He resumed moving sandbags.

Annie determined to smile. "I hear all this stuff belongs to Kramer Construction."

"Not exactly." The man's rhythm of moving sandbags remained steady.

Aha! It *was* stolen! "That's just what people say," she said.

"People should mind their own business."

"Still, it's a curious thing."

"Lady, do you have a direct question you're festering to ask?"

"Would you answer a direct question?"

"Don't think that counts as direct."

Annie pressed her lips together. She would only have one chance to ask the right question.

Her phone sang a song, making her jump. She had promised

her mother she would leave it on for a few days so her parents could reach her. This was a local number, though. She turned her back to Hard Hat Guy to answer.

"Hello?"

"Annie, it's Tom Reynolds. I just wanted to apologize one more time for what Carter did. He should never have kept your phone."

"I know. And I think he knows. Apology accepted." She glanced over her shoulder at Hard Hat Guy. The truck bed was empty, and he slammed the tailgate closed.

"I'll make sure he makes restitution."

"Thanks, Tom. I believe Carter got in over his head. I'm sure I can work through it with him." Hard Hat Guy disappeared within the plastic sheeting, taking one sandbag with him.

"Still, he needs to learn that his bad judgment has consequences. Karl is not about to let him off the hook."

"Are you out at Karl's now?"

"In my truck. Rufus is still inside. I think he hoped to make one last plea for mercy."

"I'd like to talk more later, Tom, if that's all right."

"Sure. We'll be talking a lot, I suppose."

Annie clicked the phone closed and turned around. Hard Hat Guy was nowhere in sight. She stepped toward the opening where he must have gone in. With her hand pushing back the plastic sheeting, she glanced back over her shoulder. Whatever she did, she would have to explain her choice to Rufus. She was pretty sure she knew what he would say. And it would not be good.

"They are young boys," Rufus said.

"Young men," Karl countered. "Among your people, practically grown, as I understand it."

"Among our people we seek forgiveness whenever we can. And our way is not to withhold it. Our *Ordnung* commands us to forgive."

"Don't try to convert me, Rufus."

"Of course not. But your forgiveness would free the boys to make honest restitution, rather than merely be punished."

When Karl did not retort immediately, Rufus held his breath.

"What do you have in mind?" Karl finally asked.

"They will apologize to you, of course. In person. Then they can work extra hours on the project. We can teach them something of what it means to be a man by owning up to their responsibilities."

Karl grunted. Rufus waited.

"So you still want to move forward?" Karl asked. "Together?"

"Of course. Are you willing?"

Forty-Three

June 1778

David burst into the barn. "It's over!"

Maria jumped from the stool where she was milking a cow. In the hayloft above her, Jacob pitched down a load then stilled his movement.

"When did you get back?" Jacob asked his brother.

"Just now." David drew his arm across his forehead, wiping a stripe through the grime that darkened his complexion.

"How close did you get to the city limits?"

"I was practically across. But I had delivered the last of my load. It would have looked odd to go in with an empty wagon. The merchants in the city have nothing to sell me."

"Could you really have gone in?" Maria asked.

"The Brits don't seem to care. General Howe resigned his command. Clinton's in charge and has his eye on New York. No one cares about Philadelphia."

Maria knocked over the stool in her hurry to get out of the stall. The cow mooed.

"You can't leave the cow half-milked," Jacob said. "Finish what you're doing, Maria."

"I have to go to Philadelphia." Maria righted the stool but did not sit down.

"Are you sure it's not a ruse?" Jacob jammed his pitchfork into the hay and threw down another load. "They could be trying to catch the Patriots off guard and trap them in Philadelphia."

David shook his head. "The British are packing up. Moving by sea to New York."

Jacob leaned on the pitchfork. "If Washington follows, we'll be right back where we were two years ago."

"We'll see Sarah again," David said. "We can put *Mamm*'s mind at ease."

"Ethan was there." Maria squatted and yanked on a teat. The cow's mooing intensified. "He had to be."

"Don't take your frustration out on the poor cow," Jacob told Maria. "We'll go to Philadelphia soon enough."

"It's already too late to be soon enough." Maria's hands found their rhythm again.

"The British are settled in well. They can't clear out in an afternoon. A couple of days won't make a difference at this point."

"What if it were Katie?" Maria said. "Would you still want to wait a couple of days? Ethan could be anywhere."

"Exactly. And it will be easier to look for him when the glut of troops thins out." Jacob stood the pitchfork upright in the hay. "I'll help you finish the milking."

Jacob waited three more days. He made sure the horses he and Maria would ride had fresh shoes for the rugged terrain. Maria and Katie packed saddlebags so full it took both of them to tighten the straps. David rode to surrounding farms asking about fresh news from Philadelphia. Jacob resisted Franklin's pleas that he be allowed to ride to the city, pointing out instead how much work there was for the boy to do in his father's absence.

On the fourth day, Jacob and Maria rode to Philadelphia, unencumbered by a wagon. At the outskirts of the city, they pulled the reins to take cover in a grove of black oak while they assessed the scene before them for themselves.

The armed patrol of soldiers in red coats was gone. Instead,

British troops moved about as if under orders, briskly and efficiently, but paying little attention to Americans wandering in and out of their paths. Weapons hung slack at their sides while they nailed crates shut and loaded wagons headed for British ships sprawling around the harbor across the city.

"We can go in," Maria urged. "Nothing is stopping us."

Jacob nodded. "I'll show you the way to Sarah's house."

They threaded through the streets, one behind the other. Soldiers carried goods out of private homes where officers had taken up residence, with or without the consent of owners. Some shops were boarded up, while others were open with few wares to offer.

"Looks to me like the British helped themselves to everything Philadelphia had to offer," Maria muttered.

"Now they'll go and do the same injustice in New York."

"I have half a mind to divert a wagon or two of food to people who deserve it."

"Let's find Sarah and Ethan first." Jacob nudged his horse to the right, making a turn onto a wide avenue.

Sarah's house looked untended even from down the street. Spring bushes grew wild and unshaped. Flower beds sprouted knee-high weeds. A window on the front of the house was broken and boarded over.

"We'll go around to the back," Jacob said.

There they found the door to the carriage house wide open, and the only animals within were snarling raccoons.

"She's gone, Jacobli," Maria said.

"Wait here." Jacob dismounted and handed the reins of his horse to Maria. He took his rifle with him as he walked through the covered outdoor summer kitchen and pushed open the back door of Sarah's house. Downstairs, soiled dishes dotted the tables. Upstairs, the beds looked used but in disarray. The walls were cleared of art. Even the knickknacks looked displaced.

What had they done with Sarah?

When Magdalena heard that the British were evacuating Philadelphia, her first thought was whether Patrick, the British sympathizer, might come back.

Her second thought was what might happen if he did.

Nothing, of course. She had done his bidding at sporadic intervals for a few months, captured by his good looks, but she had been *in lieb* with Nathanael in those days. What she did for Patrick was revenge Nathan would never take for himself.

Patrick could be anywhere. Philadelphia. New York. Dead in an unmarked grave. And it did not matter because Magdalena had no thought to leave the Amish families she had known all her life. She might be restless from time to time, but she belonged with her people.

"Maggie, you're not listening." Her father's voice bore through her reverie.

"I'm sorry, *Daed*." Magdalena exhaled and focused on her father's face, straining to keep track of the instructions he fired off.

"Jonas will be waiting."

"Jonas?"

Christian tilted his head. "What is wrong with you today, Magdalena?"

"Nothing." Magdalena took the reins from her father's hands and let him help her up to the seat at the front of the buggy. She remembered now. Jonas broke the axle on his buggy three days ago. The blacksmith had not repaired it yet. His only horse was limping as a result of the incident. He needed to borrow the wagon and team, and Magdalena was to deliver them. If Jonas offered to drive her home, she should accept.

Jonas Glick. His wife had died the previous year giving birth. The child perished as well. Magdalena was surprised he had not remarried already. What was he waiting for? Her own father had married again within weeks after her mother's death, and her parents had been married far longer than the Glicks had been.

Some of Magdalena's friends asked her the same question. What was she waiting for?

In a few minutes, the farm came into view. Jonas Glick leaned against the fence marking his property line. Magdalena liked the relaxed slope of his shoulders. In spite of his loss, he had none of the intensity bottled up in Nathan or the strident passion of Patrick. When he saw her coming and waved, curiosity struck.

They found Sarah, several hours later, in a narrow shop on Market Street. Jacob recognized the plain calico pattern of her dress. His mother had edged a quilt for Katie with the same fabric. Jacob remembered because Katie made a joyous fuss about having brand-new fabric in the quilt, something that had not happened again in the ten years since. Jacob did not care for the shade of green, but he did not dare tell Katie.

It had taken him too long to think of this place. Now Sarah stood in the dim light at the far end, surrounded by boxes, her hair long ago fallen from its pins in several places.

"Jacob!" Sarah dropped a handful of loose items and hurried across the shop to embrace him.

Then he stepped aside and once again Jacob witnessed the wide eyes of recognition when Sarah saw Maria for the first time in almost three decades.

The sisters locked arms around each other and swayed in tearful embrace.

"Thirty years!" Sarah murmured. "I never stopped wondering about you. We have so much to catch up on."

"We will. I promise." Maria looked up at the hammered tin ceiling. "I remember this place. It was a bookshop. Elizabeth worked here. This is where we first found her."

Jacob smiled. "The family she worked for stayed in touch over the years. Sarah lived with them for a while when she first came to Philadelphia." He gestured around. "They used to sell inks and papers. What happened?"

Sarah shifted a crate. "The British write a lot of documents. They used every drop of ink and every scrap of paper in the place. When I heard the shop had been abandoned I knew we could put it to good use."

Maria plunged a hand in a box and came up with assorted vials and corks. "Medical and surgical supplies."

"Dearer than gold these days." Sarah took from another box a thick roll of bandages. "Women are tearing their bedding into strips to send to the military hospitals."

"I used to divert goods like this," Maria said, "from British hospitals to ours."

Sarah glanced at Jacob. "As it turns out, a number of boxes have gone missing from British shipments as of late."

Maria grinned.

"What happened to your house, Sarah?" Jacob peeked in another box. "Where is Emerson?"

"The British instituted mandatory quartering for their officers. Emerson and I chose to stay with friends rather than wait on them. They hired their own Loyalist maid."

"I don't think they paid her enough. It appears she has not been there in some time."

"Sarah," Maria said, "I have a husband. He's missing. Jacob says you may know people who could track down my husband."

"Emerson knows a lot of people. We'll start looking as soon as he gets back."

The muscles in her face stretched in an unfamiliar curve. Magdalena had not done much smiling in the last few years.

But Jonas Glick made her smile.

After the Sunday night singing, he offered to take her home in a small open cart pulled by his half-lame horse. When he spoke, his eyes lit with shy wit that peppered his conversation. Magdalena wondered why she never saw his sense of humor before.

She thought he was a shy farmer, and he was.

She thought he was a grieving widower, and he was.

But he was quick-witted and resourceful and thoughtful. He looked her in the eye when they spoke. Making conversation was never hard. When he brushed her arm in the process of guiding the reins, Magdalena wondered what his embrace would feel like. If he wanted to kiss her, she would let him. Magdalena touched two fingers to her lips just at the thought.

"We've searched for four days and found nothing!" Tears welled in Maria's eyes. "Even my old network has fallen apart."

"We'll find Ethan." Jacob hoped his voice sounded certain. "Just not on this trip."

Maria paused on her horse beside Jacob and looked back at Philadelphia. "It breaks my heart to leave without him. He's here somewhere!"

"You heard what Emerson said. Many of the young men in town have joined an organized militia unit. He is fairly sure Ethan is marching to New York."

"But he is not certain. What if Emerson is wrong? What if I am giving up too early?"

"Sarah and Emerson will be in touch if they find any clues at all."

"I could go to New York and look for him there."

"And you might be wasting your time. You wrote a message. Emerson will do his best to get it to Ethan when he has reason to believe it will reach him."

"I should stay and help with the war effort. I have a lot of experience sneaking behind the British lines. No one pays attention to a woman. They'll say anything in my presence."

"It's been so good for *Mamm* to have you there...."

"I know. But Ethan is my husband."

"It's time for you to be safe, Maria."

"If Ethan is not safe, I am never safe."

Forty-Four

"Rufus, how long is this board supposed to be?" Luke Stutzman called from twenty feet away, where he stood ready with a measuring tape and handsaw.

Rufus pointed past Luke. "You have to ask Karl."

He watched as the teenager hesitated, turned around, and approached Karl. Across the outdoor space, Rufus could not hear what Karl said, but he saw Luke's head bobbing in understanding. The young man moved to a spot clear of congestion, measured the board, took the pencil from behind his ear to mark it, and got ready to saw off a few inches. Luke was doing well. Amish and *English* had arrived together at this day after all.

Rufus studied the drawings in his hands, pleased with the turnout from the town on a Saturday morning in late June. This was their first workday. Crews were digging holes for posts that would mark the trail, while others cleared rocks along the route and cut back limbs. Karl's injuries limited his ability to handle tools himself, but he was capable of giving clear instructions. Luke and a few other Amish boys worked under Karl's supervision constructing a small shelter in the open area where hikers might take refuge from rain or get out of the sun. Three picnic tables were under construction, also under Karl's eye.

The work would not be done in one day. Later volunteers would spread pea gravel along the trail to keep mud at bay on the mile and a half loop. The large boulder—Ruth's rock, in Rufus's mind—would stay right where it was. Rufus had two park benches in his workshop awaiting final sanding and staining. Eventually thick boards would frame a children's play area. Steps carved out of the earth at regular intervals would make it easy and safe for people to climb to the top of the rock and enjoy the view. That had been Rufus's intention all along. He and Joel would build a discreet fence to signal where the Beiler land started behind the rock, but they would make no real effort to keep out anyone who wandered across the boundary.

Rufus turned at the sound of a truck and found Tom and Carter getting out.

"Sorry we're late," Tom said.

"There is still much to do," Rufus said.

"Carter," Tom said, "grab a rake from the back and see if you can help along the trail."

As Carter walked away, Rufus asked, "How is he doing?"

Tom pursed his lips and nodded slowly. "Apologizing to Karl was no piece of cake. Carter was relieved when that was over. Talking to the sheriff scared him half to death. He'll be a lot less naive going forward, I'm sure. But he's not giving me a pile of excuses or pointing the finger elsewhere. He's owned up."

"They all have," Rufus said, "even Joel. He was trying to protect Carter and talk some sense into the Stutzman boys, but apparently Duncan wouldn't let up with his dares. Joel thought it was all talk, but it escalated over a weekend. He realizes he should have spoken up sooner and gotten help. This was not the way to prove he was a man."

Tom nodded in agreement.

"The sheriff told me Duncan tried to deny his involvement."

"Not for very long," Tom said. "He knew he was cornered. His father tells me Duncan won't be leaving the house on his own for a long time."

Rufus nodded. "But he promised they would both be here later today."

"And Annie?" Tom asked.

"She had a long talk with the bishop about how the Amish handle these things," Rufus said. "She's not quite satisfied on the question of why Karl keeps that stockpile where he does, but she has backed off of trying to prove anything malicious."

"The sheriff's office knows it's there. If there's foul play, they'll find it."

"I hope all they find is goodwill."

"Ha! Rufus Beiler, you do have a way of thinking the best of people." Tom gestured toward Karl and the Amish boys working on the shelter. "I don't know what you said to Karl to get him to agree to this, but it seems to be working."

"We cannot ask others to do what we are not willing to do ourselves. We are building more than a trail together."

Ruth Beiler's blue Prius was parked alongside her parents' barn. She had walked down to the work site along the path she had tamped down with her own steps over the four years she had lived in the family's home outside Westcliffe. Now she was on her knees, with hands gloved, digging out rocks that could cause someone to stumble and leaving them in a line along the side of the trail. Beside her, Elijah Capp was doing the same thing.

Elijah had not spoken much this morning, but when she knelt to begin working, he chose his place beside her.

"Shouldn't you be doing something more important?" Ruth asked. "You know how to build things."

"I am where I want to be." Elijah gripped the rock Ruth had been digging around and pulled it out of the earth.

She had broken his heart over and over in the last two years, and he kept bringing it back and offering it to her again. Ruth could not help but smile at Elijah now.

As soon as the date was set to begin work, Ruth knew she wanted to help. Lauren had come with her, claiming she had nothing better to do with her weekend, though Ruth knew perfectly well that Lauren had a term paper due on Monday for her summer semester sociology class.

"Your friend works hard," Elijah observed.

"Lauren does not have a slow speed about anything."

Lauren wore her camouflage pants and army boots tied halfway up her shins. She had gravitated toward a task that would allow her to hold a power tool, and now she gripped a cordless drill in the middle of one of the groups making picnic tables.

"I like her." Elijah spoke simply without looking up.

Ruth raised her brow. She liked Lauren quite well, too, despite their differences. But her stomach had clenched slightly at the thought of Lauren meeting her parents and Amish neighbors. Lauren did not change anything about herself to try to fit in—she did not soften her military wardrobe, she did not feminize her haircut, she did not seek out the company of women awaiting instructions from men.

Lauren was herself, no matter the setting. That was all Ruth sought for herself as well.

By now Ruth and Elijah had developed a rhythm. With a garden shovel, she loosened the dirt around rocks, and with his muscled hands, Elijah pulled them out. Ruth glanced at their mothers, who had set up a portable table together and made sure the workers had water and snacks. Franey Beiler leaned her head in toward Mrs. Capp in a way that Ruth regarded as conspiratorial.

Ruth went back to digging. She always wanted to be able to come home to visit her family, but even two determined Amish mothers could not change the realities of *Ordnung*.

"I will wait, you know," Elijah said.

Ruth had no words.

She only knew that, in this moment, she loved clearing rocks beside Elijah Capp.

Annie unloaded lumber from the back of a pickup and strapped it on a sturdy dolly with wide wheels. With a heave, she shoved the dolly toward the trailhead, where others waited to take the load to locations along the path. Stacks of beams would become stretches of protective railings to guide walkers in safety. She was already sweating through her T-shirt with the effort of the first four trips. When she felt the load lighten in the middle of her fifth trip, she knew it was Rufus whose hands captured the handles of the dolly. Annie stepped aside.

"Thank you," she said.

"You're welcome. They should have tried to get the trucks in closer."

"Too late now. We're almost finished unloading."

"You look overheated. Take a break."

Self-conscious, Annie tugged on her T-shirt to pull it away from her sticky skin. "I'm all right."

"I'll walk you back to the table to make sure you get some water."

Together, they transferred custody of the cart to someone who would drag it along the roughed-out trail.

A new confidence had settled between them in the last few weeks. The interlude Annie witnessed—but did not hear—between her parents and Rufus had wrought transformation. Annie no longer looked at every young Amish woman she met as someone more suited for Rufus than she was. Rather than fear she and Rufus could never have a future together, she began to feel that they would.

She had to complete the baptism classes first. And she had to have one more candid conversation with him to say something he might not want to hear. She did not want to say it, but she had to be completely honest.

But today was not that day.

At the Amish worship gathering the next morning, exhaustion was evident, but so was enthusiasm. In a few more weeks, the recreation area would open officially, and neither the Amish nor the *English* would feel they were intruding in each other's space. They would have brought the dream to reality together.

Annie hummed to a hymn that had become familiar to her over the last year, though she still struggled with the High German words. She held the *Ausbund*, seeking the meaning in the words, even if she could not pronounce them smoothly. Rufus had translated this one for her once.

Love will never come to nothing. Everything has an end but love. Love alone shall stand.

Love clothes us for the wedding feast because God is love and love is God.

Oh love! Oh love! Lead us with your hand and bind us together.

Annie leaned her head to one side, catching Rufus's eye as he sat among the unmarried men across from the women. Though she held her lips captive in their solemn pose, she let her eyes smile.

At the bishop's subtle signal, three teenagers stood to follow him out for the rest of the worship time. Annie stood as well, her stomach fluttering. They stepped quietly together to a rear room in the home of the family hosting worship that Sunday.

Two and a half hours later, Annie emerged from the house into the sunlight. As she expected, men and boys busied themselves with setting up tables, both inside and outside. The smells of baked ham and potato casseroles and apple pies mingled in the fragrance of June asters and columbine.

Rufus was waiting for her at the end of the driveway. She approached him and let out a nervous breath.

"You did it," he said.

"I did."

"How do you feel?"

"Overwhelmed. I've learned so much about the Amish in the last year, but baptism classes are deep!"

"It's a serious commitment in our church. Everyone wants you to be sure."

"I can tell." Annie put her fingers to her temples. "It's so much to take in."

When Rufus did not speak right away, she raised her gray eyes to the violet blue of his.

"Of course you can change your mind right up until the baptism day," he said, "but most people are sure when they start the classes."

"Don't you think I can be sure about this?"

He let another moment of time beat. "My parents think of you as a daughter, you know."

She nodded.

Another beat. "They've been through a lot."

"I'm not Ruth."

"I know."

"I wouldn't put my own parents through what they must be feeling if I weren't serious."

"Serious is not the same as sure."

"I'm sure."

He nodded and produced a smile. "Then I'm glad. Very glad."

"You'd better get used to seeing me in Amish dresses, because I'm finished with jeans and sweatshirts."

"The wardrobe change might be troublesome for your investigations."

Annie waved her hands in front of her. "I'm finished with all that, too. I don't have to have the answer to every question that crosses my brain. And I can ask for help. You'll see."

She stifled a giggle as he quickly bent and kissed her lips.

A wave passed through her, a quiver of unfinished business. Maybe he had already guessed what she needed to voice. Would that make it any easier to speak it aloud?

Rufus took her hand and led her behind a pine tree. His lips sought hers again, and she gave herself to the kiss.

Forty-Five

October 1778

"I hope you are not trifling with Jonas's affection." Christian sat in the comfortable chair by the fire. Outside the window, he watched the last sliver of light slide down behind his west pasture. "He's a worthy man."

Across the room, Magdalena turned a page of her book. Christian was fairly certain she had been going through the motions of reading all evening. The lamp burned low now, but she made no effort to raise the wick.

"Magdalena." Christian spoke in a tone he normally reserved for his younger children.

She looked up. "I heard what you said, *Daed*."

"Don't play with him. He's tender enough."

"I'm not playing with Jonas." Magdalena closed her book firmly and tucked it into the rocker beside her. "I recognize that he has many fine qualities."

"You could do worse."

"I know, *Daed*."

"He came and spoke to me today. His intentions seem clear."

"He spoke to you?"

Did she really not know the man's feelings? "There is yet time in this wedding season."

Magdalena was silent. Christian supposed she was calculating the weeks. Couples sometimes married even in early December. Was she also thinking of Nathanael? She had not spoken of him in a long time.

Christian liked Nathanael well enough. He seemed to make Magdalena happy—four years ago—and Christian would have been glad to take him into the family. Magdalena's devotion was admirable. For years, she believed Nathan would come to himself, and they would resume planning their life together. But she was twenty-one now.

"Magdalena?" he said softly.

"Yes, *Daed*. I know. It's been four months since Jonas first asked me to ride home after a singing."

Christian nodded. "Well, then, we will see what he says when he sees you next."

He read nothing in his daughter's face as she fingered the ties to her prayer *kapp*.

"I'm ready to turn in," she said. "Good night, *Daed*."

When she kissed his cheek, he felt habit more than affection.

Jacob looked up and smiled at his wife. She did not often venture into the tannery or the powder mill behind it. With his long polished stick, he stirred the mixture in the kettle hanging over the fire, wondering if he dared add more saltpeter. Bigger explosions in rifles would shoot bullets faster, and this might be a great help in the war effort.

"I hope you're being careful." Katie stretched her neck to inspect the contents of the pot without coming close to it.

Jacob lifted an eyebrow.

"I know," she said, "you're always careful."

He fixed his eyes on hers. "You don't like the tannery any more than my mother does. You must have come down here for something. What's on your mind?"

Katie nodded. "Maria is so discouraged. Maybe you should talk to her."

"I can't think what else to say." Jacob slowed his stirring. "I can't imagine what she is going through waiting to hear news of Ethan."

"I don't want to imagine what it would be like if you were missing. But I'm worried about her."

"I'll try talking to her again."

"I am afraid she is going to do something rash. You might control your explosions, but I am not as sure about Maria."

Ignoring the chaos of the kitchen on the weekly baking day, Magdalena left her stepmother and her half sisters to the task. The younger ones would grumble about why Magdalena did not have to help, but Babsi would shush them and help them learn the balance of ingredients that kept the family in bread.

Her father's admonition was clear. Because Jonas had spoken to him, Magdalena had to prepare. The next time she saw Jonas could be the conversation that changed her life.

She passed the stables and the old gelding, passed the idle cart she easily could have taken, passed the fence that framed the west pasture. She would walk ten miles today if it took that long to clear her mind. At the end of the lane, Magdalena looked in both directions, considering her options. Then she turned toward Nathan's land. She wanted to see the cabin one last time.

The miles disappeared under her feet. The cabin was in view, and then she was at the door, and then inside gazing at abandonment. Nathanael's mother had retrieved his bedding years ago, and the bare mattress was rolled to one end of the grid of rope that once supported it. Pots still hung from hooks over the dry, cold hearth, but thick dust turned their color from black to gray. One chipped plate sat in the corner of the trestle table with its rough-hewn planks. Magdalena had once imagined a happy life in this room. Then it had housed her rebellion, her outcry at the war that stole her future.

Suddenly seeing the cabin was not enough. She had to see Nathanael.

She found him in the wheat field on his own land, which he

had continued to farm with his father's help. The harvest was in, but Nathanael carried a rake to tidy whatever disturbed him as he paced the rows.

Magdalena waited for him at the end of one row. Halfway down the row he lifted his eyes and saw her, but he did not speed his steps as he once would have.

"Hello, Nathan." When she reached him, Magdalena spoke softly, searching his eyes. "I hear you had a bountiful harvest."

"A very good harvest, yes, considering the war." Nathanael stood the rake upright and leaned on it slightly. "God has shown mercy."

Magdalena twirled the loose string of her *kapp* and swallowed with decision. "We haven't had a talk in a long time."

He met her gaze. "I suppose we have moved past those days."

"Have we?" Magdalena held her breath.

"I want you to be happy, Maggie." Nathanael busied himself with the rake, breaking up clots of earth.

Did he? Then why had he abandoned her all those years ago?

"I know about Jonas," Nathan said.

Magdalena waited. She had not tried to hide Jonas from anyone.

"He will be a fine husband to you."

"You could still be a fine husband to me." Magdalena barely heard her own words.

"You would be a fool to want me."

His words stung.

Nathanael slammed the rake into a tangle of dirt, weeds, and dry remains of wheat. The ground split, shooting chunks in several directions. Magdalena instinctively stepped back.

"Nathan," she said. But he did not look up.

And he probably never would.

Jacob judged it was time to clean up and go in for dinner. The mixture in the kettle was distilled to crystals. The brimstone, tied in a linen rag and soaking in weak lye for the last hour, was ready as well. Over the next two days, he would pound the ingredients into a fine powder. Out of curiosity, he wanted to test the mixture and see for himself how much the greater measure of saltpeter increased the power of a shot. For the time being, he would carefully store the components separately.

Maria stormed into his view. "I have to leave," she said bluntly.

Jacob pressed his lips together and turned his eyes to his sister.

"I cannot sit around the farm any longer." Maria paced toward the tannery then pivoted and returned to the kettle hanging in the makeshift powder mill.

"Be careful," Jacob said. "Don't touch anything until I get the mess cleaned up."

Maria halted. "You're keeping me here against my better judgment, and now you're speaking to me like a child."

"Gunpowder is dangerous at any age."

"Yet you continue to make it."

"Maria, you don't know where Ethan is."

"I'm not going to find him sitting in Berks County."

"Give Sarah more time. She will not give up."

"I could go back to what I used to do, moving behind the British lines."

"You arrived here exhausted and malnourished."

"I am recovered. I could be still useful to the Revolution."

"You are useful here. Since John and David joined the militia, I have three farms and four families to look after, plus the tannery and the mill. I'm sending as much leather and gunpowder to the troops as I can. It's hard to find anyone to hire for the field work. A few Amish men are willing, but I can barely pay them. I need your help to keep everything running or we may have soldiers with no gunpowder."

"That's not enough for me, Jacob. The British have New York. George Washington is worn out. Maybe I could do something to bring this war to an end. It might take only one intercepted message to gain the decisive victory."

"And maybe you could get yourself killed. Where would that leave Ethan?"

"Our three brothers have all taken that risk. You take it every day in your own way with this powder." Maria swiped her fingers in frustration through the fine dust on top of a barrel.

"Maria, don't—" Jacob's warning was too late. The slight gray particles drifted to the fire.

The explosion was small, but it was enough to throw Maria off balance.

Magdalena waited for Jonas to find his words. For a well-spoken man of wit—who had already broached the subject with her father—he was breathing long and hard between phrases.

But he held her hand, and she liked the feel of his calloused palm against hers. The warmth of him. Eyes that gladly met hers. Sitting with him rather than alone.

"Will you have me?" he said at last.

Magdalena took a deep breath. She had practiced the words in her head many times. "If we ask the minister to read the banns at the next service, we can marry before the end of November."

"I do care for you, Magdalena."

She smiled. "I know."

He laid a hand against her cheek, guiding her face toward his. When his lips pressed against hers, the firmness of his kiss surprised her. Even more surprising was her response—free of hesitation, full of eagerness. Sensation flushed through her, and the years to come flashed through her mind.

Years of being married to Jonas Glick.

Their children filling the house.

Growing old together.

Jonas deepened his kiss. Magdalena welcomed it.

Forty-Six

Carter Reynolds stuck his pinky fingers into the corners of his mouth and whistled.

Immediately, the crowd hushed and heads turned toward the open tailgate where Rufus Beiler and Karl Kramer stood side by side in the back of a pickup commandeered for a makeshift platform.

Rufus looked out on the crowd. He guessed that almost half the town's population had made their way out to the recreation site on the Saturday morning in the middle of July—two hundred *English* in one place. Amish families from surrounding parts of Custer County turned out in greater numbers than Rufus anticipated. In their white shirts, black jackets, and rich, dark dresses, they bobbed in and out of clusters of *English*. Everyone was curious to see the finished work, even those who had not participated in building it.

Tom Reynolds knocked his knuckles on the side of the truck. "You have to say something, Rufus. Now or never. And speak up, for Pete's sake."

Rufus cleared his throat. "Welcome, and thank you for coming. I ask you to pay close attention to Karl Kramer now. He has a few things he'd like to say to get our celebration started."

With that, Rufus jumped down from the truck and drifted to one side of the crowd as Karl shuffled, removed his bright yellow hard hat, and expelled a sigh. Rufus took his place beside Annalise just as Karl began to speak.

He looked down at Annalise, whose eyes were forward. Her hair was the most tidy he had ever seen it, controlled by pins and captured under her white prayer *kapp*. He missed her ponytail and the days when she used to let her hair hang free. But perhaps he would one day again see her thick hay-toned blond hair shaking loose, this time for his pleasure.

Annalise looked up at him and whispered, "Has he got a long speech?"

Rufus raised an eyebrow. "I'm not sure how long it is, but you'll like it."

Her shrug held the shoulders of a new green dress against her neck. A dress she had made herself. "He's certainly surprising a lot of people lately."

Karl held his hat in front of him with both hands, his injured arms hidden under long sleeves. "I haven't always been the easiest person to get along with. That's the truth, and I know it."

Annalise grimaced and looked around. Rufus nudged her with his elbow, never breaking his somber pose.

Karl cleared his throat—twice. "A lot of you thought this day would never come. Me, working with the Amish. But it's pretty clear what we can accomplish together when we decide to."

Applause broke out, and Karl had to wait for it to subside before continuing.

"Today we're celebrating Phase 1 of turning this area into a place everyone can enjoy."

"Phase 1?" Annalise looked up at Rufus. "I thought the project was finished."

"Just listen," Rufus whispered.

"We have a beautiful nature trail," Karl said, "and a picnic spot, and benches for enjoying the view of the mountains. We even have a stargazing rock, thanks to a few young men who did not quite know what they were doing."

Nervous laughter rippled through the crowd. Karl shifted his stance.

"We framed in a playground, but many of you have heard that we ran out of funds and don't have anything to put there. That's not quite accurate."

"What is he talking about?" Annalise asked.

Rufus covered her hand with his. "Shh. Keep listening."

"Let me show you what Phase 2 is going to be." Karl reached behind him and picked up a roll of blueprints then unfurled it in one hand. "We're going to build the best children's playground in Custer County. I invite you all to come and look closely at the plans. Now, I realize you may still be wondering about the supplies we need. Some of you have wondered about a supply center I have not far from here."

"Is he looking at me?" Annalise whispered.

"Might be." Rufus twisted his lips. "Just listen."

"I have rented that land from the county. I needed a place to keep certain supplies separate from the houses I've been building. 'Why?' you might be asking."

"I certainly am," Annalise muttered.

Karl continued, "I confess my motives were not admirable in the beginning. I figured if I quoted a few dollars high and ended up with extra materials, maybe someday I could cut some serious corners on a project and increase my profit. After all, nobody makes a perfect estimate every time. Contractors always have extra supplies."

"What is this, true confessions?" Annalise asked.

"Patience, Annalise," Rufus said.

"I have decided these extra supplies will have a more noble purpose," Karl said. "We'll build a playhouse like you wouldn't believe out of the lumber and shingles. The PVC pipes will make a great jungle gym. And get ready for the biggest and best sandbox you've ever seen. Of course we'll have swings and a slide."

Rufus grinned now and looked at Annalise. Her jaw hung slack.

"Did you do this?" she asked.

"I read him the story of Zacchaeus from the Bible," Rufus said. "The rest was up to God."

"How long have you known?" Annalise asked.

"Not long. You were asking questions. Luke was asking questions. But every contractor has leftover supplies at one point or another, and it's a good guess customers don't want that stuff lying around their brand-new houses, even if they did pay for it."

"But this idea for the playground?" Annalise asked.

"That came from Karl."

Annalise looked down at her hands laced together. "And that might never have happened if I had written a blank check for the project."

"Many things require much patience."

"Thank you for being patient with me."

She lifted her face again, and it looked perfect under the *kapp*.

Annie pressed her lips together. Around her, the crowd was shifting as some moved closer to see Karl's plans for the playground and others returned to enjoying the features of the recreation area.

"Rufus," she said, "can we go for a walk?"

"Do you want to try out the trail?" he asked.

Annie shook her head. "No. I want to talk. Privately."

"All right," Rufus said, "let's walk down toward the road."

Annie turned to follow him, catching her foot on the hem of her dress. She would have to turn up the hem on this dress to wear it regularly. A year ago she never would have thought of doing that herself. She would have taken the garment to a dressmaker or, at the very least, her mother. Or, more likely, she simply would have stopped wearing it and bought something new. Much had changed in a year.

Once they were free of the crowd, Rufus let Annalise step in front of him as they made their way down the hill toward the road. Her form, even under the drape of an Amish dress, enchanted him. The way she held her shoulders. Her slender neck rising from the collarless garment. Her certain steps that made her skirt swish more than she realized. From a step or two behind her, he could feast without making her self-conscious.

How beautiful she is, he thought. How easily he could let himself imagine a future together. She would let down her hair and he could freely revel in the wonder of her loveliness. Someday their own children could romp on the playground that Karl proposed to erect, while he and Annalise sat on a bench he had crafted.

He reached for her hand, squeezing it as he fell in step beside her.

At the road, Annie inhaled heavily and let it out in controlled measures. This would not be an easy conversation. She hoped she could form her words more smoothly if they were walking and not looking at each other.

"Rufus," she said, "I made some assumptions about Karl Kramer that were not accurate."

"Many people did." His answer was mild, and she knew he had no sense of what she proposed to talk about.

"He did some bad things in the past. Last year, when he hurt you and you ended up in the hospital—"

"We don't know for sure that was Karl."

"Well, he scared the living daylights out of me one time." Annie pressed on. "All this spring, ever since I discovered that stash of supplies, I've thought the worst of Karl Kramer. I confess even I had my doubts when you said you wanted to work with him."

"Annalise," Rufus said, "I sense you are working up to something. What is it you feel you must say?"

Annie kicked the dirt. "Karl Kramer is the last person I would think could ever make me examine myself. But all this business has made me realize I've been judging him based on his past, and now it looks like he wants to be something different in the future."

"We all have pasts," Rufus said. "We carry them with us into the future."

Annie swallowed. "I don't want to carry my past into the future… into *our* future. I don't want to have secrets that might disappoint you later, when you find out."

Rufus paused in the road and turned her to look at him—just what she had hoped to avoid. "We are plain people, Annalise. You can speak plainly to me."

"I love you, Rufus," she said.

"I know. I love you, too."

She lowered her eyes to the ground. "If we marry, I want our marriage to be everything you've ever dreamed of, everything you've been waiting for."

"Annalise, what is on your heart?"

"I've. . .not been pure." She could not look at him as she said these things. "I wasn't going to church much in those days. I suppose I put my faith in a box off to the side. Jesus didn't have much to do with certain choices. I had a boyfriend in college, and we. . .we should not have, but we did."

"I see," Rufus said quietly.

Annie swallowed hard again and blew out her breath. "That's not all. I went to a technology convention once and had what the *English* would call a one-night stand. I don't think I ever even knew his last name. I have never been proud of that. I've hated myself for it." She tensed her arms and balled her fists. "Even now, I hate remembering it."

"Annalise—"

"Please, let me finish." She moistened her lips. "Last summer, when we met, I was running from my intellectual property attorney because he betrayed me and was trying to steal my business."

"I remember."

"He was also my boyfriend, and he often stayed the night. At some level, I knew it was wrong, but everybody was doing it. The box my faith was in was up on a shelf by then."

Rufus was silent, and Annie lifted her eyes to his at last.

"I don't know what assumptions you've had about my past," she added. "But I wanted you to know the truth. My faith is off the shelf now. I want to follow Jesus and be a new creation. But I can't change the past."

Those violet-blue eyes bore into her.

"If you'd rather find an Amish woman who has always had strong faith," Annie said, "I understand. You probably want someone who hasn't. . .I don't want to be in your way." Annie laughed nervously. "In case you haven't noticed, you're what the *English* would call a great catch. You could have any Amish woman you wanted."

Say you want me. Say you want me. Say you want me.

Rufus turned his head at the sound of his name, and Annie startled. Karl Kramer appeared from around a clump of bushes at the side of the road. How long had he been there? Annie wondered.

"Rufus, we can't have this party without you," Karl said. "People are asking for you."

"I'll be right there."

"You'd better be." Karl turned and began to climb the hill.

Voices and children's squeals wafted down. Annie realized she was holding her breath.

"Annalise," Rufus said, glancing up the hill.

She could see in his eyes that he wanted to say more. Dread rose up. "You'd better go," she said softly.

On the way up the hill he did not hold her hand. A thickness came over her chest, squeezing her throat.

Forty-Seven

June 1780

Jacob climbed the hill in the afternoon sun hoping he would not regret leaving his horse behind. At a brisk clip, the familiar walk from his home to the big house took barely twenty minutes.

While Maria was staying at the big house, Jacob felt less pressure to check on his mother frequently. After the gunpowder explosion threw Maria against the tannery six months ago she had no choice but to remain in Berks County while she waited for the leg to heal. Jacob had heard the bone snap. A slight limp now reminded Maria of one careless gesture, but her determination was undeterred. But Maria was gone now, and Jacob was never sure what he would find when he arrived at the clearing his parents had carved out forty years ago. His mother had not been on a horse in years, but he kept one stabled near her house just in case someone else might need it.

Maria agreed to stay with Sarah in Philadelphia, rather than chase the front lines of battle. At least there she could seek out the remnants of her own old network of subterfuge and perhaps uncover word of her missing husband.

No encouraging information had come through yet, but Jacob understood why Maria held on to hope. He had not heard from any of his brothers in almost a year. The most he could do was follow news of the battles and suppose that Joseph, John, and David were enmeshed in the fighting or working the supply lines. Jacob still manufactured gunpowder when he could find the saltpeter to keep the mill going. If he could get a load to Philadelphia, Sarah seemed to be able to feed it into channels effectively and sometimes even produce a fair price for it. He found comfort in imagining his own brothers loading their muskets with powder from his mill.

His mother was in the garden. He and Franklin helped her with the planting eight weeks ago. No doubt she was inspecting the shoots that carried the promise of bushels of vegetables. She looked unsteady to Jacob—more unsteady every day. She stumbled, and his heart lurched. He was still yards away.

Elizabeth fell. Jacob broke into a sprint.

"*Mamm!*" Jacob had his arms under her before she could sink into the soft soil.

Hours later, while his mother rested in her own bed, Jacob and Katie murmured in the kitchen.

"She should not be on her own. She should come stay with us." Katie put her hand on top of Jacob's as they sat at the table where he had eaten the meals of his boyhood.

"She has lived in this clearing since she married. She will not have it any other way."

Katie nodded. "I'll talk to Joseph's wife, and John's as well. We can all drop by more often. Some of the grandchildren are old enough to help, too."

Jacob exhaled. "I wish my brothers could make it home, even for a visit. She has not been the same since David and John decided to enlist."

"Age and heartbreak are not a productive combination."

Jacob disentangled his fingers from Katie's. "I can at least send a message to Christian, and we should let Sarah and Maria know."

Katie straightened. "What are you saying?"

"She's weaker all the time. We cannot deceive ourselves about what is coming."

"What does it say, *Daed*?"

Christian handed the letter to Magdalena, who scanned it quickly.

Magdalena held the page with thumb and forefinger on each side. "Elizabeth is failing. Jacob says she hardly gets out of bed anymore." Elizabeth was the one who gave Magdalena her first reading lesson using an old primer of Maria's.

Anxiety filled Christian's chest, the pressure building until he lifted his shoulders in three quick breaths.

"*Daed*?"

"I'm all right," he said. He could not manage more words at that moment.

Elizabeth Kallen had come into their lives through the will of his widowed father. She was not Amish and had no thought to become Amish. For years, Christian held that against her. But Christian could not imagine his boyhood without her. She had opened her heart to five motherless children. Never had she suggested he try the ways of the *English*. Except for not being baptized and joining the church—and the colorful fabrics she dressed Sarah in—Elizabeth lived as plain as any of their Amish neighbors.

Christian was only eight when his own mother died. The truth was he had far more memories of Elizabeth caring for him in maternal ways than he did of Verona Yoder Byler. He was not yet prepared to mourn Elizabeth Kallen Byler, but if Jacob's note was an accurate assessment, he had little time to ready himself for the coming reality.

"Are you going to go see her?" Magdalena asked.

"I suspect I will be sorry if I do not." Christian lowered himself into a chair. "She was always so kind."

"May I come with you?"

Christian was at a loss to know what to do with this stubborn daughter. Magdalena should have been married six months or more by now. She ought to have been busy on Jonas Glick's farm, making the place her home, perhaps waiting for a child to quicken within her.

Instead she had called off her engagement. If she could not be wife to Nathanael Buerki, she said, she would be no wife at all. Christian could barely bring himself to look Jonas Glick in the face. What was he supposed to do with a daughter unwilling to become a wife?

When Christian spoke to Babsi later that evening, she confessed she suspected she was with child again. A wagon ride over through the countryside with a passel of children had no appeal. The next day he rode out to the farms where his older sisters thrived. Although they burst into tears at the news of Elizabeth's decline, both had family pressures that would make the trip with him impossible.

"All right," Christian said that night to Magdalena, "if you still want to go, we'll leave in the morning."

They took a small wagon and a team, rather than just two mounts. Her father had seemed to want to fill the wagon with gifts but in the end settled for a dozen jugs of apple cider. He said he remembered that Elizabeth had always liked cider. *Daed* would not let Magdalena drive, however. So she opted to spend part of the journey drowsing in sun-drenched hay in the wagon's bed with the jugs.

When they crested the final hill before the Irish Creek settlement, *Daed* halted the team. Magdalena peered at the view, searching her mind for the memories of the little girl she had been on Irish Creek. She watched her father now as his face creased in longing and memory as well. He finally raised the reins again, and the team lumbered down the soft slope.

At the back door, her father knocked softly, and a moment later, Katie opened the door. Behind her, Maria and Sarah stood up from the table.

Jacob was out in the barn. Magdalena followed her *daed* into Elizabeth's bedroom and stood quietly while he watched her labored breathing.

"I need to go find Jacob," he said softly. "Will you stay with her? If she wakes, she should not be alone."

Magdalena nodded and settled into a rocker where she could watch Elizabeth. A few minutes later, Maria slipped into the room.

Magdalena stifled a sigh at the sight of the Patriot spy. Why had she even wanted to come on this trip? Her *onkel* made gunpowder, and her aunts spied on the British. She should have realized she was walking into a den of the enemy.

She bit her lip. She was not supposed to have enemies. No one knew what she had done for Patrick. And she was not sorry.

"I heard you were getting married," Maria said, her voice low and even and soothing. "Then I heard that you did not."

"He was a good man, but not the right man." Magdalena made no effort to explain that Nathanael was the right man but she could never have him.

"Then you made the right decision," Maria said.

Magdalena lifted her eyebrows slightly. No one at home thought she made the right decision.

"My family would not have understood the husband I chose," Maria said, "but I have no regret. I'm only sorry that we have been separated for two years because of this war."

Magdalena said nothing, but her throat thickened.

"Is there someone else who is the right man?" Maria asked.

Magdalena nodded. "The war has taken him away from me as well."

Maria nodded. "Then you know my heart."

They settled into silence, Magdalena considering her aunt's words. Oddly, Maria was the one who understood her best.

Elizabeth's breath grew jagged, and Maria and Magdalena leaned forward in tandem.

"Does she do that often?" Magdalena asked.

Maria shook her head. "This is different. I think you should go get your father and Jacob."

"*Daed* hoped to see her awake."

Maria pulled her lips back in a grimace. "Go get them, Magdalena. Look in the barn or the stables."

"Someone has to be with her all the time," Jacob told Christian. "Ever since she fell in the garden, we've been watching her, but every day she grew weaker."

"You've cared for her well all these years, Jacob."

"I could never approach how well she cared for all of us." Jacob rubbed his temples with both hands.

"I hope to tell her how grateful I am for the early years. I should have done it long ago instead of harboring judgment. I was a grown man with a family of my own before I could see what *Daed* saw when he married her. She never spoke against the Amish and always let me be the man I was destined to be."

A knock made them both turn to look behind them at the stable door. Magdalena stepped in. Jacob was struck afresh with how much she resembled Maria.

"Maria says you should come," Magdalena said softly.

"Elizabeth?" Christian said. Jacob watched the color drain from his brother's face.

"Just come."

Forty-Eight

October 1781

"Will you give up gunpowder now?"

Jacob looked at the upturned face of his wife as she reclined in their bed. Her hands rested on the familiar swell of her midsection.

"The war will end soon," Katie said. "Cornwallis surrendered. It's only a matter of time before the British come to terms with their defeat."

"That's all true." Jacob sat on the side of the bed and yanked off one boot. "But soldiers are not the only ones who need gunpowder. Farmers need it for blasting rock out of new fields. Hunters need ammunition for their rifles. It may still be a profitable business."

"At least you can sell it freely instead of sneaking around."

Jacob removed his other boot then sprawled across the bed in his clothes. Squalling from the loft above them made him sigh.

"It's Lisbetli," Katie said. "She's been fussy all day. She will settle down on her own."

"But if she wakes up the others, we'll have a riot on our hands." He put his hand on her belly. "Where are we going to put this babe once he doesn't need to be with you all night?"

"We always seem to manage."

"Maybe we should move to the big house."

The house at the top of the hill stood empty since Elizabeth's death. But it had once housed ten children. Jacob well remembered the spacious upstairs bedrooms.

"Or," Katie said in a tone that made Jacob catch her eyes, "we could move to North Carolina."

"North Carolina?"

"We've talked about it since before we were married. David wants to do it. Then your father died and we did not want to leave your mother. Then the war started. . . ."

"And now the war is over and *Mamm* is gone," Jacob said.

At fifty-two years of age, Christian Byler was content to leave the work of converting church benches into tables for a meal to younger men. In another month, he and Babsi would host worship and the meal that followed. Today, he stayed out of the way, huddling with a group of older men at one end of the Stutzmans' wide porch. When their conversation drifted to news of the war's end, though, Christian scowled.

"It makes no difference to us," he said. "You know this. We live apart and do not concern ourselves with matters of the *English*."

Christian saw no purpose in speculating on what changes a new American government might bring, but the faces of his friends told him they were not finished with the topic.

"They might well enact new laws and impose them on us," Joseph Stehnli said.

"There are bound to be taxes," Levi Lapp said. "The new government already owes huge sums to private investors who funded the war."

"So we'll pay our taxes but have nothing to do with it." Christian threw up his hands and left the group.

He crossed the porch and descended the stairs. On the ground, he balanced himself on the railing and closed his eyes briefly. He should not have let his hunger cause him to speak cross words. Turning, he looked up the stairs and into the house. The young men were nearly finished. Women were already putting food on some of the tables.

Christian cocked his head at the sight of Nathanael Buerki laying a board to form the last of the tables.

Nathanael was laughing. He had never stopped coming to church, but Christian had not seen Nathan smile or laugh in years.

Christian collected his plate of food and sat on the men's side of the room. He expected other family heads would gather around him, as they often did, but Nathanael was the first to take his seat across from Christian. He spoke little, which did not surprise Christian, but Christian did catch Nathanael smiling at some of the banter around him.

But more than anything, Christian saw where Nathan's eyes drifted.

To the women's side of the room.

To Magdalena.

He seemed to follow her every movement, causing Christian to do the same. She had become a lovely woman, even if she had refused to marry.

Nathanael's bass voice startled Christian. "Brother Byler, I wonder if Magdalena is going to the singing tonight."

Christian broke a piece of bread before answering. "She seldom goes. She is mindful of her age, I think." Since she had decided not to marry, she saw little purpose in the singings.

The light in Nathanael's eyes flickered. Before it sputtered out, Christian said, "Perhaps if she had an invitation. . ."

Nathanael nodded and turned his eyes again to Magdalena.

Jacob stood at the top of the hill on the fine Sunday afternoon. He was born on this land. All his children were born on this land—so far. As soon as Katie said the words aloud, they both knew they wanted to go. The new babe could be born in North Carolina.

The land was rich with much to offer. Irish Creek ran right through it. Over the years more than a hundred acres were cleared for farming, and dozens more awaited the ambitious effort of taming forest. His tannery was well-positioned, and the vats were large. Houses, barns, stables, gardens, outbuildings. Yes, the land would find appeal to many prospective buyers. But this land had been the dream his father carried from Europe close to half a century ago. Jacob's dream was North Carolina.

If the land sold quickly, they might yet move to North Carolina before the year was out. As long as they could begin the journey before a blinding snow, they could creep south away from the threat of severe weather that might bind them for the winter.

He would find land on the coast and they could drink in the ocean's beauty whenever they wished, with its spray misting across their faces. Or he would find land with saltpeter hidden under its undulating beauty and have a sure supply of the key ingredient for his powder.

First, Jacob had to wait and see if any of his brothers would straggle home from the still dismantling war. David might still want to move to North Carolina with them. But Jacob could not abandon the families of Joseph and John before their return. Joseph had made captain not long ago, so he might yet have responsibilities to discharge. Their wives had received no official notifications. If the brothers were at the final battle at Yorktown, though, painful news might still come.

With a deep breath, Jacob braced himself for the choices all the Byler brothers might make in the coming weeks.

Magdalena felt his eyes on her. Seven years ago he followed her movements in the same way, making her stomach quiver with giddiness. When he first spoke to her, at a singing, she thought she would melt into a puddle.

She was a young woman then, believing in a future. Now she was a spinster. No one had actually used the word yet, but it was not far off. Jonas Glick had been her last chance.

But now Nathan was watching her. When she drifted to one

end of the porch with a group of women—all young mothers except her—he drifted to the other end of the porch with a group of men. When she went inside to help clean up after the meal, suddenly he was there to move benches out to the waiting wagon that would take them to their next destination. When she took her little sisters for a walk up the lane to look at the horses in the pasture, Nathanael drifted along behind them.

Finally Magdalena let the little ones run ahead of her. She adjusted her pace to keep them in view but also to let Nathanael close the gap. She paused and leaned against a fence. Though not boasting the blazing heat of the summer, the October sun spilled its brilliance across the pasture. Hues of green flickered under the hooves of dozens of horses. Magdalena liked to think the beasts offered their own form of worship of their Creator while their owners were in the house singing the solemn songs of the *Ausbund.*

She kept her eyes forward, squinting into brightness. He moved into her peripheral vision, and her breath caught. He stood for a long moment, and Magdalena thought she was going to have to expel her breath in an undignified way.

Finally he spoke. "Hello, Maggie."

The weight lifted off her chest as she turned to face him. "Hello, Nathan."

They had not spoken since before she disgraced herself by breaking her engagement to Jonas Glick after the banns had been read, just days before the scheduled wedding.

"I wonder if I might pick you up for the singing tonight."

Magdalena laughed nervously and put both hands on the fence in front of her. "Will the others think we are too old?"

"Does it matter?"

He looked so earnest. He had aged since the last time she had looked at him so carefully. But surely so had she.

"I suppose not," she said.

"*Gut.*" He laid a hand on hers at the fence and lifted his eyes to the horizon. "We don't have to stay long. Perhaps after a song or two we'll leave the younger crowd to themselves and take the long way home."

Magdalena wriggled one hand so that she could hook a finger through his. "I would like that. Very much."

They stood there, side by side, silent. Magdalena labored for even breath. She had prayed so long, for so many years. He had been lost to her, a shell housing what had once been her Nathan. No matter how many times she waited patiently for him to explain what he felt, why he could not love her still, he said nothing. And then she had given up.

And now he might be coming back.

It was only one singing, but he would not have bothered if that were all that was on his heart.

And she might never know why. She did not care why. She cared only that Nathan was coming back to her.

Jacob sorted the stack of envelopes. They did not collect their mail often, but today the Kauffmans dropped it off. He let one envelope after the other fall to the kitchen table, looking for news of family members.

Sarah's handwriting jumped out at last.

"News?" Katie came into the room with one little girl on her hip and another gripping her skirt.

Nodding, Jacob tore open the letter. He scanned it then made himself slow down and read carefully.

"Maria has set out on her own," he said. "With the war ending, she would not wait another day for word of Ethan."

"He could be lost," Katie said quietly. "If he was not mustered into a unit, there might be no record of what happened."

With their two youngest children present, Katie would not speak of death directly. But every contact Maria had, every contact Sarah and Emerson had—the inquiries had led to nothing. The more months that elapsed, the more Jacob thought Ethan must have met his end. The outskirts of a battle. A British unit collecting prisoners. The slip of a horse's foot at the side of a ravine.

Jacob expelled a breath. "I would have liked to meet the man who persuaded Maria to leave us all those years ago."

"You might yet." Katie's eyes grew brighter with tears brimming in them.

"Perhaps. No doubt Maria will persist where others have given up."

"At least she waited until the fighting ended. It's safer now. She might come back to us again."

Jacob wanted to believe Katie's hope.

Forty-Nine

The weekend passed. Annie did not see Rufus alone. She had supper Sunday night with the Beilers, and Rufus took her home—with Jacob on the seat between them, prattling about a speckled egg he had found that morning.

On Monday, Rufus stopped in the shop to say he would be busy for a few days preparing to take some furniture to the Amish store in Colorado Springs.

On Tuesday, Annie did not hear from Rufus at all.

On Wednesday morning, she put on her purple dress and pedaled to the Beilers', determined to track him down. If he had decided they could not have a future, she just wanted him to tell her straight to her face. When she reached the farm, though, Sophie greeted her on the front porch with the news that Rufus and Tom had loaded three hope chests and two rockers in the back of Tom's truck to take to the furniture store in Colorado Springs. They left twenty minutes before Annie arrived.

"Come inside anyway," Sophie said. "I am just polishing tables and trying to straighten up. I would love your company."

Annie forced a smile. "Put me to work." She would rather be busy, and Mrs. Weichert was not expecting her in the shop.

"Jacob pulled a drawer out," Sophie said, waving a rag in the direction of a small desk in the corner of the dining room. "Everything fell out. The papers are a jumbled mess. Maybe you can sort them out."

"I'll certainly try." Annie sat at one end of the table with the drawer in front of her. Sophie polished at the other end.

"Looks like letters from Pennsylvania." Annie quickly stacked seven letter-sized envelopes written with the same even hand.

Sophie nodded. "Daniel writes at least once a month. Matthew sometimes sticks a note in too."

Annie had sat at the Beiler table on countless nights while Franey read news from Pennsylvania with smiles leaking out of the creases of her face. Annie found two more letters and added them to the stack. She put the envelopes in chronological order according to the postmark date and fished out a rubber band to wrap around them. She had fantasized about someday meeting Daniel and Matthew and their wives. Perhaps they would travel to Colorado for Rufus's wedding.

Annie inhaled and let her breath out through her nose. The Beiler brothers might indeed come to see Rufus get married, but she would not be the bride. Rufus's distance over the last four days made that perfectly plain. Still, she would like to hear him say it. He owed her that much.

Demut. Humility. Annie reminded herself that if she were going to be Amish, she could not proudly demand that anyone owed her anything.

The rest of the drawer's contents were assorted pads of writing paper, envelopes, stamps, black pens, and cards. Annie picked up a card made of stiff white paper, a half sheet folded once. The handwriting, in Pennsylvania Dutch, looked feminine.

Rufus's name leaped off the paper.

Rufus pushed the button that lowered the window on the passenger side of Tom's truck and let his right arm dangle outside.

"Can I tell you a secret?" Rufus said.

Tom turned toward him and raised an eyebrow.

"I hardly ever rode in a car when I was little, but I remember one time when we had to go to Philadelphia. I stuck my head out the window, straight out into the wind. My hat blew off and my mother was...well, annoyed. But I remember loving that sensation of the air rushing into my face."

Tom laughed softly. "I suppose a buggy doesn't kick up much of a wind."

"No, sir."

"Go ahead," Tom said, "stick your face out."

Rufus shook his head and pulled his arm inside. "Child's play." He put the window up.

"You never let your guard down, do you?" With one hand, Tom pulled the steering wheel left to navigate a turn.

"I'm not sure what you mean. It's ridiculous for a grown man to stick his face out the window."

"Ridiculous," Tom echoed. "As ridiculous as falling for an *English* woman?"

Rufus did not speak. He felt the flush rise in his neck.

"Annie wants you," Tom said. "Tell me you know that."

"Yes, I know that."

"She's changing her life for you."

"No, she's changing for herself."

"Hmm." Tom put both hands on the wheel and straightened himself in the seat. "For a while there, you two seemed to be an item. What happened to change that?"

Rufus turned his gaze to the colorful whir of brush and small trees outside the window.

"You and I have known each other for almost six years," Tom said. "You don't have to tell me for me to know when your mood is changing. You have something on your mind that you're not talking about."

Annalise had told him the truth. She had not been out of his thoughts for the last four days. She was a woman of strength and determination. Telling him the truth had only confirmed that in his mind.

Tom tapped the steering wheel. "I'll stop pestering you with personal questions."

"You challenge me, Tom. Today I needed it."

"Good. Now let's get back to business. Maybe I'll use the interstate this time."

Rufus grinned. "The wind in my face will be stronger that way."

Annalise deserved the truth in return. Rufus resolved to give it to her before the sun set.

"So that's what happened to that card." Sophie put down her polishing rag and took the card from Annie's hand. "Rufus was looking for this a while back. He's usually so careful with his own things, but somehow this ended up in *Mamm*'s drawer."

"What is it?"

"I don't really know. Somebody Rufus used to know, I think." Sophie pressed the card flat between her palms. "I'm curious, too, but it would be wrong to read it."

"Of course." A woman. A new letter from a woman Rufus used to know. Annie swallowed the jealousy that burned upward from her stomach. They had come so far that she almost believed it could be true. If her honesty made Rufus hesitate, she was glad to find out now.

She still had the rest of the Beilers. And she was not about to give them up. Jacob delighted her with his inquisitiveness. Franey had taken Annie to her heart. Eli's firm gentleness inspired Annie, and Lydia and Sophie received her as a sister.

"I was little," Sophie said idly. "Younger than Jacob. I think it happened right after I turned five."

"What happened right after you turned five?" Annie set aside a couple of pencil stubs to throw away.

"That's just it. I don't know what happened. I only remember that my parents were disappointed with Rufus, which hardly ever happened."

Annie straightened, attentive.

"After that," Sophie said, "Rufus stopped going to the singings."

"And he never married," Annie said softly.

"Well, not yet." One side of Sophie's mouth twisted in a smile as she glanced at Annie. "Now there's you."

Annie stacked three writing pads with the largest on the bottom. It would be up to Rufus to decide what to tell his family when the wedding they had come to expect did not happen. "I'm so glad to know your family, Sophie. You all teach me so much. I hope we'll always be friends."

"Of course we will. Why wouldn't we?" Sophie set the white card down and dipped her rag in furniture polish and scrubbed again. "You're going to be baptized. After you join the church, you and Rufus will be together, and no one can object."

"One thing at a time," Annie said. "I have a feeling the bishop would like my German to be better."

"I'll help you. We can study any afternoon you like."

"Thank you, Sophie."

"We can even start today, if you like."

Annie traced her fingers over the drawer's neatness. Sophie laid the folded white card on top of the other papers before picking up the drawer.

"Whatever happened in the past doesn't matter," Sophie said. "I judge Rufus by the man he is now, and I'm proud to call him my brother." She put her fingers to her lips. "Oops. *Hochmut*. But it's true. I only hope I find a man like Rufus some day."

"You will," Annie said. "And he'd better deserve you."

"I wouldn't have it any other way." Sophie slid the drawer into its proper space. "And don't you pay any attention to Beth Stutzman."

"What do you mean?"

"She acts like she knows something about Rufus."

"Really?"

"I don't think she does, though. She's just out of sorts because Rufus chose you."

Had he chosen her?

Fifty

May 1804

Step back, Johann." Jacob gestured away from the rifle barrel held in place by the vise.

"*Daed*, that's too much gunpowder."

"You sound like your mother," Jacob said. "She's been telling me to be careful for thirty years."

"You should be careful."

Jacob shook his head. Johann, the only Byler child to be born in North Carolina, was twenty-two. He had a solid understanding of gunpowder manufacturing. He had been helping Jacob for years. But he was his mother's son.

Jacob stuffed the barrel, tied a string to the trigger, and stepped back into his son's caution zone. He pulled the string, and the rifle splintered the air.

Jacob laughed heartily as he moved in to reload. "It's getting faster. It's almost ready."

"Almost ready?" Johann challenged. "*Daed*, you're using more saltpeter in the mix, and stuffing more mix into the barrel."

"That's the point. A faster shot will take down a deer that much more quickly, and at greater range."

"Your customers will like that."

Katie appeared behind them, pausing to lean against the stone structure Jacob used for a workshop.

"I'm sorry to bother the two of you," she said, "but I could use some help moving crates of preserves from the cellar up to the kitchen."

"I'll help you."

Johann kissed his mother's cheek, a gesture that always made Jacob smile.

"I'm sorry you had to come all the way down here to ask for help," Jacob said. "I've kept Johann too long."

"It's no problem. The day calls for a walk."

"It's a fine day," Jacob agreed.

Katie turned to go. "Be careful."

Jacob smiled and said, "I love you, too, Katie Byler."

Jacob watched mother and son traverse the gentle slope between his workshop and the house and garden. The years in North Carolina had brought them adventure and prosperity. Johann was born in their new state—just barely. The older children grew to adulthood, married, and embraced their own adventures, some of them moving west to Tennessee and Missouri. Katie was gray haired, as was he, and less nimble than in their youth. Nevertheless her beauty startled him in ordinary moments. Now she raised one hand and laid it on their tall son's back as she bent her head in to attend his words.

Jacob sifted silky gunpowder through his fingers. This was perhaps the smoothest batch he had ever ground. The saltpeter had crystallized perfectly, the brimstone softened in the lye flawlessly. Perhaps he could stuff in a few more granules than he had only moments ago.

The sound that preceded the blast told him a fraction of a second too late that he had pressed his ambition too far.

Magdalena cradled the babe in her arms. As long as she kept moving, the child slept.

Magdalena's daughter Sally, her firstborn, slept in the house, exhausted from caring for a colicky babe who was happy only while in motion. Constant indulgence would not teach the *boppli* to sleep, but Magdalena claimed a grandmother's privilege. She had walked the miles of Lancaster County since she was young, and now in her midforties, she did not complain. She still covered miles every day. It was no trouble to carry the tiny girl as she roamed through the brisk afternoon air.

The now contented child molded to Magdalena's chest. This was her first grandchild. Seven years of waiting for Nathan had found fulfillment in seven children and more than two decades together. Magdalena gave thanks every day for the life she had lost hope for.

She expected many more *kinner* would follow, and she intended to savor every moment with each one.

The years with Nathanael were not always bright. When his mind muddled, she kept the children quiet and prayed for patience. As the house filled with *kinner*, though, his heart filled with joy. He never spoke of the years they lost, and Magdalena long ago ceased wondering about them.

On this day, in this place, she held her joy in her arms and watched the child sleep. And that was enough.

Magdalena turned her steps toward her father's farm, where her daughter napped. She did not want to surrender her grandchild any sooner than she must, but the afternoon waned, and the task of preparing a meal at her own hearth awaited.

Christian heard the gentle steps on the porch and knew Magdalena had returned from her afternoon walk. He looked up from his book beside the fire as she padded into the room.

"Is Sally still sleeping?" Magdalena's voice was a low coo. The baby waved an arm once but did not wake.

"Soundly." Christian had raised enough children to know how

to manage his voice in the presence of a sleeping infant.

"I hate to wake her."

"Let her sleep a few more minutes." Christian gestured to the chair across from him and was glad to see Magdalena settle into it without protest. The marvel she held in her arms was his great-grandchild, and he would not soon tire of watching tiny gestures and the shifting faces of sleep.

"I've brought your mail." Magdalena reached under her shawl and pulled out a bundle of envelopes.

"Anything interesting?" Christian took the packet and began flipping through it.

"I did not peruse. It is your mail."

The child squeaked, and both Christian and Magdalena startled slightly. Christian lowered his voice further.

"Here's something from your *aunti* Katie."

"*Aunti* Katie? Doesn't *Onkel* Jacob usually write?"

"I haven't heard from him in almost five years." Christian stiffened and slit the envelope. He pulled a single sheath, unfolded it, and read quickly. He gasped. He had not known this particular grief would sit so heavily on his chest, making it impossible to breathe.

"He's gone."

"Gone?"

"Six weeks ago. An accident at his gunpowder mill."

"I'm sorry, *Daed*," Magdalena said softly.

"I am, too." Christian's fingers lost their grip on the sheet of coarse paper, and it fell to the floor. His spine softened, and he slumped in his chair. "Oh, Jacobli."

Fifty-One

Annie pedaled home well before suppertime. She could have stayed—she required neither invitation nor reason to be at the Beilers'. At any moment, Rufus could enter the family home and she would feel the pressure building in her chest while she waited to see if he would speak to her. The vigilance of expecting the worst wore her down, and she wanted to go home.

Annie did not pedal especially hard. When the incline challenged her balance at such a slow speed, she got off and walked the bike up the hill, taking the seat again only when she knew she could coast the rest of the way home as long as she circled the pedals a couple of times every thirty seconds.

Home—her narrow, green-shingled house with irises and daylilies, cornflowers and primroses splashed across the front. Annie leaned the bike against the side of the house, as she always did. Rufus was always after her to use the kickstand, but it was such a beat-up old bicycle to begin with that she did not see the point of worrying about scratching it. She gently kicked a pedal and watched the mechanism spin, supposing that now that Rufus was keeping his distance she would not have to concern herself with his opinions on her bicycle.

She followed the path of dilapidated concrete steps around to the front of the house and knelt to inspect the flowers. In them she saw the hope she craved. Her bulbs and flowers came from neighbors and Amish friends dividing their bounty. It was too soon to know whether they would survive the winter and burst out of the ground again next spring—green bubbles struggling to burst through earth and unbend themselves, nascent stems of promised beauty. The billowy hem of her skirt settled in the dirt as she examined bits of green and pink and violet for reassurance of her hope.

Sighing, Annie rose and circled around the house to the vegetable plot in the back. Rufus, Joel, and Jacob had dug the plot and transferred seeds from the starter plants Sophie had grown in the Beiler kitchen. Soon she would have summer squash and swiss chard and green beans. In the fall she would have sweet corn, potatoes, pumpkin, and winter squash.

And she would be proud of what she had accomplished.

No, not proud. *Demut.*

She would not be ashamed. Perhaps, she thought, that was not the same as being proud. A peaceful, simple life that helped her understand God's ways more clearly was all she wanted. If only she could learn to regard people with kindness and dignity, rather than competition and suspicion.

It was because of Rufus. Even if she did not become his wife, he had left his mark on her, and she would always be grateful for that. He was the one who challenged her to see the world—and her own life—from a new angle. Because of Rufus Beiler, she could not simply go back to Colorado Springs, accept a lucrative offer from Liam-Ryder Industries, and resume a life of determined winning.

Annie swallowed the lump in her throat and looked at her garage. Could it be made over into a small stable for a horse and small buggy? Perhaps it could be fortified, or perhaps it should be torn down and she should start over. She should have asked Rufus's opinion long ago. She still could, Annie reminded herself. Rufus Beiler had not died; he simply was not choosing her. He could still be her carpenter of choice, starting with building a back porch that did not threaten to collapse every time she stepped on it.

Annie pushed open the back door and went into her house. In the kitchen she pulled open a drawer and pulled out two items, the latest letter from Liam-Ryder Industries with a twenty percent increase in the financial offer, and a business card bearing Randy Sawyer's contact information. She ripped them both to shreds. No matter what Rufus decided, these documents had nothing to do with anything anymore. She would not continue her baptism classes with these temptations hidden in her kitchen.

The knock startled Annie. On her sofa, she roused from dozing and pushed off the light afghan. Licking her lips, she tested her coiled hair to be sure it held its form. The knock came again, sounding insistent this time. Annie leaned forward enough to see out the front window.

Dolly was there, with the buggy. Rufus's buggy.

In two seconds, she was at the door, pulling it open.

"Hello, Rufus."

"Hello, Annalise." He seemed not to know what to do with his hands and finally settled on clasping them together in front of him. "I thought we should talk."

Annie squelched the instinct to ask if he would like to come in. He would decline, as he always did when they were alone. Instead, she closed the door behind her, smoothed her skirt, and sat on the top step. When Rufus lowered his lanky form to sit beside her, her heart lurched into overdrive and she had to force herself to breathe. At least sitting side by side, he could not see the color seeping out of her face.

"I've been thinking about what you told me the other day." Rufus leaned forward, elbows on his knees.

Annie waited. Even if she had wanted to speak, she could not have.

"That took courage," he said. "I've always admired that trait in you."

He had? All this time Annie had thought Rufus regarded her as impetuous and out of control.

"You did not have to say anything. I don't think I ever would have asked."

Annie held her breath.

"There was a young woman," he began, nerves rattling in his timbre, "in Pennsylvania. I was about Joel's age. Everyone thought we would be the perfect couple. We became adept at finding ways to be alone." He shifted his weight to one foot and then the other. "I am not as pure as you think me to be, either."

"Rufus—"

He held up a hand. "I need to say more."

She nodded, stunned.

"After we had. . .well, we realized we had let our curiosity get the better of us, and that's all it was. My parents were devastated when we told them. Her parents insisted we had to marry. I felt guilty enough that I would have done it, but she refused."

In the silence that engulfed them, Annie found her voice. "Did you care for her at all?"

Slowly he shook his head. "I learned the hard way to be circumspect in all things. To avoid temptation and gossip, I even stopped going to singings."

Annie did the mental math. "But that must have been more than twelve years ago."

He nodded.

"And since then? No one?"

"No one. Ike Stutzman is not the first man with daughters to get ideas, but I did not want to make that mistake again."

"You wouldn't, Rufus," Annie said. "You understand second chances—you give other people a second chance all the time."

"I had a letter from her a few months ago," Rufus said quietly, looking away. "She never married, either."

The white card. The feminine writing. The way Sophie tactfully took the card from Annie and reminded her she should not read it.

The question blurted out before Annie could stop it. "Does she want to marry you now? After all this time?"

Rufus shook his head. "She just wanted me to know she is happy, just the way she is. She heard that I never married and hoped it was not because of her."

"And was it?"

He shook his head. "I've been waiting to feel about someone the way I feel about you. When I finally felt something. . ."

Annie giggled. "I turned out to be *English*." She tilted her head, and her prayer *kapp* slid off.

Rufus snatched the *kapp* before it hit the sidewalk. "If you had any idea how often I've wanted to kiss you. . ."

Annie chuckled. "Not nearly as many times as I've wanted you to kiss me."

"I don't think of you as *English* anymore." Rufus shuffled his feet. He turned to look at her. "You are just Annalise, with the sharp mind God gave you and the earnest heart God has been shaping in you this last year."

"You have been the one to show me that heart, Rufus."

"You are beautiful, Annalise Friesen, inside and out. If you'll still have me, I hope and pray we can have many years together."

Annie's face split into a grin. "I still have to be baptized."

He nodded.

"I promise not to run out on my baptism. I *am* going to do this."

"I have no doubt. And then we'll marry. I will do my best to make your parents know this is the best thing for you."

Annie glanced around the quiet street. Dolly nickered and shook a fetlock. Otherwise the neighborhood was clear of observers.

"Do you want to kiss me now?" Annie asked. "Because I really want you to."

"Without regret?"

"Without regret."

She put a hand on his chest and leaned in to him. His arms went around her as his mouth found her lips.

Annie moaned. Now this was the kind of kiss she had been waiting for.

Author's Note

When I started the Valley of Choice series, I began the journey of imagining the lives of my own ancestors. I have bits and pieces of information about where they lived, what property they owned, when or how they died. On these hooks I hang my story. Jacob Byler, son of pioneer Jakob Beyeler, is my ancestor. When I learned that he died in 1804 in a gunpowder mill explosion, it made all the sense in the world to me that he should be absorbed in making gunpowder for the Revolutionary War. His son Abraham was my grandfather's grandfather.

I find myself taking liberties with the real town of Westcliffe, Colorado, and for that I ask the indulgence of the people of Custer County. The setting of the series has taken on a personality of its own, but that does not mean that the true town is populated by people who are any less fine.

I find the mysterious blend of an imagined past, a possible present, and a place of so many prospects to be the perfect wrapping to hold my story of people who stand on a line that can change their futures and dare to step over it.

Taken for
ENGLISH

Dedication

For my siblings, because of the host of characters
they are and the ones they inspire.

Acknowledgments

Writing is often solitary, but I do not find it lonely. I bump into too many people on the road between idea and book to feel lonely.

The largest portion of this story came into being on Saturday mornings at a local coffee shop, with my friend Erin sitting across the table crafting her own story.

Rachelle shares her favorite books with me. Since she has terrific taste, reading these books propels me toward writing more, writing better, writing swiftly.

My family grounds me in reality while also understanding my need to withdraw to another world.

I was working on this manuscript when *Accidentally Amish*, the first in this series, released and I began to hear from readers. If I started to lag, their enthusiasm thrust me back into the game. I admit I was not quite prepared for this particular experience, but I am thankful for the cause and effect.

One

A siren screamed down the highway. Ruth Beiler turned her head half an inch toward the sound, catching the reflex before curiosity about events outside her family's home could distract her from the solemn occasion before her eyes. In a minute, the congregation would sing another hymn from the *Ausbund* and Ruth would savor every note. No matter how many times she went to an *English* church in Colorado Springs, her heart yearned for the plaintive rhythm of the Amish hymns she had grown up with. Music should have space to think, to reflect, to absorb.

And after the hymn and a prayer would come the moment that had Ruth's heart beating fast today.

Annalise Friesen was presenting herself for baptism. Joining the Amish church. This should be all Rufus needed to formally ask Annalise to marry him. If he did not, Ruth intended to have a firm conversation with her older brother.

Ruth glanced at Rufus seated across the aisle with the men. He was twenty-nine and still clean shaven—unmarried. Anyone outside the community might have thought that the small boy next to Rufus was his son, but Jacob was their littlest brother.

Next to Ruth, her mother shifted slightly in her chair, leaning forward. Normally the Beiler women chose to sit toward the back of the congregation of about sixty people, especially when the faithful gathered in their own home. But this day was different. Eli Beiler sat with bearded men at the front of the assembly on the men's side of the aisle. Rufus sat farther back, with the unmarried men, but he had taken a seat on the aisle where he could see well, with Jacob and Joel next to him. Ruth sat with her mother, Franey, and her sisters Lydia and Sophie toward the front, where they could see well but not seem ostentatious.

Because Annalise was being baptized.

Heaviness pressed against Ruth's efforts to breathe. They would not speak of it, but she was sure her mother would be remembering the same event, the fall baptism service, almost three years ago.

Ruth had knelt before the bishop as Annalise was doing today. And during the prayer preceding the baptism, with all heads bowed and eyes closed, she slipped out.

Just left. Ran. Hid. Rode with an *English* man to a bus stop and moved to Colorado Springs, where she was now a student in the university's school of nursing.

Ruth had briefly considered not being present for Annalise's baptism, but her mother would remember Ruth's baptism day whether Ruth was there or not. This was a day of joy for her dearest friend! Ruth did not want to miss a moment.

Another siren shrieked on the main highway that ran past the Beiler property outside Westcliffe, Colorado. In Colorado Springs, two sirens could mean anything. Emergency medical technicians answering a 911 call. A police car chasing a speeder. Fire trucks on the way to a kitchen grease fire. When she was driving, Ruth got out of the way of the emergency vehicles but otherwise went about her own business.

Among Custer County's thin population, sirens were rare.

Ruth heard the slight rustles behind her. Others had noticed the sirens and looked at each other, wondering.

The bishop began his prayer for the baptismal candidates.

Ruth bowed her head but kept her eyes open and watched Annalise.

Annie's heart pounded.

Not out of doubt. Not out of fear. Not with regret.

Until now she had only imagined what it might be like to truly belong to the community of the Amish. She had lived in Westcliffe for more than a year, worshiping with these families every other Sunday. Nothing in her home off Main Street ran on electricity. She had given her car to Ruth Beiler months ago. Her quilt was almost finished. Jeans and T-shirts had gone to a thrift shop in favor of the Amish dresses she had learned to sew for herself.

But this moment. This would make it all real and true and lasting. Anyone who thought she was just playing house the Amish way might drop their jaws, but Annie was going through with this.

Pressing her lips together, Annie tried to focus on the bishop's prayer. Her German still had a way to go, but she picked out the main themes. Faith. Commitment. Vows.

Annie's scalp itched under her prayer *kapp*. She ignored the sensation. The prayer ended, and she let her eyes rise enough to see what was happening. The bishop moved to the first of the baptismal candidates. Annie was one of four and the only one well out of her teen years. The deacon followed the bishop closely, carrying a wooden bucket of water. Behind him was the bishop's wife.

One by one the candidates answered the baptismal questions and made their vows.

"Do you believe and confess that Jesus Christ is God's Son?

"Do you believe and trust that you are united with a Christian church of the Lord, and do you promise obedience to God and the church?

"Do you renounce the devil, the world, and the lustfulness of your flesh and commit yourself to Christ and His church?

"Do you promise to live by the *Ordnung* of the church and to help administer them according to Christ's Word and teaching, and to abide by the truth you have accepted, thereby to live and thereby to die with help of the Lord?"

When Annie gave her final vow, the bishop's wife removed her head covering. The bishop dipped a cup into the water bucket and poured the water into his hand then poured it on Annie's head three times, in the name of the Father, the Son, and the Holy Ghost.

"Rise," the bishop said, "and be a faithful member of the church."

Annie accepted the hand of the bishop's wife, stood, turned, and grinned at the Beiler family.

A siren blared. The third one.

Rufus Beiler could not take his violet-blue eyes off Annalise.

She was a resolute woman. Whatever she decided to do, she did with her whole self. When she spoke her vows, he believed her. Even her posture had taken on a new demeanor in the weeks of her baptismal instruction. In Amish garments, she no longer looked uncertain about how to move around efficiently and gracefully. Her gray eyes and keen mind absorbed detail after detail about Amish life, and her actions moved from awkward imitation of the patterns she observed to fluid heartfelt expression of inward conviction.

Though she had come to them from the *English* world, Annalise Friesen was one of the truest people Rufus had ever known.

And the only woman he had ever loved.

The final hymn began, its tempo slightly faster as an expression of joy. The words emerged from Rufus's mind without the assistance of the hymnal, and he sang with robust belief.

In the few seconds of silence between the final note of the hymn and the bishop's first words of benediction, Rufus heard the footsteps on the front porch. A form crossed the curtainless wide window and paused.

An *English* form. Rufus did not catch enough of the movement to recognize the visitor. It was someone with the good sense not to burst into an Amish worship service, yet a messenger of urgent news. For no other reason would one of the *English* of Westcliffe approach an Amish worship service in progress.

The bishop's voice faded. The service was over. Rufus's glance bounced between Annalise and the front door.

Annalise. Of course Annalise. He moved toward her even as the congregation pressed around her with their congratulations. Many in the community harbored doubt. Rufus knew that much from overhearing tidbits of conversation not meant for his ears. "You have to be born Amish," they said.

Yet Annalise had made the same promises as the three teenagers who had been born Amish. In God's eyes, there was no distinction.

Rufus was tall enough to look over the heads of most of the gathering and catch Annalise's gray eyes. They brightened, and he knew the smile that raised her lips at that moment was meant for him. A strand of hair fell loose from her braided bun, as it always did. He hoped it always would.

He turned when someone tugged on the elbow of his black jacket.

"It's Tom Reynolds," his brother Joel said. "He says it's urgent. He's waiting on the porch."

Rufus glanced again at Annalise and then maneuvered through the congregation toward the front door. The living room windows were open to the fine September day, but the volume of the interior conversations dropped when he stepped out and closed the door behind him.

"What is it, Tom?" Rufus had counted three sirens.

"One of Karl Kramer's houses just burned."

The air went out of Rufus.

"It's the one you worked on," Tom said. "Your cabinetry. . ."

Rufus nodded. "All right. Thank you for telling me."

"I could take you out there." Tom turned a thumb toward his red pickup truck parked among the buggies.

"It's the Sabbath. And Annalise was just baptized."

The front door opened behind them. Annie stepped out.

"Did I hear my name?"

"Hello, Annie," Tom said. "Congratulations."

"Thank you." She looked from Tom to Rufus. "Why so glum? The sirens?"

"Everything will be fine," Rufus said. "One of Karl's houses burned. But the *English* have insurance for these things."

"Was anyone hurt?" Annie asked.

Tom shook his head. "Not that I've heard. It should have been empty on a Sunday."

"Then what caused the fire?" Annie moved farther out on the porch.

Tom turned his hands palms up. "That will be for the fire department to figure out."

"Custer County runs on a volunteer firefighting force," Annie said. "Do they even have forensics capability?"

"I'm sure they have someone to call in if the cause is not obvious," Tom said. "I wanted to take Rufus out there. Maybe it didn't get his cabinets."

"They are no longer my cabinets," Rufus pointed out. "The *English* will sort out who they belong to when a house is almost finished."

"I think you should go." Annie leaned against the porch's railing and looked back into the house. The transformation of the benches into tables was already under way. "Aren't you at least curious?"

"Of course."

"Then go."

"It's your baptism day, Annalise." Those irresistible eyes sank into her.

"I know," she said. "But even Jesus would take an animal out of a well on the Sabbath. You should go see how bad it is, whether you can help to salvage anything. You might reduce the sense of loss somehow."

She could see him thinking as his head turned toward the barn where the Beiler buggies were parked.

"Let Tom drive you," she said. "You'll be back soon enough. The food will still be here." *I will still be here,* she wanted to say.

Two

Tom's truck jerked to a halt. "We're still four houses away."

Rufus leaned forward and peered through the windshield. "Looks like half the emergency vehicles in the county are here."

"Might as well get out here." Tom killed the ignition.

"Are you sure we should have come? It doesn't look like we'll get any closer. We'll just be in the way."

"You have a vested interest." Tom pulled the latch to open the driver's door.

"No I don't. And it would not matter if I did."

"You may be right about the cabinets," Tom said, "but what about the peace of this community? What's going to happen when Karl Kramer finds out about this?"

Tom had a point. A year ago, the hotheaded construction contractor had no use for an Amish cabinetmaker. Rufus had stayed out of his way long enough to gain Karl's trust. Over the last few months Rufus had nurtured an unlikely relationship that drew the two of them together in a community improvement project, a joint effort between the *English* and the Amish. Karl had even gained a few popularity points and practically insisted that Rufus build the cabinets in the house now hidden by emergency vehicles.

And now this.

"He's out of town," Rufus said. "I don't know how to reach him."

"Somebody will," Tom said. "Let's get out."

They slammed the truck's doors and walked the few yards to where a crowd had assembled.

"We don't know that it's foul play." Rufus wished he had left his black jacket in the car. The warmth of the day and the smoldering remains of the fire made him sweat.

"No, we don't." Tom slid his hands into the pockets of his khaki work pants. "But if it was an accident, that means something went wrong with workmanship somewhere."

They inched through the crowd, for what purpose Rufus was unsure. Smoke filled his nostrils and hung in a wall of gray above the house. The front support of the two-story structure had collapsed, taking half the roof with it. Cinders floated on the breeze.

"The fire must be out." Tom pointed to the largest fire truck. "They're not shooting water."

Whatever was left of the house would be too smoky and water damaged to salvage. Certainly the kitchen cabinets, with their carefully sanded white oak finish, would be reduced to scrap.

Tom reached out and grabbed the shoulder of a passing firefighter. "Bryan, what happened?"

The young man turned toward them and gestured for his companion to pause as well. "Hi, Tom. This is my friend Alan."

"Tom Reynolds." Tom offered a handshake. "This is Rufus Beiler."

"All that's left is the cleanup," Bryan said. "Alan and I are here to make sure the scene is secured and the evidence is not compromised."

"Evidence?" Rufus asked. "So you think it's arson?"

"Too soon to say, but the fire chief doesn't want to take any chances in a situation like this."

Annie suspected women were hugging and congratulating her for the second or third time. Surely she had already received more embraces than there were women present during worship. Though she had a plate of food in front of her on a table in the Beilers' dining room, she hardly got to swallow a bite before someone else was tapping her on the shoulder and smiling broadly. Each time, Annie stood and allowed a pair of arms to fold around her.

"It was perfect to have your baptism here at our home."

With her teeth about to close on a forkful of ham, Annie looked up to see Franey Beiler's eyes brimming. Annie reached for Franey's hand. "I confess I'm glad it was here, too. This is where it all began for me, after all."

Annie had first met the Beilers more than a year ago when she stumbled onto their land in the dark with no idea that Amish had settled in southwestern Colorado.

"Eli and I cannot imagine our lives without you," Franey said. "I'm sure it will be only a matter of time now."

Annie tilted her head and shrugged one shoulder. She hoped Franey was right—that she and Rufus would have their banns read and be married before the end of the year. But she would wait for Rufus to decide. She had chosen to be baptized into the Amish church of her own free will. The next step was for Rufus to take.

Someone asked Franey a question, and she disappeared into the kitchen. Annie smiled at the women around her table—but hoped none of them planned to congratulate her yet again. She wished one of the Beiler girls, Lydia or Sophie, might slide into the empty chair beside her.

Instead a young stranger sat down. An unhappy young stranger with no plate of food.

"Hello. I'm Annalise."

"I know who you are," the girl said. "Everybody knows who you are."

"I suppose on my baptism day, that is true." Annie dabbed her lips with a napkin. "If we've met, I'm sorry that I've forgotten your name."

"We haven't met. I'm Leah Deitwaller. From Pennsylvania."

"Oh, the new family. Welcome."

"You don't have to say that. I don't even want to be here. And I'm not staying."

"You're ready to go home already? Have your parents eaten?"

Leah rolled her eyes. "I mean I don't want to be in Colorado. I'm going home to Pennsylvania."

"Oh." Annie doubted the girl was of age.

"Is it true that you're *English*?"

"Until a couple of hours ago that was true."

"Can you help me find out how much it would cost to take the train to Pennsylvania?"

Annie set her fork down gently and took a moment to straighten her prayer *kapp*. "Shouldn't you have this conversation with your parents?"

"I would pay my own way." Leah slumped and crossed her arms. "I just need a job. I know I'm small, but I'm seventeen—nearly eighteen. I'm old enough."

"What does your mother say about your having a job?"

Leah unfolded her arms and slapped both palms on the table. "Never mind. I just thought you might understand."

"Understand what?"

Leah stood, crossed the dining room, walked through the living room, and went out the front door.

Rufus had been gone a long time. Ruth was scraping and stacking dishes in the kitchen sink when she realized more than two hours had passed since she saw her brother step off the front porch and into Tom Reynolds's truck. Before long, the families with younger children or those who came from a greater distance would hook their horses to their buggies and begin the trek home. Because of the sparsity of families settling around Westcliffe, the church district covered a wide geographic area.

The door from the dining room swung open, and Annalise entered with a tray of dishes.

"You're not supposed to be cleaning up after your own baptism." Ruth took the stack from Annalise and began transferring plates to the sink.

"It's a ruse," Annalise said. "Elijah Capp cornered me."

"Elijah?"

Annalise narrowed her eyes. "Don't act like you don't know what he wants."

"He wants what he always wants."

"You. That's what he wants."

Ruth ran some hot water in the sink. "Perhaps I should not have come here for my internship. It's not even a real internship, just a place to work to see if it's the kind of nursing I want to do."

Annalise put both hands behind her waist and leaned against the counter next to the sink. "Right now all he wants to know is if you are going to the singing tonight."

Ruth glanced up. "Are you and Rufus going?"

"You know what Rufus says. We're too old."

"Where did he go?" Ruth asked. "Why would he leave you on your baptism day?"

"I told him to."

"How *English* of you." Ruth flattened a stray strand of her light brown hair.

Annalise nudged Ruth with one elbow. "There was a fire."

"I heard the sirens."

"Tom thought Rufus should go out there. I trust Tom's judgment about these things."

Ruth rinsed two plates and set them in the dish rack. "Did he say where it was?"

"One of Karl's houses."

Ruth exhaled. "Why does everything in this town seen to involve Karl Kramer?"

"Don't worry about it," Annalise said. "What should I tell Elijah? Better yet, go talk to Elijah yourself."

Ruth moistened her lips. "I don't think that's a good idea."

"If you're going to live in Westcliffe for the whole semester, you can't avoid Elijah."

"I know. Not completely. I'm going to be living in town with you and driving around if I need to. I'll just run into him from time to time." Ruth shook water off her hands and reached for a dish towel.

"Are you sure you don't want to live here at home with your own family?"

Ruth moved her head slowly from side to side. "I would only be flaunting my *English* ways. I can come to church and see my family, but I can't keep a car here. I can't get up from the breakfast table every day to go do something my mother does not want me to do. I can't come here in my scrubs."

Annalise reached for Ruth's hand. "I think your mother has found her peace with your decision not to join the church. She loves you. And she knows how much you love God."

"Still, I can't live here. Thank you for letting me use your spare room."

"Of course."

"I feel nervous that Rufus has been gone so long," Ruth said. "I'm going to go find him."

"What about Elijah?"

Ruth pulled off the apron covering her denim skirt and long-sleeve gray T-shirt. "Please tell him I'm not going to the singing. He has to accept that I can't."

Two fire trucks rumbled past Ruth in her blue Prius as she turned off the main highway and into the new subdivision where Karl

Kramer was building homes. Visually following the trail of smoke to the afflicted house was simple. Ruth parked the Prius and proceeded on foot to where two Custer County sheriff's cars cordoned off the end of an unfinished block.

She spotted Rufus's hat, his height lifting it above the gawkers, and she made her way toward him. He stood with Tom and two men she did not recognize who wore fire-retardant jackets and helmets.

"Ruth, what are you doing here?" Rufus had turned and seen her.

"I was looking for you."

"This is my sister, Ruth," Rufus said to the two young men.

"Bryan," one of them said.

"Alan," the other supplied.

"It's nice to meet you both." Ruth took in the scene beyond them. "Well, I guess the circumstances are not so nice."

Bryan cracked a smile. "Then I hope there will be other circumstances."

A blush rose in Ruth's neck. She felt its warmth as she met her brother's eyes.

"I don't mean to be rude." Bryan's eyes were still on Ruth. "But you are not dressed like the other Amish women I've seen."

Ruth swallowed. "I'm not baptized." She slid her palms down the side of her long skirt.

"So you're. . .not Amish?"

"It's complicated." Ruth looked away.

"Maybe another time, then."

Ruth's gut burned.

Alan raised a red locked box in one hand. "Quit your flirting, Bryan. We need to get this place secured and start collecting evidence."

Bryan nodded. "I'll take the kit."

Alan held the box beyond his grasp. "Don't think you're going in there alone and getting all the credit."

Bryan rolled his eyes. "You're so competitive."

Three

May 1892

Roast beef satiated his taste buds before he conceded the necessity to chew, which Sheriff A.G. Byler did slowly. He swallowed the bite and with deliberation took another. His lunch, though delicious, did not please him nearly as much as the movements of his wife at the other end of the kitchen table.

"Are you going to your office today?" Bess thoughtfully smoothed a length of blue twill flat against the table.

"I've managed to lollygag all morning," A.G. said. "I reckon I'd better check on the state of lawlessness in Baxter County before my afternoon nap."

"Abraham Byler, don't make jokes." Bess picked up a pair of scissors and opened and closed them three times above the fabric. "You've been gone for two weeks, and nobody trusts your deputy if things get heated."

"They knew where to send a telegram in Colorado." Stroking his pointed white beard, Abraham considered whether to indulge in his last bite of mashed potatoes before or after he finished his meat. "If Deputy Combs got in over his head, somebody would have let me know."

"Well, we're back in Arkansas now, and sometimes I think the

741

Wild West is more civilized than Baxter County." She waved the scissors again.

"You're exaggerating." He pointed at the cloth. "Are you planning to attack that innocent piece of material?"

Bess put the scissors down. "I'm trying to decide if it's enough for a romper for little Ransom. I think I've got some green that would be adorable on the twins."

"We just got home last night." A.G. scooped up the potatoes. "We haven't even been outside in the daylight, and already you're fussing about what to send to Malinda's children."

"I know their sizes now," Bess countered, "and their personalities. You don't really expect I would let that information go to waste. They grow so fast. I have to do this soon."

He nodded and smiled. "Ransom sure did laugh himself half to death playing horsey on my knee."

Bess tilted her head and raised her eyebrows. "You're as smitten as I am."

He felt the light in his own eyes. "You were a beautiful sight with those grandbabies Earl and Pearl in your arms."

"I hope Mack and Malinda find what they're looking for in Colorado, because it sure is a long way from home. I don't like being separated from my daughter. Three babies, and we only just saw them for the first time."

"They're working hard." A.G. scraped his chair back, picked up his plate, and moved to set it in the sink. "At least our boys are not too far away. We won't wait so long for the next visit to Colorado. I promise."

"I'll hold you to that." Bess pointed the scissors at him. "Will you make it to Gassville today?"

"I'll check on the tanyard and swing by the jail here in Mountain Home. Then I suppose I'll ride over to Gassville."

"I ordered some buttons at Denton's Emporium more than a month ago. Will you check on them while you're over that way?"

He dipped his head of wavy white hair. "That I can do."

Bess's face clouded. "Gassville seems to give you plenty of trouble these days."

"Child's play."

"I'm serious, Abraham. I'm anxious what news you'll hear."

"You worry too much."

A.G. caught the back screen door before it had time to slam and walked around the side of the stone bungalow out to the street. On the side of the road, he paused to inhale deeply. His promise not to wait so long to take the train back to Colorado was as much to himself as it was to Bess. He did not intend for his grandchildren to grow up not knowing who he was. They were so little they would not remember this visit when he laid eyes on them for the first time. Colorado was a long way, but it was not the edge of the world.

He exhaled and took the first steps toward the center of Mountain Home.

"Why, Sheriff Byler," a female voice said. "I didn't realize you were back in town."

Abraham smiled at Mrs. Taylor, who hung a damp rug over the railing of her front porch. "Yes, ma'am. First day home."

Mrs. Taylor fanned herself with a church bulletin. "Come Sunday I'm sure the children in your Sunday school class will be glad to see you."

"I hope so. I know I'll be glad to see them."

"Where's your horse?"

"I left him with the boys at the tanyard."

"I'm sure they'll be glad to have you back."

He sauntered toward town, reveling in the comfort of being home among the familiar landscape of northern Arkansas and ready to pit its undulating green beauty against rugged red Colorado at the first challenge. After two terms in the state legislature, the kind people of Baxter County had welcomed him back as sheriff, a post he had filled before. He was as glad to have the job back as they were to have him.

His tanyard was at the edge of town. He employed two young men to keep the hides rotating through the lye mixtures, but periodically he liked to satisfy himself that the work was done properly. An hour later, on his own horse again and just three short blocks from the sheriff's office, A.G. looked up and winced. His hope to get through his first day in peace was headed for a crash.

"You have to do something before someone gets hurt." Twenty-four-year-old Maura Woodley shook her dark curls but managed to keep her forefinger from wagging. He was the sheriff, after all.

"Well, now, Miss Woodley," the sheriff said, "let's suppose you tell me what this is all about. I've been out of town, you know." He patted the neck of his horse as he slid out of the saddle.

"I do know." Maura set her jaw. "I'm sorry not to welcome you back more graciously, but really, you must do something."

Sheriff Byler kept walking, leading the horse, and Maura fell into step beside him.

"I've left my cousin Walter with my cart," she said, glancing over her shoulder. "I can't leave him unsupervised for too long. You know what trouble he gets into."

"Has Walter been stirring things up?"

"No. It's far more serious than that."

Finally he stopped walking and turned to her. Sheriff Abraham Byler was the calmest man Maura Woodley had ever met—sometimes too calm. This situation required firm action. Maura pulled off her white gloves and gripped them both in one fist. The gloves were too small and made her fingers itch, but her mother had paid a dear price for the gloves before her death two years ago. They were hand-stitched lambskin. Maura made a pretense at wearing them because they had been her mother's.

"I don't want Belle to get hurt," she said. "She's my best friend, and I'm afraid she is going to get caught in something dreadful."

"Belle Mooney has always had a level head," the sheriff said.

"Not when it comes to John Twigg."

"Perhaps she sees something in him that you do not."

Maura slapped her gloves against an open palm. "It is more a matter of what she does not see. The man is unstable."

"Now let's not jump to conclusions."

"You know it's true as well as I do."

"Then why have you come all the way from Gassville to tell me?"

His calmness infuriated her at that moment, and she did not speak.

"It's the Dentons again, I imagine," Sheriff said.

"Yes. The Dentons and the Twiggs used to get along so well." Maura slapped her gloves again.

"John was happy working for the Dentons for a long time." Sheriff tied his horse to a post.

"Something went wrong, and his father thought giving John his own store to run was a good idea. It's getting out of hand."

"They might still sort it out." He reached a finger under his beard to scratch his chin.

"John remains an unstable sort."

"Perhaps." Byler lifted his eyes and raised his brow. "Didn't you say you left Walter with your cart?"

"That's right." Maura followed his line of vision and sighed. The thirteen-year-old was coming out of a shop. "Walter."

The boy turned red. "Sorry, Maura."

"What am I going to tell your father? And what have you done with my horse?"

"I tied him up tight. I promise."

"I asked you to stay with him."

Walter kicked a bare toe in the dirt. "I know. Sorry."

Maura turned to the sheriff. "I'd better go see about my horse and cart. My father was quite specific about what he wanted me to bring back from Mountain Home." She scowled at Walter. "Everything had better still be there."

Sheriff Byler touched her elbow. "Now, Miss Woodley, you know we don't have that kind of petty crime in Mountain Home. You say hello to your father for me."

"You can let me out in front of Denton's Emporium," Walter said as Maura drove the cart into the outskirts of Gassville, four miles from Mountain Home.

"I don't believe I'm going to let you loose again." Maura had lost Walter once already today—and had not even known it. She did not intend to fail to deliver him safely to his father now.

Maura scanned the street, looking for a good place to tie up the horse for a few minutes.

A gallop compelled them both to turn their heads. Walter pointed. "Isn't that John Twigg, the crazy man?"

"There's no need for name calling." Maura swallowed her own guilt. Walter was merely voicing what she herself believed. And he was right—it was John Twigg, riding down the middle of the street far too fast.

Twigg pulled his horse to a halt and slid off it in front of Denton's Emporium.

"He looks wild." Walter dropped off the bench of Maura's cart.

"Shh. Stay right where you are." Maura stood next to Walter and gripped his shoulder. As much as she loved Belle Mooney and as much as Belle Mooney loved John Twigg, Maura failed to see the endearing qualities of anyone in his family. They made her more nervous every time she saw them with their beady-eyed looks and harsh laughs.

Twigg calmly tied his horse to a post directly in front of the Denton Emporium then methodically removed a stick from a saddlebag.

"What's he doing?" Walter whispered.

"Shh." Maura did not take her eyes off Twigg.

Twigg pulled an arm back then thrust the stick at the chest of the horse. The beast screamed in protest, raised its forelegs, and pulled against the post.

Shoppers poked their heads out of surrounding shops. Seeing Twigg, they quickly retreated. Twigg laughed. Then he untied the horse, mounted it in the middle of its complaint, and trotted down the street to his own store.

Maura let out her breath.

"It's a message," Walter said, "for the Denton brothers."

The street was silent, and Maura considered herding Walter back into the cart to take him anywhere but where they were. Maura's father finally emerged from the emporium, a package in his arms. "Are you two all right?"

"We're fine, Daddy," Maura said.

"You look more like your mother every day," Woody Woodley said. He turned to Walter. "I told the Dentons you would sweep for them this summer. Your daddy said you needed something to keep you busy this summer."

Walter slumped. "Isn't it enough that I sweep for my own father's shop?"

"I wonder if that's wise," Maura said.

"He'll be fine," Woody said.

Maura glanced down the street. "Speaking of Walter's daddy, where is Uncle Edwin?"

"He's at Crazy Man Twigg's store, isn't he?" Walter was at full alert again. "Selling eggs."

Woody shrugged.

Maura clicked her tongue. "I wish people would not aggravate the situation by selling to Twiggs when they have been selling to the Dentons for years."

Woody moved his head from side to side. "Edwin says John Twigg is offering a better price for eggs and hens. Goose feathers, too."

"Can't he see the Twiggs do that on purpose? They're going to make people take sides. Does Edwin really want to be on the side of John Twigg in this feud?"

"Times are tight. Edwin depends on that egg money. He can't very well sell eggs in his milliner's shop."

"But selling to the Twiggs and then letting Walter work for the Dentons—that could be dangerous."

"He'll be fine," Woody repeated.

Maura held her tongue. "I should get Walter home. I'll be home to start supper soon."

Walter pointed across the street. "Who are those men?"

"They were in the emporium," Woody said. "They look harmless enough."

"Mmm." Maura narrowed the space between her eyes. "One can never be sure. I think I'll go find out."

"Now who needs to be careful?" Walter laughed.

"If they are connected to the Twiggs or the Dentons, I want to know," Maura said. The men were oddly dressed in boxy black trousers and jackets with no collars. Maura pursed her lips while she considered what their garb might mean.

"Now who's looking to get in the middle of that feud?" her father said. "You ought to get yourself properly deputized."

Walter laughed. "Ladies can't be deputized."

Maura put her hands on her hips. "But they can get to the bottom of things."

Four

"Yes, your appointment is confirmed for Friday at 3:00." Ruth tapped her pencil eraser on the desktop as she spoke into the phone. She had checked the computer screen three times. "The doctor will have your test results by then."

Ruth hung up and glanced around the clinic's empty waiting room. From a pocket in her blue scrubs, she took a key and went to unlock the front door. The first appointment of Monday morning was scheduled for fifteen minutes later. Ruth returned to the desk and double-checked that the patient files she had pulled from the drawers were in the correct order for smooth handling as patients arrived.

When she arranged for this semester-long internship, Ruth had hoped for more patient contact. She had worked as a certified nurse assistant for over two years in a nursing home and had enough of her nursing degree behind her to be qualified to draw blood and do simple lab work. So far, though, the clinic manager had kept her on the front desk most of the time. She only worked five or six hours a day. After carrying a full course load and working twenty-five hours a week at the nursing home, the reduced schedule seemed like a vacation.

It was only the second week. Surely things would pick up.

Ruth could have arranged some clinical experience in Colorado Springs, with its multiple large hospital systems and wide-ranging network of medical practices. But she had left Westcliffe because she wanted to return to a place like it someday qualified to provide a basic level of medical care. People in Colorado Springs had plenty of doctors and nurses. Amish communities often were spread out and remote, especially in new settlements like the one in southwestern Colorado. Though she had chosen to leave, unbaptized, and get her GED and enroll in college, Ruth also longed to be among her own people.

She had a hard time thinking of herself as *not* Amish, but even in scrubs and behind a desk looking at a computer monitor, she did not feel *English*, either.

The door opened and Mrs. Weichert came through it.

"Good morning." Ruth picked up Mrs. Weichert's file from the top of the stack. "Is all your information the same?"

Mrs. Weichert laughed. "I've lived in this town my whole life. I've had that store on Main Street for twenty years. Yes, my information is the same."

"Sorry. I have to ask." Ruth stood. "They'll be ready for you in just a minute."

Ruth stepped into the hall behind the desk and set Mrs. Weichert's file in a rack. The clinic manager stuck her head out of her office.

"Why don't you take the patient back?"

"Me?" Ruth's heart sped up.

"Sure. Review her list of meds and get a pulse and blood pressure."

Ruth retrieved the chart and opened the door to the waiting room. "I'll take you back, Mrs. Weichert."

In the exam room, Ruth laid the file open. Mrs. Weichert dropped her purse in a chair and sat on the exam table.

"I guess your people are pretty excited about Annie," Mrs.

Weichert said. "Her baptism and all."

Ruth clicked the point down on her pen. "It's a big step for her."

"I respect her choice, but I sure did like it better when she wore jeans to work in the shop."

"She's gotten used to the clothes," Ruth said. "We don't really let our dresses hold us back."

Mrs. Weichert scanned Ruth from head to toe. "You've made a conversion of your own."

Ruth shrugged. "Scrubs are standard." For a long time Ruth had worn skirts to work at the nursing home. Only recently had she relented and agreed to wear scrubs. She had to admit they were practical and comfortable.

"You look like you know what you're doing."

"I assure you, I do," Ruth said. "Let me start by getting your blood pressure."

Rufus took a thermos of coffee from under the bench of his open-air cart. He stroked Dolly's long nose as the horse stood obediently still in the street. Mrs. Weichert's shop had become a familiar destination for both of them. Rufus hoped the shop would be empty for a few minutes. It was noon on a Monday. Tourist traffic should be nonexistent. It was the locals Rufus wanted to avoid.

Annalise smiled when he stepped through the door, making the bell jangle, and reached under the counter to produce two mugs.

"We seemed to have formed a habit." Rufus unscrewed the top of the thermos and poured.

Annalise wrapped the fingers of both hands around the mug to sip. "Ah. I am glad becoming Amish does not mean I have to give up *kaffi*."

"Tell me," Rufus said as he picked up his own mug, "does having an Amish employee attract more tourists to the shop on the weekends?"

Annalise laughed. "I could have made a study of that if I were keeping better records."

"You might have been tempted to write a software program to analyze the data."

She shook her head. "Nope. There are no software programs in my future. I created and sold two successful companies. It's out of my system for good."

"I suppose the busy season is over now." This would be Annalise's second winter working in Mrs. Weichert's shop of unsorted small antiques, rare books, and an increasing inventory of Amish crafts.

"As long as the weather holds up we'll have traffic." She sipped her coffee. "Winter will be quieter."

"Ike Stutzman is complaining that a lantern has gone missing."

"He probably just misplaced it, or one of his daughters used it and didn't put it back."

Rufus nodded. "Most likely. But he was pitching a fit about it yesterday when I got back from the fire. Suddenly he's worried that an overturned lantern will start a fire in his barn."

"It could."

"Yes, it could. But a lantern that is simply lost is not likely to start a fire, now is it?"

"Did anyone get hold of Karl yet?" Annalise picked up a rag and wiped dust from the counter.

Rufus shook his head. "Tom was going to go by his contractor's trailer this morning and see if his assistant has a number for him."

"I heard he went to see his dying father in Virginia."

Rufus lifted his shoulders in an exaggerated shrug.

"I also heard he went to Montana to look at horses he might want to buy for his ranch."

"I couldn't say."

The shop door jangled again, and Joel Beiler stuck his head in. "We have everything ready to load at the back of Tom's store."

"I'll be right there." Rufus drained his coffee cup as his younger brother let the door close behind him.

"Joel seems to be buckling down," Annalise said.

"He is. I believe he has a knack for farming that I never had. He ordered soil nutrients through Tom's hardware store. I promised to help him get the load home."

"I suppose you should go."

Annalise's gray eyes were clear and unsullied.

"You look happy," he said. "Are you still coming to supper tomorrow?"

She nodded.

"I'll see you there." Rufus took his thermos and stepped into the sunlight, wishing he did not have to wait until tomorrow evening to see Annalise again. He never liked being away from her.

He could do something about that dilemma. She had done her part yesterday. Now it was up to him.

Ruth was out of the clinic by two o'clock and walked the few blocks to Annalise's house off Main Street. She only stayed long enough to grab a sweater and a water bottle.

And her car key.

Annalise had given her the blue Prius a few months ago as part of divesting herself of *English* ways. Ruth had surprised herself how quickly she adjusted to the freedom of going somewhere on a whim. Quick trips. Short errands. Just go and do something and come right back.

It was all very un-Amish, and Ruth was not sure any longer that using a car to be efficient with time meant a person did not value the community.

Ruth shook off the brooding. What she wanted right now was fresh air and room to move. She wanted to be on the trail that the Amish and *English* had created together over the summer. But it was five miles away, behind the property line of her family's home. Thus the car.

Just a few minutes later, she parked the Prius at the top of the trail, locked it, and dropped the key in a pocket of her scrubs. Pockets. Another convenience that did not seem the least bit detrimental. Ruth was not hiding anything, simply storing something valuable.

She took a deep breath and quickened her pace, craving the movement. In Colorado Springs, her work at the nursing home sent her up and down the halls, lifting and pushing and pulling for entire shifts. The clinic in Westcliffe simply was not large enough to be physically demanding, and this left Ruth seeking opportunities to move her entire body.

Ruth walked the trail from one end to the other, about a mile across land that began in meadow and ended in the woods behind the Beiler home. When the house came in view, Ruth turned around. Humming a tune from the *Ausbund*, she eyed the large, flat boulder at the edge of the meadow. She had climbed the footholds of that rock hundreds of time in an Amish dress. She could certainly manage it in scrubs and tennis shoes.

She stopped short when she saw a figure on the trail. He was between her and the rock, between her and the Prius. And he was looking at her.

"Ruth Beiler, right?"

The close-cropped blond hair and goatee looked familiar. "You're the firefighter," she said. "I'm sorry. I've forgotten whether you are Bryan or Alan. Yesterday you looked alike."

"We get that a lot." Bryan grinned. "I've known Alan a long time. People are never sure who is who."

"Is everything all right?" Ruth glanced past him toward her car. "At the house, I mean. Where the fire was."

"Funny you should ask." Bryan moved to close the few yards between them. "As a matter of fact, someone violated the tape this morning."

"Why would anybody do that?"

"Good question. There wasn't much there to steal." Bryan glanced at the boulder. "You ever climb that thing?"

Ruth laughed. "All the time."

"I'll race you up."

She could not resist the dare in his green eyes and sprinted toward the rock. Running without a flapping skirt between her ankles was a rich sensation. She got there first and scrambled up the back side before Bryan found his first toehold. Triumphant, she hefted herself over the top—and found Elijah Capp flattened against the rough surface. At the sight of her, he sat up.

"I'm sorry." Startled, she stumbled slightly. "I didn't see you from down below."

"Looks like you have a shadow." Elijah straightened his hat on his head and tilted it toward Bryan.

Bryan put his hands on his hips. "I don't know why I've never come up here before. The view is beautiful."

"You must be new to Westcliffe." Elijah stood now as well.

Ruth was starting to regret her outing.

"I'm Bryan Nichols." He extended a hand, which Elijah shook.

"Elijah Capp."

"Bryan and I met yesterday." Ruth felt her back teeth start to grind. "He's a firefighter."

"Well then," Elijah said, "I imagine he must be something else as well. Custer County firefighters are volunteer."

Ruth's teeth started to hurt.

"True enough," Bryan said. "I'm a cashier at the grocery store, and I'm about to be late to work."

"I suppose you'll be going, then." Elijah nodded.

"Yes, I suppose I will." Bryan turned to Ruth. "It was good to run into you. I hope I'll see you again."

He squatted and began his descent. As he loped across the meadow, Ruth wondered where he had left his car. She turned to Elijah and forced her jaw to unclench.

"You were rude, Elijah."

"What were you doing with him, Ruth? A man you only met yesterday?"

Ruth stared at Elijah. "I was not doing anything. Not that it is your business."

"I feel toward you as I always have." Elijah crossed his arms behind his back, his voice soft.

Ruth said nothing.

"You were laughing," he said. "Happy."

"I feel the joy of the Lord when I come here. You know that better than anyone."

He stepped closer. "Ruth, is your heart open to someone else?"

Annie remembered the days—years—when she pulled on shorts and expensive tennis shoes and traversed the countryside in strides measured for endurance. In her ankle-length dress and with her hair carefully pinned up, these days she aimed for a brisk power walk. Clear mountain air was irresistible after six hours in a shop almost completely dependent on artificial light. Over recent weeks, Annie had tramped down a path several feet off the highway but running alongside it. She gave her *kapp* one last tug and began swinging her arms as her feet set their pace.

Coming out of the grocery store parking lot, where Main Street met the highway, Annie looked up just in time to lurch to one side out of the path of a white horse pulling an Amish buggy. The animal was not going fast, but he seemed confused. Behind him the buggy jostled and tilted in ways that made Annie nervous.

Doing what she had seen Rufus do so many times, she reached out and slid her fingers through the bridle, pulling to slow the horse's random movement, and reached out to run her hand along his neck. A year ago Annie Friesen would not have known what a horse's neck felt like.

"Whoa there," she said. "What's going on?"

She glanced inside the buggy and saw two little boys. Neither one of them looked older than ten.

"Who is driving your buggy?" Annie tried to place their faces.

She thought she knew everyone in the congregation now, even the children, at least by sight. Except the Deitwallers. These could be Leah's little brothers. They stared at her with huge guilty brown eyes.

"What have you boys done now?" An Amish couple strode across the parking lot with two girls in their wake toting plastic grocery sacks.

Yes, the Deitwallers.

"I'm not sure what happened," Annie said, "but the boys seem to be fine."

"Of course they're fine." Mrs. Deitwaller snapped her fingers and pointed. "Girls, get in."

"What about Leah?" one of the girls asked.

"She knew she was supposed to be back here by now." Eva Deitwaller hoisted herself up to the bench beside her husband, who had the reins in his hands now. "I'm tired of chasing after her."

"Would you like me to help you look for Leah?" Annie offered.

"No need," Leah's mother said. "She wants to be treated like an adult. She can learn to show some adult responsibility the hard way."

"Will she know how to get home?" Annie asked. "I understand you haven't been here long."

"Don't worry about her. You'll discover soon enough that Leah is a dramatic child. Don't believe everything she says. I thought she would be better after we moved, but she's not." Eva met Annie's eye for the first time. "I understand you live in town. That's a strange thing for a baptized Amish woman to do."

Annie held her lips closed. She was not about to explain her relationship with Rufus to a woman she had just met. Annie hoped her days of living in town were numbered, but she could not say so with certainty. Yet.

The Deitwallers pulled out onto the highway, leaving Annie befuddled in the parking lot. She was not a parent, and she had only had one brief conversation with Leah Deitwaller, but to her analytical mind, the data did not add up to the girl's parents being so unconcerned about her welfare.

Five

Rufus sat on the wooden chair in the small office at the back of the Amish furniture store in Colorado Springs. Tom would soon be back from visiting his mother, and Rufus was not sure he would be able to hide the disappointment he felt from his friend during the seventy-five miles of highway between the Springs and Westcliffe.

"I'm sorry, Rufus. I wish the news were better." David, the store owner, rolled his pen between his palms. "I'm going to try some new advertising, but right now sales are slumping. I don't have any custom orders for you."

Rufus gave a small shrug. "Usually you like to have some pieces on the floor to stay ahead of demand."

"I know. But I still have two chests, three end tables, and a bookcase from you."

"I see." Rufus's stomach sank.

"You know I think you do beautiful work," David said. "I just cannot afford to buy anything right now."

Rufus stood. "I hope you will let me know if business picks up."

"You will be the first to know." David scratched under his nose. "If you wanted to make a few pieces to sell strictly on commission,

I could make room on the floor."

Commission. Meaning David would pay Rufus nothing unless and until a piece sold. If David's assessment was accurate, that could take months. "I'll give that some thought."

Rufus walked through the store and out into the sunlight to wait for Tom. When Tom pulled up a few minutes later and Rufus got in the truck, Tom leaned on the steering wheel and looked expectant.

"What's wrong?"

Rufus shook his head. "No new orders. He doesn't know how long it will be."

"You were selling quite a bit over the summer, weren't you?" Tom pulled the truck out of the parking lot and onto a major north–south thoroughfare through Colorado Springs heading south.

"David has given me steady work for nearly a year. It could not last forever."

"Surely it's not over. Just a lull?"

"I hope so." Rufus removed his hat and laid his head back against the headrest.

"I'll keep my eyes open," Tom said. "Maybe I'll hear of something."

"I'd appreciate that. In the meantime, I've got to wipe this gloom off my face. If you knew something was wrong, Annalise is certain to."

Rufus reined in Dolly in front of Annalise's house. The narrow green house showed its century-old age, but at least Annalise had let him pour her a new sidewalk. He no longer worried about her falling on winter ice every time he saw the walk.

She had not spoken the words aloud, even as he spent an entire Saturday repairing the concrete, but he knew she hoped she would not be in this house for another winter. Annalise wanted to be with Rufus before winter turned fierce. Every time he thought about that truth, pain clenched his chest.

He wanted Annalise. That was not the trouble. But the questions were not so easily answered.

Annalise did not have a proper post for tying up a horse, but Rufus had long ago stopped fretting about leaving Dolly untied in front of the house. She would be content to nuzzle the ground whether or not she found anything to munch on. Besides, Rufus was only going as far as the front door. He was there to pick up Annalise and take her to the Beiler home for supper.

She opened the front door with a vivid smile even before he knocked. That happened often. Her ears were programmed to hear Dolly's *clip-clop* half a mile away, Annalise claimed. In Rufus's vocabulary, *program* was not a verb. The Amish did not program anything. But Annalise had spent too many years designing software not to think in the vocabulary of her former business success.

"Ready?" Rufus met her gray eyes and drank in the welcome he saw there.

She pulled the front door closed behind her. "I'd like to make a detour if you're agreeable."

"Of course. Where to?"

She spread her arms wide. "Anywhere. I want you to teach me to drive a buggy."

One corner of Rufus's mouth went up.

"You know I'm ready. I've watched you with the bridle and harness a hundred times. I've listened to the noises you make and how Dolly responds. I know how it works."

Rufus's mother and all of his sisters had learned to drive the buggy. Most Amish women did. Annalise's request was not outlandish.

"You are suggesting that we begin now?" he said.

"Why not? We have time, don't we? I won't ask you to take me on the highway in the first lesson. We can stay on the streets here in town where Dolly won't be tempted to go too fast. And you'll be right there."

Rufus chuckled. "You've thought this through."

"That's what I do when I face a challenge. I analyze and think it through."

"Let's do it, then."

Annalise scooted ahead of him down the walk to greet Dolly before accepting Rufus's help up onto the bench. She did not need his help. Learning to accept it anyway had taken her a long time.

She picked up the reins. "I hold them this way, right?"

He covered her hands with his to adjust her position slightly and felt only confidence in the way her fingers curved and gripped.

"Look for traffic," he said.

Annalise laughed. "I drove a car for twelve years, remember? I have not completely lost my instincts."

"Then let's try a turn at the corner so we can stay off Main Street."

He watched as Annalise sucked in both lips and kept one hand beside her wrist in case he should have to take over the reins. Perhaps they should have begun with a horse-riding lesson so Annalise could feel in her body how the horse would move. He had to admit, though, that she negotiated the first turn surprisingly well.

He chided himself. It should not have surprised him. Annalise excelled at everything she put her hand to. Why should driving a buggy be any different?

She made several right turns to take them in a large square around town, bisecting Main Street twice without turning onto it. Satisfaction took on a glow in her face when she announced she was ready to try some left turns.

"Have they discovered anything more about the fire?" Annalise asked.

Though she was doing well, Rufus remained vigilant. "About what started it, no. I get the feeling they suspect arson."

"But why?"

He shook his head. "There is no clear motive, as the *English* like to say."

"And the cabinets?"

He hesitated to answer. "Well, it turns out they belonged to me after all."

"What do you mean?"

"Because the contractor had not done the final inspection and approval, he had not yet assumed the risk. In the legal sense. That is what they tell me, anyway."

"But that's not fair. The Amish do not carry insurance. Will Karl really be that unfair to you?"

"It's not Karl." He guided her wrist again, even though she did not need the help. "It's a legal point, and an insurance coverage issue."

"So you won't be paid the final portion?"

He shook his head, not wanting to speak his thoughts. It had been a big job, with cabinets in the kitchen, family room, and master bedroom. He had been counting on the final one-third of his fee, due upon final approval.

His family expected him to propose. The Amish way was to quietly have the banns read one Sunday. Even the bishop was expecting to hear from Rufus any day now.

It would all have to wait. *Gottes wille.* God's will.

"Watch out!" Rufus pulled on the reins.

Annie wrenched the reins, her hands entangled with Rufus's. Adrenaline pumped as Dolly halted on swift command and the buggy lurched forward in a moment's delay.

Leah Deitwaller had stepped into the street, her head down, something folded in her apron, oblivious to the danger.

"Something is not right with that girl." Annie made sure Rufus had a tight hold on the reins and slid off the bench. "Leah?"

The girl looked up.

"Are you all right?"

"Of course."

"I hope you made it home safely yesterday." Even as Annie spoke, she doubted. Though Leah's *kapp* was in place, the smudge on the left side was obvious. Dirt crusted the hem of her skirt.

"If you mean that farm where my parents live, no, I have not been there since yesterday morning." Leah cocked her head in an I-dare-you position, chin forward.

Whatever the dare was, Annie was not going to accept it. "We could take you."

"If I wanted to go there, I would."

"I see." Annie had not been a particularly rebellious teenager, but she had had her moments when she preferred that her parents not know where she was.

The bundle in Leah's apron moved, causing Annie to start.

"It's a kitten," Leah said. "I found him yesterday, and I'm going to keep him."

"He'll probably be helpful if your parents get mice in the barn." Annie stepped forward. The kitten looked awfully young.

"He's not a barn cat. He's going to be *my* cat."

More than twenty-four hours had passed since Annie encountered the Deitwallers at the edge of the grocery store parking lot.

"Where did you sleep last night?" Annie asked.

Leah raised her head with a sigh and stared at Annie. "You ask a lot of questions."

"I'm concerned."

"You only joined the church two days ago. I was there. This is not really your business."

"You were the one asking me questions on Sunday. Maybe you need a friend."

"I don't need a friend who believes my parents understand anything about me."

Annie felt Rufus beside her now, his light touch on her back. "I don't really know your parents," Annie said.

"I would not bother, if I were you."

"Then maybe you and I could talk, just the two of us."

"I tried talking to you on Sunday."

"Maybe we should try again."

"Maybe. But not now."

Leah brought the kitten to her cheek, pivoted, and strode toward Main Street. Annie started to go after her, but Rufus grabbed her hand.

"Let her go."

"She's in trouble," Annalise said.

"Clearly." Rufus gripped her hand. "I know you want to help, to fix whatever is wrong, but you might make things worse."

"How could they be worse?" Annalise pulled her hand out of his. "Have you spoken with her parents? I ran into them yesterday. They were not the least bit concerned about the fact that she was missing. Obviously she has not been home."

"She is not a child."

"I beg to differ."

"She looks to me to be at least sixteen."

"Seventeen. She told me yesterday over lunch."

"Same age as Joel, and we consider him grown."

"There's seventeen, and then there's seventeen. I don't think you can compare Leah to Joel."

"She doesn't want your help." Rufus held her hand again, squeezing enough to make sure she knew he had no intention of letting go.

"She reached out to me on Sunday. She's unhappy about her family's move."

"That was her parents' decision. She'll have to sort it out with them."

"They don't care. They just drove off without her yesterday. She needs someone to care about her."

Rufus led Annalise back toward the buggy. "It did not sound as if she is ready for that."

"Maybe because she does not expect it," Annalise countered. "Can't you see that?"

He nodded. "I see plenty. I see your beautiful heart. And I see her resistance."

"Where do you suppose she's been?" Annalise relented and climbed up to the bench.

Rufus released the brake. "My guess is she was used to the run of the farm in Pennsylvania."

"She's miles away from her family's farm now. Where was she? Where did she get that kitten, for instance?"

"Stray cats have kittens all the time, and there are any number of empty structures outlying Westcliffe." He paused. "Or *in* Westcliffe. I wonder where she was yesterday morning when the fire broke out?"

"In church. I talked to her myself."

"No." Rufus slowly picked up the reins as he watched Leah turn out of sight. "You talked to her over a crowded, lengthy meal. Can you be certain she was there during the service?"

Annalise turned sideways in the bench and stared, her jaw going slack. "What are you saying, Rufus?"

"I am not saying anything. I am asking questions. It is one of your favorite activities, is it not?"

"This isn't a game." Annalise crossed her arms. "What possible reason would an Amish teenage girl have for starting a fire in an *English* house?"

"I did not say I had all the answers."

Ruth turned up as well for supper on Tuesday night. Annie spotted her as she walked down the long Beiler driveway. She must have parked the Prius up near the road, under the trees, where she would not flaunt it in her mother's face. With eight-year-old Jacob trailing at her side, Annie moseyed up the drive to meet her friend.

"I didn't know you were coming!" Jacob threw himself against his sister's form.

Annie knew what that little boy hug felt like. She loved it.

"*Mamm* asked me on Sunday to come." Ruth picked up the boy under his shoulders and spun him around. "I came straight from work, after I changed my clothes."

"I love it when the whole family is here." Jacob dashed off to the chicken coop.

"We all feel that way, you know," Ruth said to Annie. "You're one of the family."

Annie flicked her eyes in Ruth's direction. "You know I love your family. Every single one of you."

"But not in exactly the same way." Ruth stuck her tongue in one cheek.

Annie kicked a stone. "No, I suppose not."

"So when will the wedding be?"

"I don't know."

"Haven't you and Rufus talked about it?"

"Not since the summer. We agreed I needed to be baptized before we could be serious. It seemed better to just leave the topic alone for a while."

"And now you're baptized."

"Two whole days." They progressed toward the house.

"And he hasn't said a word?"

Annie shook her head. "It's okay if he needs some time."

"Time? Why would he need time? It's not as if he did not see this coming."

"It's all right, Ruth."

"You could ask him. Couples talk about these things together."

"I don't think so. It's better if I wait."

Ruth reached out with an arm to squeeze Annie's shoulder.

"You know you're my sister, whatever happens."

Annie nodded.

"I never thought I would be living with you before Rufus was. He doesn't know what he's missing."

The front door opened, and Sophie stepped out. "Dinner's almost on the table."

Ruth leaned her head in toward Annie's. "Maybe tonight will be the night."

Six

May 1892

Joseph Beiler ran his thumb and forefinger along the brim of his black felt hat on the right side.

"You've been doing that since you were nine years old." Zeke Berkey leaned forward, his jaw thrust toward Joseph and his eyes wide green circles.

Joseph dropped his hand. If anyone knew his old habits, it would be the man who had been his friend for all of his twenty-five years. "I do not know why the bishop sent me on this expedition. He should have let your brother come with you."

"He is too young, and the bishop knows he's a wanderer."

"So are you." Joseph met Zeke's gaze.

Zeke nodded. "That is why you're here. And because you communicate exceptionally well in English."

Joseph looked down the main street of Gassville, Arkansas, then glanced at his and Zeke's horses tied to a post twenty feet away. "Maybe we should not have stopped here. We need land for a new settlement, not a town."

"A town helps." Zeke stood with shoulders back and chest high. "A new settlement needs something to attract settlers. If they know they can get on a train to visit their families in Pennsylvania or Ohio, that will make it easier to settle in Arkansas."

Joseph turned his head both directions to survey the town. "I do not see a depot."

"Must you always be so serious?" Zeke elbowed him. "We will investigate. It may even be fun."

"The bishop gave us a serious mission."

"He did not say we should never smile while we carry out his instructions."

Joseph flashed Zeke a half smirk.

"Now that's better," Zeke said. "We at least need to see what this town has to offer in the way of supplies. And the horses could do with a day or two of rest."

Joseph mightily resisted the urge to finger his hat. After journeying from central Tennessee to north central Arkansas, he could do with a day or two of rest himself.

"Can we afford to sleep in a real bed tonight?" Joseph asked.

Zeke grinned. "I told you to break in that saddle before taking it out on the trail."

"Ridiculing me is not helpful." Joseph reached up with both hands and straightened his hat.

"I will make inquiries about a hotel." Zeke turned to face the store behind them and looked up at its sign. "Denton Emporium. Sounds like a place that should have everything we need. Why don't you have a look around? But do not lose the horses."

"Should we not stay together?" Joseph asked. But he was muttering at Zeke's back.

Joseph sucked in his lips while he looked around to get his bearings. It did not take much to disorient him in new places— another reason the bishop should have sent someone else. The main street was only a few blocks long. Joseph allowed one finger to point from his hip at the businesses he saw as he murmured the words he read on the signs. He glanced at the sun to make sure he had his directions right. Churches, shops, and blacksmiths populated a simple grid of streets, interspersed with stretches of homes. It was not an Amish village, but as far as the *English* went, it did not look too complicated.

Joseph breathed relief.

Across the street a huddle broke up and a young woman emerged, straightened her shoulders, and kicked up road dust.

She was headed straight for Joseph. He turned his head in the direction Zeke had chosen, but his friend had disappeared from sight.

Her dark hair was efficiently bundled under a wide-brimmed purple hat above a lavender calico dress. Joseph could see her dark eyes, though, and whatever she wanted, she meant business. He ran a dry tongue over chapped lips.

"You, sir," she said. "I haven't seen you in town before."

Joseph opened his mouth, but no sound resulted. He had learned his English from doing field work beside *English* men, but he was not accustomed to speaking to *English* women.

"I don't mean to be rude." Now that she had a closer view and could see more than his hat, Maura inspected the oddly dressed young man. "But I must ask you to identify yourself and your business in Gassville."

"I am Joseph Beiler." His violet-blue eyes clouded.

"Byler?" Maura's forehead crinkled. "Are you a relative of the sheriff?"

"Sheriff?" The young man shook his head slowly.

"Yes." Maura pursed her lips. Could this man not answer a simple question? "Have you come to see the sheriff?"

"No, miss. Our people are peaceable."

Maura cocked her head. "If I might ask, what do you mean, 'our people'?"

He gestured to the pocketless black wool coat he was wearing even on a warm day. "The Amish."

"Amish? I thought you gave your name as Byler."

"Yes, Joseph Beiler." He spelled his surname.

"Just a coincidence of name, I suppose." Maura shifted her bag from one hand to the other.

"Perhaps."

"What is that accent I hear in your speech?" Maura asked. "Where are you from?"

"Tennessee."

Maura grunted. "Before that."

"Pennsylvania," he said.

"Before that, then."

"We have been in America since before your Revolutionary War."

"Then you are American, and it was your war, too. And you may as well claim the War of 1812, that horrendous mess between the states, and the whole lot."

"We have nothing to do with war. As I said, we are peaceable."

"Ah yes. So you say. Why do you sound German?"

"Our language is German."

"Mmm." Maura glanced down the street. "What happened to your friend?"

Joseph took a step back. "We are just visiting."

"Is he Amish, too?"

"Yes. Do you not know our people?"

Maura fidgeted with her handbag and extracted the white gloves, which she then clutched in one fist. "I cannot honestly say I have ever heard of the Amish." Though he had found his tongue, this man clearly was nervous, and Maura did not abide nervous people. They always had something to hide.

"Though I find your inquiry of visitors curious even for the *English*," he said, "I will answer your questions. You need only ask."

"You find me impolite." Maura waved her fist and the empty fingers of her gloves fluttered. "Your opinion does not deter me. And I am not English. My people came from Scotland."

He shifted his weight. "I apologize. I used our word for all people who are not of our faith."

771

Maura toggled her chin from side to side. "So you lump us all together, do you?"

He lifted his shoulders and blinked his eyes at the same time.

"Perhaps we deserve it," she said. "I trust our humble businesses will be able to supply your needs."

"I have no doubt we will be comfortable during our brief visit." *Brief.* That was the word she wanted to hear.

"We sometimes get troublemakers." Maura waved her gloves at Joseph again. "I just want you to know that I will not hesitate to fetch Sheriff Byler if I believe there to be trouble on the streets of Gassville."

"You will have no cause on our account," he said. "Byler is an Amish name. Perhaps your sheriff and I have something in common."

Maura laughed. "I'm not sure what your people believe, but I assure you Abraham Byler is a good Christian man. His people came from Tennessee and Mississippi, and he is in church every Sunday. The children in his Sunday school class adore him."

"I only meant to comment on the name," Joseph said. He jutted his chin down the street. "Here comes Zeke."

Joseph hoped this woman had no idea how fast his heart was beating. He had never done more than sell his mother's eggs to an *English* woman who thought keeping layers was too much bother.

"Have you made a friend already?" Zeke asked.

Only Joseph heard the jest in Zeke's tone.

"This is my traveling companion, Ezekiel Berkey," Joseph said. "I am afraid I do not yet know the name of this vigilant resident of Gassville."

She arched her back slightly.

"Perhaps vigilant is too strong," Joseph offered.

Without looking at Joseph, the woman offered a bare hand for Zeke to shake. "I am Maura Woodley. I am pleased to meet you,

Mr. Berkey. Welcome to Gassville."

"And I you." Zeke shook her hand, but his eyes moved to Joseph.

"I will not detain you further." Maura stuffed her gloves back in her bag. "The hotel is not hard to find if you choose to stay. It's just down the street. I'd better get back to my horse and cart."

They watched her leave, the two of them still and somber. She crossed the street and marched down the walkway toward a young mare that matched her hair in color and a cart Joseph had an impulse to repair.

"Vigilant?" Zeke said finally. "Is that not a harsh way to describe someone you just met?"

"It is accurate."

"Did you even go into the emporium?" Zeke asked. "Or did you spend all your time flirting with an *English*?"

Joseph scowled. "I am not flirting with anyone."

"Good. Because Hannah is waiting for you. You know that."

Joseph leaned his head to one side. "Hannah." *Maura.*

"Yes, Hannah. She is *en lieb*. What she sees in you, I will never know, but she is my sister and she wants to marry you."

Joseph knew Hannah believed this to be true. He had not known that she had spoken of it to anyone. When this journey was over, the harvest would come and then the marrying season.

Hannah was sure.

Joseph was not. But he would not tell Zeke.

"I went into a store at the other end of town." Zeke brushed his palms together three times. "It was a dusty place. A man named Twigg runs it."

"What kinds of goods does he carry?"

"I did not stay around long enough to find out. He sounded angry. He was going on about the Denton brothers who run this emporium."

Joseph fingered the brim of his hat. He had not even tried to stop. "Miss Woodley is vigilant because she is fearful of trouble.

Perhaps you have uncovered the source of her fear."

"From what I gather, the Dentons and the Twiggs both have cattle spreads along with their stores." Zeke scratched his clean-shaven chin. "If God has already blessed them so abundantly, what can they have to argue about?"

"Mountain Home is only a few miles," Joseph pointed out. "We could ride there easily."

Zeke looked around. "We are in no hurry. Let's take a room at the hotel here."

Seven

Annie pedaled harder. The five miles between her house in town and the Beiler farm inclined at a deceitfully gradual pace but inclined nevertheless. The mid-September sun was bright but not hot, for which Annie was grateful at the moment.

She was looking for Leah Deitwaller. Three days had passed since Annie encountered Leah's parents. Two days had passed since she and Rufus nearly ran Leah over. And still Leah had not returned home. Annie had heard the news not two hours ago from Beth Stutzman, who was passing on information she had heard from her mother, Edna, who had taken a basket of jams out to the new family earlier in the day. Annie recognized the process of transmission as bordering on gossip, but she had reason to believe the information was accurate. How the Deitwallers could be so unconcerned about their daughter befuddled Annie. Even if Leah were a few months older than she was and technically no longer underage, why would they not be concerned for her safety?

Annie opened her mouth wide and drew in crisp, fall mountain air and then leaned forward to put her weight on one pedal and then the other. She had made this ride enough times in the last year—except during the wintry weather—to know just how much farther her endurance had to carry her before the highway would level out. She breathed in and out, in and out, her athlete's instinct being sure her muscles received sufficient oxygen to perform.

At the edge of the Beiler land, Annie could at last cease pedaling and coast a few yards at a time. If she had to, she would pedal all the way out to the Deitwaller farm, but her intuition told her it would be a waste of time to go that far. Leah was making a point. Not a good point, not a wise point, but a statement to her parents nevertheless. She would not lurk in their backyard.

Obviously Leah had ventured into town, a good ten miles from her parents' home. But Annie doubted she was seeking shelter in town. There simply were not enough empty structures, except new construction. Annie shook off the memory of Rufus's question about Leah's whereabouts on Sunday morning.

Annie slowed alongside a fence and waved at Joel Beiler astride his horse, Brownie, in the middle of his alfalfa field. Joel took the horse to the fence. He pulled a shirtsleeve under the brim of his hat and across his forehead, sopping up perspiration.

"It's a fine day to be outside," Annie said.

Joel nodded. "Outside is where the work is. What brings you out here?"

"I'm looking for someone. Leah Deitwaller."

Joel pointed. "Five miles that way."

"Yes, I know that's where their farm is. I don't think that's where Leah is, though."

Joel gave nothing away in his expression.

"Have you seen her?" Annie sat on her bicycle seat with one foot on the ground and the other on a pedal. "Maybe you thought she was on her way somewhere?"

"Yesterday."

Annie gave a slight gasp. She had not really expected any help from Joel. "Where?"

"Walking through the meadow across the highway."

"Could you tell where she was going?"

Joel stretched his lips into a straight line. "It would just be a guess."

"Then guess! I think she's in trouble, Joel. I'm worried."

He bumped a fist softly against his chin. "She was walking west. Not sure why anyone would go that way, but there is an old mining road."

"Where? Tell me how to find it."

Joel hesitated. "I don't want to hear that you got into trouble, too."

"I'm going to keep looking either way, Joel. Just give me some directions."

He shook his head. "Let me have a few minutes. I left the cart at the south end of the field. I'll go get it."

"I'll meet you there." Annie shifted her weight and put her bicycle in motion.

"Are you sure you know where you're going?" Annie gripped the seat beneath her with both hands.

"Well, if I don't, then it's better I did not send you off on a wild goose chase by yourself."

"But do you?"

"I can't promise Leah is going to be there."

Joel swung as hard a left turn as Annie had ever seen anyone make in a horse and cart. She refused to slide on the bench.

"Fine. Just show me where you saw her yesterday and we'll figure it out from there."

Annie scanned the meadow on both sides of the narrow road that Joel had found. It was barely more than a horse trail, but she could see how in Westcliffe's history it would have been an avenue between the mines and the population. Summer was waning. Around her the meadow already had begun to brown. Leah's dress would be bright—a rich blue and a purple apron if she was wearing the same dress Annie had last seen her in. But where on this meadow could Leah have found shelter? Soon home heating

777

systems would go on at night. Even a dedicated camper would look for a way to keep warm.

"I think we found her." Joel slowed the horse.

Annie swung around to look out the other side of the cart, and there was the patch of blue and purple. Leah sat cross-legged on the ground with her head hanging almost to her lap.

Leah was crying, Annie realized. She put up a hand to signal Joel to stop then carefully exited the cart with no sudden movement. Annie glanced over her shoulder when the creak above the left wheel revealed Joel had left the cart as well. Leah's shoulders rose and fell with her sobs. Annie took one slow step at a time toward the girl. Finally, she was close enough to kneel beside her.

"Leah."

The girl's head snapped up. "What are you doing here? Can't a body have a moment of peace?"

Annie licked her lips. "It doesn't look like peace to me."

"I didn't ask you."

"Leah, let me help you." Behind Annie, Joel followed but kept his distance.

"Tell me how to take a train to Pennsylvania." Leah's eyes dared. "Get me a job in that shop you work in so I can earn train fare. You want to help me? That's what you can do."

Annie sat on the ground and said nothing.

"I suppose you want me to go to my parents." Leah sniffed.

"We could talk about it, at least."

Leah picked up a letter from her lap and waved it. "I walked into town yesterday and went to the post office. I asked if any mail was addressed to me, not to my parents, and I got this."

The letter bore a firm male hand and was written in Pennsylvania Dutch.

"Who is it from?" Annie asked quietly.

"From the only person on earth who really loves me."

"I see." Annie understood now why Leah was so desperate to return to Pennsylvania.

"He wants me to come back. We want to get married."

"You're only seventeen."

Leah rolled her eyes. "You're baptized Amish. You have to know that seventeen and Amish is not like seventeen and *English*."

It was still young, but Annie choked back her words.

"Don't say anything if you're just going to sound like my mother."

"Have you had other letters? Have you showed one to your mother?"

Leah expelled breath. "I tried. She tore it up without even taking it out of the envelope."

"I'm sorry." Annie pulled her knees up under her chin. "What if I asked you to come home with me?"

Leah's eyes widened. "To your house in town?"

Annie nodded. It would be a first step. If she could get Leah sheltered and cared for, perhaps the girl would agree to further conversation.

"It's a trick. Don't think Amish girls don't recognize tricks."

"I never said—"

Leah was on her feet and sprinting toward Brownie and the cart.

"Wait!" Annie called.

Joel sprang into action, too. But Leah had too much of a head start on them. She leaped into the cart and picked up the reins. Brownie responded to the sound she made and the signals of the reins and began a rapid trot.

Rufus looked at the newspaper folded neatly on the coffee shop table he had chosen to occupy. It was just the local Westcliffe paper, in print for over a hundred years. Rufus thought of it like the *Budget*, the Amish newspaper out of Sugarcreek, Ohio, that congregations around the nation read. It was full of news and information that might pique the curiosity of members of the community but would not interest outsiders. Rufus nudged the paper out of his way and set his coffee down.

A shadow crossed the table and Rufus looked up. "Hello, Tom."

"I'm glad you could meet." Tom sat across from Rufus. "How are you for work? I might have a lead for you."

Rufus cleared his throat. "Well, the fire has caused a setback, and you already know David has no orders for me right now."

"This could be steady work over the winter."

"I usually try to build hope chests when construction slows down."

"But you have no orders."

"God will provide."

Tom sipped coffee. "Could God provide by giving you a full-time job?"

"Full-time?"

"For a few months. A friend of mine in Cañon City keeps a carpenter on his staff, but the guy got hurt—on his own time. This is nothing dangerous. But he won't be back to work for four months."

Rufus turned the pages of a mental calendar. "Cañon City is too far. How would I get there and back every day?"

"It's not all in Cañon City. The jobs are spread around the southwest part of the state. He remodels apartment buildings, office complexes, and small hotels. You'd be installing ready-made cabinets. It's all indoors."

Rufus twisted his lips. "I don't know, Tom. I don't see how that could work."

"Granted, it would be a change for you. But my buddy's a good guy. Jeff would pay you well. And he would put you up near each job. The money could get you through the winter."

"Sleep away from home?" Among the *English*? Rufus had built cabinets for many *English* homes. Each one was a work of beauty that brought glory to God. Working as an employee of an *English* had never tempted him, though. He did not want to fall into thinking that any work was beneath him, but the thought of separating from his family—and Annalise—fed his reluctance.

"You could do this in your sleep, Rufus." Tom tilted his head back and drank the last of his coffee. "It's honest work. It's temporary, something to get you through a rough patch."

Annie lurched toward the moving buggy. "Leah!"

Joel was four strides ahead of her and broke into a sprint. If it were not for her dress, Annie could have caught him, even passed him. The rhythms of running track in high school and college still rose from her muscles when called upon, and she felt the adrenaline now. But while Annie had to use her hands to lift her hem out of the dirt, Joel pumped his limbs and ran freely.

Leah did not look back as Annie and Joel chased her up the old rutted road.

Then with a thud, Annie hit the ground. Though she caught herself on her hands, the damage was done in her right ankle. Wincing, she sat up. Even Joel was slowing down. If anything, Leah was driving faster.

Joel finally stopped and turned to look at Annie. She pushed up to her feet and started limping toward him, testing her ankle with each step.

"I'm sorry," Annie said once they were close enough to speak. "I had no idea she would do something like this."

Joel offered an arm to Annie. "How bad is your foot?"

"I used to run races on worse injuries, but that's been a few years." Leaning on his arm, she was able to move at a steady pace, but the irregular terrain made speed challenging. "I hope she won't hurt Brownie."

It was an hour later when they reached the highway and found the horse, still attached to the cart, grazing contentedly.

Leah Deitwaller was nowhere in sight.

Eight

Annie lifted her right ankle while Ruth slid a pillow beneath it and gently pressed an ice pack against the lump. "Thanks for driving me out here."

"I was coming for Sunday dinner with my family anyway." Ruth settled at the end of the couch. "Do you need anything else?"

Annie shook her head. "I can't believe I sprained my ankle chasing a buggy."

"You're lucky it's not broken."

"Lucky?" Annie smiled. "Have you become so *English* as to believe in luck?"

A smile escaped Ruth's lips. "*Gottes wille*. You are blessed that your ankle is not broken."

"It's not really too bad anymore. It's been three days, after all."

"Don't rush the healing. It takes time."

"Yes, Nurse Beiler." Annie pulled an afghan off the back of the sofa and spread it over her lap and legs. "I'm glad Brownie and the buggy were all right, but I'm worried about Leah Deitwaller."

"You can't help someone who doesn't want help," Ruth said.

"Oh, she wants help, all right. She just wants it on her terms."

Ruth checked the position of the ice pack against Annie's

ankle. "It amounts to the same thing."

"I wish I understood what her parents are thinking. Do you think they even know about the young man in Pennsylvania?"

"That's hard to say. Many Amish couples keep their feelings to themselves until they are sure that the way is clear for them to marry."

"But surely Leah would have told her parents why she did not want to move to Colorado. What if they don't know this man? What if he is from another district and they don't know that he would be a perfectly wonderful husband for their daughter?"

Ruth cocked her head.

Annie threw her hands up. "I know, I know. I'm meddling. Trying to solve a problem that is not mine to solve."

"Well," Ruth said, "I'm relieved we don't have to have that conversation again."

"You probably think I am as hardheaded as Leah."

"I didn't say that."

"If I didn't think it would hurt my foot to move that pillow, I would throw it at you."

Ruth laughed. "No more acts of *English* aggression from you. You are a baptized Amish now."

The door between the dining room and kitchen creaked open and eight-year-old Jacob appeared lugging a bag of ice. "We're going to make ice cream in the barn. Rufus says I can turn the crank."

Towering over Jacob, Rufus stood with a pan of cooked mixture.

"I love homemade ice cream." Annie met Rufus's pleased expression.

"You won't chase any runaway horses while I'm in the barn, will you?" Rufus's violet-blue eyes teased a warning.

"I think I've learned that lesson."

She watched as the two brothers—the eldest and youngest of the Beiler children, more than twenty years apart—passed through the room and out the front door.

"They'll be back for salt," Ruth predicted. "Rufus never remembers it."

"I know," Annie said.

"Speaking of Amish couples," Ruth said, "has Rufus said anything about making things official?"

Annie had thought he would move their relationship along a little more quickly now.

"Well?" Ruth prodded. "What's he thinking?"

"I wish I knew."

Rufus sent Jacob back to the house for the salt and carefully poured into the metal canister the mixture his sister Sophie had cooked on the stove. By the time his little brother returned, Rufus had the blade fixed in the vanilla goop and the lid on the canister. Together they lowered the can onto the bolt in the bottom of the wooden barrel and fastened it in place.

Jacob began to crank. What the boy lacked in physical strength he made up for in determination. Rufus decided to let Jacob give the task his best effort and see how long he lasted. Eventually, as the ice cream thickened, Jacob would need help.

The barn was the place where Rufus had first met Annalise—who of course had not known what she was getting herself into by turning up stranded among the Amish with her *English* life in a convoluted mess. He had driven her to town, where she hoped to find a ride to a location that met her expectations for civilization, someplace with a rental car business, or at least a bus station.

Only she had decided to stay overnight at Mo's motel. And then a few nights. And then half the summer.

And then she bought a house in Westcliffe and began coming to church.

Certainly Rufus was never sorry she had been so reluctant to leave. Now she seemed to have long ago given up any thought of returning to live in Colorado Springs.

She was expecting a proposal, and he was no less anxious to offer one than she was to receive it. But Annalise had given up a personal fortune to join the Amish. How could he ask her to marry him while the bottom was falling out of his business?

"Peach," Jacob said.

Rufus roused. "I'm sorry?"

"We should have made peach. It's Annalise's favorite."

"That it is." Rufus smiled. Even his little brother knew Annalise well.

The job Tom's friend offered him was only through the winter. Would it be so bad?

One by one, Ruth's family members wandered out to the barn, where she knew they would take turns cranking the ice cream. By now melted ice would be making a mess. Soon the mixture would go into the freezer so it would be ready after a light supper. Ruth would have gone out as well except that Annalise had dozed off, and Ruth did not want her to wake and find herself alone. Ruth had found her mother's mending basket and put her hands to good use while Annalise softly snored.

When she heard the purr of a motor, Ruth sat erect and looked out the front window. She did not recognize the vehicle, a gray Mitsubishi that looked to be a few years old.

But she recognized the man who emerged from the driver's side and spied the front porch.

Ruth pushed the mending basket aside, glanced at Annalise, and crossed the room before Bryan Nichols could ring the bell. She stepped out on the porch. At the last minute she decided to pull the main door closed before shutting the screen door behind her. Taking the seven steps down to the yard, Ruth looked toward the open barn door. Laughter greeted her ears and she was grateful that, for the moment, her family was absorbed in the simplicity of making ice cream.

Because they certainly would not understand the complexity of a visit from Bryan Nichols any more than Elijah Capp had understood her accidental meeting with Bryan on the trail. She put a finger to her lips and motioned for him to follow her around the far side of the house.

"What are you doing here?" Ruth asked when they were out of sight from the barn.

"I wanted to see where you live." Bryan looked around, puzzled.

"But why?" Her heart pounded. "And I don't actually live here."

"I asked someone, and they said this was the Beiler farm."

"It is." Ruth hid her nervous hands in the folds of her calf-length corduroy skirt. "My family lives here. I just came to spend Sunday with them."

"What's going on, Ruth? Why is it a big deal if I drop by?"

She blew her breath out. "It's complicated."

"I'm a college graduate and a firefighter. I understand complicated things."

"Amish complicated is different." His green eyes made something puddle deep in her gut. "Did you need something?"

"I just wanted to tell you I enjoyed running into you the other day. Maybe we could plan ahead next time and enjoy the trail together. And then I could buy you dinner."

She swallowed with deliberation. Was an *English* man asking her for a date?

The sound of a metal feed pail knocking against the side of the house made Ruth jump, though she had done nothing to feel guilty about.

"*Mamm!*"

"I thought you were in the house." Franey Beiler looked from Ruth to Bryan. "Would you like to introduce your friend?"

"This is Bryan," Ruth said. "Rufus and I met him last week out at the house that burned. He is a firefighter."

"Oh. Thank you for your service." Franey set her empty bucket in a stack of six others. "Would you like to come inside? We are about to have sandwiches and homemade ice cream."

Ruth's eyes widened. Her mother was one of the most hospitable people Ruth had ever known, even toward the *English*. But Bryan inside the house? If he were to repeat his invitation where someone might hear it—well, Ruth did not want to imagine the scene that might follow. Silently pleading, she caught Bryan's eyes and shook her head almost imperceptibly.

Annie woke to the clatter of Beilers claiming their front porch. Franey and Eli. Sophie and Lydia. Joel and Jacob.

She loved every one of them. And she knew they loved her. If Rufus did not ask her to marry him, she still had a spot in the Beiler family for as long as she wanted it. If Franey and Eli knew what was in their son's heart, they would not say.

Gottes wille.

They tumbled into the house, Jacob prancing around his father, who carried the canister of ice cream.

"Can't I just have a taste?" Jacob begged. "Just one spoonful?"

Eli shook his head. "It's too soft. And you don't want to spoil your supper."

Annie sat up and tested her ankle against the floor. Perceiving no objection to bearing weight, she stood and moved cautiously toward the door. Where were Ruth and Rufus?

Ruth stood in the long drive, speaking to someone through a vehicle window. Rufus stood at the base of the front porch steps, his arms crossed behind his back in that way that Annie knew meant he was watching the scene carefully. She stepped out on the porch.

"What's going on?" she asked.

Rufus looked up the stairs at her. "An *English* man came by to see Ruth."

"Here?"

Rufus nodded.

"You don't approve," Annie said.

"It is not for me to approve or disapprove."

"But you don't approve."

"I don't think he knew any better," Rufus said.

"Ruth would not have invited him here."

"No, I don't believe so."

"Then what is there to disapprove of?"

"You are the one who insists I disapprove."

Annie watched Ruth for a few seconds. "It looks to me that she is being polite, just as she would have learned from your parents."

"I have no doubt."

Abruptly Annie realized that whatever troubled Rufus had nothing to do with his sister. "What's wrong, Rufus?"

He shook his head. "It's nothing."

Annie knew she would get nothing else out of him tonight. But she hated the way that truth twisted her stomach.

Nine

May 1892

Joseph lay on his side, eyes closed. "Zeke?"

No response came, and Joseph wrestled with the moment when he might have sunk back into a deep sleep. He sensed the vague presence of sunlight beyond his eyelids. "Zeke."

Joseph pushed up on one elbow. He had been more than agreeable to a night in a hotel, despite the stares that came with it, but Zeke had insisted on having their own room rather than conserve cash by sharing with two *English* men. Joseph raked fingers through his bowl-cut hair and wondered how long ago Zeke had left the room. Swinging his feet to the floor forced Joseph upright and gave him a view straight out the window. The sun blazed halfway up the sky. Joseph had not slept so late since he was a boy. He slapped the thick hotel mattress in blame.

With the heels of his hands, Joseph wiped sleep from his eyes, and then he reached for his clothes. No telling what Zeke would be up to by now.

Joseph dressed, combed his hair, donned his hat, and ignored his hunger. The clerk in the lobby reported that Mr. Berkey had been down for breakfast more than two hours ago and then left the building without indicating his intentions.

Unfortunately for Joseph, the hotel's small kitchen was now closed for breakfast and at least two hours from opening for a midday meal.

He wandered into the sunlight, considering whether it was more urgent to check to see that their horses had been well cared for at the stables or to track Zeke. He opted for Zeke. The stablemen were more likely to look after the horses adequately than Zeke was to stay out of trouble.

Self-conscious, Joseph made his way down Gassville's main street looking through plate glass windows and open shop doors. Finding one Amish man among all these *English* could not prove too difficult a task. Joseph paused outside John Twigg's Mercantile, remembering Zeke's remark the day before about the man's anger and deciding not to enter. He continued a methodical yet subtle search for his friend. Eventually his walk took him back to the Denton Emporium. Instinct told Joseph to push the door open.

A number of people milled around the shop, some with lists, others inspecting the textiles. Zeke stood near the counter at the back of the store.

With the *English* woman.

"Oh, there you are." Zeke gestured for Joseph to step to the counter.

Joseph shifted his eyes from Zeke to Miss Woodley and back again, nodding at them both noncommittally.

"I came in to inquire what sorts of supplies the Dentons can order," Zeke said. "Miss Woodley overheard and has been kind enough to tell me how resourceful the owners are at procuring whatever one might want."

"I see," Joseph said. "Our needs would be simple, of course. *Guder mariye*, Miss Woodley." Good morning.

"I trust you rested well."

The pleasantry in Miss Woodley's eyes seemed sincere. Perhaps with some reflection overnight she decided that Zeke and Joseph were no threat to the fragile peace of Gassville.

A ruckus in front of the store drew Zeke and a few others to the window.

"It's Twigg!" someone called out.

"That does not look like a man with all his wits," Zeke said.

Joseph glanced at Miss Woodley, who gripped the edge of the counter with hands covered in white gloves.

"Does he have a gun?" The question came from Lee Denton, behind the counter.

Zeke shook his head. "I don't see one."

Joseph would have preferred Zeke to stay out of whatever was about to happen. There would be no explaining this to the bishop.

"He's standing in the middle of the street with his arms crossed," Zeke reported.

"He could be hiding a gun," Lee Denton said.

When the voice boomed from the street, Joseph startled.

"Denton, you fool!" hollered John Twigg. "You are hiring people to steal from my store so you can sell those goods yourself. You idiots! Did you think I would not figure it out?"

Joseph moved toward Zeke, wanting to pull him back. In the process, he glimpsed John Twigg, bareheaded and—as far as Joseph could see—unarmed. His face flamed with fury.

Maura heard voices outside yelling back at John Twigg, but she could not tell whose. If she got her hands on whoever was inciting John, she would throttle the culprit. A person would have to be half-insane to take up with John.

The man had lost all sense of reason. He was not always like this. Belle had been enamored of John for so long that she refused to acknowledge the turn in him. Maura worried what might become of Belle if she really did marry John Twigg.

"What happened to Walter?" someone asked.

Maura's stomach lurched, and she released her grip on the counter to turn and face the commotion. "He was sweeping the sidewalk out there a few minutes ago."

"Well, I don't see him now."

Before she could move to the front of the store to look out the window for herself, a *click* behind the counter made her gasp.

The sound of a shooter readying a pistol.

Lee and Ing Denton both stood behind the counter of their emporium with pistols in their hands.

"What are you doing?" she demanded. "That will not solve anything."

"If he has a gun, we have to be ready," Lee said.

"You already asked if he had a gun," Maura said. "Mr. Berkey informs us he does not."

Lee shook his head. "He said he did not see one. That's not the same."

Another *click*. Another pistol cocked.

"Ing, no." Maura slapped the counter. "This is not the way."

"He's the crazy man." Ing Denton nudged his brother out from behind the counter. Lee cocked a third pistol and led the way with a gun in each hand. Ing followed with his. Customers stepped back to clear their path to the front of the store.

Maura swallowed hard and followed them. "Has anyone spotted Walter?" She stumbled on the hem of her skirt and looked down at her shoes.

In that moment, the shots rang out.

"It's Walter!" a woman cried. "They've shot Walter in the heart."

Joseph pushed past Lee and Ing and Zeke and even Miss Woodley, oblivious to danger now, and saw Walter run past the front of the store with his hand over his chest. The boy reminded him of his younger brother, Little Jake, both gangly and fair haired, and his protective instinct kicked in.

He grabbed Walter, who was bellowing now. If the boy was screaming and running, Joseph wondered, how badly could he be hurt? Yet blood spurted between the fingers clasped over his chest.

"Make him lie down." The instruction came from Miss Woodley, but Joseph agreed. The gunshots had stopped, and even if they had not, Joseph would not abandon Miss Woodley and Walter at a time of need. Being a person of peace did not mean withholding compassion.

It was easy enough to lay Walter on the sidewalk he had been sweeping only moments ago. Maura Woodley knelt beside the boy on the other side.

"We must move his hand and see the damage." Maura's face crunched in on itself.

Walter was still thrashing his legs, but he offered no resistance when Joseph moved to pry the boy's fingers apart. Beneath them, he found no wound.

Then Maura held the fingers of Walter's left hand. "Why, he's been hit in the knuckles."

Joseph wiped the boy's knuckles with his shirtsleeve then leaned back on his heels and expelled his pent-up breath. "It looks a lot worse than it is."

"Thank you. You risked your life for my cousin."

Joseph drank in her dark eyes for the first time. All he could think of was that he hoped someone would have done the same for Little Jake. He grabbed his shirt at the shoulder seam and yanked. The sleeve came loose, and he wrapped it around Walter's bleeding hand.

"He should see the doctor," Maura said, her hands helping to wrap her cousin's fingers.

"Of course." Joseph looked up and down the street. "Which way?"

Zeke was suddenly behind him. "I know the way."

Ezekiel Berkey had not been in Gassville any longer than Joseph Beiler, but at the moment Joseph was glad for Zeke's propensity to snoop wherever he went. Joseph's eyes settled on John Twigg, and he pointed. "Someone should help him, too."

John Twigg lay in the street, bleeding from his head like a stuck pig.

"I'll go for the doctor." Zeke scooped up Walter and put him on his feet. "Follow me, Joseph."

"Why did they shoot me?" Walter asked. "And I know where the doctor is better than strangers."

"Just go, Walter," Maura said. "Let them look after you. Don't worry about John Twigg right now."

"I've seen enough hog butcherings," Walter said, "to know that a mad animal takes a long time to die. John Twigg is gonna be like that, I just know."

"Hush, Walter." Maura turned to Joseph. "If Doc Denton is not in his office, try Dr. Lindsay. He's farther away, though."

"I saw his shingle," Mr. Berkey said.

"Hurry!"

Two strangers, whom she had suspected of ill will only yesterday, had custody of Walter. The boy would be fine. For John Twigg's sake, though, Maura hoped Mr. Berkey knew the town as well as he claimed. Around the angry shopkeeper, a few people had realized the severity of his wound and stood and pointed. No one stepped forward to help him, and neither did Maura. No human being, not even John Twigg, deserved Walter's comparison to a hog butchering. But no one could help him—perhaps not even one of the doctors—and nothing Maura did would change that.

The street fell silent as the crowd realized that the Denton-Twigg feud had taken a fatal twist.

It was Belle Mooney that worried Maura now.

Ten

"Are you sure?" Outside his hardware store on Main Street on Tuesday morning, Tom Reynolds crossed his arms, puzzled.

Annie answered without hesitation. "I'll pay you twice your usual rate for taxi service."

Tom waved the offer away. "That's not necessary. If you've made up your mind, I'll take you."

"I promise not to tie up your time for a minute longer than necessary." Annie straightened the bib of her black apron. "Do you know where the Deitwaller farm is?"

"I have a vague idea."

"Good enough for me."

"I'll pull my truck around."

They found the farm thirty minutes later. Annie scanned for signs that someone was home. The land was farther out and more isolated than the Beilers', reminding Annie that most of the Amish in Custer County were farther from town. The day called for no scheduled sewing or quilting gatherings among the women, so unless Eva Deitwaller was making a visit, she would be home. As Tom eased his red pickup to a stop outside the home, Annie saw the family's buggy parked at the edge of the yard.

"You can still change your mind," Tom said.

Annie shook her head. "Wait here, please. I won't be long."

She approached the front door, set her jaw, and knocked.

Mrs. Deitwaller came to the screen door.

"Hello," Annie said. "I wonder if I might come in and talk to you." Amish hospitality would make it difficult for Eva to send her away. For extra assurance, Annie raised a hand to the door handle. Eva complied by unlatching the hook and eye.

Annie tried not to glance around the front room in too curious a manner. The invitation to sit that she hoped for did not come, so she held her hands together calmly and determined not to sound aggressive.

"I wondered if Leah is home," Annie said. "I thought I might invite her to visit the Beilers with me. They have daughters around her age."

"We know who the Beilers are." Mrs. Deitwaller pulled a dish towel off her shoulder and wiped her hands.

"Yes, of course. Sophie and Lydia are lovely girls. I thought Leah might enjoy spending more time with them."

"Well, she's not here."

"Oh?" Annie's fingers twitched. "Perhaps I could leave a note."

Mrs. Deitwaller shrugged. "If you're fishing to know whether Leah has come home, you can stop right there. She hasn't."

Annie tried to look sympathetic. "You must be concerned about her."

"She's a headstrong child. Always has been."

"But. . .where is she staying? You must be wondering if she is safe."

"No need to tell me what I must be wondering."

Annie's right forefinger began to tap. "I'm sure if the two of you sat down and talked about your differences, you could find a way through them."

"Just what do you know of our differences?"

Annie moistened her lips. "I know Leah was. . .unenthusiastic about the move to Colorado."

"We're her parents. We know what's best for her."

Annie's tongue formed sounds faster than she could stop it now. "Leah has been gone more than a week. Isn't it best for her to be somewhere safe, with people who care for her, who will listen to her?"

Even under Eva Deitwaller's long dress, Annie saw her shoes move to shoulder width apart. One hand went to a hip.

"I'll thank you not to come in here with your *English* ways," Mrs. Deitwaller said. "You're barely baptized."

Annie's spine straightened. "I gave a lot of thought and prayer to my baptism."

"What I hear is that you give a lot of thought to Rufus Beiler."

Warmth rose through Annie's face. "I was baptized because I want to be Amish. Because God called me to be Amish."

"You don't have any idea what you are getting into." Eva scoffed.

Balled into fists, Annie's hands moved to her sides, where she hid them in the folds of her skirt. "That's not true. I studied with the bishop. I worship regularly with the congregation."

"Yes, well, time will tell. But when it comes to Leah, you know nothing. She lives in her imagination. You have no idea what kind of trouble she is capable of causing."

"She seems quite sincere to me," Annie said. "She certainly is of an age to fall in love and think about her future."

"She has always made up stories of how she would like things to be rather than how they really are."

"Why would her young man write to her if he did not share her feelings?"

"I can assure you my husband will put a stop to that." Eva waved one hand. "Certainly you can see Leah does not have the maturity for that kind of relationship."

Annie dug her fists into her hips. This was going nowhere. If Leah and her mother would have a reasonable, calm conversation, they might both learn some things about each other. "I only want to help. Everyone deserves to be happy."

"You're as naive as Leah. May God help you both to come to your senses." Mrs. Deitwaller opened the door and tilted her head out toward the yard.

Annie stifled her response and marched, head up, out to Tom's truck. Inside, she slammed the door.

Tom raised a questioning eye.

"In her eyes, I'll always be taken for *English*. But she's wrong."

"Your young man was just here." Mrs. Weichert bent at the waist to rearrange the assortment of Amish jams on the shelf nearest the counter.

Annie tucked her small purse on the shelf under the counter and pushed it to the back. "Did he say what he wanted?"

"No, but he offered to unload my truck."

"I was going to do that."

"I know." Mrs. Weichert gave a slight smile. "He's just waiting for you, dear. Check the alley."

Annie hoped her *kapp* was on straight. She had slouched in Tom's truck all the way back into town, sullen and silent. She crossed the length of the shop and went into the back room. The door to the alley was propped open, and a few seconds later Rufus stepped through with a pair of upholstered dining chairs.

He set them down. "Ah. You're back. Mrs. Weichert was not sure why you were a few minutes late."

"I should have come in earlier instead of wasting my time." She scuffled toward the door. "Is there much more?"

He set the chairs beside a tower of six boxes. "This is the last of it. It's all from an estate sale in Pueblo."

"We almost always find a few things we can use."

"Annalise, why did you say you wasted your time?" He stood with one hand on a chair.

She hesitated.

"I know Leah Deitwaller has been on your mind a lot."

Annie idly stroked the faded fabric and settled her hand next to his. "If she is on her mother's mind, you would never know it. I was just there. I'm worried about Leah, but now I'm starting to wonder if her parents could be charged with neglect."

"Are you thinking of making such an allegation yourself?"

"No." She looked up into his violet-blue eyes. "I'm just grateful that the first Amish woman I met was your mother and not Leah's. We might not be standing here right now if it had been Eva Deitwaller."

"I know you want to help." He covered her fingers with his hand. "And I'm sorry if Leah's mother was harsh with you."

Annie rolled her eyes. "But I should mind my own business."

"There may be more to the Deitwallers' story than we know."

"Or Leah may be a confused young woman who is doing something foolish, even dangerous. Shouldn't somebody care?"

He squeezed her fingers, and she looked again at his face. His lips parted, as if he were about to tell her something. He closed them and moistened them without saying anything.

"Rufus, what's wrong? I'm sorry. I haven't been paying any attention to what might be bothering you."

He shook his head. "I just need to work out some business matters."

"A new project?"

He shrugged one shoulder. "Something a little different. I'm not sure it's right for me."

Rufus tugged on her hand, removing it from the chair and pulling her toward him. He glanced into the shop and then out into the alley before tilting his head to her upturned face and letting his lips linger on hers.

Annie tingled from head to toe. Rufus hardly ever kissed her, certainly not in a place where someone might walk in.

At the moment, though, she did not care. She placed her hands on his broad shoulders and deepened the kiss.

When her shift in the shop was over, Annie walked home and circled her house to the back porch. All afternoon she agitated first over Leah and then over Rufus. Leah was likely to do something rash—probably already had. Rufus likely had never made a rash decision in his life. But there was something he was not saying, something his kiss was meant to tell her.

Before going into the kitchen, Annie checked the small cupboard on the back porch where she kept a basket of garden vegetables. She could make herself a warm supper and have something waiting for Ruth later. And in the meantime, Annie would figure out what to do about Leah.

The basket was empty.

No, the basket was gone.

Ruth must have taken it inside, Annie reasoned. Then she reminded herself that the basket had been there just that morning. Annie had picked green beans before flagging down Tom Reynolds, and Ruth had left for the clinic while Annie was still in the garden.

She turned around and surveyed the yard. Then she descended the three steps and paced over to the vegetable patch. The produce had been thinning for several weeks, but Annie was sure she had bypassed a zucchini plant and one beanpole this morning because she judged she could wait another day or two before picking.

Someone had raided her garden, and Annie was pretty sure she knew who it was.

She smiled. This meant Leah Deitwaller could not be far away.

Rufus pulled open the door of the trailer that housed Kramer Construction and stepped inside the office. Karl Kramer's administrative assistant aimed her thumb toward the inner office, and Rufus stepped past her desk.

In the inner office, the foreman of Kramer Construction rose from behind Karl's desk. "Thanks for coming by."

"It is my privilege." Rufus dipped his hat. "Do you have news from Karl?"

"He has asked me to handle things for a while." The foreman gestured that Rufus should sit in the chair beside the desk.

Rufus widened his eyes. "A while? Is he well?"

"Karl is fine. He just decided to spend more time with his father in Virginia."

"I thought perhaps the fire would bring him home."

"He was angry, but that's a matter for the insurance companies now. The buyers are not sure they want to build again, and their lawyer says that our failure to meet the contract date allows them to change their minds."

"But surely under the circumstances—"

The foreman shook his head. "We're all taking a hit on this, Rufus. I wanted to tell you in person that Karl is not planning to start any new projects over the winter. He wanted to be sure you knew it was nothing personal."

Eleven

Annie straightened the stack of hard-to-find books at the back of the shop, wiping dust from each volume with a cotton rag. Some gems came through the shop, but no one would ever know it unless they stumbled on a volume on a lark of a summer's weekend. Soon the weather would turn cold, and fewer people would be happening on Westcliffe because they were out for a drive.

Once, Annie had mentioned to Mrs. Weichert that it would be an easy thing to set up a website and engage in e-commerce. If they listed with a few trade organizations and invested in some minimal online advertising, people looking for particular rare books could find the shop on the Internet. These books could go to interested buyers rather than get trucked to the Salvation Army in Pueblo, where who knows what happened to them next.

Mrs. Weichert had waved off the idea. She was content with her income and reasoned that dealers in the region knew where she was. If they couldn't be bothered to drive out to her shop, then they must not be all that curious about her inventory in any given month.

Annie had to admit it was probably just as well. Living in

Westcliffe for the last year, well away from her former high-tech life as an innovative software designer, had not completely quelled her entrepreneurial urges. But it was better for her not to be tempted to begin yet another business with computers at its heart.

With one last swipe of the rag, Annie resisted the urge to pick up a book with a faded red binding and open it. If it did not sell soon, though, she would ask for it. Its title promised a wealth of information on nineteenth-century population shifts in western Tennessee and Arkansas. In the last few months, Annie had developed a fascination with stories of people who had taken great risks that changed their lives. All the people she had known in Colorado Springs would have laughed at her curious interest, but she did not care. Wasn't it better to take a risk than just let life happen to you by never wondering what else was out there?

"I'll take those bags of clothes down to the thrift store now," Annie said.

"Thank you." Mrs. Weichert was counting bills at the cash register. "They'll try to pay you, but I don't want their money."

One in each hand, Annie hefted two black plastic garbage bags by the knots tied at the tops.

Mrs. Weichert crossed the store and picked up the red volume Annie had been eyeing. She stuck it under Annie's arm. "You might as well take this. I can tell you want to read it, and it will be next to impossible to sell."

"Thank you." It was not the first book Mrs. Weichert had stuck under Annie's arm after finding her picking it up repeatedly during her shifts.

"You can go on home after that," Mrs. Weichert said. "It looks like rain. No one will be coming in."

"All right. Thanks."

"Don't forget you have tomorrow off. My daughter will be here to help."

Mrs. Weichert held the door open, and Annie stepped out onto the sidewalk. They always took the clothes that turned up in Mrs. Weichert's shop to the thrift store three doors down. Sometimes she bought the odds and ends of an estate sale, and getting the dishes or small furniture she wanted meant she also had to take old clothes.

Vintage clothes, Annie had once corrected her employer. If they just set up one rack in the shop, she was sure they could sell them. Once again her entrepreneurial streak had raised its head, and once again Mrs. Weichert had no interest.

"What delights have you brought us today?" Carlene, perched on a stool behind the counter at the thrift store, raised her eyes and smiled.

Annie liked Carlene's natural warmth. "I'm afraid I didn't even look this time. I hope you find something worth your while."

"I remember how you used to come in here for clothes when you first came to town. You had a good eye for value."

Annie dropped the two bags behind the counter and gestured toward her Amish dress. "Now look at me."

Carlene stood up and hit a button on the cash register. "Let me give you something to take to Mrs. Weichert."

Annie raised both hands. "You know she won't take it."

"I'm not running a charity shop, you know."

"Well, neither is she." Annie scanned the shop. "Maybe I'll have a look around for old time's sake."

"There's some nice bedding in the back if you need any blankets for the winter."

Knowing that Mrs. Weichert did not expect her back, Annie was in no hurry. She ran her hand along a pile of sweaters then opened a blank journal. Farther down the aisle, she picked up a backpack that looked brand new and started checking the zippers and clasps. Voices hissed from the other side of the shelf.

"Why do I have to get a sleeping bag here?" a small boy whined.

The voice sounded like its owner was no older than Jacob Beiler. Annie dipped her head slightly to try to see him through the shelving.

"Because you are the one who lost your old sleeping bag. I'm not paying good money to replace it with something brand new."

"But I didn't!"

"I washed it and hung it on the line myself," the child's mother said. "It would be just like you to drag it off somewhere and get it dirty again. And then you didn't want to tell me the truth because you thought you would get in trouble. One way or another you're going to learn your lesson."

"But Mom," the boy insisted, "I didn't take it off the line. I'm telling you the truth. Why won't you believe me?"

"We're finished talking about this. The only reason I'm buying you another sleeping bag at all is because you were invited on that camping trip."

"I don't want to go if I have to take this dumb little kid's sleeping bag."

"You promised your friend you would go, and you will."

The woman nudged her son's shoulder toward the front of the store. She may not have believed the boy's protests, but Annie did.

"She's not here," Mrs. Weichert said when Ruth ducked her head into the antiques shop looking for Annalise. "I sent her to the thrift store and then told her she didn't need to come back."

"Thank you, Mrs. Weichert."

Ruth paced down the sidewalk to the thrift store, pulled its door open, and nearly tripped over Annalise.

"Ruth, what are you doing here?"

"I'm finished for the day, and I hear you are, too."

Annalise nodded. "I'm still not used to seeing you in scrubs."

Ruth tugged at the hem of her shirt. "I'm not sure I'm used to wearing them, either."

"They look comfortable."

"They are." Ruth grinned. "I'm in the mood for a sandwich from the bakery. Want one?"

"Sure. My stomach has been rumbling for an hour."

They crossed the street and ambled toward the other end of Main Street.

"Ruth," Annalise said, "we didn't get a chance to talk the other day. Why was that man out at the house?"

Ruth's stomach clenched. She knew Annalise was going to ask—and that was one of the reasons Ruth suggested lunch, to get this conversation out of the way.

"I suppose because he wanted my phone number." Ruth steeled herself for Annalise's response.

"An *English* man is interested in you?" Annalise's jaw dropped.

"Is that so hard to believe?" Indignation roiled in Ruth's stomach.

"Well, no, I didn't mean it like that." Annalise hid her hands under her black apron. "I just didn't think. . .well, that you would. . ."

"Be interested in an *English* man? Is that what you can't bring yourself to say?"

"Um. . .yes, actually. I know how you feel about Elijah Capp and how he feels about you."

Ruth kicked a pebble. "And you also know it's an impossible situation."

"I am not ready to concede that point."

Ruth did not want to offend Annalise by suggesting that her friend still thought like an *English* sometimes. "It's complicated, Annalise. Besides, I have done nothing to encourage Bryan Nichols. I don't think he even knows what it would mean to get involved with someone like me, or he would never have shown up at my parents' house."

Annalise nodded. "I have to agree with you there."

"It will blow over in a few days."

"Is that what you want?"

Ruth put one hand in the patch pocket of her scrubs shirt. "It's the best thing. Bryan just doesn't know it yet."

They reached the bakery. Annalise held open the door, and

Ruth moved to one of three small round tables.

"What would you like?" Ruth asked. "My treat. It's the least I can do for free rent this semester."

Annalise set her book on the table and pondered the handwritten menu. "How about roast beef on hearty whole wheat?"

"I'll order." Ruth took her debit card from a pocket. "You sit."

The bakery was empty other than Ruth and Annalise and the two employees behind the counter. Ruth ordered the sandwiches then pointed to two enormous chocolate chip cookies. She sidestepped to the end of the counter and pulled several paper napkins out of a metal dispenser. Behind her the shop's door creaked open.

When Ruth turned around, she was face-to-face with Mrs. Capp.

"Hello, Ruth." Mrs. Capp neither smiled nor scowled.

Ruth cleared her throat, looking for her voice. "Hello. How are you?"

"Fine. We are all fine."

"That's good."

"Elijah tells me you plan to be nearby for a few months."

"Just for the semester. Then I will go back to school."

"Why don't you come for supper one night?"

Ruth nearly choked on the effort it took not to let her jaw go slack. "You're kind to ask."

"I mean it. You and Elijah need some time to talk."

Ruth said nothing, unsure whether Mrs. Capp wanted her to talk to Elijah in hopes they would reunite or so Elijah would let go once and for all.

Two sturdy plates clinked against the counter behind her, and Ruth turned to see the sandwiches and cookies. She picked them up then said, "It was nice to see you."

Annalise's gray eyes were wide with curiosity. "What did she say?"

"She invited me to supper."

"Will you go?"

Ruth moistened her lips before sucking them both in.

"I'm not sure," Rufus said into the cell phone he used only for business conversations. "Might I have one more day to make a decision?"

"I'll ask Jeff if he can wait another day," Tom Reynolds said. "He seems eager to have you. You'll be a reliable worker for a change."

"I appreciate his kindness in considering me." Rufus scratched the back of his head. "But it will mean a very different schedule over the winter, and I must be certain this is God's provision. I do not want to grasp at straws out of lack of faith."

Rufus had kissed Annalise rather than talk to her about the job. It was *hochmut*, he feared, that kept him from being forthright. Pride. He wanted to provide for a woman who was more than capable of providing for herself. The kiss was meant to reassure her, while she waited for words he knew she wanted to hear.

But it might have confused her instead. It certainly confused him.

"I promise to have a decision tomorrow," Rufus said to Tom. "Being away from my family, leaving behind my own work, installing cabinets for an *English*—this is not a change I would make lightly."

"I understand," Tom said. "I'll wait to hear from you tomorrow."

Rufus closed the flip phone and set it on his workbench. When he turned to find his pencil and review his sketches for a new end table design, he saw Joel.

Rufus wiped one hand across his eyes. "I suppose you heard that."

Joel nodded. "The last bit. Enough to know you are thinking of taking a job with an *English*."

"It's not a permanent job," Rufus said. "A few weeks, a few months, perhaps. It's just hanging cabinets."

"Are you serious about it?"

Rufus used his pencil to darken the lines of his drawing. "We both know things are not going as well with the farm as we would like. My cabinetry work has had some disappointments as well."

"And you want to get married."

Rufus was silent.

"You know Annalise won't care about money. Look at everything she has given up."

"I know. But I still have to keep my business afloat."

Joel spread his hands on the workbench and leaned toward Rufus. "If you don't take it, I'd like you to recommend me."

Rufus met his brother's gaze.

"I'm serious. I've helped you hang cabinets enough times to know how to measure and get things straight."

Rufus sank into an Adirondack chair on the front porch later in the afternoon, laid the brown leather accounts book in his lap, and lifted his eyes to the Sangre de Cristo Mountains. Already snow brushed the peaks. In a few weeks, the range would be snowcapped for the duration of the winter.

He relished living in Colorado. Not once had he regretted the decision to move from Pennsylvania and join the new settlement. Though his business faced a setback at the moment, overall work had been steady for the last seven years. God's provision.

Rufus opened the accounts book then picked up the pen laid inside its spine and used it as a marker as he reviewed the small amounts still owed to him. Until now, David had always been sure he could sell whatever pieces Rufus had time to make for the store. Now Rufus faced the question of whether he himself believed the pieces would continue to sell. Could he afford to keep making them, confident he would eventually recoup his investment?

His father appeared at the bottom of the porch stairs. "I hope your business is in better shape than mine."

Rufus closed his accounts book. "Is it so bad, *Daed?*"

Eli Beiler progressed up the steps and sank into a chair beside his son. "You know the harvest from the spring planting was disappointing. The soil is so stubborn out here."

"But you've just planted the winter alfalfa. Joel is learning everything he can about soil nutrients. Things will be better in the spring."

"My faith wavers on that point, Rufus."

Rufus said nothing.

"I let Joel talk me into one more season of alfalfa before rotating the crops. What kind of doddering old man have I become that I take advice from a seventeen-year-old?"

"Farming out here is not like in Pennsylvania. You're both learning."

Eli sighed. "This could be an expensive lesson. The farm needs a few thousand in cash. I can go over my own books night and day, and I still don't see where it is going to come from. I am stretched to my limit with the bank."

"I thought you still had some reserves from the land you sold in Pennsylvania when we decided to come here."

Eli leaned forward, elbows on his knees. "I've been drawing down rapidly of late."

"I didn't realize it was that bad, *Daed.*"

"God will provide." Eli lifted his gaze to the mountains. "At the moment, I admit I have trouble imagining how."

Rufus made a decision in that moment. Annalise would just have to understand.

Twelve

Annie did not push against Ruth's hesitancy to answer questions about Bryan Nichols. They finished their sandwiches, and Ruth headed back to work at the clinic while Annie strolled home. She waved at the librarian opening up the narrow storefront branch for afternoon hours and paused to read the sale banners in the dollar store window. When she lived in Colorado Springs, Annie drove everywhere. Now she could work and shop and socialize within a few blocks of her home. She would miss that.

She assumed that when she and Rufus married they would live a few miles from town, as all the Amish families did.

Sometimes, like now, Annie wondered if she were assuming too much. Rufus still had not said a word about getting married. And she was not going to be the one to bring it up.

She turned down the ragged side street that hosted her narrow green century-old house. Outside the house next door, her neighbor stood in the front yard, hands on hips and exasperation flashing across her face.

"What's wrong, Barb?" Annie paused to see if she could help.

"Oh, nothing serious. Just aggravating." Barb flashed her eyes around the yard. "The cat's milk dish is gone."

"The one you leave on the front porch?"

Barb nodded. "If I had a dog, I would understand if it carried the dish off to bury. But cats don't do that."

"I hope it turns up."

"I don't know why I'm looking for it. Obviously someone took it. Who would be desperate enough to take a cat dish?" Barb turned to go inside her home, and Annie—her steps slowed—walked a few more yards to her own driveway. She knew one person desperate enough to take a cat dish.

The same person who would take a lantern, garden vegetables, and a sleeping bag from a clothesline. And perhaps even a cat. Had Leah Deitwaller said where she got the kitten she cradled in her apron that day? Where would she be getting milk?

Annie made up her mind. She had the whole afternoon ahead of her, and a free day tomorrow. She would get on her bicycle and look for Leah even if she had to crank those pedals for a hundred miles crisscrossing the land around Westcliffe.

She paced up the driveway to the back of the house. When she found Leah, Annie wanted to be prepared. The basket on the front of her bicycle would hold some fruit and bread with a couple of water bottles. In the kitchen she made three turkey sandwiches and grabbed an apple and a peach. No telling how hungry Leah would be.

Annie was lifting the garage door to retrieve her white three-speed bike when an old Ford Taurus pulled into the driveway. Julene Weichert got out.

"My grandmother has been taken to the hospital in Pueblo," Julene said. "Mom and I need to head over there right away. Can you watch the store?"

Annie glanced at her bike.

"I know you were supposed to have the time off." Julene dangled keys from one hand. "It might be a couple of days before we come back. Depends what we find out."

Annie gripped the bottom of the garage door and heaved it down.

Annie fidgeted around the store all Tuesday afternoon. For the most part, she simply sorted through items she knew had been on the shelves a long time, separating some to box up and rotating out some new items from the back room.

Two people came into the shop in the space of three hours. Annie chewed on her bottom lip and tapped her toes all afternoon, watching the clock and glancing out the front window every few minutes.

Leah was out there. She was somehow managing to take care of herself and a kitten, but Annie did not like the visions that floated through her head about where Leah might be holed up.

For no good reason. That was the part that burned Annie. Maybe it was unrealistic for Leah to go home to her parents. Maybe their relationship was too damaged to work things out. But was sleeping who knows where and stealing off people's porches really the best option?

Annie groaned in the late afternoon as the sky darkened. Rain. The farms and ranches surrounding Westcliffe needed the water. She had no doubt of that. Even if the rain blew through quickly, as Colorado storms often did, soggy soil would make biking around nearly impossible.

The rain did not blow through. Instead it settled into a steady, drenching rhythm. When Annie closed up the shop, she hung her sweater over her head for the dash home. Over a bowl of soup she sat at her small oval dining room table and stared out the window wondering how Leah was keeping warm. Or *if* Leah was keeping warm.

Why hadn't Mrs. Weichert simply hung the CLOSED sign as so many of the small business owners of Westcliffe did? When Annie first arrived in Westcliffe last year, she was amused by how casually people closed up their shops in the middle of the day and went on errands. And it was not as if it was the busy season for

813

the antiques shop. If someone did not come in on Wednesday and spend a great deal of money, Annie was going to be annoyed at the waste of her day.

Demut, she told herself. Humility. How prideful it was for her to think that her time was worth more than the simple task of honoring her employer's request even if no one came into the shop.

Annie was up at dawn and on her bicycle. She did not have to open the shop until ten. The open land would be too muddy for biking efficiently, especially on the hills, but she could at least try some of the areas accessible by paved roads. The new subdivision beckoned. Several houses were isolated and half-finished. Annie pedaled up Main Street, turned north on the highway, and cruised into the subdivision before the sun was fully up. She had been out there with Rufus several times to see the houses he was working on, so she knew which lots were under construction. Annie had not been there since the fire on her baptism morning, though.

She let a foot drag on the ground as she approached the burned structure. Ten days after the flames, cleanup had already begun. Annie supposed the fire department and the sheriff's office had collected whatever clues they could find, but so far she had not heard a credible account of what might have happened.

Except that someone had set the fire on purpose. According to the Westcliffe rumor mill, the fire chief seemed certain of that much.

She stopped and stared. Surely Leah could not have done this. What motive would she have? Annie shook away the thought.

The fire had burned right through the center of the house, branching off from the hall to scorch Rufus's cabinets in the various rooms. Annie could see their blackened surfaces from the end of the driveway, and grief tightened in her gut—for everyone involved in this pointless loss. At least no one had been in the home at the time.

Annie filled her lungs with fresh energy and put her bicycle in motion once again to move on to the next unoccupied house, knowing she might have only a few more minutes. Construction crews were notorious for getting an early start, and Annie did not want to face interrogation about her presence.

Inspection of three lots yielded nothing suspicious, no sign of a squatter, no residue of an unauthorized visitor. Annie headed back to town, calculating she had time for breakfast at the coffee shop before opening the store.

Between a bite of scrambled egg on a croissant and a sip of plain black coffee—she had given up her indulgence in mocha caramel grande nonfat lattes—out the window Annie saw Brownie trot by pulling the Beilers' cart, with Joel in the driver's seat.

She swallowed the coffee, abandoned her breakfast sandwich, and marched down the sidewalk in pursuit. Finally Joel saw her waving arms and stopped.

"We have to find Leah," Annie said.

Joel turned his head to the left and then to the right. "We tried that already. It didn't work out so well."

"Is that a reason to give up?" Annie widened her eyes and leaned her face toward Joel. "She's confused. That doesn't mean she doesn't need help."

"*Daed* is counting on me for help in the fields. Besides, how do you know she hasn't gone home by now? Or found a bus to. . . somewhere."

"Because my neighbor's cat bowl is missing." Annie listed the items people had reported missing in the last few days, including the food from her own back porch. "She's out there."

"She's seventeen. Almost eighteen."

"You've seen her. She's in no emotional condition to be on her own."

"I'll keep my eyes open," Joel said.

"I don't know when Mrs. Weichert will get back." Annie straightened her *kapp*. "I promised to watch the store."

"I'll try. But I don't expect to be back to town this week."

"You're resourceful. If you see her, find a way to send me a message." Annie tapped Joel's shoulder. "Otherwise I'll see you Friday when I come for supper."

On Friday after supper, Rufus took Annalise's hand and led her out to the front porch.

"I hear you are still looking for Leah Deitwaller," he said.

"Somebody should be."

"It's been twelve days." Rufus leaned against a post, not releasing her hand. "You've seen a few signs that she is around and not injured. It seems, though, that she is quite determined not to be found."

"She is about to meet her match."

Annalise looked up at him with her wide gray eyes. He squeezed her hand without speaking.

"You probably think I'm just being stubborn," Annalise said, "but this is different. I feel something. A tug. A calling. Even if she were already eighteen, I would still want to help her."

He nodded. "Then you should."

"Really? You're not going to talk me out of it? Tell me I'm being *English*?"

"How can you be *English*? You are baptized Amish."

She beamed. "You don't know how great that is to hear you say."

He took both her hands now and faced her. When he heard her intake of air, he knew he was about to disappoint her. "I need to talk to you about something."

"Of course."

"I want you to know I'm thinking of you, of us, and also of my family. I have not made this decision easily."

The light that had flickered in her eyes a moment ago was gone. He told her about the offer of employment to hang premanufactured cabinets over the winter.

"I'll be away for days at a time, even a couple of weeks."

"What about making your own cabinets?" Annalise's face

clouded. "Won't you be setting your own business back even further?"

He nodded. "Possibly. I'll work on them whenever I can be home for a few days."

"It never crossed my mind you would take this sort of job."

"Mine either. But when you pray for God's provision, you cannot spurn the form in which it comes. The income will be more certain than my own business is right now. I want to help *Daed* if I can."

"Is the farm in that much trouble?"

"We'll know more in the spring."

"That's a long way off." Annalise moved her hands and laid them on his forearms. "Won't the church help? Isn't that the Amish way?"

"They will want to, I'm sure," he said. "But everyone is trying to farm. Everyone is stretched thin. It doesn't take much for a settlement to fail."

"Surely that is not going to happen. It's been seven years, and new families arrive every few months."

"I want to do my part, and this is one way I can help."

"You do your part every single day, Rufus. Everybody knows that. I hate to see you give up your craft, the beauty you create that shows the wonder of God."

He glanced into the house, where his siblings were getting ready to play board games. "I know this is not the conversation you were hoping for right now."

She was quiet for too long. "Joel could hang cabinets," she finally said. "It doesn't have to be you."

"Joel would go. But what if he did not come back?"

"Then, God's will. Besides, Joel has told me more than once that he will be baptized when the time is right. He says he is not Ruth, that he is not going to leave."

Rufus put an arm around Annalise's shoulders and turned her to the view of the Sangre de Cristos. "Joel would not plan to leave.

His reasons would not be as noble as Ruth's. There is a difference between leaving and just not coming back."

Her hard swallow was audible, and he leaned in and kissed the top of her head.

Thirteen

May 1892

Belle Mooney charged up the street from the school.

Maura ran toward her, arms spread wide to stop Belle's progress.

"What happened?" Belle pushed against Maura's restraint. "I was at the school cleaning out my desk. I heard gunshots."

Maura closed her arms firmly around her friend. "Belle. . ."

"It's John, isn't it?"

Maura sucked in her top lip. "I'm afraid it is."

Belle thrashed and Maura's hold began to slip.

"I want to know," Belle said. "Tell me."

"It's bad, Belle. Very bad."

Belle broke free. Maura grabbed for her elbow and missed.

"I'm going to him," Belle said. "Don't keep me from him."

Belle broke into a brisk, determined pace, and Maura followed as closely as her tight shoes and long hem would allow. Belle screamed at the sight before her.

"We've sent for the doctor." Maura bunched up the fabric of her navy skirt in one hand to permit a longer stride. Bile rose within her, and she swallowed it down. John Twigg continued to bleed in the street.

Beside John, Belle fell to her knees. "John, darling, I'm here. I'm here." She pulled up the hem of her white dress and dabbed at the bleeding and then gently lifted his head into her lap.

Maura's breath caught at the tenderness before her. Belle cradled John's head, stroked his face, bent to kiss him, spoke of her love. No man had ever made Maura feel this way. No man had made her see past his flaws to what he could be. What did she know of love? Perhaps nothing. Whatever Maura thought of John Twigg, her friend loved him and would love him to the end. In Maura's mind, Belle's capacity for loyalty clanked against John's undeserving. But whatever John's faults, he did not deserve to lie in the street this way. The events of the morning did not resemble justice, Maura was sure of that much.

She glanced up the street for any sight of one of the doctors. Would those Amish men really be able to look after Walter and find a doctor? Walter would be fine, she reminded herself. He was barely hit.

John was running out of time.

Squeezing her head between her hands, Maura tried to count the minutes that had passed since the shots. She did not even know who had fired—Lee or Ing. And did it matter?

"The sheriff," Maura cried out. "Has anyone gone for Sheriff Byler?"

Maura knelt next to Belle, stretching her arms against Belle's shoulders and leaning her cheek into Belle's face. "I'm here, too."

"I'm still bleeding," Walter said.

Joseph looked again at Walter's knuckles. "It's almost stopped."

Zeke bounded ahead of them and took the steps up to Doc Denton's porch two at a time. After a quick rap on the door, he turned the knob and stepped through the opening.

Joseph raised his eyebrows in expectation. "Is this doctor related to the store owners?" he asked Walter.

Walter still cradled his injured fingers with his other hand. "Cousin or something, I think. There are so many Dentons and Twiggs around here I can't keep 'em straight."

Zeke appeared on the porch. "He's not here. Nobody is."

Joseph turned his head toward the blocks they had traversed.

"Pray for that man Twigg." Zeke thudded down the steps. "Get the boy comfortable on the porch."

Joseph swallowed as Zeke disappeared around the corner. He found a wide bench with a floral-patterned cushion on the covered porch. "This looks like a good place to wait. Do you want to lie down?"

Walter sat on the bench, and Joseph helped him swing his legs up and stretch out.

"Do you pray, Walter?"

"Sure. I guess. Doesn't everybody pray when something bad happens?"

"Shall we pray, then?"

"For John Twigg?"

"For you, of course, but yes, Mr. Twigg as well."

"No thanks." Walter popped his head up to scowl. "I'll take my chances. I'm not hurt so bad that I have to do that."

"Have you no compassion?"

"He might have my daddy snookered with his egg prices, but I don't trust him. I'd rather work for the Denton brothers any day."

Joseph leaned against the house with one shoulder. "Do you think you can protect yourself by refusing to pray?"

"I've been minding my own business. Look what it got me." Walter held up his wounded hand. "It's not fair. It's fine by me if Crazy Man Twigg gets what he deserves."

Joseph held his tongue. He had enough discussions with Little Jake while throwing hay down in the barn, away from the ears of their parents, to know that boys this age were stubborn. Even the Amish. Life was not fair. That was not God's purpose in creating. But Walter would not hear it any more than Little Jake did.

"I suppose your friend will tell Dr. Lindsay to take care of John Twigg first."

Joseph nodded slowly.

Walter grunted. "Nobody will care that I got shot, too. Even Maura didn't come with me."

Joseph cleared his throat. "Mr. Twigg's situation is quite serious, Walter."

"I know. I'm just sayin'."

They fell silent.

"What can you see?" Walter asked after a few minutes.

"Not much," Joseph said. "It is too far down the street. And there's a crowd now."

"I'll be all right here, you know. If you want to go."

Did he want to go? Joseph's people only used guns to shoot what they would eat. A gunfight in the street was beyond his understanding. But he understood that he should not leave a boy alone.

"Let me look at your hand," Joseph said. "Perhaps it needs fresh bandaging."

"Well, don't rip off your other sleeve." Walter said. "You can go inside and get bandages. Doc keeps them in the back room on the long shelf."

Joseph suddenly felt exposed and ran his hand up and down his bare arm. He sometimes rolled up his sleeves if he was working in the field with other men, but never in his life had he walked down a street with his arms bare. He unwrapped his dismembered sleeve from Walter's hand and examined the knuckles. The bleeding had stopped. Joseph pressed gently on the spot that seemed the worst.

"Hey!" Walter retracted his hand.

"Sorry." The knuckle likely was broken. "Perhaps I will have a look around for those bandages." *And some kind of splint*, Joseph thought.

"Hurry up, then." Little Jake's tone haunted Walter's voice.

Belle's shoulders trembled under Maura's touch. John Twigg's blood spilled over them both.

"Belle," Maura whispered. "I know how much you care for John."

"John, my dearest love," Belle murmured. She gently mopped the persistent wound.

"I'm sure the doctor is coming." With no such certainty, Maura forced stability into her voice. "Just a few more minutes."

Belle had held steady so far, but Maura felt the tremble morph into wracking sobs.

"We're going to get married, John," Belle managed between gasps. "You promised me. I'm holding you to it."

With one hand on the middle of Belle's back, Maura took in the scene around them. Movement had halted, as if players took their marks on a stage. No one else was within ten feet of John Twigg, but every person from every shop or office seemed to have come out and lined the streets. It was not hard to spot Zeke Berkey trotting back toward the wounded man.

He shook his head.

Maura's heart lurched as she stood to meet him.

"The doctors were both out on calls," Zeke said, his voice low. "Dr. Lindsay's son went for him."

Maura allowed herself a deep breath. "Mr. Twigg is not long for this world."

"No, I think not. *Gottes wille.*"

"What is that?"

"God's will," Zeke said.

Maura put her hands on her hips. "Pardon me, Mr. Berkey, but I am not at all persuaded that is the case."

She turned toward Belle's moan.

"I will get justice for John." Belle's voice had turned to iron. "I will find out who did this and he will hang."

823

"Belle, no." Maura knelt beside Belle again.

"It's what John would want. *Will* want. I will do everything I can."

"Right now, let's just worry about John." Maura gestured toward Zeke. "Mr. Berkey said the doctor is coming."

With heavy breath, Maura looked again at the gathered townspeople. Ing and Lee Denton stood outside their store, pistols raised, cocked, and pointed, though John Twigg was no threat now.

But he came from a large family. His father owned one of the largest ranches in Baxter County, and John would not be the only Twigg in the family's store.

"We have to do something," she whispered to Zeke.

"The doctor is—"

"Not for John. We'll have a riot on our hands any minute now. The Twiggs will do exactly what Belle is talking about—find justice on their own terms."

"You know your own town."

"Stay with Belle." Maura took charge. She stood and faced the Denton brothers. "Put those guns away."

"No, ma'am," Lee Denton said.

"Can't you see what you've already done?" Maura marched toward them. "We don't need any more bloodshed."

"That's up to the Twiggs," Ing Denton said. "But we'll be ready when they come."

Joseph hustled down the street. Walter's father had heard about the shooting and turned up looking for his son. Joseph left them both sitting on the bench outside the doctor's office, Walter's hand freshly if awkwardly bandaged. He heard Miss Woodley's voice.

"All of you," she shouted, "form a line around the emporium!"

"You want us to be target practice for the Twiggs?" one man objected.

"You're already standing in the street gawking at John," Maura said. "You might as well be useful. Line up. Lee and Ing, you stand behind the line."

"Now, Maura—"

"Do it!" she snapped, and the crowd turned itself into a human barricade.

Mesmerized by her authority, Joseph stepped into place between two men in *English* suits.

"Here they come," one of the men muttered.

From the far end of town, dust rose in robust clouds as horses' hooves churned up the road.

"Who are they?" Joseph whispered.

"John's kin. Those two in front are his brothers, Billy and Jimmy."

"Do they always ride with rifles across their saddles?" Joseph asked.

Maura took her place in the barricade, which now stretched all the way around the Denton Emporium. Joseph inched toward her.

"Your cousin," he said, "is going to be all right. His father is there now."

Maura nodded. "Thank you. Now if we can just keep anyone else from getting shot today."

Joseph watched the Twiggs circle around John. Billy slid off his horse and lowered himself into the stain of blood soaking into the street and put an arm around Belle.

"What time is it?" Maura asked.

"I do not wear a watch," Joseph answered.

"How many minutes?" she said. "How long has he been lying out there like that?"

Joseph swallowed hard. "Nigh to thirty minutes, I would say."

"That's a long time to lie in the street like a half-butchered hog."

"Does he yet live?" Joseph had supposed John was dead already.

"Honestly, I don't know. The blood stopped spurting, but there is a lot of it."

The Twigg gang circled again, staring into the line of townspeople with hard, unbending expressions.

Another horse galloped in and broke through the Twigg huddle. "It's Dr. Lindsay," someone said.

The doctor knelt with his black bag. Belle's face wrenched with hope. In only a moment, though, Dr. Lindsay looked up and shook his head. On his horse, Jimmy Twigg raised his rifle to his shoulder.

"No, Jimmy, no!" Maura screamed.

Twigg held his pose as Billy and Belle stood and stared at the crowd. "Sheriff Byler had better show up soon."

"You will *not* shoot into an innocent crowd," Maura shouted. "If Sheriff Byler catches you, he'll have reason to shoot you in the back."

Billy Twigg sauntered toward his horse and pulled his own rifle down from the mount. "He's not a shootin' sheriff, and you know it."

Fourteen

Ruth squinted at the tiny print on the form. She supposed no one actually read the stack of forms patients routinely signed when they received care in the clinic, but she was curious how the government's health care regulations over privacy and insurance translated into plain English. Even after nearly three years away from the Amish community, she was still getting used to the prevalence—even the necessity—for insurance in order to receive care. Was it not enough to be sick? It seemed to her that the *English* system left out a lot of people. She had begun to think of someday practicing her nursing skills in a setting that served people who worked hard yet still feared what it would cost to see a health care professional.

With a gasp she looked up to see the face of Bryan Nichols only inches from hers. With his arms anchored on the counter, he leaned heavily forward.

"Hello, Ruth Beiler."

Ruth pushed her rolling chair back a few inches. "Hello. Do you have an appointment?"

"No, but I'd like to make one." He grinned.

Ruth hit the space bar to wake up her computer monitor and

opened the scheduling program. "We don't have any openings today, but a doctor could see you on Thursday."

"But I don't want to see a doctor. I want to see you."

She blinked twice and met his eyes. "I'm a nursing student doing an internship. I can't see patients."

Now he laughed. "I'm not a patient. I'm just a man who would like to get to know you better. Would you have breakfast with me tomorrow?"

Ruth's belly warmed. At the university in Colorado Springs, she fell indisputably in the category of nerd—a serious student who made a solid contribution to a study group before an exam but otherwise did not socialize with many people. And certainly not men.

"Tomorrow's a church Sunday," Ruth said. "I like to go to church with my family when I'm home."

"Lunch, then."

"I'm afraid. . .well, it's the Sabbath. A family day." She was dodging him. The real question was not when she would go out with him, but whether.

"Well, you didn't seem so hot on the idea of my dropping by the house the first time I tried it, so I suppose I won't do that again." He winked. "Not yet anyway."

She blushed. Ruth could feel it. And she could not will it away. For his own good, Ruth had repeatedly told Elijah Capp that he had to let her go, but she had never done so because she imagined herself with anyone else.

"Let me cut to the chase," Bryan said. "Just tell me that you will go out with me, and then we can work on figuring out when."

Ruth shuffled some papers and glanced at the monitor, which had reverted to its screen saver of nature scenes.

Bryan caught her eye in an expectant invitation.

Ruth clicked the point of her ballpoint pen out and then in. "I'm not all that interesting."

"Let me be the judge of that. Okay?"

Ruth reached for her coffee mug, which was empty. She stared into it. "Okay."

Annie's steps slowed as she walked past the newspaper box on Main Street. It was one of those old locked boxes that took quarters and released custody of the day's news. In this case it was the week's news at stake. The Westcliffe paper, read by residents all over Custer County, only came out once a week.

Rufus did not read *English* newspapers. None of the Beilers did. As far as Annie knew, none of the Amish in Custer County or anywhere in southwestern Colorado did. They regarded the contents as *English* business that had nothing to do with them.

But that headline. How could she walk past it and not be curious?

ARSONIST PROFILED.

She was sorely tempted, and she was pretty sure she had a quarter. But when she looked down at the small bag hanging from her shoulder, she saw her green Amish dress. If someone—even an *English*—saw her dropping a coin in the slot and extracting a paper, word was certain to get back to the bishop.

Annie rolled her eyes at her own weakness and picked up speed again. It should not matter whether anyone saw her buy a paper. It did not even matter what she thought of the Amish practice of reading only their own newspapers. She had vowed to obey the leaders of the church. Her baptism was not yet two weeks old and she was already straining against its restrictions.

She reached Mrs. Weichert's shop and put the key in the lock, deciding at the same time that it was time to change the window display. Mrs. Weichert wouldn't mind. Generally the store owner gladly left that task to Annie anyway.

Annie was about to step inside when a touch on her elbow made her turn to see Trey, the newspaper editor.

"I've got some flyers here that the town council wants

distributed." Trey gripped a stack of papers in one hand. "I put them in with all the newspapers, but they'd like them in shop windows, too."

Annie held the door open. "I guess that would be all right." Mrs. Weichert could always take it down if she objected.

"Good. If you'd like, I'll put it up for you."

Annie gestured toward the front window. "What's it about?"

"The fire department is doing a controlled training burn." Trey produced a small roll of tape from a pocket. "After what happened a couple of weeks ago, they want to be sure everyone knows not to freak out when they see smoke this time."

"That sounds wise. Where will they be burning?"

"There's an old house that is a hundred years old if it's a day. You can see straight through the slats. I'm surprised a good wind didn't take it down years ago."

"Where is that?"

"At the edge of the ranch land Karl Kramer owns."

"Is he still out of town?"

"Believe so. I hear his foreman is on the phone with him practically all day every day, but Karl seems in no hurry to come back. But don't worry. They have his permission. He's been wanting to take it down anyway."

"Then I guess it's just as well." Annie tried to picture the failing structure. Gradually an image came into her mind.

"It's amazing what they can tell from investigating the scene of a fire. We've had a lot of interest in our profile of an arsonist."

Annie perked up. "I'm afraid I haven't read the article. Do they really know who did it?"

Trey pulled of a piece of tape and stuck it to the end of one finger before reaching across the display shelf to place the poster in the window.

" 'Fraid not. The article is more general."

Annie wondered if it would be against *Ordnung* to encourage him to keep talking.

"They start with establishing a motive even before they have a suspect," Trey said. "Half the time it's revenge. I never knew that."

"Me neither."

"Then of course there's simple vandalism or monetary gain. And some people do it just for the excitement."

"But how do they know the motive before they have a suspect?" Annie couldn't help asking.

"Certain patterns. A revenge burning rarely uses an ignitable liquid, for instance, because it's not well mapped out. Usually that's a firebomb."

"And the others?" Annie was simply gathering information. What could be wrong with that?

"Vandalism will often have graffiti accompanying it. If the motive is monetary gain, valuables will be missing from the scene. Fires set by someone seeking excitement will eventually develop a pattern. Someone wants attention."

"But that means there would have to be several. I hate to think of that happening around here."

"I don't suppose anyone wants to see that except the person setting the fires."

Annie shuddered at the thought. "So they don't have any theories about the fire?"

Trey pressed on one last piece of tape. "I imagine they do. Once they sort out the kind of fire it was, that will narrow down the list of suspects. But they wouldn't be saying yet, now would they?"

"I suppose not."

The door opened and Mrs. Weichert came in. "What have we got here?"

Trey set a couple of extra flyers on the counter. "It's all here. I'd better move on."

Annie watched him leave and turned to her employer. "I didn't know you would be back. How is your mother?"

"She had a heart attack, but given what it could have been, it's not too bad. They released her last night. Julene offered to stay

831

a few more days to make sure her feisty grandmother behaves herself and to arrange some help to come in."

"I'm glad it wasn't worse."

"Thanks. Now you skedaddle. You've held down the fort long enough."

Annie did not argue. It was barely ten thirty. She could spend the whole day looking for Leah if she had to. Annie picked up an extra flyer and left before Mrs. Weichert could change her mind.

Oblivious to further distraction, she dashed home, put on her most comfortable sneakers, and filled the thrift store backpack. In the days since she had first thought to take sandwiches to Leah, Annie had set aside a box of crackers, a jar of peanut butter, a loaf of wheat bread, and juice boxes she kept in the house for a treat when Jacob Beiler visited. If she could not persuade Leah to go home, she could at least take her some nourishment. At the last minute, she pulled a quart-size canning jar from the cupboard and filled it with milk.

With the backpack strapped to her shoulders, Annie set out. While her previous attempts to find Leah had been random guesses about which direction to head, this time Annie had a destination in mind. The old house Trey had described on the edge of Karl Kramer's ranch sounded just like the sort of place a lonely girl could take refuge. For years it had been abandoned and off anyone's radar.

Now it was on the radar, though. Surely firefighters would double-check to be sure no one was in the building before beginning the training burn, but Annie did not want to take any chances. Fresh adrenaline at the thought of finding Leah speeded the revolution of her pedals, even with the extra weight on her back. Still, it took her most of an hour to reach the ranch, and she was relieved to finally put one foot on the ground to steady her balance.

From the outside, Annie saw no sign the building was occupied. It looked downright unsafe to her—which was probably why it was targeted for destruction.

"Leah?" she called out. But no answer came. Annie got off the bike and laid it on the ground. The weight of the backpack had shifted, and she readjusted it as she walked closer to the old house. There was no door, only a gaping opening where one had once hung. Window frames had long ago lost their glass. Gray, brittle, weather-worn planks held a precarious balance that a large cardboard box could have rivaled.

"Leah!"

Silence.

Under any other circumstance, Annie would not have entered the house, but she had come too far not to determine whether there might be any possibility Leah was squatting here.

The room at what must have been the front of the house at one time was empty. Far from fearless for her own safety, Annie proceeded deeper into the house. At the end of a narrow hall, she found two small rooms. The one on the right was empty.

When she stepped inside the room on the left, Annie tripped on something—and immediately recognized the cat dish. Her pulse pounded as she inspected the rest of the room. A sleeping bag. A lantern. Empty mason jars. A sweater. Four apple cores.

Annie held herself still, breathless, listening for any sound of movement in the house.

Nothing.

She inventoried her options. One: go find Leah's parents and insist they come with her to this desolate, dangerous place their child had chosen. Two: report evidence of trespassing and try to force the authorities to get involved. Three: wait for Leah and insist she go home with Annie. Four: leave the backpack and go home.

Why would the Deitwallers be more likely to track their daughter just because Annie had found her? They wouldn't. Why would the authorities be interested in someone trespassing in a building scheduled for destruction in a few days and whose owner had made no complaint? They wouldn't. And why would Leah be any more likely to accept Annie's offer to help than she had been on previous attempts? She wouldn't.

Reluctantly, Annie admitted she had only one choice that made any sense. She reached into the front pocket of the backpack, where she knew she would find a small notepad and a pen.

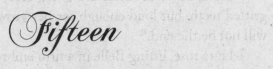

Fifteen

June 1892

"The grand jury is back."

At A.G. Byler's solemn announcement a few weeks later, the assembled residents of Gassville ceased their whispered speculations outside the Mountain Home courthouse and entered the building. By the time the jury was seated, the gallery was filled. Abraham took his seat in the inside aisle toward the back. In front of him, he saw Maura Woodley clasping hands with Belle Mooney. Nearly everyone who had been in the street on the day of the shooting was in the courtroom. He did not see the black hats of the Amish men, though they had stood outside earlier. A.G. supposed that entering a courthouse exceeded the sensibilities of their beliefs. He did not know much about them, except that one of them was named Beiler and they were looking for a possible location for an Amish settlement. They were not efficient scouts, A.G. decided, or they would have moved on by now.

The bailiff announced the judge, and silence draped the rows of spectators. The jury foreman handed a slip of paper to the bailiff, who handed it to the judge to read. All eyes were on that slip of paper as it made its way back to the jury box.

Lee and Ing Denton stood and the foreman read the verdict.

No.

The verdict was no. The grand jury did not find sufficient evidence of wrongdoing to bind over for trial.

Belle burst into sobs, and Maura held her tightly. Gasps erupted around the gallery as the judge thanked the grand jury for their service and the stoic jurymen filed out.

"The Denton brothers are going free!" Belle spoke through gritted teeth, but loud enough for her growl to turn heads. "This will not be the end."

Maura rose, lifting Belle in a firm embrace.

A.G. was not sure he wanted to meet their eyes. As a man of the law, he understood the verdict. Both men admitted shooting their pistols multiple times. With three guns firing too rapidly for witnesses to be sure, no one could prove which bullet killed John Twigg. The Dentons were on their own property, and half a dozen witnesses attested that Twigg had approached them in a menacing manner, and not for the first time. Despite John Twigg's death, A.G. believed the grand jury had made the right decision.

But the Twiggs were a vengeful family. As a man of the law, A.G. also knew Belle spoke rightly. This would not be the end.

As A.G. had supposed she would, Maura approached him. Belle still leaned heavily on her friend. Behind them, Billy and Jimmy Twigg huddled in a conspiring tangle with other Twigg men.

Deputy Combs escorted Lee and Ing out of the court as free men.

Belle's slight weight against Maura slowed her, but the sheriff was only a few feet away.

"Good morning, Sheriff," Maura said.

"Morning, ladies."

"It is not good at all," Belle said, "and I won't pretend it is."

"Now, Miss Mooney, this is an upsetting time for you," Sheriff

Byler said. "We all appreciate your loss. You have your good friend to lean on while you get through this."

Behind Maura, Jimmy Twigg took Belle's elbow. "Come with us," he said. "We think of you as part of our family."

Maura winced as Belle shifted her weight from Maura to Jimmy's arm and he escorted her away.

"I'm worried about her," Maura said to the sheriff.

"You're a loyal friend." Sheriff Byler took the end of his beard between two fingers in thought.

"Belle has always been so sensible. We always saw eye-to-eye until this. I tried to warn her away from John Twigg, but she wouldn't hear of it."

"Love is a powerful force," Sheriff said.

"But if the Twiggs use this as a reason to carry their guns a little closer. . .well, I hate to see Belle in the middle of it."

"We'll have to help her get on with her life," Sheriff said. "She still has her work as a teacher, and her father cares for her."

"But he never liked John Twigg. He has no sympathy for John's death." Maura dipped her hat in the direction Belle had gone. "You saw Jimmy. He's trying to claim Belle as one of theirs. She could lose her own family because of this."

"I hope it does not come to that." Sheriff put both hands in his trouser pockets.

"Sheriff, isn't there anything you can do?"

"What result would you be looking for, Miss Woodley? Did you want to see the Dentons bound over to trial and hanged in a public spectacle?"

"No, of course not." Maura's answer was swift. "But I wish we could do something to prevent this from going further."

"I am the sheriff," he said. "I cannot take legal action because a man's attitude strikes me as cocky. I must have at least the suspicion of a crime."

Maura expelled her breath heavily. "I fear there will be no time between suspicion and more tragedy."

They walked together to the doors and exited the building. Joseph and Zeke were waiting at the bottom of the courthouse steps.

"Thank you both for what you did on that fateful day," Maura said, "and for being here now, even though you did not feel you could come in."

Both men nodded, their black hats bobbing in counterpoint.

"The Amish do not use weapons this way," Zeke said, "but we do not turn our hearts from those who do when harm results."

Maura opened her purse and pulled out her mother's white gloves. She would not put them on. She only wanted to hold them, to having something to grip in her fist.

Joseph lifted his chin in the direction of the Denton brothers. "I would have thought they would go home immediately."

Lee and Ing approached.

"You two have been here for several weeks," Lee said. "We figure you might be looking for work."

Joseph and Zeke looked at each other; then Zeke said, "We are on a mission for our church."

"Even a mission needs money," Ing said. "We want you to work for us."

"I don't think our bishop would approve of us working in an *English* store," Joseph said.

"No, not the store," Lee said. "Clearing land on the bluff along the river."

"First thing tomorrow," Ing said. "At Denton's Ferry on the White River." He glanced at Maura. "Miss Woodley can tell you where to find it."

Maura looked at Zeke and then settled her gaze on Joseph. Every time she saw him, his violet-blue eyes pierced her concentration. Behind them, she knew, was a man of kindness and patience. She had no doubt the Amish men carried the ethic of hard work, but did they understand what the Dentons were asking? They would be taking up sides.

Joseph and Zeke had left the hotel after two nights to conserve funds. Instead, they negotiated with the livery owner in Gassville to sleep on the ground outside the stables in exchange for mucking stalls and watering horses. They were free to cook in the open air, and if it rained, they could move inside. For the extra effort of exercising horses whose owners did not call for them, Joseph and Zeke's animals would be well fed.

At daybreak the morning after the grand jury's verdict, Joseph woke and nudged Zeke. "Time to get up. We have work to do today."

Zeke turned over and punched the small pillow under his head. "I am not sure we should go. We did not promise."

"They offered a good wage," Joseph said. "Better than good. And they will pay in cash."

"You know I love an adventure," Zeke said, "but we've been here more than two weeks. We've seen all there is to see of Gassville, Mountain Home, and the land in between."

"We haven't seen everything. We haven't been out to the bluffs over the river."

Zeke sat up. "The landscape is beautiful. But there is no place to start a peaceful Amish settlement around here. Danger hangs in the air."

"What is the harm of a few more days?" Joseph tidied his bedding into a tight roll. "We cannot project our expenses if we continue west or south."

"So you believe we should continue scouting?" Zeke folded his bedroll haphazardly.

"We have not yet completed the task the bishop charged us with." Joseph put his bedroll against the wall of the stable, under the eave.

Zeke paused to lift his eyes and hands to the brightening sky. "This is the day the Lord has made."

"Let us rejoice and be glad," Joseph responded.

"Okay. We will go to Denton's Ferry and see what this work is. But we should send a letter to the bishop."

"Then we will have to wait for his response," Joseph pointed out.

"Yes, I suppose so."

Joseph nodded. They would stay in Gassville for at least a week, maybe several weeks. He wondered how Miss Maura Woodley spent her days and whether she ever used Denton's Ferry.

Zeke rummaged in their foodstuffs and produced some dry biscuits. Joseph lit a fire in the ring of stones they cooked over and prepared the coffeepot.

By seven o'clock, Zeke and Joseph sat on their horses on the thickly wooded bluff overlooking Denton's Ferry.

"It is a shame to think of clearing this land," Zeke said. "They have a thriving ranch, a popular store in town, and a prosperous ferry business on the river. What need do they have for so much wood?"

"None," Joseph answered softly. "We are stepping into the middle of their fear."

Zeke looked at Joseph full on. "You were the one who wanted to accept this work."

"I still do." Joseph dismounted and let his eyes soak up the panoramic view of the gushing foam of the White River and the lush land on the other side. "In the days of our ancestors, the men would have cleared the land along the river so that the Indians could not surprise them with their presence."

"That is what you think this is?" Zeke's horse whinnied, and he patted the animal's neck.

Joseph gripped the bridle on his mount. "If you were one of the Dentons, would you not fear ambush?"

Maura rinsed the rag then wiped down the counter one more time. The kitchen was clean. A roast was in the oven with potatoes, onions, and carrots. She had dusted every crevice of the parlor before lunch and beaten clean the rugs in the hallway. After making sure the home she shared with her father was clean and comfortable, what was left of the afternoon belonged to her. She had a few errands on Main Street.

Maura offered up a brief prayer for a peaceful, uneventful excursion and picked up her purse and a flour sack in which to carry home a few small purchases.

Walter was there with his broom in front of Denton's Emporium.

"How are your fingers?" Maura asked.

"I just saw Doc Denton this morning," Walter said. "My knuckle may be a little knobby, but I'll be good as new."

"Are the Denton brothers here today?" Maura tilted her head toward the store.

"Lee was for a while. Ing is out on the bluff with the crew they hired."

A crew that included Joseph Beiler and Zeke Berkey.

"They come and go by the back of the store and always try to have somebody with them," Walter added.

"They must be so fearful after the verdict yesterday."

Walter pointed down the street. "Wouldn't you be? Look at the Twiggs' store."

Maura peered down the street. Jimmy Twigg sat on a bench in front of the store, his rifle on his shoulder.

"He's been like that all day," Walter said. "The Dentons don't dare walk down Main Street."

"They can't live like that," Maura said.

Walter shrugged. "What else can they do?"

"There must be some other way than waiting to be shot."

Walter pointed with his chin. "Here comes one of those Amish men."

Joseph Beiler rode up the street and dismounted in front of the emporium.

"Good afternoon, Miss Woodley. Walter."

"Good afternoon, Mr. Beiler."

He looked bedraggled, weary with the evidence that he had accepted the Dentons' offer of work. Perspiration soaked his shirt—his only shirt, she knew, since he sacrificed the other to Walter's wound.

"My friend and I are low on our foodstuffs," Joseph said. "I thought I would get a few things from the emporium. Mr. Denton offered us an account as long as we are in their employ."

"Do you cook outside?" Walter wondered aloud.

Joseph laughed softly. "Cook and sleep and everything. The livery owner is generous with his water, though, so at least we can clean up."

"Mr. Beiler," Maura said, "how would you and Mr. Berkey like to have a home-cooked meal with all the trimmings?"

The widening of his eyes made her smile. "I have a roast in the oven that is far larger than my father and I require. You would make me happy if you would agree to be my guests tonight."

Joseph had done his best to rinse out his shirt and hang it in the late afternoon sun to dry. When he donned it, lingering dampness stuck to his skin in places, but he was confident that once he put on his suit jacket the moisture would not be visible. He brushed dust out of his trousers as vigorously as he could manage.

"So you insist on going?" Zeke gulped cool water from a tin cup.

"Miss Woodley offered the invitation in kindness. We should go." Joseph had already made up his mind he would go whether or not Zeke came with him.

"I do not question her motive." Zeke splashed the rest of the water on his face. "Yours concerns me."

Joseph slapped at the dust in his pants one last time. "Miss Woodley will be disappointed you did not come."

"Quite possibly she will be happy to have you to herself."

Joseph met Zeke's eye. "Then for the sake of propriety, you ought to come."

Zeke stood. "Yes, perhaps I should."

Joseph brushed his horse while he waited for Zeke to clean up and put on the shirt he had washed and left to dry the night before. They arrived at the Woodley home promptly at the appointed hour. Smiling, Maura opened the front door to welcome them.

Her scent filled the rooms. Joseph inhaled her allure above even the fragrance of the roast ready for the table. End tables held lamps but also bowls and figurines. Fabric with lively floral prints adorned the furniture. A painting hung over the fireplace. Joseph recognized the bend of the White River and the grove of trees he had helped to cut down that day.

"My mother painted that," Maura said.

"It's breathtaking." Joseph wondered if Lee and Ing Denton might someday appreciate this visual preservation of the land they were so eager to alter. His own mother would have told him that a painting was a graven image and producing one a sinful waste of time. He turned to Maura, wondering if her mother had painted Maura. "Thank you again for your kind invitation."

"It is my pleasure. Give me a moment to bring out the rest of the food and we will be ready to eat."

A man entered the front room. "Hello. I'm Woody Woodley." He extended a hand, which both Joseph and Zeke shook. "Funny name, I know. It's a childhood nickname that stuck, and I suppose I like it better than Francis."

"Thank you for welcoming us to your home," Joseph said. "I am Joseph Beiler, and this is my friend, Ezekiel Berkey."

Maura reappeared with a platter of sliced meat and a basket of rolls. "Daddy, why don't you come ask the blessing for the food?"

They stood behind their chairs, heads bowed, as Woody Woodley spoke aloud a prayer of gratitude. Joseph had never heard an *English* meal blessing before. His people prayed privately, a moment of silence before a meal rather than a rush of words. Joseph rather liked the poetic lilt of Woody's prayer. Just before the *Amen*, he lifted his eyes and found Maura smiling at him.

His lips turned up in response.

Sixteen

Annie rode in the blue Prius with Ruth to the Stutzman farm for church on Sunday morning. She had only a thin sleep Saturday night. Instead she wondered about Leah, prayed for Leah, hoped on Leah's behalf. And she crafted a speech for Leah's mother. Whatever Mrs. Deitwaller said, Annie would proceed with the next sentence of her speech. Her words would not castigate or blame or accuse. Rather, though outwardly Mrs. Deitwaller might not seem receptive, Annie believed that deep down any mother would want to know about the well-being of her child. Annie's words would reassure as much as possible.

"Leah is safe for now."

"I've made sure she has food."

"She can come and stay with me if she wants to."

"I'll let you know if I hear from her."

If Mrs. Deitwaller threw barbs about Annie's intentions, Annie would take a breath and keep going until she said it all. Then she would pray that something penetrated Mrs. Deitwaller's veneer.

The women of the congregation mingled in the Stutzman kitchen for a few minutes. Annie added her own spinach coleslaw to the broad refrigerator and helped with wiping the dishes the congregation would eat off of when the worship service was over. She chatted, still accepting congratulations on her baptism, and was mindful of each woman who entered the room.

None of them was Eva Deitwaller.

In a few minutes, it would be time for the women to take their seats on the benches on one side of the Stutzman barn, while the men prepared to process in and sit on the other side. Women and little girls and the smallest boys began drifting toward the barn. Outside the house, Annie paused to look around. A few children ceased their playing and dutifully answered their mothers' summons. The men were already informally arranging themselves in the order in which they would march in.

No Deitwallers anywhere.

Annie caught Franey Beiler's eye and said, "I notice the Deitwallers are not here. I hope they are well."

Franey scanned the assembly for herself. "I have not heard any news, but perhaps there is illness in the house."

Annie supposed that was possible. She lagged behind, though, still looking for one last buggy to come down the lane.

Rufus smiled at Annalise over the spinach coleslaw on his plate, and she returned the expression. Like most Sundays, they managed to sit at nearly adjoining tables, he with a group of men and she with women. He did not speak directly to her, but her eyes told him she heard what he would say if he could address her.

When the meal began to break up, he lost sight of her for a few minutes and supposed she had gone into the house to help wash dishes. He dutifully began dismantling the tables and benches so they could be loaded onto the wagon that would take them to the farm of the next family to host worship in two weeks.

Wherever he was headed to hang cabinets, Rufus hoped the next church service would find him seated in his usual spot for worship. By then the weather might be too cool to eat outside.

Finally the work was done. Teenagers organized a game of softball between two teams with not quite enough players and irregularly spaced bases. Younger children asked to go feed apples to the horses. Rufus's brother Jacob led the expedition to the meadow where the horses were grazing for the day.

Rufus lingered in the Stutzman front yard, speaking politely with anyone who wanted his attention but gradually moving farther from the house. He knew Annalise would be tracking his movements and arranging hers to intersect his path.

When she did, he smiled at the prayer *kapp* that was not quite straight.

"It's crooked again, isn't it?" Annalise reached up with both hands to rearrange her *kapp*. "I'm beginning to think my head is lopsided. Why else would I have such trouble pinning my *kapp* on straight?"

"You look lovely, just as you are." Rufus hoped that becoming Amish would not snuff out the quirks that drew him to her in the first place.

They walked together, staying in sight of the softball game and the horses chomping apples but carving out a private space around them.

"When do you have to go?" Annalise asked.

"Tonight."

"But it's the Sabbath."

Rufus flinched. "I know. But I have to be north of Cañon City ready to work at seven in the morning. Tom is willing to taxi me up there tonight."

She reached for his hand. "It will be so strange not to be able to picture where you are, not to think of you in your workshop humming hymns as you work."

"I can still hum from the *Ausbund*."

"I hope you will. I hope that will keep you close to us." Annalise turned to look him in the face. "Promise me that you'll call me. You can call the shop. Mrs. Weichert won't mind."

"I would need a phone," Rufus said.

"Believe me, the *English* always have phones."

"If it is God's will that I have such an opportunity, then yes, I will try to call you."

She nodded, as if satisfied. Rufus had expected a stronger insistence because she knew he would not use his own cell phone for a nonemergency call. He was not sure he would even take it with him.

Annalise's lips were slowly moving in and out. She was distracted in thought, and it was not his job that bothered her at the moment. He would not press her, though. Annalise needed no prodding to speak her mind when she was ready

As they ambled, he gradually steered her into a grove of pine trees. She may have been distracted, but Rufus had one thought on his mind that afternoon. He took both her hands so she was facing him and leaned down to find her mouth. She responded immediately, her lips surrendering their perplexed in-and-out motion to eagerly receive the press of his mouth on hers.

Rufus was on his way by now, sitting in the passenger seat of Tom Reynolds's red pickup. The grief Annie felt was not so much about his absence from her. Because she lived in town and he worked on the Beiler land or in outlying construction settings, they only saw each other once or twice a week as it was. No, her grief was that he should feel it necessary to take the job, to be isolated from his people, to be out of the rhythm of work and worship that sustained his spirit.

Would he create a new rhythm, she wondered, surrounded by *English* workers? Would he draw away to the quietness that fed his soul?

She prayed he would, and that it would be possible.

Annie sat at her dining room table, nudged up against the window, nursing a cup of tea and flipping through the red book about Tennessee and Arkansas history before going to bed. It was already late, but her thoughts had not yet fallen into the organized slots in her mind that would allow her to receive sleep. More than twenty-four hours had passed since she left the backpack for Leah—with a note. Was it remotely possible that the Deitwallers were not in church because Leah had gone home? Had Leah even opened the backpack? Did she see the flyer about the training burn? Had she already moved to a new spot without leaving a trail? Yesterday's relief at discovering where Leah was staying blackened now with the realization that, once again, Leah could be anywhere.

The small oil lamp threw a bubble of light across the table in an otherwise dark room. On the shelf above the table, where genealogy books commemorated the connection to Amish ancestors that Annie had discovered in her own family history, sat plain note cards and envelopes. Annie used them to write to her mother once a week or so. She reached for one now, but the name she wrote on the outside of the envelope was Matthew Beiler. The Beilers had left two married sons in Pennsylvania when they moved to Colorado, and Annie had seen enough letters arrive at the Beiler house from both Matthew and Daniel to know the addresses. She wrote now in a firm hand.

Then she turned to the note itself and had far less confidence about what to write. She did not even know the name of Leah Deitwaller's young man, so how could she ask Matthew about him? Franey mentioned a time or two writing to her sons about the family's new friend, Annalise Friesen, but Annie had to admit she and Matthew Beiler were strangers. She could not even be certain he would help.

All Annie wanted to know was whether this young man with whom Leah was desperate to reunite shared the girl's feelings. That information could be meaningful for knowing how to help Leah.

"*Dear Matthew,*" Annie wrote, "*My name is Annalise Friesen, and I am a friend of your family here in Colorado."*

She paused and sipped her now cold tea.

"I've met so many wonderful families during my journey into the Amish faith, and I so admire how they band together to help one another."

"Get to the point," Annie said aloud.

A shadow blurred past her outside the window, and Annie shivered involuntarily. Someone was in her driveway, moving toward the back.

Annie let the pen drop from her hand and moved into the kitchen where she kept a flashlight in a drawer. She turned on no other lights as she crept through the kitchen to the back door. Turning the knob and pulling at a snail's pace, Annie opened the solid door and now had only a flimsy screen door between herself and whoever was in her backyard. She pushed the screen door open just far enough to aim the flashlight.

"I got your note." Over her dress, Leah Deitwaller wore an oversized black hoodie with a pocket across the front.

No doubt stolen, Annie thought as she stepped out on the back porch. Leah stood at the bottom of the three short steps.

"Will you come in?" Annie said. "I want you to. I'll heat some soup."

Leah did not move. The bulge in her hoodie pocket rolled and then two green cat eyes appeared.

"I just came to say thanks." Leah stroked the kitten's head, now fully emerged from the pocket. "Especially for the milk."

"I want to help you." Annie took a cautious step toward the girl.

"I know. You don't give up easily."

"Neither do you."

"So anyway. Thanks. That's all."

"It's going to be a cold night."

"My sleeping bag is rated for twenty degrees below zero. I read the tag." Leah looked away. "I saw the flyer, too. I'll find a new place soon. You don't have to worry about me."

But Annie did worry about the girl, and she could not imagine that she would stop.

"You could stay here. I meant it when I offered. We can go back and get your things in the morning."

It had taken Annie an hour to pedal out to the dilapidated house. How long had it taken Leah to walk into town in the dark? She would be walking half the night to get back. Annie considered telling Leah about the half-written letter on the dining room table. But it would only have been to lure her inside. It was premature to imply that the letter represented any sort of promise that Leah would get what she wanted.

"Good night." Leah walked with the stretchy stealth of a cat.

Annie scampered down the steps now and around the side of the house. Leah was already halfway down the driveway, her form absorbed into the darkness.

Annie stopped chasing her and sighed. How hard could it be to get through to one teenage girl? After all, Annie had been a teenage girl once. She was not completely unfamiliar with the sensation that parents don't always understand their daughters.

A faint meow wafted across night air.

Seventeen

"hat would you like?" Bryan asked on Tuesday morning.

Ruth stood next to him in the coffee shop on Main Street. She stared at the menu written in colored chalk behind the counter, but it was a jumbled mess to her nervous eyes.

"Just coffee," she said.

"Latte? Cappuccino?"

She shook her head. "Just coffee. The coffee of the day."

"Still a simple Amish girl, eh?"

Ruth was not sure how to take that remark. The coffee of the day was an Ecuadorian deep roast, and even that sounded exotic. And if she was still a simple Amish girl, what was she doing in a coffee shop with an *English* firefighter?

"I'll get us a couple of sausage-and-egg sandwiches." Bryan pointed toward the list of breakfast foods on the left side of the menu. "How does that sound?"

"That would be great." Ruth's stomach flip-flopped relentlessly, leaving her unsure whether she could actually swallow any food. But she had said yes to a breakfast date, so it was reasonable that Bryan wanted to buy her breakfast.

He ordered, paid, and lifted some napkins from the basket

on the counter. "Where would you like to sit? Comfy chairs or a table?"

Ruth knew she ought to be able to make this simple decision. "A table, please."

Bryan led the way to a table about midway through the shop and pulled out a chair for her.

Ruth managed a smile as she sat down.

"Thank you for saying yes." Bryan took his seat across from her.

"You were kind to invite me."

He chuckled. "Stubborn more than kind, I'm afraid."

His laugh warmed her.

"Now what shall we talk about?" he said. "I promise not to say something stupid like, 'Have you always been Amish?'"

Ruth looked into his green eyes and saw the dance there. But he was not teasing her. It was a dance of curiosity.

"I'll spare you the awkwardness of asking," she said, "and just tell you that I left the Amish community almost three years ago. Our. . .that is, their education system only goes through eighth grade, and I believe God is preparing me to be a nurse. So I got my GED and enrolled at the university in Colorado Springs. I'm on a semester break while I sort out what kind of nurse."

"Really? You've been living in Colorado Springs? And to think I could have just run into you at Target or Starbucks."

Ruth sipped her still scalding coffee. "Colorado Springs is a big place."

A shop employee brought their coffee and breakfast sandwiches.

"I'll say a quick blessing for the food, if you don't mind," Bryan said.

Mind? Ruth's pulse quickened. Was Bryan an *English* with sincere faith? His words were simple but heartfelt, and at his "Amen," she heard her own voice echo the word.

"Now you," Ruth said. "Why have you come to Westcliffe?"

He took a swig of coffee and grinned. "Most people ask me why I went to Westcliffe 'of all places.'"

Ruth bit into her sandwich.

"My friend Alan and I studied firefighting in Colorado Springs, but there are no firefighting jobs available up there. Not even in Denver. We may have to go out of state, but we thought we might have better luck getting jobs if we had something to put on our resumes, so we came down here to be volunteer firefighters. Fortunately the grocery store took us both on, so we can pay the rent and eat all the almost-bad produce and cracked eggs we want."

"My friend Annalise grew up in Colorado Springs. You should talk to her sometime."

"Maybe you can introduce us."

"Perhaps. I'm staying with her while I'm figuring out my next move."

"Not with your family?"

"I went through a tough time with my family." Ruth picked at her sandwich with her fingers. "I'm not shunned or anything, because I was never baptized, but my *mamm* and I—well, it was hard. I have a driver's license and a car now, and I wear scrubs a lot of the time. So I like to go for dinner and church, but it's better if I'm not there all the time."

Abruptly someone slumped into the chair next to Bryan.

"Speak of the devil," Bryan said. "Ruth, you remember my friend Alan Wellner."

"Of course. How are you, Alan? Bryan was just telling me a bit about how you ended up in Westcliffe."

"Because we're a couple of losers who can't get grown-up jobs?" Alan took a strap off his shoulder and set a water bottle on the table before reaching for Bryan's coffee. Bryan slapped his hand away.

"It's a hard time to get a job." Ruth picked up her own coffee protectively. "It sounds like you're doing something smart with your in-between time."

"We already got to help with one fire," Alan said. "And tomorrow there's a controlled burn, so we'll get some hands-on time again."

"I saw the flyer," Ruth said. "Actually, I'm going to be there as well."

Bryan's eyebrows arched. "The fire chief is hoping there won't be too many lookey-loos."

"My supervisor thought it might be good for me to see the scene of a fire. It would just be some background for understanding what burn victims might have been through when they arrive for care."

"She probably cleared it with the chief, then."

"I'm sure she did. We'll stay out of the way. But this is big news in Westcliffe. I'm not sure how they'll keep people away if they really want to be there."

"We should see some good action." Alan tilted his chair back on two legs, hanging on to the table by his thumbs. "Did Bryan tell you he's also certified to drive the ambulance?"

Ruth caught Bryan's eye. "No, he didn't mention that."

"Only because we did not get that far before we were so rudely interrupted." Bryan glared at Alan.

"Don't give me that." Alan's chair smacked the floor, and he reached again for Bryan's coffee, this time successfully. "If you wanted privacy you would not have brought her to a coffee shop."

Bryan pasted a smile on his face. "Alan, would you like me to get you some coffee?"

"Thanks, buddy. As a matter of fact, I could use a warm-up."

"Ruth," Bryan said, "how about you?"

"I'm fine, thank you." Ruth glanced at the oversized decorative clock on the coffee shop wall. "I'll have to leave for the clinic before too much longer."

Bryan stood up. "Behave yourself, Wellner. I'll be right back."

Bryan had no sooner left the table than Alan snapped to his feet. "Dad! What are you doing here?"

Annie stood in her living room and considered the options. With Ruth staying until after Christmas, she did not have a spare bedroom, but she was determined that if Leah would agree to come and stay with her, Annie would do everything in her power to make the girl welcome. The living room was the best option.

The sofa had been new just a year ago, purchased when Annie thought of the house as a weekend getaway and before she stripped herself of her considerable financial resources. It was well constructed with comfortably deep sitting space. If she removed the loose cushions from the back, the remaining cushions were nearly as wide as a twin bed. Annie had no doubt it would be a comfortable place to sleep. But Leah would need some privacy. Annie did not know how long she might be there, and she did not want Leah to feel like she was staying in some sort of way station but in a safe, welcoming home.

Annie felt in her gut that Leah would come. It was just a matter of time.

The room was more wide than deep, stretching across the front of the house. It would be simple enough to section off one-half of the room for a small bedroom. In fact, a trifold privacy screen had just come into Mrs. Weichert's shop. It was old but not old enough for antique status, even if the meaning of the term were blurred. Mrs. Weichert was not going to want to put it out in the shop to sell. The screen had a sturdy frame, making it functional, not merely decorative.

Annie started shoving furniture around. Hardwood floors made the task reasonably simple. The front door would still open into the living room with a couple of chairs, between them an end table that Rufus had made housing a propane tank for the lamp above. The other half of the room would be screened off with the couch prepared for sleeping and another end table beside it. Annie scratched her chin as she pondered bringing down a small shelving unit from her own bedroom for Leah's use.

Upstairs, Annie cleared the shelves. From the hall closet she took a set of sheets and two blankets. They weren't the Amish quilts Leah was probably used to—Annie was still working on her first quilt—but the blankets would keep the girl warm. Remembering a pillow at the last minute, Annie carried the bedding downstairs and set the neat stack on one end of the couch before going back upstairs for the empty shelving unit.

Then she moved to the dining room table and picked up the letter she had addressed to Matthew Beiler. If she hurried, she could still catch the daily pickup time at the small post office at the end of Main Street.

"God," she said aloud, "may Your will be done. If You want me to help Leah, that's what I want to do."

A shudder shot through Ruth. Alan's countenance changed in an instant. In a fraction of a second, he went from playful and cocky to defensive and brooding. Her eyes moved from Alan to his father, then to Bryan on his way to fetch another cup of coffee, oblivious to the interruption.

This was not the way Ruth had imagined a simple breakfast date with an *English.*

"What are you doing here, Dad?"

"I had to see for myself this forsaken hole-in-the-ground of a town you chose to live in."

Alan looked at his shoes. Ruth picked up her coffee, wondering if were possible to just slip out of her chair without a fuss. The moment between father and son seemed far too intimate for onlookers. She scooted her chair back a few inches.

"Please don't go, Ruth." Alan's eyes dimmed. "Dad, this is Ruth Beiler, another resident who *chose* this town. Ruth, this is my father, Jason Wellner."

Ruth felt obliged to say something. "It's nice to—"

"We're not here to discuss anyone's choices but yours."

Jason Wellner did not even look at Ruth, who was relieved to see Bryan making his way back to the table.

"Then there's not much to say." Alan scratched the back of

his neck. "I have a job and a place to live. I'm not asking anything from you."

"This is not what your mother and I had in mind for you. It's bad enough you chose to study firefighting instead of getting a sensible business degree, but to come here? And bag groceries?"

"Look, here's Bryan." Alan pointed weakly.

"This was all his idea, wasn't it? You always did let him lead you around like a whipped puppy."

"Dad."

Ruth's belly twisted in indignation.

"Hello, Mr. Wellner." Bryan offered the fresh coffee, but Jason Wellner brushed it away.

"You're an insurance adjuster, Dad," Alan said. "You know buildings burn all the time. What's so bad about my wanting to help people when that happens?"

"There's no money in helping people." Wellner stroked his gray mustache.

"Maybe life is not about money," Bryan said.

Ruth held her breath.

"This conversation does not concern you, Bryan," Wellner said.

"Then perhaps you should have this conversation in another place." Bryan met the older man's glare.

"You're absolutely right. Alan, let's go outside."

"No." Alan sat in his chair and scooted it in. "I can get some good experience as a volunteer firefighter."

"Very well," Wellner said. "You have thirty days to come to your senses and find your room at home waiting for you. I'll use my contacts to find you a real job. After thirty days, you're on your own."

"He's already on his own." Bryan took his seat again.

A knot rose from Ruth's stomach to her throat.

Jason Wellner pivoted and strode across the coffee shop and out the door.

The trio left at the table let out a collective breath.

Eighteen

June 1892

"Why don't you let me pick it up for you?" A.G. stood at the bedroom door with his hand on the knob.

"You don't even know what I ordered." Bess Byler cast the gray hat onto the bed and picked up the blue one.

"I'm sure the clerk at Denton's Emporium will have a record of the order." A.G. stepped to the mirror and stood beside his wife. "The blue one, dear."

"Aren't you even curious what I want to pick up?"

A.G. tilted his head. "Something useful. Something we must have."

Bess slapped his forearm. "Don't tease me. I want to send some blankets to Malinda."

"For the children."

Bess donned the blue hat. "Of course for the children. It's cold in Colorado."

A.G. chuckled. "Well, it will be, I suppose." Not in the middle of June, but if he knew Bess, she was planning to add some embroidery or a new border to the blankets she was buying.

"I haven't been to Gassville since. . ." Bess fiddled with her handbag.

"Since John Twigg was shot." A.G. stilled Bess's hand then lifted her fingers to his lips. "Are you sure you want to go?"

She took her hand back and snapped the latch on her bag. "I refuse to live in fear. If I gave in to that, I would never want you to go to work."

A.G. knew Bess sometimes scrubbed the kitchen floor when he rode out to break up a fight, but she would never admit the spit shine had anything to do with his job as sheriff of Baxter County.

"The wagon is out front," he said. "I think I'll take an apple out to bribe that stubborn horse."

"I'll be right there."

He kissed her cheek. "Don't dawdle. I need to go over a few things with Deputy Combs over there, but I want to be back for one of your home-cooked dinners."

Outside, A.G. opened his palm and revealed the apple. The horse chomped into it immediately. He glanced at the trim white house with the green shutters, wishing Bess would stay home. Gassville was still jumpy. He did not want his wife in the middle of things.

Bess pulled the front door closed behind her, and A.G. gave her a one-sided smile. At sixty-three, the sight of her touched a spot inside him softer than ever.

As he tied up the mare in front of the emporium, A.G. scanned the street. The talk he had with Jimmy Twigg had successfully deterred him from sitting outside his store with a rifle aimed at the emporium, but that did not mean hostilities were calmed. If A.G. could give Bess an uneventful afternoon, though, he would take some pleasure in the day. He held the door open for her.

Inside the store, A.G. removed his hat and nodded at a few customers as he followed Bess to the counter. "Good afternoon, Leon."

Belle Mooney's father stood in the center of the main aisle

with a claw hammer in one hand.

"How is Belle?" A.G. asked the question softly, deliberately.

Leon shook his head. "How she could let herself fall into the clutches of the Twiggs, I will never understand. She hardly talks to me, even though we're living in the same house."

A.G. put both hands in his trouser pockets. He kept forgetting to mention to Bess that the left pocket had a hole in the seam. "Give Belle some time. Her loss is still fresh."

"It shouldn't be a loss at all." Leon gripped the hammer by the claw.

"Well now, that's for Belle to decide, isn't it?"

"For a man of the law, you don't have much sense of justice."

"For Belle it's a matter of the heart, Leon."

Leon grunted. A.G. patted his shoulder and moved up the aisle to where Bess was running her fingers along a bolt of pink-and-green calico.

"Why don't I go see Deputy Combs and come back for you?" A.G. said.

She looked at him out of the corner of her eye. "Yes, I suppose I might be a while."

The emporium's front door swung open before A.G. reached it, and a stranger swaggered in. A.G. slowed his pace to size him up. About six feet tall, he commanded an even larger presence. His brown suit was a recent cut. A.G. did not need his fashion-conscious wife to tell him that. Glancing at Leon, A.G. decided a welcome was in order. He extended a hand.

"I don't recall that I've had the pleasure. I'm Abraham Byler."

The man, not yet twenty-five, tilted his head and raised an eyebrow before accepting the handshake. "Jesse Roper."

A.G. heard Leon shuffle behind him, and deep in the store, Lee Denton moved behind the counter. A.G. hoped Lee was not trigger-happy enough to pull a gun on a stranger with the sheriff present.

"Leon, have you met Mr. Roper?"

"Don't you know who he is?" Leon snarled. "What kind of sheriff are you?"

"Sheriff, eh?" Jesse Roper said. "You didn't mention that."

A.G. turned his empty hands palms up. "I only meant to offer a friendly welcome."

Roper laughed and moved up the aisle, pausing here and there to inspect unlikely items. What did a young man like Roper want to do with drawers of buttons and threads? A.G. turned to follow his movements.

"He's a Twigg, you know." Leon made no effort to control his volume. "He's a grandson of Old Man Twigg. Probably a criminal."

Lee Denton stiffened. Abraham Byler winced.

"Now, Leon, nobody is looking for trouble," A.G. said. His gaze moved to Lee and held steady.

Between Roper and Denton stood Bess Byler. She had barely lifted her head at the commotion, but A.G. knew she would have absorbed every detail of the exchange.

"Mr. Denton," Bess said brightly, moving toward the counter, "I do believe I would like to look at your special-order book."

Lee mocked. "Sheriff Byler, have you considered it might save you some money if you just took your wife to New York to shop?"

"Lee, are you going to let me see that book or not?" Bess caught her husband's eye, as if to assure him she did not intend to place an order but only to dissipate tension.

Leon stared at Roper, who said, "I believe my business here is concluded. Y'all don't have the items my grandma asked for. Good day, gentlemen." He tipped his tall black hat at the Bylers and rammed a shoulder into Leon's on the way out.

For a moment no one in the shop spoke.

"Leon, are you okay?" A.G. said.

Leon grunted.

"How about you, Lee?"

Lee nodded.

"Promise me you'll keep your pistols out of this if it should turn into anything."

"You do your job, Sheriff Byler, and there will be no need for my pistols."

"The grand jury might see things differently if there is another incident."

Bess set her handbag on the counter with audible firmness. "Mr. Denton, I will thank you not to put my husband in needless danger."

Lee's shoulders sagged. "Aw, Bess, you know how I feel about you two. But I can't control everyone." He jabbed a finger toward Leon Mooney. "Him, for instance."

A.G. moved toward Leon, who was rubbing his shoulder. "Leon."

"Sheriff."

"No trouble."

"There's a town dance tonight, you know," Lee Denton said. "What if this character shows up?"

A.G. pivoted with deliberation. "Mrs. Byler, what do you say we have a night out? Dinner at the hotel and then dancing."

Bess put her fingers to her mouth in feigned shyness. "Why, Sheriff Byler."

Maura wore her mother's gloves, even though she would not last more than twenty minutes with them on.

She had tried to persuade Belle to come to the dance at the town hall. Weeks ago they had planned to attend and sewed new dresses and purchased hats from Maura's uncle Edwin's milliner shop. Belle had confessed her love for John Twigg and hoped they might announce their engagement soon—perhaps even the night of the dance.

Now Belle barely left the house and wore only dark colors. Maura had spent most of the afternoon cajoling and prodding.

She even resorted to heating Belle's iron to give her new dress a fresh press. But Belle would only shake her head.

No. No dance. Not with John Twigg in his grave and his killers unaccountable.

Maura herself did not have a date. She had one, but she broke it the previous week. If she could persuade Belle to go, it would be better to be free to be a companion to Belle, even if neither of them danced. Now Maura was on her own for the evening.

As soon as she entered the hall, Maura saw that Leon Mooney was supplementing the refreshments with a flask of his own. She licked her lips, removed her gloves, and marched toward the small round table where he sat against the wall, leaning his chair back on two legs.

He raised his flask and gave an unpersuasive grin. "So, you could not convince my daughter that she ought to come to the town dance and enjoy herself."

Maura shook her head and sat down. "I tried."

"Thank you for that, anyway."

Leon put his flask in the pocket of his suit jacket. Maura wondered how much he had consumed.

"Who are you going to dance with?" he asked.

She pressed her lips together and swallowed. "No one, I expect."

"A pretty woman like you?"

"In fact, I don't think I'll stay long. I felt obliged to come for some reason, but I wonder if I shouldn't be with Belle tonight."

"She won't have you," Leon said. "She would tell you to go home."

Maura had to agree. Still, the evening held no attraction for her now.

Leon let his chair legs down, throwing his weight on the table. "What's he doing here?"

"Who?" Maura looked around.

"Roper. Jesse Roper. I've been asking around about him. He

is Old Man Twigg's grandson, or the grandson of his brother, or something like that."

"Oh." Maura glanced at Leon's pocket. He did not disappoint. He tipped the flask all the way up this time and his head back, telling her he had emptied it.

He scraped his chair back and stood up.

"Leon." Maura put a hand on his forearm.

He shook it off. "Roper!"

The tall stranger strode slowly across the hall and halted in front of Leon, feet shoulder width apart. "Watch your mouth, Mooney."

Leon jabbed a finger in Roper's chest. "You people destroyed my daughter."

Roper knocked away Leon's arm.

"All the Twiggs are the same way," Leon said.

"My name's Roper."

"Makes no difference. You have their blood." Leon's eyes widened in fire.

Maura stood. "Leon, why don't we go get something to eat?"

"I'm not hungry." Leon stared at Jesse Roper.

Maura put on the too-small gloves just for something to do. Helpless was not her favorite feeling.

"Isn't that the sheriff?" Joseph tilted his head down the street. "Must be his wife. I don't believe I've seen them together before."

Zeke narrowed his eyes and shifted the dry goods package under his arm. "Joseph Beiler, you are giving in to distraction."

"I'm just curious. Beiler. Byler. Wouldn't you be curious if you met someone named Berkley or Buerkli?" He followed the progress of the sheriff and his wife and started walking in the same direction.

"Joseph, are you doubting your faith?"

Joseph's head snapped around. "What would make you say such a thing?"

"When the bishop chose you for this mission, you did not want to come. You came in *demut*, submission. But now I don't recognize what is in your mind."

"Have you heard from the bishop?"

Zeke stopped walking. "No."

"Then I am doing nothing wrong. I am still in submission, awaiting the bishop's will."

"We have the beans we came into town to buy," Zeke said. "We should go back to the livery and start the pot boiling."

"And now I don't recognize what is in your mind," Joseph said. "You have always been the friend to show me that God might smile once in a while."

"I still believe that." Zeke pressed his lips closed and breathed out through his nose. "All right, then. But I am hungry. I will go start the beans."

"I won't be long. I would simply like to meet my distant cousin."

Zeke laughed. "You're making up stories."

The Bylers were well down the street by now, and Joseph lengthened his stride to catch them. Everyone said his family held their heads in a distinctive way. Was it his imagination that Abraham Byler also shared this trait? Or that he seemed gentle and affectionate with his wife the way Joseph's father was with his mother?

The sheriff paused in front of the town hall and leaned his head in toward his wife, saying something that made her laugh. He held the door open for her, and the building swallowed them up.

The forbidden building. Or was it? It was just a hall. The sign tacked to the door said, Music and Dance. Perhaps it was not so different than a Sunday night singing at home. An *English* singing.

Joseph pulled the door open.

Maura nearly lost her balance scuttling away as Jesse Roper raised one giant fist, threw Leon against the wall, and held him there by the front of his shirt.

Maura gasped, and conversation around them halted. Few heads turned when the hall's door opened, but Maura felt the draft and allowed herself a glance.

"Sheriff Byler!" she called out.

Jesse Roper leaned his face within inches of Leon's and glared. "You keep your mouth shut, you brainless bigot."

"If I don't?" Leon glowered.

A stone sank in Maura's stomach. Had Leon no sense at all?

Roper responded by shaking his fist, shuddering Leon against the wall. "I'll blow your head off the next time we meet."

"The sheriff is coming." Even Maura's loud announcement did nothing to deter Roper. She tracked the sheriff's direct progress across the hall.

Sheriff Byler approached with his usual calm. "Mr. Roper, I suggest you put Mr. Mooney down now. We'll chalk this up to too much drink, shall we?"

With a downward thrust, Roper put Mooney back in his chair and turned on his heel to march out of the hall.

Mooney shook his fist. "You haven't heard the end of this."

Nineteen

Annie had hardly swallowed her breakfast on Wednesday morning before she was on her bicycle. She had no reason to go watch the training burn—other than the smoldering sensation in her stomach that Leah Deitwaller had not removed her sparse belongings after all. The pedals spun hard and fast as Annie leaned into them with all her weight to keep her speed up even on inclines. She had the day off from working at the shop and figured it was better to be sure Leah did not need further prodding than to later regret not going.

As early as Annie was, the fire department was earlier. Four water trucks circled the old house. Firefighters in full garb milled around, some still with morning coffee in their hands. Annie laid her bike down in the browning fall meadow floor well away from the house and proceeded on foot. All she wanted was to be sure, absolutely sure, that Leah was out of the house and not sleeping through the bright dawn. It would only take a minute to slip in through the front opening and look in the back rooms. If the cat bowl was gone, Annie would be certain Leah had cleared out just as she promised she would. Annie had her eye on the empty door frame now. She needed another few moments and she would clear out of the way herself.

"I'm sorry, but you can't go in there." A yellow-suited arm of a firefighter fell like a gate in front of Annie.

"I'll just be a minute," Annie said.

The helmet atop his head swung from left to right. "No, you won't. No one is going in at this point."

"You don't understand." Annie rubbed her palms together. "A young woman was squatting here. I saw her things the other night. I just want to be sure she got out."

"We walked through the house last night and again this morning. No one is in there."

"And no sign of a cat? Just a kitten? Black and white."

"No cat. No woman. No anything. It's just an abandoned structure that the owner is happy to have removed."

Annie peered at what she could see of the young man's face behind his gear. "Aren't you the man who came to see Ruth Beiler out at her family's farm?"

He snapped his head up. "I might be. Who are you?"

"Annie Friesen. Ruth and I are friends."

"Then, yes, I am the man who came to see Ruth. Bryan Nichols. She told me about you."

Annie pulled her skirt away from her hips on both sides. "I guess my story is pretty obvious. I up and joined the Amish."

"She said you're from Colorado Springs. Me, too." Bryan relaxed his posture but maintained his position between Annie and the house. "Where did you go to high school?"

"Doherty."

"Me, too. We'll have to form an alumni chapter. My friend Alan can join us."

A vague image floated through Annie's mind of what her own classmates' faces would look like if they knew she had joined the Amish church. A few of them did know, in fact, and all of them had chosen not to remain in touch. When Annie closed her Facebook and Twitter accounts, she had cut herself off from those years.

"I just want to be absolutely certain my young friend is out of the house," she said.

In the passenger seat of her supervisor's vehicle, Ruth approached the abandoned house. Already spectators were gathering in clumps, many of them sitting on the hoods of their vehicles or on blankets on the ground to await the excitement. Ruth had mixed feelings. Witnessing the burn might well impress on her the urgency of treating burn victims, but she was fairly certain she already understood that principle. In her lap was a textbook on treating burns and a checklist of standard protocol for making a patient stable enough to transport to a burn center as far away as Denver.

"Looks like we have a few minutes if you want to take a look around." Her supervisor set the emergency brake. "Let's meet back here in half an hour."

Ruth nodded and opened the passenger door, uncertain how close she wanted to go. This place was a good fifteen miles from the Beiler farm. She had had a vague notion of where Karl Kramer's ranch was, but she had no idea any structures this old remained on it. Slowly, she ambled closer and wondered where Bryan was and what his role in this event would be. In full gear, all the firefighters looked alike.

She looped around one of the water trucks and saw a ladder truck roll in and take its position. While Westcliffe and neighboring Silver Cliff together amounted to a pin dot on a map, the fire protection service based in Westcliffe served all of Custer County. Ruth knew they worked hard to keep their equipment plentiful and up to date.

It was not Bryan whom she spotted but Annalise gesturing past a firefighter. Annalise had not said anything about coming out to watch, so what was she doing here with that characteristic look of determination on her face? A few seconds passed before

Ruth realized that the firefighter staring down Annalise was Bryan Nichols.

Ruth approached.

"Here's Ruth now," Bryan said, grinning.

"Should my ears be burning?" She put her hands to her mouth at her own bad joke. "Sorry. What's going on?"

"Leah was staying here," Annalise said. "I just wanted to make sure she got out."

"And I have assured your friend that the fire department has made absolutely certain that no humans or kittens are inside this building, whether voluntarily or involuntarily."

"Then I'm sure she's out," Ruth said.

"The chief had firefighters out here all day yesterday setting up for today. No one is in this structure."

Annalise blew out her breath. "Okay, then. I won't worry anymore that you didn't let me double-check."

Another yellow-uniformed figure approached them, the pieces of his headgear in place. A deep voice boomed. "I'm afraid unauthorized personnel must vacate this area immediately."

"Of course." Ruth stepped back, pulling Annalise's elbow with her.

Bryan, however, moved toward the man and flipped up his mask. "Wellner, where have you been? The chief is about to strike your name from the training manifest."

Ruth rolled her eyes. It was Alan.

"I couldn't get away from work any sooner. I just spoke to our fearless leader." Alan tugged at his gloves. "Not only is my name on the manifest, but the chief is bouncing with joy at my mere presence. Words do not express the abounding gladness."

Ruth held her textbook against her chest with both arms. Alan showed none of the tension she had observed in the presence of his father the day before.

Alan smacked his hands together. "Are we going to burn something today or not?"

Annie looked from Ruth to Bryan to the stranger. "Hello. I'm Annie Friesen."

"Alan Wellner, future fire chief of Custer County. Pleased to meet you."

Annie couldn't help but laugh at this young man's exuberant self-confidence.

Bryan elbowed Alan. "As you can see, my friend does not lack belief in his own ability. But he's right. You ought to move farther away from the house, or the present fire chief of Custer County will be breathing down our necks."

"He's a dragon, he is," Alan said.

The foursome began slow but direct progress away from the house and past the line of fire engines.

"Isn't that your friend Capp?" Bryan asked.

Annie raised her eyes to see Elijah Capp standing behind a water truck, his feet planted shoulder width apart and his arms crossed behind his back. His brown hair fluttered in the breeze.

"I wonder what happened to his hat," Annie said.

"Hello, Elijah," Ruth said softly.

Elijah nodded.

"Looks like we have quite a turnout to watch the spectacle," Bryan said. "We'd better make it a good show."

Annie glanced at the growing crowd. She came because she was worried about Leah. It had not occurred to her that half the town would want to see this old building in flames.

"You all had better get behind the safety line now." Bryan guided the elbows of both Ruth and Annie.

"Actually, I am supposed to meet my supervisor," Ruth said. "I'll see you all later."

Ruth barely looked at Elijah, Annie noticed. But neither did she meet Bryan's eyes. She simply turned and walked around the water truck toward the area where most of the cars were parked.

"We'd better take our positions, too." Bryan nudged Alan. "We'll catch up with you guys after the drama is over."

"Nice to meet you both," Annie said. A moment later, she was left standing alone with Elijah Capp. "I came looking for Leah Deitwaller. As long as I'm here, though, I suppose I should stay and watch."

"Let's find a better vantage point," Elijah said. "We won't be able to see anything from behind these trucks once the fire starts."

"Okay." Annie followed Elijah's lead. "Should we look for your hat first?"

"My hat?"

She pointed to his bare head, uncharacteristic for an Amish man.

"My hat is not lost. I did not put it on this morning."

"Oh."

They walked together for a few yards.

"Franey Beiler tells me that your mother has repainted her kitchen cabinets. How do they look?"

"They were only half-finished the last time I saw them. I hope she is pleased, though."

Annie reached for Elijah's arm to stop his pace. "How can you not have seen your family's kitchen cabinets?"

He sighed and looked away. "I moved out."

Annie's eyes widened. "Where to?"

"An apartment. A large room and bath in an *English* house."

"When did you do this?" Annie could not make sense of what she heard. Elijah had moved out of his Amish home and had deliberately come today without his black felt hat.

"Last week, days ago." Elijah resumed walking. "I'm thinking of becoming a volunteer firefighter. What do you think?"

"Wait. Let's go back to the part about how you moved out of your family's home."

"It's better this way." Elijah kicked a rock and sent it skittering. "They will have a hard time with my decision and will have to shun me. And I don't want to be a hypocrite under their roof."

"What decision are you talking about?" Elijah Capp was one of the most devout, respectful men Annie had met in the Amish church. "What do you mean about being a hypocrite?"

He met her gaze, silent.

"Elijah—"

"It would dishonor my parents to stay where my heart no longer lies."

They had turned their backs on the old house while they walked. The sudden roar of fire startled them both, and they pivoted in tandem. Bright orange flames poured out from the center of the house and shot up billowing black smoke.

None of the firefighters moved.

"What are they waiting for?" Annie asked.

"A fire always has a head start, does it not? Perhaps they are waiting for the response time it normally takes for the engines to arrive."

"This house is a pile of dry sticks. Nothing will be left of it."

As she spoke this time, the teams went into action, each one unrolling hose and positioning themselves. Ladders appeared and rose in height.

"That house won't hold any weight," Annie insisted. "They shouldn't try to climb."

Elijah smiled. "Mainly they are trying out different hoses to see how they perform. That's why the water trucks are spaced as they are. The ladders are an extra drill to improve their time."

Annie drew her head back and stared at Elijah. "And you know this how?"

He tilted his head then straightened it. "You are not the only one who knows how to use the resources of the public library."

"Elijah Capp, have you been on the Internet?"

Twenty

$\mathcal{I}$f Elijah heard Annie's question, he refused to acknowledge it. He spread his feet and crossed his wrists in front of him, eyes forward focused on the fire. Annie stood beside him, mesmerized by both the enormity and the proximity of the inferno. Teams of firefighters rolled into action now, raising nozzles, supporting hoses, controlling the flow of water from the massive tanks.

"Did you know my parents' barn burned down when I was young?" Elijah tapped one booted foot.

"No, I never heard that." Annie watched him out of the side of her eye. "What happened?"

"Well, it wasn't an electrical fire. They were sure of that much."

Annie snorted.

"The investigators said it was a gasoline fire, but I'm not sure if they figured out where the spark came from to light it."

"It's amazing what they can determine when you think all the evidence would have burned up."

Before them, the feeble front wall of the house gave way. Annie flinched.

"I was a little boy," Elijah said. "My parents always shooed me from the room whenever anyone talked about what happened.

875

I've always wanted to know."

"You're grown now. Why don't you ask?"

He shrugged. "It was fifteen years ago. No one was hurt, not even any of the animals. As soon as the rubble was cleared away, the church came for a barn raising."

"Still. If you want to know..."

"We are not that sort of family. My family carried on. We moved out here. What's the point?"

They watched the flames. Around them, people in huddles shaded their eyes and pointed at shooting flames. Annie peered at the hurried movements of people in bulky yellow jackets and helmets, trying to pick out Bryan and Alan, the only two firefighters she knew by name and only because she had met them an hour ago. She suspected four of the figures she saw were women who did not miss a beat keeping up with the men.

"So you want to be a firefighter because of what happened to your family?" she asked.

Elijah leaned one direction and then the other without lifting his feet. "It seems a worthy cause, even as a volunteer. Perhaps especially as a volunteer."

"It takes a lot of guts. I'm not sure I could do it."

"You underestimate yourself, Annalise. Look at what you have already accomplished in your life. How can you think there is anything you could not do?"

"It's risky. Scary."

"And necessary, don't you think?"

"Well, yes," Annie admitted. "The rest of us depend on it."

"I would like to be able to do what I am willing to ask of others in this one area."

Annie waited, biding her time and rolling possible words over in her mind.

"Do Amish men become firefighters?" she finally asked. "I mean, the technology..."

Elijah turned his head and looked down at her from his height, nearly as tall as Rufus.

"No, I don't suppose they do," he said.

"So, you've made some decisions that are. . .permanent?"

He nodded. "I believe they will be."

"And Ruth?"

"I don't give up as easily as she hopes I will."

Ruth had long ago lost the thread of what her supervisor was explaining to her. She had, however, observed the fact that the woman's husband was one of the volunteer firefighters training on the back side of the structure, which explained more convincingly her belief that being present at the fire had learning value for Ruth.

The remains of a second wall surrendered, and one end of a beam that ran through the house thundered to the ground, shifting the primary direction of the blaze. Unlike the charred half-built house containing Rufus's cabinetry, nothing would be left of this one. The fire department would intentionally let the structure collapse and smolder, instead concerning themselves with ensuring flames did not spread into the meadow around the house.

Ruth cleared her throat and consulted her clipboard, trying to find her place in the oral review of procedures that her supervisor was in the midst of.

Staging area.

Triage.

Chain of command.

Safe transport.

Ruth glanced across the scene to watch Bryan Nichols in action. He was focused, attentive, on task. A few feet away and sharing Bryan's hose, Alan Wellner divided his gaze between the burning house and a clump of spectators. Ruth followed his line of sight and saw the sheriff, no doubt present to be sure the assembly on the gentle meadow slope abided by all safety precautions of the event.

The pen in her hand reminded Ruth to focus again on her list. Her supervisor had stopped speaking, though. Eyes all around the perimeter of the burn focused on the galloping flames and the disappearing structure. Slats of wood that had once been a wall popped and crumbled. Ruth covered her mouth to cough even as smoke infiltrated her nostrils. The movement of lifting her elbow transferred her gaze once again.

Annalise and Elijah stood out of earshot but close enough for Ruth to see they were conversing regularly. Annalise's hair was neatly coiled and tucked under her *kapp*. Well, perhaps not neatly. No matter how long Annalise let her blond hair grow or how many pins she used, strands always seemed to escape her efforts.

Ruth's own brown hair was pulled back and fastened simply at the back of her neck with an oversized plain brown barrette she would never have owned growing up. By Amish standards, it was ornate and might tempt the wearer to vanity. One hand went up now to check the clasp.

Standing across from them and twisting her lips in thought, Ruth's first instinct was to wonder what Annalise and Elijah would be talking about with such concentration. Were they discussing her?

She scribbled at the bottom of her checklist. So what if they were? Annalise had joined the church, after all. Soon enough Rufus would propose and they would marry. Why should she not talk to another member of the church in a public setting? They were the only two Amish people present. Annalise was probably just being friendly.

Tom Reynolds's red pickup roared into the meadow with the horn blaring as if someone had strapped a rock to it. Adrenaline surged through Ruth's midsection as Tom nudged his way past a couple of onlooking families and got as close to the security line as he could. He then jumped out of his truck and marched along the line, waving his hands at the fire chief. A moment later, the chief began pointing and shouting orders. The water supply to Bryan and Alan's hose abruptly shut off, and they began rolling the hose rapidly. Two ladders came down while a second water truck also stowed gear.

Back in his truck, Tom gunned the engine and began backing up. Ruth ran straight toward him, slapping her hands on the hood.

"What's going on, Tom?"

"A fire." Tom turned the steering wheel.

Ruth moved out of the way of the turning front left tire but would not release her grip on Tom's lowered window. "What are you talking about? The fire is right here. They have it all under control."

"Another one."

"Where?" Her heart thudded.

"An old outbuilding on the other side of the highway, about three miles out. I think it's on county land. At first I thought it was the training burn, but I realized it was the wrong side of the road."

Behind Ruth, the engine of a water truck howled. She was glued to Tom's pickup.

"Get out of the way, Ruth." Tom slapped at her fingers on his window and let his foot off the brakes. The truck rolled, and Ruth jumped back.

A moment later Bryan was behind the wheel of his water truck and rumbling through the meadow. His focus was strictly on navigating out of one fire scene and toward another. Beside him in the cab, Alan lifted three fingers in a wave. Ruth gaped at three vehicles being redeployed to the new fire even as she heard the shriek of the siren beckoning volunteers from around the county.

Ruth turned back to the fire behind her just as the final wall tumbled and remaining firefighters rushed in to fill the gaps left by the departing trucks. The glory of the construction burn was nearly extinguished, outblazed by the potential of an unattended fire in open grassland. Spectators were already jumping into their cars and turning them around toward the road.

Gripping her clipboard, Ruth ran toward her supervisor's car, where the older woman already had the ignition fired up. The clinic would need to be ready if someone were hurt.

Word of the second fire advanced through the crowd. Annie saw nothing to be gained by dashing off to watch another fire. Suddenly, though, she wondered how Elijah had gotten to this destination. She had not seen a buggy all morning, and anybody with half a brain would have kept away animals that might bolt. She turned to ask him.

He was gone, already lost from her sight.

Annie turned back to the training burn, which was fast becoming a haphazard pile of glowing half boards. Water still flowed from two trucks but with less fury. When the traffic thinned a bit more, Annie decided, she would fetch her bicycle and head back to town.

A flash of blue caught the corner of her eye, and Annie snapped her head around. Amish blue. The more she handled Amish fabrics, the more distinctive that shade became in Annie's mental palette. It was not the mass-dyed hue of a commercial manufacturer that clung to the surface of an inexpensive material, but the rich saturation that emanated from the core of tight-woven cloth.

Annie realized she was holding her breath and blew it out. Forgetting her bicycle—it was in the wrong direction—she ran after the flash of blue. At least where she thought she had seen it.

Leah had been there. Annie was sure of it. She must have left home with only the dress on her back, because every time Annie saw her, Leah wore the same hue, sometimes with a purple apron and sometimes without. But always the same blue.

At the edge of the dissipating crowd, Annie systematically scanned from left to right. When she finally spotted the girl, she was looking at her back. With her skirts gathered in her fists, Leah ran with surprising dexterity, and Annie did not think she could catch her.

Three miles. That was the rumor. The new fire was only three miles.

Annie looked again at the speed with which Leah moved and thought about the miles she knew the girl had been crisscrossing in the last two weeks. When Annie ran track in high school and was constantly training, three miles was nothing.

Would Leah set fire to another building because she had been forced out of this one? Surely not.

Rufus's words from just after the first fire rankled. *"You talked to her over a crowded, lengthy meal. Can you be certain she was there during the service?"*

Annie was just going to have to find Leah again. To be sure.

Twenty-One

June 1892

"We're shutting down for the day." The Dentons' foreman wiped a handkerchief across his perspiring brow.

Joseph and Zeke gripped the ends of a felled tree sheared of its branches, sharing its weight with Dayton Brown and Oscar Board.

"What he means," Dayton said, "is that he's too old and tired and can't stand the heat another minute."

Oscar snorted.

"We're all hot." Joseph glanced at Zeke. "I'm sure he has in mind the best interest of the entire crew."

"No doubt." Zeke's agreement came quickly.

"You Amish seem nice enough," Dayton said, "but even you can't think a half day off has anything to do with us. It's not even lunchtime. They won't pay us for the afternoon, you know."

"I do know," Joseph said.

They lugged the tree away from the edge of the bluff. Joseph had no idea what the Denton brothers planned to do with the heaps of logs cleared from their land and accumulating farther and farther from the shore. He could now stand well back from their ferry dock and see the curve of the White River. The Dentons would be able to sit on their front porches and see a horseman coming. The work would not last much longer, but Joseph and Zeke had been frugal with their pay. Whatever their journeys did not consume, they would take home to their families.

Joseph put his thumbs through his suspender straps. There was the matter of Hannah waiting for him. Perhaps in his absence someone else had sparked her interest.

She was not the flighty type.

He felt the poke in the middle of his back, Zeke's test of his nerves, and refused to flinch.

"Let's ride the crew's wagon into town," Zeke said. "We can ask at the post office for a letter."

"You go ahead." Joseph still surveyed the river. "I would like to walk and think."

"In the heat?"

"It is not so hot as the *English* believe."

"Surely there will be a letter," Zeke said. "We posed a simple question about the bishop's wishes. I am beginning to fear something has gone wrong at home that would delay his response."

"What does it matter?" Joseph murmured.

Hands on his hips, Zeke moved to stand between Joseph and the view of the river. "My friend, we can continue our scouting mission or we can go home to Tennessee. When the letter comes, we will do one or the other, but we will not linger in Gassville."

"I did not suggest we should." Joseph raised both hands to straighten his hat. When his hands came down away from his face, he imagined flinging his black felt Amish hat into the White River's current. He shook the devilish image out of his mind. "I'll see you back at the livery."

Joseph did not hurry. Eventually he would end up in town, behind the livery. He would go inside to help with the few simple chores they exchanged for the privilege of spreading their bedrolls under the night sky. But for now, he walked without specific destination. Sweat trickled between his shoulder blades.

At the crack of a pistol, Joseph dropped to the ground. Laughter followed the shot. Joseph did not find it amusing to be the target of an *English* gun. Another shot blasted a tin can. Joseph knew that sound. Even Amish boys learning to hunt for food had to practice on something. He crawled toward the shots. Making himself seen was his best hope for avoiding a stray bullet.

"Hello!" he called.

Boots shuffled against the ground.

"I'd just like to get through," Joseph shouted. He looked past the underbrush toward rows of toes reorienting toward him. Black *English* boots. "Is it safe?"

"Who's there?" a voice demanded.

Joseph stood and kept a tree between himself and the clearing ahead. "Joseph Beiler."

"Oh, the Amish man."

That was Walter's voice, Joseph was sure. What was he doing out pistol shooting?

A moment later, Walter tugged on Joseph's sleeve. "You can come out."

Joseph stepped from behind the tree in Walter's protection. Several young men stood with pistols in their hands, the tallest of them Jesse Roper. Joseph had followed Sheriff Byler into the town hall the night of the dance in time to see what Roper was capable of.

"It's just a friendly shooting match." Roper grinned. "Do you shoot?"

After John Twigg's death, Joseph had heard enough *English* talk to know that a shooting match in the woods was against the law in Baxter County.

"Well, do you shoot?" Roper asked again.

Joseph shook his head. "Only rifles, and only for food."

"So you've never fired a pistol?"

Again Joseph shook his head.

"You can use mine." Roper offered the heel of his weapon with a faint smirk.

"No thank you." Joseph scanned the group of shooters. Roper clearly was the oldest and Walter the youngest, with three in between. Joseph did not see a pistol in Walter's hand, a fact that brought some relief.

Jesse Roper fired another shot at another can. "One bullet left. It's yours if you want it."

"Try it," Walter urged. "Maybe you have a knack."

"I don't believe I will." Joseph touched his hat. As good as Roper was, Joseph was certain he was a better shot. He needed no target practice and would not fire for sport. But watching would cause no harm as long as he was behind the shooting line.

"I'll try," Walter said.

Roper laughed. "Some say I'm stupid, but I'm not that stupid."

"I'm a good shot," Walter insisted.

"Well, we're not going to find out today." Roper nodded toward one of the other men. "Your turn."

The shooter missed, which Roper found riotously amusing. In the middle of his laugher, he raised his own gun, aimed, and fired a bullet against the innocent can.

"That's it, boys. I'm hungry. Somebody owes me lunch." Roper pointed at Digger Dawson. "I believe it was you who wagered your mama's cooking."

Digger kicked up a flurry of dirt. "Yes, sir, I reckon I did."

"Let's go, then."

"Oh good," Walter said. "I'm hungry, too."

Jesse Roper shook his head. "Not you."

"Why not?"

"I don't aim to get between a boy and his daddy. You skedaddle on home. And not a word about this, you hear?"

Walter started to protest further, but Joseph caught his eye and gave the look he generally aimed at Little Jake when his brother seemed inclined to foolishness on the family farm. The boy picked up a rock and heaved it into the woods, but he left.

Jesse Roper laughed, and Joseph could not help liking the

sound. Jesse seemed to do just what he wanted at any moment. The voice of Joseph's father jumped the miles and the years to speak to Joseph words of caution, words of warning, words of the scripture about what happened to fools. Joseph had no doubt that all of the Amish and many of the *English* would cast Roper in that category. Still, watching the carelessness of Jesse's face, Joseph wondered what such abandon would feel like. Obviously Jesse could saunter into a strange town and attract a following. What did these young men see in him? A daring spirit? Fearlessness they did not dare explore themselves?

Joseph reached up and tugged his hat.

"You do that a lot, you know." Roper pointed a finger at Joseph then reached for his own hat, high and broad and black with a deep crease in the crown.

Joseph ran his hands down the front of his trousers. "I don't notice when I do it."

"It'll ruin your hat."

"It is not much of a hat to begin with." Nothing like Roper's.

Jesse threw his head back and laughed again. "You got that right. You comin' to lunch with us?"

Joseph shook his head immediately. "Thank you, but my friend will be expecting me soon."

"By all means, we don't want to make your friend jealous that you had a warm, home-cooked meal and he did not."

Joseph swallowed. He had the good sense to decline the lunch invitation because he suspected the rumor that Roper was related to the Twiggs was true.

Roper leaned over and tucked his pistol into the wide cuff of his trouser leg and fastened it in with a snap. "Put your guns away, boys. And get those cans. Your daddies won't be happy if they think I led you to the den of wickedness."

If someone in Joseph's family spoke of a den of wickedness, it would be with all seriousness. Roper found amusement in his defiance. Despite the grand jury clearing the Denton brothers, after John Twigg died, Sheriff Byler made it clear that further illegal pistol shooting would not be tolerated. Even if Jesse Roper's recent arrival meant he did not know this, the others certainly did.

Joseph watched Roper carefully pick up the jacket that matched his trousers from the bush where he had laid it. As reckless as he was toward authority, Roper was a stickler for his clothes and appearance. The young men collected pieces of the cans they had blasted and tossed them in a burlap sack, which one of them slung over his shoulder as the group ambled toward the path that would take them out of the woods and toward the ranch where Roper presumed lunch would be waiting.

None of them looked back to see that Joseph had not moved.

Joseph gave them a head start, while he briefly considered his options, and then followed. His father had taught him well to track prey through thick woods without giving himself away, and Joseph had no trouble following without causing any of the foursome to suspect their surroundings. Curiosity compelled his soundless steps. He and Zeke worked long hours on the Denton cattle ranch, but other than one dinner with Maura Woodley and her father, he had scant experience with *English* households.

It was surprisingly easy to climb a maple tree and lean comfortably into the cradle of its thick branches. From above the sight line of the home's inhabitants, Joseph had a clear view of the front porch, into the front parlor, and through to the dining room. Digger Dawson's mother scowled, but she served lunch. Fried chicken, mashed potatoes, beets, chocolate cake. The table was laid with a light blue tablecloth and adorned with a vase of daisies. The curtains were yellow with white eyelet trim and hung against pale green painted walls. Knickknack shelves and formal photographs reminded Joseph he was looking into a world not his own.

Even with the windows open to catch the breeze, Joseph heard little of the conversation, but periodically Jesse Roper erupted in laughter and the others followed in nervous imitation. Joseph was glad he had not gone in with them.

A horse trotted toward the house pulling a wagon driven by a man Joseph did not recognize. At the porch, the man climbed down and rapped on the front door.

"I've come about the pistol shooting," Joseph heard the man say when a weary-looking Mrs. Dawson opened the door.

She turned and glared toward the dining room. "It's Deputy Combs for y'all."

A moment later, Jesse Roper filled the open door frame.

"You're under arrest," Deputy Combs said, "for shooting pistols. We've had a report from an eyewitness."

Joseph's heart sank. Surely not Walter.

"All of you," Deputy Combs demanded, "come with me."

Roper spread his feet and crossed his arms. Behind him, the other shooters assembled.

Deputy Combs pointed at each one in turn. "I brought the wagon. You get on out there and let me take you into town and do this properly."

One young man came forward. "I only shot once."

"Once is against the law," Combs said. "In the wagon. If you resist, you'll only make more trouble for yourself."

One by one, Digger and his two friends slipped past Roper and straggled toward the wagon.

From his branch, Joseph watched *English* justice in process—and was once again glad he did not take hold of the pistol Roper offered.

"I do believe I will finish my lunch," Roper said.

"You're resisting arrest," Combs said. "You must come with me."

Roper whipped out his pistol and laughed. "You don't say!" He aimed the pistol, his thumb ready to cock it.

Combs turned on his heel and ran to the wagon.

Roper roared in laughter.

Twenty-Two

On Thursday, Annie and Ruth both had afternoon shifts, a coincidence that allowed them a leisurely late breakfast together. Annie laid out bacon strips on a tray to put in the oven while Ruth pulled eggs and cheddar cheese from the refrigerator and whole-wheat bread from the bread box Rufus had made for Annie.

"I'm so relieved no one was hurt in the fires yesterday." With thumb and forefinger, Annie nudged a slice of bacon to the edge of the pan to make room for one more.

"Bryan says there's definitely an arsonist." Ruth positioned two eggs between the fingers of one hand and cracked them simultaneously on the edge of a mixing bowl before reaching for two more.

"I have to learn how to do that," Annie said.

"I'll teach you sometime."

"When did you see Bryan again?"

Ruth cracked two more eggs and picked up a whisk. "Last night. He came by."

Annie pinched her eyebrows together. "How did he know where to find you?"

"I told him I was staying with you."

"He does have a habit of just showing up, doesn't he? Where was I?"

"Upstairs reading in bed already."

"That late?"

Ruth rolled her head toward Annie. "Annalise, it was eight thirty."

Annie slid the tray of bacon into the warm oven. She had to admit it was not unusual for her to be upstairs with a book by that hour. Lately it was the volume on Arkansas history. She was surprised to discover a Sheriff Abraham Byler of Baxter County, who seemed a gentle, well-loved soul.

"So what did Bryan say about the fires?" Annie asked.

"There was nothing in that shed on county land that could have sparked a fire. And it was locked. They found the padlock, and it had not been opened."

"So it caught fire from the outside."

"Except nothing around it burned." Ruth lit the burner under a frying pan. "Somebody started that fire at the back of the shed."

Annie leaned against a counter. "Is Bryan compromising the investigation by telling you this stuff?"

Ruth paled. "It's just his theory. It's nothing formal. It's not like he's the official investigator or anything."

While Ruth shredded cheese, Annie poured orange juice.

"What did you and Elijah find to talk about?" Ruth asked. "Did he mention why he was even there?"

Annie kept her back turned as she returned the orange juice pitcher to the refrigerator. "It turns out he is interested in fires. I suppose he's curious, like a lot of people. He and Bryan might actually have something in common."

"Oh." Ruth shredded with more vigor.

Annie carried the juice glasses to the table in the dining room, where she had laid out two place mats a few minutes earlier. Ruth had given her a perfect opening to say that Elijah had moved off his parents' farm and into town. In fact, the room he rented was not more than half a mile from Annie's home. She wanted Ruth to know. It might change things between Ruth and Elijah before things went further with Bryan. But shouldn't Elijah be the one to tell Ruth? Annie returned to the kitchen and took two plates from the cabinet.

"So do you really think you are going to get Leah to come and stay here?" Ruth dumped the eggs into the sizzling pan.

"I'm going to try. I hope you don't mind that I cut the living room in half to make space for her."

"Would you rather I stay somewhere else while she's here?"

"No! Of course not."

"If I weren't here, you'd have room for her."

"I *do* have room for her." Annie put a hand on her friend's shoulder while Ruth gently stirred the eggs. "And I hope that she'll soon be ready to go home."

Ruth pointed at the oven. "Don't burn my bacon."

When Annie walked through Mrs. Weichert's shop door a few hours later, the older woman was putting the telephone in its cradle. Annie smiled at the gesture. That phone had to be thirty years old, but Mrs. Weichert had no interest in updating. It was an antiques shop, after all.

"You just missed him," Mrs. Weichert said.

"Who?"

"Rufus."

Annie's stomach sank. He was not likely to call again. "What did he say?"

"He'll see you on Sunday. He'll be home all day."

Annie suppressed a grin and walked around the counter to stow her purse on the shelf underneath. A moment later, Mrs. Weichert gave her a short list of tasks for the afternoon and Annie settled into routine.

But the fire still blazed in her mind, and over and over she saw the flash of Amish blue escaping her sight. As she wiped a dust rag over the porcelain pieces and straightened up the Amish jam jars, Annie prayed for peace to come to Leah Deitwaller's heart. And she wondered if it did any good in God's eyes to pray after the fact that Leah please not be the one who was starting fires.

On Sunday afternoon Rufus put his thumbs through his suspenders and leaned a shoulder against the partial wall that divided the dining room from the living room. From this perspective, he had a clear view of Annalise, but she was not likely to see him from her seat on the sofa. For this moment—and he knew it would not last long in the busy Beiler household—she was alone. Her quilt nearly swallowed her up as she bent over her stitches. He had seen her in this pose often enough in the last few months to know that her tongue peeked out of the left corner of her lips when she was concentrating. His mother had been the one to offer to teach Annalise to quilt. A few weeks ago, typical of Annalise's independent streak, she had declared that she would finish on her own. Now she was working on the binding of a traditional Amish nine-patch quilt made from solid-colored fabrics that had once belonged to her mother. She found sentimental pleasure in bringing memories of her *English* childhood into her new life in the Amish church.

With quiet steps Rufus crossed the room and moved enough of the quilt off one end of the sofa to allow him to sit beside her. Her smile melted something at his core every time.

"The quilt is beautiful," he said.

"Well, it's not perfect, but for my first attempt, I think it's pretty good!" She laughed. "That sounds like pride. Forgive me."

"I admire what you have done and the qualities that have allowed you to do it." What he wanted to say was that he was proud of her. "It's a nice afternoon."

"Yes, it is." Annalise pulled the thread taut in preparation for another stitch.

"How would you like to take a driving lesson?"

Her fingers immediately released the quilt. "Really?"

"I'll get Dolly ready."

"I'll put this away and find my sweater."

By the time Rufus pulled the buggy to the front of the house ten minutes later, Annalise was standing on the front porch in the blue sweater his mother had knit for her last winter. While he scooted over on the bench, she clamored down the steps and around the back of the buggy, appearing on the driver's side.

When she grinned, he could not help but grin back. Most Amish women Annalise's age had been driving buggies half their lives.

Annalise straightened herself on the bench and picked up the reins. "Giddyup."

Dolly responded with gentle forward motion. Annalise tugged the reins to the left, and the horse circled the Beiler front yard. Once they traversed the long driveway and approached the main highway, Rufus felt his own foot pressing against the floor as if to slow the buggy. On her side, Annalise pulled on the reins and pushed the brake slightly too hard, and they lurched forward. Rufus only allowed himself to watch her in his peripheral vision lest the turn of his head imply any lack of confidence. Annalise managed to stop Dolly right at the edge of the road and took her time looking in both directions.

"Is it all right if we go toward town?" Annalise asked.

"Wherever you wish. You're the driver."

She giggled. "You don't know how long it's been since anyone said that to me."

"It's probably a good idea to stay on a familiar stretch of road."

"I'm a little nervous about being on the main highway."

"You can do it. You ride with me all the time."

"I won't go fast."

"Dolly will appreciate that. Sometimes I think she likes to have a Sabbath, too."

Annalise pulled the reins to the right and entered the shoulder of the highway. They traveled in silence for a few minutes.

"You're doing very well," Rufus said. And she was.

"You probably remember what happened the last time you took me out. I practically ran over Leah Deitwaller."

"But you didn't. She is the one who ran in front of you without looking. You are the one who stopped without anybody getting hurt."

"You certainly have a knack for seeing the upside of things."

"Mmm." He was not so sure. Seeing the upside of his financial bind was not what made him take a job he was beginning to think was a mistake. Hours of prayer did not give him the peace his soul sought, and being with *English* men all day made him lonely. But he had only been gone six days. Perhaps the next stretch would be better or go faster.

"I suppose you heard all about the fires." Annalise's eyes remained fixed straight ahead.

"Cars can come up faster than you think. Don't forget to check the mirrors," Rufus said. "Yes, Tom filled me in when he picked me up last night."

"Do you really think it's possible Leah set that first fire?"

He glimpsed the lovely slope of her neck as she turned her head to glance in the mirror and then over her shoulder. "Are you concerned she might have started the fire that burned the shed?"

"I don't want to think that." Annalise adjusted her grip on the reins. "But now there's more talk than ever about arson, and no one knows where Leah is most of the time."

A car whizzed by them. Annalise startled. "I see what you mean."

"Maybe we should talk about the fires another time," Rufus said.

She glanced at him. "You're probably right. Tell me about the job."

He let a few yards go by in silence.

"Rufus?"

"I may have made a mistake."

"Why?" She turned her head toward him.

"Eyes on the road."

She complied immediately but said, "Talk to me, Rufus."

"I don't want to make too much of it," he said. "It's a difficult adjustment, that's all."

"You can quit, can't you?" she said. "I mean, if you do decide it's not the right thing."

He reached up to scratch the left side of his face. "One step at a time. Tom will drive me back tonight. The next job is in the hospital in Cañon City. They are renovating a wing of offices."

"My lifetime of habit wants to tell you to do what's right for you. But I know you will always think of your family first."

He wanted to think of her first. He wanted her to be his family. But he could not speak those words while he reserved the possibility that he would choose to save his family's farm with the money meant for beginning his married life.

Ruth grinned when she looked up and saw Annalise leading Dolly into the barn. "How was the drive?"

Annalise paused next to the tack rack and moved to remove Dolly's harness.

"Let me help you with that," Ruth said.

Annalise shook her head. "No. I want to do it. I've watched you all a thousand times."

Sophie stepped out from behind Ruth. "It's easy to tangle yourself up. It's okay to accept help."

"I know," Annalise said, "but I'll learn better if I figure it out by doing."

Lydia nudged Ruth aside. "Don't you know our Annalise well enough by now to know how stubborn she is?"

"I prefer to call it determined," Annalise said. She looked up at the three sisters. "What are you all doing out in the barn, anyway?"

"Milking and mucking don't wait for the Sabbath," Ruth said.

"We're waiting for you!" Sophie said. "We want to hear all about it the minute Rufus proposes."

Annalise hefted the harness up onto its hook. "Not today, I'm afraid."

Sophie groaned. "What is wrong with that man?"

Ruth shot her sister a look. "This is between Rufus and Annalise. It's not our business."

"It's all right," Annalise said. "I know that we're going to be together. It's just a matter of time."

Sophie picked up an empty milk bucket. "We all know that. But I don't see any reason for the two of you to miss this year's wedding season."

"*Gottes wille*." Annalise straightened the dangling reins.

"Have you started making your dress yet?" Sophie swung the bucket back and forth. "I'm sure *Mamm* will help you."

"And I'm sure I'm going to need her help!" Annalise picked up a brush and began pulling it through Dolly's tangled mane.

"She wants to give you a beautiful wedding day."

Ruth took the bucket from Sophie's hands. "I'll milk. Your mind is not on it."

Sophie offered no objection, and she and Lydia closed in on Annalise while Ruth moved down to the stall where the family's only cow waited. Her jealousy shamed her. She had walked away from the Amish church and a man who loved her—and the beautiful wedding her mother would have planned for her. She had no right to envy Annalise's imminent happiness.

Twenty-Three

Ten days had passed since Annie mailed her letter to Matthew Beiler, plenty of time for him to receive Annie's letter and sit down to answer it. On Monday morning when she stopped at the Westcliffe post office to check her mail, she could not keep from imagining Matthew opening the letter, reading, and picking up a pen to respond—immediately. Annie opened her box, reached in, and extracted the pile of ads. She had not purchased with a credit card over the Internet for more than a year, and she had written to a number of vendors to have her name removed from their lists. Still, the onslaught of ads persisted. Annie fished through them for the letter she knew would be there, her mother's weekly newsy roundup, and slid it into a small outer pocket of her modest handbag. She would wait until she returned to her house to read it, and then she would take a card from the same stack she had used to write to Matthew and promptly answer her mother. Before dropping the stack in the recycling box, she shuffled through the ads one more time to make sure there was nothing from Matthew.

Out on the sidewalk, Annie could smell the yeasty fragrance of the bakery across the street and wondered if giving in to the urge to go buy a scone constituted falling into temptation. After all, she had left the house without breakfast that morning.

When she saw Elijah Capp's horse and buggy, she forgot about both her hunger and the scone. Elijah worked for a business that catered to providing and repairing Amish appliances. He had converted Annie's house, taking it off the *English* electrical grid and instead making sure the lights, furnace, stove, refrigerator, and washing machine ran on energy sources approved by the Amish district.

"Hello, Elijah." Annie stroked the neck of his horse, a habit that had grown on her since she moved to Westcliffe the previous year. "What brings you to town?"

He lifted the bakery's plain Styrofoam cup. "I have not yet gotten very good at making coffee in my new place."

"I suppose it all takes some adjusting." Annie tried to imagine what it must be like for Elijah to be living in a rented *English* room. "Where did you disappear to yesterday? I turned my head and you were gone."

"Everybody was trying to leave at once. I wanted to get my rig out of the way."

Annie nodded. That made sense. "Did you hear anything about the surprise fire?"

"I did not go over there to investigate. My landlady says it is probably a teenage pyromaniac, but I do not think that fits the pattern."

"Pattern? There's a pattern?"

"Two fires in empty structures only a few weeks apart." Elijah set his coffee on the floor of the buggy. "There might be something there."

"Do you really think so?"

"I'm sure your friend Bryan Nichols is more knowledgeable of these things."

"I only just met him that day, Elijah. He's no more my friend than he is yours."

"That's right." He hefted himself up into the buggy. "He's Ruth's friend."

Annie ran her tongue over her top lip. Whatever she knew about Ruth and Bryan—which was next to nothing—she was not going to tell Elijah.

"Where are you headed?" she asked.

"I have to drive out to the Stutzmans'. Edna claims the washing machine is not working properly."

Annie laughed. "Claims?"

Elijah tilted his head. "They have three daughters, you know."

"Can I come with you?"

"Why would you want to go to the Stutzmans'?"

Annie was not so much interested in the destination as the route Elijah might take. "I thought the ride might be nice."

"And?"

Annie kicked a rock. "And it might give me a chance to look for signs of Leah Deitwaller. She was staying in that house they burned down. Now I don't know where she went."

Elijah chortled. "I do talk to Joel, you know. I heard what happened when the two of you tracked down Leah. You could hardly walk for two days."

"We probably won't find her," Annie said. "Besides, if I'm with you, Edna won't encourage one of the girls to cook for you."

"True enough. Get in."

They were almost to the edge of the Stutzman farm and had nearly exhausted their supply of small talk. Annie was not sure how much longer they could avoid talking about Ruth, but she knew she was not going to be the one to introduce Ruth into the conversation. Her eyes soaked up the vista, the gorgeous mountains, the rolling meadows, the brilliant sunshine.

Where would a homeless, confused, Amish teenager go on a perfect fall day?

A ball of black and white flashed across the road. If Annie had not turned her head at just that moment, she would have missed it.

"Stop!"

Elijah pulled on the reins. "What's the matter?"

"The cat. I saw the cat."

"So what?"

Annie was already out of the buggy. "Did you see where it went?"

"Annalise, I am not about to chase a stray cat through open countryside."

"It's not a stray cat." Annie marched a few steps in the direction the cat had gone. "It's Leah's kitten. If the kitten is here, Leah is nearby."

"Maybe the cat got away."

"That kitten is the only living thing in Colorado that matters to her." Annie lengthened her stride. "Are you coming? We'll find her twice as fast with two sets of eyes."

"The Stutzmans are expecting me."

"You know good and well Edna probably loosened a bolt so she would have a reason to ask you to come."

"What am I supposed to do with my rig?"

"Bring it. We might need it."

Annie ignored the sigh that Elijah made no effort to disguise.

"The cat could be anywhere by now, you know," he said.

"It's a kitten. Leah dotes on it. Cats know to go where the food is."

"Amish cats are barn cats. They feed themselves or we don't keep them."

Annie glared. "Elijah Capp, stop arguing with me and turn that buggy around."

Even a fleet-footed kitten left a trace of tracks in the dust. Annie fixed on a spot where she was sure she had seen the kitten pause to circumvent a large rock and discerned the small prints.

"This way. Follow me."

Behind her, Annie heard the scuffling of the horse turning and the creak of the buggy wheels. She did not dare take her eyes off the tracks, though. They were too faint to discover again.

The kitten reappeared, poised on the first of a series of boulders. As the feline leaped from one to the other, Annie followed the probable path.

Leah Deitwaller sat atop a load of gravel in the bed of an unattended dump truck.

Annie stopped and glanced over her shoulder at Elijah, who reined in his horse.

"Whoa. What is she doing up there?" he asked.

Annie rolled her eyes. "I don't read her mind. But we have to get her to come down. It's not safe."

The kitten leaped onto a massive rear tire and splayed as if he might lose his grip. Annie sprang forward to close the yards and nabbed the kitten. The animal wriggled, but Annie held firm.

"Leah?" Annie inched along the side of the vehicle, uncertain that she had ever been this close to a dump truck.

Leah flailed her arms. "It's you again. Wherever I go, you find me."

"I care what happens to you." Annie wrapped her apron around the cat the way she had seen Leah do.

Elijah stood beside her now, speaking softly. "That has to be twelve, maybe fifteen tons of gravel. Must be a transfer truck for a major landscaping project."

"How do you know this stuff?" Annie made sure the kitten could breathe but kept it contained. "We have to get her down."

Leah shifted her position, and a spray of gravel shot off the side of the truck. "I figure that eventually this truck will go someplace where they have buses or trains."

"It will probably dump its load and go back to the quarry it came from." Elijah spoke into Annie's ear.

"It doesn't matter where it's going, because she's not going to be on it." Annie lifted her head and raised her voice. "Leah, I have your kitten. Wouldn't you like to come down and see him?"

"You keep him. I probably can't take him on the train anyway."

901

Annie blew her breath out, clueless what to say next. She only knew she must remain calm.

"I'll go around the other side and climb up." Elijah was already moving. "Just keep her talking."

"I've never had a cat," Annie said. "It might be fun to have a kitten, but this one is yours. I know he wants to be with you. He was trying to get back to you when I found him."

"He's the best kitten anyone could hope to have." Leah leaned a few inches in the direction of Annie and the cat.

"I know," Annie quickly agreed. "You deserve to have him."

"You know that I'm going to find a way to leave this wilderness."

"I just want you to be safe." Annie could not see Elijah. "I don't think you ever told me your kitten's name."

"I just call him Kitten."

"That's cute."

"You can give him another name after I'm gone."

Behind Leah, Elijah's head slowly rose above the level of the gravel. He began to crawl toward the girl.

"That doesn't look very comfortable up there," Annie said. "And I wonder if you're hungry."

Leah flinched and turned toward Elijah. "You've been trying to trick me!" She swung a foot at him and caught him in the chest.

Elijah fell out of Annie's sight.

Twenty-Four

Annie flew around the truck. Elijah lay flat on his back, moaning.

"Don't try to get up!"

"You don't have to worry about that." Elijah gasped at the effort of speaking. "My chest. She really clobbered me."

"How about your back? Can you feel everything you're supposed to feel?"

"It all hurts, so I guess so. Is she still up there?"

Annie spun around and looked to the top of the gravel heap. Leah was on all fours looking down.

"Leah Deitwaller, you do the grown-up thing and get down here right this minute!"

To Annie's shock and relief, Leah began a cautious climb down.

"Is he all right?" Leah asked. "I didn't mean to hurt anyone."

"We're going to need help. An ambulance." Constraining the kitten with one hand, Annie dug with the other in the bag still hanging from her shoulder and extracted her cell phone. She flipped it open and turned it on. A dark screen glared back at her. "Battery's dead. Elijah, did you bring a cell phone?"

He grunted. "Nope."

Leah was on the ground now and knelt beside Elijah. "I'm sorry."

Elijah closed his eyes. Annie's heart lurched.

"No! You stay conscious!"

"The sun's in my eyes, that's all."

Annie positioned herself between the sun and Elijah. "Leah, one of us has to go for help."

"You should be the one to go."

Annie was not sure which she dreaded more, the thought that if she left, Leah would bolt and abandon Elijah, or the thought that Leah might bolt with the buggy and abandon her along with Elijah.

"Annalise," Elijah said, "can I ask a question?"

"Sure."

"How many times have you handled a horse and buggy?"

"Twice."

"By yourself?"

She cleared her throat. "Never."

"Then Leah has to go."

Annie met the girl's eyes.

"Okay," Leah said, "but you have to let me take the kitten."

"Do you think she'll actually get help?" Annie sat in the dirt beside Elijah as Leah turned the buggy around and headed toward town.

"Do you think she will actually bring my horse and buggy back?"

"I'm sorry, Elijah." Annie wriggled out of her sweater and spread it across his chest. "I dragged you into this, and now you're hurt and worried about your rig."

"I'm not worried about my buggy. *Gottes wille.*"

Annie pulled her knees up, wrapped her arms around them, and propped her chin on top of the mountain they made. "I haven't quite learned to say that as freely as I ought to."

"First you have to believe it." Elijah started to lift an arm.

"Don't do that!" Annie put a hand on his wrist.

"I really think I'm fine. I'll be sore and I have a headache, but that doesn't seem so terrible. Considering."

"Considering you were kicked in the chest, fell off a gravel truck, and landed flat on your back?"

"*Ya*, that. But I landed on earth, not concrete."

"You could have a concussion. Broken ribs. Or your spinal cord—"

"I'm grateful to have such cheerful, optimistic company."

Annie clamped her lips shut.

"If you'll scratch the left side of my nose, I promise I won't try to get up."

"That bargain is more than fair." Annie used two fingers to thoroughly scratch the side of his long, narrow nose then pushed his brown hair away from his eyes.

"Thank you. That's better."

"Does your chest hurt? It looked like she kicked you right in the heart." Annie noticed that his chest did not lift high with his breaths.

Annalise reached for his wrist and put two fingers down in search of his pulse.

"Don't worry. It's still beating."

"You're taking this whole thing too lightly."

"I would shrug if you would let me."

"You will do nothing of the sort."

"Mrs. Stutzman will be in a tizzy by now."

"Oh yes, Mrs. Stutzman. The beautiful coffee cake the girls were going to serve you straight out of the oven—coincidentally—will be ruined."

"They're not so bad. You're just sensitive because Beth had her eye on Rufus. He set her straight weeks ago. You know that."

Annie picked up a pebble and tossed it several yards. "I know. But they don't seem your type, either."

"You know there's only one woman I want."

She did know. "Are you really going to leave?"

"Yes, I believe so. I cannot stay and be a hypocrite for the next sixty years."

"What if leaving doesn't change anything with Ruth?"

"I hope it will, but either way I have to go."

"Don't you believe? In what I just promised to believe and obey?"

"Are you trying to talk me into staying because you chose to join the church?"

"Of course not." She crossed her arms atop her knees. "I know you would never make this kind of decision for someone else."

"I tried that three years ago and it hasn't worked out too well." Elijah squinted at the sun. "I wish I had my hat right now, though. I left it in the buggy."

Annie readjusted her position once again to shade his face.

"If I get my horse and buggy back, I'm going to sell it."

"Really?"

"I'm going to buy a van. Tom has been teaching me to drive. He'll take me for my test."

"He's going to want you to be quite sure."

"I'm sure. You and Rufus are going to need a buggy once you're married. You won't always live on the Beiler farm."

"One step at a time." Annie raised a hand to shade her eyes and stare down the road. "Why hasn't someone at least come about this truck?"

Ruth stepped outside the grocery store and gratefully turned her face up to the sun. Late September at an elevation of eight thousand feet brought days gently sloping off the peaks of summer temperatures, but the sun comforted her nevertheless. She had walked down Main Street to the store, careful not to buy more items than she could comfortably carry the blocks back to Annalise's house. Growing up in the Amish community in Pennsylvania, Ruth rarely stepped inside a grocery store. Her family had their own milk, eggs, and vegetables, and the large church district included families of all trades. Anyone who wanted to avoid the *English* completely could do so for months at a time. Now here she was carrying two canvas bags of groceries so she could feel she was making some contribution while she stayed with Annalise.

Just as she was about to turn off onto the narrow street where Annalise's house occupied the middle of the block, a horse trotted toward her on Main Street—at a speed that lacked caution.

Elijah's horse pulled his buggy—Ruth had spent enough time in that buggy to recognize it anywhere, as much as it looked like so many others—but Elijah was not on the bench.

The driver reined in the horse and stared down at Ruth.

"Leah?"

"I remember you from the day I went to church." The girl on the bench pointed. "You're Ruth Beiler. You were the only one there not wearing the clothes of our people."

Remembering what Annie had told her about Leah Deitwaller, Ruth took care with her tone. "It's good to run into you, Leah. I see you have Elijah's buggy."

"He needs help. Is it true you're a nurse?"

Ruth's heart pushed against her chest. "I'm training to be a nurse. What happened?"

Leah licked her lips and swallowed hard.

"Leah, I want to help if I can. I need to know what happened."

"Do you have a cell phone?"

"Yes."

"Call 911."

Ruth set down the groceries on the sidewalk and yanked her phone out of the pocket of her blue scrubs shirt. "They'll want to know what happened, Leah."

"Elijah fell. Annalise says he needs an ambulance."

"Where is he?" Ruth did her best to focus while Leah described the location of the gravel truck.

As soon as she called 911 with the scant information she had, Ruth picked up her groceries and set them on the floor of the buggy.

"Do you know where Annalise's house is?"

Leah nodded.

"I'm going to run there and get my car. I would appreciate it if you could take these groceries. And you could wait there if you like. The back door is open."

Ruth spun and ran. Her car was in the driveway, unlocked, and she was in it and backing onto the street before Leah had fully negotiated the turn onto Annalise's street. Ruth had no idea whether Leah would take the groceries to the house, or whether she would stay there if she did. It might please Annalise to find her there, but if this thoughtless, headstrong girl had anything to do with how Elijah got hurt, Ruth was not as certain of her own grace. She accelerated past Elijah's buggy onto Main Street and barreled toward the main highway.

At least Annalise was with Elijah. Ruth forced herself to slow the car's speed in order to look for the old county road the Stutzmans routinely used to reach their farm. A twelve-ton gravel truck could not be that hard to find, and if Leah was telling the truth, Elijah would be sprawled on his back beside it.

Ruth saw Annalise spring to her feet before she discerned Elijah's black-and-white-clad form on the ground. She swung the car off the road and screeched to a halt.

"How did you know to come?" Annalise moved out of the way as Ruth knelt and put her ear to Elijah's chest.

Ruth put two fingers on his neck, looking for his pulse. This would be the last time she ever traveled without at least a stethoscope in her car.

"Leah found me walking home with groceries. I called for an ambulance. They should be here any minute."

"I keep telling Annalise I don't need an ambulance."

Elijah weakly nudged Ruth's hand away from his neck.

Annalise's protest was swift. "You promised not to move."

A siren wailed. "Too late," Ruth said. "It's just about here."

Annalise scrambled closer to the road and began to wave her arms.

"I'm glad you came first," Elijah whispered.

"Did Leah do this to you?" Ruth hated the tone in her own voice, but she could not help it.

"Maybe we'll talk about that later."

Ruth put the back of her hand against his cheek, telling herself it was to judge his temperature but knowing that something more than fledgling professional instincts guided her movement.

"I hate the thought that you might be seriously hurt," she said.

He gave her an impish smile. "I love that you hate it. I love *you*."

She was so relieved he was conscious, talking, smiling, trying to move. "The paramedics will be able to give you a thorough going-over, but I can almost guarantee they will take you in. Protocol. They are not going to come all the way out here and then leave because you say you don't need them."

"I do admit to having the wind knocked out of me."

A fire engine and an ambulance rolled into the meadow. Bryan Nichols stepped out of the ambulance.

Annie stood back out of the way and watched. She noticed that Ruth had moved only a few inches, crouching next to Elijah's head and leaving a hand on his shoulder while she spoke softly with Bryan as he examined Elijah. Two other responders pulled a gurney out of the back of the vehicle, rolled it across the ragged ground, and lowered it on the other side of Elijah. Ruth and the EMTs formed a wall around Elijah, and Annie could see next to nothing of what they were doing.

When Ruth pointed to her and Bryan looked over his shoulder, Annie knew she was going to have to give some account of what happened. There could only be one account. Elijah was trying to get Leah Deitwaller down off the heap of gravel, she kicked him in the chest, and he landed on his back. That was what she told Bryan a few seconds later.

"You did the right thing to keep him still and talking." Bryan jotted notes on a form on his clipboard. "He said essentially the same thing you did, so there doesn't seem to be any cognitive alteration. We'll immobilize him for transport."

"Will you take him to the clinic in town?"

Bryan shook his head. "Cañon City. The ortho doc on call at the hospital there will make sure his spine did not suffer any trauma and decide about treatment."

Ruth approached them. "I'm going with him. He needs somebody with him."

Bryan wriggled his fingers in a neutral gesture. "There's room in the back."

"What about your car?" Annie asked.

"I'll come back for it. Would you lock it for me, please?"

Annie walked over to the blue Prius that had belonged to her until a few months ago, opened the driver's door, and snapped the master lock button.

"The other rig is going back to town if you want a ride." Bryan pointed with a thumb.

"Thanks. I'll see if someone knows how to get hold of his parents."

"Good idea."

Annie paced back to Ruth and drew her into a hug. "He's going to be okay."

Ruth nodded against Annie's shoulder. "It's just the thought that maybe he won't be. I can't leave him."

"You shouldn't." Beneath her hands on Ruth's back, Annie felt her friend tremble.

They stood side by side while the EMTs slid the gurney into the ambulance. Bryan waited for Ruth with his hand on the open door.

Twenty-Five

June 1892

Sheriff Abraham Byler stood up from behind his desk in the Mountain Home jailhouse at the trampling sound of a horse's hooves overlaid with the creak and rattle of the wagon the beast pulled. He was outside the small structure by the time Deputy Combs reined in the animal. Three young men hung their sheepish heads. A.G. knew them all by name—and their daddies, too.

The deputy slung down from the wagon bench. "These are the boys who were out shooting—except Jesse Roper. He threatened me with a pistol." He jabbed his finger at the men in the wagon. "They're all witnesses. You can get their statements."

A.G. sighed. Jesse Roper had hardly been in town four days and already was a steady aggravation.

"Boys, you tell the sheriff," Combs said.

"What will happen to us if we do?" Digger asked. "All we did is a little friendly can shooting."

"Which you know good and well you were not supposed to do," A.G. said.

"Let's arrest these boys." Combs signaled that they should get out of the wagon.

"I think Roper is our real trouble," A.G. said.

"That's right!" Digger heaved himself over the side of the wagon on one arm. "He's the troublemaker."

A.G. shook his head. "I reckon he is. But that does not take you off the hook. One at a time, you tell me what you saw when Deputy Combs went to collect you." He pointed at Digger.

He listened carefully to three rapid accounts and then turned to his deputy. "What else do you want to add, Thomas?"

Deputy Combs held up his hand and opened his thumb and forefinger about three inches. "That pistol was this far from my face. It's a clear violation of the law to threaten an officer with a weapon."

"I know the law," A.G. said. He was not going to make it home while Bess's chicken was still hot tonight. "We're going to have to go talk to him."

"We weren't the only witnesses," Digger said. "One of those Amish men was there."

A.G. pressed his lips to one side. "Mmm."

"I didn't see him." Deputy Combs put both hands on his hips. "You have a lot of gall to involve an innocent man in this."

Digger pointed up. "In the maple tree outside my family's house. Must have followed from the clearing. He was there, too."

A.G. looked at the other two men. "Did either of you see him at the house?"

They shook their heads.

"I saw him!" Digger insisted. "He just about fell out of that tree when Jesse Roper waved that pistol in the deputy's face. Wish he had. Then y'all would believe me."

A.G. raised a thumb to the small jail behind him. "You three go in there and behave yourselves. I'd better find you sitting right where I left you when I get back."

"Yes, sir," they all muttered as they filed in.

A.G. pulled the door shut after them and turned to the deputy. "I'll look for the Amish man and get his story. My gut tells me we're going to need a posse to take out to the Twigg ranch. You see who is available. Try to keep Mooney out of it. And none of these boys' daddies."

They tossed some names back and forth, and Combs unhitched his horse from the wagon and saddled it.

A.G. took a deep breath and exhaled. "I will see you in one hour on the road off the Twigg ranch. Stay off their property until I get there."

Joseph splashed water from the barrel inside the stables on his face and neck and rubbed. Then he used a dipper to pour some over the top of his bare head.

"No letter?" he said, when he opened his eyes and saw Zeke's boots in the hay next to him.

"No letter."

"So we wait." Joseph toweled his face dry and ran his hands through his hair. He opened a small leather bag and considered his razor with one hand, while running the other over his three-day beard. If he did not shave soon, people would start to think he had married.

He corrected himself. The *English* would draw no such conclusion. In Gassville a man's beard meant nothing about his marital status.

"We still have to muck," Zeke said. "You'll only have to clean up again."

Joseph did not want to explain the tree sap stuck to his face and hair on the side of his head. "I was hot."

"We could go into town to eat tonight." Zeke grabbed the handles of a cart and parked it at the opening of an empty stall. "It might be cooler. We have not splurged lately."

Joseph took a pitchfork into the stall. "Maybe." He tossed soiled straw into the cart. Once. Twice. Three times, with vigor.

"Joseph, what's wrong?"

Joseph leaned on the fork. "If I tell you, you will tell me to stay out of it."

"Then perhaps you already have your answer."

Joseph raked the fork through straw with less gusto.

"*English* trouble?" Zeke prodded.

Joseph nodded. He gave Zeke the bare facts of the morning. Voices in the stable yard drew them outside. The livery owner stood talking with Sheriff Byler. One man pointed to the stables, and the other stroked his white beard as he raised his eyes toward Joseph and Zeke.

Joseph stepped forward. Zeke grabbed his arm.

"Stay out of it," Zeke said.

"He is here for me. Can you not see that?"

The sheriff approached. "Joseph Beiler?"

"I am Joseph Beiler."

"The owner tells me you are from Tennessee," Sheriff Byler said. "Perhaps we are long-lost kin."

Joseph glanced at Zeke. "I would be pleased if we were."

"Let's chew that fat another day. Right now I need to know what happened this afternoon."

Joseph repeated his account, watching the sheriff nod at intervals.

"That squares with what the others reported," Sheriff Byler said. "It seems that even Thomas Combs did not exaggerate this time."

The sheriff strode back to his horse and mounted swiftly. "We're organizing a posse to go out to the Twigg ranch," he said to the livery owner. "You are welcome to come."

"Twigg?" The owner waved his arms. "No thank you."

The sheriff looked at Zeke and Joseph. "You, too."

Zeke shook his head. "Our people do not ride in posses."

Joseph turned to the stall where his mount awaited.

Maura saw the dust cloud and heard the clatter of hooves before she discerned the individual men.

At least fifteen men on horses. It could only be a posse.

When they paused in front of her uncle's milliner's shop, Maura put a hand on Walter's shoulder.

Thomas Combs looked down from his horse. "Is your father here, Walter?"

"What is this about?" Maura held her grip on Walter's resisting shoulder.

"Just a posse, Miss Woodley. Men's work. Is Edwin here?"

"He was feelin' poorly," Walter said. "He went on down to Doc Denton's."

Thomas scowled. "Sheriff said no Dentons. Not in this business."

Walter wriggled out from under Maura's hand. "Shall I tell my daddy where to find you?"

"Hush, Walter," Maura said.

"I'll come," Walter said.

"You will do no such thing." Even as Maura chastised her cousin, she was planning her own escape from the shop. If the sheriff did not want the Dentons involved, the trouble was sure to involve the Twiggs. "Deputy Combs, I hope you resolve the matter peaceably."

"I'll settle for justice." Thomas tugged on his reins, and the blur of restless men picked up speed once again.

"Your daddy will be back soon," Maura said to Walter, grabbing his shoulder again. "Can you be on your own for ten minutes without getting into trouble?"

"I'm near full grown."

"Yes, you are." Maura's horse and cart were hitched around the corner. "So act like it."

"If you're going, I'm going." Walter shook off her hold.

"No, you are not. Your daddy will look for you right here. Promise me you'll be here."

Unarmed, Joseph Beiler was among the twenty men who thundered with Sheriff Abraham Byler into the ranch yard of Old Man Twigg. Lurking at the back edge of the posse, Joseph coughed and then covered his face with the back of his hand against the rising swirl of dirt. Around the edges of the clearing were the main house, a smokehouse, stables, and a couple of other small outbuildings.

Sheriff Byler lifted one hand as the horses responded to reins and came to a stop, their front legs thudding to the ground in final steps. He slid off his mount and scanned the posse from left to right.

"You men stay in your saddles and put those rifles away," the sheriff said, warning in his tone. "You are here in the event of a sour turn that I sincerely hope to avoid."

Shifting postures of most of the men told Joseph not everyone agreed with the sheriff's judgment, but they would comply with his instructions.

Sheriff Byler crossed the yard and approached the house, hollering in a friendly tone. "Hallo! Hallo! Anybody home?" He did not even brandish a weapon as he turned his head first toward one building and then another. Silence made him slow his steps, peering carefully. He reached the front porch of the house, put his hand on a supporting post, and looked around again. "Hallo?"

Joseph slowly moved around one side of the posse, anxious for the sheriff. He saw the rifle's end poking out through the fissure in the log smokehouse too late. The crack of the weapon swallowed up his cry of caution. Sheriff Byler lurched.

Men in the front of the posse immediately urged their horses forward into the yard and drew their weapons.

"Get the sheriff out of there!" Thomas Combs ordered.

Sheriff Byler stumbled only a few yards from the house when the rifle cracked again. This time the sheriff dropped and did not move.

Joseph responded with the rest of the men, moving into formation that would enclose the yard. Weaponless, Joseph took his horse toward the smokehouse. Two riders slung their legs out of their saddles and crouched over Byler.

"Shot twice!" one of them called out.

Jesse Roper burst from the smokehouse, dropped to his knees, and fired into the posse, first to the right, then to the left. Joseph yanked on his reins to pull his horse to the side, but the fearful animal went up on hind legs. Joseph could see a few men fumbling with their weapons, but the reflexive movement of most of the horses prevented straight shots. Bullets flew across the yard without purpose. When a cartridge lodged in the barrel of his Winchester, Roper worked the lever back and forth with cool aplomb until he cleared it.

Loge Hoppe yelped when a bullet hit his leg. Struck in the chest, Dr. Lindsay's horse crumpled beneath him. The posse fell back, out of range. With the formation broken, Roper grasped his rifle in one thick hand and loped across the yard. He climbed a split-rail fence, turned to remove his imposing black hat, grinned, and waved a final farewell as he jumped down on the other side and pumped his long legs.

Some of the posse men pressed their knees into their horses and urged them into chase.

"Let him go!" Jimmy Twigg emerged from the smokehouse, his face an angry red and his rifle seated against his shoulder. "I will blow the head off of anyone who chases him. You know I mean it."

The posse riders drew their horses to a halt. Roper disappeared into the thick woods of the Twigg property.

Joseph was afraid he would be sick. Was this *English* justice? Off his horse now, he tied the animal to a tree and turned to the throb of attention around Sheriff Byler.

Old Man Twigg's wife ran from her house to kneel over the dying sheriff. "You poor man. You poor old man."

Dr. Lindsay limped from his wounded horse to do what he could for the sheriff.

The clatter of a cart made Joseph look up. Joseph ran and

grabbed the bridle of Maura Woodley's horse, dragging against the animal's movement.

"Miss Woodley—" He did not know what to say next.

"The sheriff?" Maura said as she climbed out of her cart.

He nodded. Maura ran to the huddle and pushed aside Mrs. Twigg and several men. Joseph had seen enough of Maura Woodley before this to know she would have her way even in this situation. She took Sheriff Byler's head into her own skirt, trying to stanch the blood from his chest alongside Dr. Lindsay.

"Joseph!" she called out.

He was at her side immediately, looking into her wrenched face.

"He will not survive," she muttered. She held out her hand to him. "This should not be. This should not be."

He gripped her hand.

Twenty-Six

Elijah was strapped into the gurney. Ruth was glad that if he had an inclination to move, he would not be able to. The fact that he remained as still as he had for as long as he had was telling enough. She reached from her own seat to hold his hand. They had been circumspect around other people when they were younger. When they were alone, though, two teenagers in love held hands and stole kisses.

He was the first to confess love.

She was the first to confess doubt.

Not about whether she loved Elijah Capp. In fact, she knew she loved him months before he ever spoke the word to her. But by then, two years after finishing the eighth grade and facing the church's regulation against further schooling, she doubted that her spiritual calling was to become an adult baptized member of the Amish congregation.

She squeezed his hand and he squeezed back, a gesture that gave her some reassurance of his condition. If he were not wearing the sturdy work boot of an Amish tradesman, she might have been tempted to pinch his big toe to see if he would react. Instead, she swallowed her worst-case-scenario imaginings and smiled at him.

"I'm glad you're here." Elijah's wide eyes fixed on her face.

"I wouldn't want to be anywhere else."

A wispy recollection that she was supposed to work at the clinic that afternoon wafted through her mind. She would need to call or text someone as soon as the ambulance arrived in Cañon City, but for now she did not intend to let go of Elijah's hand.

"The orthopedist should be waiting for you as soon as we get there," she said.

"I'm sure he has actual injured people he ought to be looking after."

"And where did you get your medical degree, Dr. Capp?"

"You forget that my grandmother was a midwife."

"That should come in handy when you're ready to deliver a baby."

"I want to be there when you have our baby," he said.

The EMT sitting on the other side of Elijah perked up.

"Shh," Ruth said. "What kind of talk is that for an ambulance?"

"I have to take advantage of every opportunity to tell you how I feel." Elijah ignored the EMT. "I never know when I'll get another chance."

"I know how you feel, Elijah," Ruth whispered and avoided the EMT's eyes.

"It's going to work out for us."

His eyes shimmered till she almost could not look at them anymore. Neither could she shift her gaze. She swallowed. "You must be starting to feel sore."

"I only care what I feel for you."

The EMT shuffled his feet. "We'll be there soon," he said.

Ruth could not see Bryan from the back of the ambulance. When she looked toward the front, she saw only a wall of medications and equipment. Bryan would be concentrating on doing his job. She already knew him well enough to recognize and admire his ability to ignore distraction. Still, when the urgency wore off, what would he think about what he had witnessed between her and Elijah—or the account his partner would no doubt give him of the conversation occurring in the back while Bryan focused on safe transport?

Ruth waited alone in a small curtained area. The space seemed much larger with Elijah's patient bed missing. She had helped the triage nurse with his basic information, also providing what little she knew about the accident itself. Explaining that the Amish church, rather than insurance or a government program, would cover his medical expenses was more challenging. The *English* forms never seemed to have the right spaces for these answers.

The wait for the doctor was reasonably short, though he did what Ruth had expected him to do after conducting a basic neurological check that revealed Elijah could wiggle his fingers and toes and tell the difference between a pinch and a poke. In a clipped cadence, the doctor ticked off a list of tests for the nurse to arrange. Ruth recognized the abbreviations and knew the instructions were aimed at ruling out spinal damage before Elijah would be allowed to move more freely. While they waited for an orderly to arrive and wheel him off, Elijah had at last dozed. He roused long enough to smile at her before his gurney turned the corner and took him out of sight.

Now Ruth sat and watched the hands of the clock in the hallway of the emergency room tick. Elijah had been gone almost ninety minutes already. She would not have him come back and find the exam area empty, though, so the most she did was pace the small room a few minutes at a time. If she had to wait halfway through the night, she would.

When the curtain finally swished another thirty minutes later, it was a nurse.

"Ah. I wondered if you were still here."

"Yes. I'm waiting for my friend to come back from tests. Do you know how much longer it will be?"

"I'll try to see if I can find out where he is in the process." The nurse dragged a second chair in from the hall. "Some people are here claiming to be his parents. Judging from the way they are dressed, I believe them. They said you are not family."

"Well, no, technically not. But Elijah and I are close."

The nurse waved a hand. "You all can sort that out among yourselves. But it's against hospital policy to have three nonpatients in an ER exam area. Maybe you could use a break."

"I want to know what happens."

"I think that will be up to his parents now to decide what they want to tell you." The nurse stepped into the hall and beckoned with one hand. "You can wait out in the main waiting area if you like. No one is going to kick you out of there."

Reluctant, Ruth stood up. Already she recognized the approaching dull, heavy step of Amish boots and swish of skirts. Elijah's *daed* wore his usual somber expression with an extra furrow in his brow, and his *mamm*'s cheeks lacked their usual blush. Ruth did her best to greet them with encouragement.

"He's just away while they do some tests," she said, reaching for Mrs. Capp's hand. "I'm sorry they won't let me stay with you while you wait for him."

"We don't need you to stay with us." Mrs. Capp withdrew her hand.

"I don't think it should be too much longer."

"Thank you, Ruth, but you can go now."

"I'll just be out in the main waiting room."

"It's not necessary for you to wait. I'm sure you have other things to do."

"Of course I'll wait." Elijah's mother had never spoken to her before with such a clipped tone. "If he asks for me, will someone come and get me?"

"I think it's best if you go back to Westcliffe," Mr. Capp said. "If you want to help, you can ask the church to pray for Elijah."

Ruth looked back and forth between Elijah's parents. Close to three years had passed since she ran out on her baptism and left Elijah behind to make his vows alone. While the Capps had been confused at her choice, they never expressed anger toward her. What mattered to them was that Elijah had joined the church. Only two weeks ago, Mrs. Capp had urged Ruth to come to dinner. She understood they were concerned about their son's condition now, but that worry was underlaid with anger. They stepped into the exam area, their back to her, and pulled the curtain.

"You'll have to go to the waiting room," the nurse repeated. "His family is here now."

The words stung.

When she pushed through the door to the waiting room, Tom Reynolds stood up.

"Hello, Ruth."

"Tom, I'm glad you're here. Did you taxi the Capps?"

"Yes. I said I would wait at least until they know whether Elijah has to stay."

"I guess that depends on the test results."

"You look wiped out. How about if I see if I can find a coffee machine or something?"

She nodded. Coffee might help clear her mind, though she doubted it would fix whatever had just broken between her and the Capps.

Rufus slapped his measuring tape up against the wall, made a pinpoint dot with his pencil, and turned the tape in the other direction to make another mark. His coworkers drew two-inch-wide lines before hanging a cabinet. If they did not, they could not find their own marks. Rufus needed far less assurance that he was doing the job right. This was the first day of a two-week project renovating administrative offices in a Cañon City hospital that seemed to Rufus to require little creativity. The crew would make its way down the hallway and then back up on the other side installing identical manufactured cabinetry into identical offices painted in identical color schemes.

Rufus began to hum, hoping the hymn tune would lead him into prayer for Annalise, for his family, for the decisions he needed to make. Whatever doubts he had about his choice to take this job even on a temporary basis, he would hang every cabinet as if it were one of his custom creations. The same care and precision that expressed his gratitude in his workshop at home would do so here in the hospital and in whatever building he was sent to next. Satisfied with the accuracy of his marks, even if no one else could discern them, Rufus pulled a box cutter out of the carpenter's apron fastened around his waist and sliced through the cardboard box housing the assembly for this office, his second for the day. After inspecting the contents of the carton and satisfying himself that all the pieces were accounted for, Rufus picked up a power screwdriver and began with the hardware for the first cabinet.

His mind turned over the sign he had seen that morning across the street from the hospital in the paved-over front yard of an old house. The business within was a Realtor that claimed to specialize in commercial properties. It might be just what Rufus needed.

"Hey, Rufus!"

He looked up to welcome his assigned partner back into the room. Marcus had a habit of disappearing for curiously long periods of time, but Rufus had to admit that when he was present he was a valuable helper. He was cheerful, did not mind Rufus's humming, and did what Rufus asked him to do without looking for shortcuts.

And Marcus always returned with large Styrofoam cups of steaming coffee.

"You're going to like this one," Marcus said. "Dark. Robust. Rich."

"You found that kind of coffee in a hospital?" Rufus gratefully took hold of a cup and sipped before setting it down.

"You just have to know where to look." Marcus took a generous draft. "Ah! Smooth, eh?"

"Yes, smooth. Now let's do a smooth job of getting these cabinets up."

"Smooth transition." Marcus found a secure place to set his coffee down. "I heard another Amish dude came in through the ER a couple hours ago. Came all the way from Westcliffe in an ambulance."

Rufus dropped the bracket dangling from his fingers.

Twenty-Seven

Rufus took the stairs two at a time until he was sure he was on the ground floor and then darted through the unfamiliar hospital hallways. Stripes in the flooring and signs overhead guided his path without providing visual reassurance that he would, in fact, reach the emergency department. This was his first day working at this location, and he had not yet made sense of the building's layout. He trusted the signs until he came to a registration counter under a hanging sign announcing the ER.

"I understand you had an Amish man come in this afternoon." Rufus managed a calm tone. "I'm concerned it might be a family member."

"Your last name?" A clerk flipped over a pile of papers and looked up from behind her computer.

"Beiler." He spelled it.

"And does the family member you're looking for share your last name?"

"Yes." Joel. Or *Daed*. Had there been an accident that he would have known about if he were home on his family's farm?

The clerk clicked a few keys. "No, I don't see anyone by that name."

"Are you sure? Maybe the name was misspelled? How many Amish men would you have?"

"Sir, I cannot give you any patient information. All I can tell you is we have no one under the name you gave me."

"Thank you." Rufus wiped a hand across his forehead. When he turned away from the counter in relief, he saw Ruth huddled across the waiting room.

"Rufus!" Relief rattled her voice when she saw him. She wiped tears with the heels of both hands.

"What happened?" He sat beside her on the row of interlocking gray armless chairs and enfolded her.

"It's Elijah," she said.

Intent on understanding, Rufus listened to Ruth's account.

"What are you doing here?" she asked. "How did you get here?"

"I'm putting cabinets in offices on one of the upper floors."

"I can't believe you're here on this day of all days."

"*Gottes wille.* Is Elijah going to be all right?"

"I think so. Of course I'm concerned, but why were the Capps so cold to me? It was as if they dismissed me. Why would they tell me to go home like that?"

"He still has your heart, doesn't he?" Rufus leaned forward, elbows on his knees.

"If they think I'm trying to lure their son away, I would assure them that I have gone out of my way not to do that." Ruth ground a fist into her thigh. "That doesn't mean I stopped caring about him. He's a person, after all. Someone I've known well for many years."

"Of course you care about him. When the Capps have the reassurance that Elijah is well, they will look at things differently."

Ruth shook her head. "No, I don't think so. It's as if they are blaming me for something. I had nothing to do with what happened today. Annalise is the one who was there with Elijah, not me."

"If you have done nothing wrong, then you have nothing to fear."

"I'm not afraid. I'm hurt. And I want someone to tell me what is happening with Elijah!"

Rufus absorbed the contortions of his sister's face and wished he knew the words that would smooth them. How thick her heart must be with the burden of loving a man who belonged to a people she called her own less and less.

"Hey, dude!" Marcus dropped into a chair on the other side of Rufus. "The boss is looking for you."

Annie stared at her open back door. While she had taken to leaving it unlocked, it was not her habit to leave it standing wide open.

By the time she got back into town after the morning's drama, she had to go straight to the shop without stopping at home. In the back room, she had done her best to wash up in the old sink and brush dirt off her dress. With a sigh, she realized she had lost yet another prayer *kapp*. It could be in the meadow, snagged on a bush and billowed by wind, or it could be in the rig she had returned to town in, smashed against a floor mat. It made no difference. She would not get it back. Annie resisted the urge to inspect her face and hair in the mirror and settled for pinning her straggly braids back into place by touch alone.

By the end of the afternoon, she was ready for a hot bath and a hot meal.

And word from Ruth about Elijah's condition. Making a series of phone calls from the shop, it had taken Annie most of two hours to track down Elijah's parents and then find Tom to see if he would taxi. Mrs. Weichert, working on the month-end books, looked up periodically with concern. Annie was careful to say only that Elijah had an accident and had been taken to the hospital. For as long as possible, she hoped to leave Leah's name out of the rumors that were sure to fly around town. The truth would come out about Leah's part in the accident, but for now, just for today, Annie did not want to raise questions she could not answer.

And now her back door was standing wide open.

Annie entered her home and laid her purse on the counter inside the back door.

"Annalise?" A faint voice came from the front of the house.

"Who's there?" Still unsettled, Annie decided she would not take a makeshift kitchen weapon to greet someone who knew her name.

"It's me."

Annie progressed into the dining room. "Leah?"

The kitten shot past just then, brushing Annie's skirt on his way to the kitchen. Annie took a moment to light the small oil lamp on the dining room table. Leah came into focus scrunched into the far chair in the adjoining living room.

"Are you all right, Leah?"

The response came slowly, with deliberation. "I guess if I were, I would not have done that to Elijah."

Annie closed her eyes and offered a prayer of thanks before proceeding to sit in the other chair. "You did a great job getting help, Leah. Ruth got there even before the ambulance, and Elijah was so glad to see her."

"Is he paralyzed?"

"No," Annie answered quickly and then thought she should qualify her response. "I don't think so. They took him to a hospital just to be sure."

"Everybody is going to find out." Leah's face was suddenly slick with tears. "His family will want the church to pay his medical expenses, and everybody will know that I was the one doing something stupid, not Elijah."

Annie had no answer. What Leah said might well be true.

"My mother is right. I mess things up all the time. I can't control myself."

Annie pulled a tissue from a box on the end table between the chairs and handed it to Leah.

"But I'm not going to hurt Aaron. If I can just get to

Pennsylvania, I can change. He makes me believe in myself. No one else does that for me."

"I want to help you, too." Annie pointed across the room. "Have you looked on the other side of that screen?"

Leah shook her head. "I've just been sitting here all day. I put away the groceries Ruth bought because they needed to be in the refrigerator, but I didn't want you to think I was touching all your things."

"I would like to show you what is over there. Would you like to see?"

"It's a nice screen. Useful but pretty in a plain way."

"I'll turn on a couple of lamps so you can see better." Annie turned the switch on the propane lamp rising out of the end table. "Come over here."

Annie took Leah's hand and led her the few steps across the room. "The other lamp is over here, behind the screen. Why don't you turn it on?"

Leah gently moved the end of the screen and stepped into the bedroom-like space Annie had created.

"I told you before that you were welcome to stay with me," Annie said, "and I meant it. I've made up the couch like a bed. Your bed."

Leah's eyes widened. "How did you know I would come?"

"I prayed that you would, and I felt a peace about making up the bed. That's a kind of knowing, isn't it?"

Leah exhaled heavily. "But after today you should change your mind."

"I don't think so. God answered my prayer. You're here."

"I don't know why you want me here."

"For the same reason I wanted you to come down from the gravel. I want you to be safe."

"I can't sleep there." Leah stepped back. "I've been wearing the same dress for three weeks. I don't deserve it. I'm filthy."

"You're lovely," Annie said quickly. "As for the rest, I have plenty of hot water and a purple dress that should suit you well."

"An Amish dress?"

"Yes."

"Is that all you have now?"

"Yes. I gave away my *English* clothes months ago." Annie raised a tender hand to Leah's head. "Look, you've still got your prayer *kapp*."

"Of course. I ran away from my parents, not from God."

Annie chuckled. "You wouldn't believe how many prayer *kapps* I have lost trying to run toward God."

"I don't want to be some kind of prisoner." Leah stepped out of Annie's reach. "I could do that at my parents' house."

"I'm not trying to be a jailer. I'm trying to be a friend."

"I don't have any friends here."

"You have me."

"You can't ask me a lot of questions about where I go or what I'm doing all day. I'm not going to tell you."

Annie pressed her lips together. She had questions she did not dare ask in this tremulous moment. Was she willing to take on a distraught teenager without any boundaries? She took a slow breath of prayer.

"I'm not going to hound you," Annie said.

"You have to trust me." Leah's tone dared Annie.

"And I hope you can trust me," Annie said. "Let's start with tonight and see where we go, all right? How about a hot bath?"

Leah nodded.

Ruth accepted the coffee that Tom brought her a few minutes after Rufus returned to work. "Thank you."

"No news yet?"

She shook her head. Surely by now Elijah was back from his scans.

"Pardon me, then," Tom said. "I am going to force the issue by asking to speak to the Capps. I don't want to abandon them, but I need to know what to tell my wife about when I'll be home."

Taking his own coffee with him, Tom sauntered toward the ER desk.

The automatic doors from the outside slid open, sending a draft of cool outside air into the waiting area. Alan Wellner stepped in and immediately spied Ruth.

"I heard about your friend," he said. "I came to see if there was anything I could do to help."

She shrugged. "I'm just waiting. There should be some news soon."

"I could give you a ride back to Westcliffe."

"Thanks, but I'll be all right." Ruth was stranded, and even if Tom Reynolds had room in his truck, the Capps might not want her to ride with them. But Alan unsettled her.

"I know it was weird with my dad the other day." He took the seat Rufus had been in just moments ago and stretched out his long form, arms across the chairs on either side of him. "Stuff like that happens all the time, but it doesn't mean anything. So don't be freaked out by it."

"I'm not." Ruth sipped her coffee and moved her eyes to where Tom stood at the ER desk. "Every family is different."

"My dad is in la-la land sometimes. He'll call me next week like nothing happened."

"I hope you can work things out."

"I let it roll off my back. People sometimes do things just to make a point." Alan's fingers drummed against the back of Ruth's chair, and she stood up.

"So how long have you and Bryan known each other?" she asked.

"Long time. Best friends."

"That's great for both of you."

Mr. Capp had appeared at the desk and leaned in to speak with Tom. Ruth watched for clues about what they might be saying.

"Bryan likes you a lot." Alan grinned up at her. "He tells me these things. He thinks the whole Amish thing is fascinating, and that you're a strong woman."

"He said all that?" Ruth had only seen Bryan a couple of times and thought he understood very little about the Amish.

"He's a man who knows what he wants."

Ruth was relieved to see Tom crossing the room toward her. "Good news?"

"Yep." Tom rubbed his palms together. "They are doing the paperwork to release him now."

"He can go home?"

"Nothing's broken, everything works. And Elijah doesn't want to stay."

Relief swamped Ruth.

"I wish I could take you home, too," Tom said, "but the truck will be crowded as it is. We're going to make Elijah comfortable in the backseat and his parents will both ride in front."

"Don't worry about me." Ruth felt the absence of the car she had owned for the last few months and the independence it provided her. "I'll figure something out."

As Tom walked away, Ruth took her phone out of her pocket and dialed Mrs. Weichert's shop. No one answered. Ruth scrolled through her contact list. Most of the listings were people she knew in Colorado Springs, not Westcliffe.

"Looks like you're going to need a ride home after all." Alan stood behind her. "Good thing I'm here."

Twenty-Eight

$\mathcal{N}$o need, Alan. I can take Ruth home." Bryan took Ruth by the hand and tugged her away from Alan.

"What are you still doing here?" Ruth was grateful for Bryan's presence at that moment. "I thought you would have taken the ambulance back hours ago."

"I did. I had to finish out my volunteer shift, in case there were any more calls."

"And you came all the way back here?"

Bryan squeezed her hand. "I don't like to leave a damsel in distress."

"How did you even know she would need a ride?" Alan slid his hands into his pockets. "She could have been gone already."

"Then why are you here, buddy?" Bryan jabbed his friend's shoulder playfully. "At least I can claim some responsibility since I brought her here in the first place."

He still held her hand, and Ruth relaxed into his grip. It was an odd sensation. Elijah was the only man who had taken her hand this way before, covering her slender fingers in a grasp both affectionate and protective, and only when they were alone. Yet Ruth trusted Bryan's hold.

Alan circled them. "I was only trying to be helpful."

"Thank you for thinking of me." Ruth craned her neck to follow Alan's pacing path.

"Yeah, thanks, buddy, but I've got this one covered." Bryan released Ruth's hand and put an arm around her shoulder. "How is your friend doing?"

"His parents are here to take him home. No serious damage."

"I'm glad to hear that. His back is going to be one big bruise."

"It could have been so much worse."

"You would know. You're an almost nurse." Bryan guided her toward the door.

"I still have a ways to go with my education." Ruth looked over her shoulder at Alan. "Is your friend going to be okay?"

"Alan? He'll be fine. He goes into these moods sometimes, usually after he sees his dad."

"He drove all the way over here because he thought I might need a ride."

"He likes attention. Being a hero. But he tries too hard and it puts people off."

"So you're used to just ignoring him?"

"I learned my lesson years ago." Bryan pressed his key fob and the lights of the gray Mitsubishi came on.

"You two have a...curious relationship."

"Are you hungry?" Bryan opened the passenger door. "We could get something to eat while we're in a town with some actual options."

"I haven't had anything since breakfast." Ruth sized up Bryan's car. It was a few years old, but it was clean inside and out.

"Then we'll find a place, and I'll treat you to an early dinner."

What can you tell about a man based on his car? Ruth wondered. She hardly knew Bryan any better than she knew Alan. So far they had met in public places within blocks of where she lived and worked.

"How about there?" Ruth pointed across the street from the

parking lot to a casual dining establishment. If she decided she was uncomfortable for any reason, she would not get back in his car.

"You got it. Food coming right up." Bryan closed the car door and walked around to the driver's side.

Ruth sat facing the emergency entrance of the building. As Bryan turned the key in the ignition, the hospital doors swooshed open and an orderly pushed Elijah outside in a wheelchair. Behind, his parents carried their worried looks and studied discharge papers.

Tom pulled his vehicle to the curb, blocking Ruth's view of the Capps. While Bryan backed out of his parking space and headed out of the lot, pressure burned in Ruth's chest. Shock. Grief. Confusion. Love. Whatever it was, she ached for relief.

Rufus separated the tools that belonged to him from those his employer supplied. The end of the workday ushered in a swath of moments he dreaded.

The moment when he would decide whether to remain in the motel room he shared with an *English* man who spent his time flipping channels on the television or to seek quiet solitude elsewhere.

The moment when he would not sit down to dinner with his family.

The moment when he would not lie down in his own bed.

The moment when he would wonder what had become of Elijah Capp and have no way to find out.

The moment he would want to take his little brother to the barn to feed apples to the horses.

The moment he would wish for a glimpse of Annalise's smile, the turn of her head.

Rufus double-checked that all his own tools were accounted for in the wooden toolbox he had made himself a decade ago, then did a final visual sweep of the room. The afternoon's labor yielded a satisfactory rank of cabinets. Tomorrow a pair of young hospital publicists would move back into their remodeled work space, while Rufus and the rest of the team began on the next vacated space.

"We're getting together a group for dinner. Wanna come?" Marcus closed and latched a red metal toolbox.

"Thank you for thinking to include me, but I have an errand," Rufus said.

Marcus collected four empty Styrofoam cups to carry out of the office. "A man's got to eat. You might as well use your per diem account."

"I'm not all that hungry." Rufus picked up his toolbox. "I'll walk back to the motel later. It's not that far."

Before he left the hospital, Rufus made his way back to the emergency department, just to be sure Ruth was not still waiting for word on Elijah. A harried woman with three droopy-eyed children now occupied the seats where Rufus and Ruth had sat earlier in the afternoon. Rufus approached the desk.

"Excuse me, you had a patient named Elijah Capp today. Was he admitted to the hospital?"

A new clerk had begun a new shift, and she typed some letters into the computer. "We don't have anybody under that name."

Rufus puffed his cheeks and let out his breath. "That's good. Thank you."

He stepped on the mat that parted the sliding doors and leaned into the outside air sweetened with a flock of blue hydrangea. After a pause to get his bearings, Rufus calculated that the sign he had seen that morning must have been on the other side of the hospital and began to walk around.

Realtors worked primarily in certain geographic areas, he supposed. But southwestern Colorado was spread out, and a Realtor representing commercial property would surely have a larger region. Cañon City was not so far from Westcliffe that he could not find someone to help him.

Rufus rounded two corners of the blockish hospital and found himself where he wanted to be. The old house still had lights on inside.

Ruth ate with nearly embarrassing velocity. The potato soup was hearty, the black bread warm, the meatloaf baked to saucy perfection. Even the roasted broccoli, never Ruth's favorite vegetable, settled into her taste buds pleasantly. All day long she had thought herself too nervous to think about food

"How about some pie?" Bryan reached for the dessert menu against the wall of their booth.

"I can't eat another bite." Ruth protested with two raised hands. "But thank you for all this. The whole day is a blur. I didn't realize how much better I would feel if I ate."

"They have peach pie." Bryan wiggled his brow.

"It can't possibly be as good as my *mamm*'s."

"You'll never know if you don't taste it."

Ruth laughed. "Yes I will. Even I can't make a peach pie that tastes as good as hers. The pies here probably come out of a box in the freezer."

"Somebody had to make them and put them in a box."

She shook her head. "I'm not budging."

"I hope someday I get to taste your mother's pie."

Ruth dabbed her lips with a napkin. "Sometimes she sells them."

"That's not what I was thinking."

She knew that. She just did not know how to respond to what Bryan was hinting at.

The waitress appeared and offered coffee, which Bryan accepted. Ruth had had her fill of coffee for one day. If she had nurtured hope of sleeping that night, she should decline.

"Last chance for dessert," he said.

Ruth shook her head. The waitress poured Bryan's coffee.

"Your family seems really great." Bryan added cream to his

coffee. "I mean, from what you've said about them."

"We're not perfect."

"No family is. But it seems like they accept that you're making your own decisions without freaking out the way Alan's dad does."

"I've disappointed them, but they love me."

"How could you disappoint them by being a nurse?" Bryan clinked his spoon against the side of his mug.

"It means I can't join the church." Ruth pulled apart the remaining dark roll in the basket and nibbled one half.

"You still believe in God, don't you?"

"Very much."

"And you're trying to do something good in the world."

"Yes. But the Amish live apart. We. . .they are not concerned with the *English* world."

"Can't you be a nurse for Amish people?" Bryan held his mug by the rim, ready to raise it to his lips.

"I would very much like to serve the Amish or other groups that do not always have someone to trust when they need medical help. But I still need an *English* education."

Bryan shrugged both shoulders. "So you join another church. You keep praying. You keep serving."

Ruth gave a half smile. If he thought it was that simple, Bryan Nichols did not understand a single rudimentary fact about the Amish. "How's the coffee?"

He took a long drag on the dark liquid and set the mug down. "This Elijah guy means something to you, doesn't he?"

"A great deal." The roll was nearly crumbling between Ruth's fingers now.

"Like, you're dating him?"

"No." Definitely no.

"But you used to."

"Sort of. Yes. I guess the *English* would say so."

"My paramedic partner said he was about ready to tell you two to get a room."

Ruth looked at him blankly. "That sounds like an *English* expression."

"It is. Haven't you heard it? You know. . .when two people want to be close, they get a room."

The blush rose through her face immediately.

"I'm sorry." Bryan set his cup down abruptly and sloshed coffee onto the table. "I didn't mean. . . I would never. . . It's just what he said. He thought there was something more than friendship. Some kind of electricity."

"It's complicated."

Bryan smiled. "Now there's an *English* expression."

"One that I understand."

"I'm not doing this very well." He took the napkin from his lap and sopped up spilled coffee. "I'm trying to say that what you did for Elijah today was awesome. It tells me a lot about the kind of person you are."

Ruth's chest pressed in on her lungs. "Thank you."

"I know I'm being an idiot. But I hope I haven't blown my chance."

"Your chance?"

"To get to know you better. To become friends. To maybe, I don't know, see where things might go."

His words stunned her. "We hardly know each other, Bryan."

"Haven't you ever heard of love at first sight?" He wadded up his soggy napkin. "Okay, this is not that, exactly. It's more like first cousins once removed. . . . Or maybe perfect strangers. . . I just want a chance."

Twenty-Nine

June 1892

Maura looked at herself in the mirror while Belle Mooney fastened the stubborn buttons down the back of Maura's black dress. The buttons on the broad cuffs would be the next challenge. She had first worn the dress for her mother's funeral and only a few weeks ago for John Twigg's.

"You ought to cut the buttonholes longer and stitch them again," Belle said. "Or buy smaller buttons. Mr. Twigg carries a nice selection in his shop now."

"My mother bought these buttons at Denton's Emporium." Maura smoothed her skirt. "She had a different use in mind. I only decided to put them on this dress for her funeral."

"I wish you wouldn't trade at Denton's." Belle picked up her hat from Maura's quilted bedspread. "You know how I feel about them."

"We've both shopped there for years." Maura sat on the bed, lifted a handkerchief from the nightstand, and brushed dust off the black shoes tied around her ankles.

"That was before," Belle said. "You saw what they did to John. Vicious beasts."

Maura sucked in her lips to keep herself from speaking aloud

941

the thought racing through her mind. John Twigg had been far from innocent in the feud between the Dentons and the Twiggs. Instead, she tried another approach.

"The feud is going on too long," Maura said. "You lost John, and now the whole county has lost our sheriff."

"Because of the Twiggs. That's what you mean." Belle fingered the comb holding her hair in place, adjusting. "It's not all their fault."

Maura reached across the bed for her own hat. "Let's focus on Sheriff Byler's funeral. Half of Baxter County will be there to pay respects."

"I'm not sure I should go."

"Why on earth not?"

"None of the Twiggs are going."

"Understandably," Maura said. "They harbored the man who did this."

"Jesse Roper's mother is dead." Belle balled her fists at her sides. "Old Man Twigg is his mama's daddy. He's kin."

Maura stood slowly. "Not to you, Belle. He's not kin to you."

"Nearly. If the Dentons had not stolen my chance to marry, he would be."

Maura did not wish death for anyone, especially not the way John died. But if Belle did not open her eyes soon and see that the Twiggs were instigating harm, her own heart would freeze over in its bitterness.

"Even if he were your kin," Maura said, "he still shot the sheriff."

"Don't you think I know that?" Belle's pitch rose as her face reddened.

Maura moistened her lips. "I'm sorry, Belle. I should not have upset you. Forgive me."

"I believe I've changed my mind." Belle picked up her soft gray handbag. "I believe I will ride to Mountain Home for the service with my daddy."

"I thought we were all going together."

"You have upset me, Maura. You upset me when you try to tell me John was not the man for me. You upset me when you defend the Dentons. I will go to the funeral out of respect to Sheriff and Mrs. Byler because they have been kind to me in the past, but I will ride with Daddy."

"Even your daddy hates the Twiggs." Maura regretted the words as soon as she blurted them out.

This was Joseph's first *English* funeral and his first time in an *English* church. He did not go to the viewing the day before, but even Zeke offered no objection when Joseph said he intended to pay respects. At the church in Mountain Home, he sat at the end of a pew in the back. His black suit matched the garb of mourners, and Joseph even removed his hat and held it in his lap during a lengthy eulogy of the beloved sheriff. Joseph learned Abraham Byler had been sheriff for a long stretch then served in the state legislature before deciding he preferred to be sheriff. The county's citizens had been glad to receive him back to office.

Prayers and a homily followed, before the pews emptied to somber organ music and most of the grieved congregation trailed the carriage carrying the pine casket to the graveyard. Once again Joseph held himself to the edge of the gathering, this time his hat on his head. The brevity of the graveside service surprised him. In his community, the entire congregation would have stood for two hours of sermons and prayers. Here, the minister read from a black book, pronounced "dust to dust, ashes to ashes," and spoke words of hope and resurrection.

Bess Byler stepped forward to throw the first handful of dirt on her husband's casket as it was lowered into the gaping fresh ground wound. Two young men, whom Joseph supposed to be her sons who lived nearby, hovered at her elbows. Bess's face wrenched and paled, but she did not cry aloud.

Walter stood between his parents in a black suit he had outgrown. The ill-fitting clothes were not what captured Joseph's attention, but rather the ill-fitting expression on the boy's face as he watched the sheriff's widow release her husband to God. Walter's expression overflowed with remorse. Joseph wondered if he had even told his parents what he had done.

The assembly slowly turned and staggered back toward the church, where members of the ladies guild had stayed behind to arrange food and refreshment.

Joseph watched Maura Woodley stifle her sobs and put a gloved hand on her father's arm to gesture that he should go ahead. She remained at the grave, on her knees in the grass now. Walter stood stiff as his parents moved with the congregation.

Putting an arm around Walter's shoulders, Joseph nudged him toward Maura. "I think Walter has something he would like to say to you."

She lifted a tear-streaked face, questioning.

Walter shook his head, but Joseph kept the boy pointed toward his cousin.

"Walter?" Maura stood up.

"Jesse Roper made fun of me," Walter blurted. "He treated me like a child."

"What are you talking about?" Maura's eyes moved from Walter's to Joseph's.

"I was there when the boys were shooting cans. I'm the one who told Deputy Combs they would all be at Digger Dawson's."

Maura's breath caught. "Did you shoot?"

"No. He wouldn't let me."

"You should not have been running around with Jesse Roper, but they were breaking the law. You did nothing wrong in reporting them."

"I just wanted to get back at him."

"I grant that your motive was questionable." Maura put a hand to the side of her face.

"If I hadn't said anything, the sheriff would not have gone looking for Roper."

From Joseph's close-up viewpoint, Walter's face looked as though it might crumble into sand.

Maura glanced at the still open grave at her feet. "This is not your fault, Walter. You have some growing up to do, but you did not cause this."

Relief oozed out of Joseph. He turned Walter toward the church. "Go on. Find your parents. Let them take you home."

The boy stumbled then found his gait.

Joseph turned to Maura. "I am sorry for your loss. I did not know Sheriff Byler personally, but he seemed a kind man who only wanted peace for your people."

She nodded, and he saw her struggle to swallow. Wordless, they walked side by side toward the church but at an ever-slowing pace.

"They did not catch him, you know," Maura finally said.

"Roper?"

"Several posses went out that same day and in the days since, but he got away. How can one man escape twenty or more?"

"Perhaps he had help."

Maura ceased forward progress altogether. "Do you truly believe that?"

"It would be an explanation."

"Yes, I suppose it would. A friend of the Twiggs, a change of clothing, a borrowed horse. He could be anywhere."

"And if they do not find him?" Joseph asked. "Is it the way of your people to hunt this man down?"

Maura blew out her breath slowly. "It is our way to bring justice whenever it is possible."

"Is justice not in God's hands?"

"You ask complicated questions, Mr. Beiler."

"Do I?" Joseph meant only to understand the *English* ways.

"If he crossed Bald Dave Mountain into Missouri, he could

go into Indian Territory. Change his name. Change his whole life. Just never come back here." Maura resumed slow steps. "What must you think of this feuding? It makes little sense to me. I can only imagine what your impressions are."

"My people do not always get along," Joseph said, "but we do not shoot at each other."

"And justice when there has been a wrong?"

"Our tradition teaches forgiveness. Justice is for God to decide. Whatever happens is *Gottes wille*. God's will."

"That it is God's will for Jesse Roper to get off scot-free is a hard pill to swallow."

" 'Vengeance is mine; I will repay, saith the Lord.' "

"I can see you are quite persistent, Mr. Beiler."

"My people are persistent in peace."

Maura looked toward the church. "We should at least go in and have a cup of coffee."

"*Kaffi*," Joseph said. "I wonder if people of all churches soothe their difficult moments with a black bitter drink."

A smile escaped her lips even on this somber day. "The truth is, I do not care for coffee. I drink it to be polite."

"Perhaps they will have tea," he said.

"Or church ladies' punch."

"Lemonade with too much sugar."

She laughed, for one second, then sobered.

"I am sorry," Joseph said. "I do not make light of the occasion."

"No. Of course not." She had no doubt of his sincerity.

"Please forgive me."

"I am guilty as well. I laughed." Maura's forward motion did not display her reluctance. "Sheriff Byler was a man of good humor. He would have agreed with you about the lemonade."

"I wish I had had the opportunity to know him better."

"Even though he was an *English* lawman?"

"Even so."

"I'm so worried about Belle." Maura put one hand over her eyes for a few seconds. "I've offended her. She would not even ride to the funeral with me."

"This is a difficult day for many people," Joseph said. "You will speak again on another day."

"I am not so sure. She has always been the more sensitive one, but she has turned a new corner in refusing my company. I cannot seem to say anything right."

"Time heals many wounds."

Maura stopped again and turned fully toward Joseph. "Suppose they have been looking in the wrong places."

"For Roper?"

"Yes. I have seen an entire posse swayed by one man's assumption or conclusion. What if that one man is wrong?"

Joseph tilted his head and met her gaze. "I do not know much about posses, but would not another man speak up?"

She shook her head. "That's the point. They get something stuck in their heads and can't see past it."

"Miss Woodley, are you trying to tell me that you have an idea where the outlaw might be?"

"I might have an idea who would help a man like Roper," she said. "That's all."

"Then perhaps you should speak to Deputy Combs. I would be happy to accompany you. He's probably drinking coffee right now."

With one hand, she unpinned her hat, removed it, flipped it over in her hands, and fleetingly wondered why the Amish men never took their hats off. "I don't want to cause a stir on the day of the funeral if it turns out to be nothing. There is no point in disturbing Bess Byler on a day like today with talk of posses and criminals."

"I suppose not. It is a day to remember the sheriff."

"Besides, Thomas Combs has proven himself a coward. Nevertheless, he will insist that I should leave such thoughts to the menfolk."

"Then another day?"

"No. Today." She set her jaw and made up her mind. "We won't talk to the deputy just yet. I'm going to take my cart and make some inquiries. I would very much like it if you would come with me."

"Are you sure that would not be unseemly?"

"That I am going to investigate on my own, or that I invite an Amish man to be my companion in the endeavor?"

"Both. And I am quite sure it would be unseemly for an Amish man to involve himself in this manner."

"Do as you wish. I am going with or without you."

"Miss Woodley, I admire your spirit of independence, but—"

"Time is a-wastin', Mr. Beiler. Are you coming?"

"Where is your cart?" Joseph asked. He could not bring himself to let her drive off alone without even knowing where she intended to go.

In the field across from the church, the small, light cart Joseph had seen Maura use around town was still hitched to the dark mare that pulled it. They sat beside each other on the narrow bench, and Maura picked up the reins. Joseph's stomach tied itself into a tight knot as he wondered about the number of people who saw them leave together and how he would explain this to Zeke Berkey later. Maura urged the horse out of its malaise and turned the cart down a road Joseph and Zeke had not explored. Joseph's eyes scanned for landmarks to remember. A fallen log. A small clearing. A shed.

Maura Woodley was as competent a driver as any man Joseph had ever met. A single animal pulled her cart, but he could easily imagine her handling a team of four horses. She was small beside him, well sized to her diminutive cart but eight feet tall in her determination.

"Would I be rude to ask a question?" Joseph held the edge of the bench with one hand.

"Depends on whether it is a rude question." Maura turned, and her brown eyes danced.

He cleared his throat. "Are you certain that the deputy has not already spoken to the person you intend to interrogate?"

"*Interrogate* is a strong word, Mr. Beiler."

The road narrowed before them, yet she let the horse maintain pace with unwavering confidence.

Abruptly she pulled on the reins. "Did you see that?" She jumped out of the cart before the horse had come to a stop.

Joseph did not dare let her get out of sight. He lurched out of the cart and followed her stomping pace.

"There!" She pointed.

Joseph saw nothing.

"There! You must see it." She kept walking.

Jesse Roper's tall, broad, black hat sat on a fence post.

Thirty

*N*o more coffee.

Ruth was not sure she could ever drink coffee again without thinking about Elijah on the gurney, his mother on the rampage, and Bryan on the make.

The whole day would not have happened if Leah Deitwaller would just grow up. Coming home to find her asleep in the living room next to a low-glowing lamp and Annalise looking overly content with a cup of tea at the dining room table rattled Ruth. She went upstairs to bed as quickly and with as little conversation as possible.

In the morning Ruth waited until she was sure Annalise had left the house before she emerged from her bedroom. In the kitchen, she mixed up a pan of cinnamon rolls—Elijah's favorite. She had first made them for him when they were sixteen years old. While they were in the oven, she dressed in a simple skirt and top of plain colors and sturdy fabric. When the rolls were done, she wrapped them between cotton dish towels and whispered thanks that she had a car. Steam would still be rising from the rolls when her tires crunched the gravel in the Capp driveway.

Ruth knew Elijah might not be awake, or not able to get out

of bed to greet her without pain, but she refused to believe that his mother would be so inhospitable as to turn away the rolls she knew her son loved.

Steeling herself to be polite no matter what, Ruth pulled up to the Capp house and turned off the engine.

I just want to leave these for Elijah, she would say.

Or better, *I made these for all of you to enjoy.*

Ruth was a good cook. She knew it, and Mrs. Capp knew it. Warm rolls could help thaw whatever had frozen between the two women, and even if they did not, Ruth would be amicable to the end.

And then she would send Joel over to see how Elijah was.

Mrs. Capp was in the yard hanging sheets on the line. Ruth picked up the tray of rolls in one hand and opened the car door with the other.

"Good morning," she said. "I brought some rolls. They're still warm."

Mrs. Capp took a clothespin from between her lips. "We had breakfast hours ago."

"Of course you did." Ruth walked toward her. "A midmorning treat, perhaps?"

The older woman pulled a pillowcase from her laundry basket and snapped it on the line.

"Yesterday was a hard day for all of us," Ruth said. "But we can all give thanks that Elijah was not hurt worse."

"If you're hoping to ply him with warm rolls, you've come to the wrong place."

Ply him? "I only meant to cheer him up. I can just leave the rolls if he's sleeping."

"He's not here. He insisted we take him to that. . .place where he is staying."

Ruth's breath caught. "What do you mean, Mrs. Capp?"

"He would not even let me take care of him for one night. *One night.* Was that so much to ask?"

Ruth moved closer. She saw that Mrs. Capp had hung the last of the bedding. At the bottom of the basket were four jars of canned green beans, perhaps to weight the basket if a wind kicked up through the valley.

"Where is Elijah?" Ruth asked.

"Renting a room. In an *English* house. He has decided that is better than living with his own parents."

Ruth felt the blood drain from her face. "I didn't know anything about his moving. When did this happen?"

"Last week." Mrs. Capp stooped and picked up a jar of beans. "He saw an ad tacked up on the board in the grocery store. Some woman was looking for boarders."

Ruth knew the ad. She had looked at it herself before deciding to stay with Annalise.

"It's your influence, with all your *English* ways. Like that awful car." Mrs. Capp hurled the jar, and it smashed against the hood of Ruth's car.

Once again Ruth turned off the engine in front of a house. This time the rolls were cold and she had lost interest in them.

Mrs. Capp had muttered an apology as soon as the jar smashed, but Ruth had hustled to her car and pulled away. Elijah left his family home and moved into an *English* house. And never said a word to her. Ruth was not sure which fact stunned her more.

She sat in the car and stared at the house, trying to picture what it must be like for him to live inside, in a room, by himself.

After nearly ten minutes, during which Ruth's heart rate returned to a normal range, she got out of the car and approached the front door to ring the bell.

She rang again about a minute later. The thought that no one was inside except bruised and weary Elijah made her lean far to the right to peer between the curtains in the front room. He was in no condition to be left alone all day, but his landlady had no obligation to care for him. Ruth buzzed her lips in agreement with Mrs. Capp. Elijah should have gone where someone could look after him. Perhaps she could still persuade him to go home.

Tentatively, she rang the bell a final time and at last heard movement.

"Coming!"

It was Elijah's voice. Remorse for causing him to get out of bed scratched at her conscience.

He opened the door. "Hello, Ruth."

"May I come in?"

He took two steps back, and she entered a plain living room with furniture that looked outdated and uncomfortable. After sweeping her eyes around the room once, Ruth focused on Elijah. His hair was tousled, but he was in fresh clothes and stood fairly erect. She had pictured him more bent over.

"First of all," she said, "how are you?"

"Well enough, considering. The doctor said I could go back to work when I felt up to it."

"Take a few days. Old Amos will understand."

"I'm not very good at sitting around doing nothing."

"You should sit now." Ruth gestured toward a faded mauve sofa.

"I'm not supposed to use this room," Elijah said. "I have kitchen and laundry privileges, but otherwise just the one room and bath."

"Oh." She gained his gaze and held it. "Why didn't you tell me?"

"You try too hard to talk me out of things." He waved a hand to the hall. "You might as well come and see the room. I don't suppose we're breaking *Ordnung* now."

Ruth had never been alone in a house with Elijah. They always found each other on top of the flat rock behind the Beiler land, now part of a town park. It made her nervous to see Elijah standing up, though, so she followed his shuffling gait toward a rear bedroom.

"The room came furnished," he said.

A full-size bed, a desk, a dresser, an upholstered side chair, a rickety stand for a small television, which was turned on with the volume dialed low. On the desk Ruth saw a cell phone plugged into the wall.

"Oh, Elijah, what have you done?" Her voice was barely a whisper.

Elijah gingerly lowered himself into the side chair. "I'm not going back."

"But your family—"

"I'm not going back."

"So you're leaving the church?" Guilt swept through her, though she had done nothing to encourage this choice.

"You and I talked about this years ago. It has just taken me longer to be brave than it took you."

Ruth gulped the tide of emotion. "I think you have been very brave to keep your baptismal vows all this time."

"I did not make them lightly," he said, "and I do not break them lightly. But I am not going back."

She believed him. And she resolved to say nothing more that would suggest he should return.

"Have you spoken to the bishop?"

"Not yet. But I will."

"Your mother will hate having to shun you."

Elijah gave a careful shrug. "I don't think our district will be overly strict in their interpretation. It is not the end of the world to eat at a separate table. They can still see me if they want to."

"Do you think they will want to see you?"

"I hope so. I will want to see them."

Ruth blew out her breath.

"Do you think Rufus would like to buy my horse and buggy?" Elijah asked.

"Maybe. If he ever gets around to proposing." Ruth sat on the edge of Elijah's bed a few feet from him.

"I'll have to find a new job, of course. It probably shouldn't be in Westcliffe. I thought I would move to Colorado Springs after Christmas."

Ruth was due to return to the university in January.

"You don't have to decide that now." She ran her hands along her thighs, suddenly aware of how much she was perspiring, and looked around the room.

"Ruth."

She looked up at him.

"You can choose me or not choose me, but this I have chosen for myself."

Annie wiped her lunch plate dry and set it in the cabinet. She had looked in the living room four times already for clues about where Leah might have gone. Annie stayed up late and got up early, and still Leah slipped through her grasp.

Not that she could have stopped her.

Leah's one condition for staying last night was that Annie not ask about where she spent her days. For instance, around old sheds or gasoline cans? Annie could not ask directly, but she needed to know.

The back door opened and Annie glanced over her shoulder, hoping.

Not Leah. Ruth.

"Hey, Ruth."

"Hey, Annalise."

"I made tuna salad. Would you like some?" Annie reached for the plate she had just washed and put away.

"No thanks. I'm not hungry right now." Ruth laid her purse on the kitchen counter, next to where Annie habitually left hers.

"I feel like we should talk about yesterday," Annie said. "It all happened so fast, and then we didn't see each other all day."

"Maybe I'll just have some water." Ruth went to the refrigerator for the pitcher of chilled liquid.

Annie handed Ruth a glass.

Ruth poured and then drank. "I wasn't expecting Leah to be here last night."

"I know. I wasn't either. She was here when I came home."

"And you were ready for her."

"You knew I had set up the space. Ruth, she needs help."

"I know. I'm sorry. It's just hard to be gracious after what she did to Elijah." Ruth drained her glass.

"I understand." Annie took Ruth's empty glass and set it in the sink. "But I have to ask you one question."

"What is it?" Ruth pushed up the sleeves of her top and scratched an elbow.

"Leah doesn't just need a safe place to stay. She needs someone to help her sort things out. To sort herself out."

"Isn't that what you're trying to do?"

"I'm not qualified. She needs a mental health professional."

"So what are you asking me? I'm not a counselor, either."

"I need to know how the church feels about mental health. Am I supposed to just pray for her, or can I find someone who will see her?"

"This might be a question for the bishop."

"I don't want to ask him if it's way out of line." Annie picked up an apple from the fruit bowl on the counter and began to polish it on her sleeve. "Have you ever known anyone who saw a therapist?"

Ruth let out a long, slow breath. "Well, I've heard of people trying herbs and vitamins, along with prayer and hard work."

"But not a professional?"

"I didn't say that. Actually, I think most people—the women, at least—would agree that the mind or spirit can be ill, just the way the body can be."

"So then it's all right to see someone?"

"I said *most* people would agree. I'm pretty sure Mrs. Deitwaller is not one of them."

Annie nodded. "Leah is almost eighteen."

"But she's not. The *English* will have laws about this."

"The bishop's wife might intervene. Maybe she could talk to Mrs. Deitwaller."

Ruth rubbed her temples. "Annalise, can we talk about this another time? It's hard for me to talk about Leah. I know she needs help, but she hurt Elijah. I need some time to see past that."

"I'm sorry." Annie set the apple back in the basket. "You were amazing yesterday. I didn't get a chance to tell you that."

"You were the one who kept Elijah still while you waited for the ambulance."

"But it was you Elijah wanted to see. I could tell it meant the world to him that you rode along to the hospital."

"Did you know he moved out?" Ruth locked eyes with Annie. Annie cleared her throat.

"Annalise."

"He told me the day of the training burn. I thought he'd forgotten his hat, but he said he left it behind on purpose."

"I wish you had told me."

"Was it really mine to tell?"

Thirty-One

June 1892

Joseph and Maura clattered back to Mountain Home in the cart. He held Jesse Roper's hat on his lap, feeling its height and breadth, the broad brim, the crown creased deeply and precisely, the starched, proud shape. If Joseph's own soft black hat had ever had a distinctive shape, it had long ago dissipated into everyday practical use. It exuded nothing but simplicity and humility. He felt no affinity for what Roper had done—which Joseph had seen with his own eyes—but the confidence of the man intrigued him. His people would say it was *hochmut*, pride, that got Jesse Roper into trouble. Joseph supposed it was. But still, what might it feel like to be that sure of himself?

Maura seemed to have lost her reluctance to disturb the postburial gathering. By the time they reached the church, the crowd in the church hall had thinned. Ladies were stacking dishes and carrying them out of sight. Deputy Combs sat with Bess Byler and her two sons.

"It is too bad Malinda could not come from Colorado," Maura said. "I suppose the journey would take too much planning with twin babies and a three-year-old."

"By God's grace, her sons are with her." Carrying Roper's hat,

Joseph followed Maura's march across the hall.

Combs shot out of his chair at the sight of the hat. "Where did you get that?"

"We found it," Maura said.

Combs snapped toward Joseph. "Were you hiding evidence, Mr. Beiler?"

Joseph hardly knew how to answer the accusation and said nothing.

"Don't be ridiculous, Deputy Combs." Maura took the hat from Joseph. "I just told you we found the hat. It was sitting on a post at the edge of White Ledge Ranch, clear as day. I will not insult you by suggesting any of your men would have missed it had it been there two days ago."

Bess Byler shrugged off her sons and stood up. "Then you think somebody was sheltering Roper?"

Maura nodded. "At the very least, he was hiding out on the property."

"Looks that way, Bess," Thomas said. "I'll go out and ask some questions of the owners and any hands working the ranch."

"That was our intention." Maura gestured to Joseph. "But once we found the hat, we felt we should come right back."

Joseph was uncomfortable with Maura's use of plural pronouns. The intention had been hers and the choice to return hers.

"Maura, you should not have gone out there alone," Thomas said.

"I was not alone," she snapped back. "Mr. Beiler was with me."

"And unarmed. What good would he be?"

Joseph's spine straightened. "With all due respect, Deputy, twenty men with guns did not save your sheriff."

Bess reached out and touched Joseph's forearm. "My husband would have liked you. Even though he was a man of the law, he was not quick to resort to guns."

"Obviously Roper left his hat on purpose," Maura said. "He wanted someone to find it. Even though he was not here long, everybody knew how he flaunted that hat. He is not a man who makes mindless mistakes."

"Well, he made a mistake in shooting our sheriff." Thomas looked at the widow. "Sorry, Bess. I will get some men on this right away. We have a new starting point."

"We won't give up, Bess," Maura said. "We will bring Jesse Roper to justice."

Joseph stepped back from the group, away from the enticement of Maura Woodley's *we*.

In Gassville on the following Monday, Maura lingered outside her uncle's shop. The day was stifling. She could not decide whether she was more miserable indoors or outdoors. The task of checking her uncle's accounts for the previous month was unfinished, so she would have to return to the stuffy back room at some point. For the moment she would have welcomed the slightest hope of a breeze.

Old Man Twigg stomped down the street toward Maura, bearded and bareheaded. Maura considered retreating into the shop, but clearly he was aiming for her and would only follow.

"I heard you had my grandson's hat." Gruff hostility shot through his words.

Maura took one step back toward the shop's doorway. "I found it, if that's what you mean."

"I want it."

"I don't have it," Maura said. "You'll have to speak to Deputy Combs. It's evidence."

"It's a hat, that's all," Twigg said. "It's all I have left of my grandson, and he was all I had left of my daughter. I want it."

"As I said, you'll have to speak to Deputy Combs." Even as she spoke, Maura wondered how well Combs would stand up to Twigg. He spoke with determination about finding Sheriff Byler's killer, but Jesse Roper had not been the first person on the other side of the law to intimidate Thomas Combs.

"They sent another posse out after him, didn't they?" Twigg glared at Maura. "He's just a boy."

Maura returned the glare. A posse had ridden out Saturday night and not yet returned. "He shot the sheriff, and the way I hear it, you were there making sure he got clean away."

He harrumphed. "They won't find him."

Finally he moved on, stomping his way toward the post office.

Maura leaned against the door frame and let herself exhale heavily. Roper's mother must have been John Twigg's sister. The old man had lost two grown children in recent months. While she was sorry for the deaths, Maura refused to let that sway her feelings toward Twigg's part in the murder of a man she considered her friend as well as her sheriff.

Perspiration trickled into one eye, and she delicately wiped it clear. When she opened her eyes again, blinking three times rapidly, she started to call to Joseph across the street.

Before the sound left her mouth, she realized it was not Joseph. The man was dressed identically to Joseph and Zeke and was about Joseph's height with a similar build. But his hair was dark and trimmed shorter than Joseph's. He could be nothing other than a third Amish man in Gassville, standing in the street holding the reins of his horse.

She crossed the street to greet him. "Welcome to Gassville, Mr.—"

"Bender," the man replied. "Stephen Bender."

"Mr. Bender." Maura double-checked the cut of his black suit. "May I be so forward as to inquire whether you are seeking Mr. Beiler and Mr. Berkey?"

"*Ya,*" Bender said. "The bishop sent me. Do you know where they are lodging?"

Maura nodded. "Behind the livery. I will take you there." With one hand, Maura indicated the way.

He led his horse, and they walked the blocks to the stables at the end of Main Street. Mr. Bender was not given to conversation, Maura decided. Her attempts at offering openings for him to say more about himself were met with brief replies. She remembered Joseph's nervousness when she first approached him and how long it had taken him to find his words. She supposed that this young man was equally unaccustomed to conversing with an *English* woman. At least this time, Maura had the advantage of knowing something of the Amish people.

Joseph and Zeke sat in the shade of the livery's front overhang with tin cups of cool water. Their work helping to clear the Dentons' land was complete. While Joseph had wanted to accept the offer of work, the more trees the crew ripped out, the more he grieved the ravage of the land. Before much longer, Zeke would insist they should leave Gassville. Joseph would have to face a decision he had avoided for the last several weeks.

"Here comes your *English* friend." Zeke lifted his cup toward the street then stood up. "I believe that is our Stephen Bender with her."

Joseph set his cup down beside the bench and stood as well. There could be no doubt it was Stephen. Joseph had sold Stephen that charcoal mare himself.

"I believe you know Mr. Bender," Maura said.

"Hello, Stephen," Zeke said. "We are pleased to see you. Aren't we, Joseph?"

Joseph nodded. "Hello, Stephen. *Guder mariye*, Miss Woodley." Good morning.

Curiosity pooled in her dark eyes, and he could not resist meeting her gaze.

Stephen was already opening his saddlebag. "I brought letters from both your families. And the bishop. And Hannah sent a special letter for you, Joseph."

Stephen sorted the letters, handing Joseph a letter from his parents and the one from Hannah. To Zeke he gave news from the Berkey family and the bishop's letter.

Joseph broke the seal on the letter, written in his mother's hand, and scanned the news of the new foal and the fence line his brothers had repaired. One of her best layers had stopped producing eggs. Although the news was trivial, Joseph felt his mother's warmth. He folded the letter closed. Zeke had chosen to read the bishop's letter first.

"He is not calling us home yet," Zeke muttered.

Relief coursed through Joseph as he raised his eyes to Maura again.

"He asks for an estimate of our available resources," Zeke reported, "and has sent a little money from the church for us to continue to look for a location for a new settlement."

"Stephen, are you to carry the answer back?" Joseph asked.

"Not immediately." Stephen fastened his saddlebag closed. "The bishop felt there might be benefit in my joining you for a time."

Joseph felt Stephen's eyes on him and shifted his weight, wondering what range of topics Zeke had written about in his letter to the bishop.

"What is the news from Hannah?" Zeke nudged Joseph in the elbow. "Aren't you going to answer the letter?"

"Is Hannah your sister?" Maura asked, smiling. "Is Zeke sweet on her?"

Zeke and Stephen laughed. Joseph watched the blush in Maura's face.

"Hannah is *my* sister," Zeke explained, "and she is *en lieb* with Joseph. They are practically engaged."

"Oh. I see."

Joseph's stomach lurched. Maura's face paled in an instant, the smile gone from both eyes and lips as she looked at him.

"We are *not* practically engaged." Joseph eyes widened toward Zeke. He wished Hannah's letter would disappear from his hand.

Maura had already stepped back. "My uncle will be waiting for me to finish the accounts. I'm sure you all have much to catch up on." She nodded toward Stephen. "It was a pleasure to meet you, Mr. Bender."

Joseph moved a step toward her, but she had already turned away.

Joseph straightened his hat with both hands and turned toward Stephen. "You must have other news for us as well."

But Stephen was watching Maura. "Joseph, why did that woman look at you that way?"

"I do not know what you are talking about." Joseph stepped back to the bench in the shade and picked up his empty water cup.

"You are my friend, Joseph," Zeke said, "but I cannot encourage you in this deceit."

"What deceit?" Stephen demanded.

Zeke and Joseph stared at each other.

"What deceit?" Stephen repeated. "Does it have to do with the *English* woman?"

"Joseph has feelings for her," Zeke said.

Indignation welled in Joseph. "You speak freely of my private matters."

"We are three now," Zeke said. "We are far from our people. We must remind each other of our ways and the reasons for them."

"The bishop will not be pleased to hear this," Stephen said.

"It is not your business to tell him," Joseph said. "I have done nothing and said nothing to Miss Woodley."

"But you feel something," Zeke said.

Joseph swatted at the bishop's letter still in Zeke's hands. "You said he wants us to continue to look for land to settle on. Does he give specific instructions?"

Zeke unfolded the letter again. "He asks us to take one last trip farther west, beyond Mountain Home. Then we are to return home to give a report and recommendation. He is concerned that we have been gone from the community for too long."

The stable doors burst open behind them, and the owner emerged with two horses. "Lee Denton is organizing a fresh posse. He will be here soon for his horses."

Zeke took the horses' reins. "We will be sure he gets them."

"If you men want to ride, I can do without you for a few days."

"Thank you, but no," Zeke said.

"When are they leaving?" Joseph asked.

"As soon as they have a dozen men," the stable owner said.

Joseph looked from Zeke to Stephen. "Our work on the Dentons' ranch is finished. I will ride with the posse."

Thirty-Two

$\mathcal{R}$uth clicked open the interoffice e-mail and read the doctor's instructions:

> *Please make sure Mrs. Webb gets on the schedule with Jerusha on Friday for an initial visit. Call patient to confirm time.*

Jerusha was the counselor who came from Pueblo once a week to see patients through the clinic. She would see patients there three or four times. After that, if she thought they needed a more indefinite therapeutic relationship, she encouraged them to arrange visits to her regular practice, where open appointments would be more available.

This was already Wednesday. Friday might be full. Ruth clicked through to Jerusha's schedule and found one opening, so she located Mrs. Webb's phone number and called to offer the appointment before returning to her e-mails to look for further follow-up notes from practitioners. Before her shift ended, she also needed to confirm all the appointments for the following day.

Elijah was supposed to check in with a local doctor after a

week, but Ruth doubted he would follow that advice. She had stopped in to see him again that morning, and he was already talking about at least going into the office at the back of Old Amos's house to help with paperwork if Amos would not let him go out on calls to the Amish homes needing appliance repairs.

Leah had left Elijah's horse and buggy on the Capp farm for his parents to find. She had not known any more than Ruth did that Elijah had moved and was boarding his horse at the edge of town. Ruth's instinct was to offer to drive him out to get his buggy, but she did not want any more jars of beans broken over her hood.

As frazzled as she was, Leah had done the sensible thing with the rig. Ruth paused with her fingers over the keyboard to pray for forgiveness and compassion to rise up, because she could not muster it in her own strength.

She could at least suggest to Annalise that Jerusha might be able to help Leah. Ruth prayed again, this time for Annalise to forgive the heartless spirit of their conversation the evening before.

Ruth closed out of Jerusha's schedule and checked the sticky note of tasks she had written for herself at the beginning of her shift, scribbling out several accomplished items.

Jerusha was an *English* counselor. Would she understand enough of the Amish ways to be helpful without being offensive?

Alan Wellner. Now that was someone who should see an *English* counselor, Ruth thought. Something was not right in his soul.

"I've made some initial inquiries," Larry, the Realtor, said to Rufus on Thursday afternoon, "but I have to be honest. It's going to take some work to sell this property, if that's what you decide to do."

Rufus leaned back in the wooden chair across from the Realtor. The coffee the receptionist had offered sat untouched on the desk between them.

"What obstacles would we have to overcome?" Rufus asked.

"To begin with, the whole market is slow. I've been handling commercial properties in southwestern Colorado for twenty years, and this is about the worst I've seen."

Rufus inhaled through the sigh he wanted to let out and considered the balding, fiftyish man before him. "What else?"

"You're talking about land that may have to be rezoned to attract a commercial buyer who could invest in reasonable access. Were you planning to run a business from that location when you purchased it?"

Rufus nodded. "Also to live there." The notebook in the small desk in his bedroom on the Beiler farm held sketches of the house he wanted to build for Annalise and the new workshop where he would build cabinets and chests.

The Realtor clicked his tongue. "There's no livable structure on the land. I didn't see anything at all when I drove out there."

"I was planning to build a home." He hoped to use plans similar to the Beiler home but on a smaller scale.

"Tell me again how much you paid for it." Larry picked up a pen and pulled a yellow pad closer.

Rufus gave the figure. "Two years ago it seemed like a good value compared to what some of my people have paid for their land."

"I'm sure it was—at the time. The market is different now."

Rufus could not deny that even construction of new homes in the area had dropped off, which was part of the dilemma that brought him to this conversation. It did not surprise him to hear that properties with commercial potential also suffered. He simply never expected to face the choice before him now.

"I'm happy to take on the listing." Larry's laptop emitted a sound announcing an e-mail, and he glanced at it. "I just always like to help my clients have realistic expectations for both the process and the outcome."

"I understand."

"You haven't said why you're considering selling. But it seems to me the question is whether you want to sell so you can be out from your financial obligations as the purchaser—I assume there's a mortgage—or if you were expecting to see a profit on undeveloped land after only two years."

"I do have a mortgage, but the payments are manageable." Knowing from experience that his business could have lean times, Rufus had been careful not to overextend himself. The debatable point was whether he could afford to build a house to live in with Annalise.

"What is your equity level?"

Rufus told Larry how much he had put down on the land, combined with advance payments he made when business was strong.

"If it were a larger plot, we could look at selling off pieces, but I don't advise that."

The land was big enough for a house, a barn, a workshop, pasture for horses and a milk cow, and a vegetable garden. But Rufus had never intended to farm, so he had not looked for the expansive acres most Amish families sought.

"You have my card," Larry said. "Call me if you decide to proceed. In the meantime I will unofficially keep my ears open for anyone looking for land out that way."

"Thank you."

Larry scratched the top of his head. "Maybe you should hang on to it for another year. The market might settle as the economy improves. You could come out well."

Another year could be too late for his *daed* if Joel's land did not have a good yield.

On Friday afternoon, Annie closed up Mrs. Weichert's shop and strolled the few blocks home. She compelled herself not to rush but to walk slowly and breathe in deeply and out fully every several strides. She rolled her shoulders and moved her neck. For good or for bad, the week had brought more than its share of stress.

Elijah's injury. If she had not dragged him into the hunt for Leah, he would not have been hurt. She did not force him to climb that gravel truck, but she had not stopped him. When Annie thought about it logically, Elijah's plans to leave the church should not have come as a shock. As teenagers, Elijah and Ruth had both questioned whether they ought to be baptized. Annie knew their story. Yet she found herself conflicted about understanding his choice and being disappointed that someone she cared for was setting aside the very vows she had taken.

Ruth's frustration. On top of her ongoing emotional turmoil about her feelings for Elijah, Ruth was frustrated with Elijah's mother, with Annie, with Leah. The air in Annie's small home had become tenser than she imagined possible. These weeks of being roomies with her dear friend and future sister-in-law were supposed to be full of joy and companionship. But they weren't now.

Leah's behavior was erratic. Leah made her bed and straightened her end of the living room before she disappeared every day, but she was still gone before Annie came downstairs. Enough food was finding its way out of Annie's cupboards for her to know that Leah was eating. As the days shortened and grew cooler, Annie wanted to suggest Leah should come home before dark for her own good. But to suggest any kind of rule would shake the fragile trust that kept Leah sleeping in a safe place at night.

That afternoon Annie had dropped a vase that shattered on the shop floor. The symbolism did not escape her. When she turned off Main Street onto her street, Annie breathed prayers for insight and peace in the hearts of all around her.

And she missed Rufus.

P.S., God, she thought, *let Rufus come for a visit.*

Ruth had only four items to take through the checkout line on Friday evening. She suspected that Leah was the one absconding with Ruth's food contributions to the household, but so far she had not seen Leah awake all week, so she was not going to press the point. She was living rent-free and had enough money saved to cover her minimal expenses until Christmas, even if she had to buy the same food twice a few times.

She spotted Bryan working a cash register and debated getting in another line, but in the moment she spent wavering, the other cashier plunked an orange CLOSED sign on the conveyor belt and turned off her light. Ruth smiled as she set her items on Bryan's belt. What else could she do?

"I wondered how long it would be before you came in during my shift." Bryan slowly waved a container of yogurt over the scanner.

"I don't know what your schedule is."

"I find out every Thursday." He set the yogurt down and picked up the bag of four apples to weigh.

Ruth had never seen a checker punch in a fruit code more slowly. She glanced to make sure a line was not forming behind her.

"I'm off tomorrow night." Bryan picked up the half gallon of milk and waited for the scanner's beep. "Maybe you would let me take you to a movie."

Ruth nudged her last item, a carton of orange juice, forward. She had never been to a movie, and she did not think this was the time or place to explain that reality to Bryan. He might never understand her, she realized, but he was consistently kind.

"How about it?" Bryan finally got the juice to beep.

"How about what?" Alan Wellner swooped in and scooped up Ruth's four items, rapidly dropping them in a bag.

"None of your business, buddy." Bryan hit the TOTAL button and reported the sum to Ruth. She scanned her debit card and watched the cash drawer pop open.

"Nuts." Bryan pushed a button above the cash register, and a light blinked. "I'm out of quarters."

"You don't eat much," Alan observed.

"I don't like to buy more than I need, and I like fresh food," Ruth said.

"Frugal and healthy. I like that." Bryan grinned.

The shift manager shuffled over with a new cash drawer. "You keep running out of everything. Let's just fill you up."

"Great idea." Bryan stepped aside for the manager to swap the drawers.

"Alan," the manager said, "remember you owe me half a shift for Wednesday morning last week."

"Right." Alan tapped the side of his head.

"The next time you need to leave early, just say something instead of disappearing before we're finished with the overnight stocking."

"Yes, sir."

Last Wednesday. Something stuck in Ruth's brain, and she tilted her head as if to shake it loose.

Last Wednesday morning was the day of the planned training burn.

And the unexplained outbuilding burn.

I couldn't get away from work. Ruth was sure she had heard those words from Alan's mouth on the day of the burn. If he was not at the store, and he was not on time for the training, then where was he?

Could he have been three miles away?

Thirty-Three

Annie came down the stairs on Saturday morning and instantly knew something was different. Ruth was gone, but Annie knew she had a morning shift at the clinic. At first she thought the whimpering she heard was the kitten, but he brushed by with the casual arrogance of most cats Annie had ever known and scratched at the back door to be let out. Annie ignored the kitten's plea, uncertain whether Leah would approve and not willing to disturb the fragile peace of the household over a cat's wanderlust.

Rustling in the living room confirmed the source of the whimper. It was after eight in the morning, and Leah was still home.

Annie sucked in a deep, uncertain breath and closed the yards between the staircase in the middle of the house and the sectioned-off half of the living room. Careful to respect Leah's privacy, Annie remained on her side of the screen.

"Leah?"

The girl blew her nose but did not respond.

"Did you sleep?" Annie heard Leah come in around eleven, so she knew she was in the house all night.

Sniffles.

"Are you hungry?"

"No."

At least it was an answer.

"I could make you a cup of tea."

"Okay."

Progress.

Annie withdrew to the kitchen and started the kettle. Hopeful that Leah would accept some morning company, even without conversation, Annie took two mugs down from the shelf. She checked the kettle to make sure the water was warming and then stood in a classic impatient, foot-tapping pose, all the while listening to the noises coming from the other end of the house. The cat abandoned the quest for the outdoors and slinked back through the rooms.

At the first hint of a whistle, Annie grabbed the kettle and poured boiling water over green tea bags. She gripped one handle in each fist and followed the cat.

Leah had emerged from her bed and now sat in one of the chairs, her eyes red but dry. Annie handed her a mug and sat in the coordinating chair.

"I suppose you want to know what's going on." Leah blew on the hot tea.

"We have a deal." Annie leaned back in her chair, hoping to appear far more nonchalant than she felt. "No questions."

"So you don't want to know?"

"I'm here to listen to whatever you want to tell me." Annie's heart raced.

"It's been over a month! No letter in over a month. What if he doesn't love me anymore?"

There it was.

On top of Leah's heartbreak over being separated from her young man, she was in a panic over his lack of response. Thirteen days had passed since Annie's letter to Matthew, and she had heard nothing, either.

"I'm sorry you're hurting so much." Leah's anxiety was palpable, but Annie would not promise everything would be all right.

"Aren't you going to say *Gottes wille*? That's what everybody says to me when I'm unhappy."

"I don't think God means for us to be unhappy."

"Then why doesn't He fix things? He could make Aaron write a letter. He could make my parents understand that I love Aaron. He could give me a job so I can earn train fare to Pennsylvania. God could do lots of things, but He doesn't."

Annie moistened her lips and then hid them behind the mug of steaming tea. She hoped this disappointment would not put Leah over an edge Annie could not predict.

"So you going home for the weekend?" Marcus sliced through the bottom of a carton and stepped on it to flatten it.

"My friend should be here soon to drive me." Rufus wiped sweat off his forehead then dropped the rag in his toolbox. His small bag of personal items, removed from the motel that morning, waited for him next to the door.

"I live up toward Cripple Creek or I would have been glad to drive you home," Marcus said.

"That's kind of you. Tom doesn't mind coming."

"Who would have thought we'd finish with this place in a week? You're a speed demon when it comes to this stuff." Marcus tossed the flat box on a stack in the corner.

Rufus gave a half smile. "I've had a lot of experience with cabinets."

The door opened, and Jeff, their employer, came in. He nodded with approval. "Nice work, guys."

"Thank you," Rufus said.

"Look, this job went a lot faster than what I scheduled. I don't have things firmed up for the next job yet. I've let everybody know to plan on a few days off, and I'll call you next week and let you know where we're going to be working."

"Give a hint where?" Marcus said.

"Alamosa, probably," Jeff answered.

Marcus groaned. "That's a long drive. You have to go around half the world to get to Alamosa from here."

"We have to follow the money, my friend." Jeff gave a playful salute. "When you're finished cleaning up, you can go. Talk to you next week."

Rufus tugged on the brim of his hat in thought. Alamosa was on the other side of the Sangre de Cristo Mountains. None of the highways were a direct route on the map. On the other hand, Amish settlers were increasingly numerous in Alamosa and Monte Verde, far more than in Westcliffe. He might find a family to extend him hospitality.

His mind turned to Annalise and the land she did not know he owned. She did not know he was coming home, and now he could stay longer than just for the Sabbath.

The land meant to be home to Rufus and Annalise might keep his parents in their home. And Joel and Lydia and Sophie and Jacob. Before Annalise sold her thriving software business and gave away most of her money, she would have seen the funds the Beilers needed now as loose change. She could have solved their problems with a phone call and an electronic funds transfer.

Rufus decided to drive Annalise out to see the land. She deserved that much.

Annie put on a warm jacket and took her bike out of the garage. It was late in the afternoon, but she believed she had enough light for a long bike ride. This time she would not even mind the hills, instead anticipating a good workout to burn off the week's stress.

Leah had finally agreed to a proper hot bacon and eggs breakfast that morning, but as soon as she finished eating, she picked up the kitten and went out the back door. Annie was left with a stack of dirty dishes and a sense of dread that Leah would not return.

Garden chores called. Annie pulled in the last of the squash and stacked it in the kitchen. She cleaned the house from top to bottom, except for Ruth's room. With a broom, she thrashed at the leaves piling up on the front walkway, then found a rake in the garage and attacked the leaves on the browning grass. During and in between her efforts to find something she could control, she remembered to pray and pray again for a quiet, humble, discerning heart.

Still, she feared she would not sleep if she did not first exhaust herself. She would ride, take a hot bath, pray some more, and go to bed early before a fresh wind of discontent blew through her. Ruth had plans for the evening, though she had not said what they were, and Leah would do what Leah decided to do.

What did it mean to seek God's will? What did it mean to accept God's will? And what did it mean to do God's will? Questions tumbled without answers.

Whenever Annie went for a bike ride without a predetermined destination, her feet seemed to automatically pedal toward the Beiler home. She would be welcome, she knew, if she stopped in. But if Annie stayed too long and darkness fell, someone would have to drive her home in a buggy, and she did not want to presume on any of them. She made up her mind to ride as far as the rise in the road that would allow her to see the farm and then turn back.

She came to the rise and stopped at the highest point, prepared to look with heartfelt yearning on the scene before her.

Instead she saw smoke.

She pedaled hard down the sloping highway.

Ruth was not at all sure she had done the right thing in accepting a date with Bryan. But standing in the grocery store yesterday, she had agreed to a meal rather than a movie. Bryan said he knew a place in Walsenburg he would love to take her.

"Nothing fancy," she had insisted. "I wouldn't have anything to wear."

"You'll look great whatever you wear," he had said.

"And home early," she said.

"Right," he said. "The next day's the Sabbath."

So here she was, in the passenger seat of his Mitsubishi while he challenged the speed limit just enough to display his anticipation of the evening. In another hundred yards, they would pass her family's home.

"I don't like the way the sky looks up ahead," Bryan said.

Ruth leaned forward as they went over the rise in the road. Flames.

"Is that on your land?" Bryan accelerated.

Ruth gasped. "I think so. It looks like Joel's field."

"Is there anything in the field that could catch fire?"

"His whole crop!"

"I mean a building, an electrical wire, a can of gasoline too close to a match."

"There's an old shed. It was there when we bought the land. Joel might keep a few tools in it but nothing of value."

"We're only five miles from town. It won't take long to have an engine here."

Bryan had his phone out now and spoke calmly into it reporting the details of the fire.

Rufus was relieved to be almost home. He enjoyed talking with Tom, who had come to understand the Amish ways well during his years of taxiing for them and doing business with them through his hardware store. But Rufus was anxious to surprise his family. He probably had not even missed supper yet.

A siren wailed behind them, and Tom pulled to the shoulder of the highway. A water truck and a ladder truck whizzed past.

Tom's pickup shuddered in their wake.

Rufus put a hand on the dashboard and leaned forward. "What could be burning out here?"

"Maybe nothing," Tom said calmly. "It might just be a medical call."

The trucks were out of sight now. Tom drove past one acre of trees after another. Rufus scanned the horizon from left to right and back again.

Finally he sank back in his seat and muttered, "Joel's field."

He could hardly breathe.

Thirty-Four

Annie held Rufus's hand, not caring who might be watching, and the two of them huddled with Ruth.

"Bryan is trying to find a way to help." Ruth folded her arms across her chest, gripping her elbows. "But he's not suited up. They won't let him do much."

Annie put a hand on Ruth's back. "He knows how to be safe."

The trio stood well back from the fire, which had demolished the shed and unfurled to low-growing crop around the field. Firefighters aimed hoses and pumped water. A layer of foam quickly covered the ground, stifling the efforts of windblown embers to find fuel and burst.

"It's just about out," Rufus said.

"This is going to ruin Joel's crop, isn't it?" Annie looked a few yards to her right, where she saw Joel sitting on the ground with his knees raised and his hands hanging between them. Behind him Eli knelt with a hand on his son's shoulder. Lydia and Sophie on either side.

"The chemicals they're spraying will change the soil," Rufus said quietly. "I'm not sure what it will mean."

"It's not good." Ruth spoke sharply. "This was supposed to

be Joel's first crop. Now look. What isn't burned or ruined with chemicals has been trampled or rutted by the trucks."

"He's been working so hard." Annie's throat thickened.

"He persuaded *Daed* he could get one more crop before they let the field go fallow." Rufus scratched his cheek. "It was going to be the start of a financial stake for him."

"At least it didn't spread to the other fields," Annie said. "They'll be all right, won't they?"

"This was not an accident." Ruth took a few steps forward. "Somebody started the fire that burned your cabinets, Rufus, and somebody started the fire in that county building along the highway. Now this."

"But why would anyone come after your family?" Annie asked.

"I haven't worked that out yet. Bryan says there's always a pattern, and when this scene cools down, they'll figure out what it has in common with the others."

"The fire on the highway and this one both started in sheds," Annie mused, "but the first one was a half-built house."

"But it was empty," Ruth countered, "and the fire started in the back. At least that's what Bryan thinks. The highway shed burned from the back, too."

Annie could not keep herself from scanning the horizon, this time for a flash of purple. Leah had left the house that morning wearing the dress that had once been Ruth's and then became Annie's first Amish dress.

"Let's not get ahead of things," Rufus said. "Since this fire happened on Beiler land, surely *Daed* will receive some information about it."

"I hope they will investigate." Ruth swung her arms down to her sides, her hands still fists. "Tell *Daed* to insist."

"But what started the fire?" Jacob wanted to know. He kicked one heel softly against the leg of his chair.

Rufus was glad his mother had kept his little brother away from the fire scene, but conversation and speculation swirled around the Beiler home as Franey put a delayed supper on the table. It would be impossible for an inquisitive little boy like Jacob to understand the event that had cast a pall on the evening.

Annalise and Ruth stayed to eat, with the promise that someone would drive them home. Ruth had seemed relieved that Bryan Nichols declined Franey's invitation to stay as well. Bryan said he wanted to go to the fire station and see for himself what evidence might have been collected from the scene. Ruth, Rufus thought, was simply not ready to mix her family with an *English* young man. And perhaps to his credit, Bryan understood that now.

"We don't know how the fire started," Rufus said in answer to his brother's question. "Sometimes an event happens and we never know why."

"*Gottes wille?*" Jacob asked.

"I suppose so."

"There was nothing in that shed but a rake and a hoe," Joel insisted. "Maybe a couple of muddy rags. There was no lightning, there was no anything. Do you believe it was God's will for someone to set a fire?"

"But if it happens, then it's God's will, right?" Jacob said.

"Not this time," Joel muttered.

"Joel." Eli's calm demeanor nevertheless intoned severe caution.

Joel slumped back and pressed his lips together.

Not until the dishes had been cleared and Jacob tucked in bed did the family gather in one room again, this time in the comfort of the living room. Annalise sat on the floor between Lydia and Sophie with her knees neatly tucked to one side. She looked tired to Rufus, but he supposed all of them appeared beleaguered under the circumstances.

"I'm so glad to be home," Rufus said.

"If only you could stay more than a day this time." Seated on the couch, Franey put her tired feet on a cushion on the floor.

"As God would have it, I can," Rufus said. "We have an unexpected break in the schedule."

"That's good news." Franey reached over to an end table and picked up an envelope. "You got a letter from David's shop in Colorado Springs. Perhaps he has some orders for you."

Rufus slit the envelope and glanced through the letter. "Several customers have been in asking about my pieces. He may have some special orders after all."

"That's great news," Annalise said from across the room.

"I don't know if the time is right," Rufus said.

Joel cleared his throat. "You took the job with the *English* because you were concerned your business was dropping off. Why would you not jump at the opportunity to go back to your craft?"

Rufus glanced at Annalise, seeing the same question in her eyes.

"I've made a commitment to Jeff. He is expecting me to be available all winter."

Joel waved a hand. "Things change. For instance, today I lost my livelihood for the season. You could send me to fulfill your obligation."

"It is more difficult to live away from our people than you might realize." Rufus looked again at Annalise. Her eyes pleaded with him to stay home.

Franey shuffled her feet on the cushion. "Joel, I don't think that it is wise for you to think this way. As Rufus said, it would be difficult."

"Do you think I do not have the strength of faith that Rufus has?"

"I did not say that."

"Joel," Eli said, "are you sure you would want to do this?"

"I am probably more sure than Rufus was when he left the first time."

"And Rufus," Eli said, "do you believe it would be possible to offer a substitute for your labor?"

Rufus met his brother's eyes and let out his breath. "If I assure Jeff that Joel is capable, then, yes. I believe it is possible."

"Then I think you should stay home and Joel should go."

On Sunday morning, Ruth drove Annalise to church in the car. This time, though, she let Annalise sit forward in the congregation with the Beiler women, and Ruth dawdled in the back, near the door, and finally took a seat when she could see the men were lining up outside to process in. *Daed* was shoulder to shoulder with Ike Stutzman among the bearded married men, while Rufus and Joel marched farther back with the smooth-shaven unmarried men. Walking with the men, Jacob grinned from ear to ear. Rufus leaned over and whispered to Jacob, and the boy straightened his shoulders but maintained his exuberance.

Ruth, smiled. Rufus was old enough to be Jacob's father, and it seemed to please him to act in fatherly ways. If he did not propose to Annalise of his own accord soon, Ruth might just take it upon herself to prod her eldest brother into action. Rufus and Annalise could have their own *kinner* soon enough. *Mamm* would love having *boppli* in Colorado when she was so far from the grandchildren in Pennsylvania.

Ruth lost her place in the first hymn, stabbed with wondering how *Mamm* might receive Ruth's children someday. They would not be Amish *boppli*.

She shook off the thought. She had no aspiration to marry anytime soon, and why should she borrow worry from the future?

As the congregation assembled that morning, news of Joel's fire, as it was already deemed, dispersed through one conversation after another. Now, during the sermons, the ministers chosen to preach both focused on forgiveness and God's will. Ruth tried to concentrate and fleetingly wondered if Annalise's German had improved enough that she understood sermons without Sophie leaning in to whisper translation.

Forgiveness.

An easy enough idea to talk about, especially when it was not your friend who was kicked in the chest and not your brother whose field had burned.

Ruth could forgive. Just not yet.

During the final low, slow hymn, she slipped out of the barn housing the congregation that morning. Rufus would look after Annalise, and Ruth did not feel like facing a boisterous potluck meal or answering a barrage of questions or hearing anyone say *Gottes wille*. Instead, she walked to her car and started it, grateful for its quiet engine.

She drove to the place she always wanted to be when she was most confused, to the trail the community had created in the summer and to the monument of a rock just beyond the boundary of Beiler land. Ruth took her purse with her because it contained an item that was the main reason for her lack of concentration this morning.

It niggled at her.

Thinking that she might never get used to approaching the rock from a parking lot rather than cutting through her family's land, Ruth found the old familiar footholds. At the top, with her legs stretched out in front of her beneath her long skirt, she pulled the strap of her purse off her shoulder and opened the thrift store imitation leather brown bag.

And from its shallows she pulled a black strap to run through her fingers again.

As her stunned family made their way from the field to the house the previous evening, Ruth had idly picked up the strap. She supposed it had belonged to one of the firefighters, though what it had secured she could not surmise. It did not strike her as particularly heavy duty.

The strap was less than an inch wide, with a thin blue stripe zigzagging down the center. At one end was a broken carabiner latch.

"Ruth!"

She looked over the edge of the rock to see Elijah standing below her.

"Elijah! Are you all right?" Ruth scrambled to her feet.

"I'm fine. I'm coming up."

"No sir, you most definitely are not climbing up here today."

Confident that even six days after his fall she could move more quickly than Elijah, Ruth snatched up her purse. In a matter of seconds, she had descended and circled the rock and stood on the ground facing Elijah.

"I didn't know if you would come to church," she said.

"I thought you might be there. But if I had gone, it would give my *mamm* false hope, and I do not want to hurt her any more than I have."

Ruth looked toward the parking lot. "I see you got your buggy back. Are you sure you ought to be out by yourself yet?"

"I'm not by myself. I'm with you."

She smiled. "Technically. But you didn't know that when you came."

"I never give up hoping to find you here, in our place."

His sentimentality sluiced through her. "Elijah, I'm not sure what you want me to say."

"Yes you are."

She met his eyes then looked away. He was right. She knew what he wanted to hear, but she could not say it.

"What do you have there?" Elijah asked.

Ruth spread the strap between her hands. "I suppose you heard about the fire yesterday."

He nodded. "These days the whole town gets jumpy when we hear a siren."

"I found this."

He shrugged. "It's just a water bottle strap. The *English* use them all the time."

Ruth inhaled and took a long time to exhale.

"Ruth? What's the matter?"

"I've seen this strap before. And it doesn't belong to anyone who was at the fire yesterday."

Thirty-Five

June 1892

Joseph removed his hat long enough to drag a sleeve across his forehead and down one side of his face. A streak of gray resulted on his shirt, new dirt, as opposed to the sweat and dust of the last two days that may have permanently discolored the soft white cotton garment.

For the third time in ten days, he had ridden out with a posse chasing a fresh rumor. He doubted Deputy Combs would organize another ride. The claims people made to have seen Roper lacked substance. Some even insisted they had seen his hat, which Combs still kept locked up in the sheriff's office and for which Old Man Twigg harangued the officer on a daily basis.

Combs would surrender the hat soon. The men riding in posses would decide they could no longer afford to be away from their own shops and ranches. And the citizens of Baxter County would choose a new sheriff. Finding Jesse Roper was likely the deputy's last hope of being elected sheriff.

Joseph hung back from the posse riders who would disburse to their properties. He tugged the reins to take his horse to the edge of town. To the livery. To Zeke and Stephen and their concerned scowls and news of their own scouting jaunt. When he reached the stables, he stilled his mount and assessed the scene. The small building closest to the road looked as tidy as it always did. The owner's wife made sure the business presented well. Set back from the road, the stable's doors were open wide and Joseph could see straight through the building. Two stable boys were mucking and another was bringing fresh hay. In the yard beyond the far end, two men brushed burrs from their horses' manes. Joseph slid off his horse and led the animal around the structures.

In the rear yard, Zeke stopped brushing. "Joseph. You've come back."

"I never said I would not." Joseph straightened his hat with both hands. "And your journey? When did you return?"

"Yesterday."

"And have you found God's will for the new settlement?"

"We're going home," Stephen said. "We will give our report there."

"You must come with us," Zeke urged.

"I pray you are taking a favorable report." Joseph ignored Zeke's admonition. "The land of Baxter County has much to commend itself. Wide open acres for farming. The river nearby. A town on the railroad route."

Zeke shook his head. "You speak rightly of the virtues of the county. But this is a place of strife. Even beyond Mountain Home and Gassville, the feud between the Dentons and the Twiggs is a subject of conversation and speculation. Other families are quarreling as well. I cannot recommend to the bishop that we bring our people of peace to this region."

"Perhaps we can be an influence of peace," Joseph said.

"We seek a place to live apart," Zeke said, "not to resolve the *English* mistreatment of their own."

"The horses are nearly fully rested," Stephen said. "We will leave at first light."

Joseph held silent.

Belle Mooney covered her eyes with her hands and leaned her back on the door. On the other side, Maura Woodley pounded.

Belle breathed in and out with deliberation, lodging her weight against the door lest Maura should manage to turn the feeble lock and try to enter.

"Belle, I miss you!" Maura pleaded. "We have been friends too long for this to stand between us."

Belle moved her hands to cover her ears and began to hum the tune of "What a Friend We Have in Jesus." Never in their entire lives had she gone ten days without sharing at least a few minutes with Maura. Their mothers had been friends before their daughters were born, and it was a daily ritual for one of them to walk to the other's home on any pretense or none at all, children in tow. Maura and Belle had sustained the tradition after they came of age and after their mothers passed on.

But that was over. Maura had never understood about John. She had taken the Dentons' side.

She would leave town, Belle decided. Her mother had passed on years ago. John was gone. Her father hated the family of the man she loved. Her best friend refused to understand. She would go somewhere else, another county, even another state. Schools were everywhere. She would find a position and leave Gassville. It did not matter that she would be an old maid schoolteacher. In a new place, she could remember John in peace.

"Belle, please," Maura said, loudly now since Belle had begun to sing the hymn with full voice. "Can't we talk?"

"No!"

"I do not accept that circumstances have come to this."

"You don't accept a lot of things." Belle turned and faced the door, her open palms pressed against it now. "That's what gets you into so much trouble. I'm finished with that. I'm finished with you."

"You cannot mean that."

"Don't tell me what I mean. All my life you've been doing that."

"Belle! What has gotten into you?"

"Go away, Maura Woodley. Leave me be."

Belle exhaled at the silence that came from the outside. She heard the rustle of Maura's skirt and knew she was wearing the new petticoat they had worked on together.

"Belle Agnes Mooney," Maura said. "I will be your friend forever. That is all there is to it. I am leaving your porch, but I am not leaving you."

Silence.

"You know where to find me when you're ready."

"I will never be ready!" Belle pounded the inside of the door with one fist.

Finally she heard Maura's shoes hitting the porch steps one at a time in careful rhythm. Belle moved to a front window, stood to the side where she could not be seen from the outside, and watched the truest friend she had ever known—other than John—walk away. When Maura turned for a moment to glance at the house, Belle glided into the interior hall without looking back.

Maura did not for one minute believe what Belle said. Joseph was right. Belle needed time. She would come to her senses once her heart began to mend.

Still, Belle's words stung. Instead of turning toward home, or even toward Main Street, she let her feet carry her out of town. She walked so far she began to wonder if she should have brought the cart. No, it was better to be alone, unencumbered even by a horse that never hesitated to serve her well. At least she was wearing practical shoes, and pinched toes would not distract her from what weighed on her mind. Miles passed beneath determined steps. The closer she got to the White River, the more strongly she felt she wanted to sit on its bluff and let her heart soak in its beauty while the wind whipped cool dampness and deposited it on her clothing. Across the open ranch land, an occasional darting rabbit, cattle with fly-swatting tails, and the swarming flies of summer were the only moving beings she saw.

She cut through the woods along the inland edge of the Denton ranch, staying under the canopy of shade as much as she could. Humidity weighed down with its outrageous magnification of the heat to the point that Maura wondered if anyone would care if she meandered down the sloped side of the bluff and waded away from the river's edge. Despite her anticipation of standing in awe of the river, her heart collapsed in on itself as she moved through the Denton land and the woods thinned until she could hardly find a tree for a passing moment of shade. With horror, she realized that Ing and Lee had ravaged their own land beyond recognition. In the name of honest work, men like Ezekiel Berkey and Joseph Beiler and a dozen others from Gassville had labored to deprive the land of its enchantment.

Finally she reached the crown of the bluff and felt the movement of air swirling up from the path the river carved. Northeastern Arkansas was hardly the frontier. It had not been for some time. Trim little towns like Gassville dotted the landscape, and travelers could begin journeys in any direction in the relative comfort of a railroad car—even sleeping Pullman compartments.

Maura heard footsteps crunching behind her and spun around. "Joseph."

"It's a beautiful spot, is it not?" He tilted his hat toward the rushing water.

Maura spread her arms. "It was more beautiful before. . .how could Lee and Ing take out so many trees?"

"At first it was just going to be a few, so they could see the river from the house." Joseph moved to stand beside Maura. "Then it was a few more, and a few more."

"It's awful." She shook her head. "It's just awful. There's nothing else to say. But why should the riverfront be pretty when the county is one big gunslinging pile of hate?"

He had no response.

"I'm sorry. I don't mean to accuse you. If you hadn't wanted the work, they would have found someone else."

"True enough. But now that I see what it must look like through the eyes of someone who grew up here, perhaps I was overeager."

She sucked in her bottom lip and let it out. "I'm sure if the posse had turned up something I would have heard the news."

"Nothing," he said. "I don't believe they will ride again."

"If anyone can talk sense into them, it would be you."

"You flatter me. But my people are not given to pride, so I will only humbly respond that the men want to get back to their own businesses. Catching Mr. Roper will be up to whatever system you *English* have for such matters once a man has disappeared as undeniably as he has."

"Yet the feud continues." Maura put both hands on her hips and surveyed the water. "Old Man Twigg and Leon Mooney go after each other with hateful words practically every day in the middle of the street. It's only a matter of time before one of them carries a gun again. Why cannot we live in peace? Surely there is enough prosperity for everyone."

With her lips pressed closed, she inhaled deeply the scent of Joseph Beiler mingled with stumps and river spray. This spot would never again smell as it had before the trees were removed, but now it would at least remind her of Joseph Beiler, the most unlikely visitor she had ever welcomed to Gassville.

"Zeke is going to tell the bishop the county is too violent for a settlement of our people," Joseph said quietly.

"We should have welcomed you all with open arms. But it would seem that even the death of a man as noble and well loved as Abraham Byler cannot force people to treat each other like human beings."

"Surely the present sentiment will not last forever."

"I'm not sure I want to be around to find out." Maura surprised herself with her words. "Maybe I should just get away. Go back east. Go south. Go north. Just go someplace where people are more civilized.

"Would you really leave?" Joseph's eyes widened, and Maura's spirit stumbled under the import of what she had voiced.

If Maura Woodley would consider leaving Gassville, perhaps she would consider leaving with him. Joseph dried his clammy palms on his trousers and straightened his hat with both hands.

"Are your people truly peaceful?" she asked, her voice full of quiver.

Joseph wished he could give an unequivocal answer but settled for the truth. "We have our quarrels. We are sinners, too."

"But you stick together somehow."

"Somehow, yes. By God's grace."

"I cannot imagine God is very pleased with the likes of Gassville right now."

"God is love."

Maura paced away then returned. "You talk about the closeness of your families. The Dentons and Twiggs might say the same thing, but look what they are doing."

Joseph cleared his throat. "That is because they are motivated by pride, not submission. That changes everything."

"So why are you here, Joseph? Why are you riding with the posses?"

Joseph had asked himself the same questions a hundred times. "A man has to test his convictions. To be sure they are his own."

"And are they?"

Her brown eyes begged him for an answer that made sense. If only he had one.

"Halt or I'll shoot!" The anger in the man's voice jolted them both, and they startled. A second later they stared at the end of a pistol.

OLIVIA NEWPORT

"Ing Denton, what are you doing?" Maura roused and reached out to slap the pistol away.

"What are you doing on my land?" Ing demanded.

"I've been strolling through your land since I was a little girl."

"And what about him?" Ing thrust a finger toward Joseph.

"I suppose working on your land made me come to admire it," Joseph said.

"Well, I'm not taking any chances with those crazy Twiggs around. Get off my land. Both of you. Now."

Thirty-Six

"Yes, it's Alan's."

Bryan ran his finger along the blue zigzag as Ruth held the strap.

"But he wasn't at the fire last night." Ruth felt a tremble take hold in her knees. "Why would his water bottle strap be in our field?"

"He was definitely working at the grocery store last night."

"How can you be sure?" Elijah spoke for the first time. "Ruth says she was with you before you discovered the fire."

Ruth's stomach crunched. She had hated having to reveal that fact to Elijah. The words sounded even worse coming from his mouth.

Elijah pressed the issue. "If you weren't working, how can you be sure Alan was?"

"Alan was on the schedule," Bryan said. "The store manager was leaning on him pretty hard not to blow it off."

"Pardon me if I am being rude," Elijah said, "but that does not sound the same as being certain."

"I saw him go into the store at the start of his shift, about an hour before Ruth and I left town."

Ruth looked from Elijah to Bryan. Neither man's eyes budged from the other.

"The carabiner is broken." Ruth wound the strap around one hand. "Wouldn't his water bottle have fallen off?"

"That's hard to say," Bryan said. "Maybe he left the strap in one of the engines and it happened to fall out last night in the field."

Ruth shook her head. "The spot where I found it was not anywhere near where the engines were parked. At first I thought it might belong to one of the firefighters, but the more I thought about it, the less sense that made."

Bryan shrugged. "Then maybe I'm wrong and it's not Alan's."

"No one in my family has anything like this. Besides, it's decorative."

"So?"

"So the Amish would not so much as put a ribbon in their hair or on the band of a hat," Elijah said. "They certainly would not carry a strap like this."

"Let's not jump all over each other." Bryan put up both hands, palms out. "I want to help. But if this is Alan's strap, and you're implying that he had something to do with the fire, well, that's serious."

"I don't mean to imply anything," Ruth said. "I'm asking questions, that's all. Trying to make sense of things."

"Why don't you let me talk to Alan?" Bryan reached out with an open hand. "Let me take the strap. I could say I found it."

"I don't want you to lie," Ruth said.

"I think Ruth should hang on to it in case it turns out to be important." Elijah glared at Bryan.

"Hey, Alan is my friend. I care what happens to him. If he has something to do with the fire, I want to get to the bottom of things as much as you do."

"It's all right." Ruth put a hand on Elijah's arm. "Alan trusts Bryan, and so do I."

On Monday Ruth checked her cell phone at a frequency she would have been embarrassed to confess. It was fully charged. It was turned on. Even in the pocket of her scrubs, it would vibrate enough to alert her of activity, and even at work at the clinic she would be able to step away and at least listen to a message.

She was not sure what she expected. Bryan had said he would get to the bottom of things, but he had not promised immediate results. Only a day had passed since she let the strap drop into his hand over Elijah's objection. Although they were roommates, Bryan and Alan did not always work the same shifts at the grocery store or volunteer together at the fire station. Those schedules were in the hands of other people. In reality, they probably saw less of each other than she and Annalise did.

Ruth's clinic schedule on Monday was all day. She worked the morning at the front desk then spent the afternoon shadowing a physician's assistant. Normally she looked forward to opportunities to at least observe the medical staff rather than be buried in files and phone messages, but on Monday, her concentration had been no better than during church on Sunday. Halfway through the shadowing shift, she snagged a notepad from the front desk and forced herself to write notes in an effort to pay closer attention.

When her day ended at four o'clock, her phone had not rung all day. She took her jacket off the hook in the staff room and slid her arms into the sleeves while she weighed the pros and cons of trying to track down Bryan in person. He had never said where he lived, just that he lived with Alan, but the town was small enough that she could cruise the streets and look for his car. Or she could casually stop by the grocery store for some shampoo or something else she did not need.

No. She would not go looking for trouble. She trusted Bryan. He would find her when he knew something.

Ruth draped her purse strap over one shoulder and went out

the back door of the clinic.

When a form moved out of the shadows, Ruth sucked in her breath and stepped aside.

"What's the matter, Ruth?"

Alan.

"May I walk you home?" He produced a genial smile.

Ruth might have felt better if she could see his hands. They remained plunged into the pockets of his gray fleece-lined jacket. She glanced toward Main Street.

"A lot of people would drive to work." Alan touched her elbow now. "I suppose you people like your exercise."

You people?

"Sometimes I drive. It depends on my mood or whether I'm running late. It's only a few blocks, after all."

"You must have been on time this morning. I didn't see your car."

"I didn't know you knew my car." Ruth wished he would take his hand off her elbow as they walked.

"You could have asked me about that strap, you know."

The pit of her stomach hardened.

"I'll bet Bryan didn't tell you that we got identical straps and water bottles about two years ago."

"No, he didn't."

"They were a perk from the gym where we worked out in Colorado Springs."

"Oh. Well, that sounds healthy."

"Perhaps you miss my point."

Ruth held her tongue, grateful to be progressing toward a well-populated block.

"My point," Alan said in his easygoing tone, "is that you can't be sure that strap is mine. It could be Bryan's."

"Why would it be Bryan's? He would have just said so."

"Would he?"

She said nothing.

"I've known Bryan a long time. I would hate for you to get

hurt because things are not what you think they are." An alarm sounded on Alan's phone. "Oh, I gotta go."

He tapped her shoulder and began to sprint down Main Street.

Rufus read David's letter again before turning on the cell phone he used for business and calling the shop in Colorado Springs.

David could guarantee one hope chest larger than the ones on the store floor and was waiting to hear from another customer about a set of matching bookcases.

He set the phone down and began mental calculations. While Rufus was grateful that David carried his furniture, he needed more work. He would not miss hanging manufactured cabinets, though he would have said a proper good-bye to Marcus if he had known he would not be returning.

The workshop door was propped open. Rufus looked up when a shadow fell across his workbench and Joel was standing in the doorway.

"I just wondered if you were able to get hold of your boss." Joel's gangly arms hung from his sharp shoulders. "About the job."

Rufus lowered himself onto a stool. "You've had a day to think. Are you as sure as you were last night?"

Joel nodded. "More. I'll try again in the spring, but in the meantime I need to feel that I'm contributing something to the family."

"*Daed* is grateful for your help in all the fields, not just the one that burned."

"I'll be eighteen soon, Rufus. I need a start at something. I thought it would be farming, but now I'm not sure."

"You have better instincts for the farm than all the other Beiler sons together."

"Matthew and Daniel seem to be making a go of it. And you have your woodworking. Everything is so different here than it was in Pennsylvania. Maybe I shouldn't assume I'll farm."

"Beilers have always farmed."

"You don't. Elijah doesn't, either. I see other Amish families starting businesses. If I earned some money to get started, I could do something, too."

Rufus picked up a pencil and parked it behind his ear. "The job is yours if you want it. Jeff will call when he has the details arranged."

The cell phone on the workbench rang, and both brothers leaned toward it.

"This is another matter," Rufus said. "I'll see you at dinner."

The phone rang a second time, and a third. Rufus waited until Joel was out of earshot before picking up the call right before it went to voice mail.

"I might have a deal for you." Larry sounded upbeat.

"You said the market was slow," Rufus said.

"It is. I just stumbled onto this. My cousin in Denver mentioned a friend of his was thinking about taking up a simpler, rural life. Working from home, growing their own food, animals, the great outdoors, that sort of thing."

Rufus smiled to himself at the description that matched his life. But the smile faded in uncertainty. "What if I'm not sure I've decided to sell?"

"I'm not sure they've decided they want to buy. This is just an opportunity to strike while the iron is hot."

"I'd like some time to think."

"Of course. I'll check back with you in a couple of days."

Rufus shut the phone off, not wishing another interruption to his thoughts. He had saved for years for a solid down payment on land, and he was confident the land was a good choice for the future. Jacob was only eight. His parents were probably a dozen or more years away from having an empty nest, as the *English* liked to say. Although he and Annalise might start married life under his parents' roof, they needed a nest of their own.

It was time to take Annalise to see his dream of the future.

Thirty-Seven

Rufus tied Dolly to the tree bulging the sidewalk in front of Mrs. Weichert's shop on Wednesday afternoon. If he remembered correctly, Annalise would finish working in a few minutes. The bell jangled as he pushed through the door.

Mrs. Weichert looked up from the stack of papers she was studying behind the counter. "She's using the telephone in the storeroom. You can go on back if you like."

Rufus nodded his thanks and crossed the store. The door to the storeroom stood open, and he could see Annalise hunched over the small desk in the corner, a computer in front of her and a notepad under her hand. She looked up at him.

"Hello. I can't believe they put me on hold again."

"I thought you might like to take a drive."

"Mmm. Sounds nice. Depends on how long this takes."

"Trying to get a price on something?"

Annalise held up a finger and turned her attention back to the screen, where the image of a picture frame filled the shape.

"We think it's from the 1940s," she said into the phone. She paused to listen. "Okay, we'll wait for your call. Thank you."

Rufus crossed his arms at the wrists.

Annalise scraped the wooden chair back and stood. "A drive, you said?"

"I would even let you do the driving, if you'd like. Aren't you off soon?"

"I am." She pushed her bottom lip out. "But I have a couple of personal calls to make. Mrs. Weichert doesn't mind if I use the phone here, and it seems like the easiest thing to do."

"I'll wait."

"I'm trying to line up some appointments for Leah. I have to call Ruth at the clinic and see if she was able to get Leah into the counselor's schedule on Friday."

"After that, then."

"I'm afraid I'd only have about half an hour." Annalise stacked papers and tapped them against the desk to straighten them. "Leah sometimes comes home in the late afternoon, and I want to catch her before she decides to leave again."

This excursion was not one Rufus cared to rush. "What does your morning look like?"

"Oh! That's much better." Annalise brightened. "Would you mind so much? I could bike out to the farm so you don't have to fetch me."

"I'll come for you." They would have more time together that way. "I want to show you something. Then I'll bring you back into town."

Annalise wrote a note on a pad of yellow paper. "I'm sorry to be inattentive. I can't get my mind off Leah."

"Tomorrow is soon enough." Rufus glanced over his shoulder and saw that Mrs. Weichert was consumed with her own stack of papers. He stepped over to Annalise for a quick kiss. It deepened unexpectedly. He did not want to leave her. But if they were going to spend their lives together he had to recognize her independence for the blessing that it was.

She smiled shyly. "I didn't deserve that after turning down your delicious offer."

He dipped his head. "Tomorrow."

"I do not think it is a good idea." Elijah pressed his palms flat on the coffee shop table.

"I would be careful." Ruth countered by calmly sipping her tea.

"You already don't trust Alan. He makes you uncomfortable." With the heels of his hands on the tabletop, Elijah thumped his fingers. "Why would you want to try to attract his attention?"

Ruth looked a way for a few seconds then met Elijah's gaze. "Because I think he knows something. Or did something. And what if what I suspect is true and I did nothing?"

"The *English* have their sheriff for these things," Elijah said. "Shouldn't you report Alan?"

"And say what? That he has a suspicious strap on his water bottle?"

"You found it in the field where the fire was."

"That doesn't prove anything. Alan could say I was the one who put it there."

"Why would you have his strap?"

"The reason is not the point. Or he could say it was Bryan's strap and that Bryan is trying to frame him."

"The *English* have a strange concept of friendship." Elijah picked up his coffee at last. "And what if Alan is right about Bryan?"

"Do you mean that?" Ruth could believe that Elijah might be jealous of her friendship with Bryan, but casting accusations at Bryan was going too far.

"Bryan and Alan have been friends a long time. You've chosen to trust one and distrust the other. What if things are not what they seem?"

"If you spent any time with the two of them, you would see the difference for yourself." Ruth pushed her tea away.

Elijah reached across the table and grabbed her hand. "I'm on your side. I just want you to be safe."

Bryan was consistently calm and carried a ready smile everywhere he went. Alan was the unpredictable one, congenial one moment and elusive the next.

"No. I'm not wrong. I'm not the naive Amish girl who left the valley three years ago."

"But your *English* friends are all women," Elijah pointed out.

"I attend a large university. They have workshops about being safe." Ruth withdrew her hand from Elijah's grasp. "I have to get Alan to talk to me, and to do that I have to be friendly."

"Then let me go with you."

She shook her head. "If he suspected anything, he would be gone before he would say anything."

"I'll stay out of sight." Elijah leaned forward, elbows on the table. "I can't just turn my head and let you arrange something that might be risky. You mean too much to me."

Ruth wanted to bend across the table and touch her forehead to his, to feel his breath on her face. Instead she glanced nervously around the shop and pressed her spine against the back of her chair. "It has to be somewhere private enough to talk."

"It has to be somewhere public enough to be safe," he said. "I don't have to be able to hear what he says, but I want to be able to see you."

At last she nodded. "When I figure something out, I'll text you."

"I'll keep my phone on."

Annie tossed her mail on the dining room table and went immediately upstairs. Once again she had let her prayer *kapp* slide off her head, and this time it had landed in a puddle. Chronically seeming to need a spare one, she wanted to rinse it out and lay it to dry immediately.

From the bathroom sink at the top of the stairs, she heard the back door open and cocked her head to try to discern whose footsteps would pad through the house. Ruth moved in quiet, subtle ways, but Leah was a master of stealth. Annie laid her *kapp* flat on a towel to dry, hoping it would hold its shape. She moved into the hall.

When she heard the kitten meow, Annie knew Leah had come home. She went down the stairs immediately.

Leah stood at the table with an envelope in her hands. "Why is Aaron writing to you?"

Annie's heart pounded. "I didn't realize he had."

"He hasn't even written to me in weeks." Leah's face flushed as her pitch rose.

Annie approached Leah carefully. The girl clutched the envelope, a fist on each end, showing a neat, blockish handwriting.

"I trusted you!" Leah sliced the air with the envelope.

"And I don't want to disappoint your trust." Annie put a hand on Leah's shoulder. "I was not expecting a letter from your friend."

"I don't understand. How would he even know you?"

"He doesn't. I wrote to someone else."

"You wrote to someone about me? Who?"

"Matthew Beiler. He's Rufus's brother."

"Have you ever met him?" Leah turned the envelope over to look at the back.

"No. But when I first heard your story, I wanted to see if I could help. I wrote to Matthew to see if he knew your friend."

"I never asked you to do that. I hardly know Matthew Beiler." Annie watched Leah crumple one end of the envelope

"I didn't mean to complicate your situation."

"I didn't ask you for any of this. All I wanted was help to get to Pennsylvania."

"I know." Annie held out one hand. "May I have the letter?"

"Are you going to open it?"

Annie gently took the letter. "I don't know what it might say, Leah." Without any idea why Matthew had not simply answered her letter himself, or why Aaron would take it upon himself to write to her, Annie was reluctant to read the letter in Leah's presence.

"If he tells you why he stopped writing to me, when he didn't tell me, I don't know what I'll do."

All the more reason Annie did not want to open the letter. "Before we talk about that," she said, "I want to tell you about something."

"I need to know what that letter says!"

"I'm not trying to hide anything from you."

"Then open it."

"Leah," Annie said, "I made a call today. The clinic here in Westcliffe has a counselor who comes on Fridays. I thought maybe it would help if you talked to her."

"An *English* counselor? I didn't ask you to do that, either."

"I know."

"I just want to know what is in that letter."

"So do I. I think we should open it together with the counselor." Leah sank into a chair. "What if I don't want to?"

"The letter is addressed to me."

"But obviously it's about me."

Annie held her gaze steady. "Leah, we've worked hard to trust each other. Let's trust each other with this."

Leah pounded the table. "I want to see the letter with my own eyes."

Annie nodded. "With the counselor."

Leah rolled her eyes. "What time?"

Thirty-Eight

June 1892

Belle stuck a fork in the sizzling slice of ham, which her father expected for breakfast every morning, and turned it.

"Daddy, your breakfast is ready." She snatched the toast off the stovetop metal frame and slathered butter on it. "Daddy?"

Belle stilled her movements to listen for footsteps on the stairs. She glanced at the clock. It was early, but her father had risen with the dawn all her life. He would come down the stairs looking for his breakfast any moment. Whether or not they disagreed about John Twigg, her father expected his meals. She held the skillet above a plate and dumped the meat and then set the toast beside it. The coffee needed a couple of minutes to finish percolating.

Leon Mooney had not yet appeared by the time his breakfast was ready and laid out in tidy fashion on a green-checkered cloth on the kitchen table. Belle wiped her hands on her apron and paced down the hall that ran through the house.

"Daddy? Breakfast!"

"Wrap it up," the gruff reply came. "I'll take it with me."

"It's early. You have plenty of time to eat before going out to the ranch."

"I'll lose the trail."

Belle's stomach clenched. "What trail?" With fists lifting her skirt, Belle took the stairs like a naughty child.

"Word is Old Man Twigg moved over the state line into Missouri. Jimmy is with him. I'm fixin' to fetch them both back to Baxter County, dead or alive."

Belle stood in the doorway of her father's room. Sitting on the bed, he looked down the barrel of his Winchester. Despite the heat of summer, he wore a jacket with pockets bulging with ammunition.

"Daddy, have you lost your mind?" Belle charged into the room and gripped the barrel of the weapon.

He looked straight into her eyes. "No. You lost yours when you fell for the lies John Twigg offered you."

Belle tugged on the rifle. "That's not the way it was, and you know it."

He easily pulled the gun out of her grasp. "Don't stand there and defend his kin. You know they had a hand in shootin' the sheriff."

"Jesse Roper did that."

"And his granddaddy helped him shoot his way past the posse. I may not be able to find Roper, but I can catch Old Man Twigg and Jimmy. They've run scared, but they are not going to get off scot-free if I have anything to say about it."

"Does Deputy Combs know you are doing this?" Belle moved to stand in the doorway, even though she knew she could not physically restrain her father.

"It's none of his business." He stood up and shoved more bullets into his trouser pockets. "Missouri is not his jurisdiction."

"Daddy, please don't do this."

"The mare just got new shoes. I'll take her. I know at least three men who will ride with me if I ask them to."

"Please don't ask them to. You're going to get yourselves killed."

He slapped his hat on his head and gripped his rifle in one fist. "Now how would that be justice, child? Move."

Woody Woodley slept later and later. Maura kept her head cocked for the sound of his steps, though she doubted he would be up and moving for at least half an hour.

Woody had been seventeen years older than his wife. No one expected that he might be the one to wander through the rooms the couple had shared looking half-lost. His wife's sudden and brief illness stunned everyone in Gassville, and almost overnight Woody went from an aging but vibrant man to an elderly gentleman to whom everyone offered deference. He sold his ranch acreage to Leon Mooney. Occasionally he made rounds as a hired hand with another rancher to check on a herd, but for the most part he was content to nap and read the newspaper or one of the books Maura brought home from the small library in Mountain Home.

Maura sat alone at the unadorned kitchen table with a second cup of coffee and an open Bible. The verse her heart focused on that morning, Psalm 34:14, was simple, straightforward. "Depart from evil, and do good; seek peace, and pursue it."

The Bible spoke so simply and beautifully. The people of Gassville could fill two churches, and everyone would nod assent to these words. Why, then, could they not live at peace with each other?

The back door opened and Walter sauntered in. He inspected the empty griddle. "I don't smell any food."

"I haven't started yet."

"Uncle Woody's not up?"

"I like to make his breakfast fresh when he's ready."

"Got any blueberries? Mama just made plain griddle cakes."

"You mean your mama fed you and you're still coming here looking for breakfast?"

"That was an hour ago."

"It's time you learned to make your own pancakes."

"Women's work."

"Well, not this woman, not this time." Maura picked up her coffee cup, now nearly empty. "Pour me some coffee."

"If I do, will you make me some blueberry pancakes?"

Maura eyed him. "You might just have to take your chances on that bargain."

Walter lifted the coffeepot from the stove.

The back door flung open again, and Belle burst through. Maura nearly turned the table over getting to her feet.

"Belle! What in the—".

"Daddy's gone crazy. Just plumb crazy. I can't stop him."

Maura's heart pounded. "Stop him from what?"

"He wants to chase Old Man Twigg over the state line." Belle gasped for breath. "Dead or alive, Daddy said. He's going take other men with him if they'll go."

"What's so crazy about that?" Walter put the coffee back on the stove. "I'll go with him."

Maura flashed disapproval. "Walter, I think it would be best if you held your tongue."

Walter pulled out a chair, dropped into it, and crossed his arms to sulk.

"He's serious," Belle said. "Maura, I take back everything I said yesterday. Every word. You're the only person I can depend on. I don't think I have a friend left in this whole town."

"You have me." Maura stepped across the small kitchen and wrapped her arms around Belle. "You always have me."

"You have to help me." Belle sobbed into Maura's shoulder.

"Of course I'll help you. This madness has to stop." Maura expelled heavy breath. "I'll find Joseph. He's been riding with the men looking for Roper. He'll know where their sentiments lie."

Belle trembled. Maura nudged her toward a chair.

"You stay here," Maura said. "Walter, pour Belle some coffee. When my daddy gets up, you tell him. . .tell him I might be gone for a while."

Outside the house, Maura felt the tremble rise within her.

Joseph left his bedroll open.

"The horses are rested." Stephen pushed his spare shirt into a saddlebag. "There is nothing to keep us from going."

"Except Joseph," Zeke said. "He is not ready."

Joseph swirled the last of his coffee in a tin cup and reached for the pot hanging over the morning fire.

"Joseph," Zeke said, "if you do not come with us now, you will only have more to explain later."

"Maybe I do not have anything to explain." Joseph burned his tongue on the coffee. Zeke would not be happy with his answer.

"The bishop. Your parents. My sister. Your little brother." Zeke ticked off several more names on his fingers. "Are you planning to simply disappear from their lives?"

"Of course not." In time, Hannah would recover and marry someone more deserving of her affections, but Little Jake was a sensitive boy.

"The bishop, Joseph. Are you in submission?" Zeke poured water on the fire and kicked dirt onto the remaining embers.

"Must you ask?"

"You ask Stephen and me to leave you here. Alone. Where is the community that will guard your faith?"

"I am not saying I will never go home. Just not now." Joseph swallowed more coffee.

"This is about Miss Woodley." Stephen hung his tin utensils from a saddle strap. "You have let her cause you to stray."

Joseph's back straightened involuntarily. "If I have strayed at all, Miss Woodley is not the cause. Do not look for someone to blame where there is no one." He was loath to leave without expressing himself to Maura Woodley and awaiting her response, but no, she had not caused him to stray. He bore his own responsibility. She might yet meet the hope in his heart with her own dream of peace.

A stir in the livery yard drew all three black-suited men around to the front of the stables, Joseph first, followed by Zeke, and then Stephen with the horses. Maura Woodley sat on her restless dark mount without pulling the cart. Joseph rushed to hold its bridle.

"You must come, Joseph," she said. "Belle's father is going to get himself killed if somebody doesn't stop him. He's going over the state line after Old Man Twigg."

"What can I do?" Joseph held the horse still and looked into Maura's fiery brown eyes.

"Joseph!" Zeke's tone was as sharp as Joseph had ever heard it. "Stay out of this *English* business. It is nothing to do with you. Get your bedding and we'll go."

"You're leaving?" Maura's brow creased, and her disappointment stabbed him. "You didn't say anything."

"Where is Leon now?" Joseph focused on Maura's need rather than Zeke's indignation.

Maura waved a hand. "Gathering his forces."

Zeke swung up onto his horse. Stephen settled himself in his saddle then handed Joseph the lead to the third horse.

Galloping horses found their rhythm in the street.

"It's Leon," Maura said.

"And three others." Joseph named Leon's co-conspirators.

"Joseph." Zeke's voice carried questions, warnings, and disappointment.

"Please, Joseph," came Maura's soft plea. "They need your message of peace."

Joseph slapped the rump of Zeke's stallion. "You go without me."

On his own horse now, Joseph rode beside Maura, coughing in the swirling dust of the vengeful riders.

Thirty-Nine

"How can I drive if I don't know where I'm going?" Annie took the reins from Rufus on Thursday morning.

"Just go as if you were going to my family's house for supper. And then keep going. I'll tell you the turns."

Knowing she had at least five miles of familiar road, Annie settled in.

"Leah agreed to see a counselor," she said.

"I'm surprised," Rufus said. "But it's probably a good idea."

"And. . .I wrote to your brother Matthew about the young man Leah says she's in love with."

"Matthew? What were you hoping for?"

"Not what I got." Annie glanced at Rufus out of the side of her eye. "I thought it might help to be sure if she was reading the relationship accurately."

"And?" Rufus nudged his hat off his forehead.

"I'm not sure. Matthew didn't write me back. Leah's young man did."

"Seems like that would be reliable information. Why are you uncertain?"

"Leah found the letter before I could open it. So now we're

going to open it during her counseling session tomorrow."

"I see."

They listened to the horse clop.

Annie reminded herself to hold the reins firmly but lightly. "You think I overstepped, don't you?"

Rufus reached over and covered one of her hands with his. "I have not even spoken to Leah Deitwaller. You are the one who has taken time to try to know her. I am not sure it's up to me to say you overstepped."

She exhaled relief. "Thank you, Rufus. Ever since I was baptized, I feel so much pressure to make the right decisions."

"Have you done anything you know is against *Ordnung*?"

"No, of course not."

"Then follow your heart."

"Do you still think Leah could have started that first fire?"

"Did I sow seeds of doubt in you when I suggested it was at least possible?"

Annie shrugged. "Maybe. I've seen for myself how fast she can move and how well she stays hidden. When I caught a glimpse of her at the training burn, I wondered if she had been out to the highway."

"Have you spoken to the *English* authorities?"

"No. I don't have proof of anything. I don't even have good reason to suspect."

"Was she in Joel's field last week?"

"I didn't see her. But I was busy watching the fire."

"We all were."

"Never mind." Annie shook off the grim thought. "I just thought you should know what's been going on. Maybe you can pray for Leah and me while we open the letter tomorrow."

"Thank you for asking me to. And I'll ask you to pray for Joel."

"So he got off this morning to the new job?"

Rufus drew in a deep breath. "He was eager to go. *Mamm* was not so enthusiastic."

"My heart tells me Joel is going to be all right." Annie dared to take her eyes off the road for a quick glance at Rufus. "Are you sure you don't want to tell me where we are going?"

Rufus smiled. "Just a few more minutes."

He gave directions one turn at a time until Annie took the buggy onto a narrow stretch that was hardly more than a horse path. When even the path petered out, Rufus asked Annie to take the buggy across open meadow.

"Stop here," Rufus said finally.

Annie pulled on the reins, and Dolly slowed to a stop. "Where are we?"

Rufus scooted closer to her on the bench and put an arm around her shoulders. With the other he pointed.

"On that little ridge is where I picture the house—facing the mountains, of course. My workshop would be in back, but not so far from the house that I could not hear you call."

Annie sucked in a gale of air. "This is your land?"

He nodded.

Her eyes widened. The Sangre de Cristos beamed down from their snowcaps. The meadow, a mystery only a moment ago, sprang to life around her. She breathed in the scent of horses to come and listened to the cackling hens she would feed with their children.

He was taking such care to arrange the perfect moment.

"We'd need a barn, of course," he said. "We'll want to keep a cow and chickens."

Annie felt a grin creeping up from her toes. This would be a proposal story they could someday tell their grandchildren.

Ruth systematically—but slowly—pushed a cart up and down every aisle in the grocery store and then started again.

She knew Alan was working. He was not up front bagging, though, so he must be in the storeroom, and it was only a matter of time before he would emerge. Most of the stocking happened in the early hours while Westcliffe's population still slumbered in confidence they could buy fifty kinds of breakfast cereal or seven brands of dog food later in the day. But Ruth had been in the store at the start of the business day enough to know that some tasks remained for stockers to finish up even after carts roamed the aisles.

And Alan was one of those stockers.

Ruth put a box of tissues in her cart and moved to the frozen foods aisle to ponder the vegetables. Eventually she chose a bag of cauliflower and proceeded to the dairy aisle.

Alan was maneuvering a pallet heaped with yogurts to one side of the aisle.

"Hello, Alan." Ruth greeted him with warm eyes.

"Hi, Ruth." Alan leaned one elbow on a stack of boxes and put one hand in the pocket of his blue store apron. "I was afraid you wouldn't speak to me again. You didn't seem pleased to see me the other day."

She waved a hand. "I know you meant well."

Alan pulled a box cutter out of the apron and sliced into a carton of yogurts. "I guess we're all a little jittery about the fires."

"Yes, that's it." She reached for a container of sour cream from beside Alan's pallet. "Are you working all day?"

"I'm off around one o'clock."

"That's nice. You can still enjoy the afternoon." Ruth reached in the other direction and picked up a tub of cottage cheese. "I'm off at two today myself, but I think I'll go to the library. It would be nice to read something other than a textbook."

"I know what you mean." Alan swiftly stacked single-serving yogurt containers on the shelf and sliced open another box. "It's a little strange to be out of school and actually have a choice about what to read."

"That's what I mean!" Ruth chewed one corner of her mouth, mentally repeating cautions to remain casual. "Why don't you meet me at the library? I know it's small, but we might find something to recommend to each other."

Alan eyed her and transferred another batch of yogurt to the shelf. "Yeah. That's a good idea. I'll be there."

Her face beamed, and Rufus allowed himself a moment to bask in it. Perhaps her joy would give him the courage to hang on to the land and the future he imagined would come to be. Their children would learn to gather eggs without disturbing the hens, and Rufus would till Annalise a vegetable garden. He would come in from the workshop at lunchtime and ask how her morning had gone. For decades, they would take their morning coffee out to the front porch and stare at the Sangre de Cristos as they murmured prayers for the day.

"It's perfect, Rufus." Annalise sighed and leaned her head against his shoulder.

He opened his palm to her, and she laid her hand in it. Small, slender, feminine.

"You never even gave a hint you were buying land," Annalise said.

"I did it the summer before you came. I had some savings, and the price was right."

He knew the words she wanted to hear, and he ached to speak them.

The sound of a car engine wedged into his reverie.

Annalise turned her head, puzzled. "Who would that be?"

Rufus's suspicion sank his stomach. The car rumbled toward them and slowed to a stop.

"Rufus." Annalise sat up straight. "The side of that car has a Realtor's logo on it."

"Yes, I see."

The car stopped, and a man emerged from the driver's door while a man and a woman got out of the passenger side. The driver raised a hand to wave.

"Do you know them?" Annalise asked.

"I know Larry," Rufus said. "The driver."

"A Realtor."

"Yes."

The stone in Rufus's gut hardened another layer.

"But this is your land," Annalise said. "You just told me you bought it more than two years ago."

"Hello, Rufus," Larry called. "I didn't know you'd be out here."

If Rufus had known Larry would be coming, he certainly would not have brought Annalise out here.

"I've got some people interested in your land." Hands in his pockets, Larry moved toward the buggy. "The people from Denver. I told you about them."

"Yes, I remember."

Larry was close enough now that an introduction was mandatory.

"This is Annalise Friesen," Rufus said. *My fiancée,* he wanted to say. But he had not gotten that far when he had his opportunity.

"Glad to meet you." Larry extended a cheerful hand, which Annalise accepted. "Rufus has a great piece of land here."

"Yes, it's beautiful."

Rufus saw how hard she was working to cloak her bewilderment in hospitality. He swallowed and descended from the bench.

"Did I misunderstand you when we last spoke?" Rufus said.

"Oh, no, I realize you haven't made a decision." Larry gestured to the couple, who stood and gazed across the meadow. "And neither have they. But they came all the way from Denver. It seemed like a serendipitous opportunity to let them see what they could get if they decided to buy out this way."

"I see." Rufus glanced up at Annalise, who had shifted in the bench to look at the visiting couple.

Husband and wife stood with their arms linked now, pointing and gesturing.

And smiling.

Rufus stifled the urge to exhale his disappointment.

Forty

June 1892

$\mathcal{T}$hey can't have gotten too far." Maura trotted her horse beside Joseph's as they left the livery and headed down Main Street.

"It might be wise to pause long enough for you to draw me a map of how they might cross the state line," Joseph said.

"Why? I'll be with you." Eyes forward, Maura braced for his refusal.

"This could be dangerous, Maura."

"I asked for your help, Joseph. I did not ask you to bear the entire load."

"And if we don't find them in time? Or Leon won't listen to reason?"

"Then at least we will have tried. I want to give that much to Belle." Maura hastened the pace of her horse. "Leon has to see that the price of his choice may be his daughter."

"Right now he does not see past his anger."

"I was on the Twigg land in Missouri once, perhaps ten or twelve years ago. My parents used to be quite friendly with Old Man Twigg."

"Then I hope God has blessed you with a good memory."

"We will have no trouble asking where their property is once we start to follow the north fork of the river."

Maura kneed her horse and galloped ahead of Joseph before he could suggest again that she remain behind.

"We're close." Joseph reined in his horse and pointed to the hoofprints in the soggy ground. "Four horses, all well shoed. And not too long ago."

The winding, marshy, sometimes disappearing shoreline had made tracking the vigilantes difficult. More than once Joseph had been tempted to admit to Maura he had lost the trail. Thick woods on both sides of the White River's north fork could disguise a host of men.

Maura had not flagged, even at the hottest part of the day. Three times Joseph passed his water jug to her and insisted she drink deeply. Twice they stopped to refill the container from natural springs that began to appear with frequency. Once, he stopped to gather pine nuts and wild berries, but she wanted none of it. She cared nothing for food as long as Leon Mooney remained beyond their sight.

Finally, Joseph spied him through the trees. Joseph slid off his horse and handed the reins to Maura.

"What are you going to do?" Maura whispered.

"I'm not sure. I don't want startle him into shooting."

"Be careful!"

Joseph took a deep breath and guarded his steps through the woods. He made enough noise to be noticed but not enough to sound threatening. Mooney was alone for the moment, though the others could not be far off. Joseph continued forward, even as he realized Leon was peering into the woods, suspicious. Joseph held his empty hands up to view as he approached a man whose rifle was within reach.

"What are you doing here?" Mooney barked.

"I came to find you." Joseph paced ahead, controlled, patient. "Belle is concerned."

"Belle is blind to the truth." Mooney made no move for his gun.

"Why don't you tell me what you have in mind?" Joseph lowered himself to the ground beside Leon.

"Justice, that's all." Leon reached into a leather bag and pulled out a strip of beef jerky.

Joseph's stomach grumbled. "Our Lord asks us to forgive, Mr. Mooney."

Leon grunted. "I prefer to think I am an instrument of divine justice."

"How can any of us be sure of that?" Joseph kept his voice low.

"An eye for an eye. A Twigg for a Byler. That's the way I see it."

Joseph filled his lungs, exhaled slowly, and swallowed. "And if the response is a Mooney for a Twigg? Will that be justice? Will that bring peace?"

Mooney scoffed. "Peace. We won't have peace in Gassville as long as Old Man Twigg lives."

Joseph gestured up the river. "But he moved out of town. Is that not a sign that he is ready for peace?"

"It's a sign that he's scared, that's all. And he should be." Now Mooney picked up his rifle and tossed it from one hand to the other.

Joseph straightened his hat with both hands as he looked over his shoulder at the sound behind him. The three Gassville citizens who had followed Mooney across the state line stood with a hearty catch of crawfish.

"Looks like we'll have two more for supper," Mooney said. "You can come out, Maura. I know you're there."

Maura picked at the boiled crawfish served to her in a tin plate. It was her first food all day, and she knew she ought to try to eat it if for no other reason than to accept Leon Mooney's gruff hospitality, but the vice in her stomach made her hesitant to swallow anything.

Joseph ate slowly, she observed, but he consumed both fish and bread. He lifted his water jug and leaned toward her. "Come with me to get fresh water."

Maura set her plate aside as casually as she could manage and followed Joseph deeper into the woods. He knelt at a gurgling spring and dipped the jar's open mouth.

"These springs are all over," he said. "Mooney has his eye on one he thinks the Twiggs will use in the morning."

"How can he be sure?" Maura glanced around the woods as she knelt next to Joseph.

"It's farther upriver, at the edge of Twigg's land. They've already been up there and seen where they water the horses."

"I'm sorry, Joseph." Maura pinched her eyes between thumb and fingers. "I dragged you up here for nothing."

"You have a heart for peace, Maura. That's all you want."

"I understand that disputes will happen." Maura sank onto a boulder. "I can even accept war for a righteous cause. But this? I do not understand this burning vengeance."

Her pulse coursed harder when he took her hand in both of his, but she did not withdraw it. She looked into his violet-blue eyes, shimmering in the moonlight, as he gently stroked her palm.

"The question now," Joseph said, "is if you would like to stay the night or leave."

Maura glanced back at the four men eating fish around a dying fire. "What is it like where you live?"

He shrugged. "Not so different from here. Rivers. Woods. The handiwork of God."

"I mean your people," she said. "Your family, your church." *Hannah,* she wanted to say.

"We are people of submission." He held her hand still now. "The good of the family and the community are our greatest concern."

"I always thought Gassville was my community. But it's just a place."

He squeezed her hand. "We face our own decision now. Shall we go or stay?"

Pressure squeezed her chest as he released her hand. Joseph Beiler was like no other man she had known.

"Have we tried everything?" she said. "Is there no hope?"

"I like to believe there is always hope," Joseph said, "but we submit to God's sovereign will, even in this."

Joseph put the stopper in his jug and stood.

"If we cannot avert what Leon Mooney has fixed in his heart," Maura said, "we may be of aid when someone is hurt."

Joseph nodded. "We will stay, then. I only wish I had a bedroll to offer you."

"I will not sleep a wink anyway." Maura pointed to a wide tree. "If you talk to me, perhaps I will not say something foolish to Leon Mooney."

"Then I will be happy to talk to you."

Joseph took the blankets from under their saddles and spread them on the ground at the base of the tree Maura selected. They settled in shoulder to shoulder. Mooney and his men grew quiet, though none slept as far as Maura could see.

"Joseph," Maura said quietly, "will you be in a great deal of trouble for not going home with Zeke?"

He nodded slowly. "Some. My parents will be disappointed, and the bishop will give me a stern speech when I see him."

"And Hannah?" Maura could hardly believe the question escaped her lips.

"Hannah." Joseph took Maura's hand again. "Hannah is a sensible choice. She is eager to marry and would be eager to please her husband. Everyone believed the bishop selected me for this journey because I am sensible as well. But it turns out I am not so sensible after all."

"Because. . ."

"Because of you, Miss Woodley. When I left I was not sure Hannah Berkey was God's will for me. Now I am certain she is not."

Maura's breath caught as she stared into the darkness. "What are you saying, Joseph?"

"You have raised many questions in my heart."

Leon Mooney moved in stealth toward them. Maura stared up at him. Joseph stood.

"I want you two to promise me you will stay out of the way," Mooney said. "There's no reason to see you hurt."

"Why does anyone have to be hurt?" Maura said. "Let's go home, Leon. Home to Belle. She must be frantic with worry."

"She won't have to worry much longer. It will all be settled at daybreak."

Under cover of darkness Leon Mooney moved his entourage upriver.

Before daybreak, four men found protection behind trees at the base of a hill and carefully calculated their clearest shots.

Joseph whispered to Maura that they should stay back. But she saddled her horse and followed Mooney, and Joseph did not want to let her out of his sight.

As a pink dawn broke over the north fork of the White River, Old Man Twigg and his son Jimmy led their horses down the hill to the spring, just as Mooney had anticipated they would.

Joseph opened his arms and enfolded Maura when the rapid spray of bullets began. She put her hands over her ears and her face against his chest. Joseph watched everything.

Old Man Twigg never even had a chance to lift the rifle he carried. He fell dead with the first firing. Joseph pushed Maura to the ground and covered her as Jimmy fired back, although Joseph doubted he could see any target. In only a few more seconds, Jimmy dropped with wounds to his leg and shoulder.

Maura pushed Joseph off and sat up, weeping.

Forty-One

Rufus took the reins. Annalise offered no resistance. He clicked his tongue, and Dolly answered with forward movement directly across the meadow. Rather than turning onto the road that would take them back to the highway, though, Rufus crossed into the old mining property and halted the horse once again on open land.

"I want you to know this is not how I planned the morning." He let go of the reins and turned on the bench to face Annalise.

"What happened back there, Rufus?" Annalise's gray eyes were wide, and the day's light swam through them.

"When I was working in Cañon City," he said, "I found Larry's office. I wanted to ask some questions."

"About selling your land?"

"Possibly. I would use the money to help *Daed*."

"So why did you bring me here?" Annalise's voice dimmed.

"Because I wasn't sure. About the land. I'm sure about you, Annalise. I wanted to see you there on the land at least once. I wanted it to be the place where we choose our future together even if we do not live there."

"Rufus Beiler, are you proposing marriage?" Annalise's face cracked in a grin.

"I seem not to be very good at it—which should assure you that I have no experience with proposals."

She laughed, and Rufus let himself breathe.

"So do it," she said. "We can at least get that settled. Then we'll face the rest."

"You walked away from a fortune. You changed your whole life. I always thought I would offer a good start to married life."

"God provides."

"What if God provides by bringing a buyer for land I had not even decided to sell?"

"We'll figure it out, Rufus." She reached for his hand. "Ask me and kiss me and then we'll talk about all this."

Rufus swallowed and held both her hands now. "Annalise Friesen, I believe God wants me to be your husband. Would you have me?"

"Yes!"

The burst of joy rippled through their intertwined fingers. Rufus leaned toward Annalise's eager face and put one hand behind her neck, his fingers in the hollow of her hairline. On the first day he saw her straw-colored hair hanging loose around her lovely face, he had found her beautiful—even if she was *English*. She was no longer *English*, and the beauty of her spirit far outshone golden sun on her hair. His lips met hers, and something startling passed between them. They had known for months they wanted to be husband and wife, but this moment of deciding, of choosing, of accepting sent a jolt of electricity through their lingering kiss. Annalise put her arms around him and returned every searching softness with her own.

They separated, breathless.

"I will arrange to have the banns read," Rufus said.

"I'm not supposed to tell anyone before that, am I?"

"Traditionally, no."

"I don't know if I can keep this secret!"

"It won't be long now."

"I hope not. I very much want to marry you." Annalise stroked his arm.

"Many things are uncertain still. My land—*our* land. I always imagined we would stay with my parents over the winter and build next spring."

"We still could."

"So you want me to keep the property?"

Annalise shook her head. "I want you to do what you feel is best for us, for our family."

Our family.

She already belonged with the Beilers.

"I own my house free and clear, you know." Annie laced her fingers through his again.

Rufus stilled her moving fingers. "I would not be comfortable living in town. It is not apart."

"Of course not." Annalise was quick to speak. "I didn't mean that. I mean that the value of my house will be *ours* now. We can decide how to use it."

"You would sell your house?"

"Or rent it out for income. If I'm not going to be living there, it shouldn't sit empty."

"I know you used to have a great deal of money in your *English* life. You have already sacrificed so much."

"I have sacrificed nothing but greed and ambition," she said.

"I want you to feel secure and cared for."

"Rufus Beiler, we're going to spend our lives together. Nothing makes me feel more secure than that."

He kissed her again.

"God provides," she whispered, her breath on his neck.

Ruth tugged on the library door. By now Elijah would be seated in a reading cubicle on the other side of the main aisle. The library was a narrow space between two shops on Main Street. The number of books on the shelves at any given time was limited by the space, but Ruth had always found the two part-time librarians accommodating and helpful in placing holds on other books in the wider library system. Anything Ruth had ever requested arrived within four days.

Elijah was wearing *English* jeans and a blue work shirt he had found in the thrift store a couple of blocks down. Ruth caught a glimpse of his back—his Amish hat gone as well—and calculated that an interest in biographies would keep her within his sight. All he had to do was glance up or quietly scoot back his chair.

Ruth glanced around, relieved that Alan had not arrived first, and ambled down the main aisle, running a finger along the shelves and glancing at titles.

A moment later, the front door creaked and Alan entered. Ruth flashed him a welcoming smile then pulled a biography of Thomas Jefferson off the shelf and began to flip through it as her peripheral vision tracked Alan's movement toward her.

"Biographies, eh?"

Alan stood next to her now.

Ruth casually turned another page. "When I left Westcliffe, I had to get a GED before I could enroll at the university. I had a lot to catch up on when it came to American history."

Alan took a book from the shelf. "Alexander Hamilton. Now he was an interesting character. Some people say the whole national debt traces back to his idea to borrow private money to pay for the Revolutionary War debt."

Ruth chuckled softly. "I hope we're not still paying for the Revolutionary War."

"Your people don't believe in wars, do they?"

"Well, we believe they happen. We don't participate. It goes against our peacekeeping ways."

"Do you like to read about science?" Alan pointed with a thumb to the other side of the aisle.

"Nursing is science." Ruth closed the Jefferson book and slid it back into its place. "I suppose fire is a science category all its own."

"It definitely is." Alan pulled a book from the shelf. "No one ever seems to check this one out. I come to look at it, and it's always here."

Ruth looked over his shoulder at the photos of burning fires and shuddered. "Why don't you check it out and read it more leisurely?"

"I can't have it around the apartment. Bryan would never let me hear the end of how he got a better grade than I did when we studied origins of fire in school."

"Considering that you haven't been in Westcliffe all that long," she said, "it seems like you have seen quite a few fires already."

"I missed the last one." Alan replaced the book on the shelf. "I was at the store stacking apples and peaches."

"That's right."

"Bryan was there, though."

She nodded. "We discovered the smoke together."

"You know, it's not that hard to lay a fuse so the fire won't start right away."

Through the stacks, Ruth saw Elijah stand. She caught his brown eyes and looked away.

"You must learn all that stuff in school," she said to Alan.

"And Bryan was at the top of the class. He was a whiz with chemical reactions and retardants and all that jazz."

Ruth took a random book off the shelf. "You know him better than I do."

Alan touched her elbow then, and Ruth heard the step Elijah took. She looked up to meet Alan's gaze.

"Sometimes insiders get involved with fires." He leaned toward her. "Bryan could always calculate how much time would elapse before a certain kind of fire would explode. Exactly."

The librarian stepped into the aisle, stared at them, and put a finger to her lips. Elijah was the only other patron in the building, but the librarian could not know that Ruth wanted him to hear every word.

Ruth lowered her voice. "You're not saying Bryan had anything to do with the fires, are you?"

Alan's eyes danced, which startled Ruth. Elijah moved on the other side of the shelf.

"I think I'll stick to biographies." Ruth again began to run her finger along the spines on the biography shelves.

Alan checked the time on his cell phone. "I have to go."

Where? Ruth wondered. But she did not ask.

Alan gave a look of courteous amusement. "I hope I'll run into you again." He sauntered toward the door.

Elijah came around the stacks. "Satisfied?"

Ruth pulled the fire science book off the shelf again and ran a finger down the table of contents page. "He's been filling in the gaps."

"He wasn't trying to hide it."

She looked up and met Elijah's eyes. "It's a dare."

"I need to ask you some questions, Leah." Jerusha sat in an armchair with a notepad in her lap on Friday afternoon. "We can ask Annie to leave the room if you like."

"She can stay."

Leah looked pale to Annie. Two days of wondering about the contents of the letter had taken their toll. But at least Leah had cleaned up and was on time.

"Have you ever felt like hurting yourself or someone else?" Jerusha asked.

"Sometimes I feel like I just want to blow something up." Leah pressed her palms together. "But anyone would feel that way if they were going through what I'm going through."

"So you might want to hurt some *thing*, but not yourself or another person."

"Right."

Jerusha watched Leah. "If you felt like hurting yourself, would you tell someone?"

Leah glanced at Annie. "I guess I could tell Annalise. But I don't want to hurt myself. I just want to go to Pennsylvania. And I want to know what's in that letter she got."

"I understand. We'll get to that soon." Jerusha picked up the pen that lay on her notepad. "Why don't you tell me in your own words why you think you're here today."

"If I didn't come, Annalise would not let me see the letter."

Annie groaned inwardly and crossed and uncrossed her ankles beneath the hem of her dress.

"Is that the only reason you agreed to come?" Jerusha asked.

Leah tapped her foot steadily for about thirty seconds. "I guess not. I've been behaving strangely, I suppose."

"And why do you think that is?"

Annie calmly raised one hand to pull on a prayer *kapp* string, a habit she had developed at moments when she wanted to pray silently. The letter lay in her lap.

"My parents won't listen to me," Leah said, "and I'm anxious that I'll never get my life back."

"Your Pennsylvania life?" Jerusha wrote a quick notation.

Leah nodded.

"I understand Annie got a letter from someone in Pennsylvania you care deeply about."

Leah kept nodding.

"Perhaps we should talk about what would happen if the letter says something you don't want to hear."

Annie held her breath. This was exactly the reason she wanted Jerusha present when she broke the seal on the envelope.

"Why don't we just find out what it says?" Leah eyed the envelope in Annie's lap. "If it's good news, we don't even have to finish this conversation."

"I only want to help you be prepared either way."

Leah's eye flashed. "You've made up your mind it's bad news. You don't know that."

Jerusha held her calming pose. "No, I don't have any idea what the letter will say. I would want to help you whether or not there was a letter."

"But there *is* a letter." Leah moved her eyes from Jerusha to Annie and back again. "If I answer your questions, do you promise me we'll open the letter?"

Forty-Two

"Why don't you read it to us?" Annie handed the letter to Jerusha after nearly ninety minutes of conversation between Leah and the counselor.

"Is that all right with you, Leah?" Jerusha asked.

The girl nodded.

Annie was relieved that Leah was surprisingly calm now that the moment had arrived. After resisting Jerusha for much of the session, either actively or passively, Leah had made some remarkable and transparent insights about herself. Annie had no doubt that Jerusha would suggest that Leah see her again, but for now, Leah seemed as settled as Annie had ever seen her.

Jerusha pulled at the flap of the envelope, and it gave way easily. Annie knew it would. More than once she had—fleetingly—considered opening that flap for a preview of the letter. But she had given her word to Leah.

"That's his paper!" Leah jumped to her feet. "It's really from him."

The unfolding papers crackled in Jerusha's hands, and she reached for her reading glasses on an end table.

Dear Miss Friesen,

First of all, I wish to extend to you the right hand of fellowship. Brother Matthew Beiler has told me of your baptism and, indeed, how fond his family is of you. My heart warms with yours at your obedience and union with Christ.

I am sure you are surprised to be hearing from me rather than Matthew. I hope you don't mind that he exercised the liberty of sharing your letter with me. Although our farms are some distance apart, he took time to make the drive and seek me out. He felt that you had asked for his opinion on a matter he was not overly familiar with. That being the case, perhaps it was better to provide you with direct, reliable information.

I understand that you have not met Matthew, but I assure you that this approach is quite typical of him. I hope the day comes soon that you and Matthew will be able to meet. He mentioned that his mother's letters suggest that she hopes you will soon be a member of the Beiler family, as well as the congregation.

The most important thing I wish to say to you is that I care for Leah Deitwaller as deeply as any married man I know cares for his wife. I cannot emphasize this point enough.

Jerusha paused, and she and Annie both looked at Leah, who sank back into her chair, smearing tears across her face.

"Are you all right?" Jerusha asked.

Leah gasped a sudden intake of air. "No one believed me because of all my mistakes. But I was telling the truth."

"Do you need some water?" Annie offered her bottle.

Leah shook her head. "Just keep reading, please."

Jerusha looked back at the pages in her hands.

I respect that Leah's parents have the authority to do what they believe is best for her. Her father asked me not to write to Leah again, and I have honored his wishes. Please tell her that my heart has not changed, and I treasure the letters she sends.

Leah and I have both been baptized. I know you understand the seriousness of our commitment, since you have chosen to take the baptismal vows yourself.

I have talked with my parents at great length. After a season of prayer and searching, they have given their blessing to my union with Leah and would welcome her to their home as their daughter even if we are not able to marry immediately. I would be grateful for any assistance you can give to bring Leah to us. I believe our greatest happiness would come from receiving the blessing of Leah's parents as well, and I pray that God will reveal His will in the matter. My daed will write to Mr. Deitwaller, and we will await further word.

My heart aches for Leah and for her happiness. You have been so kind to show an interest in her and search for the truth by writing to Matthew.

Most sincerely,
Aaron Borntreger

Annie stood up and crossed to Leah's chair, kneeling in front of the girl and taking her hands. Leah sobbed.

"I was right! I was right! No one believed me, but I was right!" Leah's chest heaved. "I would never have acted so crazy if someone had believed me."

Annie's throat choked up. She had no words but only gripped Leah's trembling hands.

Jerusha folded the letter and slid it back into the envelope.

"I'll be back here next Friday," the counselor said. "I suggest that we meet again then. I wonder if we might have Leah's parents with us for at least one future session."

Annie squeezed her eyes shut. Jerusha might as well have asked for the mountains to move.

Annie held Leah's hand, which still trembled as she stood at the appointment desk in the clinic and arranged to see Jerusha again. They traversed the blocks through town and to Annie's quiet street with few words. As they made the turn off Main Street, Annie spotted Ruth coming from the other direction. Annie lifted a finger to her lips, and Ruth felt into step with them without a greeting.

Was it only yesterday that Rufus had shown her his vision of their future together? Had it only been a day since they had agreed to marry? Ruth should be the first person to hear the news—and not when the banns were read. Fatigue rolled through Annie as she pushed open the back door and the trio entered a house hushed in the shadows of a fading afternoon.

Leah moved ahead of the other two, walking in her soundless way through the house to her makeshift bedroom in the living room.

"Is she all right?" Ruth whispered.

"It's a long story."

Annie was not sure how much she could share with Ruth. The story was Leah's more than it was hers. Certainly she would not try to recount the afternoon's events while Leah was in the other room. She turned the switch on a propane lamp that sat on the end of the kitchen counter.

"I could make us something to eat," Ruth said quietly.

Annie nodded. "I'd like to freshen up."

"Maybe I'll change first, too."

When she passed through the dining room to the stairs, Annie was surprised to see Leah sitting at the table. Annie stopped so suddenly that Ruth nearly bumped her from behind. Their eyes fixed on Leah. She held a lit match between thumb and forefinger, and the oil lamp was positioned in front of her. Leah stared at the flame as the match burned down, only at the last minute touching it to the waiting oil and watching the mantle burst into brightness.

Annie moistened her lips. "Are you hungry, Leah? Ruth has offered to make some supper."

Leah gazed at the lamp. "I don't think I can eat. It's been a long afternoon."

"We'll save something for you, then. You can have it later."

The kitten grazed past Annie and jumped into Leah's lap.

"I think I'll go out." Leah held the kitten against her cheek and stood up. "I promise not to stay out late."

"All right then." What else could Annie say? "We'll leave a plate in the oven."

Leah left through the back door without speaking again.

Ruth turned to Annie. "Is it my imagination, or was she a little too fascinated with that burning match?"

Annie puffed her cheeks and blew out her breath. "It's not your imagination. She's been so sad, so confused. So angry. So hurt. I have wondered more than once whether she was capable of setting a fire as a way of acting out. I honestly don't know."

Ruth raised both hands to her temples. "You suspect Leah? Of all the fires?"

"*Suspect* is a strong word." Annalise pulled a chair from the dining room table and sat down. "I have nothing to go on except the fact that the fires happened and my extremely nonprofessional assessment of Leah's emotional state."

"I know what you mean." Ruth sat down now, too.

"You've been very patient, Ruth. I appreciate it. I know it's not easy for you to have Leah here."

"That's not what I'm talking about." Ruth pushed the burning lamp toward the middle of the table. "What you just said about the fact of the fires and a person's emotional state—I've been thinking about that, too."

Annalise furrowed her brow. "So you think Leah could really be a suspect."

"I don't know. Maybe. But I'm talking about Alan."

"Bryan's friend?"

Ruth gave in to the shiver that ran through her. "He just seems off. His father came to town one day, and the air between them was as frigid as the North Pole. And he knows a lot about fires."

"There's a big difference between two things happening coincidentally and one causing the other."

"I know." Ruth put her elbows on the table and hung her head in her hands. "We can't go around accusing everybody with emotional issues of criminal action."

"But what if it really is one of them?"

"It can't be both." Ruth raised her head and met Annalise's eyes. "They don't even know each other and have nothing in common."

"We're assuming one person started all the fires," Annalise said. "That may or not be true."

"Alan thinks it could be Bryan." Ruth hated to even speak those words aloud.

Annalise's posture snapped up. "Bryan? Your Bryan?"

"He's not 'my' Bryan. But yes."

"Aren't the two of them friends?"

"They say they are. But they're both pointing fingers at each other."

"Bryan thinks it's Alan?" Annalise asked.

Ruth shrugged. "Not exactly. After the fire in Joel's field, I found something I was sure belonged to Alan. But when Bryan asked him about it, Alan said it wasn't his. It was just a water bottle strap, but Alan made a point to tell me Bryan had one just like it, too."

"Which leaves us nowhere."

"And I don't even have the strap anymore. I gave it to Bryan."

"It sounds like you trust Bryan, and you don't trust Alan."

Ruth pulled pins from her hair and let it hang loose. "That's what my gut tells me. I tried to be friendly with Alan and see if he would talk to me, but he just points out that I don't know Bryan as well as I think I do."

"And now you have doubts?"

Ruth took a moment to think. "No. You know what? I don't."

"So we're back to Alan or Leah."

Ruth stared into the burning lamp. "Or someone we haven't even met."

Forty-Three

June 1892

Joseph hitched his horse in front of the milliner's shop, stroked the slope of the animal's face, and turned to enter the store. Walter was cleaning shelves.

"I'll be glad when school starts again," Walter mumbled. "My daddy doesn't want me to have a moment to myself."

"Being a hard worker is a fine trait." Joseph glanced around. "I wonder if Maura is here."

"You all got back day before yesterday." Walter shuffled toward Joseph and ran a rag across the shelf unconvincingly. "She still won't tell me what happened."

"It is better that way." Joseph and Maura agreed not to fuel Walter's fascination with posses and gunfights. The boy did not need to know that Leon had let Maura try to stanch the blood flow before hefting Jimmy onto a horse and tying him to the saddle for the bumpy ride back to Baxter County and reluctantly surrendering him to the care of Dr. Lindsay.

"Maura," Joseph said. "Is she here?"

Walter gestured with his head. "In the back."

A pair of dark green cloth panels separated the shop from the back room where Maura's Uncle Edwin created women's hats.

Joseph tentatively pushed a hand between the curtains.

"Maura?"

She looked up immediately and laid her pen down on the open accounts book. "What happened?"

Joseph leaned one shoulder against the wall. "Dr. Lindsay took the bullets out of Jimmy's shoulder and leg then patched him up. Deputy Combs made Jimmy promise to leave Baxter County and never show his face here again."

"It's about time the deputy found his spine." Maura puffed her cheek and exhaled. "And did Jimmy agree?"

Joseph nodded.

"What about Leon? And the others?"

"What they did was outside Baxter County," Joseph said. "The deputy can't charge them with anything."

"So it's over?" Maura stood. "Will Jimmy really leave?"

"He seemed sincere to me. Dr. Lindsay offered to take him back to Missouri in a wagon, and Jimmy is in no condition to resist."

Maura smoothed her hair back with both hands. "What Leon did was horrible. I'm not sure if I'd like to see him held accountable, or just let it all be over."

Joseph took two steps toward Maura and tapped his fingers on the edge of the desk. "That decision is not yours to make. You can't take that burden on yourself."

"Shouldn't someone?"

"*Gottes wille.*"

"God's will?"

"Yes," he said. "Can you leave it to God now?"

The muscles twitched in her face as her eyes held steady with his. They had shared an easy way with each other riding to Missouri and back. She was close enough now that he could reach out and take her hand and feel it quiver in his own. He wanted to.

He moistened his lips. "Zeke and Stephen will be nearly home by now."

"Will you be going, then?"

He searched for some sign in her face of the answer she wanted to hear. "Would you go with me?"

She was silent.

"I miss my people," Joseph said, "but the thought of leaving you weighs heavy."

She opened her mouth then closed it without speaking.

"We don't have to stay," Joseph said. "We can find another settlement. We can help to plant a settlement. You can find the life of peace you have been seeking."

Maura dropped back into the wooden chair at the desk. She had wondered if this moment might come. Even hoped it would.

Walter stuck his head through the curtains. "Are you two going to stay back here all afternoon?"

"Walter, you have work to do," Maura said.

"So do you. Daddy wants the books done today. I heard him tell you."

"I'm working on them. Please excuse us for a few more minutes."

"I'm not sure why you can't tell me what's going on."

Maura clamped her mouth closed and glared at her cousin.

"Don't tell me it's none of my business," Walter said. "I'll find out eventually. Leon Mooney will make sure."

"Then you'll just have to wait for Leon's version." The shop door jangled, and Maura heard the familiar thump of her uncle's footsteps. "There's your daddy now, Walter. Joseph and I are going to take a short walk."

With a glance toward Joseph, Maura brushed past Walter and his open mouth.

Outside, she said, "I'm sorry about Walter."

"He reminds me of Little Jake," Joseph said. "Always full of questions. You'll like him, I think."

"I'm sure I would enjoy meeting your brother," Maura said, "but the matter of leaving with you is a serious one."

"I know. I do not suggest it lightly."

Joseph straightened his hat, and Maura knew he was as nervous as she was dancing around this question. He was proposing marriage. He knew it, and she knew it.

"There is the matter of my father." Maura paced a little faster down the sidewalk. "It has been hard for him since my mother died. He depends on me."

"It seems to me a great many people depend on you," Joseph said. "Who do you let yourself depend on?"

Maura had no response. She was supposed to say God. She was supposed to depend on God, but she was not sure she could honestly say she did. And she had come to depend on Joseph, though she hesitated to admit this.

"Come with me," Joseph said, "or let me come back for you after I speak to the bishop."

"What would you tell the bishop?" And what would he tell Hannah Berkey?

"The bishop is a kind man at heart." Joseph touched her arm, causing her to slow her steps and turn toward him. "A simpler life without fearing violence from your own people—do you not want that?"

"Well, yes, I do, but—"

"And a life of faith, where your hope for peace could fill your heart?"

"In your church?" Maura asked. "Is that what you mean?"

"Do you think you could join us? We would follow the Lord together."

Maura nodded, her throat thickening.

"And a husband," he said. "Do you not want that? Do you want me?"

This was indeed a proposal.

"Joseph, I greatly admire you and have become deeply fond

of you." She nearly lost her nerve in his violet-blue eyes. "But my father. . ."

"Even the widowers among our people hire someone to keep house."

"It won't be the same." She broke the gaze and resumed walking. "And Belle. How can I leave Belle right now? She hardly knows her own mind from one day to the next. In a few weeks she is supposed to return to her duties teaching school, and I am afraid she will not be strong enough."

"Can you make her strong?" Joseph asked.

"I suppose not. But I can let her know I care for her while she makes herself strong again." Maura raised her eyes to look down the block then reached to clutch his arm. "There's Belle now. Something's wrong."

Belle hurtled toward them on foot.

"An accident." Belle put one hand on her chest as she gasped for breath. "There's been an accident."

"What happened?" Maura and Joseph spoke in tandem.

Belle looked from one to the other, seeing something between them that she had never seen before.

"A cow went over the side of a bluff." Belle focused on Maura. "My father and your father are there trying to figure out how to get to it and haul it up. But it's a full-grown cow. They need longer ropes and leverage."

"I'll go immediately," Joseph said. "Where are they?"

Belle described the location. She had run for two miles to get back to town, but a horse could close the distance in minutes.

Joseph and Maura pivoted, and the three of them marched back toward the milliner's shop.

"I'll get some rope from the livery," Joseph said.

"I'll take my cart," Maura said. "Belle, you can ride with me."

Joseph mounted his horse in one swift motion and thundered

down Main Street toward the stables. Belle lifted the hem of her skirt to keep pace with Maura as they cut down a side street to the Woodley home, where the cart and the horse occupied a small barn behind the house. Maura went through the familiar motions of hitching cart to horse, and they clattered back through town, meeting Joseph on the way.

At the bluff, Joseph jumped off his horse, a coil of rope over each arm.

"I'm going down," Belle heard her father say as he squatted at the edge of the bluff.

Belle stepped to the edge and peered. The cow lay on its side, moaning in protest. "Can't she stand up?"

"I'm going to find out." Leon Mooney tested his footing on the steep slope.

"Wait for a rope, Daddy." Belle scrambled over to Joseph, who was securing one end of a long thickly braided length to the harness of his horse. As he then tied the horse snug to a tree, Belle ran with the loop at the other end.

When she saw her father disappear from sight, she screamed.

Woody Woodley and Maura were on their knees, reaching down with their arms. Leon was beyond their grasp, caught in the branches of scrub growth.

"Daddy." Belle dangled the rope over the edge. "You should have waited for the rope, you old fool."

"I cannot afford to lose this cow." Leon's gruff reply rankled in Belle's mind. When would her father learn to think things through?

Joseph was beside her now and had taken the rope from Belle's hand. Below them, Leon wrestled with the branches and abruptly fell several feet lower.

"I'm fine," Leon reported.

Belle watched as he gripped a bush and got his feet into secure footholds.

"I'll swing the rope down," Joseph called out.

Belle held her breath as Joseph stood and wound up his arm to throw the rope wide of the bushes on the side of the bluff. As it passed him, her father reached to grab it—and missed.

This time he fell solidly on his back with a leg bent behind him, next to the groaning cow.

Belle leaned over the side precariously herself. "He's not moving."

"Give him a minute," Joseph said. "He's had the wind knocked out of him."

Finally, Leon Mooney pushed himself up on one side and attempted to stand. Instantly he howled and sank back down. Belle saw the bone protruding below his knee.

Joseph sighed. "Looks like we'll have to haul them both up now."

"If he had just waited two more minutes," Belle said, "we could have gotten him down there safely."

"Belle," Joseph said, "we'll get him up. Don't worry."

"What about the cow?"

"Let's worry about your father."

"He won't want to come up without the cow."

Joseph looked over the ledge. "Neither of them is in immediate danger, but your father is going to need a doctor to look after that leg."

"I'll go for Dr. Lindsay," Belle said. "I'll take Maura's horse."

"He's out of town." Joseph decided not to tell Belle that Dr. Lindsay was escorting Jimmy Twigg out of the county. "You'll have to go for Doc Denton."

"Doc Denton! You want me to ask a Denton to look after my father after what they did to my John?"

"It's the best thing for your father." Joseph glanced at Maura, who nodded.

"I'll go with you," Maura said.

"No." Belle looked down at her father again. "I can do it if you'll let me take your horse."

"Of course."

Belle was swiftly astride the horse with knees in its flanks. As she thundered down the road, Woody Woodley stood up. "Get another rope ready. I'll go down."

"Let me," Joseph said. He was a good forty years younger than Woody Woodley and trusted his own reflexes against Leon's rash impulses.

Forty-Four

July 1892

Maura watched her father pick up his newspaper from the sideboard in the dining room and shuffle into the front room to sit in the chair that had been his favorite since before she was born. A few years ago her mother had insisted on sending it out for new stuffing and fresh fabric, and Maura was glad she had. The alternative had been to haul the chair to a trash heap. At least this way Woody Woodley got to enjoy its familiarity.

She saw the stoop in his shoulders, more pronounced since Leon's rash retribution against the Twiggs had drawn her into harm's way and his equally impulsive attempt to single-handedly rescue a fallen cow had raised Woody's heart rate for an entire afternoon. From the doorway between the dining room and the kitchen, Maura watched him settle into the chair, pick up his glasses from the end table that had been a wedding present from her grandparents, and scan once again the same newspaper he had read from start to finish over his breakfast five hours earlier. He was likely to spend the entire afternoon there, and she would never know what thoughts passed through his mind.

He was tired. And alone. He had plenty of longtime friends in Baxter County, but Maura knew they did not fill the void her mother's death had left. She did not pretend that she filled it, either, but she was his daughter. As much as she could not stand the thought of Joseph's departure, neither could she imagine leaving her father. Joseph would have to understand. After all, the ties of family bound his community together.

Maura was not entitled to any hold on Joseph. Already he had stayed several days longer than he should have, hoping for a change of her heart. But there would be none.

She could not leave her father.

She could not leave Belle.

Perhaps Joseph would return to Tennessee and find happiness with Hannah Berkey after all.

Maura pushed the swinging door open and went through to the kitchen. Leon Mooney's leg was broken in two places. Belle had hardly left his bedside in the last four days, refusing several offers of assistance from Gassville residents. Maura could not do much to make Belle's emotional tumult easier, but she could at least spare Belle having to worry about food. She laid a towel in the bottom of a basket and began to arrange small covered dishes in the flat bottom.

She glanced at the clock. In five hours Joseph Beiler would appear at her front door for the meal to which she had invited him.

Outside her father's bedroom, Belle took the sodden handkerchief from her skirt pocket and dabbed at her eyes for at least the twentieth time that day.

How could she have thought that caring for her father while he recovered from his injury would somehow bring them closer? She had been a fool about so many things in the last year.

The bell to the front door rang.

"Whoever that is, tell them to go away," Leon barked.

Belle straightened her shoulders and stuffed her handkerchief back in her pocket. "I will make sure you are not disturbed."

"Take these dishes away. I don't want to eat this rot."

Belle went into the bedroom to retrieve the tray she had only brought up only ten minutes earlier. The bell rang again.

"Didn't I tell you to make them go away?"

"One thing at a time." Belle lifted the tray from the bed.

"Don't give me back talk."

"No sir." Belle left the room as swiftly as possible. In the hall, she set the tray on a table and flew down the stairs to answer the door before the bell could ring again. She opened the door to Maura and another basket of food.

Belle forced a smile. "Hello, Maura." She stepped aside so Maura could enter.

"You must think I'm trying to feed an army." Maura lifted the basket, and Belle took it from her. "I just want to help, and I don't know what else to do."

Belle burst into tears. "You're trying to fix something that can't be fixed."

Maura enfolded Belle in her arms, and Belle did not protest. "Is he not any better?"

Belle wiped her tears with the back of one hand. "He has only been immobile for four days, and already he has pointed out my every failure in how I care for him."

"He is lucky he has you."

Fearful that their voices would waft up the staircase, Belle led the way to the kitchen. "I thought he would calm down. He hated the thought that I wanted to marry John Twigg, and that's impossible now. Then he made sure I could never have anything to do with Old Man Twigg and chased off John's brothers."

"I'm sorry that he cannot see the tenderness of your heart," Maura whispered. "I'm sorry that *I* could not see the tenderness of your heart."

"Why can't my father ever leave well enough alone?" Belle set the basket on the kitchen counter and began to unpack it. "I have nothing left of the family I thought I would spend my life with, and that's not enough. How long is he going to punish me?"

"This business between the Twiggs and the Dentons—"

"A feud," Belle said. "You can call it what it is."

Maura turned her palms up. "It wasn't always that way. The people of Gassville remember better days."

"But no one will ever forget that it was a Twigg who shot Sheriff Byler." Belle opened the icebox and set a plate of ham slices inside.

Maura fiddled with the edge of the towel lining the basket.

Belle reached for her handkerchief again. "I think maybe you're the only friend I have left in this town."

"I'm sure that's not true," Maura said. "You teach half the children in town. So many families know how lucky they are to have you in the classroom. You'll see. Things will be better once school starts in the fall. Gassville will see better days again."

Belle looked at Maura's face for the first time since she arrived. Maura was saying the right words, but the sentiment was absent from her countenance.

"What about Joseph?" Belle asked. "Are you. . .will you go with him?"

"He wants me to."

"Love is powerful."

"But not simple."

Maura's roast was tender and juicy, just as it should be. Her baking powder biscuits were lofty and fluffy. The green beans had a just-picked flavor that made Joseph homesick. The potatoes were free of lumps and nearly floating in butter, just the way Joseph liked them.

Yet the pall over the meal nearly strangled him.

Maura's eyes followed her father's movements more than anything else. No matter how many times Joseph tried to catch her glance, she had another place to look, something to fetch from the kitchen, a dish to pass. By the time she brought out cherry pie and coffee, the three of them were eating in near silence.

Woody dabbed his lips one last time and scraped back his chair. "I believe I will retire early. You young people enjoy the evening."

"Are you all right, Daddy?" Maura asked.

"I'm fine. Just tired."

Joseph waited until Woody was well on his way up the stairs before speaking.

"Come with me, Maura. Your father would want you to be happy."

"How could I be happy without him?" Maura stacked the dessert dishes.

Joseph stilled her motion with both of his hands. "Can you be happy without me?"

Tears welled in her eyes. "I understand that you can't stay in Gassville," she said. "You've tried our *English* ways. They are not your ways. But my father. . .and Belle."

"You haven't answered the question."

She looked away, refusing to meet his eye. "No. Probably not happy. But I will have a fulfilling life."

Joseph cleared his throat. "In case you should have any uncertainty, I want you to know I feel the same. I know I cannot remain here, but without you. . ."

"Hannah is waiting for you. She loves you, and she knows the ways of your people."

He shook his head. "I will not marry Hannah Berkey."

"You should."

"No, I shouldn't. She deserves better."

"Better than you? She will not find such a man."

"She deserves a better love than I would give her. She would know my heart was elsewhere." Joseph laid his hands in his lap under the generous drop of the tablecloth. "I will set out tomorrow. First thing."

Maura exhaled. "I know you must go."

"But I will come back. Belle's father will get well. They will find their way back to each other. With time she will believe that happiness is possible once again."

"Perhaps. And my father?"

"I pray God makes His will clear."

Forty-Five

A tap on the shoulder made Ruth turn around just as she finished ordering her sandwich at the Main Street bakery on Saturday.

"Bryan! Hi."

"I hope I didn't startle you."

"No. I'm sorry I didn't see you come in." Ruth gestured to the handwritten menu above the counter. "Are you going to have something to eat?"

"I think I will. Let me buy your lunch, too." Bryan asked for a roast beef on rye. "We never got to have the dinner I promised you in Walsenburg."

The clerk took the twenty-dollar bill Bryan offered and counted back change. Ruth and Bryan moved to one of the small tables to wait for their food.

"The bread is so good here," Ruth said. "I confess it's better than anything I make."

"I'm glad I ran into you." Bryan pulled two napkins from the dispenser on the table. "I've been wanting to talk to you about a couple of things."

"Oh?" Ruth hung her purse on the back of the chair.

"I'd still like to take you to dinner—a proper date."

"You just bought my lunch. Thank you, by the way."

"You're welcome. But I'd still like to spend more time getting to know you."

The clerk came around the end of the corner and set their plates in front of them. Ruth rearranged the two halves of her ham sandwich and the dill pickle.

"Maybe it's just as well we didn't go to dinner," she said. The last thing she wanted to do was hurt Bryan Nichols. "My life is... well, a little inside out right now."

Bryan bit into his sandwich and chewed, not moving his eyes off Ruth. After he swallowed, he said, "Is this because of what Alan said to you?"

"What do you mean?" Hoping to appear less nervous than she felt, Ruth bit into her own sandwich.

"He flipped out about that water strap. He said he was going to make sure you knew it could just as well be mine. I couldn't talk any sense into him."

"He did make that point rather adamantly."

"You don't believe him, do you?"

She set her sandwich down and put her hands in her lap, where it would be less obvious that she could not hold them still. "No, I don't. I've learned to trust my own impressions about people. And I trust you."

"Good."

"Alan makes me unsettled, though. I think I might talk to the sheriff."

"I'll go with you," Bryan said quickly. "As soon as we finish eating."

Ruth perked up. "Really?"

"That strap is a small thing, but I know it's not mine. I haven't been able to get it out of my head."

"I'd love to have you come with me," Ruth said. "It might mean something coming from a person who actually knows Alan."

"It's the right thing."

She smiled. "You're a good man, Bryan Nichols."

"I am glad to hear you say that. I hope it means you will reschedule dinner." He chomped into his sandwich again.

"I'd better not." Ruth winced inwardly. "It wouldn't be right."

Bryan chewed slowly. "It's Elijah Capp, isn't it?"

"Yes," she answered. "And I don't think it will ever be anyone else."

"Are you sure you don't want to back out?" Elijah asked.

"Why?" was Annie's retort. "Do you want to back out?"

"I didn't say that."

"You're giving up your only mode of transportation."

"Amos has a buggy for the business." Elijah stroked the horse's neck one last time. "I'm not sure how much longer he'll let me work for him since he knows I'm leaving the church, but he'll let me use the buggy until the time comes."

Annie signed the check. The price of a horse and buggy would make a serious dent in her bank account once the check cleared, but it was time. She could not ride her bicycle around the hills all winter.

"Are you sure Rufus is going to understand this?" Elijah folded the check in half without looking at it and tucked it into his shirt pocket.

"Is there something about your horse that you don't want Rufus to know?"

"Of course not."

"Then leave Rufus to me. I want to surprise him."

"Taking care of an animal is a lot of responsibility."

"Save the lecture for your own *kinner* someday." Annie ran her hands along her new pitchfork. "I've mucked enough stalls with the Beiler sisters to have some idea what I'm doing."

Elijah grabbed the strapping around a bale of hay and tossed it onto the floor of the garage. "I wish you'd let me come by and do it for you."

"I don't want to get dependent. You won't be here much longer."

"Until I go, then. I won't leave before Ruth does."

"I'm sure she doesn't want you to." Annie surrendered the pitchfork, and Elijah used it to spread hay.

"Are you sure you're ready to drive on your own?"

"I have to do it sometime, don't I?" Annie kicked at the hay, remembering the first time she stumbled into the Beiler barn accidentally and hardly knew what to make of the horses and cow and buggies she saw there. Whatever Rufus decided about his property, she could at least bring this much to their marriage. It was an old horse and an old buggy. He could not object that she had splurged unnecessarily.

"What have we got here?" Ruth paused at the end of the driveway. "Is this what I think it is?"

"*Ya*." Annie took the horse brush off the hook where Elijah had hung it and began running it through the horse's mane.

"The garage is a barn now?"

"The lot is zoned for horse property. I hope you don't mind parking the car in the driveway."

Ruth grinned. "If Elijah was going to sell to anybody, I'm glad it's you."

Annie looked from Ruth to Elijah. Their eyes locked on each other. If ever two people belonged together, it was Ruth and Elijah.

Ruth's phone rang, and she reached into her bag to find it and look at the caller ID. "It's the sheriff."

"I have Alan Wellner here," the sheriff intoned.

"But I only just spoke to you a few minutes ago." Ruth's chest tightened. "I didn't realize things would move so fast."

"Don't worry," the sheriff said. "We didn't have to make a scene. We found him at home, and he agreed to come in for questioning under his own volition."

"That's good, I guess."

"It's very good."

Ruth took in the puzzled expressions on the faces of Annalise and Elijah. She had not yet told either of them that she had decided to talk to the sheriff.

"What are you charging him with?" Ruth was almost afraid to hear the answer. At least no one had been hurt in any of the fires.

"Nothing yet. We don't know that Wellner did anything. We have only the opinions of you and Mr. Nichols that he might have."

"Yes. Right. Sorry."

"I made it clear this was not an arrest. We'd only like to have Mr. Wellner answer a few simple questions to determine if we consider him a person of interest. The thing is, he said he won't talk to us unless he gets to talk to you first."

"Me?" Panic welled. "I thought you weren't going to tell him where the lead came from."

"We didn't."

Ruth swallowed her anxiety. Alan must have figured it out for himself. If they had asked him about the strap, it would not have been difficult.

"You'll be perfectly safe," the sheriff said. "I'll have an armed officer in the room with you at all times, and I'll watch through the glass."

"I don't want him to get hurt," Ruth said.

"We all hope it won't come to that. He seems calm for now, just adamant that he must speak to you."

"What if I don't come?" The phone trembled in Ruth's hand. What had seemed like the obvious next step a few hours ago at the bakery with Bryan now felt like a personal risk she had failed to calculate.

"If we can't get him to talk, we may have to let him go. Unless we can get a psych hold. That might get us a couple of days."

Ruth had seen enough television shows to know what a psychiatric hold was. She looked up at the befuddled Elijah and Annalise.

"Can I bring my friends with me?"

"Bring anybody you want," the sheriff said, "but he wants to talk to you, nobody else."

Ruth's mouth had gone more completely dry than she had ever experienced.

"I'll be there in a few minutes." She clicked the phone closed.

Elijah stood the pitchfork on end in the hay. "Wherever you are going, I am going."

Ruth let out her pent-up breath. "I wouldn't have it any other way."

Ruth clenched Elijah's hand unabashedly as the two of them and Annalise walked to the sheriff's office.

"Do you have any idea why he is so emphatic about speaking with you?" the sheriff asked when she walked through the door.

"None whatsoever." Unless he was going to threaten her. Or Bryan. Or Elijah.

"What is the nature of your relationship?"

Ruth scrunched up her face. "We don't have a relationship. Alan is a friend of someone I met a few weeks ago—Bryan Nichols. He was here with me earlier. I already told you everything I know."

"An officer is with Mr. Nichols now trying to verify the existence of the water bottle strap."

"Can I just get this over with?" Ruth returned Elijah's squeeze on her hand.

"Your friends can have a seat and wait here."

Reluctantly, Ruth disentangled her fingers from Elijah's. At least he would have Annalise with him and Ruth could be sure he would be there when she emerged. She followed the sheriff into a sparse side room, where she found Alan seated on one side of a metal table. Just as the sheriff had promised, an armed officer stood against one wall.

The sheriff pulled a digital recorder out of his shirt pocket. "Mr. Wellner, would you have an objection if we recorded your conversation with Miss Beiler?"

Alan met Ruth's eyes finally. "Ruth, do you mind?"

She shook her head, not trusting her voice.

"Go ahead," Alan said.

The sheriff put the device on the table and pressed a button. "I'll be just outside," he said to Ruth.

Ruth nodded, still mute, and the sheriff left. She tried not to let her eyes drift to the officer against the wall.

Alan smiled his broad, affable grin. "Am I making you nervous?"

She moistened her lips. "A little."

"I wonder what you must think of me. I don't blame you. If the tables were reversed, my imagination would be running wild."

"I just want the fires to stop," Ruth said. "I hope we can help make that happen."

"When we were kids," Alan said, "Bryan was the one fascinated with matches." His lips turned up. "Surprised? I tried to tell you that you don't know him very well."

"Matches are dangerous," Ruth said, "but even Amish children are sometimes curious."

"Bryan used to start fires in a metal trash can so he could time how long it took him to put them out."

Ruth sat motionless, feet together under the table and hands in her lap. "He told me that he'd always wanted to be a firefighter."

"Sometimes there is a fine line between being a fire starter and a firefighter."

Ruth had no response.

Alan leaned back nonchalantly in his chair, tipping it precariously as Ruth had seen him do before.

"My father was furious when I said I wanted to study fire science rather than business." Alan let his chair legs fall to the floor with a clank. "Well. You saw how he is. Imagine living with that all the time."

"I'm sorry you did not get along with your father."

"Instead of applying to an elitist four-year college, I enrolled at the community college. They have a great program."

"I've heard that."

"It's true." Alan scraped his chair back a few inches.

Ruth was relieved to see that the officer behind Alan had taken note of his movement.

"Maybe I wanted to be found out," Alan said. "Maybe I dropped that water bottle strap on purpose. Did you ever think of that?"

"So it was your strap."

"You are more observant than I gave you credit for. How many people would pay attention to something like that?"

Ruth refused to divert her gaze. "You did drop it when you set the fire in Joel's field."

He slapped the table. "Why, yes, I did. I was supposed to discover that fire, but you and Bryan turned up first."

"And the others?" Ruth hoped she was asking questions that might be useful to the sheriff.

"I made sure no one would get hurt. Only empty structures with space around them."

Ruth waited.

"I tried to vary things just enough to break the patterns we learned about in school."

She waited some more, mindful of the recorder on the table.

"If my father could see that I was doing something important, he would get off my back and let me follow my own career."

"So you were going to solve the arson case." The light went on in Ruth's mind. "You were going to set Bryan up. You wanted to be the hero who put out the fire, and then you wanted to expose Bryan as the one who set the fires. That's why you wanted to make me doubt him."

"I miscalculated you," Alan said. "I did not want to believe you were anything more than a naive Amish girl."

The knot in Ruth's throat was about to choke her.

Forty-Six

Ruth sat at Annalise's dining room table with her chair scooted toward Elijah's and one arm linked through his elbow. She was not sure when she would be able to let go.

"You were so courageous." Annalise carried a pot of coffee in one hand and three mugs by the handles in the other. She set everything in the middle of the table.

"I wish I could do something to help Alan." Ruth used her free hand to pull a mug closer.

Annalise poured coffee. "I think you did."

"I wish he didn't have to go to prison."

Elijah patted her arm. "I understand sometimes the *English* work out a deal of some sort."

"If he cooperates," Annalise said, "the charges might not be as severe as they could be. Either way, I suspect he'll get some mental health help."

"I hope so." Ruth poured cream in her coffee.

"I've been reading a book about Arkansas history," Annalise said. "There was a Sheriff Byler who was killed by an outlaw. Well, I suppose killing the sheriff is what made him an outlaw. They sent out posses, but he got away. From what I read, they would have hanged him on the spot if they'd caught him. I like to think that law enforcement is more humane now, while still keeping people safe. If Alan needs help, that's what he should get."

"And Leah?" Elijah asked. "Do you think she will cooperate with getting help?"

Annalise nodded. "It's her best hope for getting what she wants—to go to Pennsylvania with her parents' blessing."

Ruth took a long swallow of coffee and set her mug down. "We should go out to the house for supper."

Annalise glanced at the clock on the wall. Her eyes lit. "We have time to help set the table. Franey won't mind the extra mouths. I'll drive."

"Oh, no, no, no." Ruth waved her free hand. "It will be dark soon, and you don't have enough experience driving a buggy at night. We'll take the car, and I will drive."

Annalise pouted. Ruth picked up her coffee.

"Word will get around town quickly that the sheriff has detained Alan," Ruth said. "I realize my parents might not have any reason to go into town for quite a while, but I want them to hear about what happened from me."

"I agree," Annalise said. "And I'd love to tell Rufus about how things went with Leah."

Ruth realized she was going to have to let go of Elijah to drive.

"I'll check on the horse." Elijah pushed his chair back. "Perhaps you can drop me at my new place."

Ruth clenched his arm. "You're not coming to supper with us?"

"Would you like me to?"

She lost herself in his eyes, so relieved to have him near.

"They won't approve of the decision I've made." Elijah put his hands in his jeans pockets. "I don't want to cause trouble."

"They're going to have to get used to it." Ruth stood and pulled Elijah to his feet. "I think they will be pleased that we are going to be a package deal after all."

Elijah grinned.

Annalise gasped. "Is it all settled?"

Ruth chuckled. "We haven't even talked about it yet. But I don't think there will be much to discuss."

Elijah cleared his throat. "Now if Rufus would just get it through his head that it is God's will for him to propose to you."

Ruth caught the smile that Annalise tried to obfuscate. "He has, hasn't he?"

Annalise nodded.

Ruth finally let go of Elijah in order to embrace her friend. "Why didn't you say anything?"

"It only happened yesterday. And you can't say anything! He wants to be traditional and wait until the banns are read."

As Ruth backed the car out of the driveway a few minutes later, Leah approached on the sidewalk. Ruth stopped and rolled her window down.

Leah leaned in. "I came home this afternoon and there was a horse in the garage."

"There still is." Annalise leaned forward from the backseat. "He's mine. The buggy, too. You probably recognize it. You drove it."

"Don't remind me." Leah rolled her eyes. "I'm so sorry for all the trouble I caused that day."

Ruth pushed the button for the automatic unlock of the back door. "Why don't you get in? We're going out to my family's farm."

Leah's eyes widened. "Why would you invite me?"

"I think you'll be interested to hear some of the things we're going to talk about." Ruth reached behind her seat and pushed open the door from the inside. "Besides, they are your people, your church. You should get to know them."

"Wait a minute," Annalise said from the backseat. "I have one condition."

Ruth scrunched up her forehead.

Annalise put a finger to her lips. "No one says a word, not one word, about the horse in my garage. I want to surprise Rufus when the time is right."

A week later, Annie felt as if tectonic plates had shifted.

A public defender representing Alan struck a deal with authorities that would assure he got the help he needed. And Alan wrote an article for the local newspaper apologizing to the entire town for the disruption and anxiety he caused. His father refused to see him, but his mother had driven down from Colorado Springs to make sure he knew she had not given up on him.

Leah had eaten breakfast and dinner with Annie every day for the past week. She still wandered during the day, but she accepted a jacket from Annie and came home before dark every day. During Friday's session with Jerusha she nodded agreement to let Ruth drive her to Pueblo to see the counselor in her office once a week and not to try to leave Colorado before they both agreed she was ready for the life waiting for her in Pennsylvania. Annie would make sure the counseling bills were paid.

Just after ten on Saturday morning, Leah brought the horse in from the small pasture behind Annie's house.

"Are you sure you don't want me to drive?" the girl asked.

Annie patted the side of the horse's neck and slipped the bridle over his head. "I admit I'm glad to have an experienced buggy driver with me, but I feel ready."

"It's ten miles—twice as far as the Beilers'."

"I know. You can help me harness the horse to the buggy."

Together they positioned the horse in front of the buggy and double-checked the arrangement of leather straps.

"Let's go." Annie hoisted herself up onto the buggy bench and took the reins in her hands.

Leah climbed up beside her and let out a protracted, well-managed sigh.

"Nervous?" Annie asked.

The girl nodded. "I've been practicing in my head all day what I'm going to say."

Jerusha had encouraged Leah to make an initial overture toward peace with her parents as a first step.

"Did you mail your letter to Aaron?"

"Yesterday." Leah rubbed her trembling hands across the fabric of her lap. "And I'm going to keep on writing even if he doesn't write back."

"He wants to respect your *daed*." Annie signaled the horse to begin the trek.

"I know. And I love him for it. It shows me how much he wants to be a man of respect."

"I do want to make one stop," Annie said.

Leah smiled with one side of her mouth. "Rufus?"

"Yes, Rufus."

An hour later, Annie turned her rig into the long Beiler driveway. Eight-year-old Jacob looked up from where he was scattering chicken feed. He dropped the bucket of food and lit across the clearing to Rufus's workshop. Annie did not try to stop him. By the time Rufus emerged from his work, Annie had parked the buggy and was leaning casually against its frame.

"Good morning." Rufus looked around. "Where has Elijah gone off to so quickly?"

"Elijah is not here," Annie said.

Rufus grinned. "He's a brave man to loan you his horse and buggy."

"He didn't loan it to me. He sold it to me."

Rufus planted his feet and crossed his arms. "Annalise Friesen, what have you done?"

"We're going to need our own rig." She moved toward him. Little Jacob dashed to the house. Annie knew in a matter of moments Franey and the girls would scramble down the porch steps to see for themselves what Jacob was even now describing to them. "No matter where we live, we'll need a buggy."

Rufus's violet-blue eyes, inherited through ten generations, shone in the cerulean of the Colorado sky.

Annie stepped closer. "I trust you to make the right decision about the land and where we live and how we make our livelihood—and even when to marry. If you want to wait, we'll wait." She paused to point at the buggy. "But you don't have to face anything alone. I'm not going anywhere. This is my down payment on our future."

She wished he would kiss her then, and she knew he wanted to, but the screen door snapped open and footsteps tumbled down the wooden steps. Rufus touched his hat and nodded ever so slightly, and she saw the flash of approval roll through his complexion.

When Annalise had gone and the commotion settled, Rufus saddled Dolly. In a leather bag he had carried for years, he packed his sketch pad, two charcoal pencils, and three apples for the horse. After nearly seven years on the farm, he knew its boundaries well. He could recall from memory the surveyor's legal description of the property he and his father had chosen when they pooled their resources to buy land and erect a sprawling house for the eight members of the Beiler family who joined the new settlement.

He rode now around the perimeter of the land and then followed the horse paths that cut through it, dividing fields. His parents always talked about someday building a *dawdi* house where they would retire to enjoy grandchildren by day before sending them back to the main house and their parents—whoever that would be—when they tired of them. Joel would take over the farm, Rufus had always assumed. He had a much richer love of the soil than Rufus did, and it was too early to say what Jacob might like to do.

But the land could sustain a third house. If he situated it at the far corner, it would not interfere with the crop rotations and irrigation rows.

Rufus slid out of the saddle and stood to gaze at the line where the land met the sky. In his pad, he sketched the layout of the farm and drew rectangles for the existing buildings. He marked off where a new house could sit, with its front porch soaking up the vista of the Sangre de Cristos just as the main house did.

For now he and Annalise would be happy living on the farm with his parents. Rufus did not know if Larry's Denver clients would choose to make an offer on his land. He did not know if the land might sit empty for two years or five years. He did not know if the farm would turn the corner toward financial stability. He did not know if he would build a home on the land he had purchased or here on the corner of the farm.

When the time was right, he would build Annalise a house, and wherever it was, it would be the right place because Annalise would be there and their children would be there. Time would reveal *Gottes wille*, and Rufus only wished to stand in that place.

Annie took the buggy over the final ridge and pulled on the reins slightly to slow the horse's gait down the gentle slope onto the Deitwaller farm.

"You're coming with me, aren't you?" Leah asked. "Into the house, I mean."

"If that's what you want." Annie intended all along to be at Leah's side. Unlike her last encounter with Leah's mother, this time Annie was armed with the truth, and she was prepared to step in if Leah's composure diminished.

Leah sat forward on the bench. "There are my brothers. What rascals. I'm sure they are supposed to be doing chores."

The boys, tumbling over each other on an empty wagon bed, had spotted the buggy and now stood still to watch the arrival.

"*Mamm!*" The older one turned toward the house and hollered. "It's Leah!"

Annie slowed the rig and pulled alongside the boys.

"Have you come home?" the younger boy asked.

"I've come to talk," Leah answered calmly. "Do you know where *Daed* is?"

"In the barn."

"Will you please go get him?"

Both boys sprinted toward the barn. The screen door creaked open, and Annie looked up to see Eva Deitwaller standing in front of the house with a mixing bowl in her hands.

"*Daed* will want to finish what he's doing." Leah slowly climbed down from the buggy bench. "He likes to do one thing at a time."

Annie noticed Leah glance toward the barn rather than move closer to her mother. The scene reminded Annie of a standoff in a B-rated cowboy film, the sort of thing she and her sister used to laugh at on Saturday afternoons when they were kids. This time, though, Annie felt the tension, wondering who would make the first move.

Leah's father finally emerged from the barn. In no rush, he paced across the yard, halting only when he was within a few feet of his daughter. As if on cue, his wife now approached. Beside Annie, Leah tensed.

"You look well." Mr. Deitwaller inspected Leah, who wore a freshly laundered dress and crisp prayer *kapp*.

"You're thin." Mrs. Deitwaller examined Leah from head to toe. "I suppose that's what comes from living like a wild animal."

"Leah is not a wild animal." Annie took a half step forward.

Leah stopped her. "I've been staying with Annalise. I'm going to stay there until I'm ready to go to Pennsylvania."

"You've still got that nonsense on your mind?" Mrs. Deitwaller scowled. "I've got work to do, so if you've come to say something then just say it."

"I know you asked Aaron not to write to me, and he has respected your wishes. But he has written to Annalise. His parents have invited me to live in their home."

"I won't have it."

"In three weeks I'll be eighteen." Leah's jaw was set. "I'm going to work hard to make better decisions, and I don't want to hurt anyone. But Aaron wants me, and his parents want me, and I want to go. I have come to ask your blessing."

"You'll do no such thing." Mrs. Deitwaller shook a finger in Leah's face. "You'll not have our blessing."

Leah's features strained against the assault, and her breathing quickened as she clenched her hands behind her back.

Annie spoke softly. "Your daughter is going to go. Wouldn't it be better if she left on peaceable terms? That's all she asks."

"This matter does not concern you." Mrs. Deitwaller glared at Annie.

"Eva." Mr. Deitwaller had only to speak one word in that tone to silence his wife. "I am the head of this household. It is my decision whether to give Leah my blessing. Everyone deserves forgiveness. And love."

Annie intertwined her arm with Leah's. The girl trembled as her father stepped toward her and kissed her cheek.

Forty-Seven

July 1892

The night yawned deep and dark, taunting Joseph with every wakeful shift on top of his bedroll. In the midsummer heat, he lay watching the moon's progression across the sky. He both yearned for the release daybreak would bring him and dreaded the finality.

No. Not finality. Maura would change her mind. The weeks since his arrival in Gassville seemed to him a lifetime away from the ways of his people, but to Maura they would have been brief and muddled with anxiety, frustration, confusion.

Joseph rolled onto his side and tucked a hand under his neck. A brush of pink teased his flittering eye open, and he sat up with a sigh. The moment could not be far off now, but first he would start the day with prayer. For Maura. For Belle. For Woody. Even for Leon Mooney. And for Hannah and Little Jake.

For the light of God's gracious will and hearts ready to see it and accept it. He breathed deeply and began to speak his prayers softly.

When he opened his eyes, dawn had broken with sufficient light for Joseph to gather his belongings and slide the stable door open and lead his horse out. He took the steed to the trough and pumped water. While the animal drank, Joseph slapped the blanket over the horse's back and filled the saddlebags.

"Joseph."

He spun at the sound of her voice, and Maura stepped from the early morning gray.

"I couldn't sleep all night," she said.

He straightened his hat with both hands. "I was awake as well."

"I wanted to see you one more time."

The sun lit her from behind, casting a glow around her that would have been angelic if his heart were not cracking. Joseph was unable to speak.

"I'm worried for you," Maura said. "You're going to face judgment, and it is all my fault."

"No. No." He stepped toward her and held out a hand.

"There's no telling what Zeke will have told everyone by the time you get home."

"Stephen will have the bigger mouth." Maura's hand felt so small in his. Joseph tightened his hold.

"What does it matter? Either way, it's the same in the end."

He shifted his hand to intertwine his fingers with hers. She offered her other hand.

"It is true that some of my people will say I was foolish to get involved with the *English*, that I fell into temptation. They will say God's will brought me back from the brink."

"And you?" Maura searched his face. "What will you say?"

Joseph felt the tremble in her fingers laced through his. "I have no regrets."

He leaned in to kiss her. She offered soft, eager lips, and he owned them until they were both breathless.

"Joseph," she murmured when they stepped apart.

"Shh." He put a finger on her lips. "I will be back. Those are the last words I want you to hear from me."

She kissed his fingertips but said nothing. Joseph swung into the saddle and trotted his horse out of the stable yard. He did not dare look back.

Belle hung her handbag over one arm and a basket over the other.

The cupboards were getting bare. The Twigg store, where she had shopped for months, was closed. No one from the family was left to run it. Driving over to Mountain Home to buy the sugar and eggs she needed immediately would take longer than Belle was willing to leave her father alone. He was liable to be foolish enough to try to get out of bed on his own. Returning home promptly would require that she shop at the Denton Emporium—though she was tempted to discover how long it would take her father to worry about her absence.

Outside the emporium, only moments after it opened for the day, Belle shoved down the knot in her throat. She pushed open the door and stepped inside. Ing Denton eyed her from behind the counter. Ignoring the pressure in her chest, Belle paced slowly up the center aisle toward the basket of eggs she knew from years of experience would be sitting on a small table. She found a mixture of brown and white, glanced at the price, resolved to start keeping laying hens again, and listened idly to the conversation of two women.

"Yes, I'm starting any day now."

"But why would Woody Woodley hire a housekeeper? Maura is more than capable."

"Oh, don't tell me you haven't noticed she has a young man. He's from over in Tennessee. They'll be married before you know it."

Belle's heart nearly stopped. Maura had said nothing to her about leaving with Joseph!

But neither had she said she would not go.

Belle stomped through the store. Her father would have to wait.

She found Maura sitting in the Woodley kitchen. The breakfast dishes were still in the sink. Maura's eyes swelled and reddened with the tears she could not hold back.

"Maura, why didn't you tell me?" Belle demanded.

Maura stared at her. "What haven't I told you?"

"I thought Joseph was leaving."

"He did. I said good-bye this morning."

"I don't understand."

"Belle, what are you talking about?" Maura wiped her nose with a handkerchief.

"You're getting married."

"I'm what?"

"Did you think that because I lost John I could not be happy for you?"

"Belle, I'm not getting married. I told you, Joseph left a few hours ago."

"Then why has your father hired a housekeeper?"

"What?" Maura was on her feet now.

"I heard it with my own ears at Dentons'. Widow Sacks claims that she is going to start working for your father any day now."

The kitchen door opened, and Woody Woodley entered. "What is all the commotion about?"

"Daddy," Maura said slowly, "have you engaged the services of a housekeeper?"

"Why, yes. Mrs. Sacks and I came to an agreement yesterday. She will come in the afternoons to tidy up and make sure I have some dinner. I'm sure I can get my own breakfast. I'm not a doddering old man quite yet."

"You might have said something," Maura said.

Woody pulled out a kitchen chair and sat in it. "Maura, you've done a wonderful job of looking after me since your ma died. I admit I still miss her every day. But when your Joseph came out to rescue Leon Mooney, I saw in your eyes that you feel about him the way I felt about your mother."

"But I never told you I was leaving."

"It's just a matter of time. If it is not Joseph Beiler, it will be someone else—but I think you would be crazy as a loon not to accept a fine man like that."

Belle reached out and gripped Maura's hand. "One of us should be happy. I had my chance at love. You should have yours. Do you want Joseph?"

Joseph's kiss still lingered. Maura had not allowed food or drink to pass her lips for fear of losing his taste.

"Yes," she said. "Yes! I want Joseph Beiler."

"Then let's get you packed."

"Now?"

"Of course now. How much of a head start does he have?"

Maura looked at the clock, her bottom lip trembling. "About three hours."

"That's not so long. You're a good rider."

"I don't know the way."

"He'll follow the train tracks where there is no road. Everyone does."

Maura stared at Belle.

"It's one of the few useful things my father has said to me in the last year." Belle grabbed Maura by the elbow and pushed her out of the kitchen. "I'll get your horse. You get whatever you can stuff in the saddlebags. Wear sensible shoes."

Maura stumbled to her bedroom, unprepared for these rapid choices. She picked up the photo of her mother and slid it out of the frame then snatched up the too-small gloves. Then she gasped at her own thoughtlessness. Joseph's people would accept neither the photo nor the gloves, and she did not intend to cause him any more discomfiture than would already await him when she rode into his community with him.

From a hook in the wardrobe, she took a simple dark calico dress and rolled it into a bundle. Sitting on the bed, she took Belle's advice and changed her shoes. A black shawl was her final selection. She heard her father's steps in the hall and looked up to see him.

"You're fixin' to leave, then."

She nodded. "We'll be back. Joseph won't keep me from you."

"Come back a married woman, and you will make your daddy happy."

Maura smiled. "I can do that." She stepped across the room and kissed her father's cheek.

Joseph had already dawdled too long at the watering hole outside the railroad station in a small eastern Arkansas town. The horse had had its fill of refreshment and so had Joseph. A few other travelers had mounted and trotted away, leaving him alone. He knew he ought to be making better time, but somehow he could not make himself hurry.

He was stroking his horse's neck when he heard the thundering gallop approaching from the west. A shaft of sunlight distorted the view. Joseph thought his eyes were playing tricks, making him see what he hoped to see. The horse and rider emerged from lines of streaming brilliance and settled into a constant form.

Maura.

Her dark hair, with no hat, had lost its pins in the wind. She leaned forward, low and tight in the saddle, her knees unrelenting in the horse's side.

Joseph stepped into the road that paralleled the iron rails, spread his arms wide, tilted his head back so far his hat fell off, and laughed with glee. Moments later, Maura Woodley was in his arms. His heart, his future.

He kissed her and reveled in her eagerness to share his life.

Forty-Eight

"Are you sure you wouldn't like to be at church?" Ruth grinned at Annalise over breakfast on Sunday.

"It does feel odd not to be there." Annalise poured herself a third cup of coffee. "But Rufus wants to do things the traditional Lancaster way, and he says the bride does not come to church on the day the banns are published."

"He's right," Ruth said, "but we're a long way from Lancaster. Each district has its own traditions."

"I want it to be perfect for Rufus. I just want him to be happy."

Elijah helped himself to a second cinnamon roll. "He's marrying you. What else does he need?"

"Is the date set?" Ruth asked. "The first Thursday in November?"

Annalise nodded.

"You have a lot of sewing to do!"

Annalise twisted in a sly smile. "I bought the fabric for the dresses weeks ago."

Ruth grinned. "What color?"

"Purple. To remind me of the first Amish dress I ever wore, your purple dress." Annalise sipped her coffee. "Thank you both for keeping me company this morning."

"You haven't eaten anything." Ruth put a roll on a plate and set it in front of Annalise. "It's nice that Leah went to church—and that you let her take the buggy."

"Leah and I have come to an understanding of the heart. Of course I let her." Annalise stood and picked up her coffee, leaving the roll untouched. "I'm restless. I think I'll go sit on the front steps."

"Rufus will be along soon enough to tell you how it went." Ruth handed the plate to Annalise. "Distract yourself by eating."

Annalise ignored the plate and ambled through the house and out the front door. Ruth looked out the front window at a used seven-passenger minivan parked in front of the house.

"I can't believe you got a license to drive a car and did not tell me."

Elijah shrugged. "You got one. Why shouldn't I?"

"So you'll taxi?"

"At least for the next couple of months." Elijah picked up the roll Annalise had abandoned. "Tom is always saying he has more taxi business than he has time for and still run his hardware store properly. And I'll have room for a family."

Ruth lifted the lid on the coffee carafe to confirm her suspicion that it was empty. "I guess I'll be here alone with Leah after Annalise and Rufus get married."

"When will she go to Pennsylvania?"

"After Christmas, she thinks. She promised Jerusha a few weeks of regular sessions before she makes a major change. Yesterday her father agreed to help her with train fare."

"I suppose she and Aaron will marry soon enough."

"Even if they wait until next fall, at least they'll be together." Ruth picked at the remains of the roll on her own plate. "Elijah?"

"Yes?"

"What will our wedding be like?"

His countenance transformed. "Our wedding?"

"We're going to get married, aren't we?" Ruth dabbed at her mouth with a napkin. "I've turned you down so many times. I hope you're going to ask one more time."

Elijah stood and pulled Ruth to her feet then held both her hands. "Ruth Beiler, our wedding will be anything you want it to be."

She wrapped her arms around his neck and waited, watching his face as he lowered his mouth to her and kissed her with the longest, most delicious kiss they had ever shared.

"I still want to finish my degree," she said when they broke for air. He kissed her again.

"That means we'll have to be in Colorado Springs."

He sought her lips again.

"It's not going to be easy. It took me a long time to get used to living in the *English* world."

This time he put a finger on her lips before kissing her yet again.

The bench at the base of the Beiler staircase was a tight fit for six people adorned in new wedding clothes. Even if Annie wanted to move her arms freely, she would not have been able to. Crunched between Sophie and Lydia Beiler, her attendants wearing clothing identical to hers, Annie tried to keep her white cape and apron from becoming crumpled before the ceremony. She would have neither photograph nor ring nor pressed flowers to remember this day by. Instead, she breathed in every detail around her, committing as much to memory as her brain would hold.

She could not even get a good look at Rufus at the other end of the bench, where he was flanked by his brother Joel and Levi Staub, one of the young men Rufus employed when he could afford to take on extra help. She would have liked to get a better view of his new black suit and bow tie before the formalities began. Wedding guests had been arriving for most of an hour already. They slowly made their way past the bench where the wedding party were seated, shaking hands and offering congratulations. Annie listened for the lilt in Rufus's voice as he greeted the members of the church district by name, her chest swelling with the assurance that she would hear that voice for the rest of her life and have the joy of calling him husband. After offering their greetings, the men circled around and returned to the outdoors, while the women took their coats and shawls upstairs to the master bedroom set aside for their fellowship before the wedding.

Leah stepped through the front door of the Beiler home. Annie smiled as the girl crossed the room and then stood to kiss her cheek.

"I'm so glad you could come," Annie said.

"You're so kind to invite me. I only wish you could be at my wedding someday."

"These are my new sisters." Annie gestured to Sophie and Lydia. "I hope you will get to know them before you leave for Pennsylvania."

Behind Leah came Ruth and Elijah in unadorned simple *English* clothing. Although the bishop had advised that they should refrain from coming to church in the wake of Elijah's decision to forsake his baptismal vows and leave the congregation, they were welcome as wedding guests. Annie could not think what to say to Ruth in such a moment. When they met each other two summers ago, who could have known they would become such dear friends—and sisters-in-law? Elijah somberly shook her hand, and a wordless peace passed between them. Annie knew Elijah would lay down his life for Ruth. Whatever awaited them in the *English* world, they would face it together.

Annie hardly sat down again before her eyes listed to the next group to enter and filled with tears. She looked past Lydia and Joel to Rufus and saw that his eyes were fixed on the same sight.

"They came." She swallowed her sob. "I wasn't sure if they would."

Rufus smiled, his violet-blue eyes sparkling.

Annie wanted to run to the front door, but she held her dignified position and waited for the guests to come to her.

Her parents. Her sister. The family who had been so confused last summer by her choice to join the Amish church but who had taken Rufus into their hearts. Her parents' acceptance of the man she loved so deeply, evident by their presence on this occasion, made her knees go weak in gratitude. Annie embraced each one in turn, clasping their shoulders and feeling their heartbeats.

Ruth had walked Annie through every detail that would follow, and now she focused as much as she could through tear-brimmed eyes on the procedures.

The arrival of the bishop, who would preside at the ceremony.

The seating of her parents and Rufus's parents, who loved her as their own daughter.

The entry of the young people, some of them looking at each other with yearning before they went their separate ways, the men to sit with the men and the women to sit with the women.

A hymn began, and Annie and Rufus followed the bishop to a room that had been prepared for them to hear his words of encouragement in Christian marriage. By the time they returned to the main rooms, the congregation was singing a second hymn. The wedding party took their seats in six matching chairs. Annie and the Beiler sisters faced Rufus and his side sitters.

A sermon.

A silent prayer.

A reading from the Bible.

And the bishop's words, "What God hath joined together let not man put asunder."

The main sermon.

And the bishop's words, "If any here has objection, he now has opportunity to make it manifest."

Annie smiled at Rufus as no one made manifest any objection, and the bishop said, "If you are still minded the same, you may now come forth in the name of the Lord."

Rufus offered his hand and she took it, walking forward to stand before the bishop.

"Can you confess, brother," the bishop intoned, "that you accept this our sister as your wife, and that you will not leave her until death separates you? And do you believe that this is from the Lord and that you have come thus far by your faith and prayers?"

Rufus left not an instant of hesitation. "Yes."

The bishop turned to Annie and asked the same question. Softly, confidently, she answered, "Yes."

The bishop spoke again to Rufus, and then to Annie with the same question to which Rufus had given a somber answer.

"Because you have confessed, sister, that you want to take this our brother for your husband, do you promise to be loyal to him and care for him if he may have adversity, affliction, sickness, weakness, or faintheartedness—which are many infirmities that are among poor mankind—as is appropriate for a Christian, God-fearing wife?"

Annie's pulse pounded. "Yes."

The bishop took Annie's right hand and placed it in Rufus's right hand. "The God of Abraham, Isaac, and Jacob be with you and give His rich blessing upon you and be merciful to you. May you have the blessing of God for a good beginning, a steadfast middle, and a blessed end, this all in and through Jesus Christ. Amen."

Annie squeezed Rufus's hand, free of doubt and full of certainty that she had indeed come to this moment by faith and prayer.

Author's Note

The Valley of Choice series began with imagining the lives of people who lived three centuries ago and discovering a personal connection to them. This third story in the set comes closer to me generationally. The historical thread is based on what happened to my grandfather's grandfather, the first sheriff of Baxter County, surrounded by some embellished historical characters and a cast of people who never lived but might have. And now I've come to the end of the three stories feeling enriched by this foray into history and reflecting on the themes that follow us through the centuries and into our contemporary lives. Anger. Hurt. Grief. Vengeance. Forgiveness. Love.

I have again taken liberties with the region around Westcliffe, Colorado, in creating this confluence of what might have happened long ago and what might yet be waiting to greet us in our lives as we confront these same themes. May you name these experiences as they occur in the circumstances of your life—as they do for all of us—and find the blessing of stepping into a land of grace.

Olivia Newport's novels twist through time to find where faith and passions meet. Her husband and two twenty-something children provide welcome distraction from the people stomping through her head on their way into her books. She chases joy in stunning Colorado at the foot of the Rockies, where daylilies grow as tall as she is.

Also by Olivia Newport...